THE GRAY BLADE

LAST OF THE HOLY HOUND TRILOGY

M.N.M. Abbott

ACKNOWLEGEMENTS

A very special thanks to all those who live to see others smile and who also share my love for adventure. Read on and see what else my land of magic has in store this time around. Thank you family, friends, and everyone else who helped me to get this far with my dreams.

As far as specifics go, I want to thank David for making this second installment possible. Then I have a very big thank you for Lynda and "Cally." If it weren't for you two I would have been lost at the very start.

Thank you all.

God Bless!

The Realm of Magic
N
KEY
Bridge Ferry Manor Ruins Road
Town City Fort Castle Spire
King's Peak
Crescent Remains
Lost Roads
Elf Wood
Tanoaks
Plexus
Dargadia
Ft. Redu
Broad River
The Great Wastes
Ft. Wight
White Sea Desert
Eskrana
Kati Jungle
Ebony Range
Mortigad
Lorison
Bebidin
Ulla Lake
Zsu

Introduction
INTO THE STORM

Night had fallen and with it had come a ferocious storm. Thunder clapped, and a streak of lightning lit up the green landscape of Dargadia while raindrops fell like bullets. Together, the two ran into the howling wind, heading for the closest village. As the lighting flashed again, Adwen's soaking wet fur glistened like quicksilver. Her tail whipped, and her violet eyes glowed, gazing into the distance.

Oryn was close by, sprinting with the Greatsword set across his back. It swung with the cadence of his stride, and despite the weight of the six-foot blade he was not slowed. His body had become even more powerful since being marked a fortnight before. Every day brought more strength and a brighter shine to his emerald green eyes. The sky tonight was engulfed by rain-laden clouds, so he needn't worry about the four moons of the magical realm. He would not be forced to become his new hound self tonight.

Since the time of Adwen's murder and rebirth into a body full of light powers, she gave no thought to the moons. She could change at will now and traded that worry for a new load of concerns. Being the heir of the Master Knight, she was the only one who could help destroy the gathering witches, undead and demons. She was the only hope for the Kingdoms of Day. With the Order's protective halls behind them, danger lay in wait. The alliance of the kingdoms had been forged, and their attention was turned to defending all fronts in the White Sea Desert, the jungle plateau lands of Eskrana, as well as Dargadia.

Having once been a knight from the Order of the Master Knights, Oryn was used to traveling at length and into intense battles. But Adwen, though she was the heir and his superior, had once known the life of a normal girl. She had been born into the realm of logic, opposite of the magical world. The day before graduating from high school there was a fateful encounter that ended with her being cast into the land of magic, miracles and monsters.

Only after dying and being mysteriously revived had she learned of her heritage and ties to the Order of knights. She was their prophesied leader, messenger and defender. More proof of her bloodline lay in the fact that Oryn had been marked by her during a confrontation with the Red Cult witches. Now he was a part of her journey of self-discovery and renewal.

He had been forced to leave his human life behind. No longer a fragile mortal, he shared the same weaknesses to evil weapons. Though he was proud to be at her side, he still could not forgive himself for the wrongs he had committed. Memories of doing her harm were difficult to bear as his dire secret tortured him daily. Oryn loved her and hoped that she would never learn this.

Refraining from giving more furtive glances, he forced himself to look ahead. He was her subordinate and servant, so he refocused and continued running.

Chapter 1
HOLY HOUND

After covering many miles and spending hours in the rain they spied dozens of lit windows. Their nocturnal vision allowed them to see the whole town nestled at the bottom of the hill with about twenty homes, a few shops and an inn.

Oryn turned to Adwen wondering how she wished to proceed.

The white hound-being stood to her height of seven feet and then shrank into her less beastly shape. At a height of five-foot-eight, her white head of hair and golden bangs were soaked, as were her grey and golden battle garments.

After examining the small town and pondering to herself, Adwen advised him, "Go ahead and visit the inn. If you get them to sell a room, we could stay the night. This weather isn't going to let up until morning. I'll meet you there after I look around for any demons that might be hiding out."

Nodding, he watched his leader pull the enchanted white cloth hood over her head and vanish. Even though she was completely invisible, he sensed her departing for the streets. Her bare feet left small prints, which were quickly washed away by the weather.

Eyeing the glowing windows of the inn, he hoped for the best and prepared for the worst.

The barroom of the Strapping Lad Inn was relatively quiet. Only a few villagers were drinking tonight, and some casually played cards, sharing a story or two. But once the front door opened to let in a stranger they all looked up, curious to see who had been out in the rain.

The traveler stepped past the threshold and closed the door. Putting down the hood of his cowhide jacket, he looked quite young, no more than twenty-two years of age. He had an abnormally beardless face, and his brown hair was short with cheek-length bangs, dripping from the fresh downpour. Standing at six-feet-two, he shook off some water before setting his large sword down alongside the rest of the visitors' weapons.

Not knowing where he was from, the other guests left him alone and watched wearily. Judging from the size of his weapon, he had incredible strength. Everything in his appearance was strong, from his masculine jaw and long features to his confident controlled stride. No one took notice of the glow in his eyes, and they decided he seemed human enough. No longer concerned with the visitor, they minded their own business.

Oryn approached the counter across the way and called, "Innkeeper, do you have a room to spare?"

Handing a mug of beer to another customer, the bearded man looked him over before saying, "We do indeed, if you can pay your way into it."

Before leaving the Order's fortress with Adwen, his old comrades had given him what gold they could spare, which turned out to be a lot. Dropping the bloated bag on the table, he showed that there was business to be done.

Coming closer, the stout and sturdy man nodded in approval. "I suppose you'll want a room for one then?"

Oryn shook his head and corrected him: "A room for two, if you have it."

Raising an eyebrow and chuckling, the man looked past his shoulder. "That's an expensive buy, and you look very alone to be claiming two beds."

"I shall be joined shortly. What will the price be?"

"That's twenty gold pieces."

The usual cost for two beds was half that, and Oryn was insulted. He scowled dangerously and tried to keep his eyes from glowing too brightly. If they became aware that Oryn was less than human, the deal could be ruined.

Unafraid, but recognizing the guest's displeasure, the man shook his head. "I did say it was expensive. If you don't wish to pay then you may go and knock on another door for a place to stay."

If Oryn were still a knight in armor, he wouldn't be treated so poorly, but he would rather not say who he really was. Counting out the coins, he chose to pay with money rather than verbal confrontation. Most of the kingdom knew his name and believed he was dead. But if they knew he had been hiding and for selfish motives, then he would rather they never found that their hero from the Order still breathed.

Once more the door opened, and a stranger stepped inside to

escape the storm. To avoid startling anyone, Adwen's hood was down, making her very visible. Everyone watched her shake the rain from herself, but Oryn did not turn to look until after his deal was closed. He had caught her scent the instant she had set foot in the doorway.

Finished slinging the rain from her clothing and hair like an animal, she saw an empty table and went to rest her feet. She ignored the glares, knowing that they didn't trust inhuman beings. Completely unwelcome but otherwise unperturbed, Adwen pulled out a chair and plopped down with a sigh.

Breathing in deep through her nose, she tested the air and smelled the humans. No matter how much they feared or hated her, it was her duty to protect them all. So when three men left their chairs to approach, she let the breath go and didn't bother turning to look. The sixth sense allowed her to feel their presence surrounding the table.

They stood over her expressing their disapproval. One was bigger and smelled of burning metal: obviously a blacksmith. He cleared his throat until she looked him in the eye.

When she finally met his glare, he warned, "Inhuman beings aren't welcome. It would be better if you stayed the night in a tree."

Another smelled of manure: a stable hand. He cracked his knuckles and grumbled, "Creatures like you shouldn't be in here."

Then the third, the blacksmith's apprentice called Adwen something that Oryn found intolerable. "Get up, monster. It's time to leave."

Scowling, he approached from behind and made sure that his presence was known. "Go back to your drinks, now."

All of them turned.

Indicating Adwen, the blacksmith demanded, "Is this thing with you?"

Clenching his fists, Oryn refrained from lashing out. One vengeful hit could prove fatal for any of them. Keeping the anger caged, he sneered, "It would be unwise to ignore my offer. I say again, return to your drinks."

The blacksmith and his protégé left her alone but did not leave. Going up to Oryn, they rounded on him. "If you invited this animal in and thought you'd be welcome, you are sorely mistaken. Get out and take it with you."

"I have already paid my way, and I intend to have what is due," he informed them, stepping past to join Adwen and the stable hand.

"Then reclaim your coin from the innkeeper," smelly horse keeper said. "This animal will not be spending the night, and neither shall you." Turning his back, he reached for Adwen's arm.

In the moment before he touched her, Oryn's anger broke loose. With blinding speed he grabbed him by the hair, causing him to cry out, and swiftly planted his face into the table. Pressing him down firmly, Oryn listened to him gasp and wail at the pain of a broken nose.

The others moved to defend him, but froze when the stranger quickly looked over his shoulder. Both eyes were bright like balls of fire. The green glow startled them, and they thought twice. Realizing he wasn't as normal as previously thought, they took a few steps back and wondered what to do about the pair of inhuman creatures.

Glaring at the two humans, Oryn dared them to try to stop him.

But then he heard Adwen speak: "Let him go."

Keeping an eye on the men, he glanced at her.

She told him a second time using her softest tone, "Let him go."

The sound of her voice quelled some of his rage. Slowly, he raised the man's head up and gave a venomous look before tossing him into his friends. They caught his weight and gaped as Adwen joined in facing them.

Shaking her head, she addressed them: "I'm sorry for what's been happening but we're not responsible. We're only staying for the night and leaving first thing tomorrow. You won't have to see us again."

"That may be the case, but it does not matter," the innkeeper said. "I shall count out your coins and let you take them on your way."

Raising an eyebrow she cocked her head. "What if we gave you a few more coins? How would you feel?"

Oryn's brow furrowed, but he held his tongue hoping that the offer would work. The thought of giving more money to the bigots soured his already bitter mood.

Surprised, the innkeeper considered the deal. Everyone waited as he thought it over. "Ten coins more, no less."

Adwen was well aware that it was borderline robbery. Turning to her tall and very angry friend, she waited to see if he could agree to the terms. They were his coins after all.

Red in the face but under control, he would have loved for this to have happened while he was still a knight. Glancing at her again, he saw she was waiting for his approval.

Soon after, he replied with much disdain, "Done."

Fuming and seething, he opened the door to let his feminine leader enter first. Upon closing it, he stalked to the end of the room beginning to pace. Everything inside of him wished to go back down and thrash each and every one of them senseless. The outrage at how they treated the heir burned in him until it showed in the shine of his eyes.

Adwen usually didn't sleep in beds, but since he had paid an unfair bargain to get her one she felt driven to humor him. Sitting back onto the mattress, she watched him pace. Then she shook her head and asked, "Are you going to do that all night? Take it easy. We got the room."

He never used to pace and suddenly realized why: More of his human traits and attributes were being replaced with animal actions.

Coming to an abrupt stop, Oryn clenched his fists. "Yes, after they took almost half the coins."

Feeling horrible and partly responsible, she grimaced. "Sorry."

He did not blame her for the misfortune and attempted to dispel her guilt. "You have no cause for shame in this. They were thieves and thugs at best."

Nodding, she felt better. "Well, how about you settle down? We went through the trouble of getting in. It would be a waste if you didn't kick back and relax."

Oryn's eyes flashed, and he replied, "They may come while we sleep."

Adwen chuckled and smiled. "Don't worry about it. I'm standing watch. You know that I need less sleep than you. Stop wasting your energy and just lie down already." She thought he was being very silly.

Knowing she was right, he gave in and obliged her.

Watching him, she asked, "Do you miss being a knight that much?"

Keeping himself from meeting her eyes by gazing at the ceiling, he thought of telling the truth but lied. "Very much so." He enjoyed being with his old comrades, but he did not miss them. Being with her was all he could ever ask for.

"Well, when all of this is over, you can go back to working with them again. I've heard them talk about you. You're their hero."

Another twinge of guilt hit him, but he did not react. He didn't deserve the title.

Sensing his reaction, she let it go and thought of something different to ask. "Oryn?"

"What is it?"

"While we were in the hall of elders, I saw something on the floor. It was this little dot. Light was reflecting out of it and distracting me. What was it?"

Realizing right away what she was describing, he breathed a sigh. "There is an entire legend surrounding what you saw."

Hearing him mention a legend got her attention, and she moved to sit on the edge of the mattress, listening intently like a child at bedtime. "Tell me. What's the story?"

He could see her expression out of the corner of his eye, and her sweet face made his heart melt. No longer angry, he forgot the lost coins and began the tale. "Darien was not the only hero of Dargadia. No one knows if the stories are true, but there is evidence that, perhaps, some have authenticity."

"There was once a powerful man with a beautiful face. He had an encounter with a vampire and was bitten. He failed to kill the creature within seven days time and became one himself. After defeating the undead responsible for his fate, he went into the plains, waiting for the sun to finish him off, but it was not meant to be. The light of day spared him. He had become a day walker.

"Dubbed Evrox, he rode a black steed and defended all of eastern Dargadia from the forces of Mortigad. The name is Elvish and means eclipse eyes. As he never fed on humans, the bright rings that newly bitten men have did not disappear. They say that he once set foot into the hall of the Master Knights. He was seeking their blessing and intended to be their spy in the dark lands. No human could ever invade the black kingdom, and so he hoped to serve.

"They condemned him. Summoning the guards to take him, the elders spurned him for being what he was. And as a sign for all, he expressed pain. Shedding a single tear, it was not of blood as normal vampires have. Only good vampires may shed tears of diamond. Casting it before the elder's feet, he left it behind to show what a terrible wrong had been committed."

Oryn shook his head.

"There are many other stories of his exploits, but that is the one considered to be true. No others can be proved."

Adwen was thoughtful and mused, "It sounds a lot like what almost happened to you. If I hadn't shown up, the elders would have condemned you, too. Even when you showed them that I was the heir, they tried to anyway."

"The elders have never been lenient on the disobedient," he admitted.

"That's not a good excuse to kill you. Do you think so?"

He didn't respond. When they first met, he had taken his knife and sword to her on more than one occasion. She had forgiven him, but he still loathed himself over it. From his standpoint he deserved endless torment alone for what he had done.

His silence let her know how he felt. Rolling her eyes, she flopped down and thought of what to do. A flash of golden color crossed her eyes, and she knew what would work best for soothing his inner turmoil. Closing her eyes, she started to hum a soft lullaby.

The sound reached him, and his eyelids grew heavy until he was fast asleep and dreaming.

"You found the bags and rope?" the blacksmith asked.

Insulted, the cobbler replied, "Do you think me a fool? Of course I did. How else are we to restrain them and toss them out?"

The local trader shushed them into silence and hissed, "Keep it down. They could hear your blathering and be expecting us. Shut your mouths and keep your wits about you."

Easing the door open to the dark room, they heard a soft growling. Raising the candle a little higher they could make out the inhuman male, fast asleep and rumbling like a beast. The female was missing, so they looked everywhere including the ceiling. She was nowhere in sight, so they moved closer and prepared to pounce on the unsuspecting creature.

But once they were up close they stalled, none too eager for a beating. Once he woke, they knew the creature would not be submissive.

"You grab his head once I bind his feet," the trader whispered.

Not agreeing to the plan, the blacksmith hissed, "No. He will rip my arms off. You get his head while I get his feet."

"I'll do it," snapped the cobbler. "Just shut your holes and get to it."

The three took their positions and prepared to act.

Just when the trader reached for Oryn's ankles with a cord in hand the cobbler gasped. The others looked up at the sound and were perplexed.

The large sack had been put over his head and tied. While he grappled with the bag, the man with the cord felt something grab his wrists, tying them behind his back. Grunting, he tried to fight against the invisible attacker.

Seeing his company being restrained, the blacksmith headed for the door, attempting to escape. No sooner did he reach the threshold than his feet went out from under him, and his face hit the floor. As he was swiftly dragged inside, he struggled but to no avail.

At the bottom of the stairs the rest of the men waited for their return. When the creatures were handed over, they would receive a beating they would not forget.

Someone heard footsteps and struggling and assumed that the inhuman beings were being dragged along. "Hurry up, will ya? We haven't got all night."

Then they saw an odd spectacle. Two of the men were floating along while the third fell and rolled. After tumbling down the many wooden steps, he landed in a heap at their feet. Everyone gaped and backed away as the two drifted down side by side and then dropped onto their friend. Each of them moaned.

Adwen removed her hood and gave them all a start when she suddenly became visible to their eyes. Shaking her head in disappointment she asked, "Do you need more coins in order to let us sleep?" When they were unresponsive she heaved a heavy sigh and turned away, headed upstairs.

Dawn came, and Oryn felt much better after a peaceful rest. The first thing he thought of was her, so he glanced at the other bed. She wasn't there. He looked to the window and all around, but Adwen was still nowhere in sight. Wondering where she could be, he sniffed the air and could tell she was close. Then he realized where she was and sat up, turning over to check the floor.

As suspected, she was prone on the hardwood boards. She appeared to be asleep and was placid in her state of rest. He loved watching her face whenever she slept and always wondered what she could be dreaming.

"They turned up at about midnight," she said.

Alarmed that she had been awake the entire time, he was thankful she hadn't seen the look on his face. His heart had leaped into his throat when she spoke, but he calmed himself. "As I thought they would."

Leaving the room behind for the stairs, he followed her to the front door. They passed three men covered in bruises, and he smelled traces of Adwen's scent on them. As they were going out he wore a small smile knowing what must have happened.

Everyone in the town was out and about for the day running errands and earning their keep. While cutting through the streets and continuing east, many from the prior evening recognized them and followed, eager to have them leave. Carrying tools and heavy instruments for work, they saw them off to the edge of the forest.

One called out before they could get too far, "You wouldn't be so bold coming into town if Sir Oryn was still living!"

Adwen stopped. Turning back to stare, she growled to her friend so that the humans wouldn't understand. "Tell them."

His jaw clenched as he express his opinion of the idea with a glance.

When he refused, her eyes glowed brighter and she growled, "Then I will."

"NO!" he snapped.

Her brow furrowed, and she growled much softer, "Then tell them who you are."

The small mob was observing them when he turned around and wondered if he would attack.

Grappling with his own tongue, he forced himself to utter, "I have seen him."

They murmured and one called out, "When? Where did you see him, beast?"

Adwen turned to watch and saw their looks of confusion while her companion fought to form the words.

Swallowing hard, he replied, "In the looking glass. I saw him in the looking glass." Then as they gasped, he darted away for the trees, disappearing amid the boughs and the thicket.

He ran and ran, putting the townsfolk as far behind him as he could. Not willing to wait and hear their responses, he couldn't bring himself to stay and watch their looks of outrage. Fighting his way through the underbrush, he panted from running and finally stopped to catch his breath.

Bracing against the trunk of an old elm, he gasped for air as his heart pounded. More shame washed over him as he realized that he had fled. His fear of their scorn had gotten the best of him, so he had run away. Cursing himself for his cowardice, he breathed deeply, recovering after the cowardly retreat.

A soft growl came from behind: "You didn't need to do that."

Recognizing her scent, he hesitantly looked back at Adwen.

In her white hound form, she dipped her head below the branch of a blooming cherry tree. Hundreds of pink blossoms shaded her lean body while she watched him. The golden blaze between her violet eyes shone in a patch of light as she gave him a look of concern. When he didn't reply, she gave another gentle growl, "You didn't need to run."

No longer panting, he looked away. "What would be the point?"

Cocking her head and flattening her ears, she whined, "They weren't angry."

Oryn blinked but did not turn to face her.

Changing into her woman form, she left the shade of the cherry tree saying, "They were happy. You should have seen their faces. Why did you run away?"

"I forsook them for vengeance," he snapped, turning around at last. Glaring, he continued, "You know how I have shamed myself. I would rather they think me dead than let them know I had abandoned my duties to the Order. They would be gravely disappointed and their hopes dashed regarding my honor."

"They don't care about that. Once they knew who they were looking at, they were excited. Knowing that you had been in town gave them hope. You should have told them as soon as you went into the inn."

He was silent. Then he stared and firmly asked, "And what of you?"

His counter was a strong one. Growing angry, Adwen also glared. Eyes glowing brightly, she clenched her jaw.

"If your presence were made known, their hope would be tenfold compared to what my title would bring. The heir of the Master Knight is who they should be rallying behind not the shameful knight they once praised."

Pursing her lips, the glow of her stare threatened to spark into flame.

Unafraid, he knew she would not harm him for speaking the truth.

Very displeased, she stated, "It's a deal then. Whenever we go into town, we will introduce ourselves fully. But if one of us won't, the other will do the introducing for both." She also disliked the attention of the populace for personal reasons, but it seemed this was the best thing. Dargadia's people needed hope.

He also disliked the plan. Then again, it suited him.

"Agreed."

The sun was sinking, and neither of their moods had improved. Hiking and occasionally running through the woods, the two did not discuss their thoughts. Adwen was frustrated but cooling down while he relentlessly abused himself. What a coward he had been, fleeing like a whipped dog.

As darkness fell on the land, they stopped by a strong flowing creek. There she left him alone by the deep end, removing his jacket and boots to wait for the four moons. Once the full orange moon changed him into his true form they would press on.

Reaching into the current, it was cool to the touch and tasted fresh as he drank. He took a few more scoops to quench his thirst before splashing some on his head, combing his finger through his hair. The sensation on his scalp was more soothing than he remembered, and he knew that more of his human side was disappearing. Denying the need to scratch, he gazed at the doubled reflection on the water.

His face was in the rippling surface with the beastly silhouette surrounding it. For now he was not completely human and well on his way to being something else. What was he really? Their breed had never been seen before. What could they be called? Frowning at both images of himself, he felt the full moon was close to being revealed.

Eyes glowing brighter, his veins swelled with blood as his heart quickened. It didn't frighten him like it used to. The pain involved with changing was the least of his concerns. What worried him was his nature. More animal behaviors were forming inside him, and he feared that perhaps not all of the new ones would be as harmless as nervous scratching. Fixated on the water, he wondered if Adwen had experienced the same fears while going through this stage.

Lost in bleak ponderings, the moon came out at the same instant he was pushed. Falling headlong into the creek, he felt surprise and the excruciating crunching of bones. Struggling to hold his breath under the surface, Oryn could not tell which way was up. Muscles swelled and stretched with the rest of him, filling in his strong build. As the change was almost completed, he found the open air and gasped, snarling and coughing violently.

Once the water expelled from his lungs, he faced the shore and found Adwen in her hound form crouched over shriveling demon remains. The man-sized monster turned to mush beneath her.

She snarled at Oryn in the current while he swam back, "What is the matter with you? You didn't hear it coming?"

Ignoring her, he crawled onto shore, coughing harder.

"I've noticed you, Oryn," she snarled and gnashed her jaws angrily. "Something's got you distracted. What's wrong, and what will it take to snap you out of it?"

Not willing to answer, he ignored her and moved to stand upright. Just as he did her clawed hand clutched him by the throat, pinning him to the side of a broad tree. Her hound body was smaller and much more feminine than his, but her strength was far greater. Holding him tight, she snarled, and their eyes met.

Realizing that Adwen was going to look into his heart he quickly averted his gaze. He couldn't let her see inside. She would know his secret.

Snarling louder as she tried to get a look at his eyes, he refused to give her the chance. Fed up with his stubbornness she took control of his movements at will.

Oryn felt his body suddenly stop taking commands from his mind. His eyes widened in horror as she made him face her. Adwen let go so he could take a knee, and he was helpless against her. Though she was staring raptly back at him, she did not peer into his being.

Holding him still with her power, she growled, "I can make you do whatever I want; remember that. Go ahead and keep your secrets from me. I'm going to give you the chance to solve your problems yourself, but if you can't get your head sorted out, I will look inside and see what the matter is."

He possessed power over his own breathing, so he gulped, and his breath came in heavy, startled gasps.

Adwen smelled his fear and felt remorse for being the cause. Ceasing her snarling, she looked on him with pity. "I don't like the fact that I can do this, but I think I have power over you for a reason."

Gulping again, he felt her ease her grasp and waited for her to finish.

"I will only take control to protect you, even if it's from yourself," she said. "I would like to think that my power over you is so that I can help." Putting her ears back, she was apologetic.

Still frightened by what she had done, he found himself forgiving her. Dropping his gaze before she could recognize his affection, he growled, "As you command."

An eerie and alarming shriek reached their ears, making them look off through the trees. There were more vile creatures gathered not far away.

More demons like the one she had recently killed were raiding a town and screeching madly in their excited spree. Attacking any townspeople they could find, they bit into their flesh and sucked them dry. Called Creepers, they scrambled out of the shadows, made visible to the humans by the magic in the air that hung about them as a black mist. Appearing as lanky black things with large fanged heads, they stalked and loped around, hunting and chasing villagers.

A woman fell in the street and cried out when one of the dozens reached for her. It was about to clutch her ankle with crooked claws when a white set of claws batted it away, sending it rolling.

Gasping, the woman got to her feet and fled as Adwen roared, drawing the attention of the nasty things.

They were everywhere, crawling along rooftops and climbing

across walls. Like monstrous, tailless geckos, the monsters came at her and Oryn in the cobbled town square. Swarming, the abominations forgot the humans entirely.

Pouncing on another one of the Creepers, Adwen ripped it apart, and her companion used the Rose Thorne sword to hew others in half.

Focused on his work, it eased Oryn's mind to be in battle again. Taking three down in one full swing, he whirled around to find five more. Swiftly, he destroyed four of them and the last lunged for his legs.

Kicking it back with one padded foot, he heard Adwen yelp.

It made his heart wrench, and he found her fighting a larger demon called a Wretch. He moved to go help her, but three more of the eight-foot fiends came out to stop him.

Black as pitch with spikes and tendrils on their backs, the things were obviously much stronger than their cohorts. He was being encircled by them and the Creepers, but he had a worse problem. While he carried on killing the last of the smaller pests, the full moon was blotted out by clouds.

In moments he was no longer the same height as them. When the demons did attack, he found that his strength was impaired by his shape as well. Swinging the six-foot weapon to defend himself, he missed one demon, which dropped down and slunk under the attack. It slashed at his leg, dealing deep, bloody gashes and making him cry out.

Staggering, he jumped away to avoid the others, waiting for his wound to heal. When he got the opportunity, he glanced at the injury and was alarmed. The flesh still bled and did not mend. Then he understood that their evil claws were one more thing he was vulnerable to.

A Wretch lunged again, trying to cut him across the chest.

When he missed completely, he sensed the others approaching in time to duck and whirl out of the way. Quickly, he stole a glance at the moon. It would be coming back soon, but probably not soon enough. A huge demon was racing in, and he held up the sword sideways to stop it.

His bare feet scraped across the stones until they were raw as the Wretch pushed against the sword in his hands. The demon gripping the blade attempted to crush him down as the others circled in from either side. Continuing to resist, Oryn was gradually forced to the ground. His strength was not enough, and eventually he found himself on one knee.

Then the full moon emerged.

His bellow swiftly turned into a roar as he transformed and sliced the head off of the demon. While getting to his padded feet, the two bit the sides of his neck. Their ethereal jaws sunk into his living flesh, and he yelped, feeling them sucking his blood, draining him.

Before they could sap too much of his strength, he managed to slice one in half. It fell away, turning to mush and ooze as he crumpled back to his knees. The third was a moment from draining the last of his life away.

Oryn's vision blurred. Feeling faint, he clutched his blessed weapon tight, releasing a mighty roar and plunging it into the final Wretch.

When it was gone, he almost was as well. Both ears drooped, and his eyes were dim as he was on the brink of unconsciousness. He could barely sense that during his scuffle, Adwen had slain the last of the fiends. All of the shadowy monsters were scummy stains on the ground, and he found the mind to get up.

Dragging the Rose Thorne across the cobbled street, he blearily limped for the stone fountain. Slumping down to rest against the side, he breathed in shallow gasps. The last thing that registered in his thoughts was Adwen's scent as she came near.

Looking down at him, she knew he had passed out. With the damage he had taken, she wasn't surprised. Only a few of the demons had managed to touch her, and she had minor scrapes from the battle. Shrinking into her woman form, she shook her head and went to fetch his jacket and boots on the outskirts of town. Once the sun came up he would heal. Oryn would be just fine.

He smelled dawn. The air was warming, early birds chirped and there was the smell of dew on rock and grass. He picked up the scent of many humans, too. Water was splashing behind him in the fountain, and he eventually opened his eyes.

Some of his strength had returned in the night, and his injuries didn't hurt so badly. The sunlight was awash over the homes as he sat. Soon he saw movement in the windows as people were looking out. Even though he was in his human shape, he knew they weren't fooled. They knew what he was. Taking a deep breath, he sat up against the side of the stone pool.

Blinking to make his tired eyes focus in the shrinking twilight, the dawn behind him played tricks with his vision. Light and shadow made seeing difficult for his nocturnal sight until a man left the dark of a doorway to investigate.

When he came closer and the sun shone on his face, he seemed familiar to Oryn. An expression of curiosity and intrigue was on the human's face. Then Oryn realized that the man had only one arm. He came even closer, and they recognized each other.

The man smiled and finally spoke. "Oryn? By the stars, is it you?"

Oryn had heard at the Order that Darek, one of his closer comrades, had left for home after the loss of his limb. "More or less," he replied. He could see the jubilant look in his friend's weary face, as he knew the truth.

Then the look turned to shock as he spotted Adwen walking along the rim of the fountain pool. The dawn's first light had been dancing across her body making her difficult to see against the sun. Now that she was perfectly visible, he gaped and thanked them both. "The two of you came at the proper time. Any later and we never would have lasted the night."

Adwen smiled softly. "You're welcome."

He managed to smile back and then addressed his old friend: "I never thought that I'd ever see you again." Chuckling, he added, "Then again, I never would have expected to find you fighting alongside a Holy Hound."

The term struck Adwen as interesting, and she cocked her head. "Holy Hound?"

Darek watched her smile to herself, contemplating the title.

Oryn found his jacket and boots sitting beside him. Putting them on, he heard other people chattering in corners and through open windows. Getting to his feet and grabbing up the Rose Thorne, he frowned and turned away. "We must be going."

Before Adwen could interject, Darek expressed her opinion.

Putting his one hand on his shoulder to stop him, he said, "Please, don't run, Brother! Please. Stay a while."

Frozen in place, he was surprised to be called Brother once again. Turning to look his good friend in the eye, he had nothing to say.

Adwen spoke for him. "We have a little time to spare."

"Good," he replied, sounding relieved. "Who is this friend of yours, sir?"

He didn't say but looked at her to see if she would keep their bargain.

Taking a breath and speaking so that all could hear, she forced herself to announce, "I am Adwen, the Tame One and heir to the Master Knight."

Everyone was thankful, most were thrilled, and only a few were skeptical. Inviting them into the local tavern, the villagers planned to celebrate their success and Adwen's unexpected arrival. Most everyone wanted the chance to meet the heir before she could depart for another town.

They gave her a seat at the bar counter where everyone could see her face and greet her with gifts she couldn't take or accept. Happy whether she took the things or not, the simple and the wiser of the humans enjoyed her company. Whenever she smiled, it surprised her that they weren't fearful of her fangs.

Meanwhile, Oryn was contented to sit in private beside the window. Feeling the touch of the sun on his face kept him calm as the busy chatter battered his sensitive hearing. Thinking about how he had almost run for a second time upset him, and he continued to brood. Chastising himself further, he was lost in thought.

As he recalled it all, his hand came up without his noticing, scratching behind his head at an imaginary itch.

He had to make himself stand his ground before them, he thought. Sick and tired of feeling so cowardly, he was determined not to let it happen again. After years of being a knight, how could he let himself turn tail so easily? How could he run? He would not let himself be so ...

That's when he noticed his scratching and froze. What was he doing?

Making a fist, he methodically took it away, forcing it to rest on the table. As Darek took a seat across from him, he wondered how he could refrain from animal habits if he couldn't notice them happening.

Darek had witnessed him scratching and noted the ashamed expression he wore. Remembering how his old captain of the Order used to feel toward inhuman creatures, he asked, "Has this new way of living changed your opinion on beasts and magical things, sir?"

Not knowing how to react, he searched him before answering, "Wouldn't it you?"

Chuckling, he stated, "I've been wed to a woman who can make things float and fly about the rooms of my home." When he received a surprised look, he added, "You never knew I was a married man, due to the fact that I knew what would become of it. Most inside the Order are unaware."

"Then what are you looking to say? I am well aware of the tyrant I was. What do you intend to ask of me now?"

This was obviously a changed Oryn he was speaking to. He never used to be so close to humble. It was clear that the new perspective had caused him a world of hurt. "You fought valiantly against those shadows, Brother."

This made him give pause, putting a stopper on his frustration he glanced away.

Shaking his head, he smiled. "I still can hardly believe you've been with the heir for all this time."

"Less than half that. I shamed myself for leaving you all behind."

"Perhaps and perhaps not. But you are here. Not only that, but I see the change in you. Something has killed your hate. Though you've gotten stronger, I see something warm in your look."

Grimacing, he was annoyed that even Darek could notice and directed his attention out the window.

When Oryn seemed even more put out, Darek raised an eyebrow and pondered. Giving the Tame One a glance, he guessed what had changed the general's heart.

She was leaving the crowd of villagers to approach, so he chuckled and told his disgruntled friend, "Well, I shall let you two be alone a while."

Even further aggravated, he seethed and waited for him to go and her to take his place. He was contented to wait, look out at the bubbling fountain through the glass.

Giving a sigh of relief, she said, "It feels like I can breathe again. That was like a circus."

He didn't reply, maintaining his stare to the outside, where some villagers were mourning those who had not survived the attack.

"Well," she said, "that wasn't so bad, was it? Your friend made it pretty easy with the introductions."

Oryn didn't respond right away. Looking off into space, he asked, "What is it that you fear from them? Why would you prefer the people's ignorance to their recognition?"

The question surprised her, and she frowned. "Through most of my first life, aside from a few friends and family, if anyone was paying attention to me it was because they wanted to hurt me somehow. After so many years of it, I sort of, I don't know. Being ignored makes me feel safe. I guess you could say, if you beat a dog enough it'll either flinch or bite. I flinch."

He understood. Then he struggled to keep from scratching as he considered his next words, wondering whether they would expose his feelings. "You should have nothing to fear of recognition. Only more shall come. It is due to you."

Shifting in her seat, she felt uncomfortable at the thought of more people coming up to her with questions, requests and gifts. The gestures were confusing, as she had never known how to receive them. The concept was alien, and his indirect compliment nearly made her blush.

Soon both of them were watching out the window. Of the numerous inhabitants, nearly twenty had died. Adwen was disappointed with herself for not arriving sooner. The sight of the fallen put a knot in her stomach. This could not be allowed to happen in every village. Motivated by the visual incentive, she told her companion, "It's time to go. We can't stay much longer."

Chapter 2
FIGHTING SHADOWS

Darek shared what he knew about other towns. No one had traveled from the west to do trade in their shops since two days before. This, according to him, was very unusual. Not wanting to waste time, Adwen thanked him, and the two were off.

The woods were thick, and using the highway cut down on travel time. Daylight boosted their endurance, and it was near dusk by the time they grew tired. Oryn was healed, but his energy was not completely restored. During their hard push, Adwen made sure to remind him that after inspecting the next village he must hunt. What they had confronted the night before was only a small horde, and they would surely find things much worse ahead.

Catching the first scent of the next village's homes, she slowed, and he did as well. Coming to a stop, she frowned and turned to her friend. "I know that you're not fully recovered, but we don't have time to let you to hunt until after we take a look. Something's telling me that this isn't going to be pretty, so keep your head on straight. I don't need to tell you that night is coming. If there're any demons, they will be stronger in the dark."

"Understood."

"Okay, then. Let's do this." A dark stillness was in the air as they entered Vanguard. More than a year ago, Oryn had been a knight passing through on a quest and had seen busy streets. Everything was quiet. Their ears were pricked, and the loudest thing they heard was their own thoughts.

The town was dead. Shriveled remains of humans cluttered every alley and lay crumpled by doorsteps. Windows hung open like lifeless eyes, letting them both smell the odor from corpses inside. Bodies of men were clutching weapons that had served them poorly, while women were never far from the smallest among the dead.

As they stalked around the deathly town square in search of demons, both were hoping to detect survivors. Darkness had fallen, and only their brilliant eyes were alight amid the shadowy ghost town. After an hour of looking, she became daring and wanted very much to see another living being.

Speaking for the first time, she called out, "Hello! Is anyone there?" There was no answer, and she called again, "If it's not safe for you to speak, do something to tell us that you can hear."

Nothing was the reply.

Oryn sighed and followed a she turned to go elsewhere.

Then they heard glass shatter. It had been somewhere on the other side of the wide-open square. Not foolish enough to bolt for the origin of the sound, she led her companion closer.

To be ready for an ambush, Oryn took the weapon from his back and kept a wary watch for his powerful leader. A few of the shadows seemed too solid to trust, and he kept them in his sights. His own sixth sense was becoming more attuned, and he knew that their progress was being observed by many eyes, both good and bad.

Stopping a few yards short of the tavern, Adwen studied the boarded windows and the entrance. Smells of death were far too overwhelming and covered those of living occupants. Unable to see or smell them, she trusted her sixth sense that there were frightened humans inside.

"You don't need to be afraid," she assured them. "We're here to help. I know the demons are still here, but you're going to have to trust us. It will be much easier for us to protect you if we can see you all."

They detected movement and heard hushed whispers. The scent of fear rose before there was more movement, and a stranger came to the door. A wary man cracked it and peered out. He could see their silhouettes and their eyes. In spite of his fear, he widened the opening to invite them in.

Adwen was calm and composed as she entered with her counterpart diligently watching both of their backs. Only once the door had shut did he stop eyeing the shadows that he was sure had moved.

A candle was revealed, and many sets of eyes blinked at the new arrivals.

Very relieved to see eighteen survivors, she smiled a little.

The daring man who had answered the door came forward and was hopeful. "It's so good that you've come. What is your name, and who has sent you?"

"I am Adwen, the Tame One. I am the heir of the Master Knight."

Three women gasped, and some murmured quietly amongst themselves.

While they stared in awe, she looked to her friend. There was nowhere for him to run.

As he was preparing to announce himself, a few stares made him pause. Quickly, he reminded himself of how ashamed he would feel for being cowardly. The idea gave him the gumption he was searching for and spoke up: "My name is Sir Oryn Conrad, servant to the heir of Darien."

The impact of his declaration was obvious, as their expressions lit up and most smiled back from their shadowy corners. Everyone was overjoyed.

Once the man found his speech, he hurriedly spoke to Adwen: "Tame One, you must be ready. They will be coming for us soon."

"I know. We can take it from here. Help everyone to the middle of the room. Set all of the chairs and tables out of the way. We need all of you to stay close. When they show up it will make it easier to stop them."

He nodded. "Right away, Tame One. We'll get to it."

As he left to have others prepare, she turned to Oryn and smiled.

Stunned by the people's reactions, he was left speechless. She had said what the people would feel at hearing his name, but he hadn't realized what he himself would feel at their reaction. They were so frightened moments before. Now they had a light in their expressions. He had given them hope, and seeing it squelched his fear at last.

Then Oryn heard her whisper, "I told you so."

As they sat and waited by the wall, she explained, "They need human blood to stay in this world. What they've been doing is initially feeding on what they need in a town. Once they consume what they need, they do this: They hem the survivors in and keep them like a food store. We're going to have to kill all of the demons that show themselves before these villagers can escape. Otherwise they will be followed. I need you to take a position on one side of the room while I take the other."

He nodded. "As you command." Striding over to his place, he put his mind in a meditative focus using the breathing ritual.

This was not going to be easy, she thought. If they swarmed the way she was anticipating, it would be impossible to stop them all. She and Oryn would live, but there was so little to be done for the humans.

Glancing back, she spied a small girl among them. Her mother was lending what little food she could offer. When the child looked at Adwen, she felt tears swelling in her eyes. How was she going to save them? Giving up was not an option. Simply letting it happen would be much worse.

Even now she could tell the Creepers were gathering and getting ready to enter through shadows in corners and cubbies of the bar. A small spark of hope was still in her saying that there was a chance.

Getting to her feet, she called to the people: "They're about to attack. All of you must not run. Stay where you are and don't move. Do exactly as I say when I say it. Be ready!"

A few candles had been lit earlier, and the little lights were beginning to flicker. Then they went out, and some of the villagers whimpered. Only Adwen and Oryn could see until she allowed her body to emit a soft glow, revealing most of the space.

Her eyes shifted and searched while she felt the darkness building. It was all around, and her hands became balled fists. There were going to be too many. Loud screeching and wailing from every corner made the humans scream, and the first wave of Creepers spewed out.

Oryn was holding his own while they came, and he slaughtered them like rabbits.

Appearing from all sides, the red-eyed shadow monsters bombarded them. She destroyed two with a single kick, and four more took their place rushing for the humans.

She cried in anger, "No you don't!"

Sliding into their path and using her fists, she bashed their faces in and killed them in time to leap over the people. Even more were attacking from another angle.

The humans recoiled from the demons screaming at the top of their lungs as Oryn began to roar and transform. A full moon had risen outside, and his expanding body shredded the jacket and boots.

Neither of them had time or the ability to restore calm. With so many enemies coming at once, there wasn't a spare moment to say a word.

Suddenly a Creeper got past Oryn as he was still changing. It pounced on a man and was fighting to bite him. As the hound warrior was about to rescue the human, a gaggle of the things pounced on him.

Killing another Creeper, Adwen stole a glance and saw what was happening. Her eyes were wide as saucers, and she clenched her small fangs. A fresh wave of demons were about to spew out, and she cried at the top of her voice, "*No!*"

Then everything changed. Suddenly everyone was safe. The demons were all destroyed, and not one of the humans was harmed. They all were getting up, shouting and cheering their thanks. As they smiled and went to praise her, she shook her head and blinked a few times. What had happened?

Adwen massaged her temple, ignoring the people, and tried to understand why she had had another lapse in her thoughts. All that she could recall was yelling to the people to close their eyes. Then she did something she had never done with her powers before. Forcing balls of light into her hands, she clapped once to smash them together. It created a flash-bang that destroyed more than half of the monsters. Those that were not eradicated were stunned, and Oryn had aided her in finishing them.

He was beside her and knew that she was confused. Her eyes had been solid gold for the duration of the event, and she was hardly remembering anything. It had happened before, and he had made a promise not to tell her what he knew. A being with golden eyes was helping guide her. Whenever there was no time to lose, the being would have no choice but to take control of her body and actions. This would mean that Adwen would have, if at all, a fuzzy recollection of what had transpired.

She glanced up at his hound face, wondering why she couldn't remember. He didn't comment. There was no need. He only gave her an approving look.

The humans were clamoring over her so much that she held up a hand hoping they would give her room. To her astonishment, they all started to step back, quietly listening to what she would say.

Still completely confounded by the victory, she forced herself to let it go. "Everyone, I'm so sorry that we didn't get here sooner. Come with us, and we will take you as far as the western edge of town. All of you must go west as far as you can. Go to Plexus if you are able. There is the safest place in Dargadia."

One man asked, "Why can you not take us there?"

"Because this isn't the first place that has been attacked. We have to keep going east and liberate more survivors in captured towns. The Creeper demons can only follow you as far as their reach extends. They won't be able to track you from here after what I've done."

Realizing what she knew, she paused. How did she know that her power had cut off the edge of the enemy's territory? Swallowing, she refocused and added, "After we leave you, warn everyone that you meet to go west. Let's get moving before they can send more demons and try to feed again."

Before she could open the door, a man came forward to reassure her. "Do not be sorry, Tame One." When she glanced back he added, "We are simply thankful that you came."

The gesture touched her, and the other nods of agreement reinforced his claim. Seeing so many smiles gave her peace. Feeling better, she led them out.

Oryn could detect the strong scent of deer. It had been an hour since letting the humans continue alone, and it was time for his hunt. He was so weak during the battle in the village that even a small band of Creepers had tackled him to the ground. Leaving his sword with Adwen, he prowled along among the trees.

Stopping for a moment to think, he almost started to scratch but forced his claws to brush back his bangs. He kept his human hair and eye color regardless of his shape.

The villagers had been pleased to see him. With the fear of public slander gone from his mind, only one fear remained. The last time he had hunted, he had momentarily gone wild once he had his prey. This was the perfect opportunity to practice controlling his animal instincts, if he could.

Sensing that it wasn't much farther to his prey, he brought his attention back to the present. He would attempt to use his breathing technique for focus. Hopefully it would help.

A buck and four does were in a clearing, munching on grass. As he glimpsed them, he closed his eyes. Keeping calm, he breathed in a set rhythm, meditating until his mind was set on a single goal. The deer were his target. All that he would sense was their sounds and movements; nothing else mattered.

Opening his eyes, he peered around the tree at the small herd.

He locked onto the closest one. Oryn refused to consider the buck or two of the does that were obviously expecting fawns. The nearest doe was strong and perfect for his needs. Crouching low, he crept closer.

None of the five could hear his approach. His self-induced trance held as he crept along. He judged that his speed was greater than that of the deer he was stalking. It was as good as his. Without realizing, he gradually went onto all fours.

Without warning, the wind turned on him.

The deer's heads and ears snapped up at the scent to look around, and in the blink of an eye they were bounding away.

All of his focus remained on his chosen target. She ducked and weaved between the underbrush, but he gained on her. Very rapidly, he closed the gap. Leaping through the air, he pounced and listened to her scream.

His trance was still maintained as he held the doe, kicking and crying out. Totally focused, he held her tight. His fangs closed around her neck, first locking down, and then making her go quiet very suddenly.

Breathing in the exact rhythm, he was mauling her and ripping at the skin over her haunch. He was just swallowing the first bite by the time he realized what was happening.

Horrified, he gasped and froze. Standing upright, Oryn reeled backed from the bloody kill until he collided with a sturdy tree. Gazing with wide eyes at the dead doe, he couldn't believe that he had failed again. His breathing ritual for focus was not aiding him at all in controlling his animal side. Snarling, he cursed himself for not realizing beforehand. Going into that focus allows instinct to take over. His ears flattened, and he growled, grasping his head in his claws. "What am I to do?"

There was nothing to do about it, he told himself. Going back to the body, he still had to consume it. And again, he felt the animal inside want to lunge for the flesh.

Refraining, he attempted to reassure himself with a positive thought. At least, as a Holy Hound, he did not need human flesh to survive. Feeling contented with his lot for the moment, eating his fill was a little less upsetting.

Afterward, as he was walking back, a storm rolled in to blot out the sky, filling the air with flashes and rumbling. Without shoes on his feet, he had to endure stepping across pointed sticks and stray rocks. Adwen soon came into view, and the rain began to fall. She was waiting with a small donation from the people.

His dragon-skin trousers were handling his changes well, but he happily accepted the secondhand jacket and boots. They fit comfortably, and he set the Rose Thorne across his back again. Heaving a disappointed sigh, he turned to go.

"Wait," she said. "Are you doing okay?"

Not willing to tell her the embarrassing truth, he grimaced. "Well enough to leave this place. Why do I concern you now?"

"There's a lot of blood all over your face." Seeing him attempt to hide his alarmed expression, she knew something was wrong and watched as he cleaned most of the mess away with a wet sleeve. Wanting very much to make things easier, she gently reminded, "Whenever you're ready to talk I'll listen."

Determined not to make eye contact, he gazed out into the wood. Her kindness was both soothing and agonizing. At once he felt the powerful need to turn and hold her close. Keeping those emotions well hidden, he appreciated the offer and confidently replied, "I am prepared for travel. Lead on."

"Then let's go."

Rain was coming down in sheets when they left the tree line for the wide open plains. Headed for their next destination, the wind and rain were at their backs for a change. Racing across the rolling terrain with the weather pushing them forward would have otherwise excited them if it weren't for the recent events.

Both were lost in their thoughts of personal struggles. Soaking wet and driven to seek out the enemy, Adwen and Oryn continued toward the eastern horizon.

She was in her hound form, bounding alongside. Forcing herself to forget her problems, she looked to her friend. Why was he so shaken? It was most definitely not the battle, so what was it?

When she was about to bark out a question, her eyes caught a glimpse of something farther out. There were ten riders fleeing for their lives. All around were demons, lunging from atop wicked mounts that resembled living horses.

Barking loudly, she got Oryn's attention. "Look over there!"

He did and was surprised. He sneered, eyes glowing brightly.

Catching up with the death race was not difficult. The horses were exhausted and on the brink of collapse.

A devilish rider reined his sinister mount into bumping an opponent, making the horse whinny and nearly stumble. The Demon Knight laughed, and it sounded like a series of guttural croaks.

When it drew a dark sword and was about to cut down a human, Adwen pounced.

The evil rider and creature cried out as she came down and roared, slashing and biting until they vanished into nothing. Leaping off before she could be left behind, she locked eyes with a human and saw for the first time that they were knights.

Oryn had come to the realization as well, running between the horses until he was beside the leader. Just as the head of the formation noticed him, Adwen transformed and jumped up to join him on the horse.

He was about to draw his weapon but heard her say, "I'm here to help!" Pointing at her companion, she instructed, "Follow him. He will lead you through a narrow rock formation and a set of ruins. Trust him and don't look back."

When he finally nodded she leaped up high, transformed and landed on a run behind the group of weary knights. Two Demon Knights were there, and she snarled.

Both laughed, and one summoned a jagged spear to take care of her.

Snarling even louder, she barked before sinking her jaws into one of its mount's forelegs. The evil thing cried out as she destroyed the limb and it crashed.

Adwen heard a loud snap, and a pitch black arrow narrowly missed her head.

She looked back as the other demon prepared to fire another.

Barking angrily, she avoided a second arrow, pulling away to rejoin the living riders.

Oryn was taking them through the pass and shutting down the enemy's ability to attack from the side. With the Demon Knights on their heels, he led the company between many high jutting rocks.

Six of the dark riders were still in pursuit and contending with a very angry Adwen as one had grazed her shoulder with an arrow. Her gaze burned brightly as she avoided another, leaping up high to race along a lofty tier.

All of them summoned bows to shoot her down and quickly honed their aim.

Barking and gnashing her jaws, she suddenly spotted a large section of rock that appeared loose. Amused, she picked up the pace.

The demons watched her pull away. As she was leaping across the pass, they tried to strike her out of the sky. Their arrows clipped her body but didn't stop her from reaching the other side.

No sooner did she touch down than the rocks gave way. Leaping back to the ground, she barked excitedly as the rockslide made the monsters bellow. They were not destroyed, but they could no longer follow. With the pursuers blocked, she caught up with knights and Oryn.

He heard her bark beside him, "I couldn't kill them all, but they're gone for now."

Slightly winded, he replied, "We're still being followed. Something is in the sky." Then he heard her yelp and looked in time to see her being lifted high up into the darkness.

A massive and powerful flying demon, a Dred, had her in its talons, screeching as it took her higher. Both wings effortlessly took her into the storm.

Caught by surprise, she fought back ferociously, desperate to make it let go.

Irritated by her struggle, it hovered beneath the flashing lightning, arching its long, serpentine neck to bite her with tusk-like teeth.

Not sure what else to do, its bulky jaws were about to snap down when Adwen formed light in her claws and smashed them together.

The resulting explosion blinded and stung the Dred, and it dropped her, shrieking.

Falling through the chaotic winds, she tucked at the last second, rolling hard and fast down the back side of a hill. Once she came to a stop and shook off the dizziness, she started running, hoping the thing wouldn't try to snatch her again.

The knights were not far, and she joined them as they were just leaving the narrow pass. Pulling up alongside her friend once more, she growled, "There'd better be only one of those!"

"The things won't be chasing much longer," he replied.

All of them saw a hazy glow coming from the east. With the storm just beginning to subside, dawn helped brush back the night. They heard no more evil screaming and felt no dark presence while they continued. Within the hour the rain had gone and the sun was ascending, driving out the shadows for a time.

Finally coming to a stop, the company watched Adwen turn to face them, shifting into her woman shape. Their leader removed his helm and announced, "I am Sergeant Gerick Melrose. We are thankful to you, beasts. What are your names?"

Stepping forward, she replied, "My name is Adwen, the Tame One."

Then before she could finish two rode up and took out their swords. "We have heard of you, foul monster! Come have some silver steel for your breakfast!"

Brushing back his hood, Oryn got between her and the sword tips, shouting angrily, "Let her be and show some respect! She has saved your lives, imbeciles!"

They were about to strike when the leader cried out, "Stand down!"

Falling silent, they looked over and saw he was gazing at the green-eyed being.

When Oryn looked up, the Sergeant nearly gasped. Climbing down from his horse he asked, "Don't I know you?"

Recalling many spars with the knight, he stated flatly, "Not if you're as great a fool as your subordinates." Then he glared to show just how he felt about the situation.

Recognizing the look instantly, he called to his knights, "Keep your swords sheathed or I'll have your hands for the dogs. It is Sir Oryn!"

They murmured, and the Sergeant went closer. "Many apologies, sir."

One cried out, "What is Sir Oryn doing running about with a monster?"

Enraged, Oryn bellowed, "She is the heir to the Master Knight!" No one spoke, and he shouted again, "Even if she were not, how dare you turn on the one who has delivered you from death? To the pit with you and your fear-scrambled brains!"

Not about to let him go any further, Adwen cut his rant short. "Take it easy!"

He was obedient and shut his mouth but did not stop seething.

While the sergeant was still gaping at her, she stated, "The Kingdoms of Day are uniting, and we're going to liberate as many towns as we can. We need to know everything that you can tell us."

Clearing his throat, he answered, "Yes, well, the state of things is foul. Most places west of the Broad River are emptied. Many commoners have taken up refuge at Nellore."

Worried, but relieved to hear of more survivors, she asked, "What about on the other side?"

Each of the men either shifted in his saddle or murmured.

"It is lost. Every village has been ransacked, and things far worse than what chased us claim the towns." He pointed to the distance, a dark smoggy haze hung over the woods. "There are so many that darkness remains even in the day."

"Is there any chance of finding survivors?"

"Those who we saw were going for Fort Wight. If any good people still breathe, they would be there. It is no good seeking them out, Tame One. A powerful demon is in control of those shadows. He slew more than half of my men. And what's more, we destroyed the two crossings over the river. The ferries are gone."

Reeling at his news, Adwen thought about her options and replied, "We'll be going there anyway. No matter what, we have to save whoever we can. We would be rescuing innocent people, as well as taking away the enemy's food supply and power. Having a ready supply of human blood gives them strength and a farther reach."

The sergeant was disappointed that she was going but was reassured by her determination. Giving a small smile, he saluted with a fist across his chest. "May the Light Spirits always watch over you, Tame One. And thank you again for your courage."

Adwen nodded and smiled while she walked past.

Oryn was following close behind until the sergeant called, "General?" Frowning, he said, "I am deeply sorry for my men's actions."

He grimaced at the others then stated, "I would have done the same. Keep your pride and be gone. Get to the Order before more trouble finds you."

Walking away, Oryn overheard him reprimanding the two who had advanced on Adwen. They would be punished once they reached the safety of the halls. Oryn was also livid, but what he had said was true; he would have done the same a year ago.

Chapter 3
DISTRACTED

As they continued at a walk, she asked, "What did you say to them?"

The knights were far behind, headed for the safety of the fortress, and Oryn hardly realized that Adwen had asked a question. Once he did, he answered, "Nothing of any importance. I bid them farewell." He hefted the sword strap up higher on his shoulder. It fit him much better in his other form.

Sensing that he didn't wish to press the issue, she fell silent.

Above them was a clear sky, and beneath their feet was mud and wild grass. With such a beautiful view, it was not difficult for Adwen to distract herself from the thought of reaching eastern Dargadia. Finding a way across the river would pose a problem in itself, but knowing that horrible things were waiting made her shiver. Quickly, she looked to the beautiful flowers and green things in order to forget. She would deal with the troubles when the time came.

Then as she was just beginning to feel better, her companion ruined it for her. Frowning, he prompted, "What is your plan once we cross the Broad River?"

Groaning in aggravation, she sounded anxious. "I'm really trying not to think about that right now. It's just going to stress me out, so I'll worry about it later."

His frown became a grimace as he watched her. "There must be a plan."

Sighing heavily, she let her shoulders sag. "I know that."

"Then what do you intend to do?" After spending so many years commanding knights, he was attempting to prepare her. Inevitably, she would be issuing them orders, and they would need constant instruction. His pushing was his way of helping.

Not happy with the focus of the conversation, Adwen gave in a little. "We'll try to cross it at the north-most point, where it is narrow. Then we'll go south and southeast to Fort Wight."

"Shall we investigate other towns along the way?"

Very annoyed, she pressed her black lips together until they formed a thin line. She glared up at him as he gave his inscrutable expression. After a few seconds she was half tempted to look into his heart. It would be an easy way to get back at him for being so stubborn and irritating. Then she knew it would be a cheap shot and decided against the idea.

Looking away and shaking her head, Adwen finally replied, "Yeah, sure. We could do that, but only the ones we pass along the way. There's no point in wasting time stopping if there are survivors waiting at the fort. We can't take too long."

"Very well."

Now that her mind was permanently stuck on concerns, she thought of an odd question. A few moments passed, and she asked, "Have you been sleeping? I mean, have you had any weird dreams lately?"

What she said made him curious and a little concerned. "Not anything out of the ordinary. Why do you ask?"

"The past few times since we got to the Order I've been ... I'm not sure, but I think I might be having visions in my sleep."

Simultaneously, they sensed something dark approaching from behind and looked back, eyeing the last hill.

She growled with snarl-like wrinkles flaring on the ridge of her nose. Then the six Demon Knights came into view, and she changed into her true self.

Oryn was about to take up his sword but heard her barking, "No time! Run!" Off on a sprint, he did what he could to keep up with Adwen, heading for a series of rocky shelves amid the lazy rolling landscape. The demons had timed their attack with the clouds that came from nowhere. Until the sun could come out, they would be on equal footing with their enemies.

She let Oryn catch up, and he was barely keeping the pace. Then he heard her bark as they continued to flee. "Don't stop, and stay on course for the woods. Don't you dare slow down!"

Too busy gasping to answer with words, he gave a nod.

Very angry from the last encounter, the fiends soon gained on them. Their targets were weaving between earthy formations, making a clear shot with arrows impossible. Growing impatient, they bellowed at their shadowy mounts to go faster. Again, they gained and could just make out Oryn with the Rose Thorne on his back.

As they were passing another larger shelf, Adwen pounced on the demon bringing up the rear. She had missed the rider, but buried her fangs into his mount.

It cried out, and she didn't stop mauling until it was dead and turning to plasma. Standing on the dark and purple goop, she snarled and bared her fangs at the rider.

Amused by her ambush, it tilted its head, summoning a cruel whip. Snapping it in the air before her nose, she nearly flinched, and her growls grew louder.

Stalking around the fiend, she gnashed her fangs. When it snapped at her once more, she lunged.

Much quicker than she could anticipate, the whip came back out to wrap around her neck. Chuckling horribly, the demon used his dark leash to slam her into a boulder.

She yelped, but was unfazed. Rebounding as swiftly as possible, she raced back to try again.

When she came in closer the demon pulled out a jagged sword. Then as she leaped it prepared to gut her.

They collided, and she yelped and snarled. Both went tumbling through the turf until she was on top. Lifting her jaws from the monster's face, she panted and stood, pulling the evil weapon from her arm. It burned terribly in her flesh and equally as bad in her grip. Howling and yelping, she took it out and threw it away.

Gripping her weeping wound, she saw the last five returning. Wrinkling her muzzle into a hard snarl, she stared them down, biding her time for the proper moment. She would wound one or all of the mounts and head for the woods. Like most demons, they had strict rules to abide by while in the living worlds. Their territory was the plains. Reaching the safety of the trees was all she needed to escape.

They were nearly upon her. Oryn jumped down from a rock, landing before her. He swung his long blade back and bellowed, lunging for the demons.

They were forced to leap over, narrowly avoiding the lethal swing.

She and Oryn stood back to back. He glared and she growled at the demons, daring them to make a second pass. All five circled and brandished evil weapons, though none made a move. As one was contemplating an attack, it looked to the sky.

They all hissed or cursed in their harsh language, shielding their faces from the sun. It shone brightly, and the demons were weakened.

Four turned to ride away, and one pointed a sword at her, speaking with a sharp and warning tone.

Only she understood and barked back, "And I'll be ready for you!"

Disappearing beyond the folds of the earth, they didn't dare fight her while the sun was out, weakening them and healing Adwen.

Changing into her woman shape, she faced Oryn as he was putting his weapon away. Shaking her head and giving a disappointed expression, she warned, "Don't do that again. I was going to cut their legs out from under them. You were supposed to be waiting for me in the forest."

If anyone could decipher his expression, they would have needed telepathy to aid them as his face was devoid of emotion. Hiding his feelings and thoughts well, he replied, "You were outnumbered when they left me to turn back. I heard you cry out and considered the chance that you needed aid. No one can afford you to be slain."

Heaving a sigh, she rolled her eyes and accepted the excuse. "Fine. But next time don't turn back unless I actually call for you." Then she decided to make sure he would obey and added, "And that's an order."

"As you command."

Throughout the day, they ran, jumped and hiked toward the river. Once they found the waterfront, they would follow it north, simply because it was safer. The power of demons is weakened by strong flowing waters. An ambush would not be likely so close to the powerful current.

With night falling upon them, it was time to stop for rest. She announced to her companion, "We'll sleep in two shifts. Which would you rather have?"

"I shall take the first. Moonrise would wake me."

For a while Adwen was silent and thinking to herself. Then she sounded forlorn. "Everything's been so crazy that I never got the chance to talk to you about it. I'm so sorry for what happened. I don't even know really how it happened, but I didn't mean to mark you."

Not responding, he settled down beneath a tree.

His silence worried her, and she bit her lip.

At last he stated without looking back, "There is no need to apologize. You intended to save me from falling to my doom. There is no reason for you to regret." Adwen was unaware that Oryn had already been through this conversation. He had already forgiven her, in a manner. Wanting to wait for the moon, he went about removing his boots and jacket.

Thankful for his forgiveness, she still felt remorseful and offered, "I can keep you from feeling the pain if you want."

Recalling the last time she did put a bitter taste in his mouth. She had been wounded at the time and nearly killed herself as a result. Keeping him from feeling the pain of the transformation would mean her taking it upon herself. Shaking his head, he turned her down.

"There is no need for that, either. You endured it alone, and I shall do the same. Do not pity me." Then he looked at her, trying his best to be obscure. "You know very well how I deserve this."

"No, you don't; not anymore."

His heart skipped a beat as she said it, and he scowled, boring his eyes into her. He could not disagree more and glowered. "You are far too forgiving."

Taking up a resting spot nearby, she was becoming annoyed by his stubborn nature. "When are you going to let that go? Yeah, I think you messed up a couple of times. But that life you had is over and done with." Frowning, she urged him, "Let it go. If you were supposed to get more punishment, I would have let the high elder have you, so knock it off. Stop acting like a beaten dog."

Abashed and insulted, his eyes glowed brightly in anger. Holding his tongue, he chose to help end the pointless discussion. They obviously weren't coming to an agreement anytime soon. Seeing her turn away for sleep, he scowled at her back.

His howls never woke her when he eventually changed. Undisturbed, her mind was absorbed in a deep and powerful sleep.

Breathing heavily, Oryn relaxed, settling back for more rest and to continue the watch. Taking a second to look at her, he wondered how she could forgive him so easily.

Casting the thought aside, Oryn lifted his jaws to the sky. There were so many stars out that the dark heavens looked like a blanket sewn with diamonds and ebony. Taking a deep breath through his nose, he smelled all of the forest about them. Scents from the river were in the air, as the waterside was less than a mile away. They would cross it tomorrow.

He wondered what kind of horrors they would find. Surely, there were worse things awaiting them. How could he best prepare himself? As he was about to rethink his prior battles with Creepers and Wretches, Adwen cried out in her sleep.

Sitting bolt upright, she screamed, "*No!*" Panting and sweating, she held a hand to her mouth. Eyes wide, tears were rolling down her face.

Startled and alarmed, Oryn waited a moment before growling, "What has happened?"

Unable to reply, she cupped both hands over her mouth. The look of horror didn't leave her, and she gasped again, struggling to hold back a sob.

"Adwen?"

He forgot all of his anger the instant she locked eyes with him. Those violet eyes made his heart melt, and he fought to keep from seeming too soft. Patiently, he listened as she gathered the will to speak.

Breaking eye contact, her eyes became even wider as she realized something and whispered, "I messed it up!" Gasping again, she swallowed a sob and murmured, "I messed up so bad!"

Not wanting to press her too hard, he waited for her to explain.

Gulping, she breathed a little easier and asked, "Remember how I said I thought I was having visions?"

"Yes."

Getting a grip, she went on, "They were about this woman. It wasn't fantastic or anything. I'd just see her doing things like cleaning the kitchen or walking down the street. It was a blond woman from my world." She shook her head. "I hope I don't have any more visions about her."

"Why?"

Her gaze drifted even lower. "Because ... I saw her die."

Shocked, he didn't have a response for the statement.

"I was supposed to find her before it was too late," she explained through a building sob. "I was so distracted that I didn't understand until it was too late."

All he wanted to do was console her. Keeping emotion out of his sounds, he growled, "It is but one life. One has died while you were fighting to save many more. The one is a small price and of little importance."

"No." Locking eyes with him yet again, she gasped, "She was very important. I can feel it. I was supposed to find her."

The news was not what he had expected. Rethinking his approach of comforting her without showing too much feeling, Oryn replied, "Then let it go."

She shot him an angry glance.

He knew he was being somewhat hypocritical, but wanted her to not be so harsh with herself. "The mistake was a miscalculation. Learn, so that it shall not be repeated. It was nothing that you intended to allow."

Seeing his point, she stopped glaring and realized he was right. Still shaken, she shuddered. There had been so much blood. A thick blade was used. The woman hadn't even had the chance to scream or make a sound. A mental image of her vacant stare made Adwen sick to her stomach. Now that it was almost impossible to return to sleep, she started her watch early.

Chapter 4
ASCENDANCE

Up above them hung the sun, while at their feet lay the water's edge, splashing on the shore. Out over the distant bank was a thick dark mist. Like a cloud of permanent night, it had settled over the forest. Adwen frowned, knowing that hordes of demons were the cause. Their presence was so strong that they corrupted the magic in the air, blacking out everything.

Hiking north, she kept an eye on the other side. In spite of the dread, she wanted to reach that place as quickly as possible. She was desperate to free any survivors they could find. Then she wondered if there would be any by the time they got there.

Oryn was silently thinking over how to properly combat the demons they had faced. The Creepers were simple enough to deal with, but a single Wretch was more than a handful. As he was trying to come up with a plan for confronting more, he began to scratch the back of his head.

Quickly realizing what he was doing, he balled the hand into a fist, taking it away. Clenching his teeth, glaring at the unruly arm, he couldn't understand why he was losing control of his habits. Then he wondered if she had noticed and glanced at her furtively.

She had stopped walking a moment before and was a ways behind. Going to join her, he heard her ask, "Do you think we could try swimming there?"

After studying the water, he shook his head. "The current is too strong, and the distance is too far."

Groaning, she complained, "It would be really nice to just go straight across. Going north to get to the other side is going to take way too long."

He was going to tell her to be patient, but they both heard something that sounded like leaves rustling.

Adwen was quite sure someone had spoken in a strange language. Eyeing the bushes, she called, "Is somebody there?"

The odd leafy sound came again, and Oryn watched her squint at the greenery. "I'm sorry. I couldn't hear you very well. What did you say?"

A young face peered from around the closest tree, watching apprehensively.

Oryn almost reached for his weapon, but stopped when he realized what it was.

Adwen called to the tree nymph, "Don't worry. He won't hurt you."

The dryad's brown face flowed with the same colors as its hiding place. Then as it smiled, the dark hues turned to a leafy green. Stepping out into the light, the nature spirit spoke again.

Only Adwen understood and replied, "Really? That's awesome! What do we do?"

Try as he might, Oryn couldn't make sense of the tree being's language.

Growing even more excited, Adwen turned to him and explained, "We can go across right now! All we have to do is ask permission!"

Wondering if she had suddenly gone mad, he studied her. "Ask the river permission to cross?"

Rolling her eyes and shrugging, she chuckled. "Well, not really. I have to call up the sirens and ask them if we can." Turning back to the helpful dryad, she smiled. "Thank you so much. Take care!"

Its giggle sounded like the rustling of a leafy branch, as it jumped back into the old sycamore. It vanished into the solid bark as if it were water.

After laughing at Oryn's surprised expression, she went to the river.

Crouching low, she leaned down to dip her fingertip into the surface. Then she swished it around in a series of sloshing and splashing motions.

Going to her side, he asked, "What are you doing?"

"The sounds I'm making are their language. If this is what they hear, they're more likely to come up and talk. It's like knocking on a front door."

"But you do know what you are saying?"

"Yeah, I can understand them."

She took her hand from the water and waited. Seconds passed, and she folded her arms, eyeing the surface.

Then the water rippled as three watery women came up to meet her. Their bodies were semitransparent like the river and decorated with shells and reeds. Two studied them critically while the third spoke in a burbling tone.

"Hi, and thank you for coming," Adwen replied. "We need to get across, and I was hoping you could help out. As you can see, there's trouble over there."

As she pointed to the darkness over the woods, they looked, and the one spoke again, cocking her head.

"I know how you feel about the humans, but if they die then you would be next." She sighed and assured them, "We can stop the demons. Please, help us. We need to get to the other side."

The three drifted farther away to convene in private, giving occasional glances.

Adwen was patient and sure that they would help, but Oryn was irritated. Sirens always had been known for allowing innocent humans to die because of their differences. They were a fickle lot.

Returning to speak again, they played with their adornments as their leader spoke. Her expression was sly and calculating.

Groaning to herself, Adwen rolled her eyes. "I can try."

Being dismissive, the spirit bubbled.

"Fine! I'll do it, but I don't know how long it'll take to get. You'll just have to wait."

Appeased, the spirit smiled, and another came to present a drift log.

Sighing she waded into the water, and Oryn asked as he followed, "What was the bargain?"

"Nothing."

"You promised them something. What was it?"

Rolling her eyes, she answered, "They all want red lilies for their hair."

She had worried him for nothing, and he grimaced. The way she had acted made him think it was a bargain for a life. "How is that a problem? They are fairly common in Dargadia if you know where to search."

She shushed him and whispered, "Don't let them know that! They might want me to get more! They asked for ten of them! I'm not going to waste my time being their personal errand girl!"

Clearing his throat, he looked away and tried not to scoff.

The spirits bid their watery farewells, and she warned him, "You might want to hold on a little tighter."

Just as he grasped onto the sides, the river began to swell. Beneath them the water bulged up high until they were nearly sixty feet over level ground. An excited grin split her face, and Oryn gasped as they were suddenly launched forward.

The wind whipped through their hair, and she laughed and whooped. To her it was no different than riding a rollercoaster. Lacking any such experience, Oryn clenched his teeth and held on for dear life. Travelling by means of a giant wave was not what he had been expecting.

In a matter of minutes they were making their final approach, and the wave began to roll, crest and then crash onto itself. Gently, they were brought to the edge of dry land, and the water put them on their feet in the shallows. Completely silent and shocked by what had happened, Oryn clung to the log.

When he looked over at his leader, she was watching his face. First she smiled and then burst out laughing at his alarmed expression. Leaving the log, she laughed all of the way to shore. "If only Toth could have been here to do that. His face plus yours would have been a riot! Now he's going to miss out on all the fun."

"Guarding and advising King Lorvan is a lofty task. It is good he is not here. He may have grown powerful, but these demons would be too much for him." Then he thought of how horrified the half elf would have been to ride the wave. He surely would have had an odd facial expression.

Leaving the river behind, they entered the dark fog.

After fifteen yards most detail was hard to make out. Their nocturnal vision allowed them to see in the thick darkness, but not as well as in true nighttime. Enveloped by the black, the woods already were showing signs of decay. With no sun shining through, grass was wilting and flowers were limp and dying.

The trees were vacant of animal life. No birds sang. No insects flew. The wildlife had evacuated the area completely. Adwen ducked below a branch, and Oryn stayed close, watching out for any threats to his commander.

Then she abruptly halted and sniffed.

He came alongside and followed suit. A rank odor was in the air. He had smelled it before but couldn't place the scent.

"You smell that?" she asked with a dark tone.

"What is it?"

"Demons. Lots of them. It smells like burning tires." Then she growled. "It stinks." Taking another sample of the air, she started off in a different direction, following the smell of death.

When they had gone farther, she whispered, "Where do you think we are?"

Pondering for a moment, he eventually concluded, "I believe we are approaching Gulden, the north-most town beside the river."

"Well, then we better be ready."

"What do you propose?"

"At first we go in together. Then if we have to, and all is clear, we'll split up."

He was certain that all would not be clear. "As you command."

"Okay, let's go."

Upon reaching the outer wall, she discovered on her own that Gulden was surrounded by high timbers. Skirting the barrier, they found the wide-open gate. Inside was quiet like the forest, and the darkness was lifted enough to see farther out. The streets were empty. Nothing moved, and every window was as black as the shrouded sky. When no demons made themselves visible, they entered.

Very warily, the two moved toward the plaza and still detected no impending danger. Not only were there no signs of life, there also were no bodies in sight. Coming to a halt in the heart of town, Adwen and Oryn studied the empty surroundings. Where were the dead?

"All right," she whispered. "I can't tell if there's anything alive. We have to split up."

He didn't stop scanning for danger and responded, "Agreed."

"If there's any trouble you can't handle, call. They could be anywhere. I don't think they know we're here just yet. If they attack, head for the temple over there." She gestured to halfway across the large town. "Either way, we meet there after searching each half of the town. Good luck."

Parting ways, Adwen went left, and he went the opposite way.

Weaving along the narrow alleys, she sniffed and searched for anyone who might be hiding and waiting to be found. Good or bad, she planned to find them and take care of them, whatever way was appropriate.

Soon Adwen found herself following the scent of rot. It piqued her curiosity, and she sniffed again. Moving very cautiously, she quickened her pace with the rise of the odor.

Encountering no demons on the way, she came across a large tavern. The scent grew even more intense, and she checked both ends of the street before crossing. Going to the closed door, she knocked lightly and waited.

There was no reply. Looking over her shoulders for enemies, she gave the door a solemn look and bit her lip. Gut instinct told her what awaited and made her feel sick at the thought. Ignoring the feeling, she gripped the handle and eased the door open.

When it was fully open her eyes watered and she stepped back.

With some difficulty, she gathered the will to tear her gaze from the sight. She had found the last of the townspeople. There was little point in checking for survivors among them. Gasping at the stink and the horror, Adwen held her tears at bay and moved on.

At almost every corner Oryn stopped to observe his surroundings. The stench of demons was getting thicker, but he pressed forward and constantly stayed aware. Reaching another street through an alley, he paused and sniffed, peering down both directions. The street appeared perfectly clear.

Then as he approached the other side, the stink intensified.

Sensing movement to the right, he darted for the next corner. He waited a moment in his new hiding place before furtively checking to see if it was Adwen.

It was obviously not. A Wretch had come out from another alley and was sniffing through its short snout. Ducking back, he was sure it could detect him. Then he heard the eight-foot monstrosity stepping closer and backed away behind a high stack of crates. Hidden even better, he waited and listened to its movements.

It was closing in on his alley, and he took the sword from his back. Getting ready for a battle, he waited, eyeing the corner of the wooden boxes. A few seconds passed, and his sixth sense helped him to feel eyes watching his back. Nothing was moving to attack, and he glanced through a broken window, half expecting a Creeper. His eyes widened as he saw a young boy hiding behind overturned furniture, gazing out at him. For a long moment they stared at each other in surprise and confusion. The window was much too small to climb through.

The Wretch passed by Oryn's hiding place, and he carefully stole a look. All he saw was the long amphibious tail, gradually disappearing as it stalked along. Relieved and seeing his opportunity, Oryn crept to the side of the street, keeping the sword low behind him. Once more, he peered out to see that the demon wasn't looking, and he darted inside the small home.

Instantly he saw the overturned furniture and quietly moved to find the child. Crouched down low, he came around the obstructions, and the boy was frightened by the sight of his glowing eyes in the dark. When the boy recoiled from Oryn's reach, Oryn whispered, "Be calm. It is all right."

Then they both froze at the sound of a loud hiss.

Realizing that the demon was returning, he gestured to be silent. Backing away, he hid himself behind a tall cabinet.

He heard it sniffing as it entered and slowly stepped closer. Heavy footfalls became louder, and it sniffed again. Then it noticed the boy, hissed louder and caused the child to scream.

Swiftly, Oryn drove the Rose Thorne into the demon's back. It wailed when he gave the blade a twist before cutting it down completely. The fiend was turning to a puddle of goo, and Oryn reached out for the boy again. This time the child jumped into his arms.

Leaving the house, he checked for danger and was about to ask the child's name. The words were quickly swallowed as there was another hiss. Giving a start, they gaped up at the Wretch crouching on the rooftop, watching intently.

It cocked its horned head and wailed. The call was repeated everywhere as others were alerted to their presence.

A sudden jolt of adrenalin surged through the warrior as he set the sword across his back and ran. With the boy in his arms, he darted around tight corners, and the monsters followed across the rooftops. Even more demons were alerted by the commotion and joined in the pursuit, howling and screeching.

The temple was not far, and Oryn had managed to pull away from the horde, but as he rounded a corner they came to a halt. More evil beings were heading them off. Oryn glanced behind him, and the pursuers were closing them in. Then he looked up at the temple roof ledge. It was forty feet high, and he was about to jump to the next closest building, but it was covered in demons. Giving the temple ledge another judging glance, he clenched his jaw. He couldn't jump that high, not as he was.

Glaring at the rushing swarms, Oryn warned the boy, "Hold on to me! Hold on and don't let go!"

As he did, Oryn reached inside to find his other self. Reaching into his mind, he tried to find the way. When the powerful enemies were nearly on them, he bellowed, and it soon became a resounding roar. The boy gasped and whimpered as Oryn's neck suddenly became thick and covered in fur. His height shot up, his roar ended, and he leaped, leaving the monsters behind on the ground.

Air whistled by his long hound ears, and he reached for the edge of the stone shingles. He nearly came up high enough to clear it, but his chest caught on the brink. The sudden stop made the boy lose his grip, and he scrambled to get away.

Oryn's claws screamed across the stone tablets as he slid and started to fall. Snarling, he desperately held on and skidded to a stop until his arms and jaws were all that kept him from dropping. He could hear the demons calling at him and knew they would soon climb. The ledge reached out too far from the building to kick himself up the rest of the way.

To his great surprise, the boy brushed aside his fear and reached to help him. Moving close enough to grasp his head, he pulled.

Not wanting to let the child fall with him, he was careful in continuing. Finding a little traction, he made another attempt to climb. In a few moments his chest was over the ledge, and then his whole torso. After crawling up the rest of the way, he gave the child a thankful look. He smiled in return and let Oryn take him into his arms.

The temple bell tower was close by, and he moved closer to peer down inside. It was a long way to the bottom. Hearing the monsters coming after them, he held the boy close and grabbed hold of the strong rope. Leaping into the dark, his weight caused the bell to toll throughout the descent.

Loud ringing fell with them, and he landed easily inside the silent temple. The boy didn't let go as Oryn growled and prowled along the corridor, following the scent of death. Reaching the temple hall, they found dozens of bodies strewn over the floor. Shielding the child from the sight, he huffed in disappointment.

Glass suddenly broke in a nearby room, and he took up the Rose Thorne, anticipating more demons. He waited and was relieved to see Adwen.

Seeing him as his hound self, she was shocked and then smiled, putting a hand on her hip. "Well, what do you know?"

She didn't take notice that Oryn's tail was swinging back and forth contentedly. Very glad to see her, he let her take the boy.

Smiling, she asked, "Where did you find him?"

Gesturing with his jaws, he said, "Hiding in a demolished home."

Adwen smiled to the child, and the expression abruptly turned into a frown as she sensed the monsters that were about to attack. Going to a large decorative urn, she let him inside it and covered the top saying, "Stay quiet, and we'll get you out once it's over."

He didn't object and silently nodded as she closed him in.

Going to her companion's side, she chuckled. "I was wondering when you would figure out how to change."

Hearing more glass breaking, he replied, "I haven't any idea how I managed."

Both Adwen's eyes flashed with golden color, and she chuckled. "You passed your test. Part of the test was to want the change to happen. As for everything else, I'll explain after we clean up." Grinning broadly, she stood in wait for the enemies.

Flattening his ears back, Oryn's tail swung in a playful manner, and he gripped the Greatsword, relishing the moment. The only thing he enjoyed more than battle was battling alongside her. When the first Wretch burst into the open, he roared excitedly, "Come at me!"

His challenge was answered by that one and many more from out of the dark. They came in fast, and Adwen created another flash bang. Blinded and stunned, the large monsters were easily dealt with. In the first few minutes, most of them were cut down.

Adwen transformed and slashed them to ribbons of purple slop with her claws. As much as their attacks stung her and Oryn, her hands gave out even more devastating blows. Biting and clawing while he swung and slashed, they tore down their numbers with little effort. The Wretches howled and screamed in anguish, being destroyed one by one and turned into sickly puddles on the floor.

When the last of them was liquefied, the darkness began to lift. After all of the fiends were gone, sunlight began to stream through the shattered sills and stained glass. Feeling triumphant, they looked to each other.

Adwen started to smile and then laughed out loud.

He marveled at her and listened as the joyous sounds echoed around him. With the demons in Gulden banished, the Dargadian town was liberated.

Strolling along the road through the forest, Adwen spoke with the boy in her arms. "So, Garret, where did you last see your family?"

To Oryn's surprise, the answer was not as anticipated. "I saw them cross the river. I couldn't go with them."

"Why not?"

The more Oryn listened in on the conversation, the more he felt something about the boy was odd. His big ears flattened as he wondered what he was missing.

"I don't know. I was stuck here."

She smiled and told him, "Then we're just going to have to help you find them."

Approaching the river where the burned remains of the docks sat, she swished her toes in the water and waited.

The sirens surfaced, glaring.

Adwen cleared her throat and greeted them: "Hi again." Her smile did nothing to sway their composure. "I'm sorry, but we got caught up in something. We need to go back to the other side one more time."

The leader of the spirits ranted, and it sounded like a roiling current.

"I know I promised, and I do promise to find the lilies. Just give me a chance to do my job, too."

Even though the watery beings were put out, they brought the drift log forward.

Adwen turned to her friend and asked, "So are you going to change back or do you want to visit town like this?"

The prospect alarmed him. "I ... how is it done?"

Shaking her head and rolling her eyes, she chuckled, "It's easy. Just will it. That's how you changed the first time, wasn't it?"

To him the concept sounded too simple. Taking a breath, he focused on what he wanted. Right away, his form shrank as the fur and claws smoothly disappeared. Once his jaws recoiled into his more human face, he was thoughtful and asked, "Has the ability to control the change always been as simple as wanting it?" If he could have ended the nights of pain this easily, he would have made an attempt much sooner.

Her eyes flashed gold, and she replied, "No, not really. You had to pass a test. That's the catch. Anyhow, let's go." Helping the boy onto her back, she smiled. "Get ready to hold on!"

Clinging to the log once more, they waited and watched the river swell. All of them held on tight as the wave launched them forward. The young boy cried out, and Adwen squealed with delight.

Oryn clenched his teeth and closed his eyes to wait out the ride. He enjoyed hearing her laugh but had a great dislike of being thrown. Wind whipping through his hair pleased him enough to tolerate the odd experience, and only once he felt their sloping descent and heard the wave breaking, did he open his eyes.

Their bare feet found solid ground in the shallows, and Adwen started straight for the shore. Chuckling, she asked, "Was that fun or what, Garret?"

The boy giggled in agreement. She was still walking away and didn't notice her companion behind her, staggering.

Oryn's vision was swimming, and his other senses were erratic. Leaving the log, he swayed and stumbled, trying to follow. As he left the water's edge his whole body felt like it was flowing. A surging energy was coursing through him. Unable to stand or focus, he was alarmed and dropped to his knees. Nearly falling onto his face, he caught himself in time. Panting and alarmed, he called out, "Adwen?"

Looking back, she saw his eyes glowing solid green. Setting the boy down, she was more curious than worried. Knowing what was happening, she wondered how it would end. Standing quietly, Adwen observed his new changes.

At last, his senses became clearer and sharper than ever before. The energy settled within, and he took a breath. Everything was intense, and he thought for a moment that he could be in his hound form. Looking down at his hands, he found that he was not but also found a set of dark gloves. His eyes dilated, and his sight allowed him to count the grains of sand amid the dirt and dust.

Flexing his body and standing, he felt as strong as when in his hound form. Looking himself over, he was wearing a set of dark garments with deep green markings.

The Rose Thorne had vanished, and as he was searching for it, Adwen came closer. "You can summon or dismiss the sword whenever you want now."

As his feral eyes locked onto her face, he gave an unintentional growl of confusion. "What has happened?"

Standing before him and studying his enchanted garments, she replied with a shrug, "It's like I said: you passed your test. Let's keep going."

Before she could turn away, his hands snatched her by the shoulders, and he snarled and snapped in alarm, "What's happened to me?"

At first she was surprised but quickly expressed her disapproval.

Getting a grip on himself, he forced his hands to release.

Gazing sternly into his alarmed look, she explained, "You passed your test and the Light Spirits have granted you power. What you felt was magic, transforming every last sinew of your being. Your body harbors light. You don't have as much as I do, but it is in you now. The last part of you that was human is gone."

Horrified, he couldn't find the will to breathe.

"Congratulations. Welcome to becoming a Holy Hound."

Disturbed, he felt unsteady. His eyes fell to the ground and he let the truth set in. All of his human side was gone? The thought made him ill.

Seeing his reaction made her feel a twinge of guilt.

Realizing Adwen was coming closer, he looked up at her sympathetic face. She was reaching up with both hands toward him. Frozen and wondering what she intended to do, Oryn held his breath again, hoping she might kiss him.

Reaching for his bangs, she combed them out of his face. Studying his enhanced features, she admired his strong jaw, seeing how much more powerful his cheek bones appeared. His bite could snap bones, by her estimate. Brushing back at his hairline, she reached a little farther and touched his ears. Her fingers felt around them, soothing his internal fears. Just as he was feeling calm, she felt further up to their elf-like points.

Feeling the new shape snapped him out of it, and he was surprised. Pulling away and feeling them, he heard her giggle at his reaction.

Smiling and doing her best not to burst out laughing, she smiled. "It's going to be okay. You can put up that hood if you like."

She left him to pick up the child as he noticed the longer fangs in his mouth and touched them with his fingers. Still very disturbed, he attempted to be calm, donned his new hood and rushed to catch up.

Approaching the buildings of the town made Oryn wary. His eyes constantly shifted as he sniffed, attempting to detect any threats. Another growl escaped him, and he muttered, "Enemies are watching."

"They can't hurt us. Just calm down and relax. Your senses are going to feel overwhelming for a while until you adjust. For now, take it easy. They're only people. They're scared of us."

He was not calmed and continued to glare at closed windows overlooking the street. This riverside town was very quiet, and his instincts told him there were no demons. Many humans were hiding, and some were contemplating an attack. He knew it and growled quietly to himself.

Going farther inland, they came across a cemetery. Oryn was hardly paying attention as Adwen started through, wandering between the old and the new additions to the plot of ancient ground. Only when the little boy spoke did he realize where they were. "There they are!" he cried out excitedly.

Adwen let him down to meet a man and woman standing not far away. His mother held him close, and Oryn locked eyes with the proud father. Instinctively, he sniffed to pick up his scent. At last he understood why the boy seemed so strange. The three didn't have a scent. The little family smiled and waved happily as a light filled their forms. When the bright light faded, they were gone.

Smiling in contentment, she turned to see his eyes dilating.

A deep growl came from him as he gave her a befuddled look. Shaking her head, she led the way out and back to the streets.

"I held him. How could he have been a spirit if I could touch him?"

"It's what we are. What we are allows us to interact with everyone.

Our job is not just to protect the living. We have to protect everything. Helping spirits caught in limbo is a part of what we do."

Under normal circumstances he would ask how she knew this, but there was no point. Adwen didn't even know how she came by this knowledge. Somehow, she simply knew the answers to these odd questions. Holding his tongue, he followed.

In the cobbled street, a man came toward them with dark circles under his eyes. The weary-faced villager was in good health and strong, but they could smell his fear, no matter how confident his stride.

Coming to the edge of the smooth stone roadway, they watched him approach. Oryn's eyes narrowed, and Adwen calmly observed his manner.

A few paces away, he stopped. After studying the dark and green-clad figure, he was unconcerned by him and looked to Adwen. She was obviously not human, and he grimaced. Working his bearded jaw, he spat on the ground and asked, "What kind of nerve does a creature like you need to set foot into our town?"

Being cordial and soft with her tone, she replied, "I'm sorry for intruding. We're only passing through."

He didn't respond directly. Angrier than before, he sneered, "You have no right to come here. Were you in there ... looking to feed on our dead?"

Oryn grew angry, and she shook her head, gently answering, "No. We ..."

But he cut her off: "Don't tell lies to us, monster!"

Windows were opening, revealing dozens of archers. All of the common folk looked very tired. Each face was fearful and even more determined.

Going closer to Adwen, the man glowered. "You cannot leave. First you will pay for the deaths of our innocent children."

She was aghast and didn't know how to react. Her words weren't getting through like they usually did with good people. They had too much fear in their hearts for her speech to help them see reason. The man before her wouldn't listen.

"And you!" he cried at Oryn. "You shall be caned for hours for bringing this despicable animal!"

Trying once more to calm the human, she soothed, "We're here to help. There ..."

Then she fell silent as he suddenly struck her face with the back of his hand.

As her head jerked from the hit, Oryn's eyes widened, and he roared in outrage. Snatching up the man by the front of his shirt, his hand instantly became claws covered in dark fur. Swiftly transforming, he lifted him high and roared again into his face.

The man wailed in horror, and two archers fired. One was off target and headed straight for the man's blanched face. Before it could kill him, Adwen's hand snatched it out of the air. Landing nimbly on her feet, she stared at the rest of the humans, watching their astonished expressions.

Meanwhile, Oryn was far too fixated on the man in his clutches. His fur coat now had dog markings, and his black mask was twisted into an intense snarl. The blacker fur encircling his eyes made the green stand out, terrifying the villager further. Still rumbling with thunderous growls, he finally heard Adwen quietly snap, "What are you doing? Look at yourself!"

He glanced at his arms and ceased his sounds.

"Put him down, nicely," she ordered, keeping her eyes on the archers.

Disappointed by not being allowed to throw the insufferable cretin, he took a deep breath and reverted to his much more human shape. After changing completely, he found the will to set the man on his feet.

The stranger backed way, gaping at Adwen in shock.

Both Oryn and Adwen realized a moment later that the second arrow had struck her in the gut. Pulling it out with ease, she tossed both arrows aside.

She looked the man in the eye and spoke calmly and very clearly. "We do not mean to upset you, and we did not come to eat your dead. I'm sorry, and if you excuse me, we have other places to be. This place is no longer safe. Go to Plexus. Travel through the woods and do not go to the plains. Demons are roaming there." Giving them a final disappointed glance, she said, "Goodbye and good luck."

As she passed the villager, Oryn was close behind, growling dangerously.

Together they returned to the river. After calling up the sirens once more, they soon reached the other side and stood on solid ground.

When they were far enough away so the water beings could not hear, she rounded on him. "What were you thinking? You could tell they were scared, and you know very well that they can't hurt us! What is the matter with you? Everything was under control until you blew up and lashed out like that! And why did you change in front of them?"

"That was not my intention!"

"What was your intention? After he hit me you ..."

He gave her a look of aggravation, but there was glint of another feeling in his eyes. When she saw it he looked away, but it was too late.

Stunned, she gave pause. All of this time, she had thought he didn't like others harming her because she was the heir. She wasn't completely sure, but Adwen had a good idea of what his feelings toward her really were.

Attempting to cover his tracks, he said, "The human was rude and a coward. I failed to keep his words from affecting my actions. It shall not happen again."

Studying his face as he looked elsewhere, she wasn't angry anymore. Understanding, she nodded. "Okay. Well, let's keep moving. We have a lot of ground to cover before we get to rest."

Adwen's mind was swimming. He was attracted to her? That explained a lot, she thought to herself. Then she had a sudden idea and stated, "I think I know what made you lose control of your change back there."

He didn't reply, glaring straight ahead at nothing.

"It's just a guess, but I think your ability to change could be linked a little to your emotions. When you went off ..."

Stopping to cut her short with a retort, his rage swelled. He barely staved off the change and snarled through his words and lengthening fangs, "I am well in control!"

Pressing her lips together, she frowned and nodded. "If you say so."

They continued in silence. She knew he was having trouble dealing with his feelings and the new instincts at the same time. Thinking even more about it, she was certain that inside, he was a complete mess. Not being human anymore was hard enough, but accepting the fact along with everything else must be torture. Leaving him alone, she decided it was better to let Oryn ask for help rather than offer it. He was in too much pain at the moment to accept any.

Chapter 5
FERAL CALL

Running through most of the day helped to sort out more intriguing thoughts. While Oryn did what he could to think of nothing, she was still surprised to consider the idea that he was infatuated. There were so many times she could recall when she should have realized. For whatever reason, she hadn't. For now he refused to look her in the eye and wouldn't utter a word. Since the knight was always so reclusive with his feelings and opinions, even with the evidence, Adwen was not completely sure if he was falling for her. At the moment, it was only a theory.

Cutting southeast, they headed for Fort Wight. Most of the way was clear with bright sunshine. As night was starting to fall the black fog came into view. Going any farther was out of the question so they prepared to rest and wait out the night for dawn. When the sun was up again they would search in the thick dark.

There was a pleasant green clearing that smelled strongly of honeysuckle. With the sweet scent and the clear view to the open sky, it was an ideal place for sleep. Adwen was studying the flowery vines over the tree trunks, waiting to see if her friend would attempt to break the silence. After a long while, she could see that he would not, and stated, "These flowers are a good sign."

Prowling around for a place to settle down, he didn't reply.

She watched him eye the base of a trunk. Then, to her confusion and surprise, he circled twice before sitting on the soft turf.

Oryn pulled the hood up over his face and heaved a heavy sigh, growling lightly.

Very concerned, she didn't know whether he realized what he had done or not. When she had gone through some of her last major transformations, the instincts and animal habits had been minor. Glancing up at the first few stars, she bit her lower lip and picked out the words to say. "I'll stand the first watch", she murmured, knowing he could easily hear. "I'll wake you at midnight or so."

Yet again, he did not respond.

As he began to dream everything was distorted, colorless shapes. Lost in a primal hunt through thick underbrush, he sensed his prey and stalked even closer.

It all suddenly fell away as he awoke to a soft sound. With the hood over his eyes, Oryn used his nose to sense Adwen standing over him. He could also detect her concern. Conversation was not inviting so he growled quietly in acknowledgement.

Frowning, she whispered, "It's your turn. See you in the morning."

Sitting upright, he breathed in deep. Her scent melded with the honeysuckle, and for a moment, it overwhelmed him. Oryn was thankful for the large hood to disguise his face. Wide awake, he brushed back the hood as she laid down to sleep across the clearing.

Watching her turn away, his mind was empty, and with his face enveloped by her intoxicating aroma, it was impossible to keep from gazing. He closed his eyes, sniffing the lovely scent. He started getting up to go lay with her, but paused.

Oryn forced himself to sit back down. Every part of him wanted to be close enough to touch her copper tan skin. Swallowing hard, the heartache set in and swelled until it practically choked him. He could never have her or allow himself to make any attempt. Not only had he wronged her before, but he was her subordinate and servant. That fact alone made it wrong.

Firmly decided on the matter, it was time to keep a proper vigil. He had let himself be distracted again. Frustration caused him to growl and glare at the forest. Some animals still remained in the quiet trees. He could smell bluebirds and a squirrel snoozing amid the boughs. The sixth sense let him know that dozens of other living things called this clearing home.

The hours dragged by, but he didn't care. Senses on full alert, he was constantly aware of anything that moved within fifty feet. There was the occasional cricket or mouse rustling leaves in their passing, but for the longest time there was nothing. Then his ears pricked at the sound of a larger creature through the brush. He felt it approaching off to the side and his bright green eyes dilated, staring raptly at a moving bush, sniffing for the scent.

An old boar plodded out into the open, snorting and rummaging for bugs.

It hadn't seen him yet and he locked onto the animal. Completely silent, he shifted his weight into a crouch and slowly inched forward. His breathing shallow, his heart pounding, he slunk a few inches further. Seeing how stout the boar was made him salivate. As it suddenly looked up, he froze and didn't draw breath.

For a long moment they gazed at one another. He thought he could hear a faint voice calling telling him to stop, but he ignored it. Locked onto the surprised pig, he swallowed and waited to see if it would run. He wanted it to run. It would make catching and feeding on it so much more enjoyable.

Then it snorted and took off.

He was just starting to lunge when the voice became a desperate yell inside his head. Realizing that it was his own thoughts, he stopped dead and became sick. Taking back control, Oryn felt terrible dread. For those few moments he had not been himself. He breathed a slow, shuddering breath and returned to his post.

As he sat, he struggled to determine exactly when he had lost to the instincts. When had he lost control? Everything was a blur of smells in his memory and he grasped his head in his hands. Snarling quietly, he struggled to root out the pieces of his psyche that were still his. What part of him was the animal and which was not? He couldn't tell anymore. Who was he? What was he?

Defeated and sick with worry, he silently tucked his troubled thoughts aside. There was still a watch to be held. He had to protect Adwen as she slept. Whether he was a beast or a man, guarding her was at the forefront of both sides of his mind.

Dawn arrived and Adwen heard a short rumbling growl. Coming round, she found Oryn standing close by, hood drawn and gazing out at nothing. He wouldn't look at her as she turned over. His face was blank, but there was a disturbed expression in his eyes. After studying him a moment, she murmured, "Ready to go?"

His gaze shifted as he thought it over, and gave a small nod.

She wondered what was upsetting him so badly, but chose not to ask. Getting to her feet, she quietly led the way toward the darkness.

This place had obviously been shrouded for a much longer time than the first they visited. Leaves were falling in the dreary doldrums and the ground stank like a warm autumn. Dying greenery filled their senses with decaying smells and their eyes strained to see through the thickets and dense shadow. The two maintained a flying sprint, darting around obstacles and ducking under reeking boughs of dead greens.

More than an hour passed by the time they caught the scent of death and demons. The odor was subtle and drew them to where the darkness lifted a little. Slowing to a walk, they came to a stop to stare at the walls of Fort Wight. Gates closed tighter than a prison cell and empty watch posts made it seem as if it could already be devoid of life.

They stalked closer to the towering barrier and Adwen felt that there were indeed survivors here. Running her hands over the solid stones, there was no way to grip. Jumping to the edge would be difficult, considering the height was about fifty feet by her estimate. She approached the giant timber gates to scratch at the sturdy wood. Judging the surface, it pleased her. When she turned to convene with her companion, she gaped.

Oryn was distracted by a place on the wall where an animal had left a marking. He did nothing more than investigate, but he growled under his breath, sniffing at it.

Her concern was peaked and she frowned. When he didn't stop, she quietly asked, "Are you alright?"

Interrupted at last, he came to his senses and let the spot alone. He grimaced under his hood and didn't reply, continuing to brood.

Adwen could see he hadn't realized what he was doing. Alarmed and worried about his state, she thought it best to confront him a little.

"Oryn?"

Silent as ever, he gave a growl of acknowledgment.

Her frown only deepened. "Oryn? I need to know if you're okay."

He nodded.

Biting her lip, she wasn't convinced, "I need to hear you say it. Speak."

The last word sounded so much like an animal command, his fists clenched and the black leather gloves groaned. Taking a second to fume and roil at his self, he murmured angrily, "I am well enough to continue. Lead on."

Still not convinced, there was little she could do. "Okay. We're going to climb up from here. Can you do that?"

Checking the feel of the gates himself, he replied, "I can manage."

She watched as he began, his powerful hands crunching into the fibers, creating hand holds. Shaking her head, Adwen easily caught up, digging her sharp nails into the timbers. They were both more than powerful enough and scaled the way to the top. Peering over at the streets and houses, everything was in a haze and appeared empty. Neither of them was fooled.

Her eyes glowed and narrowed suspiciously. "There's something bad here."

Though he heard, he continued to search for enemies in tight corners.

"This is like a nest. We won't be splitting up this time. They would overwhelm us way too fast", she warned. "Stick close and we'll head for the town square and market. Starting the search there would be best. What do you say?"

Thinking it over, he struggled to focus and take his thoughts off of the dark facets. He finally replied, "That...that will do. Lead on."

Adwen didn't like the prospect of entering with Oryn in such a bad way. Giving him a questioning look, she knew he was barely holding together. It was plain for her to see that his mind was a disarray of instincts, emotions and fear. Could she trust him to be calm and stay in control? As far as she could tell, there was no time to spare for his troubles. It would have to wait. Heaving a sigh, she went over the side and he followed just behind.

The scent of demons was thick. For whatever reason, they did not attack or come out of hiding. They simply remained in their small hideaways, biding their time and letting them go deeper into town.

Adwen didn't like the feeling but Oryn had her back, both taking notice of all the places that Creepers could pour out. Even though the demons stayed tucked away, the two knew that incredible numbers were throughout Fort Wight. There was another presence they could detect and it was something far worse.

Entering a sizable open block with small trees, wilted by the dark and stale air, she sniffed and came to a halt. When she took another sniff, her friend mimicked her.

"There are people here", she whispered.

Oryn growled quietly to himself, eyeing a shuttered window he thought had moved.

Sure that there would be no harm in the action; she called out, "Hello!"

A second passed and a few more windows showed signs of movement.

Feeling eyes on them, she called, "We're here to help."

A voice cried from a doorway, accusingly. "How could you possibly help?"

Her companion's head was on a swivel, carefully keeping track of how many places he found movement. The survivors of the town were many and everywhere.

"We're here to liberate this town", she answered. "Come out, so we can talk."

There was silence. Then a shifty eyed stranger stepped into a doorway before them. His clothes were filthy from lengthy use and his beard was like a rat's nest. Half starved and wary, he cautiously left the threshold for the open cobbled square. He was curious.

As he came closer, Oryn turned to observe. Straight away he didn't trust him and barely kept from snarling. He stunk like a homeless drunk. Alcohol was on his breath, a trustworthy indicator of why he was so daring.

Adwen didn't like the look of him either, but knew all of the others were watching. How she received this man would dictate their welcome. Taking a calming breath, she smiled and waited for him to speak.

Standing before her, his eyes searched hers. Smirking, he asked, "How would a weird little elf help us? Huh? You going to carry the lot of us over and out to day light?"

Oryn glared at him while she shook her head and replied, "We're going to kill the demons." A few windows started to open as more began to watch and listen.

The stranger burst out laughing and it filled the plaza. Calming enough to speak, he chuckled, "You can't do a thing about this." Then a thought occurred to him and he smiled slyly with his eyes wandering along her form, studying her curves, lean legs, and eventually settled on her breasts.

Licking his chapped lips, he chuckled again and added, "I could show you a safe place to hide. Come. I'll show it to you." Reaching out a hand for hers, he leaned closer and took a step.

Adwen didn't like his idea, but she did move to let him have her hand. As soon as he tried anything obscene she would flip him over. Everything was perfectly under control; for the moment.

As his hand drifted nearer, Oryn's eyes were growing dilated. Locked onto the greasy, smelly, and callused fingers, a quiet growl escaped his throat. Then his gaze moved to his eyes and he knew exactly what was on his mind.

Instinct suddenly took over, and he lunged. Darting between them, he batted the filthy hand away, glaring and clenching his teeth.

Drunk and very angry, the man quickly retaliated and took a swing.

The fist was easily avoided. As the second swing was thrown, he lunged again. With blinding speed, Oryn snarled and sunk his fangs into his forearm, knocking him to the ground. Crying out in alarm and surprise, the man could only watch as he bit down harder and was about to rip his arm off.

Just as he was starting to thrash, Adwen cried out, "*Oryn!*"

Her voice rang around the square and in his ears, making him freeze where he was. Blinking once, he stopped glaring and a look of horror took its place. Gaping back at the human, he tasted fresh blood filling his mouth. In his shock, the sound of villagers coming out with weapons was dulled.

Swiftly, he let go and jumped back, staring. What had he done? Holding a fist to his lips, he continued to gape. Someone was calling him a monster from a lofty window. Grimacing and silently cursing himself, he wiped the blood from his lips.

Adwen's firm words reached him, "Get back."

He did as she bid and took a few steps back to her side. Ashamed and very afraid of what he had done, he had nothing to say.

More villagers were crowding into the open with weapons and she shook her head. Disappointed, but not surprised, she stated quietly, "We're going to have to take care of this problem once this is over."

As they were surrounded by more than forty angry people, he stood his ground and felt sicker. Conceding to the fact that he was out of control, he grimly replied, "Agreed."

The screaming drunk was quickly carried off and more shouting villagers brandished sharp blades. Daring them to attack again, they closed in.

Soon a strong looking man came forward. His long dark hair hung about his shoulders and his beard was thick. What caught Adwen's attention was his gaze. It was sharp and she could tell he was their leader.

Raising his sword, he signaled for silence. Once he had it, he glared at Adwen and asked, "Who are you and why have you come, Creature?"

Locking eyes with him, she announced, "I am Adwen Andredan, the Tame One and heir to Darien Andredan, the Master Knight. We are here to liberate this town."

A stillness settle among them and some blinked in confusion. The man soaked in the information and chose to believe the claim. "What of your companion? What was the name you called him?" He was curious and thought he had recognized it.

Glancing over at her friend, she waited for him to react.

For a moment his instincts got in the way. He was sizing up the human and waiting to see if he would try and touch her. Prepared to rip him apart, he pushed back at the powerful urges and searched for the proper response. Only after convincing his self that the human would not approach, he managed to say, "She called me Oryn. My name is Oryn Conrad."

Many of the people gaped and their leader, at last, noticed the golden Andredan symbol on his left forearm. Relieved by the news, he commanded the mob, "Stay your weapons!" When some didn't adhere, he shouted, "For the sake of the white oak! Put your things down! They are not our enemies!"

Seeing their submission cooled Oryn's wilder side and Adwen was relieved. Smiling, she addressed him, "Thank you. I'm so sorry for what happened. I..."

He raised a hand and cut her off with an apology of his own, "He is a cretin and deserved it. I believe that aiding our survival would be enough to make amends for such a thing. He should have been held back."

Happy that he was so forgiving, she still felt remorseful for not stopping her own counterpart. Giving a wry smile, she asked, "Is there a place indoors where we can talk? Staying out here for too long would not be a good idea."

He promptly nodded, "Of course. It's this way, Tame One."

As they were led along to the local tavern a few men tried to go close and ask her questions. When they came within an arm's reach they jumped back at the sound of Oryn's snarls and growls.

Stopping a moment, their leader scorned them, "Keep your distance you dolts! Let them be and give them room. He's liable to take you heads off if you can't tell!"

Forgetting her, they saw him glaring and thought the order was a wise one.

Continuing, Adwen gave her friend a look. He failed to notice and she saw no point in trying to talk sense into him. The instincts were much more commanding than her words. In his mind he was protecting her. There was little to stop him from seeing these humans as a potential threat so she let him be.

Once they were safely inside, the man brought them to the bar counter and introduced himself. "My name is Sysco. We have been trapped here in this darkness for a fortnight. There is little food left. How far does this nasty black cloud reach?"

"It's mostly over the homes and towns", she explained, "A mile or two in any direction is where you can find open sky."

He looked relieved and smiled, nodding.

"Now tell me, what kind of demon is hiding here? Something powerful is in this town and I need to know anything of use."

While they talked, Oryn willed himself to walk away. Prowling off to a vacant space, the humans gave him a wide berth. He sighed deeply, relieved to feel the primal instincts relaxing. Glad to be moderately in control of his own thoughts, he frowned and pondered. He gazed blankly at the floor, folding his arms and leaning back against the wall.

He was losing the battle over his identity. These driving instincts were intense and snuck up on him worse than any Creeper. For a moment he wondered if his bite would mark the man, but quickly dashed the thought. Only Adwen had that power. He was not the heir, and he was most certainly not cursed. All the same, he had almost ripped him to pieces.

Recalling the moment that he came to, he felt sicker. He couldn't stop himself anymore. He was losing his mind to the animal side. How would he stop himself in the future from attacking a human?

There was a small movement in the corner of his vision and he growled, snapping his eyes to the spot. Locking onto two frightened little girls, he watched as they recoiled from his stare. Cooling his surprised instincts, he gulped as he thought of how easy it would be for him to accidentally kill them. It would be far too easy. Giving a shudder and looking ashamed, Oryn tore his eyes from the pair.

Seeing Adwen sitting alone in a chair by a window, he chose to join her and ask for relief, if she could give it. She was the only hope he had for sanity.

Arms firmly folded across his chest, he took refuge in the corner at her side. For a while, he stood in the dark place, thinking over his words. She said nothing, simply watching the empty plaza as he struggled with his thoughts.

Looking very afraid, he whispered, "I am losing to this."

Without turning her head, she sighed, "I know."

"How do I take back my mind?" he murmured, "I'm losing myself."

When she spoke again her tone was firm, yet consoling. "You don't need to be afraid. You will not disappear." Turning to look at him, her eyes were a brilliant gold. "I will not let that happen."

Scowling, he replied, "I was beginning to wonder when you would next speak."

The golden eyes wore a sly smile. "For as much wondering as you do, you haven't the mind to ever make a decision. It's one of your faults that I enjoy most. You are both clever and dull witted." She beamed and chuckled softly.

His eyes glowed angrily and he sneered, "You allowed me to bite that man."

Her sweet smile wilted into a frown and she shook her head, "It was the only way to make you see. Unless you saw how powerless you have become there would be no other way to make you believe. Now that you know and understand, when the time comes, you can be helped."

Growling, he retorted, "Vagabond or no, there was no need to let harm befall him."

She scoffed and restrained a laugh, "You are being quite the hypocrite and a liar. Even still, you would like to see harm come to him for what he wished to do to me."

He ceased his growling and frowned. It was true. "Tell me," he asked, "Why did you kiss me before? What was the purpose?"

The glow of her eyes grew with her smile. She whispered, "The heart wants what the heart wants. That cannot be denied."

It was an obvious riddle and he was not pleased. "How long until you make yourself known to her?" he asked. "How much longer do I play the charade and lie?"

Turning her golden eyes back to the glass, she sighed, "Soon enough."

Impatient, he growled and his gaze shined dangerously, "If you harm her when you show her..."

Snapping her eyes back to his, she swiftly interjected. "And what would you do?"

Not happy with the point, he listened.

The mysterious being was slightly entertained, "Would you think to tell her of me before the proper time? That, I promise, would do far more harm than good. She is not ready to know of me yet. Keep this fact in mind when next you intend to argue with me. In comparison to me *you* are a pup."

Oryn didn't enjoy the shot and grimaced.

With a kinder tone, she added, "Once this demon commander is dealt with, your problem will be next."

"How powerful is this enemy?"

She didn't answer right away. "He can be defeated, but for Adwen, he is a close match in this setting. Without sunlight we are at a great disadvantage. She could easily lose."

He asked, "She intends to face this alone?" He liked this plan even less than being referred to as a pup.

"You must protect the people", she explained. "These enemies, as you well know, do not play fair. I have little doubts of their intent to win. Especially if it looks as if their leader shall lose, they will kill everyone to keep them from being set free."

"What if I were to lose control", he growled softly to keep others from understanding. "I could potentially lose sight of my task."

She was not worried. "If given a strong command you will not fail to adhere. Have no fear of that. Summon your sword by willing it into you grasp when you must. Do not leave the villagers alone for any reason."

He hesitated to agree to the last, "As you command."

Frowning, she went on, "There is one more thing I need from you."

Not liking the tone, he replied, "Name it."

"For this battle, do not fight your instincts." When she sensed his alarm, she soothed, "It will be alright. Trust them. Let them take over if you must, but do not refuse them when the fight is on. These strong instincts know your abilities far better than you. You have power." Smiling, she added, "There is a power in you. You have kept it hidden for far too long."

Grimacing, he knew what she was talking about.

"I saw it when I first looked into you", she explained. "You've tucked your wondrous gift away for so long you nearly forgot it was there. I am telling you now that you still possess this beautiful talent."

Ignoring the compliments, he stated, "You never answered my question."

"Which one?" she asked.

Oryn was firm. "Who are you? Name yourself."

She smiled. Letting him wait a while, she thought to herself and said, "I thought you already figured that out. I didn't lie when I said you know me."

Frustrated, he growled, "I grow weary of your riddles!"

Entertained, she answered, "I grow bored with you not guessing correctly."

The reply both irritated and humored him. He knew he was being teased.

"But will you promise to trust your instincts for now?" she asked, "If you do not, then I cannot assure you this shall end well. Please promise."

After taking a moment to admire her, he swallowed his fear and answered, "Done."

The golden eyes smiled at the clear glass window, and then, the color change to violet. Adwen resurface and her expression was calculating, "After I take care of this demon problem I'll help you fix yours."

Glad to see her back, he was also glad to see she hadn't noticed the lapse in her thoughts. She didn't need to be frightened by that before a battle. Feeling reassured by both Adwen and the golden eyes, he was prepared and ready.

She lingered indoors a while longer, focusing herself and none too thrilled to face the horrors waiting just outside. Once Sysco had all of the villagers congregated safely in the tavern, it was time. The brave leader of the survivors opened the door at her approach and she hesitated for one last time, took a steady breath, and went out.

Adwen stalked through the cobbled plaza, judging the deceivingly empty buildings. Her enemy was watching, she knew, and tried to decide how to get them into the open. Playing hide and seek with a high ranking demon was not something she had in mind. One way or another, she would have them come to her.

Stopping in the heart of the square, she brushed at the dust with her bare foot and was interested by the feel. She knelt to take up a small hand full. Clutching the granules tight, she stood and thoughtfully sniffed. Then after taking a longer whiff, she glared at the vacant rooftops and aggressively slung the dust into the air. Her sample had reeked of human blood and dark energy. This foe was not weak.

Gazing out the window, Oryn watched and waited. He was afraid of what was to come and his instincts were as primal as ever. The creature that he was felt the strong need to be obedient, despite the powerful urge to go after her. Thankful that the instincts were cooperating with his goals, he continued to follow her with his eyes.

"She cannot defeat this thing alone."

Sysco's sudden appearance surprised him and his focus quickly snapped to the side. The man was momentarily startled, but both calmed and relaxed. Oryn said nothing in return and went back to watching Adwen.

He whispered so not to worry the others anymore than they already were. "This demon is not as simple as the others", he warned. "It had come before the sun was blotted out and consumed everything with his power. It is far too strong." Then he murmured, "You should go to her."

For once, he sided with his unwavering instincts and forced himself to reply, "She commanded that I stay and so I stay." After speaking it aloud he wasn't sure if it was he or the animal that answered; perhaps both.

Now in a more urging tone, he almost begged, "She shall need your aid."

His fists clench and a thunderous growl rumbled in his throat, making the man step back. Glaring at him, both he and the instincts rumbled in human and animal speech, "*She said to stay and so I stay!*"

Sysco was instantly reproachful, "If you insist. What shall I do to prepare?"

Cooling the instincts, Oryn thought about it and replied, "Light candles."

"We have lit most of what remain", he explained, still shaken by his glare.

Simply wishing to not be badgered, he sneered, "Then light the rest."

Gulping, he nodded, "As you wish."

With the irritating human busy elsewhere, he could go back to watching Adwen. She seemed ready, but his instincts knew she was in great danger. Sensing the terrible darkness about to come down on her, he gave an unintentional whimper.

Narrowing her luminous eyes at the silent town, she cried out loud and her words echoed, "I know you can see me, Demon! I also know you can hear me! Come out and fight! What are you waiting for?"

A moment came and went, and just when she didn't think there would be a reply, a dark presence stirred in the air. Her gaze burned brighter and she braced herself as thousands of voices spoke as one from every shadow and empty space. The demon speech buzzed and hummed like the raspy throats of crows and rustling ragged wings. No one but her understood the demon language, same as with any other spirit she encountered.

When the ringing guttural sounds ceased, she stood still and wondered how to provoke it. Gulping, she didn't like the idea of making it mad, but have limited options. "I'm not as weak as you say, and whoever told you I was foolish is probably right. I'm not afraid of you!"

The darkness in Fort Wight chuckled like a stormy sky. It knew she was lying.

"Laugh all you want, but I'm pretty sure your boss wouldn't like to hear you were too scared to fight me while I was practically sitting in your lap", she goaded. "I never thought I'd come across a cowardly demon!" Right away, she wished she hadn't said it.

Hissing was everywhere and the feel of the air thickened. Adwen soon sensed movement throughout the streets and tucked away places as the darkness in the sky intensified. Watching the darkening air, she soon realized that thousands upon thousands of small shadows were darting out and up like a flock of black swallows. They swooped and swarmed like a storm of hungry locus, swirling and moving in to engulf the plaza and her with it.

Swiftly transforming, she forced condensed light into her claws, waiting for the intimidating numbers to attack. Baring her fangs and flattening her ears, she snarled and watched the swarm as it suddenly came sweeping down in a rush of screeches and little wings.

Adwen slammed the bright orbs together and the pure flash bang erupted. Her powers destroyed the closest winged shadows, but hardly fazed the rest and they struck like a cascade of claws. The hundreds that reached her bit, cut, and tore at her body, utterly overwhelming her. It felt as if she was on fire and she howled.

Oryn couldn't contain his rush of emotions, "*No!*"

His feelings were exploding inside and he transformed. It was unavoidable and the startled villagers recoiled, clinging to one another and crying out at the sight of him.

Then there was more screaming and he turned to find Creepers spilling out from the corners. Snarling, he summoned the Rose Thorne and leaped in to cut them to pieces. More appeared in other corners, but his increased speed and agility helped to make short work of them. After he slew the first few, the villagers lost all fear of him, seeing that he was very much on their side. Keeping together and away from the walls, they held their candles close, quivering and watching wide eyed as Oryn held the sinister things at bay.

Outside, Adwen snapped and slashed at the tiny demons, only killing a couple and making room for more to come in. Desperate to shake them off, she snarled and yelped, thrashed and rolled. Then she found the ground and ran to get away.

Her speed helped to escape the swirling cloud. They were hot on her tail, but she pulled away, racing around and out of reach. Her fur was bloody and torn, soaked with silver. The shining liquid trailed behind as she darted to and fro, avoiding more harm.

There were too many to dodge them forever and she made a mad dash for a tall building. Racing straight up it, the nasty flying things were just behind, chasing her up towards the shrouded sky. Adwen reached the highest point and leaped.

As she was airborne, the masses flew at her at once.

Working quickly, she made a second flash bang. Several dozens were blasted into nothingness and the multitudes found her long before the blinding light faded. Biting and scratching even more fiercely, they shredded her as she fell back to earth.

Yelping and thrashing against the onslaught, she failed to land on her feet and hit the cobbled stones. The impact did nothing while the many mouths and claws pierced her shimmering flesh. Batting and snapping and kicking, she struggled to fight back. A few moments passed before the things receded.

Then she heard laughter. Opening her eyes and turning over, she saw the swarm melding into a solid being a few feet away. His chuckles sent a shiver through her and she snarled, gnashing her jaws in defiance. The demon lieutenant brandished a cruel sword and continued to laugh at her weakness.

Like lightning, she lunged and took a bite at his shoulder. To her frustration and disappointment, she got a mouth full of small demons, hardly doing any damage. Landing on all fours, she flanked him and tried for his face, a dark imitation of a skull.

Dodging her fangs, he laughed and sliced her across the back.

Yelping, she managed to land on her feet and not to fall. Adwen landed on her feet, whirled around and stood in time to face his attack.

He came close and she slashed for his head. The second before she could land the strike, he cut her side and split apart to avoid the set of claws. Adwen buckled over howling and the demon rematerialized just behind, laughing. Then he swung again.

Rolling to avoid another devastating blow, she ducked and backed farther away while he continuously sliced and swung.

The commotion in the tavern settled as the waves of smaller demons ebbed. As soon as they were gone, Oryn took his chance to see Adwen's progress. When he realized how badly she was losing it was even more difficult to keep from leaving his post. Eyes wide and ears back, he clenched his jaws as another strike landed on her. His instincts made him whimper and snarl. He flinched and twitched, desperately wanting to disobey.

He watched her quickly disappear and reappear a few yard farther way. Her flash jump put her out of reach of the demon's weapon, and she made a blinding flash bang.

Then to his complete horror, she failed to avoid a jab to the gut. The light had done little to stall the fiend and he ran her through.

Oryn roared. All instincts took over and he made the sword vanish. Dashing for the door, he slammed it open, nearly ripping it from the hinges.

The demon laughed as she coughed and gasped, silver dribbling from her gut and open jaws. Letting her fall, he took the dark blade from her flesh to stand over her, chuckling triumphantly.

She laid quivering and bleeding on the stones at his feet. Turning over the sword, he prepared to plunge it into her heart and finish the job.

A loud howl rolled around the quiet plaza and rang in the network of dead streets.

Surprised, the demon paused. Forgetting Adwen for the moment, the demon lieutenant turned round. He glared at Oryn standing outside the tavern.

His eyes glowed brighter and he howled again. Nose to the air, he howled a clear tone and let it out as loud as he could, filling all of Fort Wight with his sound. It winded him and the effort of what he had done sapped him. Finished with the short song, he crumpled and dropped to all fours, gasping and panting. Once he had his breath back, he raised his head and snarled.

Amused, the demon chuckled and spoke with a cold harshness, *"You cry for her? Do not fret. You shall join her soon."*

A soft growl came from behind, "He wasn't crying."

The demon's blackened eyes widened. He had made a very foolish mistake and realized it far too late.

Adwen was mostly revitalized by the power her friend granted her. On her feet once again, she plunged her claws deep into the demon's body. She roared and it bellowed as her white light purged every piece of him. The dark energy that didn't dissipate twisted and turned to pale particles that shimmered and withered to nothing. The demon fell and burst into a spray of many evanescent fragments.

Panting and watching the last of him go she realized that everywhere was growing brighter. In a matter of moments, warm sunshine was filling the square, illuminating the homes and stores. A breeze brushed past and she breathed it in. Shifting into her woman form, she let it out as a glad sigh.

Then the people in the tavern began to laugh and cheer.

She heard them and smiled.

As she stood in the daylight, Oryn was relieved. His tail swung from side to side and he barked once for her attention.

She looked at him and her smile grew. If he hadn't healed her with his strength everything would have been over. Then she noticed that something wasn't quite right, as he didn't stand and bound to her side. Confused, she watched as he slowed and crept closer.

He gently nosed her arm and sniffed. Then he whimpered, "You're hurt."

To her complete surprise, he tried to clean the blood from her scratches. Licking her bare arm, he growled softly, content in tending to her wounds.

Adwen was befuddled and took a moment to watch. He wasn't pulling out of his feral state and she felt terribly sorry for him. Giving a sad look she whispered, "You really are losing to it, aren't you?"

Busy licking, he didn't answer and continued.

As she tried to touch his jaws and tame him down, he lovingly sniffed her palms. Soon he was licking them as well. She tried to get his attention and gently shushed, holding his head. He sat crouched before her and sniffed her face. Then his long tongue came out as he attempted to kiss her face, but she held him just out of reach. When he finally gave up the idea of cleaning her injuries, he quietly stared back into her eyes with an animal's adoration.

Looking into his much simpler gaze, she knew what to do. At first she pressed her lips together, knowing he wasn't going to be pleased. While she still had his undivided attention, she whispered softly, "Come back."

Shortly after the words were said, his breath caught in his throat and his pupils were pin pricks in his eyes. Then his ears flattened and he snapped up to stand at attention, heart racing. Recalling what he had just done embarrassed him almost as much as it frightened him. He had been completely feral. Not only that, but now there was no doubt that she knew his dreaded secret.

She watched him stare out at nothing, almost quivering with shock and fear.

His eyes shifted and he mustered the will to growl apologetically, "Forgive me.... I...." Then he fell silent and closed his eyes in shame.

Adwen understood. More concerned that he couldn't control his actions, she tried to be reassuring. "It is okay. We're going to get this taken care of." Looking past him at the astonished faces of the villagers, she added, "You can wait here if you like. This won't take long."

His tail tucked and wrapped about his leg as she passed him. Swallowing and short of breath, he didn't dare to move. He could feel the eyes on his back and even more embarrassment washed over him. Oryn felt humiliated tenfold compared to when his men had first found him, and he hadn't thought it possible to be so.

No longer willing to trust any of the instinct that had betrayed him, he waited. Adwen was giving the humans instructions of how to make it across the Broad River to safety. Her voice was his one comfort. As he stood by, he let it and the sun distract him.

Chapter 6
WHAT TAMES THE SAVAGE BEAST

With Fort Wight cleared out and the humans far behind, they walked in a relative silence. Adwen was very sympathetic toward her friend. His problems were much more complex than she had initially guessed. This was going to take a little time and a lot of attention to sort out. Glancing back at him as he followed through the trees, she frowned.

Oryn trailed a ways behind, his thoughts half panic and half shock, pondering his recent actions and mistakes. There had to be a way to take himself back and reassume command of his actions. His ears remained flattened and his gaze low.

A sturdy tree bough got in his way, and he ducked down. He dropped to all fours and continued, forgetting to stand, and was too wrapped up in his frantic anxiety. Hanging his head as he went, his tail curled and tucked at the recollection of biting the human. Remembering Adwen shouting his name filled him with regret and even more remorse. He was out of his mind.

He whimpered as recurring thoughts convinced him that he was a bad dog and his master was angry. Cowering down, the tail curled tighter about his leg, and he crept along like her sullen shadow. When she stopped, he did, too, keeping his distance.

"It's going to be okay," she soothed and noticed how he flinched at her initial words. "You're not in trouble. I'm not mad at you."

Taking the chance, he looked up. Seeing her smile softly was a comfort.

She was well aware that the instincts were in control again. Not as much as before, but he was very much an animal for the moment. It would alarm him to be pulled back to the surface, so she let him alone. Tapping her thigh, she kindly invited him to her side.

He hesitated at first, but thankfully took the offer. Going close, he felt her hand touch his back and didn't glance or react. She stroked his neck, quelling his nerves, and guided him farther into the forest.

Taking her time to reach their destination, Adwen could taste his sadness whenever it resurfaced and would soothe him, running her nails through the short coat on his shoulder. She studied his handsome dark markings and kept him as contented as possible, thinking of a way to set him right.

Hours passed while they wandered in the stillness. She was lost in her brainstorming and he in her scent and touch. He contemplated giving her a thank-you kiss to show his appreciation but chose to keep his tongue where it was. The last thing he wanted was for her to stop combing at the back of his neck. It relaxed him so well that if they hadn't been walking he could easily have fallen asleep.

At sunset they arrived at the location of a world gate. Waiting for it to materialize fully, she turned to her lowly friend.

"Are you ready to go?"

He hardly comprehended the question and sniffed at the portal, cocking his head. Oryn looked up at her, wondering what she meant. Whatever she intended didn't really matter. His tail gave a slight wag. He trusted her.

She smiled and saw his eyes light up, happy to see a smile on her face. The world of logic was her ideal place to teach him. Taking him from the world of magic and swords and putting him into the realm of cars and bright lights was going to be a shock to his animal senses. Scratching behind his ear, she watched him close his eyes. Hoping for the best, Adwen brought him to the grand glowing sphere of light and led him through to the other side.

They were engulfed in the shadow of a dark alley. It was already night in her old home town, and automotive exhaust was the first thing they smelled. Adwen prepared for Oryn's reactions, ready to restrain him if the need arose. It was important that he try to take control on his own.

Roaring traffic and flashing headlights at the end of the ally startled him. He reared and stood, ears erect and eyes wide. Smells of garbage cans and chemicals confounded him, as distant alarms and horns threatened to send him into a panic. Reeling from the sounds, he stepped back, ready to bolt and unsure of where to go. The strange sounds and smells were everywhere. Where was the quiet forest? What were these metal beasts, racing along like demons with glowing eyes? Which way was he supposed to escape?

Then he heard her voice: "Everything's all right, Oryn."

Gasping and panting, he gaped at her. His ears were still up and his eyes dilated madly, but he maintained his attention on her face. Fleeing was out of the question. That would mean leaving her side. Gazing even longer, he found the will to brush back the confounded animal. He blinked hard and was able to be calmer.

It pleased her that he was present again and started for the sidewalk.

Seeing her leaving alarmed him. Too afraid of what he would do out in the open, he whined and restrained a yelp. "Wait!"

Stopping to look back, she smiled and asked, "What's the matter?"

"I ..." he blinked and his ears drooped. "I'm not safe."

She shook her head. "You won't hurt anyone. So long as I can see you, I can take control of your motions. I can stop you from doing anything. Come on."

He felt a little more daring and moved to join her.

Then she chuckled lightly and held up a hand. "Wait."

It worried him and he stopped. "What is wrong?"

Adwen gave him a warm smile. "Don't you think you should change first?"

He blinked. For a while he couldn't recall how. He had to dig deep into his thoughts, searching for what he used to be ¾ the shape of a man? At first the concept of being that was absurd to his instincts. Pushing the animal aside more forcefully, he remembered what he had been at the start of the day. Focusing with all his might, he changed into his human form.

When it was over, he checked to see if he had succeeded. The rest of his garments were back, and he felt small. Flexing his strong hands, his hound mind was disturbed by the loss of his claws. Then he saw Adwen walking away again and was instantly afraid. Letting out a growl, Oryn swiftly moved to the level concrete slabs.

A loud car blew past, its wind striking him and messing his short hair and long bangs. The initial shock made him freeze as another came and quickly went.

The instincts were screaming and thrashing, urging him to run for his life. More bright light flashed on him before another car flew by, and he clenched his eyes shut. Gritting his teeth and smaller fangs at the loud honking things, he fought against the urge to panic. He couldn't let himself run. More wind and light hit him on the curb, and he winced and gritted his teeth harder.

Adwen quietly slipped her hand into his and waited.

He felt her gentle touch, and the sounds seemed dull. Relaxing his tensed body, he carefully opened his eyes. He gave a small furtive glance to see her expression. Realizing that he was shuddering like a leaf helped, and he licked his lips, attempting to be calm.

He was doing well, she thought to herself. A few more moments passed, and he was under control by the time the crosswalk signal illuminated. Going into the street, she let her hand slowly slip away.

At first he watched and eyed the stationary line of rumbling cars.

Stopping halfway, she laughed and called to him, "Come on!"

Oryn gulped. Telling himself to ignore the bright, growling machines, he locked onto his leader and bravely went forward. His tough boots padded on the black tar and rock as he felt exposed in the strong glow of the headlights.

He was about to reach her when a driver suddenly honked.

Freezing, he turned and glared angrily at the laughing teenagers.

"Hey!" the boy jeered. "What're you doing, freak? It's not Halloween yet!"

They laughed at his medieval-looking clothing, and he snarled.

It entertained them more, and Adwen called again: "Ignore them."

Giving the lot one last glare, he left and successfully reached the sidewalk.

His leader was pleased. "You're doing well so far."

Realizing what she had said made him uneasy. "Are you putting me through this gauntlet of distractions for your own amusement?"

"Absolutely not," she assured him. "I'm trying to help you."

"How is this madness to help me?"

She was more than happy to elaborate as they continued down three more blocks. "You have more than one thing to sort out. First off, I'm pretty sure you're having trouble telling when you or your instincts are dominant. As a knight, and because of who you are, you were too used to letting your instincts guide you. But now those have been swapped out for wilder ones. You can't let them be dominant. You were so used to hiding your thoughts and ignoring your emotions that the wild animal mannerisms started taking over."

He didn't like being told he was hiding from anything but made no comment.

"When you adjust to the instincts a little better, we can take care of the other problem."

For a while they were quiet, and he wondered what she was insinuating. Growing curious, he couldn't help but ask, "What is the other problem you're referring too?"

"Well, your change is linked to your emotions. Wouldn't you like to have more control of your shape?"

He was unsure of her vague statement. Grimacing and leery of the answer, he asked, "You intend to do what with my emotions?"

She bit her lip and thought about it. Then she shook her head and smiled. "Your emotions are a little *out of whack*. You ignore them, and what you have become needs an understanding of emotions. All of your power, movements and talents are linked to it. Ignoring your emotions makes room for instinct to take over, and we both know the result of that."

Though he didn't like the explanation, it made sense. For most of his life he had never given credit to strong feelings except anger. They weren't important. But if what she said were true, that emotions were paramount for taking back control, he could stomach the experience?

Then he saw her blushing furiously. Glowering and growing irritated, he knew the reason. He didn't feel like asking any further questions regarding emotion. It was demoralizing.

The animal in his head had become submissive for so long that he was already feeling waves of relief. He continued to follow her into a large lot of cars outside a busy establishment. Before he could ask what it was, the odor of alcohol and vomit blew their way. The bar was loud, and vagabonds were flowing in and out continuously. Disgusted by the scene, he sneered, "Tell me you don't intent to enter."

She laughed. "Of course not! This place is too smelly."

Stopping to observe her studying the cars, he couldn't help but think she had something overly exciting in mind. While traveling with Adwen, he had learned very quickly that she loved an Adrenaline rush as much as laughing. He held his tongue, dreading what she had in store.

At last she settled her attention on a long Cadillac with glistening rims, decked out in studs and outlandish designs. Giving the sedan and the building a sly look, she murmured, "Well I think it's safe to say this is our ride." Tossing Oryn a mischievous smile, she blew a kiss at the driver-side door.

Its headlights flashed, a chirping came from the thing as the security system turned off, and the door opened wide, inviting her to get inside. She grinned back at her friend and raised an eyebrow. "Are you going to stay here or come along?" Tapping the roof lightly, she caused the front passenger door to pop ajar, as well.

Knowing she was up to no good, he shook his head, sighed and went around to his seat. Once he climbed in, the door closed itself and locked.

Being trapped suddenly made his instincts flare. He gaped at the door. Realizing that he was breathing heavily, he fought to restore his calm. He managed to get a grip as Adwen buckled up and said, "I figured you'd be upset by that. You're doing better, aren't you?"

Sitting back and giving a disapproving glance, he replied, "As far as I can see."

"Then let's go for a spin." She gripped the wheel as the engine purred. They backed out and turned onto the road, joining the flow of cars through town.

Oryn had seen vehicles once before while he was still human, but the wild instincts were making his first ride in one nerve-racking. Everything was flying past and seemed to come from nowhere. Gripping the side door and the broad cup holder, he was looking for a solid thing to latch his attention onto.

After the first five minutes, Adwen noticed him clinging to the interior. She whispered directions at the console, and it chirped in acknowledgment. The GPS came up and plotted a course for her request.

Letting go of the wheel, she turned and asked, "Would some music help?"

Surprised by her sudden question, he blinked and muttered, "What?"

Smiling, she turned on the radio. A loud rapper's voice blared, making him jump, and she quickly apologized over the obnoxious noise. "I'm sorry! I should have known this garbage would be the first thing on! Give me a few seconds. I know exactly what to play!"

He was pleased when she lowered the volume and turned a dial, making the voices garble and mix with static or the occasional silence. He wasn't terrified anymore and found himself being thankful for the strange distraction. Waiting a little longer, he listened as she found her favorite station. A singer was wailing, and Oryn's brow furrowed at the sound.

Adwen sighed contentedly. "That's more like it."

Listening to the odd song with whining guitars and heavy drum beats, he didn't know what to make of it. What was relaxing about this style of tune? "What is this? Where is it coming from?"

"It's all electrical recordings. It's a machine repeating a song that was played by a band almost thirty years ago."

Hearing the raspy singer doing his duet with the guitar remained puzzling. Confused by her choice, he asked, "Why do you like this type of sound?"

"Listen to the song. This is a rock love song. Listen to the tone of the guitar and the singer. It's one of the most passionate ones ever written." Then she hummed along, rapping her hands on the leather steering wheel.

Oryn listened more carefully. "His words are passionate, but singing with a passionate sound requires a much softer voice."

"Not necessarily. He's singing from the heart, and you can hear it if you listen. This guy is ..." She stopped to give him a searching look. "Hey, wait a minute. What do you know about singing?"

Gazing solemnly out the window at passing scenery, he ignored the question and sighed. "Where are we heading?"

Her sly smile returned, and she allowed the change of topic. "You'll like it. Don't worry."

They were entering the riverside park. Monolithic pines stood tall, blocking out the sight of busy streets and making the green rolling hills by the water feel secluded. On the other shore was a series of resorts built to imitate log cabins, windows lit by glowing bulbs. Yellow and white light shone on the water below, giving the strong-flowing river many sets of bright eyes.

Coming to a full stop under a lamppost, the car purred and revved before shutting down. Oryn scanned the scene and could feel the animal growing eager. It wanted to go for a blissful run. He wished to be turned loose. The thing almost seized control, but he restrained it. Putting a mental leash on himself as the door opened, he climbed out and relished the fresh air.

He could still hear the distant traffic, but the riverside was much more peaceful. Looking around at the city park, there were plenty of flowers and play sets for children. It wasn't difficult for him to figure out what the strange structures were once he spied the swings. Adwen was right; he liked this place.

She took a seat on the lengthy nose of the car, and the rock station DJ put on another rowdy hit. The guitar jammed, and the singer screamed out the opening lines like a banshee. Her eyes shone with amusement as he turned with an astounded look. Her friend obviously didn't know how to listen to rock-and-roll. When he continued to stare, she smiled and patted the hood. "Come and have a seat."

The animal liked the idea, and his emotions also pushed to accept, but he frowned and looked away. "I feel no need."

Cocking her head, her smile grew. "It's really warm. Are you sure?"

He was in no mood to be teased. Angry with his great need to sit close to her, he growled and snapped, "Why have we come here?"

Giving up, she shrugged and answered, "To wait. I don't know how long it'll be, so you should go ahead and make yourself comfortable. This could take hours."

Glaring back, he grumbled, "And why do we wait?"

She wouldn't say. All she did was smile with the most impish expression, as if she had done something very wrong and was quite pleased with herself. Strumming her sharp nails on the dark paint, she tossed the car a sly glance.

Catching the hint that the car was part of the ploy, he rolled the thoughts around, looking for the most likely conclusion. After only a few moments of thinking and watching her playful grin, the answer came to mind. He gave her a less-than-amused look. "I'm certain the owner of this thing will want it back once he finds it missing."

Still grinning from pointed ear to pointed ear, she answered, "Yup."

The calm situation was obviously not going to last, and that fact was disappointing. His ears already had pricked at the sound of another car cruising slowly along.

Adwen recognized the black-and-white coloration, then a golden flash crossed her eyes, and she was suddenly urgent.

"Oryn! Disguise your ears and fangs!"

"How and why?" he growled, eyeing the two faces through the windshield.

"Will it like your usual change! Hurry up!"

He did as she said just before the two police officers were near enough to see their faces. When they stopped at sixty yards away in the lot, Adwen slid casually from the hood, and the radio turned off. She put on her most innocent act, standing beside her friend, meeting the cops as they approached.

The first had a thick mustache and a sizable gut, as she would expect from any man who drank coffee with their bagels and donuts. She knew he ate them because she could pick up the smell of the crumbs hiding on his bushy upper lip. By her calculation, they must have been interrupted during break time to answer this call. Typical of his looks, he was the predictable and irritating model of the man in blue.

"How are you two doing tonight?" he asked, looking them up and down, studying their stance and strange apparel.

Oryn did all he could to keep from growling, disliking the officer's posture. It seemed aggressive, and Oryn's instincts wanted to make the man back off. At least, he thought, it was the instincts that felt that.

Unlike him, Adwen was casual and friendly. "Doing all right. Thanks. How are you doing, Officer?"

The second cop spoke, and she recognized the voice. "Nice costumes. Homemade or did you get them from out of town?"

Gazing in surprise at her old high school crush, she nearly

laughed. He wasn't a tall man and stood at a height of five-foot-five with a tough build. His mahogany eyes were sharp while he studied her perplexed expression, readjusting his police hat. As he did, she spied the small patch of hairs that grew out white amid the black, which he colored red for style. He didn't recognize Adwen at all and didn't approve; he never had.

Putting aside the small shock, she shrugged. "Oh, I bought a few pieces here and there to put it all together. Thank you."

His tubby partner readjusted his belt, eyeballing Oryn, distrusting the dangerous glint in his green eyes. "What are you two doing here at this time of night?"

Waving a dismissive hand and rolling her violet eyes, she formed a white lie: "Everybody at the house was being too crazy. We needed a quiet place to practice our parts for the play."

Both officers exchanged looks.

Groaning in false disappointment, she explained, "The Shakespeare festival! You know ... *A Midsummer Night's Dream*?"

"Really? What parts are you playing?"

He had her. She always had loved fantasy stories, but not once had she seen or studied the play. Avoiding the question, she acted impatient. "Are we not supposed to be here or something? We have lots of work to do!" Gesturing to her companion, she added with a sigh, "He can't remember any of his lines, and it's going to take forever."

They weren't fooled and saw through the ploy. Regardless, her old crush nodded at the Cadillac. "Nice car. Yours?"

Now she was prepared and glad he asked. "Absolutely not! Do I look like I'd drive a ride with rims like these? No. A friend of ours that has this gangster complex wanted to drink, so we volunteered to be sober drivers and dropped him off. We're planning to pick him up after last call. That's two in the morning, right?"

Completely unconvinced, as she knew they would be, the two looked at the plates and shifted their stances. "That's a shame," said the one, readjusting the belt again. "This car was just reported stolen."

Acting out her best stunned expression, Oryn watched her become openly outraged. "I don't believe this! Why? He was plastered, wasn't he?"

Both cops smiled, entertained by her series of lies. It would have been mildly convincing if they hadn't known the facts. "We talked with the owner. He was very sober and pretty upset."

Her old crush took the cuffs from his hip, shaking his head and trying not to laugh. "Nice try. You guys are going to have to come with us. Turn around, put your hands on the hood and spread your feet. We don't want to have any trouble."

Adwen appeared disappointed until she turned and put her hands on the car. A look of satisfaction played across her face, and she listened as he came closer. Glancing back at her friend, she watched for his reaction.

He refused to submit and stood his ground, glaring at the cuffs in the human's hands. When the officer reached for her, the instincts nearly made him snarl and lunge, but he refrained. The urge was incredible and made him shudder in anger. Then the officer took both her hands and forced her face into the hood.

The other cop watched Oryn the entire time and didn't know what to think when his eyes flashed bright green. A hint of black colors scrolled across his face in that moment, but he thought it was a trick of the lamp lights. No matter what he thought he saw, the stranger was still showing obvious signs of aggression.

As the cuffs were squeezed tight, she smiled up at him. His increased control pleased her, and she ignored the cop as he recited her rights, allowing him to take her away. His eyes followed them to the police cruiser, and the plump cop started to approach, coaxing him to do the same.

Now that Oryn's first training session was nearly done, Adwen decided to have a little more fun. Walking along, she said back to the man, "So, Jack Towers, did you really follow through with marrying Ashley Alhouse?"

The question shocked him, but he didn't reply. Opening the back door, he gave her a searching look.

She turned and locked eyes with him, smiling, shaking her head of silver and golden hair. "Don't tell me you're the only one who can't recognize me?"

Scowling and disturbed by her knowledge, inch-long incisors, and pointed ears, he snapped, "Shut up and get in the car."

He still hadn't figured out who she was. When they last met, her appearance was very ordinary, with brown hair, blue eyes, a fair complexion and slightly different facial features. None of that had mattered when her family and others had seen her changed. They all knew almost instantly who she used to be: Shari Gates.

That was who she had been before being pushed off a cliff into a river. After going over a raging waterfall and disappearing into the realm of magic, everyone thought she had drowned. No one knew that she lived for three more weeks in another world.

Seeing little point in refreshing Jack's memory, she shrugged and quietly got inside. The door slammed shut, and she watched Oryn dealing with the other human. Once he could prove he understood his instincts, she would end this. For now, she sat and smiled.

The cop was growing steadily more agitated. "Don't resist or you'll be looking at a charge of resisting arrest. Do exactly what she did, and you could get to walk, so long as the judge likes you. Come on. Put your hands on the car."

He was very angry and confused. Keeping just out of reach, he looked to Adwen inside the cruiser, wondering what she wanted. Restraining himself from transforming was difficult, and the animal side wanted to bark and snarl. That wouldn't do, and he stayed quiet, glancing at her and glaring at the humans. Soon both cops were demanding that he obey. To his surprise, he was able to stay calm, despite his angry instincts and feelings.

This appeased his feminine leader. A loud crunch and the screech of metal came from the car, making the men forget Oryn completely. She had kicked the door and snapped it off, sending it flying across the pavement.

Oryn took his chance to vanish into the shadows as they stared at Adwen climbing out, smiling.

With the restraints still on, she chuckled. "Sorry about that, but I just remembered I left the stove on at the house." Snapping the chain on the cuffs, the two gaped as she peeled the metal away like old Band-Aids. She tossed the cuffs aside with a clatter and giggled, racing into the darkness.

Jack and his partner were jaw-dropped.

"That better not come out of my paycheck," Jack said. "You want to call this in?"

"Yeah, sure. Just after I figure out what I saw."

Halfway across the park, Oryn climbed up high into a darkened pine and came to a sturdy limb. He perched and observed the two police officers. After a few moments, as he heard them talking, he heard Adwen join him.

Higher up on the other side, she sat and smiled a wide grin.

He growled curiously. "Are these a manner of knight or guard?"

"No, but pretty close. They're police officers. Their job is to protect the law. That means some people don't like them."

He growled in agreement. Watching Jack as he marveled at the damaged car, Adwen confessed, "You know, I used to be crazy about that guy."

Realizing who she meant, he was shocked, and his heart skipped a beat. Without thinking, he asked, "You still have these *crazy* feelings for him?"

She didn't laugh, knowing what he must be thinking. "Not really. I actually don't know why I thought he was cute." She shrugged. "It was nothing but a phase."

Glancing at her, he wondered whether she was insinuating that his feelings were no different. He asked with a note of worry, "How do you know the feelings weren't true?"

She pondered for a moment. "I think I was so wrapped up in his looks and talents that I didn't care if I knew who he really was. Now that I've had the chance to see his eyes clearly, he's obviously not my type." Then she sighed. "He never liked me very much anyway."

Oryn growled, studying the overconfident human. "Did he harm you?"

Hearing the tone of his voice, she looked at him and saw his expression. He had flattered her, but she also knew the instincts had tricked him into asking. "Are you okay down there?"

His attention snapped to her, and a moment later he mentally wrestled the animal into submission. Snarling in frustration, he glowered. "I'm still losing to it!"

"Don't beat yourself up. You are doing just fine. You passed that test so easily I think you're ready for the crash course."

The wording was strange and sounded very violent. He stopped snarling to gape at her in alarm, hoping she was joking.

Seeing his look, she understood and started to laugh. "No, no, no! It's not like it sounds! I mean that you can skip ahead to the final test in a really challenging environment." Still laughing, Adwen dropped backward and landed on the ground below.

Shaking his head, he paused to take a last look at the human. She had liked him? Why? Before he could turn away, he saw something that made him glare.

Three small flying demons were beginning to circle in, drawing closer to the lamppost. He watched curiously and was even more surprised that the one human could hear the wing beats. Oryn gave a small dry laugh. Though his human eyes couldn't see them, Jack's ears told him where they were, while his partner remained oblivious.

Oryn stayed long enough to watch one demon land on the post and douse the light. Jack was looking around in confusion at the sounds as his partner was busy calling in their recent report to see him. Perhaps, Oryn thought, Adwen had liked only the talents, as she had claimed, and not the character. Believing her words, leaving the tree felt easier.

Going deeper into town away from the river, they darted over rooftops, avoiding the streets and detection. Only twice were they glimpsed, but the skeptical humans easily dismissed the brief sighting as a trick of the light. Running after her and leaping through the air made controlling the instincts simple. Most of the distractions were on the ground, where they failed to pose a problem.

She brought him to a dark dead-end alley. On the street was bright neon, full of loud people, and the muffled pounding of amplified music. The two stood just short of the light's reach, and she pointed out a large line of people that led to a rope and burly guards. The guards would let a few in the building at a time as others departed for the night.

"This is called a night club," she told Oryn. "This is your big test."

Not liking the look of the guards, he asked, "What does one do here? Fight?"

A laugh escaped her, and she blushed. "Sometimes, but that's how you get thrown out. People go to clubs to have fun, drink and maybe dance."

He didn't understand and was unimpressed. "I fail to see the point."

"Well, I failed to mention the details. Inside is close quarters with lots of humans, loud music, drunks, slutty girls, guys looking for a fight and ..." Adwen stopped when she saw the disturbed look of revelation on his face.

With everything put that way, he cleared his throat and asked, "What of the guards by the front? How do we get by without confrontation?"

She nodded at a couple dressed in racy attire. People waiting patiently in line groaned and booed as the guard let them cut ahead and go inside. Adwen watched Oryn frown at the spectacle and elaborated: "The owners of the clubs have rules for which people get in. Some clubs let those with a better appeal skip ahead."

"What do you suggest?"

"Look at the guys about to be let in with those girls." She laughed as they also cut ahead. "Make your clothes mimic them a little. What would you want to wear that's nice and close to that style?"

He took a moment to study the scene and make up his mind.

Closing his eyes, he focused. His clothes and armor rippled and twisted. The boots became polished black shoes, and his dark trousers and sash became black slacks with a belt. A dark green collared shirt rippled and settled on his lean frame, and he looked down once it was over.

Enjoying the sheer ease of changing his clothes, he liked the ensemble but turned to seek his commander's approval. Brushing back his hair, he asked, "Would this be appropriate or shall ..." He nearly gasped, and his eyes bulged.

Adwen was now wearing a silky dress that reached past the knee. Two small straps kept it from falling, the front was low, and the back rivaled it entirely. As if that weren't enough, the side of the thin fabric was open up along her thigh to the hip, showing off the glow of her copper skin. She brushed at her hair, shrank her fangs and ears to acceptable shapes, smiling dreamily.

Once he noticed that his mouth was hanging open, he swiftly looked away.

She saw and blushed. "Are you okay?"

He cleared his throat. "Is that garment necessary?"

"Don't tell me you don't like it."

It did not repel him in the slightest. Accompanying her as she was would be very distracting, and he wasn't sure whether he could cope. Already he was struggling to keep control of his emotions and not change shape. Coughing awkwardly, he asked, "Is this fashion ..." he swallowed the knot in his throat, "... appropriate?"

She rolled her eyes and gestured to the street again.

Four scantily clad women were nearing the rope, and he could make out their very petite undergarments. They happily flirted with the guards and giggled when the door opened for them. Compared to the odd troupe, Adwen now seemed conservative.

Clenching his jaw, there was little else he could use as an excuse to stall.

"You look good," she exclaimed. "Let's go! Try having a little fun, and it won't be as bad. Come on!"

He gaped as she was practically dancing to the end of the line. Bracing himself, Oryn took a breath and followed. She kept the lead, and he didn't try to catch up; he was in no hurry to enter the pounding building. It sounded like a madhouse with the insane laughter he heard whenever the doors opened. His eyes fell on her, and he took a moment to study the slope of her smooth back and then a little lower. There were no thoughts in his head as he was oddly transfixed.

Then he gasped, tripping on the curb. Stunned and realizing what he had been doing, he cursed himself under his breath and heard her snigger.

Restraining her laughter, she had a guess as to why he had failed to notice the drop. This was going to be fun.

Grumbling to himself, he thought it better to stay beside her, where he could control his unruly eyes. He was clenching his teeth and looking very surly by the time the duo reached the rope. She gently hung on his arm, causing him to gasp and nearly transform.

Approaching the two bouncers, she smiled. At first they noticed she had no shoes, but decided to let them through anyway. They could afford to let this one slip by.

Oryn paid no attention, fighting with all his might to avoid shifting into his other shape. He could see very clearly why she had called this a crash course. He could metaphorically crash at any moment and ruin everything. The animal was only mildly unsettled by the commotion inside, but his emotions were on the verge of exploding. Every desire and urge he could think of was taunting and driving him to the brink of insanity.

They pushed past the throng, and she picked a table in a dark corner. It was still very loud and chaotic there, but it was as close as her friend would get to any sanctuary. Taking her seat across from him on a tall stool, she leaned on the table to be heard over the deafening music.

He was about to look at her but quickly chose not to. Too much of her chest was visible to him from that angle.

"Now you understand?" she asked.

Blinking at the strobes and shrill noises, he replied, "Quite well."

"Let me know if you think you can't handle it. You can handle this, right?"

"Perhaps." He struggled to be heard over the racket. "I believe so."

"Good! Because I want to have some fun while I have the chance!"

With that, she left him for the open floor. At first he was alarmed by her departure, but he remained seated. Chasing her through this mob was not something he would enjoy. With nothing else to do, he watched her dance.

Some people stopped what they were doing to watch Adwen sway and swing to the rhythm. Flexing and jiving, she became the beat and moved to the tune. She closed her eyes and became lost, dancing like a wild fire. A few girls joined her, enthralled to see her jubilant moves and body language, feeding off her energy like cold beggars by a hot blaze. They were laughing, living the moment.

It helped him to see her dancing. For a while he stared, admiring her sweet style. Then he heard part of a nearby conversation and glared. A few men were admiring her too, and making comments about her body that sparked his rage. Fuming, he made sure not to get too angry. He could lose his human disguise in an instant.

When he next looked for her, she was gone. Scanning the many faces, he spotted her by the man choosing the music, bobbing his head like a drunken bird. She spoke with him for a few moments, and he didn't seem cooperative, at first. Then she cocked her head and gave him the big-eyed begging expression that Oryn figured was one of her dog-like attributes. The man laughed and then nodded, giving in to the look.

Smiling, Adwen skipped and sidestepped through the people to-ward his hiding place by the wall. Seeing her coming closer, his heart started to hammer. Staring was something he could no longer help, and he had to consciously keep breathing. She looked so innocent, like a flower, yet smelled so much more alluring amid the humans; she was a diamond among common gems.

Going to him, she waited a few feet away, smiling. A moment passed, and he realized she wanted him to join her. He grimaced. The sight of her alone threatened to make him change. To touch or smell her up close would be too much to handle, and he was going to de-cline.

Movement caught her eye, and she turned to watch one of the crude men stepping forward. First he went to Oryn, leaned over and said with a smile, "Don't bother getting up. I've got this one."

His friends laughed as the man moved toward her.

Oryn's face twisted into a furious sneer, his eyes bright like small infernos as he flew from his seat. He swiftly brushed the man aside and got between them, glaring and growling in a threatening display. Though he managed to hold back the change, his instincts were very aggravated.

The man held up his hands. "Wow, man! Sorry. It was a joke!" Backing away, the man wondered how anyone's eyes could glow like that.

Before Oryn could do anything else, Adwen found his hand and held it. When he felt her grasp, Oryn gave a final snarl and led her out onto the floor. Another song was starting, and it obviously wasn't pop or hip-hop. He brought her into the open, and some people were caught off guard by the sound of a swooning guitar intro.

Immediately, he realized what he'd done and frowned. Had she known that the man would provoke him into accepting her invitation to dance?

She laughed. "Please, don't tell me you had the guts to take me out here and don't know how to dance?"

He hadn't thought it out that far. "I'm not ignorant to the art, but this song is not to my taste."

Listening to the melody of the metal ballad, she shrugged. "Would it be easier if I took control first?"

Frightened by the idea, he had never liked any of the times she chose his motions for him. But this was a very different predicament. Embarrassed, nervous and looking for an escape, he licked his lips and thought it over. Grimacing and deliberately avoiding her eyes, he replied fearfully, "Do as you will."

Her expression was kind as she laced her fingers into one of his hands, and he waited for her to actually take control.

When nothing happened, he stole a look at her face. Adwen was not using her powers. He simply couldn't look away from the pair of sparkling violet eyes.

"Ready?" she asked.

He hesitated but gave a short nod.

It was so sudden that he gasped as his free hand went to brace Adwen's side and she moved them both as one. For the first few seconds of their dance, he thought this wasn't so bad. He realized the thought was too soon when she pressed closer, laying her head on his shoulder. His heart was screaming in his chest as he smelled and felt her body. For reasons he couldn't begin to understand, he hadn't changed.

She thought he wanted to be this close and couldn't understand why he was still unnerved. Perhaps it was because she was controlling his steps. To put him at ease, she had him turn his head and lifted hers to whisper in his ear. "You don't need to be afraid. It's just training."

His eyes wandered while she spoke, listening to every word like it was a confession of something secret and invoking. When she continued, her soothing voice was a hypnotic spell, though there was nothing magical or binding about it.

"Listen. Feel the sounds. Ignore the lyrics and hear the voice. Every beat is a step in time to a dance for the heart and soul. That is how we move. I move to a song, and so can you. My song is liquid and wild with white fire and water. Your song must be from the heart, as well."

She smiled, and he felt warm breath on his ear. "You said that a soft voice is used for expressing passion. Forget that. Listen. Do you hear it? This man's voice slips somewhere between the folds of a harsh, daring and powerful love. I've watched you fight, and if you were to meld those feelings, you would be unmatched. Do you feel the song inside you now?"

His look was distant, eyes half cast from the longing. Oryn was enchanted by her careless whispers and gave a nod.

"Let it fill you. Let your heart go, and see where it takes you. My heart guides me through every move. Now let yours do the same."

Oryn closed his eyes and sighed. Then he moved.

Taking the lead, he swept her to and fro in a sway. His movements were smooth, confident and in time with the driving melody. Bystanders stopped to watch as they danced together in a wash of red and purple neon.

She laughed a little when he twirled her and pulled her back, sweeping her into a swinging step. He simply let himself go, feeling the song. It had become the only thing. There were no thoughts, no instincts, fear or reason to ignore the need to hold her close. All they did was move, matching each other, step for step.

The beat became his heart when he pressed her close again, and she returned his deep green gaze. He wasn't hiding the look anymore. She knew how he felt. She had been right. His face seemed so gentle and warm that it amazed and captured her. Now it was her turn to feel a terrible longing, laying her head on his shoulder again.

As the song came to a close, he somehow knew. Picking up the pace, he swung, spun and then twirled her out and back into a sweeping, passionate dip. Looking down into her face, he watched her beam and smile.

When everyone began to whoop and applaud, Oryn realized something as they smiled back at each other. She had relinquished control. He had done it on his own.

He watched her face, and then she was serious. With the force of a tackle, she knocked him far back and rolled away, as the glass from the skylight shattered.

Everyone inside gasped or cried out in surprise when shards rained down, but only a rare few could see the demon that landed amid the mess. In the world of magic, Creepers were dark and roughly the size of a man. Without magic in the air to make them black and visible to all, they were a little bigger and very colorful.

Crouching like a demented rainbow, the monster screamed at Adwen.

Getting to her feet, she sneered and smoothed out her dress. Glaring at the demon, she spat. "Figures. Of course they'd send in a Clown to crash the party."

It lunged, and she dodged, sidling away and leaping through the broken skylight to the roof. The demon leaped after her.

Oryn was stunned at first but gathered himself and went after them. The night was clear, and he found that she and the fiend had taken the battle to a building rooftop across the street. He watched as she still seemed to be dancing, whipping about and delivering strong kicks. Obviously, she was playing around. A moment later Adwen shifted into her battle garments, letting her ears and fangs grow out, and finished it off.

There was another climbing up to attack her, but he heard one coming his way. He had seen it at the corner of his vision and watched it bounding closer. As the thing jumped from another rooftop, Oryn's head was empty, and his chest was still writhing with the beat of the song he'd danced to.

When the Clown was flying through the air toward him, he let the song fill his mind and every limb. He summoned the Rose Thorne in a flash of gold, and whipped and lunged with a mighty swing. The feeling was wonderful and liberating like no other. His blade caught the thing, decimating it in one stroke. A cloud of black passed him as he killed it and heaved a sigh of proud accomplishment. He felt balanced.

Turning to see Adwen smiling from across the way, he was in control. The instincts were nothing but a wisp of an afterthought. She gestured with her head to follow and turned to dash away. Thrilled, he dismissed the weapon and leaped over the street, crowded with alarmed humans.

Heading into the wind, the two jumped from rooftop to rooftop, racing through the night. She brought him to a quiet side of town, with a street of closed shopping centers, lit by small spotlights showing off suits and dresses on expressive mannequins. No one else was around to witness them drop down onto the sidewalk, and Oryn altered his magical clothes back into traveling garments and armor.

Oryn was curious now that his senses weren't a distraction, so he studied the strange world. Beside him was a sheet of glass, encasing a male dummy with a suit and tie. He admired the style and approved of the look. Before he could make his clothes match, the reflection made him pause.

Adwen saw the reflection, too, and joined in gazing at the image of a hound.

He grimaced at the face that was really his, disappointed that it was no longer layered over a human one. Saddened, he asked, "Why is it that you appear as you are, while ... all I ever find is this?"

She touched his shoulder, and the image shifted to his physical form.

Confused, he turned to her.

"I know why," she admitted, taking her hand away and letting the reflection change to what it had been. Shaking her head, she frowned. "I see me as I am in the glass because that's simply how I see myself. You see yourself as an animal. Am I wrong?"

Thinking about it for a moment, he realized that she was right. Oryn looked at himself and found no reason to see his image any other way.

"Until you can see yourself for who or what you really are," she explained somberly, "this is what you'll see in the mirror. Don't worry about it too much. You still have a lot of time to learn."

Shaking his head, he couldn't understand. "How? What brand of magic is this?"

"It's our magic. We have light magic. That is the power of truth. What you think you believe you are is what you will see. That also applies to your appearance. If your heart or mind was ill and twisted, you would look sickly." Adwen shook her head and smiled, "You are doing just fine. You look healthy. There's nothing wrong with you, and there's no reason to worry."

They looked at each other in the glass a moment longer, and she smiled. "Let's get going," she said. "I know a good place to spend the night."

Chapter 7
CODE 187

Winds brought sweet smells from dozens of unknown places. Running and leaping freely, keeping out of the light, they crossed the town. All the humans remained ignorant of their liberating sprint. Adwen laughed and sensed her closest friend, following and watching the expressions playing on her face. A dog barked warnings from his yard when they dashed past. It was like a game for that short space in time, one they were playing together.

She was taking him to her favorite park. The place was past the city limits by the river, tucked in a neat little valley where the city lights couldn't reach. Adwen could remember how green it was in spring; ducks swam in the pond under the decorative wooden bridge, while white clouds trailed through the blue sky. It would feel like a haven at night, and she was eager to see if it was still the same.

On the way, they came to a segregated plot of ground. It rested on a hill, protected by a tall metallic fence. She slowed when the local monument stole her attention. Then her heart thumped harder with a sick sense of alarm.

Oryn watched her lick her lips nervously, staring at the distant graveyard.

Swallowing her dislike of visiting such sites, she murmured, "This should only take a minute. There's something I have to check."

They could have leaped over, but it felt more respectful to enter by the main gate. Adwen's shuddering breaths came slowly. Her eyes scanned the standing stones. There were many, and most were older than the oak standing watch in the back like a noble sentry.

Smooth gravel shifted and crunched underfoot. She was reading the tombstones as she went, searching for what she recalled reading in a vision more than a year ago. It was like a ghost in her head, and she realized the marker was bigger. There had been wings. Fear gripped her as she saw the few grave markers with a similar shape. It had to be here, she thought. No matter how much the idea frightened her, she had to find it.

Oryn wasn't entirely sure why they had come here. Feeling her dread, he thought to ask, but stopped himself when she froze.

There it was. A stone angel knelt on a perch, smiling. She went close and crouched down beneath the gaze of the lovely statue. Touching the brass plaque filled her with a surreal emotion that escaped description. Everything about it had felt like a dream until now that she could see and feel it under her fingertips. It was so cold and real.

Curiosity made him step closer. Frowning, he asked, "Who was Shari Gates?"

Removing her hand from the memorial, she sighed. "I told you the name some time ago."

He couldn't recall.

There was the salty taste of tears, and she smiled, wiping her face. Giving a wry laugh, she reminded him, "That was my name before I found the realm of magic, Toth and you. Remember when you asked me who I really was?"

It all came back very clearly, and he clenched his fists. "I recall," he whispered, ashamed of the memory. He had held a knife to her throat.

She wiped more bittersweet tears away. "There's no way my parents could have paid for something this nice." She shook her head and chuckled. "My grandparents probably had something to do with it. They were always visiting. Every year, they gave me and my brother and sister birthday and Christmas cards with checks. I could never understand how they always had the spare dollars compared to my parents."

"Do they know?"

"No. Well ... yes, they do. Only my mom, dad and my siblings know I'm still running around. I saw them all just before going back to start visiting the Kingdoms of Day with you and Toth. They had to run. Someone was trying to hunt them down. I'm pretty sure they're in hiding somewhere."

He studied the stone over the grave with no bones inside. Admiring the face of the stone angel, he lowered his gaze to her and saw the similarity. She had a solemnly caring expression like the smooth rock. He locked eyes with her. "It seems they care for you very much."

Catching another long glimpse of his warm stare, she smiled. A light tugging sensation was in her chest, so she looked away and bit her lip. "We should go now. This is a good place, but I've never liked graveyards. There's too much of a death aura. I like living things a lot better."

Adwen walked down the gravel path, while he lingered, studying the wonderful parting gift her family had granted. They must love her deeply, he thought. He quietly read the inscription and thought it was suiting. "The angel with a heart of gold," he murmured. A smile came as he turned and silently departed.

Dozing in the giant sycamore was both satisfying and precarious. He managed not to fall during the night, much to his surprise. But when a pointy nail prodded his neck, he mistook it for an insect bite. Swatting angrily, he turned and almost went over. Both eyes snapped open as he kept himself from falling, lying back along a strong row of sweeping branches, splashed by pools of daylight.

Adwen was crouched over him, and he looked up in surprise. After a moment of studying her expression, he found a hint of worry.

"Hey," she greeted him.

He didn't like the smell of her feelings. Sitting up, he crouched low and turned to confront her. She was still quietly thinking and biting her lip, another indicator that something was troubling her.

"What has happened?"

"I had another dream last night."

"Of her?"

She scoffed and gave a wry smile. "I wish."

"No games. I haven't the patience for them. What did you see?"

"Well ... I saw someone else this time. They're still alive for now, and I think we're going to have to work fast to save this one. I got lucky, and the dream showed a few dangers around him."

"Who?"

She bit her lip again and sighed. "This is going to get complicated really fast. And it's not going to be too easy. We need to keep him calm and ..."

"*Who?*"

"Jack Towers. He's about to be in a lot of trouble."

Police Officer Jack Towers was in his favorite bomber jacket and at his favorite café with his lovely, doting wife, Ashley Towers. They owned a cozy little house on the quiet side of town, away from where local troublemakers gathered. He was smiling, listening as the love of his life shared cookies and a creamy brew of chocolate mocha.

Adwen and Oryn sat at a table, across the street in a neighboring café. They had to drink water to remain inconspicuous, casually discussing how to act. Their sharp eyes could read the Towers' lips through both sheets of glass and at such a distance.

Dressed in a grey and golden vest and skirt, Adwen's hair was neatly tied back, with the golden bangs still side swept and wavy. Taking a sip from her glass, she continued, "You're going to have to look as human as you can, for as long as you can."

Wearing a sharp suit and dark green tie, Oryn's hair was smartly slicked back. "Is there a purpose for my deception?"

Watching Jack laughing with Ashley, she smiled and felt sorry for him already. Looking her companion in the eye, she explained, "When I first went to your world, I didn't react very well. I was terrified and very confused. The only thing that made it easier was having someone in common to confide in. I need you to let him confide in you. You need to be his touchstone."

"But why must I hide my true nature?"

"Because if he knew what you really were, he wouldn't trust you. He already knows I'm out of the ordinary, so you're the only other option. Will you be able to pull this off?"

Glancing across the street, he huffed, "Undoubtedly. You seem sure he will be joining us. Why must he come along?"

She didn't like the idea either, but leaving him to die would feel like murder. "The enemy wants him to die. I know they want him dead ... and I want to know why. I have reason to think they'll try it tonight."

Narrowing his eyes at the foolhardy human, Oryn grumbled, "He is going to be trouble. I've seen men with his look many times before. He is self-serving."

"He's a cop. He serves himself the same way you did as a knight. He can learn to get over it."

"Not likely. Bringing him into this is dangerous."

"I don't like it either."

Then her tone changed, and Golden Eyes came forward. "He is already a part of this."

Glaring at the being, he shot a look. "How could he be? You would be ripping him from his home. I'm certain that is something Adwen wishes not to do, yet you force her. How dare you, Golden Eyes?"

Angry, Golden Eyes glared back. "Do not mistake her decision for something I've influenced. We have both made the decision. When I make a choice for her, the color you see washes over her eyes. You know this. Neither of us wishes any harm to befall the human, no matter how foolish he is. The only way we may protect him is to take him from here. You know this."

"What will come for him?"

Firm and still angry, her gaze was unblinking. "A fate worse than death. When his heart has stopped, a demon commander shall steal his soul. That is what befell the last person we failed to save. We shall not allow it to happen a second time!"

Conceding, he nodded. "Then there is no avoiding this."

"No, there is no alternative. He shall come with us. Do as she said and hide your ears, fangs and fur. Using your strength before him will not alert him to your breed. He lacks the intuition to perceive what it could mean."

Then both eyes turned violet. She had left again, and Adwen returned. "He's a jerk, but he could end up being useful. I don't really know why, but I've always thought he was more talented than he seemed."

"If you believe so. What shall I do to assist?"

Realizing she hadn't told him, she half choked on her next sip of water. "Oh! You will wait. Stay in the park. I sensed a world gate there. Once I go to him, you can't let anyone see you. Stay out of the open, and don't try to help me." Then she hastily added, "Unless a demon like the one from Fort Wight shows up of course!"

A smile splayed across his amused face. He would have helped regardless.

"All right, are you ready for this?"

"Mostly," he replied, lost in her eyes.

She blushed under his beaming gaze. "Me too. Let's get going."

Another twenty minutes with his sweet wife was all Jack wanted. He got that, and after giving her a gentle kiss, he hopped onto his flashy motorcycle. It was time to go to work.

The station wasn't far. Most of the places he liked to go weren't far from it, and he liked that. Some days, he would purposefully take the long way, testing the power of his bike where he knew his coworkers wouldn't catch him in the act. As a man of the law, he respected it – to a certain extent.

Rolling into his personal parking space behind the brick building, he took off his helmet and saw his friends smoking nearby. One raised an eyebrow, making him chuckle. They all knew how far beyond the speed limit Jack liked to go.

"Darn right I was speeding, Officer Williamson." Kicking out the bike stand, he took the helmet to the lockers.

He was nearly in uniform when his partner came through the

door. Recognizing him in the corner of his vision, Jack shook his head and called out, buttoning the last few buttons. "You're late again, Dan."

"What are you going to do, Officer? Shoot me?"

"Don't need to. I know where you sleep."

Both chuckled.

Dan started to get dressed, as Jack went for another cup of coffee. Even though he already had enjoyed his daily cup with his wife, another from the station was an ingrained habit he couldn't deny. Caffeine hardly did anything to his system. It was the bitter black flavor he enjoyed.

A friend was passing him to raid the coffee machine, as well. The red-headed policeman fitted the precautionary holder around the paper cup, held it under the spout and raised an eyebrow. "Well, hello. I could have sworn you were sitting there yesterday, too."

Jack scoffed, "How did you ever work with Dan and not put your own gun to your head? He stinks, he's dumb, and then there's how many hours he wants to spend at the donut gig. It's because of cops like him that we get the fat donut eater rep. Dan's ... I swear! The moron's killing me." Taking another sip of espresso, he drowned out another slander he didn't need to say. He would save it for later, when it would be more comical. Perhaps he would go against the chief's direct orders and say it to Dan's face, as he really wanted to.

Officer Malone plucked a straw from a small bin, shrugging and chuckling. "He's transferring soon, and Chief's hoping you'll get him to be more ... never mind. There's no way anyone's going to make him into a police station poster child." He took a sip and quickly scorched his tongue.

"Want me to put an ice cube in that for you, sweetheart?"

Shrugging off the burning sensation in his mouth, he retorted, "I see a small regulation breaker on your head, Officer Towers. How do you get away with putting that punk coloring in your hair?"

Playing with the small patch of red hair centered on his brow, he grinned. "I can hide it undercover. That's something you've never figured out how to pull off yet, buddy. Don't hate me because I know how to be cool. You're jealous of my skills." Then an idea came and he had a sly look. "Want to make a bet?"

"Not a chance! My wife's about to shoot me with my own issued bullets because of the last one you pulled at the picnic!"

Recalling how he got to drive Malone's GT for five minutes at the park made him laugh. "The look on her face was great. She wouldn't stop screaming and hitting you while you were making those smoking donuts."

Seeing his chance to make a pun, Jack remarked. "You wish you could make her scream like that. It just goes to show that I'm the master." Before Malone could take some quick revenge, Jack saw Dan and escaped. "Time to clock in and check out!" Avoiding a fist, he jumped and left for the lot.

They had been given another cruiser, as the other was still being repaired. The hinges on the back door had snapped when the freakish girl kicked her way free. How she had done it baffled them, but now she was gone, and they were in search of a place to park and catch hell-raisers. There were so many places perfect for apprehending speeders, but those quickly became boring. For a while they sat near the superstore parking lot, passing the time before moving on.

Dan sat in the passenger seat, playing with his mustache. "Would shaving it off make me look younger? I've been thinking about it for the last few days and can't decide. It's like trying to pick sunny side up or over easy."

Irritated, Jack wanted to say that either way wouldn't change that he was a fat moron. What he did say was, "Keep it, and you'll look like a porn director. Loose it and you'll ..." He trailed off, refraining from saying he would look like an obese infant with an IQ of 65.

The idea of looking like a porn director was welcome. "Hey, you're right!" He stopped judging the mustache to admire the sheer bushiness in the side mirror.

Rolling his eyes and sneering, he turned the ignition. Tacos and burritos sounded like a tolerable dinner. They wouldn't be going inside after the last time. It didn't matter how long the line of cars was. Standing and waiting would take even longer. He never liked wasting time for anything, least of all food. After getting his hot burrito and Dan his dozen tacos, they left for more patrolling.

Gangs had started to form, as more families moved north from California. Some parents couldn't afford to let their children stay connected to the riffraff, but others couldn't afford to live in California at all. This meant that hoodlums and criminal teens would find ways to maintain loyalties to old deals and oaths. That created a lot of work for police.

Twice, the pair stopped to deal with punks loitering by drugstores and hawk shops. It usually didn't take much effort to make them leave, but Jack found ways of getting some respect. He didn't get much from them for being a cop, but he understood how they thought. Firsthand experience served him well.

Inevitably, the sun set, and inevitably, Dan was hungry for donuts. Shortly after dark, they were taking up space in the local pastry shop. While Jack had black coffee and attempted to daydream of his wife, his partner ordered three confectionaries. He was feasting on them and letting useless words pour out with petty crumbs. His terrible table manners sickened his superior on multiple levels.

Seeming thoughtful, he said, "I think I should be a detective."

"Really," Jack murmured, uninterested yet bored enough to hear him out. "How's that?"

"I think I could solve mysteries. You know that massacre that happened in New York a while back?"

Sometime in the past few months, a slaughter had taken place in a mob casino. The only survivors had been one mob soldier, a woman and her little girl. Neither the mom nor the girl was harmed, while the two dozen other occupants of the building looked like Freddy Kruger had come to visit.

"You think you can figure that mess out?" Jack scoffed. "Sherlock Holmes would have his hands full just trying to decipher the first floor."

"No, I'm pretty sure I know how it went." He devoured another donut as he pondered. "The witnesses were unharmed and said they saw an animal and a man just walking through like nobody's business. They said that he caused the whole thing and up and left when it was over. He didn't say a thing and just kept on going."

Jack was wondering how Dan could suddenly sound so smart for a change. Curious how far he could go sounding intelligent on the matter, he asked, "Well? What do you think happened?"

"You need to have an open mind for that! You see, the guy they saw was covered from head to toe in blood. None of it was his. He had no weapons, no guns. The couple hundred rounds that were fired belonged to the mob. So I think: How does a man walk into a firefight unarmed, kill them all and walk out without a single scratch to show for it? I say ..."

"You say ... what?"

Giving a very clever and eerie smile, he replied, "That was no man. That was ..."

Their radio's interrupted: "Zone 17 dispatch, 1050 in progress."

Getting up to hurry to the police car, Jack rolled his eyes and called back, "This is Unit 5. We've got it. Same thing again?" There had been domestic disputes in a rural area like clockwork every week.

It was usually the same home.

"What do you think?" the radio replied. "Code 2, Unit 5."

The officers kept the sirens off and let the lights blink red, white and blue. It was getting late, and it was the middle of the week. This meant that most of the locals were either away or minding their own business. This area was known for some gang activity. Many residents kept their windows closed and doors locked tight.

Coasting along the dark street for the call, Jack reiterated, "Once we stop and get out, I need you to let me do the talking. If the kids were hit this time, we've got to take him in. I don't want to let this bastard get away from the charges just because his wife is too scared."

"Why can't I have a say?"

"Because of what you did the last time. You let him get to you. Breaking up his personal property because you're pissed won't help. I need you on your best behavior so we can nail this guy."

Disappointed, he frowned and murmured, "Whatever you say, Towers."

After pulling alongside the sidewalk, they peered out their windows, examining the home. The lights were out, and it looked quiet. Worried and confused, Jack picked up the radio and called in, "Radio, this is Unit 5."

"Go."

"You sure the call was for the same place?"

"Yes, Unit 5. Do your job, Unit 5!"

"Whatever you say." Finished questioning the irritable dispatcher, Jack instructed his counterpart: "Stand by the car so that they can see I'm not alone. All I need you to do is be an added pressure."

"How about I hold the twelve-gauge?" he asked, pulling the shotgun from beside him, smiling stupidly. "That would put pressure on him to cool off on the little lady."

"Put that down! No, you can't flash him a twelve-gauge! I want to put pressure on him, not threaten him! Read your manual and look up 'unnecessary force!' That's the quickest way to let him get away again! Quit being a waste of space and be a real police officer!" Leaving the car and slamming the door, Jack didn't wait for a reaction.

Dan let the stupid look fade and wore an expression of sly expectancy. He didn't put the gun away. Smiling, he heaved a sigh of contentment and murmured, "You smart-mouth punk." To his satisfaction, when he also left the car, Officer Towers never looked back, or knew Dan still had the shotgun in his grasp.

Walking casually to the nose of the cruiser, Dan judged the distance. It was going to be twenty yards in a few seconds. There wasn't much time left. Being quiet and steady, he used his hours of practice on the range, lifting the weapon. Once it was firmly planted into the crook of his shoulder, he took aim. He had put a round in the chamber the other day in preparation.

He fitted his callused finger on the trigger, touching it the same way his tongue licked his lower lip. This was an easy shot. It would go relatively unnoticed on this side of town. Gunshots were not uncommon here in the middle of the night. Should he shoot him in the back? No, he thought. It should be in the head. That way it would be a closed-casket funeral. He wouldn't have to see Jack's mug ever again.

Jack was growing wary as he neared the doorstep. This was the quietest call to a domestic dispute he had ever answered. Clearing his throat and about to knock, a gun blast went off and a hole appeared in the door, inches beside his head. Instinctively, he pulled his gun from the holster and spun around, looking for the threat.

Dan's shotgun was on the ground, smoking. He crumpled and fell like a sack of potatoes beside it, his cranium having been smashed in. The strange girl's violet eyes flashed, and she gazed at Jack with the look of a wild animal. In a moment the blood and brain matter was gone from her knuckles and she took a step back. She didn't run, but stared, watching for Jack's next move.

Stunned and angry, he called out along his raised arms and pistol, "Get down! I said get down, damn it!"

Adwen blinked, slowly raising her hands. She didn't move to obey.

"Get on the ground!" he bellowed louder.

She ignored his yelling and only watched his eyes, and she cocked her head.

Jack watched her turn toward the patrol car, and what she did next was even more alarming.

Using both hands, she reached through the grill to snatch out the siren speakers. The metal was like wet paper to her. Easy as plucking grapes off a vine, she tore the equipment out and dropped it to the pavement.

Jack saw the parts land in the pool of his partner's blood. The realization of what the dark liquid was brought him out of it, and he squeezed the trigger.

The girl was lightning. His first bullet whizzed past her ear, and she jumped to dodge the second. Her bare feet touched down on the roof of the cruiser, and she glared. When he didn't fire a third time, she snarled and growled.

Stunned again, he gaped and muttered, "What the?" There was nothing he could think to do, as she ripped the lights off of the top, lobbing the plastic and wires across the street. She was not afraid. The stripping of his sirens and lights was not a threat, but he couldn't fathom her actions.

To his complete confusion, she seemed to relax before dropping to the pavement and turning to walk away. Her bare feet hardly made a sound on the road.

Taking back control of his shuddering limbs, Officer Towers dashed to his partner. He was dead. A void the size of a small fist was in the back of his skull, letting the contents flow out like black porridge. Stowing his Beretta pistol, he opened the car and practically ripped the radio off the consol. "Dispatch, this is Unit 5, Code 5150!" He fumbled with the receiver and added, "Code 187! In pursuit along ..." he checked to see that Adwen hadn't vanished. She was still strolling down the way. "... North on Alder to First Street and requesting backup!"

The radio swiftly answered, "Unit 5, describe the target."

"Uh..." he swallowed and watched her walking under a lamp post, "White hair, tan skin, black lips and ..."

The radio quickly cut him off: "Unit 5, do not engage! I repeat, do not engage! Remain at current position!"

He wasn't listening and didn't respond. Very angry as he revved the engine, he pulled away and made a U-turn. This freak wasn't going to get away twice.

Without glancing back, Adwen knew what mindset Jack was in and began her little game. She gradually picked up the pace and moved to the sidewalk. Her feet were moving faster and faster, as he was pulling forward to match her speed.

Jack felt his foot pushing on the gas more than he thought was normal. After following her to the next block, he snuck a peek at the speedometer. It read thirty-four and climbing. Swearing under his breath, there was no reasonable explanation for this situation. The strange girl was not slowing down and not about to tire. He could see her smiling.

He blazed through two stop signs while keeping up, and when they reached Fifth Street, the speed was tipping closer to fifty miles per hour. But as soon as they came to Sixth, she hung a right, and Jack cursed. His tires squealed, and the sparse traffic swerved to avoid a collision. In seconds, he caught up with her again.

Then she looked over and locked eyes with him. He glared and tried to read her expression. She seemed almost satisfied by something. As he was wondering what it might be, he saw the traffic that blocked his path and spat out choice words.

Hitting the brakes, he tried not to crash, but he had been doing fifty-five with her. Having no other alternative to a collision, he swerved onto a lawn, tearing up the sod. Jack was relieved to narrowly avoid an accident and punched the gas, calling in his progress and location.

Adwen took him to the next block. The city courthouse steps were pure white and very broad, as she remembered, but she had never walked on them. Deciding to take them for the first time, she turned right again and dashed toward the top of the steps.

Jack was just behind and screeched to a halt, calling in the location before getting out after her. Running up the steps, she wasn't going as fast as before, but steadily getting away. Pulling out his gun, he aimed and called out, "*Stop!*"

She ignored him and continued to approach the building's towering columns.

Very irritated and determined, Jack pulled the trigger. His bullet hit the pillar nearest to her, and she stopped at last. Though she didn't turn around, he continued up and commanded, "Now! Get on the ground, right now!"

To his surprise, she lifted her hands and proceeded to kneel. Just as the first few backup units arrived, she lay flat on the cool stone.

Panting and aiming at her head, he seethed. "Make one move, and you'll get a hole in the head, too, freak. Stay quiet and stay down."

Glancing furtively at a large hedge, she locked eyes with a set of green ones. Adwen lifted an eyebrow at her friend. Oryn's expression was impatient, but he would do as she had instructed. He would not interfere.

Eight other officers came to assist, and half of them ascended the steps of the courthouse. As they came closer, Jack warned them, "She's not armed, but don't let her move. She's extremely dangerous! Cuff her ankles and carry her to the car." He reminded himself that she could easily snap the restraints. Before he could warn them of that, she was already double cuffed and being carried away. The odd girl continued to smile but did not fight back. What was her game?

He holstered his pistol and followed back to his damaged vehicle. Watching the other officers driving her off to the station, something was itching at the back of his mind. She was weird, but he had the feeling he was missing something. Unsettled and unsatisfied, Jack looked at his patrol car's white hood. Blood was splattered across it at an angle. Seeing it reminded him that Dan was dead and that he was angry, but why did seeing the piece of evidence confuse him more? What was missing?

"We got her," Malone reassured him, coming around from behind the car. "We've got her, and she isn't going anywhere."

Jack was glad to see Malone, but again, there was something odd. Tired from the Adrenaline crash, he asked, "What is going on?"

Officer Malone put an arm around him and steered him to his car. "Nothing, Officer Towers. A perpetrator assaulted and murdered a fellow officer in a routine call. Come on. We've got more coffee at the station. Take it easy. We got her, and she isn't going to get away with this."

Taking his seat in the front, he buckled the belt. What was he missing?

Chapter 8
NO EVIDENCE, NO WITNESSES

Seated and cuffed to an uncomfortable aluminum chair, Adwen rolled her eyes again without saying a word. This was boring.

Officer Malone's face was almost the same shade as his hair. Seated beside his partner, Officer Higgins, he restrained his wearing patience and asked again, "Why did you kill Officer Spengler?"

Staring off into space was getting even more boring, so she made eye contact for the first time. The question was the same as the last, but she wanted something out of this interrogation, so she waited for the opportunity. She knew better than to wait too long. Time could be against her for this odd game.

Glaring at her, he asked, "Do you think you'll be getting out of this? We have everything we need to put you away for the rest of your life. Cop killers don't get very much sympathy. Talking is the only way to lighten your sentence."

Now she could not help but smile.

His partner was enraged and couldn't hold back. Slamming his fists on the table, he bellowed, "Answer the officer, murderer!"

Looking him in the eye, she was surprised and sympathetic. Frowning, she sniffed the air and whispered, "You haven't been eating or sleeping well, have you, Officer?"

Fear gripped him, and his heart skipped a beat. He hadn't had a peaceful night in almost a month.

With Higgins quiet, Malone asked, "What did you say to him?"

She scowled and shook her head. "That's private." Adwen truly pitied the man who was now starting to shiver with fear. The smell of werewolf was coming from him. The only way he could be saved was by her hands destroying his body. She hoped to get the chance before leaving. It was either death by her, or the demon manipulating his anger would eventually drive him mad and send him into the void forever.

Glancing between them, he left the matter alone and continued: "Your fingerprints are being processed as we speak. There is photo and video evidence. DNA from the crime scene is the only thing we really need to put you away. Any judge will take a look at what we have and ... I don't really need to repeat myself, do I?"

Heaving a sigh, she said, "I don't know what you want, Officer. Maybe if you could make yourself clear ..."

"A written statement. I've already told you! It's right there in front of you! Write out your official statement of what occurred and ..."

She shrugged in an asking way to Officer Higgins. He got up, apprehensively, to temporarily remove the cuffs. She picked up the pen, studying the form.

He waited in silence and watched as she wrote.

Once finished, she handed it to him, and winked while being cuffed.

Her statement read, "Could you please repeat the question?"

Balling it up and tossing it away, Malone's face was the same purple as aged wine. Clearing his throat and struggling to remain calm, he said, "You're not making things better for yourself, missy."

"And you don't understand why I'm even here. This is one big mess. What do you really want from me, Officer? Do you want a lie?"

His glare momentarily flickered to alarm. Rethinking the approach, he asked, "What? What, missy, do you want?"

Putting away the smile, she frowned and answered, "Jack Towers."

"You want to kill him, too?"

Sighing heavily and rolling her eyes, she groaned. Then she scowled. "No, I don't. I don't want to kill anyone. I want to talk."

"Then talk to me! You don't get to talk to Officer Towers! He doesn't want to see you until an appointed court date!"

"No."

"We have all of the evidence. We have you in cuffs! What do you have that makes you think you'll get your way?"

Her eyes glowed softly, and she replied coolly, "All of the control."

The man and the unwitting werewolf gaped and started to laugh.

"You have nothing," she added confidently.

"Of course we do," Higgins said. "You heard the Officer."

Cocking her head, she asked slyly, "Where's a picture of me? Can I see it?"

He was still chuckling as Malone became straight-faced. Leaving his seat, Higgins told her, "I'll be right back, freak. I'll get your mug shots in a second.

"What?" he asked as Malone put a death grip on his wrist.

Making him sit again, he snapped, "She doesn't get anything."

A sweet smile spread across Adwen's face as feigned innocence. "I'm sorry, Officer, but is there a problem with my pictures?"

Shooting her a sharp glare, Malone sneered, "No, there isn't, murderer!"

Higgins was confused, while she was clearly entertained. "What would be wrong with the pictures?"

Sensing that he was a good and unfortunate soul, and after glancing at the other officer, she cocked her head. "I don't know. I think the details might be hard to make out. I'm not very photogenic." Then she winked and smiled mischievously.

Sipping at his coffee again, Jack recalled her smile. When she was running she could have easily lost him. She was going fifty miles an hour and not even breaking a sweat. She had led him to the courthouse. What was she doing? What did she want? He frowned and took another sip.

The door opened, and Higgins leaned inside. Dark circles beneath his eyes seemed to be part of a new fashion statement in the department. Not paying Higgins' unhealthy appearance any mind, Jack was about to get up.

Malone and the department chief followed, closing the door to the briefing room behind them. The thin, pale man was frowning — not an indicator to anything out of the ordinary. Being his usual and disgruntled self, he motioned for Jack to remain seated and listen.

As the two officers stood by, looking disturbed and very disappointed, Jack became angry. "Please, Chief, don't tell me she's slipping out of this." The old man clenched his jaw.

Clearing his throat, the Chief spoke while staring along his narrow nose: "We have no viable evidence against her. None of what we've gathered can be of use."

Jack roiled with anger and glared.

"There were no fingerprints at the scene," the Chief said without emotion. "Her fingers leave no prints anywhere, not even with the ink on them."

Shaking and holding his head, Jack murmured, "And the pictures?"

"Those are useless, as well. All of them are or appear to be overexposed. At best, we get a white ghostly outline with no definition. The same effect is in the video footage, as well. We have nothing."

Clenching his hands and glaring at them all, Jack glowered. "I saw her hand come out of the back of his head! I saw the blood on her fist! There is evidence! There's blood on her hands!"

All three exchanged glances before the old man shook his head. "There was nothing on her. Even after swabbing ten different times, we found nothing of use."

Jack's frustration overflowed and he yelled, "I don't believe this!"

Higgins murmured, "Calm down. We have a way of getting a written confession. We had to cut a deal with her, though."

He looked up and frowned, shaking his head. "It doesn't have to do with me, does it? You didn't just use me as a bargaining piece?"

Malone sighed. "She wants to talk. That's all."

"She's psychotic! What's worse ... she's dangerous! You all just decided to sell me?"

The chief cleared his throat with finality and firmly stated, "If we are to prosecute her to the full extent of the law ... we must have a written confession."

"Were there any other witnesses?" Jack asked. "There had to have been more witnesses."

"None," Malone admitted. "No one else had any idea what happened or saw anything. This is the only thing we've got. If we don't get this, she walks. You know that the word of one policeman isn't enough. Just talk to her."

"How long?"

"She wanted five minutes," Higgins replied. "But we got her to settle for three."

Seeing no way out, Jack was tired and wanted to be with his wife. Getting to his feet and downing the last of the espresso, he crushed the cup. "Well, let's get this over with and book her."

Malone and the chief headed for the video surveillance room to wait, and Higgins walked Officer Towers to her. The interview room was an eight-by-six space with no windows and carpeted walls. Only a camera and microphone allowed others to hear from the outside. Standing before the closed door, he turned and asked, "So are you going to wait for her to kill me so that you have a real way to convict her?"

The dark-haired officer scoffed and checked that no one else was listening. Leaning closer, he murmured reassuringly, "To be honest, I don't think she's as crazy or homicidal as she seems. You're safe, Towers. Good luck."

He didn't know what to make of the remark or the shifty way he had whispered it. Deciding to bite the bullet at last, Jack's hand grasped the door handle.

Adwen had smelled him the moment he had approached the room. Well collected and focused, she watched him frown and take a seat across from her.

For the first few seconds, he glared, and she appeared satisfied.

She was the first to speak: "Hey."

Not willing to wait for anything further, he leaned forward in his seat and sneered, "Look, I don't want to talk to you. You are a murderer. I saw you kill my partner, Dan Spangler. I want nothing to do with you or any weird crack-head ideas."

She didn't move. Simply listening, she was placid and unperturbed.

Disturbed by her violet eyes, among other things, he snapped, "What do you want? Why are you here? Who are you?"

For a brief moment, her eyes moved to the camera and microphone. "To start, I don't have long, so listen very carefully."

He glared, but she had his attention.

"Why do you think your partner is dead? Why were you sent to a house with no one inside? Why haven't they shown you the footage of how the officer died?"

The questions made him blink and feel uneasy.

"Not all of your friends are very good friends, Jack. Don't tell them anything I am about to say. They want a reason to kill you, sooner rather than later. Watch your back and trust no one."

Confused and disturbed, he spat, "Why would my own department want me dead? What the hell are you getting at? You are crazy! You're sick in the head!"

She shook her head. "I know how this seems, Jack. You have to believe me, or you'll be dead before this night is out. Find the video, but if they find out you saw it, they will kill you. They'll be interrupting us in a few seconds. The microphone feed is screwing up pretty bad. They can't hear any of this."

"What are you doing? What is going on? Who are you?"

She could smell them coming. "You knew me. Look into the gates and the waterfall."

The cryptic riddle angered him. "What's that supposed to mean?"

A knock was at the door, and Higgins peered inside. "Towers? Come out here a minute." He glanced at Adwen searchingly.

Jack departed for the hall, the door closed, and she stared at the far wall, smiling.

"Are you okay? What happened in there? You look like somebody stole your wife and burned your house."

Caught in a daze, he gave a confused look. "What? I wasn't even in there for two minutes. What's going on?"

Shaking his head, he admitted quietly, "The camera and microphone ... they didn't catch hardly anything. All they got was garbles and static. Are you okay?"

Feeling disturbed, he thought fast. What did he need to do?

Higgins was worried. "Do you need help?"

Shaking his head he forced a chuckle and pretended to be well. "I'm fine. She's crazier than a meth head on mushrooms. She just got to me a little."

Not knowing whether to take Jack's word or not, Higgins suggested, "Go to the briefing room. Get some coffee and relax."

"Sure. Let me know as soon as you get that written statement." Turning away, he wondered how to go about his private investigation. Too much of what she had said was making sense. He had to find the recording from his cruiser.

Passing through the security doors using his badge, he easily found the evidence storage. The one problem he had was that there weren't many ways of seeing the evidence without being watched. If what the insane girl had said were true, then checking it out under his name in the logs would be signing his own death certificate.

He loitered close by and waited. Checking his watch, it was nearly midnight. For the past week he had been badgering the officer in charge of the space for not doing his job right. Being careful, he approached the window to speak with the simpleton. "Hey, Osborne. I hate to be the bearer of bad news, but ..." he leaned closer and whispered, "Soto's just busted into your locker again."

"What? Do me a favor and keep an eye on things!"

Being a pain to seem in character, he laughed. "What do I get for it?"

"You jerk-off! Please, just watch the stuff!"

He was forcefully given the keys, as the officer waddled away in a hurry.

Smiling to himself, Jack went inside and closed everything to keep out witnesses. If his guess was right, the pathetic blob wouldn't have even logged the thumb drive.

He proceeded to rifle through files and bins, but to no avail. It wasn't there. Why wasn't it in the evidence room? Growing angry and worried, he remembered.

Malone had been by the trunk of his car at the courthouse.

By the time Osborne returned, Jack had set everything back to the way it was before. Playing with the keys, he laughed and greeted the angry officer. "Sorry for the false alarm! If you had seen the look on your face, you'd be laughing, too! Don't lie."

Osborne snatched the things back and spat, "You prick!"

With that disaster over, it was time to find Officer Malone's personal locker.

Adwen stared back into Malone's beat-red face, smiling innocently. Suppressing a laugh, she replied, "You promised me three minutes, and you broke your end of the bargain. When I have a lawyer present, I'll sign anything you want. That's my new deal, and I'm not settling for less."

"What in the world are you playing at?" he raged. "What do you think you're doing?"

"Take it easy," Higgins urged for a change of pace, attempting to calm his superior. "Let's just lock her up and call it a night. We'll get her in the morning."

Roiling and thinking it over, he glared at her and pointed a shaking finger. "This isn't over, freak!"

She allowed them to put her in a cell on the bottom floor. Passing through the halls and down the elevator went silently and without incident. Both men kept a wary eye on their perpetrator and didn't dare to let go for even a second. Everyone who saw her was stunned by her odd appearance but didn't remark. She was aware that one or two of them knew who she was. Time for Jack was steadily running out.

Stepping quietly into the cell, she watched as Malone turned to go.

When Higgins didn't move, the officer paused and asked, "We have to talk to the chief. What are you doing?"

Giving a shrug and a grimace, he snapped, "I'm watching the lunatic! What does it look like? Do you want to let her be alone when all of the cameras are screwed?"

He had a valid point. Tossing her a scowl, he nodded. "She doesn't leave here unless I come back. Got it?"

"I don't like touching her," Higgins said. "Go already!"

Not having much of a choice, Officer Malone left them alone.

Once he was gone, Higgins cautiously approached the bars.

Adwen studied his eyes the same way he did hers.

"What are you?" he asked.

Pitying the officer, she was frowning and answered honestly: "I don't really know. But we call ourselves Holy Hounds."

Afraid, he asked, "There's more than one of you?"

She frowned and asked, "You're hurt?"

He swallowed the knot in his throat and lifted his hands, showing a pair of scorched palms. It had been difficult to touch her and not scream while bringing her along. Very afraid, he gripped the cool steel bars and asked, "What's happening? What's wrong with me? You know. Please. How do I make it stop?"

It pained her to see his anguish. She replied somberly, "You're very sick. There aren't very many things anyone can do for you. It's only going to get worse."

Eager for any relief, he pleaded, "Please! Please, help me. What can you do? The nightmares are getting worse. I haven't slept in three days. All I want to eat is ..." Tears swelled in his brown bloodshot eyes, and he laid his head on his knuckles.

Her heart ached to watch him. "There's only one way you can get out of this. You don't want to hear it, but it's better than everything else that can happen."

Higgins locked eyes with her and was afraid. Choking on a sob, he said, "I'm going to die."

Trying to be of some comfort, she smiled sweetly. "It's not so bad. I would know. So long as I do it, you'll be set free. I promise it is the best way."

Composing himself, he asked, "What do you want with Towers?"

There was nothing to fear in sharing what she knew. "He's a good man in a very difficult situation. I want to make sure he doesn't have to die. What's coming is bad. I've seen traces of the darkness throughout the offices and officers of this department. I have to get him away from here."

Concerned for his friend, he shook his head, "What are you doing here? Why don't you just take him and get away?"

"Because If I just took him before he could see what was happening here, he would never believe me and never trust me. Before he can leave, he needs to see the truth for himself."

Satisfied, Higgins dried his eyes and seemed to come to a decision. "So I take it you would like some help with watching him?"

Adwen smiled in an understanding way. "I would help you out anyway, but that would be really nice, too. Helping us will be a big benefit to you. Come closer."

He leaned against the cold metal that caged her. She looked into his eyes and warned, "Don't be afraid. I'm going to look and see what kind of man you really are."

"Will it hurt?"

She only smiled and made her eyes glow.

Jack's stomach had flipped when he found the small portable drive. After picking open Malone's locker, he had found it hidden in the shaving kit. Now he was sitting at his personal computer. Did he dare to watch the footage? Discovering it in the locker alone was an indicator of how far the conspiracy went, but if this showed what he thought it did, then he would have to leave the building very soon.

The plastic and metal made a small click as it went into the USB port. Anxious, he opened the video viewing window on the screen and waited. When it loaded, he had to fast-forward through hours of feed. As he found the images of the quiet street, he let the video slow to normal speed.

As the patrol car pulled up to the curb, he heard the arguing. There was something Dan had mumbled before he got out, as well. A moment passed, and he saw Dan in front of the hood. The black-and-white second-by-second video showed the officer sighting along the shotgun. After a moment of aiming for Jack's head at the doorstep, a white shape with no definition flew in from the side, killing Dan instantly.

Shaking, he fumbled with the mouse and closed out the window. She had saved his life. Dan had tried to murder him in cold blood.

Focusing, Jack remembered calling in and the radio asking what she looked like. After describing her, they had known who she was.

Jack's face went pale, and his eyes grew large. There was one more thing to sort through. Pulling up a search engine on the internet, he typed in "*The gates and the waterfall.*"

He had many results. Most didn't stand out, having to do with cartoons or natural conservation. Then his eyes came across "Gates drowns in Hell's Gate Falls."

Clicking on the link showed a local news article. It was more than a year ago, and he looked at the high school photo of a young girl. As soon as he saw the face it all came back like it was yesterday. He had been a chaperon on a graduation hike. The girl in the picture was a part of his team when he proposed to Ashley.

Something about the picture was familiar. After a few more seconds of studying, he sat back and felt shocked. Somehow, it was the same girl he had just spoken with. Now he understood how she knew so much. He really had known her.

His mind was a whirl of paranoia and alarm. When a hand clapped down on his shoulder, he was shocked and gasped, "*Jeez!*" Putting a hand to his head, he huffed and tried to calm down. "Trying to give me a heart attack?" Quick as he could, Jack casually deleted the window and smiled back at Higgins.

"A little jumpy after dealing with the lunatic?" Higgins asked.

Leery of the conversation, he moved to stand. "Kind of. I just …"

He fell silent as Higgins kept him seated and held up a finger to stay quiet.

Both checked the doorway and saw no one.

Higgins shushed him again when he was about to speak and pulled up a blank text document on the computer. Using the keyboard to share a more private conversation, he entered "She's not crazy."

Jack nodded and entered, "I know. I need to leave."

"Don't talk to Malone," Higgins typed. "Not safe. She can help you get out and hide."

Giving him a perplexed frown, he entered, "You coming along?"

He licked his lips and thought. Swallowing, he slowly entered. "Can't."

As Jack was going to type his own response, Higgins stopped him.

He hastily added, "No time! Follow me and look natural, or we're both dead."

Closing the window and turning off the computer, Higgins laughed and crowed so that others could hear, "Hah! I haven't heard that one before, Towers! Your wife's a keeper."

Smiling and taking the drive with him, Jack replied, "Well, I am the master."

Continuing the casual and bland banter, they escaped down the hall and reached the elevator unhindered. With privacy mostly restored, Jack turned and whispered, "Why do you look like the guy from those war movies?"

Feigning a cough for the camera, he replied, "Which guy?"

Faking an itch below his nose, he covered his lips and said, "The one who knows he's the sacrificial lamb."

Higgins smiled, gazing at the closed elevator doors.

"Come on," Jack urged, "You don't need to stay here. Take this." He showed him the thumb drive. "Show this to the chief. Then …" A long and terrible side glance from Higgins was enough to make Jack throw out the idea. Now he was afraid of how far the conspiracy really went. Worried of what could happen to his friend, he urged again, "Come with me."

"I can't," Higgins voice cracked as he restrained tears.

It alarmed Jack, and he snapped, "David! You don't need to be a martyr!"

An incredibly strong hand gripped his throat. With inhuman strength, Higgins lifted him up, and his eyes glinted red. "*I can't do that, Jack!*" A moment passed, and he regained control.

When he was free again, Jack coughed and sputtered for air, gaping at Higgins. How could he be that strong? He wasn't that big of a man?

Apologetic, Higgins grimaced. "Don't push me. I'm not doing very well."

Leaning heavily on the handrail, Jack coughed out a weak laugh. "Could have warned me a bit sooner."

The unexpected humor brought a warm smile to Higgins' face. "Once she gets you out of here you need to listen to her," he told Jack. "It could save your life."

Exiting the elevator, Jack whispered, "If you say so."

Going around to the cell, they found it apparently empty.

Higgins noted Jack's anxious expression and called out, "I know you're still there. Did you forget that I can smell you, too?"

Her laugh echoed in the quiet prison. "Just being cautious." Then she put back her white hood and reappeared before them, smiling broadly.

While Officer Towers was tongue-tied, his friend asked, "Are you ready? They're probably on to me already. You could just force your way out."

She bent the bars like chicken wire and joined them on the outside. "No. This way is better for everyone. Let's get on with it, Officer."

Jack gaped, and Higgins chuckled at his expression.

Both posed as guards, taking her up and then toward the back doors. As they went, Higgins told off a few people who had attempted to stop them. With one look or a word, his frightening glare would scare them back. Jack took a moment to get his helmet and jacket from the lockers.

When the three miraculously reached the parking lot, Adwen warned them, "We've only got a few moments before they come pouring out. Jack, get on the bike. I need to talk to your friend for a second."

Jack gave her a searching look but did as she instructed.

As she turned to face Higgins, he was shuddering and breathing slowly for calm. Smiling, he asked, "So this is it, huh?"

"Yes. Any regrets or requests?"

A weak laugh escaped him. "Take care of him. It's a good thing me and my girl never had kids, but Jack's a good man. He's rough around the edges, but ..."

"Most guys are. Are you ready?"

He gulped and nodded, "Just promise me one thing: Keep that big mouth safe and get those guys who are doing this, whoever they are."

She nodded solemnly. "I promise, I'll try my best."

Jack had his helmet and jacket on. He kicked the ignition hard, making the bike start to purr beneath him. Looking over, he saw Higgins' face. He was crying and smiling.

Then a small light filled Adwen's hands. She held them up and quickly drove them into his chest in a flash.

"*No!*" he bellowed through his helmet.

The police officer's body was instantly incinerated by a white light, and the police inside the building who saw it came rushing. Guns drawn, they yelled and came after them.

Jack made the tires scream and spin until he was well on his way to escape. Adwen jumped and landed on the motorcycle seat behind him. Balancing on the back, she snarled at the humans firing their nine -millimeter pistols. Jack and Adwen sped out of the lot together and quickly found the road, picking up more speed.

He wished she had not saved his life. Shaking his head, he yelled over the roar of the wind and the motorcycle, "You killed him! You murdered him!"

"I gave him the only way out. He's happy now. Go to the park where you first found me. No matter what happens, keep heading for that spot."

They both heard the sound of wings as a large flight of demons swooped down. Alarmed by the familiar beating, he asked, "What is that?"

"Don't worry about it. There's nothing you can do except drive faster."

Whirring sirens were getting steadily louder, and she smiled.

"What's your ingenious plan for them, freak?"

"Don't worry about them either and keep going! Don't look back! No matter what, don't look back!"

He felt the bike jar as she jumped, and he heard a loud roar that

couldn't have been from a car. Then it was followed by the screaming of tires and brakes. Chuckling inside the helmet, he wondered what she must have done to stop them.

Something screeched as it swooped and clawed his shoulders, slicing the back of his jacket. He wasn't hurt, but he cried out in surprise. Holding on tight, he opened the throttle to pour on the speed and keep away from the invisible things chasing him.

The park was in sight, and relief started to fill him. While crossing the bridge, the street lamps fizzled out, and he knew it had something to do with the flying things. He leaned into the sweeping turn and entered along the sloping pavement. In seconds, he reached the spot and the solitary lamppost. Without the sound of beating wings, he found he was even more afraid. Where had they gone?

Removing the helmet and dismounting, he searched all around for anything. There was no one. There were no sounds aside from the river and his nervous breathing. He could hear a light thumping, and thought it was his heart.

Behind him the thumping grew louder, and then a whoosh came.

Turning around in fright, he saw the back of a tall man dressed in black and green swinging a large sword. It stuck something invisible and a loud screeching filled his ears. When he finally turned, they locked eyes. It was the same man who had been with the girl before. His green gaze scrutinized him, sizing him up. When he was done, he seemed unimpressed and even more disgusted.

Swallowing his shock, he didn't know how to react.

Oryn glowered. "She sent you alone? How far behind is she?"

Before he could get a word out, the girl came dashing in. Her expression was tense, and her tone was hurried. "We have to get out of here, like, right now!"

"What has happened?" the swordsman asked.

Shaking her head, she summed it up. "I heard a few things that didn't sound very good. After I busted up their cars, I heard the radio say they were calling in their boss. Whoever that is, I don't think we want to see him. Come on."

She grasped Jack by the wrist and hauled him along down the steep grassy slope to the river's edge. Oryn was following and keeping a sharp eye out for danger.

Jack didn't like being handled so roughly but didn't have the urge to struggle. Instead he asked, "What were the flying things? Why didn't they follow into the park?"

Headed for the underside of the tall bridge, she explained, "In a world without much magic, or in the living worlds in general, demons have strict rules and boundaries. For them to have presence and influence, they have to abide by territorial rules. They didn't come closer because weaker demons can't get too close to a strong current of water. It messes with their physiology too much. But if they stayed back, that could mean something worse is looking to pay a visit."

As the three reached the darker shadows, Jack wrenched free. She didn't try to stop him, and he thought of turning back. When he found the glaring swordsman in his way, he paused. This one didn't look nearly as patient as the weird girl. As a warm glow started to pool over them, he glance over his shoulder and was surprised.

A giant sphere of light was rippling out of nowhere.

Oryn pushed him gently toward it, and he tried to resist. "Wow, hold on! What the hell is that thing? What's going on here?"

She was quick to respond: "There's no time to explain. After we go through, I'll tell you everything. First we have to get out of here."

"Not until you tell me what that thing is!" he cried, pointing at the portal.

She was going to answer, but the air caught in her throat, and her eyes widened.

Everyone turned and looked down along the shore.

Standing a few yards from the water was a figure. He was darker than the surrounding nighttime shadows. The being exuded a domineering tone of evil. His eyes were hollow, and he narrowed them, tilting his spiked head that seemed to be a sum of many slivers and thorns. The rest of his form was just as sharp and threatening, but he didn't move to attack. The powerful demon studied the crew, curious and meticulous in his observing.

When she heard him chuckling, her heart skipped a beat and she cried, "Go!"

In a swift step, Oryn snagged Jack by his bomber jacket and leaped through the shimmering gateway to the magical realm.

She stayed behind for only a moment longer to get a good look at what was watching her. With so many slivers and spikes making up his shape, she couldn't tell for sure, but she thought he might be smiling. Disturbed by this meeting, Adwen turned her back on him and vanished into the glow.

Chapter 9
A FAIR WARNING

After taking a long tumble down a sand dune in the dark, Jack righted himself and cried out at the top of his voice, "What is this?" He could just make out both of his new companions in the bright moonlight and looked up at the sky. The sight of four moons made him stagger and almost stumble. Confounded, he dropped onto his backside in the grains of white sand.

Adwen moved to stand beside him. "There's a lot you don't know, Jack. Things are only going to get weirder from here on in."

He gave her an alarmed expression and said nothing.

"Take it easy and breathe." she said. "This is a place you've never heard of in your entire life. Right now we're somewhere in the White Sea Desert."

Taking a breath and swallowing, he asked, "How did we get here?"

The two exchanged glances, and she smiled, while he shook his head in disbelief. She laughed lightly and said, "It's called magic. There's a lot of it here, so we need to start looking for civilization. When the sun comes up, you'll roast in the heat."

He got to his feet. No matter how much she explained, it was still too confusing. What was this place? Had they really traveled into a different world? That couldn't be possible.

Then Adwen noticed his handgun. Quickly, before Jack could react, she snatched it out of the holster.

She was backing away, and he cried out in anger, "Hey! Give that back! What do you think you're doing? Give it back before you hurt yourself!"

"I know what a gun is, Jack Towers. Or don't you know who I am yet? I thought you'd be smart enough to figure out my play on words at the least."

"I know exactly who you are! Shari Gates! Now give me the gun!"

Her gaze narrowed. Shaking her head, she held the barrel to the ground in the proper safe handling she remembered. Her father had taught her all about guns when she was seven years old. With a hard tone in her voice, she said, "Shari is dead. Call me Adwen. She died three weeks after going over the waterfall." Then her eyes turned gold. "I am what was left after her untimely demise. Make no mistake. The girl is dead and gone."

Questioning her sanity, he thought before responding. "Well ... Adwen ... can I please have the gun back?"

Oryn continued to stand by and observe. What would he do now that he had no control? Would he be a coward or a fool?

She read his face. Then Adwen calmly explained, "I want to test something. When I died, I was in this world. Someone shot me between the eyes with a gun close to this caliber. All I want to do is fire off one shot. After that, I'll give it back. Is that all right with you?"

He still thought she was crazy, but nodded. "Hurry up and get it over with."

Raising it and aiming for a small rock, she squeezed the trigger.

The shot rang out, and the rock went flying as she felt the metal in her grasp change in texture. Holding it before her eyes, she watched the weapon rust over and deteriorate into red dust at their feet. In seconds, the gun was gone, and she cocked her head.

"Interesting," she muttered.

Jack was outraged. "What did you do? What happened to my gun?"

"I didn't do anything. That was the magic of this world. Apparently you can't bring technology into this realm. It's kind of comforting knowing the enemy can't cheat." She turned to Oryn. "What do you think about this?"

Oryn shook his head. "It is a blessing. Such weapons would deal untold harm."

"What now, *Adwen*?" Jack snapped. "Now that I don't have a gun, or anything else for that matter, what am I supposed to do?"

Going closer, she sighed and said, "Trust me."

Once she introduced her traveling companions to each other, they were able to find the vast Ulla Lake and went north in search of the Lorisans. Along the way, a pair of scouts dressed in red cloth and armor rode out to meet them. It was almost sunrise, and in the dawn light, Jack could see the true colors of their clothing. He stared in disbelief when they approached.

"You have got to be joking." he chuckled while studying the Roman-styled attire.

Oryn glared at him, disliking his rudeness.

"I am Adwen, heir of Darien, and I'm back to see how King Loggias is doing. Can you escort us to the city?"

They instantly bowed their heads upon recognizing the name, and the policeman scoffed, "This is nuts."

Again, Oryn glared. He very much wanted to teach Jack a lesson in manners and minding his tongue.

"Of course, Lady Adwen!" one called down. "The king has been hoping you would return soon. He has been wishing to show some of his preparations to you for approval. It is this way."

The other rider dismounted to let her have his horse, which she accepted.

When they reached the city walls, they saw the activity of workers and weapon smiths everywhere. Messengers were running about, relaying messages and orders for materials between forgers and ore traders. Adwen and Oryn were pleased, while Jack remained silent for the duration of the walk.

Seeing the Lorisans at work helped Jack grasp how real the situation was. This really was another world. Seeing a man driving a cart with a subdued beast caged inside caught his eye. When the monstrous minotaur turned and snorted at him, he gaped. What other insane things were waiting to be found?

Beside the coliseum sat the palace. Inside was lined with sculptures and ancient pottery, depicting the deaths of demons and the rise of warriors. They were brought to the small garden to wait, and the servants offered fresh water.

"Thank you." Adwen smiled at the woman and accepted the cup, drinking down the cool contents.

Oryn declined silently, and Jack thankfully took one. "Thanks," he nodded and then asked, "Who's paying you? What kind of prank is this?"

They were confused by what he had asked and exchanged looks.

Adwen rolled her eyes and made a soft growl, covertly addressing Oryn. "You better talk to him."

When Oryn glowered, she gave him a firm look. He cleared his throat loudly. As Jack made eye contact, he explained, "This is no game. This is not your world. These are servants of the King of the Lorisans, not players in an elaborate joke on your behalf."

Forgetting the women, Jack frowned and asked Oryn, "Who are you anyway? Are you her boyfriend or something?"

Oryn glared and replied as Adwen suppressed a laugh. "I am her servant. I do her bidding and stand watch over her while she sleeps."

Then Jack laughed and came to a conclusion. "Oh! I get it! Now I know why you're so stuck up! You're her slave!" Leaning closer to whisper, he added in an undertone, "I'd be pretty pissed off too if I had to work for her. She's psycho!"

Oryn's eye twitched, and he balled up a fist. With a little effort, he kept his eyes from glowing brighter and cleared his throat. Holding a cool composure was difficult when he wished to strike someone down, but he maintained control. "I hope that in time you will learn to understand what you have stepped into," he whispered back. "You have not an inkling of it. Mind yourself and do not underestimate her." As Jack scoffed and stepped back smiling, Oryn wished he could have warned Jack to not underestimate him, too.

"Ah! Adwen the Tame One has returned to my doorstep!" crowed the tall powerful king. He took brisk strides to meet them and nodded his bearded face to her, "Come! I have much for you to see! It should please you very much to see your horned berserkers!"

Unlike the last time they saw the coliseum arena, the expansive stands were devoid of spectators. All of the commotion was on the ground, where creatures from the desert were being carefully trained.

"What do you think?" the king asked.

She was surprised to be seeing the minotaur so cooperative and the fire drakes taking orders. Shaking her head, she replied, "How did you get them to play along?"

He gave a few booming guffaws. "I have skills and knowledge with these beasts, Lady Adwen. You should know better than I that these creatures are far more intelligent than they seem at first glance. They can be taught and shown how to be effective soldiers for your army."

"Do they know what they're fighting for?" she asked, watching an angry bull creature. "Or are you just trying to tame them?"

"The minotaur can speak, and I have tried to explain. Most of these creatures understand and are more than willing to commit once a little freedom is granted in return. The conformed creatures are allowed to take to the streets. There are only a few now, but soon there will be many. We have a barracks especially for them and another for the drakes. Those are even more enthusiastic when given food for their efforts."

The king's presentation was suddenly interrupted. A minotaur was ignoring commands and growing angry, roaring and bellowing.

Adwen saw the imminent danger and quickly uttered, "Excuse me!" Then she leaped down from the fifteen-foot-high sidelines.

Everyone watched her slide in between the man and the creature. It roared and quickly tried to run her through with his long black horns.

Just as the trainer leaped to safety, Adwen snarled. Catching the two points with her hands, she let the beast push her back. His eye slanted, and he snorted in her face past the thick nose ring.

Then to Jack's shock and alarm, she roared and transformed.

Oryn, meanwhile, enjoyed Jack's reaction.

Snapping her jaws in the thing's face, she swung him over onto his back. He was so stunned by her strength that he held still and gaped. With her nose almost to his, she crept around to crouch low on his broad open chest. Gnashing her teeth, she snarled, "What are you doing?"

He snorted and spoke the best he could with his animal tongue: "I don't want to fight. It's not my war!"

"Of course it is! What do you think will happen after the undead and demons kill the last of the humans?" After giving him a moment to think, she growled, "You will be next. Don't try to fool yourself that it will be any other way. For now, everyone, including your breed, needs to fight. Without you and the rest, we will all fall. Now get up and give your kind credit! You're a proud race! Act like it!"

Enraged, he roared and tried to throw her off, but she left shallow cuts across his nose to make him freeze.

"Think about it!" she roared back. "Think about a world without light! Imagine a desert with no sun, water or wind! You live and breathe for those things! If for nothing else, fight for that!" She backed off to let him stand.

When he got up, he grunted, "What makes you think the humans matter? Why should I fight with them? They are stupid!"

Changing back into her woman form, she stated firmly, "Your kind can be stupid, too! What makes the real difference is if you make the right decision when it counts. Indifference will not change anything. Fight for your kind. Make a deal with the king." They looked back at King Loggias. He was beaming past his folded arms.

"Talk with him. And if you can, go and tell the others what is happening. Tell them ... all of us need to be a part of this ... or everything will be gone."

He bowed his head. "They will not want to listen."

"Trying counts. Do whatever you can." As he looked up, she smiled. "I look forward to being beside you on the battlefield. You're strong. Think about what I said, and good luck to you."

Jack stared and backed away as she leaped and landed beside them.

Reading the fear and uncertainty in Jack's eyes, she waited for him to speak.

He glanced between the king and Oryn, wondering why they weren't surprised. Very slowly, he relaxed. Clearing his throat, he looked at Adwen as if he had never seen her before. Regaining control of himself, he murmured, "So, you're a werewolf or something?"

King Loggias chuckled, and Oryn's face was expressionless.

She shook her head. "Not really. I'm different. Someone in the kingdom of Dargadia called me a Holy Hound." Chuckling, she added with a shrug, "It kind of fits."

Not sure of what to think, he smiled back with great difficulty and replied, "There are other places besides this?"

The king answered for her, "Yes, indeed! There are four other kingdoms!"

"We've been getting ready," she indicated all around with her hands, "as you can see. There's a war going on. I know this is going to sound really crazy, but I'm helping to defend all of the kingdoms and buy them some time."

Jack almost laughed. "A war? "You? You're organizing forces for a war? A war against whom?"

"Against the forces of darkness," Oryn stated flatly, making Jack turn around to look him in the eye. "They are coming."

Still unsure whether this was still some strange joke, he asked, "So are these *dark forces* part of the reason my partner tried to kill me?"

Adwen nodded. "That's right."

"What about Higgins? Why did he have to die then?"

She frowned.

"You did murder him," he muttered darkly.

"It wasn't like that. He didn't have the choices you do. The easiest way to explain is that your friend was already dead. I set him free."

Jack was about to retort but thought better of it. The king was glaring at him angrily.

"Whatever differences you have with the Tame One, I have not the place to say, but you must understand that she is likely to be right," the king warned Jack. "Be careful when you oppose her word. She does the bidding for much greater things. Even slanders toward her can have consequences."

Oryn restrained a smile. The king had taken the words out of his mouth.

All of the sudden, Adwen's eyes flashed gold, and she turned to the king. "Excuse me, Your Highness?"

"What may I do for you, Tame One?"

"We need to see the guardian's chamber."

Jack was hungry. With all the coffee and no food since the cheap burrito, he was beginning to starve. A servant was sent to fetch him some bread and fruit. In seconds it was at his fingertips, and in minutes they were on their way down through hidden passageways.

Secret chambers connected the coliseum with a quiet cavern that once held water. It had gone dry long ago, and walkways let them travel deep into the earth.

It seemed apparent to Jack that there had been a big misunderstanding. If everyone in this odd world was listening to what this weird girl was saying, then they were obviously in for a big letdown. Frowning to himself, he waited for his knowledge of her to prove true. No matter what kind of animal she had been turned into, she was still Shari. She was simply nobody.

After a few minutes of walking, they came to the entrance to a broad, dark cavern. He could see a stretch of stone that led out and disappeared outside of the pools of torchlight. Though he stopped, Adwen kept walking.

He was going to ask, but Oryn cut him off and tried to reassure him. It came out sounding like boredom. "All is well. Follow her. She will keep you safe."

Taking a moment, he tried to read the swordsman. What was going through his mind? Sure, he took orders from the oddball, but what was his deal? Jack sensed that Oryn was hiding something. With a searching look, Jack said, "Go ahead and stay, I guess. Some servant you are. You won't even follow her in there. Why should I?"

Shrouding his anger with forced calm, Oryn replied, "I am not meant to join you. What is to occur here is between you and her. Be wiser than you have been. I give you this advice, and heed it: Take her words *very* seriously. If you do not, you will come to regret it."

"Is that a threat?"

Oryn's expression went blank to hide the mounting wrath. "No. It is a guarantee."

"And I'm thinking you know this from personal experience." Shaking his head, he chuckled and entered the shadows.

As soon as he was gone, King Loggias joined Oryn. "Why would she cater to this brute's needs? He is a fool."

Oryn shook his head and thought how to answer. "I was a fool once. When you last saw me, I was learning that fact. I continued to learn as misfortune broke me down." Then a gleam of vengeance filled his eyes. "I can only hope this piece of fodder has a similar falling out. I shall wait and see. I have the patience for that inevitability."

The king's thick chuckle was directed into the dark. His eyes sparkled, knowing where the man was walking. "I second your feelings, warrior."

With the torch-lit entrance too far behind to brighten the cavern, the lack of light left Jack blind. He felt around with his toes and outstretched hands. He could sense the vastness of the space. Brushing his shoe farther to the side, he gasped upon finding an edge. Adwen gave a soft laugh. "It's not that funny. I can't see anything. How far is the drop?"

"Pretty far. I can't even see the bottom."

Nervous, he licked his lips. "Great."

Her voice echoed. "Keep going straight. You're almost there."

"What's in here?"

She wouldn't answer.

A flicker in his mind told him she must be smiling. He didn't know how he knew, but she was definitely smiling. Frowning at the intense darkness, he asked, "What's so funny anyway?"

"The look on your face. Go four more feet. It's right here."

After a few more seconds of blind walking and searching, he reached her. "Now what?"

Adwen laughed and spoke to someone else close by. "Give him some light. Show it to him."

A loud bird shriek made the cop flinch. "He is blind anyhow!"

"Just give him some light, please."

The guardian hesitated and hooted at last, "Very well."

Light filled the void, as the creature's body glowed with soft pearly shades of white and opal colors. Moth markings dotted its proud breast, and the large eye spots glistened over them. As the giant guardian folded its wings, Jack gasped and couldn't move. For whatever reason, he was not afraid. It was so beautiful.

The owl hooted again, lowering its head to get a closer look. "You can see me, can't you, little human?"

Jack blinked, not comprehending anything that it had said, in awe of the creature.

"And yet, you are blind." It hooted again, bobbing its luminous face. "Blind to everything."

Adwen interrupted: "Are you going to let him see it, or what?"

Sitting upright and fluffing itself, it shrieked, "You are too impatient."

Realizing she understood its language, Jack was intrigued. "What did it say?"

"That doesn't matter. Check this out."

For the first time, he noticed the golden chest, covered in weaving designs that seemed to ripple and roll like waves. Going close, he studied the flowing metal. "Wow," he gasped. Then he touched the seamless surface.

Bright light filled every groove and indentation. Then the glow faded, and the disguised lid opened wide.

Both he and Adwen curiously peered inside. Resting on a red silk cloth were twin daggers. The weapons' gilded hilts and guards glimmered, and white cutting edges seemed to mimic fangs. It was not difficult to guess that the treasures were as deadly as they were alluring.

Concern tugged at her and she told Jack, "You can take them if you want." Then she saw his hand about to reach and added hastily, "Wait!"

He had been fixated onto the weapons, and her fearful voice made him think twice. Giving her a questioning look, he asked, "Why? What happens if I take them?"

"This is the realm of magic, Jack. These daggers belonged to a special hero. He gave them to someone so that that person could be one of his warriors. I am the descendent, his heir. I really don't think you want to take these."

"Why not?"

"Because if you take these, you will become tied to this world. The chance to return to the life you knew will be gone. You will never be able to go back to being who you were before. Do you understand what I'm trying to say?"

Nodding, he replied, "Yeah, I know. Here's one question: When Higgins helped you and me, why did you kill him? He was a good man. He deserved a chance. Why save me and not him?"

She didn't reply.

"I'll make you a deal," Jack said, frowning and pointing into the chest. "If you can tell me the truth and exactly why you had to kill my friend, I'll leave them in the box. So let's try this one more time. Why did you kill David Marshal Higgins?"

"Even if I told you the truth, you wouldn't listen to me."

A twinge of disappointment settled in his gut. He really wanted to know why, but she was obviously being stubborn. Breathing a sad sigh he nodded. "I thought you wouldn't have the guts to tell me."

She couldn't tell him yet. Letting a tear roll, she knew that telling him what Higgins had become would make no difference. So she watched him admire the second treasure of Darien.

He shook his head and added, "But you got one thing right." Gently, he lifted the two relics from the chest, taking note of how sharp they were. Jack judged the weight of one, liking the smooth feel and balance. Then he chuckled, still feeling remorse at the same time that Higgins couldn't see this with him. "I can definitely use these. I've been playing with knives for a long time." He fitted both blades under his belt on either hip.

Adwen gazed somberly at the ground, and the guardian lifted its wings. "The treasure has been claimed," it said. "Farewell, and let the light granted by the eternal spirits guide you." The body of the being became as brilliant as the sun, shining throughout the cavern until there was nothing else. Even Adwen was momentarily blinded by the brightness, until it settled and softened. The light diminished almost entirely. Only a tiny glow remained and sat in the chest.

Curious and surprised, Jack blinked. The two stared in wonder at the little candle, bemused. "Is this what it really was?" he asked.

"No. The owl left it for you so you can see where you're going."

He thought she could be insinuating something, but decided not to respond. She led the way back along the narrow stretch of stone, rejoining the others.

When they reached the tunnel, she passed Oryn and the king, and kept walking. Not even Oryn tried to stop her, knowing that the only thing that could soothe her now was the feeling of sunlight on her skin. But as Jack came out of the utter darkness with his candle, Oryn blocked his path. They glared at each other.

The king called back from along the tunnel, "Sir Oryn?"

Not taking his eyes off of the police officer, Oryn replied, "Give us a moment."

With Adwen and the king gone, Oryn restrained the need to snarl or make his eyes glow. He held his anger and disdain at bay and asked, "What are you doing? I heard what she said to you. Why did you not listen?"

"Think about it. I knew her before you did. I know what she's really like. When she was in school, do you know what kind of person she was?"

With an expression devoid of emotion, he listened.

"It doesn't matter what she calls herself," Jack explained. "In school, she let everyone tease her and treat her like a rug. She never had the courage to defend herself. She let them walk all over her and never stood up for herself, ever. How do you think this *war* is going to end when your leader is a loser?"

Maintaining his unreadable gaze, Oryn sighed.

"Shari is a geek," Jack said. "She doesn't have a clue. And everyone knows that people never change. No matter what happens, we all stay the same. Your Adwen is always going to be the same cowardly, awkward, pathetic, introverted, overcomplicated weakling that she was as Shari Gates. That won't ever change."

Aside from a firmly bridled rage towards the man, Oryn felt a flicker of pity. If he knew the Light Spirits the way he thought he did, then they would make this human eat his words off a platter. Oryn continued to remain as quiet and composed as before.

Jack chuckled. "You're good. I've never seen anyone stay this calm when someone's bad mouthing their favorite girl. Don't take it personal." He became serious. "I like you. I'm trying to save you from a big disappointment. You'll learn."

"I have allowed you to say your piece," he replied politely. "Now hear mine."

Crossing his arms, Jack waited with mock expectancy.

"Adwen told you that Shari is dead. That was no lie. I knew the girl before her passing. I made the same mistake in expecting the very same characteristics. Shari was a girl full of uncertainty and fear, but you never witnessed what I have. Before her death, she learned true courage."

Jack suppressed a laugh.

Oryn glowered and showed a small portion of his feelings. "Adwen has given you fair warning. Yet you did not heed it. You see her as a fool, simply because that is all you recall of her. Now hear my fair warning: If you do not see her for what she is, before too long, you will suffer ... just as I did. Open your eyes before it is too late, but it could very well already be."

"If it is, then you'd be wasting your breath by lecturing me. I don't see you wearing the daddy pants, so how about we cut the crap. I'm not like you. I'm not her personal slave. When I've seen enough of this crazy world, I'm going home. When I get there, I'm going to take my wife and go far away, where we'll never see either of you again."

"You've forgotten her warning," Oryn reminded him.

"I'm not scared of her mumbo jumbo! Having a pair of pretty knives is not going to make me stay here. You wait and see."

They started along the underground path together. Both sets of footfalls rebounded off of the stone walls like small whispers, and Oryn muttered, "You're going to pay dearly for your words."

"Just wait and see. You're the one who's going to look like an idiot. Not me."

Scowling, Oryn growled quietly to himself, "We'll see."

The king and Adwen waited near one of the many inlets into the coliseum. Letting the warm rays of daylight wash over her, it cooled her worries, though it did not remove them entirely. She was afraid of what was going to happen now that Jack was already making reckless decisions. How was she to help him when he wouldn't take her seriously?

King Loggias breathed a hefty sigh, enjoying the breeze. "Lady Adwen, how else may I be of service to you?"

Lost in her fearful pondering, she didn't hear or reply.

"Lady? What troubles you?"

"What do I do?"

"Lady?"

Gazing out into space, she muttered, "What do I do, Your Highness? Jack won't hear me or understand, no matter what I do. My voice won't reach him like it does with other good people. What do I do with him?"

"That is not my place to say, Lady."

Locking eyes with him, she was almost pleading. "What would you do? If you couldn't tell someone the truth because they won't believe it, how would you try to help and protect them?"

Taking the question, he grimaced and thought it over. "I would allow him to make mistakes. This man is not in his own world. While in this one, he is like a child. Shield him from mortal harm, but let him discover where the thorns lie on his own. He must learn where it is best not to tread."

"And?"

"And when he causes trouble, like with any child, you give him a consequence. This man must learn to respect you, among other things. He has very little regard for the things around him. Yet he is not a complete fool." The king nodded. "After running across enough thistles, he will understand you. He cannot hear the truth of your voice because he has chosen to be deaf to it. I hear you. I know you speak truths. He has simply chosen not to listen. But I assure you, in time he will learn."

"How do you know?"

"Because, my Lady, no otherworldly man could romp about in an unfamiliar land without finding his share of trouble!" He laughed heartily. "He will have to learn to hear and trust you, just as when you led him through the dark."

At last, she looked calm and a small smile tugged at the corners of her mouth. "Thank you, Your Highness."

The sound of footsteps coming along the tunnel caught her ear just before Jack's voice, "Where to now, *Tame One*? Going to do more sightseeing?" As they came out into the light Adwen noted the look on Oryn's face. Even though his expression was blank, she knew he was angry. There was no point in asking why.

Being patient with the cop, she answered, "No. Oryn and I still have work to do. We need to go back to Dargadia."

"Ah, my Lady!" the king proudly announced. "We have uncovered one of the kingdom gates! It is through a hidden passage in my palace. Come!"

He and one of his servants led the way, while Adwen and Oryn trailed some distance behind, holding a discreet conversation. Speaking in hushed growls to each other, they discussed what to do. They passed through the first arch of the palace, and the many footfalls masked their animal speech.

"We cannot keep him in our company if we are to liberate towns," Oryn advised. "He must be left someplace secure."

"I already thought of leaving him at the Order," she growled. "The only problem with that is what the elders might do. There's no telling what kind of trouble he'll start without someone to watch him."

"Castle Gailarien," Oryn growled back. "With the king's many eyes and Toth, he should be well looked after. If the point of bringing him along was to keep him alive, then letting him tag along like useless luggage would be a step backward."

"I know. We'll go to the castle then. After that, we can sort out where to go from there."

"Agreed."

Jack thought he had heard something growling behind him. Turning his attention away from the eerie candle in his hand, he glanced over his shoulder. All he could see was Adwen and Oryn, staring directly ahead at nothing in particular.

Adwen glanced at Jack and asked, "Is there something else you want me to explain, or do you still think I'm crazy?"

"Were you just growling at me?"

Her look was sarcastic as she cocked her head. "Maybe. If that's a problem then let me know. It happens fairly often."

Shaking his head, he was unimpressed. "Don't growl at me or I'll get a rolled-up newspaper. You don't want me to smack you across the nose." Jack felt disturbed and looked away to continue following the king.

She and Oryn exchanged entertained glances.

After passing through many more halls, pillars and lattice covered in grape vines, they found a passage to the treasury. The king counted out the torch brackets until the seventh one and gave it a firm twist to the side. As it made a satisfying click, a hidden door opened up at their backs, unveiling the way.

"Here is where I leave you, Lady Adwen. There is much more preparing to oversee. Farewell to you."

She smiled and nodded. "Thank you. And good luck dealing with the minotaur. I hope you can convince more of them to band together. Try other ways besides poaching them, now that you have a few to be messengers."

"I shall do what I can."

Oryn nodded on his way into the dimly lit passage.

The king chuckled and shook his head, then stopped when Jack was handing him the small candle. Raising an eyebrow at his searching expression, he asked, "Do you not want to keep that? A guardian spirit left it as a parting gift."

Trying not to offend a king, he shrugged and grimaced. "Well, Your Highness, I don't really need it. Could you keep it for me?"

Taking it and examining Jack's eyes, the king replied, "Believe me when I say, you need a light more than I do. I wish you the best."

Frowning, Jack touched two fingers to his tongue. Pinching out the small white flame, he made the king grimace. "I can see just fine. Thank you, Your Highness."

When Jack was down the tunnel, King Loggias closed the door. Shaking his head at the candle and the extinguished wick, he felt a twinge of anger. How could he put out the last flame of a Light Spirit's servant? "What an ignorant man he is," he muttered darkly. What was to become of Jack, he could only speculate.

Chapter 10
NO CHOICE

Jack Towers was following close behind, expecting either Adwen or Oryn to turn and say something. He knew he had bothered her by taking the blades but was absolutely sure she was only upset that he wouldn't believe her threats. There was no way he was going to be manipulated by false warnings. Did she really think he was that stupid?

Oryn was difficult to read, but Jack had a good idea of how he felt. Jack had made him angry while in the underground tunnels. Of that he was sure, but what was keeping him so cool? He was hiding something, and that idea was unsettling. Keeping up with their confident strides was a chore, just like keeping himself from speaking his mind.

He wanted to call her the lame one, but what he said was, "Hey, Tame One. Are you going to keep me in the dark or tell me how I fit into this war? Why did you save my life anyway?"

She didn't say and kept walking through the dim pools of torchlight as Oryn shot him a discreet look.

A feeling of uncertainty and suspicion grew, curdling in his stomach like maggots, as he waited for a response that wasn't coming. With the feeling came anger, and it almost made him snap, but he stopped. Light was washing down a set of stone steps at the end of a dark chamber. The kingdom gate was beneath an arch, inlaid with gold like curving leafy branches. It rippled and shone brightly enough for even him to avoid the rough formations on the floor.

They quietly ascended, and when the liquid light of the portal was just before them, he tried again: "Why did you stop them from killing me?" His angry tone echoed all around in the gloom, making her halt.

When she finally turned around, her face was as blank as Oryn's. Adwen's tone was soft, tired and pained. "Because I knew they were coming for you." She shook her head. "I don't know why they were after you, but I couldn't knowingly let you die, so I got in the way."

"These dark forces want me dead? Why do you think they want me dead? What is it that you two won't tell me?"

Her companion found the self restraint to keep out of the argument.

Frowning, she answered, "I don't have any idea why they would want you to die, Jack. You haven't shown yourself to be a threat to either side. There's nothing to tell."

"Yes I have!"

The two stared in surprise.

He shrugged and his outrage grew. "You stopped them! You got in the way, and now they'll keep coming after me. Am I right?"

Then Golden Eyes glared. Jack seemed confused, and she snapped, "We haven't time for this. Be glad that you still breathe, and come along!" As her eyes returned to violet, she softened and frowned. "I'm sure you can figure it out as we go." With that, she turned and went through.

Oryn paused long enough to scowl and disappeared into the light, as well.

Alarmed by what he saw, he murmured, "She's out of her mind." A moment later he realized the light was fading. His stomach somersaulted, and he quickly leaped into the glow so that he would not be left behind.

Reaching the other side instantly, Jack came rushing out across green grass in a blaze of sunshine. Blinded, he skidded to a stop, shading his face. "Ah! What the ...?"

The travelers stood in a grassy field, full of blossoms. A flock of birds took flight from a tree, as Adwen scaled it to get their bearings. By the time Jack stopped shielding his eyes, she was already climbing down. Jumping the rest of the way, she told them, "From my estimate, we're somewhere by the high cliffs. We need to go south."

Shaking his head, Jack said, "No." When they froze and glared, he wasn't afraid and went on. "I'm not following until you say where you're taking me."

Rolling her eyes and sighing, she stepped closer. "This isn't how it's going to be, is it? You're going to have to trust me. I'm taking you to someplace safe. You're going to stay with some friends of mine for a few days until things are situated."

"Then what? What about my life? What about my wife? What happens to Ashley?"

"What did you think I meant by situated? I'm doing the best I can to keep you safe, as Higgins made me promise. I can't call off this war for you, but I can do things within reason to make sure you and she are safe. Now come on. We can stop at the nearest village for food."

Not pleased at the mentioning of his friend, he glanced between her serious expression and Oryn's blank stare, and heaved a sigh.

"Fine. Let's get going then."

The hike was not short. Tired and struggling to keep up, the police officer panted and brushed by another low-hanging branch. He glowered, as his two guides were always out of earshot. Every so often he could catch a word or two, but nothing that hinted to what the topic was. For all he knew, they were discussing the weather. Jack continued to combat the dense foliage.

"Why did you say you would seek out his wife?" Oryn asked disappointedly.

"You weren't listening to me were you?"

He gave a searching look.

"I never said I'd be going to find her. All I said was that I'd do what I could to keep them both safe."

After thinking it over, he almost laughed. "You don't intend to do anything?"

"Actually, I've been avoiding the topic of when he's going back home on purpose. So long as he stays here, our enemies will have no reason to touch her. She doesn't know anything, so she's safe. Ashley just needs to stay ignorant."

"Are you certain?"

The golden color flashed across her eyes, and she nodded. "I'm sure. Whatever happens, so long as Jack doesn't go back to the realm of logic, they won't do anything to harm Ashley Towers. They have bigger fish to fry."

Shaking his head, a feeling of pity came over him. "When do you intend to tell him this? He will inevitably deduce your plan and become a problem. Hiding the fact shall only fuel his loathing. You risk making him your enemy."

She sighed and became sullen.

He was looking for a reply and raised an eyebrow. "Adwen?"

Grimacing, she answered in a depressive tone, "He was never my friend."

Anger threatened to spark inside Oryn, as he asked, "What has he done?"

"He just ... he always counted me out of everything. When I still thought he was cute, I only saw the good aspects of who he was. I wouldn't be able to stop myself from ..." she had a look of discomfort. "I couldn't stop looking at him. The one time I got the guts to even talk to him was when he was having a bad day. I tried to comfort him."

When she didn't continue, he gently prodded, "And then ...?"

"And he ..." she sighed. "He yelled at me to get lost and said he didn't want anything to do with a loser like me."

Oryn's eyes glowed, and he snarled softly to himself.

"He wasn't like the others. He didn't go out of his way to hurt me, throwing garbage or spitting." Shaking her head and forcing a wry smile, she admitted, "I set myself up to be shot down. I couldn't see what kind of person he really was underneath it all. That was my mistake."

"It is no excuse for cruelty. Once more, you have gone out of your way to aid him. And once more, he spurns your open hand. What you did was nothing to condemn, and the same can be said even now. Do not let his foul tongue cut you, or I doubt you could stop me from cutting it out."

A few laughs from her cooled some of his heated feelings.

Entertained by the offer, she smiled, shaking her soft head of hair. "You don't need to do that. He's my responsibility, and I don't think cutting him up would do much. Jack's as tough as he is annoying. Don't hurt him ..." She gave him a big smile that made her eyes sparkle. "And that's an order."

Staring off at nothing, he remained silent.

"Oryn? You won't hurt him, will you?"

Heaving a sigh, he answered at last, "Only when it is warranted."

Another laugh escaped her. "I guess I can live with that. Just keep him in one piece and alive if you do."

"Hey," they both heard the cop's voice echo to them. "Wait! I'm stuck!"

Oryn glowered, while Adwen struggled not to laugh.

Jack had managed to get tangled in a few vines. The ropy growth was tough, and it took a few moments of awkward struggling to remember his new weapons. Taking up one of the daggers, he easily sliced his way free.

Satisfied and glad to be out of the snare, he planted a happy kiss on the golden hand guard and put it away. "You were thinking about leaving me in the man-eating plant, weren't you?" he joked as he rejoined them. "How about including me in the conversation so you know I'm not falling behind. The last thing I want is to get lost here."

She rolled her eyes. "Well, if you did, you'd be one step closer to knowing what I've had to deal with. I won't lose you, and you can't lose me. I can smell your scent from a mile off. Come on. We're almost to the town."

Both watched as she stalked off through the trees, and Oryn stared silently at the cop, looking for an ounce of compassion.

Jack chuckled. "If I didn't know any better, I would think I was getting to her. What do you think?"

Oryn didn't reply. After staring for a moment longer, he turned and went on.

Seeing and hearing her reaction was fun, but what was Oryn's look about? A little confused, Jack tried to catch up with their long-legged strides.

Once he found them again, the stone and timber buildings that made up the town stood before him. People were everywhere, milling about and minding their business until they came into the streets. Whoever saw Adwen and Oryn smiled, as others studied Jack curiously. A few girls giggled at his uniform.

Chuckling and shaking his head, he tagged along to the tavern.

Oryn opened the door for her, and someone called out, "The Tame One is here!"

In seconds, a crowd had engulfed the trio and began to usher them to the bar.

"What has happened across the river?" one asked, and another called, "Are the demons still coming? What will you do?"

Soon they were seated, and she shushed them, trying to get a breath of fresh air. The smells and sounds were overwhelming. "Calm down, please! I can't answer every question." To her surprise, they hushed, and she continued. "I went across the Broad River. Those who were still alive have been set free and are making their way here. Once we leave, we will be going to fight elsewhere."

A woman cried, "What of my son! He was a guard in Fort Wight! Does he live?"

Not knowing how to reply, Adwen said, "The only survivors from the other side had taken refuge there. I don't know if he was among them, but nearly fifty people left for the westbound highways." Then she had an idea. "Was his name Sysco?"

The woman smiled and sobbed. "Yes! Is he living? Please, tell me!"

Adwen beamed and nodded. "He was leading them. He promised me he would get them to the city of Plexus."

While the villagers cheered and asked more questions, Jack was offered some strong-smelling alcohol by the bartender. Not liking the flavor after having a taste, he gagged and asked, "I don't have any money, but do you have anything to eat?"

Gesturing to her, he laughed. "If you're traveling in the Tame One's company then all of my services are free, lad! Shall it be cheese and bread?"

Curious, he asked, "Do you have any meat to go with that?"

In the blink of an eye, the bartender had what Jack had asked for. "Help yourself!"

Jack's stomach grumbled at the sight of fresh-baked bread. Taking out one of the trusty daggers, he went about making his lunch.

The hefty bartender stared, as Jack sliced open the small loaf and layered the meat and cheese inside. He was thoroughly entertained. "That's not a bad idea! Why didn't I think of that?" His laughs continued, and the cop bit into his simple meal.

Two villagers started for the swordsman. "Some said Sir Oryn is traveling with the heir!" one of them said. "Are you him, sir?"

Without uttering a sound, he nodded.

Jack chuckled as they began to banter, nudging him with an elbow. When Oryn glanced, he swallowed a bite and asked, "I take it you are as much of a celebrity as she is."

He only stared with a blank expression and refused to commune with him.

The cop rolled his eyes and took another bite.

After what Adwen said of this human's treatment, it was difficult to fulfill his role as Jack's touchstone. Now all he wanted was to see the scoffing man suffer. He knew it was coming very soon. That was the only thought that kept him from losing control and tossing him out like a street urchin. His instincts told him that Jack's first lesson was fast approaching, and he couldn't help but smile.

As he did, Jack noticed and felt a shiver crawl up his spine. This was his first time seeing the ghost of a smile on the swordsman, and he didn't like it very much. Putting his attention into filling his empty stomach helped relieve the sudden unease. Adwen's personal bodyguard seemed scarier with every passing minute.

Adwen was still taking questions from various concerned villagers but answering vaguely. She didn't want to unsettle them or give the wrong ideas. Gradually, her senses began to tingle. A familiar itching sensation was in the back of her mind, urging her to be alert. Oryn also experienced the feeling, and both ignored the clamor, watching the windows.

The door crashed open wide, and a man with blood running down his face cried, "The Cult!" Everyone silenced immediately and gaped.

"The witches are here! Tame One! The Red Cult is here!"

The bloodied man was about to fall, and the crowd parted so that Adwen could rush forward and catch him. Parts of his body were burned by dark magic, and others bled through stab wounds. Jack gaped and set aside his food to follow Oryn to where she knelt, holding him.

Blood was in his mouth and he apologized: "Forgive me. They sent me to make you come. I'm sorry, Tame One."

She shushed him, horrified by his mortal wounds. "You didn't do anything wrong. Relax. I'll take care of them."

The stranger attempted to smile, but his next breath was his last. He coughed and gagged, both eyes rolled back and slowly closed.

Laying him gently down, she grew angrier. Adwen glared out through the open threshold at a dark assembly of figures robed in crimson and black. None was attacking. The witches waited for her to come meet them. She was not about to disappoint.

Snarling and eyes glowing, she stood and addressed the onlookers behind her: "Everyone! If there is a way to get out of this town, find it! Don't get in the way, and run as far from here as you can! The Red Cult is mine! Go!"

She strode to the porch, as the people poured out the windows like fleeing animals. Oryn was at her side, ready to summon his sword, and Jack was close behind.

"These are witches?" Jack asked her as he caught up. "How many are you going to let me fight?" Taking out his daggers, the cop was eager to test them out in a real fight.

Without taking her eye off of the vile troop, she growled and snarled to her tall counterpart, "I don't want him to be part of this mix. Make sure he stays here."

Before Jack could say anything more, Oryn's fist tapped his temple, knocking him out and to the porch. He fell in a heap, and his daggers clattered on the floorboards, as Adwen led the way down.

She practically screamed from the steps at the dark assembly, *"If a fight was what you wanted, all you had to do was knock! But no! You had to push me!"*

As she was yelling, Oryn was scanning the orderly mob for Nadeen. He still had a score to settle for the things she had done to Adwen. Last he had seen of the Blood Red Witch, she was lost in the chaos and panic at the Crescent Remains. For the moment, the rotten woman was nowhere to be seen, so he snarled. The beautiful hag couldn't be far.

"We have a reputation to uphold," their leader called out and laughed. "I'm afraid that simply knocking would not suffice! We are all curious, Tame One! Show us what you can do!"

"Gladly!"

Roaring in a fit of rage, she transformed, and Oryn summoned the Rose Thorne. The witches launched a bombardment of burning spells, and the duo parted to avoid the strikes, flanking them like trained cattle dogs.

A few black spells landed on her white fur, but they only managed to aggravate her further. She gnashed her fangs, leaping into the formation to rip them apart. Those that her claws and jaws found screamed as they died, and others cut and stabbed in retaliation. Avoiding the worst of their attacks, the pain only enraged her further.

Oryn cut them down like stalks of wheat, spilling black witch and warlock blood across the cobbled street. In moments, he was covered in their vile fluids and prepared to claim more. He remained in his human disguise and roared, cleaving enemies in half as far as his six-foot blade would reach.

As always, when blood and filth came in contact with Adwen's body, it turned to dust before falling away. Only she stayed unsullied amid the mess of gore and evil spells. More cult members were coming out of hiding with demon-steel weapons. They launched arrows from a distance, not caring if their own were struck.

When the first two volleys landed, both Adwen and Oryn were surprised and clipped by multiple arrows. She bobbed and weaved, as he jumped and rolled to escape the next set of deadly points, looking for an opening in the assault.

Half a dozen villagers had taken to the rooftops with bows of their own and shot down angrily. The witches were surprised at first but soon retaliated. With only a few spells, they set the buildings ablaze with red flames, laughing maniacally.

For the small moment that the arrows stopped flying, Adwen was able to reach the witches. In a single leap and a flash–jump, she appeared behind them and commenced to tearing their numbers down. They screamed and cut her with dark weapons, drawing her silvery blood, but she didn't care. Oryn was also making them pay for setting evil flames to the town, slaughtering as many cult members as he could.

Jack smelled smoke. As he came to, screams were permeating the air, helping to bring him around. The side of his head ached, and he gritted his teeth. When he looked out past the tavern porch, most everything was bathed in blood or flames.

When he finally saw the swordsman, he was soaked in dark crimson, swinging his giant sword back and forth. Horrified by the sight of him and what he had done, the cop gasped, "Holy ..." but he stopped as he heard Adwen roaring.

She was perfectly clean and twice as fierce. He flinched as her claws quickly disemboweled a warlock and swatted the head from another. For a moment it was hard to imagine she was really Shari. Gaping when she took a slice across a thigh, bled silver and killed the offender, he couldn't believe what he was seeing.

He grabbed his daggers from the porch and stood, surveying the rest of the battleground. Homes burned, and a few villagers attempted to put out the flames, as others fired arrows at the dark intruders. Everywhere was screaming, blood, fear and fire. The utter chaos confounded him, but he willed his mind to not panic.

Billowing smoke turned the sky dark in patches and stained the afternoon sun red like the ground. Then Jack squinted at a figure on a rooftop. The smoke half hid her from view, but he could see a woman with flowing black hair. Her red dress flapped in the breeze and rolled like the smoke that swirled about. Jack's gut twisted, as he saw her lifting a pitch-black longbow, covered in barbs and human bones. She was notching a lengthy shaft with big raven feathers and a spiny steel head.

Leaving the tavern for the small plaza, he watched her. Then his worries were confirmed when she drew back on the tight string. His eyes darted between her weapon and Adwen's turned back. Oryn was far too distracted to see, and no one else noticed.

Cursing under his breath, he stowed the blades and fought to reach the white hound.

Nadeen's black eyes glistened in the brief patch of light. A sickly smile lifted the pale cheeks on her face, and she honed in on Adwen, waiting for the perfect shot. She adored this arrow she had made with the help of her demon lover. It was sure to break Adwen down, render her unconscious and weaken her will. The thought broadened her smile into a sadistic grin. A shot to the heart was what she really wanted, so she waited a moment longer.

Panting and sprinting as fast as possible, Jack called out, "Look out! Look out!"

Adwen didn't hear and dropped to all fours to strike low at her enemies.

Seeing no other way, and out of options, he ran at her.

When the sound of Jack's yells reached Oryn's ears, he finished the last witch in his way and turned. First he saw the cop rushing for Adwen but then saw Nadeen perched on a roof across the way, taking aim. Before he could think to take a step, Nadeen fired at his unwary leader, and he gasped in dismay.

In the last second, Jack stopped on a dime, facing the head witch and her arrow. His expression was fearful but determined. Then he felt something bite into him. Stunned by the force of the hit, he fell back and almost onto Adwen.

Sensing him, she jumped away, whipping around in time to see his body land on the ground. Her eyes widened, pupils dilated, and she snarled in outrage. When his eyes closed, she looked up at Nadeen and roared.

Rearing to stand over the wounded human, another roar rushed out of her with a fearsome eagle call. Her eyes continuously alternated between gold and violet, growing brighter all of the while. Oryn rushed to her side, but she hardly noticed through the burning rage. It filled her from the inside and doubled over and over until the burning grew her power even higher.

Then her vision was awash with rippling white flames as they flowed out and enveloped her entirely. Roaring again, white fire filled her up and spewed out her eyes and mouth again, covering her body. Wherever she bled glowed like molten gold, and her jaws gnashed at the terrified hag and her doll face.

Her friend knelt by the fallen cop and examined where the arrow was through his abdomen. Quickly snapping the shaft to a shorter length, he saw what was happening to his commander and gaped. The white flames had consumed her but did not burn the coat or her skin. While she snarled and growled, the waving tongues of her light grew. He had never seen his leader this angry and almost flinched when her fiery eyes locked with his. Would she attack him?

Adwen's vision was shaded with the colors that danced in her eyes. She hardly realized she was speaking to Oryn and couldn't grasp her own thoughts.

He listened as either Adwen or Golden Eyes snarled, "*Get out of here! Take him to the ruins in the plains!*"

Thinking of the demon riders, he hesitantly asked, "What if the enemy sees us fleeing through the plains? It would render ..."

When she interrupted her eyes blazed bright hot gold, roaring, "*Go! Go to the high rocks by the ruins to wait! Now go!*"

Oryn scooped up Jack's limp form in a hurry and didn't look back, as she roared.

To Adwen, everything seemed to be a blur of sight and sound. Nothing made sense, like a dream she was struggling to straighten out into perceivable form. All she knew was what she felt. Her white fire quenched the red witch's flames and left the innocent untouched. As she bounded and roared, the power she wielded devoured the corrupted humans, burning them into nothing in seconds.

A few arrows were fired at her, but when they met with the light and fire, they evaporated like water. Sensing the assault, she turned and snarled.

By the time Oryn reached the last hill before the plains, he finally looked back. The white wildfire was blanketing the town, purging any dark intruders while shielding the villagers. He saw a few bursts of light that he knew was her flash-bangs and heard her cry again and staved off a shudder. Jack groaned, and Oryn looked to see if he was waking. His eyes fluttered but remained shut. Grimacing at Jack's state, Oryn turned his back on the rescued town and ran.

The wide-open spaces were quiet. Racing over the grassy terrain with the wind at his back, Oryn reached the rocky land formations in hours. Night was upon them, and the human was not about to improve. Oryn gently held him and leaped up along the rough earthy shelves. As he thought he would, he found a dry cave and took him inside.

Sniffing only once told him it was safe and empty. Around a bend and in the dark, his eyes spotted a patch of level ground. He laid Jack down and unbuttoned his jacket and blood-soaked uniform. When his strong bare chest and gut were unveiled, Oryn clenched his jaw at the sight. The place where the arrow went through was bleeding and purple at the edges. The tip had been dipped in a demon's essence.

He was about to pull it out, but the sound of Adwen's roar outside gave him a start. There was a bright white flash as he went out, but he saw through it and spied her form, attacking trees and large rocks at random below.

The flames weren't dancing on her anymore but burned in her violet eyes. Snarling and barking, she unleashed her vengeance on another tree, snapping it. As it fell with a crash she heard Oryn's voice, "What are you doing? Calm yourself before you alert them to our hiding place!"

When she whipped around, he froze and glared while she snarled, "Then let them come!"

He frowned, maintaining his accusing look.

The longer she saw his expression, the more she cooled. What was left of her fire settled inside, and she huffed, transforming into her woman form. Shaking her head and scowling, she added, "It would be a good way to vent some frustration."

He led her to their small hideaway and admitted darkly when they reached the mouth, "It would be a miracle if he lasts the night."

With the rage gone, she was somber, and her tone was fearful. "How bad is it?"

Knowing she would only blame herself, he chose not to answer. After giving a stern look, he said, "The arrow he took was meant for you."

"What? How do you know? Why did he ...?"

"First and foremost, its tip was covered in demon's blood. You would have been poisoned. He saved you."

"What made him get in the way? Was he shoved?"

Oryn shook his head grimly. "It surprises me as much as you. He willingly chose his fate."

"We can't move him from here, can we?"

"No. He is fading. Carrying him off now would only wear him faster. He has perhaps an hour at the most."

Clenching her fists, the reality set in, and she loathed herself. Tears blurred her vision, as she shook and whispered, "I promised. I promised, and I screwed it up."

Oryn barely stopped himself from drawing her close and shifted his stance instead. Being firm, he attempted to end Adwen's self abuse: "He made his own choice. There was nothing to be done. You cannot save every life you promise to protect."

She swallowed the sob, glared back and snapped, "I keep my promises!" Then she calmed and let the tears roll, shaking her head. "It was his friend's last request."

He sighed and finally asked, "Why did you destroy him?"

Wiping at her eyes, she murmured under the arm, "He was marked. In a few days he was going to be a werewolf for the first time. I just couldn't tell Jack." Finished drying her face, she gazed sadly into the cave.

Looking into the quiet stillness, Oryn understood why she hadn't told Jack. He wouldn't have listened to or comprehended the explanation. Oryn watched in silence as she went into the cave. He didn't follow and felt it was best. Picking out a disguised perch, he stood guard and served as her lookout.

She could smell the demon blood along with that of the human. Once she saw Jack lying so still, the tears couldn't be stopped. Cupping a hand to her mouth, she kept herself quiet and sat beside him. After taking a moment to get control of her emotions, his right hand was closest, and she held it to feel for a pulse. It was faint, and he didn't stir. Setting his hand down again, a few more tears fell, landing on her lap.

Her lips quivered while she whispered, "I'm sorry. I didn't see her coming."

There were no signs of life from the cop besides his shallow breathing.

"I should have known it was a trap. I should have grabbed you and run out of there or ... something."

Jack remained unresponsive.

Closing her eyes tight, she tried not to sob, and her voice cracked. "I really did promise your friend to keep you safe, Jack. I'll tell you why I did what I did. He was ..."

The arrow was not in Jack's body anymore. It was lying beside her.

She smelled more fresh blood and tasted it on her lips. Touching them with her fingertips, she found red on them upon inspecting. Then she saw his arm. Her eyes bulged, and her heart pounded like mad.

Oryn was still crouched by the ledge outside, vigilantly studying the lay of the land. No movement caught his eye, and everything seemed clear. He sighed, feeling hopeful that no one had followed either of them to this place.

Adwen's scream reached his ears like the shriek of nails on glass. As he whipped around, she was transforming and ripping out of the cave and down the rocky slope. In a split second she disappeared into the trees and was gone.

He didn't bother trying to follow and sighed, shaking his head. Glancing back through the entrance, the thought of a proper burial came to mind. Simply leaving his body out for the insects and carrion beasts didn't seem right, even for this man. He had, in fact, sacrificed himself to keep Adwen alive. Going in to fetch the corpse, he shook his head once more.

The first thing he noticed was the arrow left on the ground. Small pieces of soft flesh were caught in the harsh barbs where it lay, in a pool of blood from another wound. When he noticed the sleeve on the body's right arm pulled back an idea dawned on him. Oryn knelt down low to investigate the new injury. It was a bite mark from a small set of fangs, cutting deep into his forearm.

As soon as he realized why she had bolted and fled, he was surprised. Then he felt remorse for her, which was quickly replaced by intrigue and steadily rising entertainment. For a moment, he was disgusted that Jack would be a permanent part of this war, but he let the disappointment go. He watched as the bleeding began to slow and stop. Both wounds were on the way to mending.

Buttoning the police officer's sleeve and up the front of his uniform, Oryn was expectant. A small smile lit up his face, and his eyes glowed. Very soon, this whelp was going to see his prior warnings come to life, all at once.

Chapter 11
OTHER RESPONSIBILITIES

Adwen ran. There was nothing else she could think to do. After unknowingly harming another person for the second time, all her fears were being relived. What had she done? Had she marked him, too? Even though she didn't know, she ran anyway.

Bolting through the trees and headed who knows where, her fear remained. Why was she having blackouts? Was someone controlling her? Was the enemy doing this to her? Panting and bounding past dense thickets of brambles and bushes, she didn't want to stop until she felt lost. Once her nose picked up traces of salt and brine, there was little chance of losing her way. The coast was about fifteen miles out.

Howling miserably at her inability to escape her fear, Adwen ended the pointless attempt. Finding an opening amid the wind-bent trees was easy, and she transformed, grasped her hair and dropped to her knees. Screaming and sobbing out her internal anguish felt liberating. The tears were blinding. All she saw was a landscaped blurred and misshapen by past storms and countless gales. It felt like a small sanctuary with the leaning trees blocking out the rest of the world while she cried harder.

After a while of sobbing, she sensed her three friends before she saw them. They had no scent, as always. The three spirits of order took the form of three human girls wearing white robes. A spirit with blond hair laid a comforting hand on Adwen's shuddering shoulder.

The being representing peace cooed and soothed her. "It is all right. No wrong has been done, Adwen." When no reply came, Pearl knelt down to embrace Adwen's shaking, weeping form.

Red-haired and fiery, the being of justice folded her arms. "Jack has made his choices, and now he must live with them." Judy frowned and shook her head. "You kept your promise. He will live."

What she had said hit Adwen like a bolt of lightning, and she screamed, "*At what cost?*" Then the sobbing continued, and Pearl tried to shush her, stroking the back of her hair and giving the spirit of justice an accusing look.

Using a soft, commanding tone, the black-haired spirit of law instructed, "Adwen? Stand up. You must speak with us and be spoken to." Lacey shook her head and added, "There is no more hiding. What has happened cannot be undone and was meant to be."

As Pearl helped Adwen stand, she sobbed in the being's arms. "That's why I was supposed to find him, wasn't it? This was why the darkness wanted him to die?"

When their eyes finally met, the three nodded in answer.

"This one is going to take a bit of work before he's ready to accept the responsibility of his new role," Judy warned. "This warrior is as bitter as the last once was, but he will have little to console himself with. Sir Oryn had ways to get around the pain and fear of leaving the past behind."

Lacey nodded again and agreed. "Jack will be difficult to work with, but eventually, he will fulfill his destiny. Be forgiving when need be." Then the spirit grimaced and shook her head. "But you must find the will to give him punishment. He will not come to your call easily."

The cautions worried Adwen, and she glanced at Pearl, who nodded and murmured, "Jack Towers is going to be very stubborn. Do not be cruel. Be harsh. For his heart to find peace, he must find the way to forgive and move forward. No matter how cold or how many terrible things he says and does ... have faith. He will learn."

Gulping down a few tears, she asked warily, "What's happening to me? Why wasn't I aware when I marked Oryn or Jack?"

The spirits exchanged discreet glances, while Adwen gazed at the ground, listening to their awkward hesitation.

"Be confident in this knowledge, Adwen," Judy advised. "None of your actions have been dark, and they have been in the best interests of all. What you have done, though while not entirely present, is the bidding of the Light Spirits. You are their warrior and servant. As you are, they would not allow you to do evil. Have no fear of doing wrong. They will not let you dabble in that."

Feeling calmer, she dried the last tears from her bright eyes. Some unease remained, but she breathed easy. Studying each of their encouraging expressions, she murmured, "Could I ask you guys for a favor?"

They smiled, and Pearl answered with her soft voice, "Of course."

Licking her black lips, a bad feeling had started to bother her ever since sighting the powerful demon in the park. She was worried. "Could you ... keep an eye on my family? Can you keep them safe while I'm away?"

Lacey blinked, Judy frowned, and Pearl looked away.

Their reactions alarmed her. "What's wrong?"

Quick to keep Adwen calm, Lacey reassured her, "They are well."

"We can keep an eye on them," an unusually shifty Judy said, "but we can't be with them all of the time."

Pearl was frowning when their white and golden-haired friend asked, "Why not?"

Locking eyes with her, the blond spirit of order forced a small smile. "Well ... we are the Horai. We have a lot of work to do. For you to succeed, we must go to many places and cannot be at all of them at once. You are not the only one who needs looking after and protecting. Guiding two different warriors is not so easy."

Now her curiosity was equal with her worry. "Who is the other you're talking about? Who else is fighting?"

"That is not important now," Lacey answered. "You have work to do, as well."

Adwen nodded and put away her sadness. Looking back at the proud beings, she announced, "I guess I'll wait here for them to find me. This place feels safe enough for dealing with Jack. He isn't going to be very happy when he sees me again. I'm not going to let him view me as weak anymore. ... Never again."

The Horai were pleased and Lacey nodded. "We believe you. Farewell."

A moment later, they were gone, and Adwen was alone.

A Change of Plans

High in a secluded, wind-whipped and barren mountain pass, Nadeen strutted into the dark. The click and crunch of her tall heels reverberated along the narrow cave entrance. When it was far too difficult to see, she summoned a ball of red fire to light the way and smiled, scanning the shadows. Her perfect porcelain skin caught the flickering glow, bathing her face and chest in a bloody hue. She relished the color.

A flight of stairs took her higher and opened up to a cold chamber. Dark chains hung from the walls past deformed black pillars of rock, dangling like dead snakes. She ignored her lovely restraints. What had her rapt attention was the figure seated in the back on a long sacrificial table. Candelabras were on either side of him, glowing brightly, like his white speckled eyes.

Sycan's smirk made her swoon and shiver. The demon's young face captured her, as did the rest of his powerful body, hidden beneath the folds of his black and red human-skin leather clothing. Ascending another set of steps, she went closer to play with his wine-red hair. He was so terrifyingly handsome to the witch that there was no question why she had sold her body and soul to him.

But as she was reaching to touch his face, his smile vanished, and his hands moved with blinding speed. In a flash, he had her wrists and held her still. Frowning into her face, the whites around his pale eyes turned black. Clenching his jagged shark-like teeth, he asked coolly, "Well? How did it go, dearest Nadeen?"

She gulped and was taken aback. Fluttering her eyes, she replied, "All went well, my lover. It is going well."

A thunderous growl came rumbling from him and he sneered, "If that were the case, then you would not be so quiet. You'd be giddy to have her here and ready to be sent into the nothingness of oblivion! So I have a simpler question. What went wrong?"

Utter terror made her bottom lip tremble. "That man – the one who wears a dark blue uniform."

The demon stopped sneering and was disappointed with where this was going. Frowning and rolling his eyes, he calmly asked, "He got in the way, didn't he?" When she nodded, he tossed her hands away and sighed. Sycan shook his head and lay back on the stone slab, folding his arms. "And I actually thought for a moment that the general's men would do a better job than my own." He ticked his tongue in disapproval.

The witch was looking for a way to make him proud of her and gladly told him, "The man was mortally wounded by my hand, lover! All is well! He is no longer a threat!"

An instant later, the demon was up and pounced. He grasped her by the throat and kept her head from striking the ground, making her cringe and giggle with fright. She was terrified, and she loved it.

He snarled in her face and bellowed with his youthful human's voice, "If he already possessed a treasure from Darien's private collection, then your shot ensured his joining her ranks! I told you specifically not to let him be harmed! Now she will be stronger because of your failures!" He let go and stood.

She gazed up, horrified that she had done all of that to set back her master. Gaping and trembling on the floor, she attempted not to squirm under is glare.

Then Sycan's face became surprised. He smiled and chuckled at the dark.

Worried that he could have something in mind for her, she asked, "What will you do, my lover?"

Grinning, he reached and helped her up. "I have a new idea. This one is going to be twice as fun. It should work very well."

Wondering if she was being brushed aside, she batted her eyes and pouted. "Do you have a role for me to play?"

He blinked at her in surprise and shook his head. "Oh, but of course, my pet! You will have a very important role for the big finish! I haven't forgotten you!"

Enthralled, she chortled, "Oh, lover! You tease. You did too nearly forget to include me." She didn't care and smiled a saccharine smile.

He chuckled again, drawing her closer by her chin. "Your role is going to be at my side through every step. This way, you can learn how not to make the same mistakes again."

"Do you promise?" she whispered with eyes half cast in pleasure.

A slow growl vibrated in his throat, he flung her onto the stone slab and crouched low over her as she laughed. Her ebony painted nails combed through his hair while he sniffed and licked her neck with his blue forked tongue. Moving up to her ear, he whispered darkly, "You know I will, Nadeen. You are mine to do with as I please."

Chapter 12
COMEUPPANCE

With the last hours of the night, Oryn found a creek in which to bathe. For the cleaning, he was in his hound form and to dry off he rigorously shook the water from his short coat. He remained just outside the cave for the rest of the waning dark before dawn, thinking about how to contend with Jack. Once Jack woke, there was little doubt that he would ask questions.

Running the series of possibilities through his mind, it was all too amusing. Should he feel pity and warn him of what was coming? Glancing furtively into the cave, he scoffed and shook his head.

Inside the quiet confines, Jack felt uncomfortable on the solid ground. Groaning, he turned over onto his side and winced at the soreness. He hurt all over. Lying on the hard rock and dirt left his muscles stiff, making him grimace and groan again.

Sitting up was even more unpleasant. He gasped, hugging at his sides. A second later, he was feeling better and sighed, glancing around. The cave was too dark to make out any details past the entrance, where dawn's first light spilled in. Forcing himself to his feet, he never saw the large dry patches of blood underfoot. When he made his way toward the light, his shoe kicked the arrow aside. His sight wasn't capable of seeing the signs throughout the shadows, showing how close he had come to death.

Going to stand in the warm sunshine, he heaved a sigh and was glad it didn't hurt. The air was crisp, same as the mornings in his world when he would be jogging. He already missed Ashley too much.

"How do you feel?" Oryn prompted in a cool tone.

He chuckled dryly and grumbled past the grogginess, "Chipper."

Raising a curious eyebrow, the swordsman asked, "Is this your form of sarcasm or genuine honesty?"

The cop stretched his stiff body and soon regretted it as his gut ached. Gritting his teeth at the dull pain, he remembered this man was from a world where some words didn't exist. "It's sarcasm. I feel like a pile of week-old dog crap." Looking down at himself for the first time, he found a silver dollar sized hole in his shirt and a stain.

The splotchy area was still damp and he wiped at it. Sticky half-dried blood was on his fingers. Confused, he asked, "All of this is mine?"

Perfectly nonchalant and prepared, Oryn yawned to hide his smile. "All of it. Every drop, but nothing to worry about. As you can plainly see, you've mended."

He was astounded at the amount of blood down his front. "I could have died! How am I still alive? What happened?"

When he looked his way, Oryn shrugged. "Magic."

Jack narrowed his gaze and studied Oryn's green eyes. Something was up. The blank expression was firmly set in place like a mask, but Oryn's eyes had a glint to them. Looking the swordsman up and down, he asked, "What's going on? Where's Adwen?"

Getting up, Oryn pointed to the south. "We may find her in that general direction. Are you well enough to travel?"

Unsure, he cocked an eyebrow. "How long was I out?"

"The entire night."

"Why did she run off without you?"

Oryn was prepared. "She had other business to attend to, and I was left to stand guard." A smile was unavoidable.

Frowning, Jack knew he hadn't touched on the right subject and was even more suspicious. "What was her other business?"

"She wouldn't say. I am as curious as you. Are you well enough to join me in seeking her?"

"Do you think she went to get my wife?" This was a thought that already made his day feel better.

Oryn shook his head, and disappointment tugged down at Jack's shoulders. "I highly doubt that is the case," Oryn said. "But I assure you, she would be safe regardless. Come along."

When Jack started after the tall swordsman, all he wanted to do was clobber him. What was he hiding? At that moment, he saw how high up they were and gaped at the rough, narrow path. Beginning to follow, he called, "How did we get here anyway?"

Oryn was doing his best to go slow, finding the smoothest of the narrow trails. If he showed off how easily he could leap across the rocky shelves, the coming night wouldn't be nearly as entertaining. Balancing, and faking the precariousness, he replied, "Magic. She used her power to bring us here and escape our enemies. Come along."

There was nothing Jack could use to argue with that answer, no matter how much he felt that it was somehow a lie. Letting the feeling go, Jack went down using the same paths. The rest looked too loose to hold his weight anyway.

They cut across a few short acres of the plains, and Oryn was glad they did not come across demons while in their territory. With that one fear out of the way, all he had left to think of was how much he couldn't wait for sundown. He had stolen a look at the sky while entering the small mountains that shielded the plains from the sea. Two crescents were visible shortly after noon – the red and orange. Tonight the full one would be the green moon. Drawing his attention back to tracking Adwen, he restrained a chuckle and moved on.

Jack had noticed him studying the sky and took a look for himself. Besides the two colorful moons, there was nothing out of the ordinary. Scowling after the swordsman, he kept his mouth shut and followed into denser woods. Soon the terrain became rough and forced them to hike up and then trudge back down. After a few hours, the cop became impatient and suspicious once more.

"Hey, something just occurred to me after almost thirty miles of following you to nowhere."

Unperturbed, Oryn replied, "What has?"

"How do you know where she is? How do you know that this is the way she went?"

Heaving a sigh, he decided to answer. Showing him the golden Andredan symbol on his left forearm, he explained, "This is her emblem. With this mark on me, I am a chosen warrior to do her bidding. I share a small link with her. I can sense that she went this way. It is something felt, rather than seen." As he was about to start off again, the police officer stopped him.

"Wait a minute."

Slightly worried that Jack might have caught on, Oryn turn and asked, "Is there a problem?"

Taking up the two daggers, he examined them saying, "These have the same mark. And what are these other marks by the handles?"

There was no need for Oryn to read them. He had studied the weapons while he was still a knight, serving the Order. Despite that, he accepted them and pointed to the old inscriptions. "This is the weapon's name. Notice the other has a different one. You are in possession of the twin daggers of love."

The cop rolled his eyes and groaned. "Great. That figures."

Oryn glared. "This one," he said as he pointed to the first, "is named Heart. And that one is named Soul."

When Jack took them back, some of the embarrassment of the weapons' titles went away, and he almost felt in awe. Admiring them, he thought about thanking Oryn for translating. "Who did they used to belong to?"

Watching Jack placing them through the gaps between his belt and the loops, the idea that this scum owned them threatened to make him puke.

He maintained a calm, but disappointed tone. "They first belonged to a woman. She was a powerful sorceress who used white energy to heal. Despite her beauty and gifts, her rage was fearsome, like a howling winter storm in a mountain pass." Then as their eyes met, he shook his head and frowned. "You don't deserve them."

Jack was stunned, as the warrior walked away. Looking between the swordsman and the weapons, Jack understood the reasoning, but why tell him straight out? Feeling ashamed to be carrying the daggers, he was quiet. What reply could he have? He was just a city cop, running around with two magical blades that used to be in the hands of a white sorceress. Shrugging off the feeling of shame, he forced it from his mind. Shaking his head, he continued to follow in silence.

Another hour of hiking went by and Jack spoke again. "Hey, where can I get some food? I haven't had anything since that disaster."

Not stopping or giving a glance, Oryn replied, "You will have to tolerate that for a little longer. Things are not as convenient here."

"I haven't seen you eat anything yet. Aren't you hungry at all?"

This conversation could blow Oryn's cover. Remaining calm, he lied: "While you healed in the night, I found a berry bush. Adwen catches most of our food in the wilds. When she is with us, she may catch a deer or a large hare."

The cop was still inquisitive. "How do you cook out in this without pots?"

Oryn hid his unease and rolled his eyes. "Magic. Do you intend to question me for the entire journey, or shall I cast a silencing enchantment on you?" To his surprise, Jack fell for the empty threat.

Taken aback, but unafraid, he backed off. "Sorry! Just curious! For the first time, I'm seeing real magic in another world. Give me break."

As they found level ground again, the sun was beginning to set, and Oryn couldn't help but notice. Slowing enough to enjoy the brilliant wash of colors on the sky, he also noted how clear it was. The green moon was nowhere in sight, but it would rise. Glancing at Jack, he seemed completely unaware and also enjoyed the sunset.

"Man, I wish I had my camera."

Admiring the warm glow a little longer, Oryn asked, "Why do you wish for it?"

"My wife, Ashley. She loves pictures of sunsets."

For a brief second, Oryn felt a twinge of remorse. Putting it away, there was no turning back now for Jack. Watching his expression in the light, it was peaceful and deceivingly friendly. He shook his head for the umpteenth time that day. "Come along. We have a little farther to go."

Jack smiled at the light as it faded and grumbled, "That's what you keep saying."

With dusk turning the sky black and bringing out the stars, night quickly arrived. They hadn't seen any sign of Adwen yet, and the cop's stomach was growling loudly enough for Oryn to hear. It was all he could do to keep from commenting.

When his stomach groaned again, Jack asked, "You can hear that, right?"

Glancing at the sky, he muttered, "Somewhat."

"I'm starving. Where is she? You've been leading me all over creation for the entire day! What is going on?"

Keeping his cool, he replied, "We shall stop for rest here."

The swordsman was settling down by a fallen tree, and the lack of an explanation irritated Jack further. "I've been letting you lead me on, and now I'm tired, I'm hungry, and I'm fed up with your smiling! What's so funny?"

Realizing that his smile had returned, the thought hadn't crossed his mind to put on a blank expression. Watching Jack carefully and glancing at the sky, Oryn warned, "You really should relax yourself. As you said, you are tired and hungry. Wasting your energy on being put out will only make things worse than they seem. Sit someplace a while."

Glaring angrily, Jack clenched his fists. "I know there's a reason for that smile, and I'm sick of you messing with me! What are you hiding? I'm not an idiot!"

"This is no joke. Rest for you would be best. Be calm and rest yourself."

"I will not calm down!" "Tell me what is so funny!"

Oryn raised an eyebrow as if to ask, or what? Being civil, but no longer smiling, he replied, "Your ignorance. Your complete ignorance to everything is what is so amusing to me. I wish to ask, Officer Towers, how does a man live so long with such a blind way of seeing the world? How can you look at another being and not see who they truly are?"

Jack was outraged. "Is this about her? I already told you who she really is! She's a stupid girl who doesn't know who she is! Shari is clueless and weak! Why can't *you* see her for what she really is?"

Shaking his head, Oryn almost pitied Jack for his imminent comeuppance. "You are wrong, Jack. You are seeing only what you wish to see. Adwen is strong and forgiving. People can change if they learn to see the world through new eyes. She has. I have. Soon ... you will, as well. I'll ask you once more: Sit and rest."

Worried that something terrible was happening, Jack's breathing was heavy, and he couldn't understand why. As beads of fine sweat formed on his brow, he murmured, "What are you talking about? What is she doing?"

Tilting his head back and taking a deep breath, Oryn closed his eyes and wished to know what Adwen was up to. After a moment, he got the sense that she was waiting. Looking back into Jack's frightened face, the reply was calm. "She is waiting for us. A few more hours of traveling, and we will find her. Is something the matter?"

Jack's entire body was pouring with sweat, and his head ached. The pounding of his increasing blood pressure echoed in his ears with the rhythm of his heartbeat. Blinking blearily at the intensity, he groaned and staggered, grasping his face. Small popping and burning sensations were flooding his every limb.

Feeling his capillaries and blood vessels expanding alarmed him, and he gasped. "What did you do? What's happening? Ah! Make it stop!"

Watching him collapse on the soil brought Oryn's smile back, but after another moment of relishing the spectacle, he smelled demons. He became serious and got to his feet, summoning the Greatsword into his grasp. As Jack continued to writhe and gasp, Oryn stood over him, eyes aglow, scanning the surrounding forest. The scent thickened, giving a rough indicator of how many were about to arrive.

Desperate to end the mind-bending pain, the cop found Oryn's heels and latched a death grip onto one ankle. He could hardly see through the agony, though his eyes were now glowing in the dark. Gasping and shuddering, he groaned, "Make it stop. I'm sorry I messed with you in the tunnels. Just take it away."

As the first Creepers were coming into the open, Oryn pulled free and snapped, "I can't take the pain away, and it won't stop until it has run its course! Now do as I say! Stay calm, and stay down!"

The demons lunged, shrieking and snapping until Oryn severed their heads. One came from the side, and it was kicked away, while he spilled the guts of another. Regardless of what manner they were slain, they turned to purple puddles at his feet. The attacks were relentless and came from all sides.

Clutching his sides and groaning, Jack wasn't sure what he had said. As he thought the pain couldn't get any worse, it did. Every part, bone, organ and sinew screamed and he did, as well. Stretching and crunching dulled his senses to the battle and completely filled his mind. Thrashing and contorting from what he felt his body going through, there was nothing to do but wail and cry.

A second of the experience passed like a dragging hour. When it was past, his screams became roars and howls, confusing and panicking him even more. He tried to scramble away, and his growing claws pulled him through the dirt. Then another second went by, and his spine crunched and ground on itself, forcing him to stop and roar again.

Expanding sides and limbs split the seams of his uniform and his jacket, and eventually snapped the belt, letting the blades fall away with the rest of his clothes. The bones in his face seemed to break, bend and elongate, as he howled and couldn't see Oryn close by, fending off the waves of monsters.

Lost in the excruciating transformation, Jack's skin felt like it was on fire. Black fur grew out all over him, getting thicker and longer. After nearly five minutes of slowly changing, it was about to be over, but his panic remained. His hearing caught the sounds of the demons' gnashing teeth and screeching as they died. It spurred him to move, and he was off on a bound through the trees.

Killing the last of the ethereal vermin, Oryn saw Jack fleeing and snarled.

Darting around like mad, fear and confusion drove Jack on. Before he could get far, something blocked his path and hit him like a homerun swing. His attempt to escape ended, and he was bowled over backward, gasping, panting and reeling from the hit. When he turned over and raised his head, it was the swordsman. The flat of his blade had knocked him back with little effort.

Glaring down at the muscular black beast with a spot of red hair on its brow line, Oryn was firm and commanding. "Calm yourself before I hit you hard enough to make you sleep the night away! Get control of your actions and be calm!"

Angry and still alarmed, he roared back in defiance.

"Silence, you stupid fool! You'll alert more demons to us!"

On the verge of more panic, Jack gnashed his jaws and snarled, "What did she do to me? What's happening?"

In an attempt to make him think clearly, Oryn answered, "I comprehend your feelings on the matter, but if you wish to ..."

"What do you know? You don't have any idea ..."

In an instant, Oryn transformed fully and roared down into Jack's face, forcing him to fall silent and gape. Then, while Jack was still frozen by shock, Oryn rumbled dangerously, "I know plenty more than you do!"

Jack couldn't breathe. At last, he gulped and sat, staring wide-eyed, as the massive creature returned to being the swordsman. Now he wasn't hiding his pointed ears and fangs, allowing Jack to see what he really was. Jack was shaken.

"Come along," Oryn growled with his eyes glowing brightly, "Come and fetch your daggers before you forget them. You're sure to need them in the future."

Far too stunned to do anything else, Jack followed, creeping along on all fours. His senses were sharp. He heard everything but couldn't react. His claws and paws padded along in Oryn's wake and back to the clearing where the daggers lay. Trying to get a grip, he looked up at Oryn's stern gaze. There was no sympathy.

Unable to think of another question, he moaned, "Why?" Then he was angry and snarled, "You knew! Why didn't you tell me?"

Done hiding any feelings from the brute, he snapped, "Would you have listened?"

Jack froze.

Then he spat out a command: "Now pick them up and stand. We haven't long before they send hundreds more onto us."

The idea sounded simple enough, but when he tried to stand, his legs felt awkward. He made the attempt to stay up twice. Falling back to all fours for the second time, he yelped in frustration, *"I can't!"*

Irritated and running out of patience, Oryn clenched his inch-long fangs and growled, "Stop being a pathetic twit! Use the tail for balance!"

"The what?" Then he looked back and found the long bushy extension of his spine. Seeing it made him yelp again, *"What the ...?"*

Oryn's anger sparked, and he bore down on Jack, changing into his monstrous self. Snapping and snarling, he barked in outrage, "*We haven't the time! Bring them in your jaws! Grab them up and hurry!*"

Jack's mind was still too numbed by shock, and he couldn't think to argue. He used his teeth to gather up the weapons by the grips.

Oryn reverted to his less-intimidating shape, and they ran south. They were following a scent Jack couldn't identify. It smelled good, and then he realized the scent was Adwen's. He moaned again in self pity and aggravation that he had been so easily fooled. The swordsman hound had played him like a violin.

Chapter 13
WORLD OF WOE

The full green moon loomed overhead, and dawn was a few short hours away. Both warriors sped along the trail, ignoring other smells. Oryn kept his nose busy detecting Adwen's scent, his ears pricked for enemies, and his eyes on both the dim horizon and the brutish looking black hound. Much like his own hound form, Jack kept his eye color and human hair. Jack was not as large as Oryn but possessed a more muscular build. He will have to be strong, he thought, if he's going to keep up in the weeks to come.

Jack was still numb. Thinking over everything that Adwen's servant had said, it made more and more sense. His strong jaws clenched around the daggers, and he growled. He wasn't sure what he was going to do, but he would do something. There had to be a way out of this. There had to be.

A hunter's cabin was nestled deep in the forest, secluded from everything. The strong, bearded man lived happily with his son, and both were sleeping when there was a knock at their door. As a precaution, he instructed the teen with a hand to get the crossbow ready and opened the entry enough to see a stranger on the doorstep.

With the sunrise at his back, Oryn saw the young man with the loaded weapon. He stayed quiet, waiting for them to speak first. It would keep things orderly.

Leery of the visitor's glowing green eyes, he frowned and asked gruffly, "What's your name, and what do you want?"

Carefully, Oryn replied, "I'm passing through, and I must ask a favor." Lifting and tilting his left forearm enough to show his mark, he added, "As for my name, I believe you could guess at that."

Spotting the golden emblem made the man's eyes widen, and he smiled. "Well, well! Sir Oryn is at my door? What could I do for you at this hour?" His son lowered the crossbow and came closer to hear.

Oryn's gaze judged the size of the two humans. "My companion is in need of a change of clothes. A single set would do if ...”

“Whatever you need, sir,” the son said. “Which of us is he closer to in size?”

He nodded to the son. “He is near your height and girth. Thank you.”

“No, Sir Oryn,” the hunter said. “Thanks are due to you and the Tame One.”

The forest was growing steadily brighter, and Jack felt more degraded and exposed than at any other time in his life. In his human form, he waited quietly, hiding by a broad tree, loathing everything in sight. Being completely bare in the woods with only his gold ring was a nightmare, but he wasn’t waking.

His senses were already sharper. Taking another breath, he rolled his eyes. He could smell Oryn coming back with something to wear.

Soft sounds of boots on soil announced Oryn’s arrival. Approaching until they could both see each other through the brush, Oryn stopped and tossed a set of clothing and boots over the bush.

Catching the shirt and breeches, Jack asked, “You can’t cast any enchantments, can you?”

“None at all.”

Jack huffed and shook his head, going about dressing himself. As he was belting the trousers to his waist, he saw something on his right forearm. The sight of the mark sent a chill through him and put a sick knot in his stomach. He swallowed and gaped. Thinking he might be able to rub the golden design from his skin, he scratched and brushed rigorously but to no avail. When he failed, he gave Oryn an alarmed look.

Oryn had been watching and knew what Jack had been doing. Frowning, he looked away.

The Andredan emblem remained unchanged by Jack’s efforts. At last, leaving it alone, he was shaking and fumbling to get the shirt over his head. He understood what the mark meant, thanks to the green-eyed hound, and was growing anxious and very angry. Snatching the boots from the bush, where they had landed, they were a close enough fit for his feet.

“We are nearly there,” Oryn calmly advised, as Jack came storming out from behind the natural screen, stowing the daggers on his belt. “Any questions you have you may ask her.”

Now equipped with his own heightened sense of smell, Jack

stomped past and sneered, "I have lots of questions." He kept following the scent trail. It was getting stronger.

Her smell took them to a rut path that wound, twisted, rose and fell with the earth. Eventually the scent became difficult to make out at the edge of a meadow. Thick greens and other animal odors masked hers. Frustrated, Jack searched around and crouched low, trying to find her footprints. There were none.

While he was growing even further aggravated, Oryn stepped forward. Scanning the broad opening, he felt eyes watching. His senses were much sharper than Jack's, so he closed his eyes and took a deep whiff. Along with the aroma of every plant and animal that had been passing through in the past hour, Adwen's scent was there as well.

Getting up, Jack noticed his sniffing. "Where is she?"

After a moment of staring around, Oryn eventually nodded to the edge of the clearing behind him.

She was stepping out from the fading shadows under the trees and into the warm daylight, where her hood could not keep her invisible. Pulling the white cloth back, she came close, frowning and watching Jack's reaction. When there were only a few yards between them, she stopped, studying his eyes.

No matter how pained his gaze was, his face was furious. He glared back and shuddered, restraining the need to wring her neck. Keeping his voice low and controlled, he asked, "What did you do to me?"

Afraid of how he would respond, she hesitated. "I had to. I didn't have a choice, Jack. I'm sorry." Her heart sank, as his face turned beet red.

"You're sorry?"

Adwen felt horrible, and tears almost came. She held them back and listened as Jack continued into an unbridled harangue.

"You killed my friend!" he cried and waved his arms at the scenery. "You brought me to this insane place! Then you turned me into a monster! What are you sorry for, freak? Isn't this what you wanted while you were stalking me in high school?"

Shaking her head, she murmured, "It's not like that. I admit it: I had a crush on you, and I didn't know what to do about it. That was then. If you think that I would still feel that way about you now, then you have another thing coming. I didn't do this on purpose, and I didn't do it for myself."

"Then who did you do it for, huh? What reason could you possibly have to make me ... into this?"

"I made a promise."

He nodded and scowled. "Yeah, Higgins. You killed him so he couldn't tell me what you were going to do to me."

At last, Oryn had had enough of listening to Jack's cold shots. "Of course she didn't, you lowlife scum! Have you learned nothing yet?"

"Then why?" Jack bellowed. "*Why?*"

Her eyes were glassy and bright, as her soft voice cracked. "You were dying, Jack." His eyes locked with hers, and she shook her head. "What was I supposed to do? Sit back and watch you bleed out? We took you to safety and ..."

"You bit me to save my life?" Her silence confirmed the theory, and he added, "Then you probably should have sat back and watched me die. I didn't even get a chance to make a choice."

"Neither did I. I didn't get to choose. Oryn didn't either. My promise to your friend was to keep you alive and safe, nothing more."

This news did not soothe Jack. "Thank you. Thank you for keeping the promise you made to my murdered friend. In all honesty, I actually do appreciate that. Now I need you to take this back. Take it away and take me home, right now."

Adwen's battle against her own tears was lost. She shook her head.

Jack's anger got the better of him. He lunged and grabbed her arms, yelling into her face, "Take it back! Take your stupid sign off of me!"

Oryn was about to sort things out in his own way, but Adwen gave him a discreet hand signal to stay back. Oryn's eyes were bright and his fangs clenched, enraged that Jack dared to handle her so roughly.

Her tears slowed, and she was calm enough to speak again. "I can't. I would if I could, but I can't. I'm sorry."

Jack's expression turned to one of terror. His grip on her slackened, and he gaped. Somehow he knew she was telling the truth. After letting go, he stared at the ground, thinking of what to do. When he made up his mind, he turned and started hiking north.

She called after him, "Where are you going?"

Jack didn't turn around or stop. "Home! I'm going to find one of those gateways, and I'm going back to the real world."

Her stomach was in knots, as she forced herself to tell him, "I'm the only one who can take you through them." As he stopped dead, she added sadly, "They only appear when I get close to them."

Alarmed and about to panic, he came stomping back and yelled, "Then take me back! Take me back! You have no reason to keep me here! You already said I mean nothing to you, so let me go! Take me home, Adwen!" He was in her face, horrified and outraged that she was his only hope.

Shaking her head, she replied, "I can't."

"Can't or won't?"

"If I let you go back, they will follow you to your home, if they aren't watching your house already. Then when your guard is down, they'll kill you and anyone who ever mattered to you. All of your friends, family and Ashley will be hunted down. My family is being hunted as we speak." She shook her head, and more tears tumbled down. "And I don't have the time to spare. I can't go back and find them, because I would be putting them in danger. The only way you or I can protect the ones who matter is to stay here and fight."

For the first time, Jack was listening and hearing the truth, but he didn't want to. "No. No. Take me home. Please, just take me back."

His fear provoked a sob from her. "You can't go back until this is over. If you love Ashley as much as I think you do, then you want to stay for her sake. They won't touch her while you're here. I don't love you in any sense of the word, but I will take care of you the best I can. I'm doing this for her and you ... even though you're a jerk."

The more Jack looked into her eyes, the more he knew she was telling the truth, and the more he felt sick inside. It couldn't be this way. He couldn't be trapped. There had to be a way out. He staggered back a few more steps and turned away.

Adwen knew she could stop him and force him to come walking back. Instead, she let the tears roll out and allowed him to run.

As he was disappearing into the trees, Oryn asked, "What are your plans?"

It was a long moment before she quietly replied, "I'm going to give him a little time to accept things. We'll go and get him by sunset and move on. If he finds trouble, I'll know where to find him."

Oryn nodded and pondered a moment. "I had thought I knew the reason he saved your life, but it has since been disproved."

Wiping her eyes, she faced him. "What was it?"

"I thought it was for selfish motives. But that can't be. He was completely unaware that only you could open the gateways. If he did not aid you for that reason, then why did he?"

She sighed and dried the rest of her face. "I think the reason he saved me is the same one that he was marked for. Just like you, he has his flaws, but ..."

Not bothering to finish, she led the way out of the clearing and into the dense, coastal forest.

Bright rays sliced through the bowing trees, and Jack kept running. His sense of smell picked up everything and made him want to go faster. He could smell sea salt, algae, dry tree bark and whatever happened to be living in the leafy boughs. Each scent continued to remind him of what he was running from and couldn't escape. It stayed with him, and he ran even faster.

He was in a nightmare, trapped in a strange world full of monsters and stuck with the odd library nerd from school. Not only that, but because of her, he was now no different from the rest of the monsters. This had to be a dream. None of this could possibly be real.

Panting and out of breath, there wasn't enough energy left in him to continue. He slowed to a staggering walk and dropped to his knees, gasping for air. Everything Adwen had said came back to ring in his head. What was going to happen to Ashley? Then the most painful thought crossed his mind: He hadn't even gotten the chance to say goodbye.

Jack shuddered and cried out his anguish at the trees. Completely alone, there were just his sobs and a breeze. This couldn't be happening, he thought. It had to be a long drawn-out hallucination.

In between gasps and sobs, he thought he heard a voice. When he finally recognized the sound, he stopped to listen. His breathing was loud and he strained for the distant tones of a frightened woman. Getting up, he looked to the coast and the source. Then his eyes widened and his heart all but stopped. He murmured, "Ashley?"

Getting up, he looked to the coast and the source. Then his eyes widened, and his heart all but stopped. He murmured, "Ashley?"

Her screams were faint. "Jack! Jack, where are you?"

"I'm coming!" he ran for her voice. "Hold on!"

The more she screamed his name and cried out, the more he quickened his pace. Adrenalin pumping and bent on rescuing her, he sprinted for the sea. He couldn't find her scent, but her shrieks of fear and pain were more than enough to lead him on. The plants and trees blocked his way up ahead, but he wasn't about to slow. Her voice guided him, and he burst through, only to find a sheer drop. With no room to recover, he skidded and cursed to himself before slipping over the side.

Landing on solid ground knocked the wind from his lungs. He coughed and wheezed, gazing up at the ledge. The fall was thirty feet. When his breath came back, he realized he shouldn't be awake or even alive.

Then he heard her voice again. It was weak and not far. "Jack ... please hurry."

His eyes snapped to a small cave entrance. Seeing how close it was made his heart leap, and he struggled to right himself. He could smell someone inside, and he thought it could be her. Recovering from the fall, he slowly went inside. "Ashley?"

Her voice whispered, "Jack ..."

Going further into the dark, his vision was cut down to almost nothing. A faint red glow was around a bend in the cave, and he froze. It was coming closer. Something didn't feel right, and he called out quieter, "Ashley?"

The first thing he saw was a woman's hand holding a ball of red fire. As the rest of Nadeen came into view, she smiled and used Ashley's voice again: "Hello, Jack."

Recognizing her, he didn't know what to do and was stunned. Then his back became rigid, and he smelled someone else. He heard light, methodical footfalls behind. They came up close and stopped. The senses in him warned that something terrible was watching his back. The fear held him paralyzed. A small part of his mind alerted him that the thing was grinning with rows of wicked teeth. Gulping, he attempted to look.

Everything went black. When Jack came to, he was back on the topside above the cave. The witch in red was gone, along with whatever had been breathing down his neck in the confined space.

He picked himself up, glowered at the place and trudged away.

While he was stalking off, Nadeen and Sycan came out of hiding, side by side. She fawned over the demon, tracing his chest with a pointed nail. Sycan hardly noticed, busy watching the newest addition to Adwen's team wander through the trees. Proud of his own handiwork, he chuckled and smiled.

This all had to be an illusion. Maybe he had had a nervous breakdown. It made sense. That would mean that all of this was imagined.

Jack rolled his eyes. Hours of walking were behind him, and he seemed to be getting nowhere. When he finally found the defenses surrounding a town, his first words were: "I need a drink."

During the afternoon hours, the main gates were busy, and he easily merged with the crowd. Chuckling to himself, Jack thought that in reality this must be a sidewalk. But as he was passing through, a guard noticed his odd hairstyle.

Stopping him with an outstretched arm, the armored soldier got his attention: "Hold! Who are you, stranger, and what is your business here?" Jack's appearance was relatively normal besides the dyed hairs.

He stared back and tried to think of what this could be. Deciding that it must be a bum asking for a smoke, he replied with a scoff, "Give me a break, okay? I just want to get a drink. Is that fine with you?"

The guard narrowed his gaze and studied him closely. His hair was a mess, he needed a shave, and there o threat and irritated by his insolence, the guard dismissed him with a wave and a glare. "Move along."

"Thank you." Shaking his head, Jack was glad to get away at last. He hated street-side panhandlers; especially pushy ones.

Walking casually along the street, Jack saw shops selling traveling goods, jewelry, clothes, saddles, special wards against evil spirits and lastly, ale at the local tavern. He took his time in finding the place, and passersby gave him curious looks, but they didn't matter. He ignored them easily, went up the steps and opened the door.

The smell inside made him curse quietly. Closing the door, he dealt with the stinks of alcohol and sweaty human bodies. After convincing himself that the intense odor was due to bad bar cleanliness, a vacant space at the counter appeared. He claimed it and waited for his nose to slowly adapt to the stale air full of odors.

A barmaid came to his side and saw the discomfort in his expression. Brushing the brown curls aside, she was concerned. "Sir, are you well?"

He raised a hand and replied, frowning at the burning in his sinuses. "I'm fine. My allergies kick up when I'm exposed to lots of dust. Can I get a drink, please?"

She curtsied smartly and smiled. "Of course, sir."

Turning and resting his arms on the bar, he heard the man beside him chuckle. "She's a right sweet one. Just by looking at a man, she knows what he likes."

Jack misinterpreted what the man had said and laughed dryly. "I'll bet she does."

The stranger asked merrily, "What might your name be, sir? I can't recall ever seeing your face before."

"Jack," he answered, instantly disliking the stink from him. "For now, I'm out on business." The maid kindly handed him a mug of bitter mead. As soon as he took a swig, he liked it and took another gulp.

The other bar patron was amused and curious. "Call me Morris. I could help you find your way if you have need. What sort of business are you dealing in?"

Thoroughly enjoying the mead, Jack wiped the foam from his mouth with a sleeve and scoffed. "Nothing personal, but my business isn't any of yours. I'm just passing through. I had a really rough night." Hoping he had deterred the stranger from continuing the conversation, he returned to drinking.

"I did not intend to pry. You seem like an interesting fellow."

Finishing off his first mug, he asked for another and frowned. "Things just haven't been going well for me lately."

The man nodded and agreed, "These are dark times."

"I call it bad luck."

"I've had some bad luck, myself. From the look of you, I doubt I could come close to your troubles."

Beginning to feel the alcohol's effects, Jack puffed. "You don't know the half of it. I haven't been able to see my wife in the last four days. I don't know if I'll ever see her again." After swigging again, he shook his head ruefully. "I was two weeks from having my bachelor's."

Not knowing what to make of his last statement, Morris patted Jack's shoulder and raised an eyebrow. "You do seem to have your share of misfortunes."

Thinking about that fact helped Jack to finish his second mug. Feeling pleasantly drunk, Jack replied, "To make it all worse, I'm pretty sure I'm losing my mind." Tapping his temple, a dry laugh escaped him. "I think everything around me is some messed-up trip. Nothing I see right now is real. Somehow and sometime in the last week, I guess, I was too stressed, and I snapped."

Listening to this testimony made Morris leery. "Well, Jack, what do you see when you look about this place?"

Jack looked around briefly and blandly relayed his perspective: "I see lots of people dressed up in old garments like dark-age peasants, maids lighting candles, and you're dressed about the same way as them. Pretty crazy, huh?" He chuckled and asked for a third mug, knowing that the strange alcohol was robbing him of all sense.

What Jack had described was exactly what the bearded stranger saw, as well. Chuckling to himself, he said, "My friend, I see all that you described. It is truly there."

Jack wiped more foam from his lips and was confused. "That's

not possible. None of this could be real. This isn't old-age Europe."
Then he chuckled and took a long drink.

Now it was the man's turn to be confused. "What is Europe?"

The response caused Jack to choke on his mead and erupt with laughter. "How drunk are you?"

"Not so much as you. You're not accustomed to this drink, are you?"

Inspecting the inside of his empty third mug, he laughed and asked, "What is this anyway? Doesn't taste like beer."

Taking the handle and smelling the rim, he had a taste and informed him, "You've been drinking Peter's Dapple Root mead. This is right strong stuff and expensive. I do hope you have the coin to pay for it."

Attempting not to laugh, Jack replied, "I'll tell you what. I'm going to check my pockets. If this is an illusion, then my wallet will be there, and I'll buy both our drinks. If it's not ..." He chuckled at the thought, "Then I guess this is real and I'm really screwed."

Morris didn't like the way things seemed to be going and watched as Jack reached inside his pockets. He reached around inside his clothes. When his search was over, he chuckled and asked the barkeeper for another round.

"Well," Morris asked warily, "you found it?"

Jack started to laugh and almost cry.

The barkeeper stood by holding the fourth round in his hand and listening for his answer. He had been paying attention to their conversation. It did not please him.

With the two waiting, he almost sobbed and shook his head. Glancing out the window, it was past sunset and he muttered, "I guess this is really ... really real." He heard the bartender whistle for his friends.

The next thing he knew, they had him by the shoulders, dragging him out into the street. Tossing him down the steps and onto the cobbled stones, they were just behind, brandishing scarred knuckles.

Street torches had been lit in town for the night. They illuminated the walkways and cast multiple shadows about the feet of everyone. Four men encircled him and waited for him to stand.

Inebriated and not happy to be thrown down the stairs, he groaned and glared at one of the burly men. "That wasn't necessary, was it?"

The man came forward to grasp the front of his shirt and didn't reply. Instead, one planted a large fist into Jack's face, rocking his head back.

Wearing a bloody and broken nose, Jack gasped and took another strike to the gut. It knocked the wind out of him, and he couldn't breathe.

His attacker stepped back and said, "If you wish to drink, then you are expected to pay. This is simple business. If you don't have coins, you leave with broken bones."

Another man kicked Jack while he was bent over.

It was a punishing blow, and he collapsed, coughing and gasping.

A third gripped his hair and pulled up to look into his face. "If you can't pay us with gold, then you can pay us with your teeth."

Bright lights flashed before his eyes, and it took a moment for Jack to realize he had been hit again. Sprawled out prone in the street, everything was spinning. A couple dozen people watched, and the four men were entertained and impressed that Jack was getting back up.

He took a breath and staggered, looking around. His skin felt hot, and he could hear his pulse beating faster. All four men came forward as he grasped his head, groaning. The pressure was building. He knew what it meant and the many punches and kicks added to his pain. One of the four moons was rising full.

While falling to the ground, Jack caught a glimpse of the sky. The green moon was by the mountain range, slowly slipping out of hiding to make his bones ache. His beatings were magnified and eventually dulled. More fists punished his body, but he hardly cared. It was about to happen again.

The pressure peaked; he wailed in agony and lashed out, sweeping one attacker off of his feet. He kicked another in the chest and sent him flying ten yards back, and the remaining two saw that something was happening to Jack. They put some distance between them, not liking what they were witnessing.

His changes made him shudder and shake. He turned over and tried to find his footing. Making a getaway was no longer possible, and he watched his hands. Seeing bones stretching under his skin and the black fur sprouting frightened him, and he couldn't hear the villagers getting their bows. His bellows and groans were quickly becoming howls in his throat.

Random stings pinched in his sides and back. The transformation continued and distracted him from the several arrows buried in his flesh. His clothes stretched and ripped at the seams but didn't fall away like before. They weren't as tight of a fit compared to his destroyed police uniform. With the belt snapped, the blades on the ground and the rest barely holding together, he roared at the pain of his face and spine elongating at once.

People were screaming and running away, as his changes were nearly finished. Eight silver-tipped arrows had hit their marks, but he wasn't dead.

It hurt terribly. He snarled as the changes ended and swatted a set of claws at the protruding shafts. His desperate move to get rid of the stings snapped three in half. Jack thrashed and shuddered, disliking the feeling of the metal cutting inside. He was yelping and snapping on all fours when another volley was launched.

The few arrows that would have hit him were swatted out of the air by Adwen as she darted from a nearby alley. She left the villagers stunned and called out firmly, "Put your weapons down! He is not your enemy!"

They did not fire again, but as Jack discovered his ability to stand, her claim was difficult to believe. Very angry and in pain, he snarled and was going to lunge for the nearest archer.

His attempt was quickly halted as Oryn leaped onto Jack's back full of arrows and wrapped an arm around his thick neck. The sudden added weight was enough to put Jack off balance. Caught in the powerful strangle hold, he stumbled backward and reached for Oryn.

When his claws had hardly touched Oryn's garments, Oryn squeezed harder, cutting off all air and blood flow. Very angry, the warrior's eyes blazed green, and he growled into Jack's ear, "You have a choice. Calm yourself and remain still, or you shall remain asleep for the night. I can put you out now. Make your choice."

Jack's vision was blurring, and he stopped resisting. The pressure around his neck released, but the initial relief came too soon. He yelped as the much more experienced hound grasped one of his ears and squeezed. The hand pulled and guided him down, making him growl and whine. He was obedient and lay flat on the ground.

A villager called out, "You monsters have no place here! Be gone!"

Everyone else cheered in approval, but Adwen replied, "We will leave. Don't worry about that. Tell me, what did he do?" She shot an angry glance at the black hound as her friend was making him cry out, extracting the arrows.

One of the bartender's companions came forward, "That bloody brute drank three mugs worth of our best and didn't have the money to pay! Then he attacked us all!" Some around him nodded, and others spat curses.

She rolled her eyes. "How much did they cost?"

"Three gold coins each. Take him and get out of our village!"

When everyone started to cheer again and spit out more than words, they suddenly fell silent at the sound of Oryn's angry roar. It echoed around and rendered them completely quiet.

Outraged, he pulled the last arrow from Jack's back and bellowed out, *"Hold your tongues! Anyone else who dares to spit at the heir of Darien shall deal with me!"*

"And who are you?" one shouted, unconvinced.

"I am Sir Oryn, you fool!"

Some laughed, making him all the angrier. When Jack tried to get up, Oryn pressed him back down with a boot across his neck. If Oryn were any angrier, he would lose control and change, as well.

Keeping her cool, Adwen went to him and held out a hand. "Can I have ten coins so we can get this over with?"

He gave her a perplexed look. Ever since becoming a full Holy Hound he hadn't seen the bag of coins. "They have gone." She sighed and shook her head. "No they haven't. Just about anything you can carry on yourself, you can summon and dismiss. Cough it up."

A moment later he magically summoned the bag of gold into his hand and was counting out the number.

She went to one of the bartender's men. Others backed away in fright, but he stayed frozen and stared into her eyes. She held the money out and politely explained, "I'm sorry we've given you trouble, but here's what we owe plus another coin for peace of mind."

Taking them, he sized her up and snorted, "You're not the heir of the Master Knight. Who are you, beast?"

"I am the heir. My friend is Sir Oryn, and we are leaving. You should too."

Then she firmly addressed everyone, and unlike with Oryn, they listened to her powerful voice. "The demons and witches are on the move. They are attacking towns to the north and have all but destroyed everything east of the river. Go far from hear and to Plexus. You will all be much safer there where the knights can be close. If you do listen to my warning and leave, avoid the plains. The demons have knights of their own, and that is their territory. Good luck and let the Light Spirits protect you. Goodbye."

Most of the crowd was tongue-tied, and some attempted to pour out apologies. She ignored them and turned to her companions. Her close friend appeared pleased with how things ended, while Jack glared up defiantly. She knew he wasn't completely accepting of what was happening yet, though she had hoped for better.

"What are you looking at?" he growled from under Oryn's boot.

"Are you ready to go, or would you like to embarrass yourself some more?" she asked.

"How about calling off your attack dog first?"

With a look, she told Oryn to step off, and they watched Jack stand.

He got up and stood upright. It was getting easier as he adjusted to his strange body, and he took a few steps toward her. The first were awkward, but he grew steadily more confident. At last he was before her, glaring down into her searching eyes. Thinking that she was vulnerable in her woman form, he lifted a set of claws, about to deliver a full-armed backhand.

She frowned and waited until his arm was in motion. When his knuckles were about to connect with her face, she took control of his body at will.

To his horror, her eyes glowed, and his whole body froze in midswing. Breathing rapidly and confused, he gaped. Against his will, he stood at attention and slowly took a knee. He tried to fight back, but it was no use. The only thing he could still control was his breathing and facial expressions.

His ears flattened, as he heard Oryn scoff, but Adwen was not amused. She went closer, glaring and reaching for one of his hands. Despite the angry tone of her voice, her expression was calm. Guiding his hand up for emphasis, she informed her new warrior, "I'm going to treat you no differently than Oryn. If you push me, I can and will control you."

Fear and panic swelled up inside him, as his own hand was grasping his throat. He couldn't stop it from squeezing. The grip was not hard enough to cause pain or hinder blood flow, but only frighten. Unable to look away, he stared back, and she went on: "I have the power to make you do anything I want. I can take your pain and make it my own, or I can make you show me what is inside your heart of hearts. Respect that, and we can start getting along just fine. We have work to do. We've held back for you long enough. Let's stop playing around and get going."

As control returned to Jack, he fell over and scrambled backward, panting.

Being kind, she picked up his daggers and offered them to him.

He hesitantly took them, still stunned and horrified.

Unlike in the past with Oryn, she felt little pity for causing him fear. "Come along. It's time to run."

Chapter 14
MADE KNOWN

Jack's wounds healed as they ran. It did not amaze him. The bleeding had stopped before they took to the woods, heading west to avoid the open plains. There was no reason to visit castle Gailarien, and the south seemed well. Adwen led the way, heading for Plexus and the Order of the Master Knights. Jack followed close behind, panting with the daggers in his jaws and working hard to keep up.

Both she and Oryn were in their hound forms, side by side. As they continued on, Oryn growled, "Why would you not see the king while the castle was so near? He shall need to be warned of the looming danger. With eastern Dargadia emptied, the castle could be the enemy's next goal. If King Lorvan falls, the kingdom will be thrown into chaos."

"He's fine. If there was something bad coming for the castle, I'm pretty sure he would know it before anyone else. The king's got a sharp mind and has lots of friends. Either way, I can sense that he's safe for now."

"Then if I may, I have one final inquiry." He glanced back. "Why return to the Order with *him*?"

Jack glared, lacking the breath to spare for a retort.

She glanced at Jack also and turned back toward what lay ahead. The terrain was rough and demanded all of their attention. "He needs to understand what we do. The best place I can think of to teach him is there."

With his ears pinned back, Oryn rumbled, "With all due respect, I do not think it wise to expose him to that yet. The elders or others could lead him astray by feeding him lies."

"I can hear that!" Jack barked past his mouthful.

"You and I are going to talk after dawn," she barked back at Jack. Ignoring his snarls and returning to the prior conversation, she growled, "I see your point, but that can't be avoided forever. He'll have to learn on the fly. We both know that putting other responsibilities on hold for him would not be right."

Oryn's ears flattened even more in disdain as he growled in agreement.

"We're going to have to make do and be careful," she growled.

"So, Adwen," Jack prompted irritably, tying a knot on the side of his half-shredded pants to prevent them from falling off, "what are we going to talk about?"

The moon had set, and sunrise was upon them. Adwen chose to stop in a secluded field of tall grass. Odd rocky formations stood all around in the dawn light, some as tall as trees.

She and Oryn were in their more human forms. While Oryn stalked around, sniffing and making sure the area was clear of enemies, she faced their angry companion.

Sitting on a smaller rock, she gestured to another. He sat down heavily, scowling.

"Before we get some rest, I'm going to try and explain as much as I can about what is happening inside and around you," she began. "This realm is different, but very similar to ours. Right now you're breathing in magic. Dargadia is rich with it. If the demons take it, they can turn everything black and kill everyone. Our war is your war, because I'm convinced that once they have this place ... they'll come for ours in a hurry."

"What do they want our world for if this one has so much power? What makes you so sure?"

"Forget the witches and the undead hordes. It's really the demons who are running the show. They manipulate the witches into helping open doorways into the living worlds. From what I can tell, the undead are only looking for a way to block out the sun. They're mostly trapped inside their land, where the light never gets through, but the demons ... consuming is what they do. They are empty beings. They want, lust and crave everything. We have the power to stop them dead in their tracks. That's why they want you, Oryn and me out of the picture. We are the one threat that stands in their way."

Jack absorbed the information and blinked. His expression was unmoved and impatient. "All right, so what's happening to me? I have the same mark he does. Are my ears going to look that funny, too, or do I have other options?"

Oryn was more than a hundred feet away and heard every word. He and Adwen exchanged glances, and he shook his head before continuing his scouting.

Patiently, Adwen answered, "He started out the same way as you. He was a knight for the Order and their captain. We both had to go through a lot before reaching this stage. The stronger you get, the more your outer appearance changes. As you progress your senses get sharper, your changes get shorter, and things get a little more bearable. There is only one ..."

"What's the catch? Don't sugar-coat it. Just tell me."

"The only way that you can progress is if you can accept the changes. The only way to make it easier and less painful is to embrace what has been given to you. Until you do that and pass your test, you will be miserable."

He scoffed.

Narrowing her gaze, she asked flatly, "Get the picture?"

"I think I get it. If I accept being a monster, then I'll be one. And if I fight it, you'll keep hurting me. Am I close?"

She heaved a sigh. "It doesn't work that way." Leaning forward, her eyes glowed, and she murmured, "Unlike you, I had to endure this alone, with no one to give me a hint. I am genuinely trying to help you. Becoming what we are is no longer avoidable. You've passed the point of no return, Jack. Trying to fight the changes is like trying to fall up or keep from breathing. All you'll accomplish in the end is to hurt yourself more than necessary. When you hurt so much that you want to die, no one is going to be responsible for it except you. Adapt, Officer Towers. Adapt as fast as you can, before the instincts start to develop."

"The instincts?"

"I doubt you will have such a hard time with them compared to Oryn, but if you want to know what it's like to forget who you are, then ask him. He can teach you a lot."

Now Jack felt afraid. He gulped and glared. "How do I get out of this? I know you can't lie to me, so what can I do to get set free?"

She was surprised. "What took you so long to figure that out?"

"Back in the town. They all believed you. I believed you. When you tell the truth to anyone who's willing to listen, they can hear it. I heard it when you told me you wouldn't let me see Ashley until this war is over. But I can, can't I?"

"Yes and no. The only way you can get past me and to her is to make a deal, a sort of bet."

His eyes lit up and glowed for a moment, as his heart leaped. "What kind of bet?"

"It has to involve a challenge. We both name the terms, agree on them, and if you win, I'll have no choice but to let you have your way. But the challenge must be something we both can agree on. If we can't agree to that and the terms, then there is no deal."

Oryn came to wait close by, listening as Jack made his choices.

Rubbing his hands together in anticipation, Jack smiled, "Okay! Now we're talking! I want a fight. No magic and no changing."

Entertained by the development, she smiled. "No weapons." When he gave her a suspicious look, she explained, "Those weapons are technically mine. They can't hurt you or Oryn. It would be pointless to use them for a fight."

Jack's chuckle darkened. "Who said anything about fighting this stuck-up stiff?"

The insult made Oryn's green eyes glow, and he relished the thought of fighting him.

Adwen's entertained expression melted. She shook her head. "You'd be better off fighting him than me, Jack. With him, your odds of winning are at least slim."

"I don't want to fight him. I want to fight you, one on one, mono a mono. If I win, you let me go and take me back to Ashley. Does that sit okay with you ... *Tame One*?"

"If those are your terms, I'm cool with that."

Her consent put a smile on his face.

Becoming stern, she glared. "Now here are my terms. If you lose, you will not return to the realm of logic until I deem you ready and trustworthy. Lastly and mostly, you will never challenge me again."

Hearing her terms made Jack's smile fade.

"Are the terms good enough for you, Officer Towers?"

His smile revived, and he scoffed again. "That's fine by me. When do we fight?"

"Right now if you like. I'm leaving the ball in your court, as far as time and place is concerned. What do you want?"

"I want to get this over with and go home." Jack stood and went to gather up his weapons. Facing her, he chuckled, holding the cutting edges. "You're lucky, you know. If I could use these to fight you, it'd make things end so much faster." Finished with his sentence, he threw them both at a nearby tree where they struck and held fast in the bark.

Adwen was not impressed. She left her seat to stand by Oryn. "You know this isn't a fight to the death, Jack. I won't kill you, and you don't have the skill or weapons to do anything to me." Turning on her heel, she added, "Why would you choose to fight me anyway? It's the second worst choice you've made so far."

"Because I've figured it all out. I challenged you because I know you. This is all just a bad dream. If I beat you, then I get to wake up."

She shook her head and frowned, pitying him.

But he went on: "And even if this is real life and not my personal nightmare, there's no way I could lose to a naïve, dumb girl like you."

All pity was evaporated by burning anger, and she glared. Her eyes were bright like windows into a furnace.

Oryn was equally angered. As Jack was preparing himself, Oryn growled quietly into her ear, "I have a request to make."

Adwen clenched her fists and replied in a deadly tone, "Don't bother. I don't plan on being light with him." The snarl-like wrinkles were flaring on the ridge of her nose, while she growled, flexing and crackling her knuckles.

"Are you ready?" Jack called out.

She cracked her neck and answered, "Sure, but how about I make one small change to the brawling rules."

"What'd you have in mind?"

She opened her arms in an inviting display. "How about a free-bee? One free hit at me to start things off?"

Chuckling to himself, Oryn didn't know whether to be cross with her or entertained. The prospect put a bad flavor in his mouth, but he knew it was going to be the only hit Jack would get. He turned and stalked off to watch from a safe distance. There was no telling how long Adwen would draw this out. His only hope was that she would make it slow and painful for Jack.

"Well?" she prompted. "What do you say?"

The suggestion made Jack uneasy. After contemplating the idea, he asked, "What's the catch this time?"

"No catch. Once you get your free hit, the battle begins. Think of it as a gift for your troubles."

"In that case," he murmured as he approached. To him, it wasn't sportsmanlike to accept a free hit, but she did owe him for the grief she had caused. Standing before her, he studied the blank expression she wore. Her face was so vaguely similar to Shari's that it was disturbing. Jack had never approved of striking a woman, but he sighed and shrugged. This was not a woman.

He swiftly made a fist and put everything he had into the motion. His knuckles connected with her cheek, bowling her over in the waist-high grass. When he didn't see her get up, he chuckled at Oryn.

The swordsman's faint, disturbing smile had returned.

After wondering why, he looked for Adwen and couldn't find her.

She had vanished into the thick greenery. Grass rustled all around as he heard her moving, but she was too fast for his sight to catch. Whipping around wildly, Jack tried to keep her from getting an easy ambush.

His valiant efforts counted for nothing. By the time he smelled her standing just behind him, it was too late. He swung around with a fist for her other cheek, and she caught it like a softball before getting a firm hold on his throat. She acted quickly to keep him from using his free hand to resist and looked deep into his eyes.

He was immobilized as Adwen looked into his heart. When she had seen enough of his inner self, she lobbed him a couple yards away.

Bellowing in outrage, he picked himself up and called out when she was gone again, "I said no magic! You broke the rules!"

He heard her voice reverberating all around between the rocks. "That wasn't magic, Jack. That was an ability, a talent. You have a few hidden skills yourself."

Spying her perched high on a towering rock, he called, "What did you do?"

"I know why you hate the thought of being trapped here, Jack. I understand you completely now. This fight won't end until you can't move."

"Come down here so we can finish this! What are you doing?"

Closing her eyes, she took a deep breath. "Your favorite smell aside from her skin is what you wake up to every Sunday. She makes your coffee dark, and the strong aroma wafts up the stairs along with her perfume. It fills your senses, warms your heart and gives you more than enough reason to get out of bed."

Alarmed and outraged, the description was so perfect that he snapped, "*Stay out of my head!*"

He jumped and tried to reach her, but he didn't have the strength. Slipping back to the ground after leaping only ten feet, he seethed and glared.

"I can't get into your head. I looked into your heart. I know what you love and hate. I know your deepest darkest fears. Right now, your second greatest fear is never seeing her smile or feeling her warmth."

"*And I hate you,*" he raged, struggling to find a way to get at her.

"No, you don't. As much as you think you do, you don't. You hate wife beaters, child molesters and especially corrupt government officials. In short, you hate society's criminals and the lawyers who set them free. At the worst, I'm an annoyance to you because I stand in your way. You're afraid that I can keep you from getting back home. Before I come down and face you, I'm going to make a promise. And just in case you don't already know, I keep my promises."

"What's your promise, freak?"

"I promise you, Jack Towers, that you will see Ashley again, alive and well. Of all the things that my instincts are saying, one of the strongest is that you will be reunited with her, even if only for a short time. I promise ... you will meet with her again in the future."

Not knowing whether to be outraged or thankful, he scowled, "Stop messing with my head and just fight me already!"

He was unable to understand her angry snarl. "Have it your way!" In a flash of light, she was on the ground beside him, growling.

Never having seen her flash-jump before, he was caught off guard and startled. That passed quickly, and he readied a punch for her nose.

She was too fast. Before he could even draw his arm back, her palm already hit his chest. The power behind the strike sent him flying into a large pillar of stone. He gasped for air, clutching his now-fractured sternum, glaring at her. The fact that he hadn't seen the hit coming made him rethink his challenge, but it was too late. He could see it in the brightness of her eyes.

She was running at him, and he tucked and rolled out of the way. His evasive maneuver worked, and she flew past to collide with the stone.

Her feet landed against the solid rock and she bounded off to pounce. She snatched him by the arm, put her momentum into a roll and used it to launch Jack into another pillar.

There was a crunch as two ribs cracked in his side, and he fell back down, crying out in pain and surprise. He knew she would be coming again and forced himself to stand, holding up his fists, watching her confident advance through the tall grass. She kept strutting closer, and he backed away, not taking his eyes off of her. When she was within reach, he took two quick jabs, and she avoided them both, still advancing.

In desperation, he threw a punch at her gut, and his stomach bottomed out when she caught his wrist. There was only enough time to be fearful and blink before she twirled and flipped him through the air.

Landing hard on his back, the pains from his injuries made him bellow.

She stood by, waiting for him to get up, as she knew he would.

Softly, she said, "I'm going to give you all of the opportunities I can to end this. You can either throw in the towel, or I can put you out."

He coughed lightly, and some blood came out, but he managed to turn over and make it to his knees. Jack was not going to stop.

Shaking her head, she continued, "I know you won't give in. I'm giving you the option. I'm offering back whatever control I can, because the truth is that all three of us would rather be someplace else, doing something else. We didn't get to choose to be involved in this war, but we are. I'm giving you the choice, Jack. Do you or do you not submit?"

Finding his balance, his legs were strong enough for him to stand. It hurt to breathe, and he coughed, shaking his head. Glaring, he murmured, "No."

Her face showed no visible emotion, though her heart sank at the predictable reply. She took no pleasure in delivering a full-armed backhand to his jaw.

His battered body flew back and rolled through the grass, half stunned.

It was a moment before she could see him trying to get up again. Each movement was weaker.

She approached again and waited. "Sooner or later, you will have to take orders from me. I understand how you feel about that. I know you can't do that yet because you don't respect me. That's fine." He coughed and wheezed, getting to his knees as she went on: "You're doing this because of Ashley; your feelings for her border on obsession."

Lifting his head to scowl, Jack fought to rise and found it much harder than before. He was relentless and gradually found the willpower.

Watching his bloody face, as he stood once more, she murmured, "Don't forget my promise, Jack. You will be with her again. So long as you keep her in your heart, it is a guarantee. The one thing you must learn to ignore is your one greatest fear. Forget the fear of never getting another chance ... to hear her voice say your name."

Hearing her say it aloud enraged him. Purposefully and with what little energy he had left, he spat a mixture of blood and saliva into her face.

Oryn remained on the sidelines and clenched his fangs.

Jack was glaring, and Adwen didn't blink or react straight away. The spatters fell away a moment after as dust, and she felt nothing. No thoughts crossed her mind as she stared into his eyes, reading the cold anger and blatant defiance.

At last, she asked yet again, "Do you submit?"

He took a painful breath and wheezed, "No."

Immediately her fist struck his chest, sending him backward into another stone pillar. She gently caught him by the neck to keep him from falling and watched his eyes roll. Holding him upright against the natural pillar, she waited, observing his will to resist.

The pain kept him barely conscious, and he slowly focused his vision onto her.

Still feeling and thinking nothing, Adwen asked, "Do you submit?"

Jack tried to swallow and choked on his own blood and saliva.

He coughed for a while, but she was patient.

His breaths came in shallow gasps, but he sneered and muttered, "No."

Nodding, she replied softly, "All right." Adwen carefully set his feet over level ground to let him stand on his own.

He swayed but refused to topple over, maintaining his angry stare. All of the strength he had left was being dedicated to being steady. Coughing lightly and wheezing, his eyes watched her sizing him up.

Adwen sighed. This deal was binding. If either of them broke it, the other would have full rights to give out punishment. Having had enough of seeing Jack suffer, she jumped up, swung and delivered a roundhouse kick.

She struck him in the head, causing him to tumble and cartwheel through the grass. As his body rolled to a stop, he was already unconscious. The damage he had suffered would take all day and into the night to heal. Leaving him alone where he fell, Adwen listened to Oryn's casual movements as he came to her side.

Oryn told her, "That was a generous offer."

"What?"

"The free strike against you. I would not have been so kind. You may think him foolish for choosing you over me, but I say he was fortunate."

"What would you have done?"

His eyes glowed when he scoffed at Jack's motionless form. "After breaking his legs, I would make him watch me snap his fingers, one by one."

She shook her head and nearly smiled. Oryn was not lying. "I guess I was going soft on him after all."

Oryn resisted putting his arms around her and said, "This place is secure. No foul things will find us here. I shall stand the first watch. Rest yourself."

"Thank you." Then she gave Jack a last glance.

Seeing her look Jack's way, Oryn frowned and added, "Save your pity for when the fool has none for himself."

"Okay."

Both felt a longing as they parted ways – her to sleep and him to stand guard. They would not be free to travel until their third member was ready and capable of carrying himself. It would be a while.

It was the intense pain and pressure that woke Jack in the evening.

He became conscious just as the changes began, thrashing and writhing. He hugged his sides. The broken bones had all but mended but were still very sore. With the addition of his injuries, the transition was beyond excruciating. He couldn't tell which way was up or down through the sensations of growing flesh and fur, and bending bones.

His howling irritated Oryn as he sat with Adwen over her fresh kill. She had just returned with the dead doe and was about to remove the skin when a full moon rose.

Both were in their hound forms, and her ears were folded back. Oryn's were flattened much more to show his displeasure.

"His noises are far worse than either of ours ever were," he growled.

"It's because he's fighting it."

"I'm well aware of that. And the sooner he accepts his fate, the better. It would ensure that I don't render him unconscious before each rising."

Suddenly the howling stopped.

They exchanged surprised looks, and Oryn went to see Jack.

Oryn took a few steps until he could see that Jack's changes were nearly completed, but he wasn't moving. Astounded and disappointed, he growled, "He fought the change too much. The pain caused him to faint." Hungry for fresh venison, Oryn snarled, turning away. "Pathetic fool."

A short while later, Jack started to come around. He could smell blood besides his own and tried to move. It hurt, and he yelped. His injuries convinced him to remain lying down. Baring his fangs and panting, he let his body relax. No matter how much he wanted to cry, it wasn't going to happen. He was in too much pain and didn't want to let them hear. He could smell them both and heard the sounds of ripping and crunching through the grass.

Not knowing what they were doing made him anxious, but he continued to listen. A few minutes of worrying passed, and he couldn't guess at what they could be preparing. When he heard and smelled Adwen coming, he expected the worst.

Her hand brushed aside the grass, and she was in her tan elf-like form. There was a large strip of raw flesh in her other hand and a pitying look in her eyes as she knelt down. She bit her lip and thought before saying, "This will help."

Watching her set the cut before him, he was wary. The length of back strap was still bloody. Wrinkling his muzzle, he growled, "That's disgusting. How's this supposed to help me?"

She frowned. "You'd be surprised. I had to learn the hard way, and it wasn't easy. I almost starved to death eating what I used to. The things you used to eat can't sustain you anymore. This is all you need besides water and sunlight to survive."

"You've got to be pulling my leg. I'm not eating that. No way. I'm not like you. I'm not going to give up and turn into an animal."

Her look became even more sullen. "That's exactly what I said when I was at your stage. Even if there were anything else to offer you, this is the only thing that will help to heal your wounds faster. You're hungry. Don't lie."

Pinning his ears back, he growled in defiance.

"Adapt, Jack. There's no running from this. You won't find a back door or a loophole worth taking to get out. Trust me. This is the only way."

As Adwen was walking away, he glanced at the generous portion and felt ill. She was right on all points. Most of all, he was very hungry. Looking at the back strap made his stomach squeamish, though it wasn't the sight or smell that made him sick. The scent of the deer flesh was making his mouth water.

He whimpered and fought against the need to taste it. Was this what she had meant when she mentioned developing instincts? It was horrible. His mind and feelings were being contradictory, tearing him in two. Licking the drool from his jaws, he had a staring contest with her offering. When his stomach growled, begging him to reconsider, he knew he was losing.

Deciding to have a small taste, he hoped nothing terrible would come of it. Jack carefully reached out his tongue, got a lick of the moist venison and sucked it back in to judge the sampling. He was aware that hunger made it seem sweeter than it actually was, but it didn't matter.

The gracious serving was more tempting than before.

He whined to himself. He didn't want anything to do with it, while the rest of him continuously urged him to take it all. Lacking the ability to move elsewhere without excruciating pain, he could only whimper. Seeing and smelling it under his nose and well within reach was torture. He whimpered again.

The following dawn left everything covered in a blanket of dew. Oryn woke to find Adwen in her woman form, perched on the tallest standing stone. She continued to bask in the first golden rays and smiled while the light danced like fire on her skin.

Getting up to speak with her, he paused. The light felt so warm and soothing. Looking at himself, the same solar-flare effect was playing across his body, as well. He relished it, letting the dawn's first light fill him with warmth. It lasted until the sun finally rose, climbing higher into the sky. Deciding to hold his questions for later, he turned to see Jack's condition.

In his more human shape, Oryn waded through the damp grass to the place where the cop had been. It was empty. Jack was gone, and the long blades of green were smashed down where his bulk had slept. Then Oryn noticed the splotch of blood where Adwen had set the piece from her kill. Nothing was left, and he felt mildly surprised. Taking a moment to glance around, he found Jack at the edge of the clearing, pulling his daggers from the tree.

Jack's mood had not improved. He easily pulled the points free and instantly felt a difference. His body was stronger. The battle wounds were healed, proving that Adwen's advice involving eating raw meat was true, though he already knew she hadn't been lying. It was concrete evidence that he still refused to accept. The dark circles beneath his eyes were worse, and the state of his clothes was as unbecoming as his unshaven face.

The knot in his waistband had come undone when he changed, making it possible to repeat the process again. Once he noticed the tear in the back where his tail had breached, he worked his jaw and sighed. There was nothing he could do to remedy that defect. Much like his change of diet, he would have to grit his teeth and bear it. His attention shifted to Adwen as he heard her approach and glared at her.

"Let's get going," she called out.

Oryn was already going to her and stole a glance to see if Jack would follow.

Jack scoffed. That green-eyed suck-up was always catering to her, just like a blindly devoted mutt. He wasn't going to be so easy, he thought. He wasn't going to roll over for her the way he did. Stowing the blades on either hip, there was no point in disobeying, so he started to join them.

With the sun lighting the way from a clear blue sky, the trio hiked west and then north. They had made good progress the night they had run. Now Adwen kept their pace slow and steady. The Order wasn't more than three days away. She was hoping to give Jack a fair chance. He was resisting but slowly adjusting. What she wanted was something more. Jack needed to understand.

At around noon, she held back to walk beside him, attempting to coach him. "How are you feeling?"

Avoiding eye contact, he ignored her.

She thought to herself, wondering what else to say. "There's a lot you need to know about the Order. When we get there, some of the knights will respect you, and others won't. If my guess is right, the whole place could be divided. The knights are governed by strict rules, enforced by a panel of fifty elders. Most of them don't like me very much."

Rolling his eyes, he huffed, trudging on.

"We have friends there," she gently continued. "Sir Peregrine is the captain, and he has plenty of loyalty. You'll be meeting him and others."

Still refusing to look at her, he muttered, "You know very well that I don't get along with losers. Anybody who listens to you is someone I want nothing to do with."

Frowning, she shook her head in disappointment and left to rejoin Oryn.

Jack rolled his eyes again. What was she trying to prove?

Three more times in the day, she fell back to offer Jack guidance or help. Each attempt she made lasted longer and only ended when she knew he wouldn't take in anymore. By sunset, she managed to tell him of the Red Cult, the Alliance of Day and their current objective: buying everyone more time.

Hearing her voice was becoming aggravating. The kind tones were like buzzing flies to his ears after the second lecture, and he wanted to swat her away. Only knowing what she could do in response kept him from lashing out. It wasn't worth the trouble, he assured himself. Even though he didn't want to listen, it wasn't something he felt like being crushed over. Having broken bones was still more unpleasant.

She found them a cozy clearing among the trees for the night. Jack was glad when she didn't object to him resting just out of sight so he didn't have to see her. Trying to ignore her voice, he removed his shirt and checked the soles of his feet. It had been two days since the boots were destroyed, and he missed them. He spent the next hour using a dagger point to dig out splinters, quietly swearing.

Both Adwen and Oryn knew it wouldn't be long before he could interpret animal speech while not transformed. To hold a more private conversation, she growled softly and sat on the soft ground. "I'm worried. He's looking horrible, and I don't understand what's wrong. Something's not right with him."

"He's being a self-pitying brute," Oryn growled. "Let him be."

She sighed, lying back with her arms behind her head.

Then there was a glint in Oryn's eye. "I could help him to see clearly."

"Don't. Making him mad will probably make it worse. He needs to feel peaceful. Beating him to a pulp won't work."

Claiming his place and sitting back against a solid tree trunk, he growled, "Teaching the men of the Order to fear me made way for their eventual respect. Having a forceful hand is paramount when grooming a warrior."

"I don't know," she growled, propping herself up to sit cross-legged. "I just don't think that would be the way to go about this. He's hurting. It needs to stop."

While working to remove the final irritating sliver, Jack froze and blinked. He had understood her last growl. Forgetting his feet altogether, his ears were pricked and tuned into their beastly language.

Oryn was insistent: "Your warrior is simpering as we speak, and you let him. In doing so, you allow him to find ways of undermining your authority. Show him how to respect you. Force his nose into the dirt when he next utters slanders. Teach him respect."

Anger lit like a fire in Jack's gut, and he listened carefully for her reply.

There was a long pause as she was thinking. "No. That won't work. That worked for you and the knights, but Jack is different. His heart is aching. He's afraid and angry. Even though he believes in a strong set of moral codes, they're not the same as yours."

Oryn's snarl was mixed with a dry scoff. "That self-serving fool has a code?"

"Jack believes in justice."

Hearing the rebuttal settled Jack's hatred into a light simmer. For the moment, he was not irritated by hearing her voice and listened more. He was still angry with her, but he wanted to know whether she knew him as well as she had claimed.

"He loves Ashley very much, but he's a dedicated lawman," she panted, and it sounded like a subtle laugh. "When he cools down and gets used to things, he's going to be great. When I looked into his heart, I saw how much he respects you."

"He has hinted to me at that," Oryn rumbled. "I cannot imagine why."

Hearing her panting laugh made Jack curious.

"He sees the warrior spirit in you. He can see the part of you that he admires in the friends he's had. He knows you love to fight."

Adwen was right, and Jack smiled, while Oryn was unmoved.

"Then why is it that he cannot see the same strength in you?" Oryn growled back. "He has witnessed your power and kind nature. What else must he see? Must he see you die before he will believe in your ability and intent?"

"There's nothing either of us can do about that. Trusting you and me is his decision."

Jack heard her pause and a more confident voice added, "Jack is ill. He lets fear and hate breed within. If it is not squelched, he may become consumed by it."

Oryn's reply was low and accusing: "And yet you have done nothing. What do you wish to accomplish by this meeting ... Golden Eyes?"

"Answer me this: Would you choose your words more wisely if he could hear what was being said?"

The question made Jack uneasy. He couldn't help but wonder whether she knew he was eavesdropping. Holding perfectly still, it was a while before he realized he was holding his breath.

Glaring, Oryn rumbled, "It would change nothing. What do you want now?"

His irritation made her smile. "I am merely ensuring that all is well."

"You're bluffing. You cannot fool me anymore with your riddles. I know you are speaking in double truths!"

"If you are so sure then tell me what my bluff is."

Oryn's growl made Jack nervous. "Don't toy with me! You're planning something. You only speak when you mean to set the stage! It was you who urged me to let my instincts swallow me whole! I have not forgotten that!"

She heaved a heavy sigh and became firm: "What would have happened if you had not? What would have become of her if you had not let the animal out?" He was quiet, and she continued, "Everything would have been lost in one fell swoop. I have kept my promises and she hers. You are no longer battling the instincts, are you?"

Glaring, he growled, "No. They have been quelled."

Golden Eyes was contented. "Good. The beast has been tamed, and now all that remains is breaking his shackles."

"I tire of this," Oryn groaned. "Speak plainly."

"All right."

Weary and a little less angry, Oryn asked, "How much longer?"

"...Very little."

"Will she be harmed?"

Her pause was long.

Jack couldn't tell what they were discussing, but it didn't sound good. His face was sweaty, and he absentmindedly wiped the moisture away.

At last, she replied, "She is going to need you."

Oryn's fists clenched, and his heart sank.

Even Golden Eyes sounded worried. "You will be there for her, won't you?"

He sighed, working his jaw. At last, he nodded. "Yes."

When she smiled thankfully, the full orange moon came out from behind the mountains. Their companion's changes erupted, and his hollers and howls signaled the end of the conversation. Golden Eyes slipped away, and Adwen's violet eyes blinked when she became aware of the commotion. She couldn't tell whether there had been another lapse in her thoughts.

Doing what she could to speak over Jack's sounds of pain, Adwen announced, "I'm going to sleep. Wake me for my turn."

Oryn shook his head. "Sleep the night away. I have no need."

She could tell he was unsettled but chose to let it go. "Okay."

Then he whispered too quietly for anyone to hear, "Peaceful dreams to you." Jack's sounds helped to drown out his words. Quiet was soon restored, and she went into a deep sleep.

With no distractions, his troubled thoughts remained. What did Golden Eyes know? He watched Adwen while she dreamed. Something was going to happen to her, and the eerie being wouldn't tell. Oryn couldn't stop brooding over the unknown, aware only that he couldn't begin to guess.

In his human form, Jack murmured, "Oryn?" When that failed, he tried a little harder to wake him. "Hey! Hey!"

Dawn had come, and Jack was dressed in his even more tattered clothes. It had occurred to him that prodding would do the trick but didn't know if there would be consequences. Brushing at his thin beard, he was hesitant to try.

At last, he huffed and lightly tapped Oryn's shoulder. He was instantly pounced upon and being snarled at.

His eyes gleamed bright green, but he realized that Jack had only been trying to wake him. "What is it?"

Jack was panting from the sudden shock. He took a breath and replied, "She made us both fall asleep. She's gone."

Keeping a hold of Jack's shirt, Oryn stood and brought him upright as well. Looking around, he confirmed that Adwen was gone. He could vaguely recall her humming a soft tune.

"Hey," Jack asked warily, "are you going to let go?"

Taking his hands back, Oryn was leery of the situation. "How long did you wait to wake me?"

"Not long. Maybe a minute," he answered, while scratching the back of his head. It itched horribly, and he thought it could be fleas. "As soon as I got up and saw she was gone. What's happening?"

Oryn's eyes shifted while he thought. "Come along." He picked up her scent and quietly added, "Don't utter a word and keep close."

It was too early to be difficult, and seeing Oryn worried made him uneasy. He kept his tongue tied, lips securely closed and listened for any sign of her. Everything in this realm was still strange, but Adwen disappearing and her servant looking anxious put him on edge.

With Jack watching his back, Oryn followed the scent through the trees. The sun had risen more than an hour before and was shining down between the boughs into streams. She had come this way long before sunrise. He could tell by the faintness of her trail. This did nothing to settle his disquiet, but he had the sense that she wasn't far.

A wide meadow gradually came into view. It seemed peaceful, and they crept along the scent that drew them closer. Then Oryn saw movement and held up a hand, halting his companion. Both stared at her, strolling through the high grass.

"Hold," he whispered to Jack. "Do not approach until I've seen that all is well."

Hands out at her sides, she felt the stems and green blades brush past, tickling her palms and outstretched fingers. It and the daylight soothed her as the next breeze came. Pausing, she chose enjoy the cool air blowing past. It was hypnotic, and she sighed, closing her eyes, smiling. Even though she could hear Oryn coming near, there was no reason to respond. She already knew who it was.

Joining her, Oryn stood and studied her face. She appeared well. He still felt that something was amiss so he softly asked, "What is your command?"

Her smile brightened and she replied, "To be at peace and feel the wind."

"Adwen?"

Golden Eyes glanced sidelong at him, raising an eyebrow at his surprise. "Do you not enjoy the touch of the sun and the wind?"

After shooting a small anxious glance at Jack, he hissed, "What are you doing?"

She scoffed and gave a sly smile. "What have I done now to vex you? Are you not happy to see me in such a lovely setting for a change?"

"Don't toy with me!" he snapped in a hushed tone, knowing that their third party was approaching. "This one will not help to keep your secret! Do not show him!"

"What's going on?" Jack asked, suspicious of the way Oryn had been acting with her. "Are you two going to keep whispering, or are you going to include me?"

Oryn glowered, as the strange being looked his way.

She could see their ragged warrior was unnerved by her eyes glowing gold. Turning to face him, she was watching his expression carefully. "You look as if you have something to ask."

Jack immediately knew that this wasn't Adwen. She was pouring with genuine confidence, and the sparkle in her gaze hinted that she was being crafty. Slowly shaking his head, he answered with a note of uncertainty, "Not really."

She frowned and growled in warning, "Lying is unbecoming, and so is eavesdropping, warrior."

Both servants were surprised.

"All right," Jack said. "Who are you? You're not her, so what's going on?"

Golden Eyes blinked. "Who are you?" she countered. "Basking in anger, pain and fear? What is your goal?"

Her questions confused and annoyed him. "You're worse than she is. I know you smell like her, but who are you?"

Looking into his eyes made Jack step back, and she became straight faced. After studying him, she replied, "Out of sight, I glimmer and shine. I race to fly, but I cross no line. All of my power flows through what sees. Neither of you know me except by these." And she indicated her eyes with two pointed nails.

Jack sneered, "You're just as cryptic as a Rubik's cube, aren't you?"

"Life is a divine riddle."

Jack grew even more agitated.

Flatly, she added, "Live with it."

Oryn could see the beginnings of a fight in the making. The more that occurred without Adwen's knowledge would be all the more terrifying when she realized the fact. It was slowly occurring to Oryn that this eerie being had something harsh in store. Hoping to restore some calm, he cleared his throat. She didn't move, and he spoke up: "The day is passing us by. We must keep moving."

Her stare never faltered as she answered, "It is, and we shall." Turning away, she started north at a brisk walk.

The two exchanged wary looks, and Jack was first to speak. Astounded by what was happening, his tone was accusing: "When were you going to let me know that she was possessed?"

Both began to follow, and Oryn muttered warningly, "Much like the rest of her, this is not as simple as it seems. This creature has a sharp wit. You've tried Adwen before. Do not try this one."

"Do you even know who that is?" he didn't bother to keep his voice low, "Who or what is it? What does it want?"

Oryn's gaze shone brightly. "It has told you more than me. It has given you the answer in a riddle."

"That's just great. We're following a severely bipolar monster. What comes next, a gang of munchkins and the yellow brick road?"

Oryn shook his head and ignored the angry mutterings that followed. To him, this was quickly turning into a disaster. What was Jack going to say or do? Worse yet, what was Golden Eyes planning?

This was the longest Oryn had ever witnessed Golden Eyes taking control of Adwen's body and thoughts. The day wore on, and few words were spoken. Rough land formations and green forests gradually leveled out into sloping hills, crowned with trees and other growing things. Noon passed them by, and no trace of their enemies gave them cause for worry. Their only concern was the mounting tension.

Golden Eyes remained at the head of their trek. She never said a word or glanced back, silently watching and listening, while they continued on. Her two cautious shadows occasionally held conversations that were hushed and abrupt. Jack would whisper questions, and if Oryn felt there was no harm, he would answer.

Dreary clouds blotted out the sky, casting the land in shades of grey. With evening on the way, Oryn grew ever more wary.

"I hate riddles," Jack muttered and asked, "Do you know what she meant?"

Oryn's judging gaze was still on her, as he shook his head. "I am not fond of word puzzles, either. From my experience, most everything this being says is a riddle. She keeps many secrets and shares only what is needed."

"Right," the sarcastic tone drawled from his mouth. "So mysterious."

Oryn grimaced at Jack's rude reply, knowing she could hear. Seeing Jack demolished once again would be entertaining, but Adwen would surely resurface sooner or later. The fewer occurrences before then, the better it would be for her.

Oryn was not nearly as angry as he was concerned. "Disrespecting Adwen has a cost, but this being is not the same. She knows things that neither you nor I can perceive. When dealing with her, you must be humble or risk being made humble."

Jack's eyes brightened and glowed, causing Oryn's worries to swell. "You just gave me an idea," Jack said and increased his stride to catch up with her, calling out, "Hey! Hey, Goldie! I have a few questions to ask you."

Scowling and sure of an impending conflict, Oryn stayed at his heels and muttered, "Simpering fool." He didn't make an effort to stop him, but he observed.

"What's your real name?" he prompted and matched her stride. "What's your name? I know it can't be Golden Eyes."

"What you think you know is trivial. My name is none of your concern. Think more in regard to your future in this war."

Not about to be brushed aside so easily, Jack got in her way, forcing her to stop.

She frowned and stared him down, waiting.

"You're not her. I mean, you're somebody else, right?"

Golden Eyes seemed irritated and replied, "What is your real question?"

"I want to know if you're someone else. Because if you are, I want to set a challenge."

Oryn's throat clenched, and he had to cough in order to breathe freely. Alarmed by the turn of events, he made to step between them, growling through clenched teeth at their overzealous companion. "Do not do this!"

Golden Eyes blocked him with an outstretched arm, and he obediently stepped aside. All the while, her gaze was locked with Jack's defiant, mahogany eyes. The only question she posed was direct and cold. "Would the stakes remain the same, or did you have another bargain in mind?"

Anxious and apprehensive of what was coming, Jack wet his lips and nodded. "Yeah, but the only thing that changes is the rules. I'm adding no use of abilities and making the request to be ..."

She frowned. "You wish to fight as your true self, in your new body."

The wording put a knot in his throat, and he gulped. He didn't like how she had said the fact so plainly, and it made him grimace. "That's right. No special abilities or anything weird. I want a regular fight."

"I'm unsure whether you and I are at an understanding. You are asking for a raw and unbridled brawl against me?"

Jack hesitated. Oryn's facial expression was in his peripheral vision; he was none too pleased. The nervous look made Jack think twice. In the end, his decision was chosen by the bitter feelings building in the pit of his stomach. Glowering and forcing the reproachful thoughts out, he answered, "Yes. That's exactly what I want."

Seeming disappointed, she studied him and replied, "Done. We battle here in this open field, now."

Jack was as confused as Oryn and scoffed. "Hold on! How is that going to happen when it's cloudy? It's not even night time!"

Golden Eyes leaned in close and whispered, "I grow in power every day. I can arrange this with little trouble. Do you wish to fight now or not at all?"

His bitter feelings forced out an almost unintentional reply: "Of course now!"

Even further disappointed, she pressed a hand to his chest, and he couldn't move. Then she forced his body to change. There was no pain and little discomfort, but it startled him, and he restrained a few yelps, clenching his growing jaws.

The process was short. Taking her hand from his utterly destroyed shirt, she transformed as well, taking methodical backward steps. "I await your signal to begin," she growled and her eyes glowed brightly. "Dawdle for too long and I shall begin it myself."

He was unsure, watching her stalking to the far side of the wide space.

They could smell rain coming, and Oryn was past being unsettled. When he met Jack's eyes, he shook his head, turning away to wait by the vague forest line. A lonely tree with dense, fanning branches would serve him well once the raindrops started to fall. Going to its strong trunk, he leaned a shoulder against it and folded his arms.

A loud barking brought Jack's attention back to the present, as he was lost in thought. "Time is nearly out! There is no backing down now!"

Ears flattened to the sides of his head, he barked, "Give me a minute!"

Her jaws were wrinkled into a deadly snarl, showing her teeth, but she waited.

Jack could feel his hound body shuddering. He wanted to beat her but had doubts that he could. What was her weakness? Those eyes were beautiful and sharp like his twin daggers. The doubt was pitted against his disdain for both identities who occupied the white creature. Forgetting what Adwen had done to him the other day, he grew more confident.

Taking one of the weapons from his sides, he held it up for her to see.

Her jaws gnashed, and she snarled, flexing her claws in anticipation.

He held up the second in the other hand, watching her wild and angry body language. Clenching his own jaws and reaching for the nerve, he found it and forcefully threw both points into the ground. They sunk down until the hilts struck topsoil.

Golden Eyes roared.

He snarled and started bearing down on her. His padded feet ripped gouges into the earth as his claws gripped, slinging small clods and weeds.

She bounded out to meet him on all fours, growling through bared teeth.

Racing for each other, her jaws opened to lunge, and he leaped high at the last second. Jack landed on all fours behind her, and they swiftly began to circle, darting over the grass. He could see that her speed greatly surpassed his and that she was veering directly for him.

Turning into Golden Eyes' attack was his only option, as there was no point in turning tail. For the second time, they ran for one another, and both leaped. Her fangs snagged his arm, and the combined momentum made their bodies contort and flip on impact. Only she managed to land on all fours.

Before Jack could react, she released and lunged, closing her maw around his tender side.

He roared in surprise and agony, kicking and whimpering. In desperation, he grabbed her ear and threw powerful punches into her face.

She barked, snarled and stopped mauling to toss him aside.

After being bitten and thrown as easily as a rodent, he gasped and picked himself up. His wound was pouring red, staining the tattered remains of his trousers. He cringed at the pain and warily clenched his jaws.

The light of her eyes was a burning glow. No pity could be found in them. She leaped, and he threw a fist for her nose.

Landing on two feet, she ducked and slashed across his face, leaving red ribbons.

It stung, but he wouldn't let it distract him. Jack tried and failed to land another blow when she ducked, throwing a punch of her own. Taking the hit to the gut, he buckled over in time to receive a cruel uppercut, bowling him over backward.

As he had suspected, his body was much stronger than before. The black hound swiftly turned over and lunged with his own fangs for her leg. He snapped his jaws shut and only found air as she leaped over the attack.

Jack whirled around and yelped when she came back to snap up one of his feet. He was helpless, as she crushed his bones and his howls rang in the open battleground.

She snarled and bit down again before throwing him over her shoulder.

Yelps and growls followed, as he tumbled. Resisting the need to cringe was difficult, while he was forced to hunker down, now that he could not stand. Still defiant as ever, he snarled back at her luminous glare. "Is that the best you've got? Huh?"

Golden Eyes' gaze narrowed, and her ears flattened. "What is your best, warrior? Shows of witless defiance? I have given you my riddle, and now I give you your own. What suckles at hate and drives with fear festering in a tender heart? Answer me that, and this punishment shall end."

"I hate riddles! Stop playing games with me!"

"Don't fight me with your hate. Fight with your heart."

His mind went to a mental image of Ashley. More shuddering racked his body. Waves of heartache made him groan, but a sudden spark of desperate anger made him roar. "I'll never give in to you, freak!"

Instantly, her demeanor turned to outrage, and she snapped and snarled.

Jack saw her lunging and leaped aside.

She redirected herself. On the rebound, she pounced and clamped her jaws around the back of his neck, pinning him down. No matter how much he flailed and clawed back at her nose and muzzle, she wouldn't let go. When she wouldn't react to his efforts, he paused and stole a glance at her.

Golden Eyes was glaring back, and her growl was like building thunder.

Fear gripped him, and he realized what was going to happen.

Her fangs drove deep into his flesh. Holding tight, she swung his weight up high and slammed him back into the ground. He yelped and barked, and to his compete horror, she did it again. The sickly sensation of many bones breaking filled him, and she smashed his body into the hard earth a third time.

Jack was dazed and in agony. While he was unable to fight back, she roughly thrashed him in her jaws until there was a small snap and a yelp.

For the first time since the start, Oryn was alarmed and gaped.

The black hound no longer moved, and she stood over him, growling. His mahogany eyes were open wide, staring back in utter horror.

"You shall heal in due time," Golden Eyes said. "Here is a new lesson on what your body can do. The first things that heal are what matter most to your anatomy. You are kept living by the magic that has been bestowed upon you. Only dark beings and weaponry may deal fatal blows to us. Most of your bones are broken, internal organs are bruised or ruptured, and as you can plainly see, I have snapped your neck. You cannot feel anything but the stings to your face, can you not?"

He blinked, unable to make a sound.

"Imagine, if you will, what is to come when the first thing to heal is your severed spine? Learn from this meeting. I do not wish to repeat it."

Standing upright, she transformed and left him lying alone with the load of disturbing knowledge.

Jack could only wait, blinking and breathing in shallow gasps.

Oryn went out to meet her halfway, gazing in shock at what she had done. Her look was rueful, as she started to walk past, but he got in her way. "What have you done? Is he living?"

Disappointed and solemn, she quietly replied, "He lives and will mend. Until then, there is little to be done." The first raindrops fell around them, and she added, "Leave him where he is. Let the elements lick his wounds." She continued to walk away.

Oryn tossed a frustrated glance at Jack and glowered. "And what of your wounds?"

She had stopped walking a moment before he called out. Turning back to face him, her face was terrified and confounded.

Then he saw that her eyes were violet. His heart skipped a beat at seeing her back and knowing what must be going through her mind. The last she had been aware was the night before, when she fell asleep. He watched the emotions growing in her expression. As he was giving her a pitying look, she turned and fled.

Adwen sobbed and didn't stop sprinting for a mile. This lapse was longer than any other. There was no recollection of waking or going anywhere. Tears streaking her face, she found a large tree with an empty hollow by its base. Ducking and quickly slipping inside, she sat and hugged her legs to herself.

She couldn't understand what was happening or why, and not knowing was most painful. More and more sobs made her shudder and quake. With her face buried into her knees, she could barely hear someone coming. Quiet footfalls were crunching on dead leaves and brittle pine needles. They were getting louder until they stopped short of her hiding place.

Oryn's scent filled her senses when he knelt down, peering inside. Her eyes were full of fresh tears, and she looked up, struggling to keep her voice from cracking. Very much afraid, she whispered, "Something's wrong with me."

His eyes moved, but the rest of him did not. Unafraid, he waited patiently.

When she remembered how he looked at her before she ran, her eyes became wide. Almost too terrified to asked, she whimpered, "What's wrong with me? What did I do to him?" Salty tears continued to trickle down, as she held her breath for the answer.

He thought long and hard. Gently, he murmured, "You gave him what was warranted, nothing more."

She sobbed harder, shaking all over. Voice muffled as her face was buried again, she whined, "What's controlling me? I don't know what to do. I can't even trust myself anymore."

It saddened him to see her this way. His deep rumbling growl had a consoling tone: "You have nothing to fear."

Holding off more tears, she asked with a questioning look, "What's controlling me? I know you know. Please ... tell me ... please."

Hesitating initially, he kept his voice low and assuring. "It is a good thing. There is no need to fear."

Her face was pained, and she fought the need to continue crying.

Quietly and slowly, he held out a hand, waiting for her to take it.

Every part of her wanted to stay hidden in the small shelter. There was no assurance that she would be herself when she stepped out. Tearing her gaze from the inviting gesture, she looked up into his eyes. They were so soft and warm. Seeing him wearing his heart on his sleeve gave her a little courage. Closing her own eyes and swallowing some of her fears, she hesitantly put her hand in his.

Holding her slender fingers, he coaxed and guided her out.

She was not completely willing and shuddered when she was standing in the open. Tears still streaked her face, collecting at her chin.

He could see her trembling. This one time, he chose to ignore his ingrained knightly professionalism. Oryn reached out and slowly wiped the teardrops away. With the watery substance in his hand, he made a tight fist around them as if they were precious.

Adwen watched and glanced up into his face again. Her shuddering did not cease, but lessened. Licking her lips, she took a deep breath, steadier than before. "Is he all right?"

Rain drizzled lightly on their heads, and he replied, "He will be."

She didn't like the answer, but nodded. "Okay. What did I do?"

He watched her eyes and did not plan to tell. "Night shall come shortly. I'm sure most of our company is in need of rest."

Blinking in the light downpour, she did not refute the response. "Yeah, I guess so."

He took her nonverbal hint to lead the way.

She was not in the mood for blazing the trail. With the ordeal ended, everything felt numb and empty. She didn't want to think or plan the next course of action. For the next few hours at least, she would leave that to her closest ally and dearest friend.

Chapter 15
WHAT WE DO

Misty rain fell while they sat beneath the ancient tree that Oryn had chosen for shelter. It shaded them from the depressing weather, as they occasionally gazed out at the motionless black form, lying in the open field. Jack was left in his hound shape to heal, and the cool wind and rain slowly soaked his thick fur.

Lying back against the smooth bark, Adwen studied her bare toes, feeling utterly overwhelmed.

More than an hour had passed, and Oryn glanced at her and frowned. He didn't want to ask but felt an obligation to do so, "What shall you do once he recovers?"

She didn't reply and continued to stare off into space.

Watching the dazed expression she wore, he waited, not wanting to press her.

Though she didn't want to think, an idea surfaced and she murmured, "Talk."

At that moment, Jack's paralysis faded, and all feeling returned. The sensations of so many shattered bones and pulverized insides registered in his mind with full force. Blinding agony caused him to gasp repeatedly, fighting for breath, and he wailed.

His cry made Adwen feel sick, while Oryn clenched his jaw, throwing the miserable brute a frustrated look.

Attempting to ignore the sound, she muttered, "What do I say?"

Continuing to glower at the black hound, he shook his head. "Whatever you deem he must hear. Lie if you must. It matters not."

She grimaced and watched the rainfall. "Yes, it does."

Turning his attention back to her, the disdain slipped away, and he softened. After rethinking the answer, his tone was reassuring. "Sight, at times, can hold more value than sound."

She looked to where Jack lay, shuddering and crying. "I hope you're right. It doesn't look like he's going to feel like cooperating anytime soon."

"It would not be a stretch for you to aid him in cooperating."

Not liking the idea of assuming control of Jack's actions, Adwen was instantly uncomfortable. "I can't do that. It would make things worse."

"Something must be done. To let the day pass without keeping him a part of this would be a grave mistake."

"Yeah." Thinking on possible solutions, a long silence followed. Eventually, she had an idea.

The worst of the pain lasted into the night. Gouges were in the dirt nearby, where he had clawed and ripped up clods in response to his anguish. The last of the storm was dissipating, stings and aches continued to subside, and he breathed easier.

Jack had feeling but couldn't muster the mind to feel. He shut off his angry thoughts when they went to the two Holy Hounds. Even though he wanted very much to imagine seeing and feeling Ashley in his arms, he couldn't cope with that thought, either. Knowing he still wasn't free to go made recalling her face almost as agonizing as contending with Adwen and her other side. Once the emotions threatened to swallow him whole, he wiped them from his mind.

The light mist left, and fog settled about him. When the rain had gone, he could smell Adwen approaching, and hearing her voice didn't stir any anger.

His daggers in one hand, she combed back her hair with the other. She sighed, letting the sensation have a calming effect. "Can you move?"

"That's a stupid question."

"How's that?"

"I don't want to." Lifting his jaws from the turf, he scowled back at her with flattened ears. "Then again ... why don't you just make me?"

Her gaze lowered, as she thought of how to reply.

"What do you want now?" He rumbled. "What do you want from me? Submission?"

"If I remember correctly, you haven't been submissive. Anyway, that's not what I want. Slaves are submissive. Dogs are submissive."

Jack glared, wondering what the point was.

"All I want is an understanding," she continued. "You don't know what you are. You don't know your role. This new way of life is not simple or easy to understand. Contrary to what many people might think, we are not animals. We have strong instincts like beasts, yes. But are we low-level creatures?"

When she stopped and watched his apprehensive expression, he growled, "What am I? Tell me the big, special, fantastic end and point."

Her eyes glowed brighter and she replied. "I'm going to show you."

Jack prowled close behind with most of his wounds healed. Adwen led him through the trees under the heavily clouded night sky and brought him to the edge of a river embankment. There, his leader stopped and examined the steep grade.

He sniffed, while his tail swished sharply. A chill crawled up his spine and settled at the back of his strong neck, making the long hairs stand.

"Why are we stopping?"

"Relax," she whispered, "We need to be quiet."

Folding his ears back, Jack kept his sounds hushed. "What is it?"

"Relax."

Looking upriver gave him a bad feeling. "This doesn't feel right. What are we doing here?"

She waited until his eyes met hers to reassure him. "Settle down. Your instincts are getting stronger."

"Something's coming this way, right?"

Leaning back against a spruce, Adwen asked, "What do you think when you hear the word *monster*? What comes to mind?"

Pausing to think, he growled, "I think of the boogey man? Why?"

"That's close enough I guess."

"This isn't funny. What's going on?"

Her gaze drifted along the steady current. "When you see it, try not to be afraid. I brought you here to learn. Watch what it does and how it moves. You'll know it when it comes."

Jack disliked the cryptic advice. He wanted to know what was causing his anxiety. The instincts were forcing him to stare raptly up along the river, and as the sense of danger grew, he saw movement and couldn't help but growl.

A filthy man in clothes more shredded than his own slowly trudged through the mist beside the water's edge, sobbing. He muttered to himself, blubbering and clutching at his head, covered with matted hair. Then the disturbed stranger wailed mournfully at the woods.

His cry unsettled Jack. Not knowing whether to be fearful or concerned, the black hound observed the man as he crouched on the shore. He dipped his bearded chin in the cool water to drink.

"Is that a man?" Jack asked with a whine.

Both continued to observe the pitiable thing, and she whispered, "You know it's not. That used to be a man. A lot like us, he has beastly instincts that drive him. Many traits separate this creature from us. One is its nature."

Unable to keep the water down, the man abruptly vomited it back up. He sobbed louder, wailing and cringing.

"What's wrong with him? Is he sick?"

"You could say that. Since he still had the mind to clothe himself, I'd guess he's been this way for less than a month, maybe two weeks. He's slipping into insanity. He can't eat what he wants to. He can't even drink water anymore. This man probably hasn't slept in a few days. The thing that makes him mad is the demon sealed into his body. It will never leave. It cannot. The only thing that drives him now is hunger. He is a monster."

Jack absorbed her words, watching the pathetic thing cry.

The night began to brighten. Clouds drifted away, unveiling the stars.

When the man saw the heavens coming into view, his sobs became violent screams of terror. The four moons appeared at last, and one was full, as always. Seeing the glow made the stranger quake and quiver. In the moment that the full golden moon came into view, he screamed and began to contort in the mist.

Jack's eyes bulged in sickened surprise.

The changes were hideous. While bones repeatedly broke and twisted under the skin, his face turned a searing red, blistered and bled. Soon his eyelids were melted away, along with his lips, as evil jaws stretched out. Screams became roars and howls, hair was replaced by fur, and his body bent as it enlarged. Then it ended, and the werewolf howled.

"Well," Jack quietly growled, "what now?"

She didn't answer.

He turned to look, and she was gone. Both his daggers were left behind, stuck into the tree trunk. "Hey!" he whimpered, keeping quiet enough to avoid alerting the monster. "Are you crazy enough to leave me alone with this thing? Where are you?" Giving up, he turned back to watching the werewolf. It was sniffing the ground. After a short while, it was testing the air.

Jack's stomach turned over when he realized the wind was blowing

at his back. When it looked up the slope and saw him, the red, beady eyes shone.

His ears dipped, and he growled out a curse under his breath.

The three-hundred pound werewolf snarled and broke into a bound.

Snatching the blades from the bark, Jack snarled and backed away swearing.

In a matter of seconds, the thing was racing up over the side, gnashing its jaws.

"Stay away from me!" Jack barked, holding his daggers tight.

It rumbled like thunder, "*Fight me, little hound. Don't be scared.*" The monster roared and leaped to pounce.

Thinking fast, Jack switched his grip on a blade and threw the point. Then he ducked and narrowly rolled out of the way.

The werewolf snarled. It stood and turned with the weapon imbedded hilt-deep in the top of his shoulder. Angry at the inability to use the one arm, it tried to pull the dagger out. The pierced flesh smoked, and his hand sizzled on contact. Unable to remove the relic, it roared at Jack in outrage.

Alarmed and not knowing what else to do, Jack snarled and swiftly threw the second. The dagger flew and made a direct hit between the monster's eyes. The werewolf fell instantly and toppled to the ground with a thud.

Panting heavily and his heart racing, Jack cautiously went closer. The werewolf was obviously dead. He took the daggers out of the remains and flinched when it began to change back into the man. Watching the monster turn into a tragic figure made him nauseous.

"You did what you had to do," Adwen said as she let down her white hood, revealing herself beside him.

He had smelled her and wasn't startled by her appearance. "This is a werewolf, isn't it?"

"That's right," she murmured, going to stand over the body, gazing down with remorse. "You, Oryn and I can do what no one else can for things like this. In any other case, when a werewolf dies, the human soul is dragged down to the void, a place ruled by demons."

As she smiled back at her servant, a ghostly figure leaned out from behind her. The soul of the dead man smiled at Jack as well, causing him to gape.

Adwen glanced at the spirit and smiled.

A moment passed, the man nodded in thanks, and a soft white glow filled him. When the light had gone, so was he.

She continued to smile at Jack's dazed expression. "You set him free. That is what we do as Holy Hounds, Jack. We protect the living and liberate poor souls."

Jack's eyes shifted while he thought.

Watching him consider the prospect, she softly added, "Now you know why your friend was smiling."

Jack's thinking ground to a screeching halt, and he stared back in shock.

She crouched low and turned over the departed man's remains. Combing the messy hair out of his solemn face, she elaborated: "Men who have the curse show a few symptoms. They have heightened aggression; insomnia gives them dark circles around their eyes; and paranoia. One easy sign - if you know how to look - is in their eyes. There's a red glint in their pupils. It's a lot easier to see when they're showing aggression."

Becoming disturbed, Jack growled quietly and felt dazed. "Higgins had it."

After folding the man's arms over his heart, she stood. "I hope this has helped you. There's so much to do, and things are going to be hard. I need to know if you understand what I did for Higgins. Can you understand what we're really fighting for?"

He thought for a long while. Then his ears flattened and he grumbled, "You couldn't have explained this sooner?"

"That wouldn't have stopped you, Jack. Would you have comprehended what a werewolf is? Most everyone from our world has seen too many movies. No one understands that they're possessed, doomed souls. Then again, would you have even listened?"

"I ..." He growled with hesitance. "I don't know. This is crazy. I'm having trouble believing it now, and it's right in front of me."

"This is very important. I need you to let go of what's happened the last few days. I want this to be a new start."

Returning her gaze, he wasn't sure if he could.

"We need you. We can't do this without your help. I understand what you're leaving behind, and I don't have control over that. What is it going to take to help you accept this?"

Jack was torn. He wanted to be angry but resisted. Struggling to say what was really on his mind, he growled, "Tell me if Higgins was really cursed. Was he going to end up like this?"

She was taken aback. "Why?"

"I need to hear you say it. I'll know if you're telling me the truth, so say it."

"Higgins had the werewolf curse. He was going to change for the first time in a few days."

Hearing the truth subdued Jack's anger. Now feeling a sense of disquiet, he scratched the back of his neck at an uncomfortable itch. Finished clawing, he was embarrassed. "Thank you, for saving my friend."

She smiled. "We should be at the Order tomorrow. Are you ready to deal with the knights? Your senses are going to make being around humans a little uncomfortable."

"Keep your promise, and things should go sweet as a nut."

Adwen nodded and shrugged. "Well, I haven't failed to keep one yet. Let's go before Oryn gets impatient. He's worse than you when things take too long."

Recalling being alone with her more powerful servant made him growl. "I've had a few chances to analyze his anger problem."

Scoffing and trying not to giggle, she warned, "You have no idea. Hopefully you won't screw up enough to see what he can really be like. He's been nice to you so far."

Her warnings were honest, and the knowledge made him shiver.

Oryn smelled them long before he saw them walking back through the field. Jack didn't appear harmed, and there was no scent of blood. It intrigued him. Adwen had promised she would let him fight alone. He hadn't expected the fool to handle his first werewolf so easily.

"He did it! Not a scratch!"

Giving a scoff, Oryn replied, "You're certain you had no part in that? Did he have no assistance?"

"Sounds like you missed me, Cujo," Jack growled as he approached while twirling one of the daggers playfully.

Both glared at each other challengingly, and Adwen took notice. "Whoa! Cool down, you two. We're staying put for the night. Don't start getting under each other's skin just yet."

Giving her a glance, the black hound shrugged and stalked off to find a place to rest. He wasn't intimidated by the green-eyed glare anymore. Jack secretly hoped to get the chance to see if Oryn was as macho as he made out to be.

Clenching his jaw as the brute left, Oryn growled.

"He did all right," she said. "Give him a break."

"I had hoped the same as you. But I sense that our companion is not any better for the lesson."

Her expression showed a mutual feeling. "I had to try. He knows now, so there's no excuse for being vengeful."

Growling more softly, he replied with a tone of warning, "He is dangerous!"

"Maybe, but he's one of us. There's no other way for him to go." Seeing Oryn still displeased, she added, "Look, I'll make you a promise." She had his attention and continued: "From here on, if he does do something wrong, anything at all, you get to take care of him. Does that make you happy?"

Oryn rolled the thought around for a long while. It was a handsome offer. Being given the full right to beat Jack into complete submission sounded very alluring. There was no reason to object, but he enjoyed toying with the thought before agreeing. Frowning at the idea of Jack causing more trouble, he muttered darkly, "Done."

The sun was high the following day when the trio spotted Plexus and the Order across the vast fields and farmlands. Hardly a moment passed without Jack's questions and frequent comments. Oryn was silently annoyed, as Adwen continued to roll her eyes and answer as best she could.

Jack was in his human form once again and curious to know more about the realm of magic, but he also enjoyed being irritating. Seeing how others reacted to stress helped him learn the way that they functioned. He would spend some time poking and prodding with sharp quips and bold statements to find out exactly whom he was dealing with. The green-eyed Holy Hound was still somewhat of a mystery but not complicated.

Adwen had his undivided attention. The dominant violet-eyed version was easy enough to read, but her other side was what interested him. Somewhere just beneath the surface of Adwen lurked the elusive mind of something powerful. Jack didn't need to ask whether it was keeping an eye on him. Jack knew that Golden Eyes was listening and watching all of the time. Not understanding the harsh personality made him uncertain and curious. Being curious, for Jack, meant throwing caution to the wind. He wanted to know who this being was.

"So if you're the prophesied leader for the knights, then that means you have your own room there, right? Do we get our own suites, too?"

Oryn clenched his teeth, as his patience wore thin, resisting the need to break Jack's jaw. Jack's talking was incessant, and the questions were slowly becoming more personal.

Hoping to provoke Golden Eyes into making a show, Jack continued his casual integration. Admiring the farmlands and the distant towering spires, he mused aloud, "There's something I've been wondering. With all of this going on and dealing with the Order elders, what do you do to relax? Do the two of you pick a day or an hour to play a game or something?"

Getting the sense that he was probing for something, Adwen remained placid and raised an eyebrow. "We don't go out on dates, Jack. There's no time for chilling in the sunshine, so I'm sorry to burst your bubble, but we're not dating."

Jack chuckled. "I wasn't talking about you and Captain Stiff over here." He gave the disgruntled warrior a curious glance. Oryn was scowling; his expression warned not to press the subject.

Leading the way, and not worried that her stronger companion was hanging back beside him, Adwen replied with a tone of uncertainty, "Are you talking about the king? I've only met him two times, and he's way old. What are you asking?"

Both warriors quietly eyed each other. While Oryn continued to scowl, Jack smiled slyly. He wondered whether Oryn's look was a credible warning. Should he ask her his next question? He was far too curious to see the results.

Watching Oryn closely, he prepared to reach for the daggers at the first hint of an attack. Jack wetted his lips in anticipation and smiled. "You know who I'm talking about. You know? Golden ..."

Oryn's fist flew so fast that Jack did not see him move. An instant later, Jack was knocked out and sprawled out on the dirt road.

Adwen heard the punch and paused. Turning around, she stared down at his bloody face and then at the culprit.

The knight quickly hid his furious expression and watched her, wondering whether she had heard too much. Holding his breath, he waited.

She studied the blank look and knew he had tried to hide something. It disturbed her, but she brushed the worry aside. Heaving a sigh, she shrugged. "Well, now you have to carry him."

Oryn scowled, shaking his head. "Better than to listen to him."

A few hours later they reached the city gates. Common travelers, filtering through the gates in a constant stream, gave the trio shocked and uncertain looks. While Oryn had their unconscious third member on one shoulder, his leader led the way.

Four armed guards saluted sharply when the trio passed, and she sighed. Adwen doubted she would ever be used to that kind of recognition. "We're going to need to wake him up and get him ready. Where should we take care of that?"

Her servant thought for a moment and spied an open barrel of water by an alley. Crossing the cobbled street, they ignored more stares from strangers. He laid down the load, gripped Jack firmly by the back of the neck, and dunked his face into the water.

A moment later, Jack was thrashing, and Oryn released him.

Coughing and sputtering, Jack gagged and sat back in the quiet alley. Once he could breathe, he glared up with two black eyes and a broken nose. It had been crushed earlier and was mostly healed. "You have no sense of humor, do you?" He coughed again and stood, examining the tall city buildings and walls. "So this is Plexus? What now?"

Adwen shrugged. "Well, you could do me a favor and close your eyes for a moment. I have a small surprise."

Unsure and not knowing how else to react, Jack gave a hesitant shrug. "All right."

The instant that he had shut his eyes, she leaned in close and breathed on him.

He felt the warmth and jumped, opening his eyes, "Whoa! What the ...?"

They watched as the shredded remains of his clothes shifted into a presentable set of grey and golden garments. At first, he was astounded but then shook his head, rolling his eyes. "You waited until now to do this?"

"Sorry. I have full control over your shape, but clothes and other things are different. My energy can only transform those temporarily. I'm a lot stronger, so that should last maybe forty-eight hours. Enjoy it while it lasts."

"Sure, but grey and gold aren't my colors."

Oryn glowered, while she shook her head.

A warm welcome came from every angle on the way to the hall of the Master Knights. People greeted them and showered them with blessings and praise. Try as Adwen might, she could not acknowledge every kind gesture.

Leaving the open streets for the enclosed grounds of the main entrance was a relief. The knights rode in and out through a broader arch, while a small garden grew before the double doors. All three were thankful for the garden's softer smells.

Jack massaged his sinuses and blinked a pair of watering eyes. "You weren't kidding about visiting cities with these senses. These people reek."

"You'll adjust after a while," Adwen insisted. "The smell of humans is nasty in general. They taste just as bad, so be prepared if you end up biting into one."

"You sound like you think I'm going to turn wild. I'm not an animal."

Oryn gave a dry laugh and added, "Yet."

A pair of guards saluted as the trio passed and reached the threshold. Coming to a stop, Adwen sighed and turned to confront her clashing warriors. Once the two finished glaring at each other, she became serious.

"This is where you put your differences aside. When we're here, we have to hold our act together. The elders have people watching all of the time. After we leave, you can fight it out for a few hours and get it out of your systems. For now, knock it off and behave yourselves." She glanced between Oryn's firm expression and Jack's clever smile. "All right. Let's go."

Pushing past the entrance, she brought them along a torch-lit passage to the grand hall. Strong sunrays spilled down from many small skylights, giving the broad space a dim glow. The trio's newest addition admired the sheer vastness until he heard a loud voice calling.

A vivacious Captain Sir Peregrine spotted them from another exit and burst into laughter. His lively voice echoed, "Tame One! Sir Oryn! You've returned so soon!" He met them halfway and saluted sharply. "It is good to see you well, Adwen, and ..." Getting a better look at his old comrade, he spied his pointed ears and nodded, smiling. "Well, well, well. It seems you've found yourself a more elfish appearance. Who is your new friend, and what could I possibly do to serve you all?"

"This is Police Officer Jack Towers," Adwen replied. "Jack, this is Sir Peregrine Gallegos, captain of the Order."

Reaching out, the knight shook hands with him and beamed. "Good to see another strong one joining the lot. You're in good care, Sir Towers. How might I help you this day?"

Jack felt the scruffy beard around his jaw. "Do you have a barber handy?"

"Oops!" Adwen was embarrassed. "I'm sorry. I completely forgot."

One of her pointed nails swiftly prodded Jack's cheek and he withdrew. "Wow! Stop that!" A moment later, he paused and felt his face. The skin was smooth with no stubble. He was thankful but wished she had warned him in advance.

Turning to the captain, she smiled. "So, Sir Peregrine ..."

Holding up a hand, he said, "Now, Lady Adwen, I'm quite fond of my beard, and I like it where it is, thank you."

She struggled not to laugh. "No, I can only do that with them. I was going to ask how things were going here. What have the elders been up to?"

"Nothing too outrageous of late," he said and became serious. "But I do believe there is a matter that needs your personal attention. If you will, please come with me to the tower library. The king awaits you."

"What? He's still here?" she asked as they broke into brisk strides. "Is he all right? He told me he would be at Castle Gailarien in two or three days."

"He wishes to speak with you in private on the matter and has told me nothing. But I do know he is troubled. Something is afoot."

No one spoke further on the subject, as they made their way to the tower. Cavernous marble halls gradually shrank to spacious stone walkways with torches and open railings along either side. On a higher tier, they came to a door, and the captain of the knights knocked.

"Enter," a voice beckoned.

Sir Peregrine opened the door and announced, "Your Highness, Lady Adwen and her company are here to see you."

King Lorvan turned his weathered face from the window, relieved at the news. "Let them in! Come, all of you." His white beard flecked with blond shone silvery in the dim lighting, and his aquamarine eyes sparkled with a liveliness that defied age. Wearing robes of scarlet and gold, he welcomed Adwen with open arms.

She dipped her head, while the captain left and closed the door on the way out.

"It is good to see you, Lady. How have you fared thus far?"

"We've sent the survivors we could find across Broad River, Your Highness. You were right about finding stronger demons. We're lucky enough to be standing here. Speaking of that, what are you doing here?"

A look of dread filled him, and his lips pressed together hard. Clearing his throat, he hesitated. "I'm afraid that I've received bad tidings."

The three waited.

"I have received a letter, by way of a trusted friend. He arrived the morning I intended to set out." He seemed to show his age as he admitted, "Castle Gailarien has fallen into dark hands."

Adwen and Oryn gaped, while Jack simply comprehended it was bad news.

"It fell silently. Whoever infiltrated the defenses knew of the secret passages. My informer was a witness. Unbeknownst to the people, the castle is now filled with vile things."

Taking another step closer, Adwen was alarmed. "You own some of the writings – the ones written about me – don't you?"

"What are you worried about a bunch of books for?" Jack asked warily, wondering how severe the situation was. "What writings?"

Gulping, she already knew the king's answer, as his gazed lowered.

"The leaders in the realm of magic all have writings telling everything about me," Adwen said. "Not all of the information was kept in one place. But if they have one book, they could know too much. This is bad."

"How?" Jack asked, still not comprehending the problem. "How bad is this?"

"It is catastrophic," King Lorvan murmured. "They may know her secret weaknesses before she discovers them for herself. With enough knowledge, they could destroy her and bring an end to everything. If Lady Adwen falls, all will fall. My texts of her arrival were very descriptive of her traits."

"What would they know if they found the writings?" she asked, growing more anxious. "What was in the text exactly?"

The king shook his head. "I'm very sorry, Lady. I cannot recall what was written. I may only assure you that they would know too much by reading my portion."

As dread was weighing down on their shoulders, a more cheery voice called from the other side of the racks and shelves. "But we have knowledge, as well!"

Everyone looked, as a blond young man with long pointed ears came out with an armful of scrolls. Wearing a set of purple and golden robes, the king's half-elf advisor tapped the patch over his left eye and smiled. "You may yet catch them on their blind side before they catch you on your own! I've found quite a lot of useful things since you departed! You should have a look for yourselves."

Adwen and Oryn were glad for the interruption from their old friend. "Well, Toth, I'm hoping you can back up that tall talk," Adwen chided. "What did you find?"

They joined him around a table, as he set the collection down. "I've found the scrolls telling of the stronger demons. They come in a variety of forms with different weaknesses. Each one is difficult to slay for one reason or another. Take this blighter for example." He rolled out a scroll to show a small illustration and descriptive texts. "This is the demon named Furor. His being is made up of many small flying fragments of shadow."

Adwen and Oryn exchanged looks, and she raised an eyebrow. "So what would this one's weakness be? How would you kill that thing?"

"Well ..." He read what was before him and shook his head. "This one is unusually resilient to direct sunlight for a demon. There is no real weakness to speak of. A run-in with this dark lieutenant would be rather sticky. The only time he may be harmed is while he is in his more solid form."

"I sure could have used that tip."

Toth beamed at her and mused, "So, you've already dealt with the dark swarm? You destroyed the demon, I hope?"

"Yeah, and barely. What other demons have you found stuff about?" Then she thought better and asked, "What about one with splinters and thorns all over the place?"

The half-elf's expression turned from enthusiastic to disturbed. Without a word he went to fetch another scroll and laid it out for all to see.

Instantly recognizing the detailed illustration, she exclaimed, "That's him!"

Going white in the face, Toth asked, "You saw this? Where? What was the demon doing?"

Toth's dismay was unsettling. Adwen eyed her friend warily. "Why?"

Licking dry lips, the king's advisor explained, "This is General Guillot, the sliver of darkness. Where did you see this?"

"He was in my world," Adwen told him. "We saw him standing by the river."

"And? What else?"

"He didn't really do anything. He watched us go through a realm gate and didn't try to stop us. All he did was smile. At least I think he did."

"I saw it, too," Jack said.

Everyone's attention fell on Jack, while Adwen and Oryn were bemused.

"I couldn't see the flying things, but I saw that," Jack added. "I saw a dark shadow with sharp edges. Why did I see him and not the others?"

"Because," Toth said with a shudder, "this demon is simply that powerful. Its power is so immense that anyone who dares to look will see solid darkness. General Guillot has but a single equal."

"Sycan," Oryn muttered darkly, "the White-Eyed Demon."

Adwen and Jack were curious as Toth replied, "He is mentioned in other scrolls, but I have yet to find the texts telling of that fiend."

Grimacing, Oryn blinked. "I know it. No knight may call themselves a werewolf slayer without knowing." Approaching a high wall of shelves bloated with tomes, he spied the black-bound book and brought it to the table, "Sycan is the last of the first six werewolves. This demon is the most treacherous and has brought about more suffering and horrors than any other before or since."

"How is that possible?" Adwen asked.

Lending the book to Toth, Oryn continued, "It was he who brought about the Red Cult. It was he who taught them to do what they do. He is and has always been their teacher and leader."

They listened after Toth read only a single page: "Sycan had the dealings in the deaths of the other five so that he might claim their power. This demon has the power of six-fold." Shaking his head at the terrible truth, Toth continued, "He is intelligent and chaotic in nature. He is only slightly hindered by silver weapons. It says the creature's most human disguise is in the image of the Master Knight himself. It was his way of mocking Darien and the Light Spirits. It also says that, if he so wished, he could take his true form."

"What do you mean by true form?" Adwen asked. "He can look like a man, and I'm pretty sure he can look like a bigger werewolf. What is his true form?"

Closing the binding, Toth shuddered again. "All demons have a true form. If it occupies a living body, you cannot see it. Their true form is a reflection of their nature. General Guillot is sharp, rigid and precise. That is that demon's nature. I cannot begin to grasp what Sycan's true form could be, if or when he has it."

"No one has ever seen his true shape," Oryn added.

"I hate to ask," Jack said, "but why hasn't anyone seen it?"

"Because," Oryn replied, "he's never had the need to use it."

Adwen was still anxious to know more about the evil general. "But what was Guillot doing in my world? Why would he be there instead of here?"

"I cannot guess at that mystery, either," Toth replied. "Why he would be there is beyond me. He was not intent on attacking you, and that gives reason to suspect he has something else in store. As for how he came to be there, it is no secret that you are not the only one who travels betwixt the realms. The dark armies have been doing so for eons."

Adwen and Oryn were unsettled, and the king remained thoughtful.

Jack pondered to himself.

"Sycan is going to be as terrible, if not more so, than the rest of the dark forces," Toth said. "He was your ancestors' greatest nemesis. Guillot may be the general of the demon army, but the white-eyed abomination knows no bounds. He possesses excessive power with very few limits, if any exist for him. He even has the power to go between the two realms of the living."

The small party stood in silence for a moment. Adwen had learned enough for now. She knew who her two greatest enemies were but wondered what they could know about her. There was a sick sensation in the pit of her stomach. The demons had the king's texts.

Gulping down the unease, she asked Toth, "So do you have any good news?"

He chuckled. "I'd almost forgotten." Presenting yet another scroll, it contained the image of a knight and four warriors in flashy armor.

She smiled back and muttered, "Let me guess. This is Darien and his four sworn?"

"It is indeed," Toth answered and read aloud: "Darien, the good light, gathered four to his side in the dawning of darkness. Granting them a gift and a new beginning at the bidding of the Light Spirits, their strength became great by melding with his. Each warrior answered his call and accepted one of four tokens, binding their fates. At the untimely dusk of their lives, he would intervene, and their lives would begin anew. From the time they received his mark of good light forward, they served the purpose of the spirits." Toth looked up from the scroll and smiled at her astonished face.

Adwen realized what it meant and looked at her two servants. When she recalled how to speak properly, she said, "Okay. That explains a lot."

Having a small grasp on the underlying meaning, Jack studied her shocked expression. "What? What is it saying?"

Clearing her throat, she spoke to her warriors, "It's something else I have in common with the Master Knight. Both of you were going to die in some unnatural way. The only reason you didn't is because you both accepted the weapons. That's the only reason I was able to mark either of you and not anyone else. By claiming the weapons of Darien, you signed an unwritten contract to work with me and share your strengths."

Toth and the king only then realized that Jack must be marked, as well. "You've joined her calling as well?" Toth asked Jack, becoming cheerful once more. "You are very fortunate."

Jack glared. "I don't know what you're talking about."

"It is fortunate that you were destined to be one of her sworn warriors," Toth assured him and interpreted the bitter look. "Despite the pains it has brought you, this is a chance, an opportunity."

"How is this supposed to be an opportunity? If you know what happens when the moons come out, tell me why you would see this as a good thing?"

"I have read through this scroll thoroughly. It says that each warrior would have a personal matter left unsettled if they had not accepted," Toth explained. "Each warrior who accepts the responsibility has unfinished business and has been offered the chance to set things to right. Rather than perish, they were allowed the power and time to correct a wrong in their previous life – to fix an oversight."

Turning his attention to Adwen, Toth continued: "This is good for you to learn. For gaining more power quickly, adding a warrior to your side is the key. You are meant to do this as Darien did. In order to defeat General Guillot or Sycan, and even who they could be serving, you shall need four warriors. Each of them must pass a test of the heart. Once the four have passed and become full-fledged warriors, you shall have the power to succeed. Only then will you be ready to face the greatest of your enemies."

Two knights escorted Jack to the city weapon smith. As he followed the men through the streets, shielding his nose from harsher odors, they were glad to point out the finer points of Plexus.

"And the back streets lie in that direction," Dynic said while pointing. "There is a popular spot for the knights. A tavern can be found rather close to a brothel down the way. Do you take to either?"

Barely paying attention, Jack grimaced and showed him the ring on his left hand. "I'm married. What do you think?"

Dynic's older brother, Raglan, slugged Dynic's shoulder. "Dolt! We've known the man for hardly an hour, and you've already insulted him." He turned to their guest, while Dynic groaned and massaged the deadened arm. "My sincere apologies, Sir Jack. Ah! Here we are then! This blacksmith is talented in crafting weapons and armor."

The younger knight recovered and assured him further, "He shall take measurements of you and then the daggers. After a few hours, you shall have a proper way of carrying them along."

"How is that supposed to work when I change almost eight pant sizes every night?" Jack asked skeptically, entering the shop with the knights. "I'll destroy whatever he makes for me once a moon is full."

The brothers exchanged looks and chuckled. "Trust us, sir," Raglan assured him. "This man is gifted in his craft."

Smells of hot metal and ash reached Jack and almost made him gag.

A burly bearded smith paused in his work with red-hot metal and called a greeting: "Good day to you, sirs. What might I do you for?" He dipped the steel into a trough of water, causing steam to fly.

While the man set aside his tools to approach, Raglan explained, "We have a warrior bearing the mark of Andredan, sir. He is in need of very special assistance."

The smith was surprised and dipped his head to Jack. "Sir! It is an honor to have you in my shop. What shall I be making for you?"

Offering up his daggers, Jack decided to trust the knights. "I need a way of wearing these. The catch is that I won't be the same size when a full moon shows."

"Oh." The smith felt his beard, pondering. "So you'll need something that will stretch rather than give way." After playing with his chin hairs a little longer, he chuckled. "I believe I have just the thing in mind."

Jack allowed the smith to measure his waist and thighs. Before leaving the blades behind for sheath measurements, he was promised an expandable harness in a few short hours. He was thankful, but his mind was on other things.

Walking through the streets alone, remembering what was explained by Toth, the half-elf made him feel like a moron. Adwen had warned him what could happen if he took the daggers. He was stunned to learn that, yet again, she had proved him wrong.

Then he recalled that Toth had said his being marked meant that he had unfinished business. What unfinished business? What oversight? His life had been perfect until Adwen showed up. This was ridiculous. What could be so wrong with his past life that he should continue living this way in order to fix it? He had everything he could ever want. He had everything he could ever need.

Growing angrier, he wanted even more to go home and leave this behind. This was not supposed to be his life. This was a nightmare. He wanted to wake up and go home. He wanted Ashley to be in his arms again. What he wouldn't give for that.

He was lost in his turmoil until a familiar smell reached him. Coming to an abrupt stop on a cobbled sidewalk, Jack glanced down a shadowed alley corner. Glaring at the empty narrows, he went closer, waiting to see movement. A tingling feeling in his mind said that someone was there. They were waiting.

The smell was much stronger in the shade, and he coolly walked farther into the secluded space. His instincts told him danger was close. Whoever was hiding ahead was amused. Bits of trash cluttered the walkway, and he wasn't deterred. Reaching the next turn, he stepped past and paused.

A woman stood some distance away, wearing a grinning wicked cat mask, crested with purple feathers and a jewel. After watching him for a while, Nadeen removed the mask that had helped her elude detection.

Jack sneered.

Chapter 16
UNDERHANDED

While Jack was out with the knights, Adwen and Oryn discussed with King Lorvan and Toth how to act, now that Castle Gailarien was taken. The elders of the Order were still unaware, and the decision was unanimous: They had to be informed.

With grim expressions, Adwen took brisk strides through the halls with Oryn alongside. Neither was eager to interact with the fifty old men. Those who saw them smiled and then stepped aside. Both Holy Hounds gave off a strong sense of disdain.

Strutting around another marble pillar, she growled softly, "I hope this goes better than my gut tells me."

"I sense the same as you. This could be a confrontation, like the last time."

"Any suggestions? What should I expect once I tell them?"

"I think they shall be distressed." His frown became a sneer. "Then I suspect they shall attempt to take control of the situation. Those who truly believe you to be the heir may make an effort to impress. I doubt many will make such an attempt."

"You sound pretty sure."

"I'm quite confident of this."

Rolling her eyes, she snarled quietly, "In that case, I'll need to put on a confident-leader act. The last thing I want is them to think I'll roll over."

The air suddenly filled with a shrill bird cry, "Child of Andredan!"

They stopped, as a firebird with a sweeping tail of flames glided through an arch. Malik the phoenix trilled again, as he touched down on Adwen's outstretched arm, blinking his hot blue eyes. "I have dire news! There are foul winds blowing!"

Not pleased by the addition of trouble, she groaned, "That's great. Let me guess: General Guillot is waiting outside the gates and wants a one-on-one?"

Her personal messenger was irritated by the response. Shrieking angrily, the bird fluffed his red and golden feathers. "I have worked tirelessly in your absence! Now is not the time for humor!"

Taken aback, Adwen exclaimed, "Take it easy! I'm only half joking! What's wrong now?"

It took the better part of an hour for the council to assemble in the elder hall. The monstrous flight of benches echoed with mumbles and whispers, while Adwen and Oryn stood below. With the grand balcony view to their left, a breeze tumbled through, rustling their hair and Malik's soft plumage. The Phoenix continued to relay everything he knew, detail by miniscule detail.

Most of the elders couldn't tell that the firebird was speaking with her. The few who could were wary and suspicious. Since she had left and appointed the creature as their overseer; they wondered what kind of report he would give her. Even though the men hadn't been able to talk to the mystical avian, they knew the creature disliked them.

With the other forty-nine seated, High Elder Mamalis was ready to begin the council meeting. The thin old man wore white and red robes with the golden markings of the Order. He watched as Adwen listened to the bird. Then he turned his attention to Oryn, who was listening, as well.

The high elder grimaced. It was hard to imagine that this elf-like creature had once been his most dependable knight. This had once been a dignified and honorable man in armor, not a beast masquerading as a man with pointed ears. How much of the knight was left, he wondered?

Oryn had sensed the high elder's gaze and locked eyes with him.

Unsettled by the brilliant glow in his eyes, the elder's grimace became a frown. Oryn's eyes were much like an animal's. His look was as sharp and calculating as ever, but Sir Oryn was obviously nothing close to human. After clearing his throat, the elder raised a hand for silence.

The last few murmurs hushed, and Mamalis spoke: "This council has been called by Adwen Andredan, The Tame One. All are present and await the words to be presented to their ears." Nodding while carefully concealing his disdain, he addressed her: "The council's eyes are upon you, Tame One."

Adwen nodded. "Thank you." She wasn't fooled, and neither was Oryn. The withered faces were bitter and suspicious, analyzing them with biased attitudes. Clearing her throat, she spoke with her powerfully magnified voice: "I have called you all here for one reason. I wish to keep you informed of everything that we know. As of a few days ago, the last survivors east of Broad River have been liberated. I have warned villages closest to that territory to move to Plexus. The demons are growing stronger and have claimed the plains."

She hesitated and added, "Castle Gailarien has been taken." The elders gasped, and some mumbled to each other as she went on. "The king's texts have been taken along with it, and we will not be able to reclaim them."

An elder stood and shouted, "Why have you not protected the king's castle? You run to the borders and risk foundations closer to home! What is the meaning of this?"

Oryn grew angry and growled, while Adwen held up a hand. "Please, listen and wait until I'm through explaining."

"What is there to explain?" Another interjected, as more elders got to their feet. "You have allowed the enemy to take the castle of our king!"

A deep and angry roar from Oryn thundered throughout the sizable chamber, causing all to fall quiet and many to retake their seats.

When they were hesitant to speak out again, Adwen gave him a glance. He nodded to her and glared at the assembly.

She was thankful and continued her announcements: "I have also been told that a large force is building in a mountain pass to the north. If we attempt to liberate the castle, we will lose our entire northern border. I cannot let that happen."

A high-ranking elder near Mamalis stood and called, "The knights can squelch that battalion of monsters. You may reclaim the castle, while they cut down the assault. Castle Gailarien must be taken back."

Adwen frowned and shook her head. "The knights cannot stand alone in the mountains. There are three-hundred strong waiting there. An army of demons and werewolves is steadily reaching closer for Dargadia. What's worse, Sycan is leading them. Malik, the Phoenix has seen him."

This time the high elder couldn't restrain himself. In a mixture of fear and anger, he cried out, "Your bird lies! It was written that the White-Eyed Demon perished long ago! It is impossible!"

Malik shrieked in outrage, and Oryn whispered to Adwen.

Her eyes shifted, and she growled at the bird to silence him. With quiet restored, she replied, "A predecessor of yours replaced those texts with lies to comfort younger generations. Sycan still exists. The Red Cult witches are proof of that."

Each of the elders exchanged worried looks, and Mamalis was shaken. Clearing his throat to keep his voice from cracking, the old man asked, "What do you intend? Surely, the two of you cannot face the numbers alone."

She shrugged and staved off a smile. "Three hundred to two doesn't sound fair. You're right. That's why we're taking my newest warrior with us. A hundred monsters for each of us should be better odds."

The high elder grimaced. "With all due respect, Tame One, this is not the time or place for jests. How do you intend to defeat the three-hundred fiends?"

Her eyes glowed brighter, as her small smile became an angry scowl. "You have no faith in me, do you?"

Maintaining his firm expression, Mamalis gulped.

"We will destroy the enemies in the mountain pass," Adwen told the assembly. "And when we come back, you and I can discuss what it means to believe in the powers of light."

The fifty elders shifted in their seats, as her angry stare drifted across the stands.

Returning her glare to the high elder, she announced, "This council is over."

In the highest room of the fortress tower, Adwen, Oryn, the captain and the high elder discussed the best means for countering their enemy. The airy chamber had a single entrance, no chairs, and a large model of the region resting on a stone table. Malik joined them and scattered small embers down to mark the locations of adversaries.

After glaring at the hot cluster in the mountains, Adwen turned her attention to the lights set on the castle's location. Shaking her head, she leaned heavily against the edge and sighed.

The High Elder inquired, "The elders, I'm sure, are as curious as our king to know if you have learned anything of the Princess Eyrie. Have you discovered her whereabouts?"

Studying the lay of the model, she murmured disappointedly, "Nothing yet."

"You understand that she must be found. Even if this war is won, the king is without a proper heir to the throne."

Being pressured wore some of Adwen's patience thin. "I know that. I get it. It's going to have to wait. First, these demons and were-wolves have to go. They have her locked away. It's just a matter of time before we find out where." Taking a deep breath and righting her posture, Adwen turned to Oryn and Captain Sir Peregrine. "What approach do you think we should take? I think the cliffs from either side of the pass would be perfect. They wouldn't see us coming until it was too late."

"Possibly, but in the end, it would matter little," Sir Peregrine replied. "If your feathered friend has counted correctly, an ambush from you would only aid in the initial killing of a few."

Oryn agreed, but added, "Yet, the element of surprise would prevent the masses from assaulting us quickly. With enough forest cover, our attack could go largely overlooked for a few minutes."

"Yeah," Adwen chuckled wryly. "Up until the alarm is sounded, and all of them come running. One thing's for sure: This isn't going to be easy." Thinking it over, she eventually concluded, "We'll stay downwind and under cover in case they have flying scouts. We'll flank them when they reach this narrow pass. Waiting for moonrise should give us even more time to cut them down. A hundred or so werewolves transforming at once is a big distraction."

The captain cautioned, "The terrain there is very uneven."

"Even better," Adwen replied. "We have the edge when we have obstacles to maneuver around. It's as good as things are going to get."

Mamalis was somewhat contented with the proposal.

Beside her, Oryn nodded and enjoyed her knowledge of battle tactics. "It is a plausible strategy. We shall have to set out shortly if we are to beat our enemy to the location."

A sudden knock at the chamber door caught all of them by surprise. All was quiet, until Adwen realized it was her obligation as highest ranking in the room to call out in answer. Feeling awkward, she replied, "Enter."

Dynic opened the door to let in Jack, who now wore his daggers in leather sheaths on either thigh. The harness was made of tough dragon leather that would stretch and never snap or tear. Along with the handy device, he had been given dark brown breeches and a vest made of the same durable skins. He strolled closer as the door closed behind him and chuckled at their silent looks. "Don't stop the party just because I showed up. What did I miss?"

While he studied the model of the territories, Adwen and Oryn couldn't help but notice something was out of the ordinary. Though he seemed his usual casual self, Jack had darker circles beneath his eyes. As Oryn was closest, he discreetly sniffed for a hint to the cause. There was nothing besides the smells of the city and a blacksmith shop. Still uneasy, he shot Adwen a look, and she returned it.

Jack realized what his green-eyed counterpart had done and

shrugged. "What? You need a bath as bad as I do, so don't even start. What are we doing now anyway?"

Seeing little point in pursuing the unmentioned topic, Adwen answered, "We are going into the mountains tonight."

"So we're going on another hiking trip," he chuckled, while everyone stared. He then pointed out the cluster of embers in the miniature mountain range. "I take it that's where the picnic is going to be. That is where we're heading, isn't it?"

Adwen nodded. "That is where we're going."

"I'm assuming all of those pretty lights are the party guests to your next big bash."

"Yes, Jack," Adwen replied dryly. "I'm giving them all surprise invitations."

He understood that the embers represented enemies and made an effort to count them. "I'm seeing twelve. Oh, wait, fourteen. Are you expecting to host for a party of sixty?" When she gave him a blank look and no response, he offered, "Seventy-five?" His stomach seemed to slowly disappear, as it dawned on him that the number was far higher than he wanted to guess.

When he didn't ask again, she told him, "We are going to fight around three-hundred demons and werewolves."

For a long moment, Jack gaped, then smiled and restrained the need to laugh. Gripping Oryn's shoulder merrily, he smiled and pointed to their commander. "You see that? That is how to have a sense of humor. What are you waiting for? You should be taking notes!"

Oryn shook him off and glared.

"This is serious," Adwen said, folding her arms.

"She's good," Jack continued. "Really, Cujo, I don't understand how you have such a good comedic role model and still not even know how to laugh."

Adwen rolled her eyes at him, growing irritated by his immaturity. "We're leaving for that pass within an hour."

Thinking for a moment, Jack offered another question: "How many knights are going with us, four-hundred?"

"The three of us are going alone. The knights are staying here."

Jack smiled admiringly and shook his head. "You know you have a real talent. If I didn't know any better, I'd think you were being completely dead serious."

Captain Sir Peregrine exchanged confounded looks with the high elder, while Oryn grimaced until his jaw clenched. It was all he could do to keep his hands to himself.

Adwen, maintaining a controlled demeanor, eyed her childish warrior and addressed him as clearly as possible: "Jack, I am only going to say this once. I know you don't care, but I'm going to say it anyway, so listen carefully."

He gave her his undivided attention.

"Shut up."

As preparation for the imminent battle, Adwen made it a point that each of them ate their fill before departing. She and Oryn left Jack to feast on raw pheasant near the food cellars, while they took hefty cuts of beef to the northern battlements. The privacy atop the fortress wall served a dual purpose. It kept knights from being disturbed by seeing their old comrade consuming meat like a beast, and it allowed the pair the freedom to discuss a very important topic: Jack.

Both were in their hound forms, and Oryn was first to finish feeding. Licking his jaws to clean away remaining morsels, he glared at the distant mountaintops. "This is far more dangerous than it need be. It would be best to leave him behind. You have noticed what I have, as well. Something in him cannot be trusted."

"We can't leave him. We won't be able to pull this off without him."

Turning his glare from the mountains and to her violet gaze, he growled firmly, "With all due respect, might I remind you of what occurred the times you took an unfit warrior into battle. The first, I was too weak. The second, I was hardly in control of my own thoughts and actions. Both battles were nearly lost. You must understand that you cannot afford to continue taking the same risk."

Finally through with her meal, Adwen folded her ears back and was defensive. "Excuse me, but we won both fights – one because you weren't in control. Jack is coming with us."

"I have experience with this mistake," Oryn warned and shifted into his more human shape. He shook his head and was much sterner. "I have seen what becomes of those who continue to repeat the same folly. To take the risk again is a gamble. Every instance that you do, you increase the chance of failure. You cannot sway me on this."

Adwen heaved a long sigh and shook her muzzle. "I understand what you're saying. You're right, but you cannot change my mind, either. There was a good reason that I took those risks and why I'm going to take it again this time."

Oryn's frustration mounted, causing his eyes to glow brightly. "What reason could you possibly have to justify such foolishness when you know it to be so?"

Someone as knowledgeable as Oryn questioning her decisions usually made her think twice. But no matter how right Adwen knew he was, it set a fire in her that he was questioning something she felt strongly about. Instead of being unsure, she grew angry.

Clenching her fangs, she glared. "If you stop thinking about how much you dislike him for one second, you'll know why." Adwen brought her eyes down, level with his, and growled, "Because we don't have time."

Oryn clenched his jaw hard and chose to hold his tongue.

She studied his look of disapproval, growling deeply, "But after taking that into consideration, can you think of a better solution? If you do, I'm all ears."

He was thinking to himself when her eyes changed to gold and Golden Eyes took control in order to reassure him.

"Have you completely forgotten I am present, knight? Just as I have before, I will not allow for her or her warriors to fall. I have the keenest of instincts among us. I sense the best course of actions to be taken. I can detect which is the right path. Can you name a time I have not set the stage for victory?"

His brow furrowed, as his grimace deepened.

Being much gentler, the cryptic being vaguely said, "It is apparent that both of you must learn the same lesson I've been attempting to teach."

Oryn wasn't in the mood to play into her riddle.

Then she cooled. "I have given every reason to, but neither of you have found the will to trust in me. Soon you will learn."

Golden Eyes allowed Adwen to return. Blinking hard, she held a clawed hand to her head and looked confused. She was instantly disturbed and whined, "Did it just happen again?"

It took every ounce of control he could muster to not show pity. He knew it would unsettle her even more.

Her ears were set back and her tail tucked. She wanted these lapses to stop far more than ever. It felt as if she were losing her mind. Desperate for an escape from her greatest worry, Adwen found comfort in Oryn's strong tone.

"There is no other alternative," Oryn said. "If we were to do anything besides face this threat, too many lives would be lost. You are right. Jack cannot be left behind. We shall need his strength. To eliminate them all, he must join us."

At first, she was comforted but was alarmed soon afterward.

"What aren't you telling me? You keep dodging my questions!" She snarled and yelped in his face, growing more anxious with each moment. "Tell me what's happening to me!"

He was silent.

Yowling miserably, she was close to crying, "Tell me!"

His heart ached at the sound, but he forced himself to reply, "We must move now, or we will lose what we cannot afford."

A few hours later, darkness fell as the three hounds ran far from Plexus and the Order. Only once did they spy a flying Dred demon scouting overhead. They managed to stay out of sight and continue north, closer to the monstrous horde of abominations.

Clouds were few overhead, and the spring air was cool. The earth was soft, masking the footfalls from the marching horde's many sets of feet and dark claws. Brief scents from human villages assured them that they were a few short miles from having a grand feast. Wretches hissed to each other, as the werewolf men salivated uncontrollably. Though they wanted to bolt toward their prey, their leader had been clear when he warned what would happen if they broke formation.

The ground became broken and uneven. Volcanic rock formations stood everywhere, forcing them to meander around. Only slightly hindered by the earthy obstacles, not one among the horde could detect the three sets of eyes watching from a high ledge.

After spotting the masses moving along the lower valleys, the trio determined that keeping to higher ground would be best. Two-hundred Wretches prowled alongside half as many naked werewolf men.

Adwen put Jack into his hound form long before the moons arrived. She had gained the ability once he joined their team, and it no longer bothered him that she could force his body to shift with a touch. He always changed back the following sunrise, and her ability never caused him the pain that the four moons brought on.

From a lofty hiding place on the cliff face, they gazed down at the disorderly march through the rocky mountain valley. The three hid in the shadows and bided their time. Once moonrise came, they would strike. There were only minutes left to wait.

Jack gaped down his snout at the large numbers of enemies. With few trees amid the volcanic rock formations, it was easy to see what the trio was up against. Jack disliked the scene as much as he feared they would be jumping from their eighty-foot high ledge. It occurred to him that he might land safely, but he didn't wish to find out too soon.

Forcing his brilliant mahogany eyes to study the prowling shapes instead of the intimidating drop, he folded both ears back. "Adwen, I want to take back all of those times I called you crazy. After further analysis, you have just graduated to completely psychotic."

She and Oryn remained in their more human shapes to wait. They stared at the opposition, as well. Both were scanning everywhere for the fiend, Sycan. Malik couldn't have been mistaken. The phoenix had seen the monster on many occasions alongside the Master Knight. He was here, they knew, though there was no sign of his whereabouts. Wretches and hungry madmen were the only visible adversaries.

"When the first werewolves howl, we're going in," Adwen told her warriors with a note of hesitance.

Jack grew nervous, as he sensed that the time was drawing near. "Okay, so do I take down the monsters with the big teeth or the ones with red eyes?"

Adwen and Oryn silently frowned at him as he crouched by the edge.

Then he whined, "Just a simple question. Anyway, what if I run into that demon with white eyes? Should I try to kill him, or tell a funny joke so he laughs?"

Oryn was irritated by this brainless banter, while Adwen was too anxious to care.

She continued studying the valley full of monstrosities and eventually replied, "If you see him, run. Get as far away from him as you can, and let me know where he is. I doubt either of you would stand a chance against this thing. If he really is as powerful as the demon general, I should face him alone."

In shock at what she was commanding, Oryn's gaze snapped directly to her determined expression.

"I'm the strongest and the fastest," she said. "If he can't reach you two and use you against me, I can try and outmaneuver him in a fight."

Oryn struggled to hold his tongue. He wanted to argue that he was not a liability in combat. Then he conceded that she could be right. Nodding, he said, "Lest we forget who we are dealing with."

Adwen grimaced and murmured, "I haven't yet. The longer we sit here and watch this, the more I get a bad feeling. Something about this doesn't seem right."

Oryn glared at the horde, eyes glowing brightly. "I sense the same. Our enemy is the founder of underhanded dealings. Now that I have seen this assembly, I have the impression that we are expected."

A chill coursed through her and their new companion.

"Why send werewolves when Wretches are obviously so abundant?" Oryn continued, brooding as he spoke. "Any number of those demons would be enough to decimate the villages in the foothills. Werewolves added to the attack present an obvious weakness. That is the same weakness we seek to exploit. It seems to me that this is a trap, a ploy for luring us closer."

She balled her fists, feeling the sharp claws pressing into her palms. "If this is a trap, they set out some good bait. Either we go and kill these, taking their invitation, or hundreds die. This does look like a trap."

Jack turned his jaws to stare at her. Grumbling anxiously, he asked, "And you still want to go in? You really are psychotic."

Ignoring the comment, she added, "This seems vaguely familiar, too. Bait we have no choice but to go for, laid in a trap we can't see beforehand. Any idea what to keep an eye out for once this fight is on?"

Oryn was quiet for a long moment. He calculated all that they knew, thinking hard. Shaking his head, he said, "I suspect our true opponent will reveal himself once we are weakened. We may be strong, but set against these numbers, our strength will be whittled steadily down. Once they deem we are easy to take, they will come."

A deep breath of the cool air helped Adwen ease some of the tension. "It's kind of funny," she murmured wryly. "I thought for a while that this might be a fair fight."

Suddenly, dozens of eerie howling cries echoed through the pass, and the three clenched their teeth. Knowing Jack would be hesitant, she forced him to leap first, and he yelped. Adwen instantly went after him, with Oryn close behind, both transforming into their true selves as they fell down through the air.

Jack clenched his jaws tight and struggled to control the descent. Air rushing past him ruffled his fur coat and rustled his new vest. Watching the ground rushing up to meet him made his stomach flutter, as he braced for a bone-crushing impact.

To his astonishment, his body absorbed the shock easily. After nearly losing his balance and catching himself, he realized he had landed not far from two towering Wretches. They hissed, as he gulped and reached for his daggers.

A second later, Oryn arrived, knifing his sword through one demon, followed by Adwen pouncing on the other and ripping its throat to ribbons.

Jack gaped at how quickly they had killed the dark creatures.

Still crouched over the disintegrating remains, she snarled to him over the echoing of a hundred howls, "Keep up!"

Both blades in hand, Jack clenched his jaws nervously and sprinted after them.

Adwen forged the way through the valley and into the heart of the loosely formed ranks. She swiftly led them to the plot of ground they had spied from atop the cliff. As she bounded, Oryn quickly slaughtered enemies that were within reach of his sword.

The hideous bodies toppled almost at once, and Jack nearly tripped over a bloody corpse that fell in his way. "You did that on purpose," he barked angrily.

Once they arrived at their chosen battlefield, Adwen worked to clear the area, making room for her to continue darting to and fro.

Her two warriors came to a stop on a mound. Oryn hewed one of the spiked demons in half, letting Jack take on two transforming werewolves.

The brutes were easy to kill with quick slices and stabs. When they were dealt with, Jack barked and growled, "Have you ever been in a situation like this before?"

Oryn ignored his questioning and eyed a band of demons that were approaching.

Another werewolf lunged for Jack.

After using one of his powerful fists to punch its nose and stun it, he stabbed it through the ear and kicked it away. Recollecting himself, Jack barked again, "You seem too calm. It gives me the idea you've been against these kinds of odds before."

Oryn finished the first of the demons coming his way and snarled, "End your senseless inquiry and keep your thoughts on the task at hand!"

"All right. Sorry for trying to get to know you."

Meanwhile, Adwen was utilizing her raw speed and agility. Several Wretches chased her about, and she did her best to remain just ahead. She raced past many small volcanic boulders until she found a notably taller formation. Dashing straight up the porous rock surface to the sky, Adwen lured the creatures into her trap.

In midair she whirled around to face them head on. The first collided with her, and she didn't wait to tear it apart. Acting quickly, she caught hold of the second that dared to follow too closely and carried on with her aerial assault.

A third waited just below, as gravity brought her back to earth. Her claws and jaws full of sharp teeth were the quicker as she landed, sinking them into the ethereal beast's head and neck. Adwen destroyed it in seconds, but failed to see another rushing in at full speed.

It pounced, and they both went rolling in a tangle of screeching and snarling. The Wretch managed to leave a set of shallow scratches on her side before she won the feral brawl. She remained unfazed by her weeping silvery wounds. There was no time to be concerned with pain. Her companions were being overwhelmed.

Completely surrounded by a wall of evil jaws, Oryn and Jack were covered in bites and gashes that bled all over. Despite the pain and loss of blood, both fought relentlessly against the seemingly endless waves of demons. They remained back to back and worked to keep enough ground to defend themselves.

Jack was holding his own but naturally the quickest to weaken. He wasn't nearly as strong as his superiors and lacked the endurance Oryn possessed for battle. For the first time in a long while, he hadn't the moment to form a remark on their situation. This was ridiculous, he thought. How did Adwen expect them to survive this? Everything about this mission was suicidal.

When he was on the verge of speaking his mind with a few small whines, slashing claws dashed the thought from his mind and left three marks on the side of his head. The black hound yelped in surprise before quickly retaliating.

Adwen redirected her efforts to where her warriors were hemmed in. The two didn't relax when she began to thin out their closer opposition, knowing better than to let their guard down. There were so many more still arriving. Everywhere was the sound of screeching fiends about to strike.

Oryn swung his blade, occasionally missing his targets because of fatigue. Behind him, Jack jabbed and stabbed whatever came close enough to take on. They were tired and growing weaker. Out of determination to win and to keep their lives, they didn't dare think of giving in an inch.

During her bounding and slashing at dark enemies, Adwen found her fair share of battle wounds. Few of the injuries sapped her energy, which she was desperate to save for later. In the back of her mind, she remembered that she would have to meet Sycan. The white-eyed last of the first six werewolves could show up at any moment. He would be at his best, and she wanted to keep a hold on her precious strength.

But once the rare sound of Oryn yelping in pain hit her ears, she felt her stomach churn. Aside from the fact that he was terribly hurt, it was the confirmation that she would not be allowed to save herself for later. Leaping between her warriors, she created a flash-bang to buy them a few seconds.

Only the three were not blinded or deafened by the blast of compressed light. Nearly a dozen demons were killed by their weapons and strength before the white glow faded away. Adwen's eyes flashed gold. As always, she was unaware of the momentary change but blinked at the sudden idea that had come from nowhere. For the first time, she dreaded acting upon the mysteriously helpful solution. It would mean spending all but the last of her strength.

Listening to more yelps from Oryn and Jack put her quandary to rest. She clenched her jaws. As she cast aside thoughts of what was to come, she released all feeling entirely in order to perform the newly learned use of her powers.

Pain faded as sight blurred, sound dulled to her ears, and all she felt was warmth. Heat pooled and flooded her every limb until her form glowed brighter. The light she gave off encircled her companions, stopping their bleeding. Adwen continued to lose herself in the warmth that came from deep inside her core, bringing forth all of the light she could muster. She soon illuminated the whole of the mountain pass.

The grass began to ripple and bend away, while her raw energy surged out in all directions. It rustled Oryn's and Jack's fur, tossing about their hair, while they watched the demons begin to shield their eyes, moving back from the intensifying glow.

Then a blast like a thunderclap came from Adwen's body, as blinding white light engulfed her form. It knocked the two warriors to their knees, as they braced against the heat and force that threatened to blow them away. Any surviving werewolves howled in agony at the burning. Their eyes were put out by the light, while Wretch bodies withered and were ripped to pieces.

Defiant of the force, Oryn tried hard to look at her amid the complete whiteness. His eyes weren't harmed, but he struggled to focus on her. What he could see was nearly impossible to make out. He squinted harder and was confused. What he could see didn't seem like her hound shape, yet it was too large to be her womanly form. Before he had a chance to guess what was masked by white light, the eerie details shifted. Adwen's hound body returned to plain view, as she closed off the power inside.

As predicted, she felt very drained but still had strength enough to fight without using more light. If she spent too much now, she would likely collapse. The more she carefully tucked away her energy, the more her surroundings were revealed.

Scattered, writhing werewolves howled and cried at their seared bodies, completely blind and totally vulnerable. All of the Wretches were gone. Not even purple puddles of muck were left behind. Despite the clamor from the fallen, she was alerted to a presence. The terrain before Adwen was dotted with the remaining werewolves, and her fur bristled and stood the farther she looked ahead.

Then she saw the figure. A titan of a black beast stood over a hundred yards away, staring intently at her. His height was close to that of the trees, and he licked his wicked jaws. It was impossible for the creature to hide the double set of incisors while he wiped them with his blue, forked tongue. Along with the strange tongue, fangs and immense size, what set him apart from his lesser brethren was his very wolf-like head. A long scar ran diagonally across his head and between his two white, speckled eyes.

Adwen was alarmed at first. Then she snarled and lunged, leaving her warriors behind. No sooner did she move than Sycan bolted away, and Adwen learned that her nemesis was very swift for his size. It frightened her, but she did not let the fact be a deterrent.

Sycan's gigantic shape was also notably agile. He ducked and weaved as he bounded through the thin forest, hardly touching any of the earthy blockades. Branches on bushes and trees shook violently with the force of the wind at his passing.

Adwen eventually caught his scent, and her eyes widened with realization. This was the smell of her murderer. Now knowing who was responsible for her death blotted out what was left of her fear. A loud snarl escaped her wrinkled jaws, and she found the will to accelerate. She wasn't going to let him get away a second time.

Their race brought them to an opening surrounded by standing volcanic rocks. She leaped high through the air and landed a short distance ahead of Sycan, forcing him to stop abruptly. He stared with what appeared to be a mixture of intrigue and delight, while she snarled up at him.

The last of the first six stood up to his full height of thirteen feet, and Adwen gnashed her fangs defiantly. "Where's Princess Eyrie?

Where is she?"

Sycan didn't say a word. Cocking his horrible head to one side, he gave an equally hideous chuckle.

In outrage, she roared and lunged for his legs. He quickly side-stepped and swatted with one enormous hand, narrowly missing her before she returned for a second attempt to leave a mark. Adwen darted for his ribs with her claws out and ready to reach into his flesh.

This time his hit landed. The demonic being swatted her out of the air hard, making her yelp.

Adwen tumbled violently and rolled over a hundred feet away. Once she finally came to a stop, she picked herself up. Four large silver gashes were across her chest and throat, weeping droplets like windowsills during a hard rain. Shaking from weakness and pain, she glared at the fleshy demon, unwilling to submit.

Thundering laughter boomed from Sycan's throat and through his grinning jaws.

She could see how outmatched she was but still refused to consider a retreat. Taking a few deep breaths and focusing her remaining energy, she snarled and raced back in to attack. Approaching him at full speed, she leaped and flash-jumped to avoid his open hand full of claws. He missed, as she reappeared just behind and sunk her fangs into his love handle, growling and thrashing ravenously.

Sycan roared in surprise and reached to rip her off, but Adwen was already gone.

Leaping back, she landed and flash-jumped again. This time she leaped up high, kicking and pummeling his jaws. As he tried to react, she repeated her tactic of evading and rebounding. Again and again, Adwen assaulted her enemy while avoiding his massive swats and swings.

Her barrage of fists and clawed kicks began to overwhelm and anger the demon. Soon he was confused by her rapid disappearing and reappearing from every angle, landing repetitive strikes to his head and muzzle. She knew she was gaining the advantage and didn't relent. Kicking harder and punching with even more determination, she knocked him off balance.

When he finally toppled over, momentarily stunned, Adwen saw her chance. Sycan's great girth stumbled backward until he fell with a resounding thud on soil and rock. She went with him and gripped a handful of his wine-red mane for leverage. Her right hand filled with her remaining powers as she prepared to knife it deep into his core. The demon was all but finished.

But a heavy fist struck the side of her head. Distracted, but unhindered, Adwen barked in surprise and looked over her shoulder.

Jack bared his fangs at her, ready to attack again.

She snarled, enraged and made him freeze where he stood.

The demon recovered and swiftly snatched Adwen up in one hand. Clutching her by her head and shoulders, Sycan mercilessly smashed her into the earth over and over again. When she continued to yelp, he dropped her and crushed her body with a giant fist. Then she was quiet.

Completely weakened and beaten, Adwen blacked out and reverted to her woman form. She lay motionless.

Sycan took a moment to study her until he deemed she couldn't fight any longer. Once satisfied, he turned to face Jack. He grinned at the confused little Holy Hound. Then he gave him an immense backhand.

The black hound collided with a rock and fell unconscious.

When he lay motionless, as well, the giant werewolf laughed manically. His laughter echoed around the valley.

The ringing guffaws masked the sound of Oryn's paws driving him forward to strike. Coming up from behind, he leaped and readied to take off the monster's head with one stroke. His fangs were bared in anger, while he flew through the air toward the unsuspecting fiend.

A lengthy demon-steel chain whipped through the air. It snatched the last standing Holy Hound around the middle and ripped him away from his target. Oryn swiftly made his sword vanish and vainly reached to untangle himself. He gripped the chains as they swung him up high.

Then he yelped, as he was slammed into the ground and bashed against nearby stones. Oryn fought to remain conscious, but the chain wouldn't stop. Eventually he succumbed, and everything went black.

When the three creatures were all silenced, Sycan reverted to his deceptively human shape. He smiled, watching as Nadeen came out from hiding, clutching the other end of the black chain.

Oryn could smell cold, dry stones. As he came back to full consciousness, scents from a number of humans reached him where he lay. Even when he was fully aware that he was bound in chains and his jaws were free, he remained still with his eyes closed. Sycan's scent was faint, hinting that the demon had left the cave some time ago. Oryn was alone with whoever else happened to be in this dreary hideaway.

His ears detected at least eight pairs of human feet quietly strolling about the space. He smelled burning and evil magic, as the Red Cult continued to light candles along the walls with their vile powers. Though he was tempted to steal a look at his surroundings, Oryn was patient in waiting for an opportunity. Countless minutes dragged by, and he continued to bide his time. None had strayed close to where he was bound. Even if he couldn't get them all, he wanted to at the least kill one before they executed him. He could smell Adwen, and Jack's scent was even stronger.

Fewer of the Red Cult members were moving about, and it grew quieter, until a single set of shoes were clicking on stone. They came closer.

A second after Nadeen came to a stop before Oryn, he rushed her, jaws open wide. The unbreakable chain that fed from a port in the wall magically retracted on its own to keep him from reaching the witch. His huge fangs snapped dangerously close to her face, as she smiled.

After struggling to reach her a second time, Oryn clearly saw it was impossible and snarled defiantly. He stared her down, shrugging against the enchanted steel restraint that pinned his arms to his sides.

"How wonderful it is to see you again" She chortled and smiled sickeningly. "Your new body is just as impressive as your last. And before you say anything rude, I'd think more carefully about the consequences."

Gripping a crevice on the ground by the claws on his feet, he continued to resist the chain. Struggling to reach the witch, he gave a thunderous growl, gnashing his jaws. "I have no fear of your hand, hag. Whatever you do to me will show how weak you truly are."

Red-robed followers of the cult chuckled, as Nadeen's smile grew more sadistic. Turning, she strutted to where Jack was in chains. He was in his human form once more and did not fight his restraints. On his knees and head bowed somberly, he sat in silence.

Oryn's eyes narrowed, while the witch went to run her painted nails through Jack's messy hair.

"You've done so well. Why are you not happy?"

Oryn's pupils dilated in mounting wrath, and his jaws clenched.

"You lied," Jack murmured accusingly. "You said you'd let me go home."

Nadeen sighed. "Oh, you silly little creature, I did not lie to you. Of course you will go home. Your home is going to be at my doorstep on a chain. You shall be my new pet when this is done. Don't fret. I'll remember to feed you scraps with very few maggots to squirm in your belly."

She began to laugh haughtily, and Jack pulled away from her hand, sneering.

Forgetting Nadeen altogether, Oryn lunged in Jack's direction. He hit the end of his chain, barking madly, "You insufferable fool! You've doomed us all for your selfish wants and heartaches! If my hands ever get hold of your flea-bitten hide, I'm going to snap whatever bones you have that Adwen has not already! I shall make you wish you were mortal enough to die like the cur you are!"

When his raging faltered, Oryn noticed the witch strutting away. Passing the cult members lining the hall, she ascended to a stone altar, where Adwen lay unconscious.

Red-flamed candelabras stood at her head and feet, splashing bloody lights across her prone, motionless form. She appeared asleep and peaceful, unaware of the terrible danger approaching. Nadeen let her nails scrape across the stone slab, as she strolled casually around to the other side, watching Oryn's reactions.

As the witch stopped at Adwen's side, a warlock presented a small chest and opened it. First she took out a vial filled with a black serum.

Seeing Oryn's uncertain expression, she cooed and batted her eyelashes. "Oh, do not worry. This will not harm her. This shall keep her in sleep." Then she laughed softy and dripped the contents on Adwen's forehead. The foul liquid evaporated quickly, and Nadeen turned back to the chest and took out a second item.

The instant Oryn saw the flash of demon-steel he whined, "No."

Nadeen brandished the serrated dagger, licking her upper lip, enjoying Oryn's failure to hide his horror. She had been longing for this.

Fear in Oryn quickly gave way to complete panic, and he fought to get loose. Seeing Nadeen studying Adwen's vulnerable chest sent him into hysterics, and he barked and flailed in an attempt to break free.

"No! I'll kill you, hag! If you lay a finger on her, I'll kill you!"

Desperate and unable to do anything except fight the chain, he glimpsed Nadeen taking aim at Adwen's heart and was maddened.

"Let me free, cowards!" He thrashed around and ran to the end of his chain barking in a crazed fit. "Let me free! I'll kill you! I'll kill you! I'll kill you!"

With a sickening thud, the black blade cut into Adwen's body.

Jack shuddered at the sound, and Oryn felt as if his own chest had been run through. He let out a miserable howl. "No!"

Nadeen continued to saw at Adwen's chest, gritting her teeth at the apparent chore.

The gruesome sight held Oryn's attention, and his sorrow threatened to crush him. He couldn't look away. It was impossible. No matter how much he wanted to, he was unable to avert his gaze.

Silver and green trickled down Adwen's sides to the stone surface. Suddenly a small shimmer could be seen coming from the gaping cavity. The witch gasped in awe, as Oryn found breathing difficult. Even Jack raised his head to watch Nadeen reach inside. After a moment of fighting something loose, the light grew brighter.

Everyone watched, as Nadeen pulled it free and held up the smooth, pulsating portion of golden flesh. A feeling of shock was as great as Oryn's despair, as he realized the golden thing dripping with silver was Adwen's heart.

He quivered and felt sick seeing it in the woman's greedy clutches. Oryn shuddered, as grief gripped his insides and he howled. The deafening sound echoed around the dark chamber: "Adwen!"

A sudden bright flash came from the heart. At that moment, it vanished from the witch's hand and instantly returned to its rightful place.

In the blink of an eye, Adwen's hand swiftly latched onto one of Nadeen's silver-drenched wrists.

The evil woman gasped and saw Adwen's pure golden eyes upon her. The light from the heart soon dimmed and disappeared, as her silvery essence refilled the void in her chest.

When the hole was gone, Adwen's body quickly transformed as she stood, holding up the witch to roar in her face. A few of the robed witches and warlocks fled, while the rest scrambled to form ranks and draw weapons.

Two or three who could cast spells prepared to fling fireballs.

Adwen lobbed Nadeen across the hall to their feet just as evil magic and arrows flew toward the altar.

Stepping gracefully down, Golden Eyes flash-jumped a short distance to avoid the projectiles. Now on level ground, she took a step forward as the cult prepared another volley.

The white creature's hands filled with light. When she clapped hard, the powerful light explosion temporarily blinded all but the eyes of the Holy Hounds. In seconds, the lesser cult members were lying dead, killed by quick swipes from her claws.

Nadeen recovered and stood, gaping around at the mess. She realized too late that the white creature was standing behind her. The witch whirled around only to be ensnared by the throat.

Golden Eyes held her close in one hand, glaring down into her soulless black eyes. Only showing a hint of wrath, she rumbled, "You dared to touch the heart of gold. I have seen into you, Nadeen. Though you fear Sycan, there is another whom you fear more. Who is it that you fear most of all? Who is it that commands the general and the white-eyed abomination? Name him."

The witch mustered her breath and spat into her face.

Golden Eyes' gaze narrowed. She glared, growling quietly, "Very well. Even for one such as you, I have the gift of mercy."

Nadeen scoffed and smiled. "That was always your kind's weakness."

"There shall be no pain for you, for there is none in nothingness."

Nadeen's sadistic smile quickly faded.

The hand that held the witch began to glow. In a last-ditch effort, Nadeen tried to pry her way free. When the light grew brighter and she couldn't escape, she screamed. Her body suddenly exploded into a cloud of dust, while her final cry rang in the dark cavern.

Satisfied, Golden Eyes shifted Adwen's body into its more human shape.

With the witch gone and no one to command the bewitched steel chains, the heavy bonds collapsed. Though the two warriors were freed, they couldn't find the mind to move. Jack was astounded and speechless.

Oryn was breathless. When Adwen slowly turned and smiled, Oryn's legs gave way, and he slumped to his knees. Her shining golden eyes seemed to smile as softly as her supple black lips. His breaths were shallow. Moments ago, it appeared she was destroyed. Now she was before him, her face level with his jaws. Oryn felt his heart flutter, as she reached with both hands to hold his face and stroke his muzzle. He was filled with relief to see her alive and stayed silent as she caressed him.

Golden Eyes quietly soothed, "Thank you. Did I not tell you all would be well?"

He was still too stunned and did not reply.

She admired him for a moment, then glanced at her second warrior and frowned.

Jack shuddered.

Done showing kindness to her loyal companion, she turned to deal with the traitor. Angry, she stepped across the cold mountain stone, eyes burning. She held him still with her power. He wouldn't move, and she made certain that he couldn't if he changed his mind.

Standing over Jack while he stared back in fear, she spoke harshly: "Any number of slanders or swears could define you, Jack Towers. Using them would be a waste of breath because all and none touch the surface of your character. You have betrayed me."

He shook and tried to speak, but no words would come.

"I saved you from being condemned to eternal suffering. I sheltered you from absolute evil, and in turn, you forsook me." Golden Eyes shook her head. "You betrayed me for your own fear."

Before he could say anything, she beat him to his own explanation. "But I know you attacked me because of what ails you. For giving in to your fear and wrath, I shall give you yet another punishment."

His eyes widened in horror.

"But because you traded everything because of your love, you will be forgiven in time. For now, this is what must be."

Her hand reached for his forehead and Jack fought against her hold. Seeing her open hand about to lay on his face, he struggled harder, gasping and sweating as he vainly resisted the indomitable magical bond. He was frozen on his knees, helpless.

She touched him, and he began to cry out at the top of his lungs. A mind-blowing pain exploded within. His body began to shift. Bones crunched, muscles ripped, and skin stretched, sprouting thick black fur. Claws grew out along with fangs in his lengthening skull under her palm. He howled, blinded by pain. Then she let him collapse in an unconscious heap at her feet.

Golden Eyes scowled down at him before calling to Oryn, "Bring him. Even now, he shall not be left behind. Jack is still our own. It is time to leave this accursed place."

Without a word, Oryn lifted the limp creature up and hefted him onto one shoulder.

The two took the only exit, a long dark tunnel full of dripping moisture and the echoing of wind from the other end. Oryn was forced to duck at a few places and made a point to let Jack's head knock into the ceiling whenever possible. It eased some of his frustration. It would have to do until he had the time to fulfill his most recent vow. He was pondering on what to do first when there was a light was up ahead.

The dawn greeted them, as they came out onto the windy ledge. They could see a hidden set of steps in the earth that led down to the forest. They were in the foothills of the mountains, not far from where they had made their stand the night before. Golden Eyes allowed the sun to mend her wounds completely, soaking up the rays like rain into the earth.

Her body shimmered by the first light of day, while Oryn purposefully dropped Jack carelessly. The brute landed with a loud thud and still did not wake or stir as the green-eyed hound shifted into his more human shape. After studying the black hound, he asked his commander, "How long is he to remain this way?"

She continued to gaze in silence at the sunrise with her back turned.

Curious to know, he asked again, "How long, Golden Eyes?"

His question was the first thing Adwen heard, as she came back to full awareness. She blinked at the sunrise, confused. The last thing she could recall was brawling with Sycan at night. Daylight confounded her, and she noted the surroundings, while a feeling of anxiety swelled in her chest. How long was this lapse? Adwen wondered what she must have done this time and dreaded to know.

Oryn watched, as she cautiously turned to look at him. When he saw that her eyes were violet and reproachful, he watched her closely, preparing for her reactions. There was no telling what she could remember from minutes ago. Either way, none of this would please her.

Her eyes searched his briefly. She caught a hint of concern, though he tried to mask it. Then she looked at Jack, and her eyes dilated, while she attempted to grasp what she was seeing. After glancing at the rising sun and back again, her heart pounded, and she began to shudder. Unable to recall what had happened, she grasped her head and squeezed her eyes shut, clenching her teeth as a few tears fell. There was only one explanation for how Jack could be locked into his hound body.

Oryn could smell tears and sense her anguish. As he was going to step closer, Adwen cried out, and the sound echoed off of the mountains. She swiftly bolted away and leaped down the rocky embankment.

Alarmed, Oryn darted after her.

He jumped into the denser trees and sprinted as fast as he could to catch up. Adwen's scent was strong enough to follow, and he quickly spotted her running away. It was apparent she didn't think he would come after her, as she was clearly not going at her fastest. Weaving amid the broad trunks and leafy bushes, he cut off her escape.

Adwen slid to a dead halt. On the brink of tears, her frustration and alarm caused her to holler at his unyielding expression. When he didn't move, she clenched her fangs and glared.

"What are your intentions?" he asked, hiding any sign of pity.

She screamed, "Stop it!"

Oryn was taken aback but did not soften.

Growing angrier, she seethed: "Tell me what's happening to me. You called it something. I know you know what's going on. No more secrets. What keeps taking control of me? Tell me!"

He wanted to tell her everything. As he was about to speak, Golden Eyes came forward long enough to give him a look of warning. Oryn glared back at the stern being until Adwen was present again.

"Tell me!" Tears rolled down her cheeks.

His fists clenched, and he made his decision. "You have nothing to fear."

Restraining a sob, she pleaded, "What is it?"

"I do not know. It has only sought to further our quest and ensure victory. It empowers and strengthens you."

"Why?" The tears fell freely. "What does it want? Why does it do this to me? Why is it here, in me?"

Oryn relaxed his expression and sighed. "I asked, and it would not be clear. It speaks in an endless stream of riddles." He paused a moment before asking, "What are your intentions?"

"Go back to the Order."

Once he understood, he was questioning: "You would flee from this? As the heir, you must return to your task. Without your efforts, all of ours would be for naught."

"I'm not running. I have to know what's wrong with me. I don't care how helpful it is. I'm going to find out what this thing is and why it's here. It's something I'm going to have to do by myself."

"When shall you return? And in the meantime, what do you wish for the cur in our midst?"

"I don't know how long." Then she frowned and gazed at her feet. "I'm leaving him with you. Keep him at the Order. I'll need to talk to him when I get back." She did not say anymore.

Oryn wished she would stay but could never think of getting in the way of something she wanted this badly. There were no more questions to ask, so he gave a salute, smartly bringing his right forearm across his chest.

Adwen saw the gesture but did not know how to respond. As she was about to pass around him, Adwen hesitantly glanced up to see his face. He appeared soldier-like with a relatively blank expression. Dropping her eyes, she skirted around and started running through the forest.

When she was gone, he gradually let the salute fall. His expression softened into one of concern. Again, he wished she wouldn't go. He missed her company already. Then he assured himself that she would return soon. Adwen would succeed in solving the mystery of Golden Eyes and come back to continue their quest.

His thoughts then went to those regarding his own prerogative. A scowl furrowed his brow, his eyes burned brightly, and he let out a low and terrible growl.

Chapter 17
IN SPITE OF EVERYTHING

"He is a menace. He ought to be flogged, burned, and have his head bashed in for good measure." Sir Peregrine glowered at the edge of the pit of doom. "You amaze me, sir, allowing this insufferable maggot to live. You have changed much, but I did not expect you to ever be tolerant of fools or traitors."

It was almost noon, and the captain of the Order stood beside his predecessor with a dozen other knights. All of them were glaring down from the stands to where Jack was chained. The most deadly training arena in the Order fortress with its twelve barred gates was devoid of monsters. One gate would let in apprentices to be tested for the right to be a knight, and the rest of the gates were for releasing their challenges.

The disgruntled knights stood atop one of the half-dozen archer's posts, observing the unconscious black brute. Oryn had found the strongest chain they possessed and clapped the large iron one around Jack's thick neck like a collar. It was locked, and the key gotten rid of, to be sure he stayed put. His powerful tether was fifteen feet in length, with the other end secured to a stone in the middle of the twenty-foot deep fighting pit.

"His life is not mine to take," Oryn said. "Or else I would have no hesitation with dispatching him. Death is better than he deserves. My intent is to display that readily and with no remorse."

A few men chuckled, and Sir Peregrine offered his own knife with a smile. "Then you would want this. Old habits die hard, my friend. Surely, this is still your favorite tool for educating scum?"

Oryn shook his head. "Not in this instance. This calls for a tool that preaches a point all its own. A very clear meaning must be made here."

All of the knights smiled.

Eventually, Jack began to stir. Sitting himself up and grasping his aching head, he clenched his teeth and finally opened his eyes. The light dazzled him for a moment. He glanced around, and his mutter came out as a low growl. "Looks like she finally sent me to hell."

Once he heard himself, he gasped and quickly examined his hands. He was still in his hound shape. Jack took a confused double-take at himself and the daytime sky, beginning to panic. It was noon, and he had not returned to his human shape. Would he ever, he wondered fearfully?

Jack next realized that the daggers were missing and that a steel ring was around his neck. It was locked, and he fought to pry off the restraint. It wouldn't bend or give way. Giving up, he turned his attention to the chain to search for a possible weakness. His anxious eyes swiftly followed the heavy links to where the chain was firmly set into a boulder. Just as he noticed a figure atop the large rock, something cold and unforgiving struck the side of his jaws, bowling him over in the dirt.

Oryn tossed aside the steel mace and stepped down to approach Jack, who was howling and clutching his bloody muzzle. Oryn took pleasure in seeing Jack writhe but wore a bone chilling scowl.

"What was that?" Jack yelped and snarled. "What did you hit me with, a rock?"

The sarcastic humor irritated Oryn. He delivered an angry kick to Jack's gut to shut him up. It knocked the wind from his lungs, leaving him gasping and stunned. Taking a firm hold of one of Jack's big ears, he squeezed and spoke into it with clenched teeth and glowing eyes.

"Count yourself lucky that I am not able to take your life. Then again, that would spare you from what I have in store. You are the greatest fool I have ever encountered, and so you shall have my worst."

Finished, he planted a fist into Jack's lower back. The force slammed his burly body to the ground and made him yelp.

"The more sounds you make, the longer this lesson will last."

Jack found his breath and growled, "Lesson? How are you supposed to teach me when you haven't learned anything yet? You don't see what she's done to you!"

The closer Oryn came, the further Jack scurried away until his chain was almost taut. Oryn's eyes burned bright green, as he grasped the chain and pulled hard, sending Jack sliding back into the boulder.

Jack didn't yelp and ignored the pain. Picking himself up at Oryn's approach, Jack clenched his battered jaws, snarling, "She's turned you into her pet! You only hate me because she makes you! Don't you see it? She's using you! You're letting her manipulate you through that bond!"

Oryn punched him in the side of the head, knocking him down into a submissive crouch. He stood over him and glowered. "I've heard enough vile words from you." Ready to continue, he grasped the shackle around his neck and made a tight fist.

Jack was not intimidated, and their angry gazes met. "No one is going to control me!" He snarled as his eyes flashed.

Sensing an unusual energy, Oryn paused to stare. He had seen something.

The knights observing from above couldn't help but wonder why he had stopped. One called down, "What are you waiting for, sir? Crush the mangy mongrel!"

As Oryn continued to bear over Jack with a raised fist, Jack took the chance to make a remark: "So you get it now?"

Oryn remained frozen, thinking and studying his subordinate's face. What he had glimpsed had gone, but the sense grew stronger. His instincts were tingling, making him all the more suspicious. Oryn was unable to shake the feeling and chose to do as the powerful instincts demanded. He used his grip on the chain and forced Jack down, stepping on the links to hold him there.

"What are you doing?" Jack protested loudly, snapping and growling. "Have you totally lost it? Get off me!"

Oryn ignored the sounds and examined Jack's body. His black-gloved hands searched his sides for anything until he reached his back. The space between his shoulder blades had his attention. Narrowing his gaze, he touched Jack's spine.

Something moved under the skin and fur, and Jack seemed unaware. "Stop touching me, you lunatic!"

When the thing moved again, Oryn swiftly clutched at it and pulled.

Jack howled and yelped in pain, "Let go of me!"

Then Oryn understood what he was dealing with and pulled harder. Jack's skin stayed intact, while Oryn pried at the squirming parasite. It slowly came loose, and the dark creature's form sizzled and smoked where the light touched it. Jack fell unconscious, and Oryn held up the fat, black demon bug.

Its four sharp arms flailed, the tentacle-like antennae whipped madly, and its bloated abdomen pulsated in agony. The knights watched, as Oryn snarled, clenching his fangs. With the sun shining so brightly, it wasn't long before the bug disintegrated and burned like a piece of paper on a fire.

When nothing was left, Oryn glanced at Jack and pondered quietly to himself. He felt an odd sense of relief but was troubled. Was it possible he had misjudged Jack?

An hour later, Jack started to come around. He was dizzy and groaned as he picked himself up. He sat and took a good look at his surroundings. Feeling lost and disoriented, he sensed a presence. Oryn was sitting on a boulder behind him, observing with that familiar unreadable expression.

They watched each other, and Jack was naturally first to break the silence. Unable to recall much of the last week since first being marked, he grumbled hesitantly, "I get the impression that I messed up recently?"

Oryn was stoic in his reply: "Few would disagree."

"What is this place? Why am I stuck like this during the day?"

"This is the Ring of Trials. Most knights call it the Pit of Doom. She left you trapped in this form as a punishment for your crimes."

Gaping back, Jack grumbled, "Then I must have messed up worse than usual."

"Indeed. Why did you do it? Tell me what drove you to that, and do not lie."

"I can honestly say that you would know better than me."

Oryn's gaze narrowed. "Then I shall refresh your memory. Nadeen, the Red Witch, spoke to you. She fed you lies about taking you back to your world."

At first Jack was more confused. "What? Who is ...?" Then he began to recall the conversation with a dark-eyed woman in red.

Oryn saw his dog features show distress. As his ears folded back, and the tail tucked of its own accord, Oryn asked, "Now do you recall?"

Jack did not answer.

The quiet amused Oryn. "So you do possess the skill of silence."

His remark brought Jack back to the present. "Very funny, Fido, but you still need to fine-tune your jokes. That wasn't even a knee-slapper."

"Answer my question, or I will share more of my poor humor."

Feeling his mostly healed muzzle, Jack replied, "I don't think that's called for. I can't think of why I made a deal with that witch. All I remember is being angry. I can remember bits and pieces. The angrier I was, the harder it is for me to remember it."

"You were infected."

Jack looked back in alarm. "Infected? Infected by what? Worms?"

"There is a weak demon known as Spite. If it can bury itself in a host, then over time, it feeds off of dark emotions. Once strong enough, the parasite can puppeteer the host by using hate and fear. That was what I ripped from your body no more than an hour ago."

Memories continued to slowly piece together in Jack's mind. He could remember turning on Adwen in the mountain pass. It put a sick sensation in the pit of his stomach. What else had he done wrong?

Eventually, he thought of the first fight with Adwen. The instant that he remembered throwing a fist for her cheek, he felt sick. Jack grasped his head and fought with the horrible realization. He couldn't have. He wouldn't have. Why would he do it, he wondered angrily?

Oryn watched him driving his claws into his own head, growling pitifully. "What is it that you recall?"

"I hit her?" Jack was in disbelief and then admitted to himself. "I hit her. I actually hit her." A snarl of utter frustration escaped him.

"You did so with enthusiasm. From where I stood, it looked as if you took great pleasure in the act."

"No! That's not me!"

Not pleased with the tone he used, Oryn gave a rumbling growl of warning.

Turning to glare and clenching clawed fists, he growled back, "You really think that I would ever hit a girl?"

"It didn't surprise me."

Every hair on Jack's body bristled, his jaws clenched to expose sharp fangs, and his mahogany eyes glowed bright hot. He stood upright, glaring down at Oryn's serious expression. The urge to attack was strong, but his head was clear, and he somehow knew that he was being tested. As with the recent times that he had sensed things in his mind, he ignored this occurrence, dismissing it as imaginary.

There was little doubt the green-eyed warrior was unafraid. This time, Jack thought before he spoke.

"I want to make something clear," Jack rumbled. "Because of what I know, I would never ever hit a woman. All my life I've known girls who were abused or worse. I stopped being a street punk to be a cop so I could try and do something about it. Nothing gets under my skin more than hearing about some scumbag beating up a woman."

Oryn was as unreadable as before.

Jack had yet another mental sense of what he was thinking and grumbled. "Do you want to rub my nose in the rest of how I've messed up, or are you done messing with me?"

Oryn huffed and raised an eyebrow. "You are not as feebleminded as I had thought. Perhaps there is hope for you after all."

"More hope than for your sense of humor."

The corner of Oryn's mouth tugged into a faint ghost of a smile. His bright green eyes sparkled. "Then, as you once suggested, I shall practice. Do you hunger for something from the food cellars?"

Not getting where this was going, Jack cocked one ear. "Yeah."

At that, Oryn scoffed and replied, "I will return shortly."

Jack watched the warrior stroll across the arena. "That's it? How is that funny to you? That isn't even a joke!"

Oryn paused to glance back. "Do you not see our audience?"

At last, Jack noticed the captain and his men by the entrance to the Pit of Doom. Each of them had a weapon of some kind and looked eager to use it. They were only remaining at a distance because of Oryn.

Jack's ears drooped. "Okay, you're funny. That was a good one! I'm not really that hungry, you know. What are you doing? You don't have to ... Oryn?"

As Oryn disappeared through the tall timber gate, Sir Peregrine led his men inside.

Jack gulped hard and stepped back, while the surly band stalked nearer with sharp blades and loaded crossbows. Knowing they wouldn't understand a word, he backed up against the boulder and gave them the most pathetic look possible. It was embarrassing to him, looking at them like a whipped puppy. Swallowing what little pride he had left, Jack did everything he could to communicate how sorry he was.

Sir Peregrine stood a short distance away and pointed his sword at Jack's throat. When he gulped again, he spoke with a deadly tone: "Your betrayal is inexcusable. Know this. If you make another foul play against the heir or Sir Oryn, neither of them will stop me from gutting you like the vermin you are. Do you understand my words?"

He nodded rigorously and whimpered, "I get it."

The captain chuckled darkly and put his sword away.

They turned to go, and Jack began to relax. Sitting down, he sighed and stared at the ground. He had been sure they were going to attack.

An arrow suddenly struck the ground by his clawed toes, causing him to jump and yelp. The knights' guffaws filled the arena, as he tried to calm himself.

Jack gave them a dirty look, as they went out and couldn't help but be somewhat amused. His tail flicked behind him. "No one here knows how to be a comedian. What a bunch of meatheads."

Guilt resurfaced once he was alone. How could he have allowed himself to be such a monster? He had to make this up somehow. What would Ashley think of all this? The thought saddened him greatly. He missed her so much. The least he could ask was to know if she were safe. Was Adwen right? Would he see her again?

Shaking his muzzle, he thought she would be more than disappointed with him if she knew what he had done. Jack wouldn't blame her if she never wanted to see him again. There was no other conclusion. He had no choice but to try to redeem himself, if in no one else's sight, at least in his own.

Chapter 18
CHASING GHOSTS

The mountain wind was cold, like water rushing through the vacant valleys and billowing over trees. The harsh northern mountain range was devoid of human influence. There were few places level enough to build a home. Nature and magic ruled the quiet passes crowned with snow.

Strong sunlight gave Adwen the endurance to run throughout the day without rest. It was bright enough to restore her power quicker than she could spend it. Never tired or out of breath, she sprinted with her wild silvery hair flowing in the breeze.

The chill deepened as the day began to close, but she was impervious to cold or heat. What did bother her was a simple question: How was she to get this controlling being to communicate with her? She used the time to ponder the mystery.

If this thing could take hold while she was unaware, then how could she make it face her? What could it possibly want? Could it influence her in other ways?

Adwen remembered the times when oddly helpful and unusual ideas would dawn on her. They had seemed to come from nowhere. Had they? Becoming sure that they were from the strange being, she thought hard. If it could tell Adwen what it wanted, then she could potentially sense what it wished.

As she raised her eyes and gazed at King's Peak, she knew instantly. The mountain was more than twice the height of the others. It was also the first unusual thing she had seen upon arriving in the magical realm. This being, whatever it was, wanted her to go to that mountain. She could feel a powerful pull that seemed to be drawing her toward the place.

Then Adwen thought of a way to test her theory. Not wanting to help what was manipulating her, she chose to go where it did not. She turned west and took brisk strides through old dead leaves.

Adwen smiled to herself and glanced at the mountain on her right. The being wouldn't like this. Sighing deeply, she looked straight ahead, proud of her clever choice. A half-second later, she stopped dead.

King's Peak was no longer to her right. It lay before her once more.

Before the panic could overwhelm her, she examined the tracks in the mess of leaves and branches. She clearly saw where she had stopped heading west, backtracked to where she turned, and then began walking north again.

Utter helplessness threatened to crush her, and tears swelled in her violet eyes. She didn't want to do what the being wanted. What did it have waiting for her at the mountain? She doubted it was anything good. The being had been very helpful, but manipulation was not a tactic she approved of.

There was no other choice. She had to continue to the summit.

Pines grew taller and dominated the terrain at the base of the mountain. Many rutted paths twisted upward. Adwen followed them for a time until blankets of snow swallowed them whole. Strong winds whipped up and occasionally tossed long streams of powder and crystals.

The scenery made her recall her first night in the realm of magic. White carpets decked out the forest, and frosty plants glittered in the rising moonlight. The three crescents of red, orange and green were dominated by the light of the full golden moon overhead. All four made the land appear to be made of diamonds. It was all so eerie and familiar. Unlike her last excursion through the Dargadian snow, she was equipped with well-honed instincts. This time, she knew she was not alone.

Despite that fact, she kept running. The sixth sense warned that a stalker was in the area. She wasn't worried by the smell of strong dark magic. It was distant.

Then Adwen detected a second evil stalker ahead and came to a halt in knee-high powder. She took a moment to scan the area and see if these enemies were visible. Eventually she noticed tracks in the snow. Large paw prints that resembled a cat's led off in several directions. Each print was two feet wide and appeared to be melted, as if something hot had touched down.

Adwen was instantly wary. Two powerful demons in the night would not be a fair fight by any means. According to her instincts, these demons were each strong enough to subdue her. The magic in this place was old and deep. These creatures could have been prowling this territory for a long time, absorbing enough to sustain themselves. She couldn't stay put for long. If these were Hell Cats, as she could only assume by the evidence, they more than likely knew she was here.

As she deduced it was time to move, she felt eyes watching from behind. Adwen prepared for a brawl and made tight fists. Then she whirled around in the snow and glared at what was approaching.

It was not a Hell Cat. Wind was blowing harder across the face of the mountain and threw the snow in thick, wispy flurries, obscuring details. Adwen's eyes grew wide, and fear gripped her as she saw a glowing golden figure a hundred paces away. The solitary thing was transparent and walked coolly up the steep grade as though there was no resistance. The energy coming from the spirit was immense. Adwen was no match, and that thought made her insides churn.

Abruptly changing tactics, she turned and ran up the mountainside to escape. For the moment, a pair of Hell Cats was much less threatening. Adwen's rapid footfalls were quiet in the soft white drifts. She weaved between the trees as fast as possible, even though the powerful being was falling farther behind. Its energy dwindled as it vanished into thin air, but she didn't think it was gone for good.

Spotting movement ahead, she froze in her tracks and quickly dove far downwind, hiding herself behind a mound of snow. The leap for cover was just in time to avoid the detection of the Hell Cat. It thought it smelled something and stalked over to investigate.

Her hiding place was closer than she preferred. She could hear the sound of searing hot feet landing on snow, melting it on contact. Curiosity eventually got the better of her, and she stole a peek. She was able to feel the creature's power and was not surprised by its size and intimidating appearance.

The ethereal beast was seven feet tall at the shoulders and black with orange stripes like a tiger. Its fangs were like a saber-toothed cat, reaching far out from under the upper lip. From horned nose to barbed tail tip, the Hell Cat was covered in black and red flames that the wind could not snuff out. It growled angrily as it smelled her tracks, flicking its long tail.

A roar echoed up the mountainside, causing Adwen to duck. The Hell Cat answered its partner before bounding away. They were aware of Adwen and would start their hunt shortly. Once the demon was out of sight, Adwen bolted, searching for a sure way to avoid the monsters of King's Peak.

Adwen ran. With every step she took, the weather seemed to worsen. Clouds rolled in, blotting out the starry sky. Swirling snow on the gusts made traveling precarious, as she could hardly see obstacles underfoot. Even though she tripped on a few rocks, she never fell.

The Hell Cats roared up along the obscured slope, and she heard their ominous calls. Their supernatural senses could pick up faint traces of her energy wherever she stepped. No earthly elements would stop them from finding the trail. It was a matter of time before they would catch up.

The incline of the mountain grew steeper. Adwen thought of transforming in order to move more quickly. Her energy was better concealed in woman form, and only traces were left where she walked. It was too great a risk, so she chose to remain as she was.

Pondering the dilemma was a distraction. By the time she came to her senses, the powerful transparent entity had rematerialized ahead. Details were more obscured than before, as Adwen nearly stumbled over hidden rocks. Sighting the figure sent her into a panic, and she raced away down the mountain, far from where she knew the demons were approaching.

Downhill skipping and sprinting took her past more trees and through snowdrifts that were almost waist high. She avoided the deeper mounds, looking for safety. It was plain that there was no hiding from any of her hunters. If she paced herself, she thought, and lasted until morning, the sunlight could help her fight off the demons.

The ground began to level off, and Adwen was going to pour on the speed. Then she realized the ground was about to drop off. She came to a sliding stop just short of a ledge. Her heavy panting and the howling wind filled her ears, as she peered over and down into the storm. The violent blizzard made seeing the bottom impossible. She doubted any fall would be harmful, but she was not in the mood for a rough landing. There would be no climbing down, so she turned to go.

Adwen took a few strides through the wind and frost and then became paralyzed. Fear held her in place once she saw the transparent spirit again. It strode closer, cutting off her escape routes. To the left or right were sheer drops along the jutting length of stone and ice that stretched from the mountainside. There was nowhere to run.

As the being continued to approach, Adwen slowly backed away, clenching her fists at her sides. Soon she found herself cornered against the ledge. If she had to, she would fight. The power radiating from her rightfully confident opponent was almost double the strength she possessed. Now that there was no alternative, Adwen faced her fear with firm defiance.

Fewer snow flurries blew past to hinder her view of the golden figure. It was no taller than she was and just as lean. When there were no more than ten paces between them, the being stopped and stared in silence.

Adwen was confused and anxious. It was just standing there, watching. The spirit was difficult for even her eyes to discern because of its transparent form. This couldn't be a ghost. She could see ghosts as plain as living people. What was this?

Then her eyesight adapted to the foul conditions. Her mind grasped the appearance of the spirit. It was a lightly armored woman with pointed ears. Flowing hair reached as far as her shoulder blades, and a cloth was draped about her neck. The spirit's face was striking, eyes sharp, her stance strong, and she had no shoes.

Apart from the apparel, the golden being looked exactly like Adwen.

Adwen was stunned until the spirit held out a hand. The inviting gesture wasn't expected, and the surprise made Adwen all the more wary. She recoiled, clenching her teeth and small fangs, growling.

The being wasn't moved. It continued to hold the offering pose, waiting.

A long moment went by, and neither acted. Wind howled about them. Snow came in sideways in a wild whiteout. Adwen didn't know what to do, as the powerful golden being still held out an open hand.

Adwen flinched at the echoing roars of two Hell Cats. More than ever, she considered jumping off the ledge. The fall would be merciful, whereas the demons would not. She was running out of options by the second, but she didn't leap or run and kept a wary eye on the mysterious spirit.

The spirit also sensed the demons coming through the storm. Turning its head, the being glimpsed the fiery brutes stalking closer. When she returned her attention to Adwen, the calm expression was gone. The spirit's face showed great urgency.

The being's expression confounded Adwen to the point that she hardly noticed the demons. Was it trying to tell her something? What did it want?

Once she locked eyes with the being, a realization dawned on her. It wasn't like the many times before. This was no subconscious message. Adwen realized what was happening. The fear was gone. The demons meant nothing to her now. She stood tall, smiled, and opened her arms to the golden form.

The specter's shape instantly flew forward. At the same time that they collided in an explosion of golden light, the demons leaped. Adwen's body was encased by the pure energy when the creatures lunged for her, and all three went off the edge.

She and the monsters fought during their freefall. The first to reach her received a vicious slash across the eyes from her glowing hands. Blinded and enraged, it roared before Adwen's body whirled and kicked downward, sending the Hell Cat faster in its descent.

The second demon swatted a set of claws, gnashing oversized fangs. When it missed, it roared and swung its barbed tail after her.

Adwen slashed at the spiked tip, shredding it easily. The demon yowled, while its purple blood flew upward, and she guided herself in close. She grasped the creature's dark skin on its chest. Where she touched sizzled and smoked, burning the Hell Cat. It roared over and over as she delivered punch after punch. When it tried to bite, she struck the jaws with all her might, stunning the desperate demon.

During their fall, Adwen was eventually over her enemy, attacking relentlessly. A frozen lake loomed below them. The blinded monster's body hit the thick ice with such force that its hot body crashed through into the freezing water. Steam and fragments flew in every direction before the two plunged into the cold dark lake.

"Where am I?"

"You ought to know. You're the one who brought us here."

All surroundings were blurred and dark. Direction did not exist, as Adwen was confused by the lack of solid ground, though she was standing on a seemingly invisible floor. This place had no horizon and only space. Unsure of how to react, she studied Golden Eyes.

"I brought us here?" Adwen asked. "Where is here, exactly?"

The golden form smiled softly and tapped one temple.

She was aghast. "We're in my head?" Looking around again, an embarrassed smile came over her. "I wouldn't have expected it to be this empty. Jack would get a good laugh."

Golden Eyes couldn't help but let out a small chortle. "We are in your subconscious. It only seems empty because you are not dreaming."

"So, who are you?"

Golden Eyes shook her head and replied, "You don't need to ask. We could only be here this way if you truly knew. Say it aloud."

"You're my inner self."

Smiling, she shrugged. "That is close enough. In essence you are correct. I am your heart, Adwen. I am the center of your strength. Not only that, but I am the way you receive direct instruction from the great light."

"You mean the Light Spirits. This doesn't make sense."

Golden Eyes cocked her head.

"How are you separate from the rest of me?" Adwen asked. "If you're my heart, then why are we having this conversation? I'm pretty sure I'm not schizophrenic."

"This happened upon your death. Only an immortal weapon would have the power to sever your soul. While you were still composed of living flesh, what brought about your demise was of evil make."

"Demon steel," Adwen murmured darkly.

"Correct. Sycan more than likely forged his own personal weapon for the deed. Ever since, I have worked to fulfill my original purpose of being your guide. I formed my own identity as Golden Eyes, but this awkward partnership is no longer sufficient. You ... we ... have a purpose to serve. You cannot hold all of the power at hand, and I simply cannot be allowed to take dominion over this body of ours. You are the thinker and I the leader. To continue these quests, this must be changed."

"What are you asking?"

"I am not asking. I am informing. What you see before you is a ghost of who you are meant to be. As those of the living lands must, you have found yourself. I cannot act on your behalf any longer. I cannot make this choice for you, either."

Adwen was stunned.

"I now ask you, Adwen. When you make your decision I shall still be, but not. I will disappear, and you will be made whole. Adwen, do you accept your own identity?"

After a moment of silence, she was about to answer.

The sky over the mountain lake was calmer, and the wind was like a soft whisper. It whistled through the tree boughs and swept across the thick ice, covered by a blanket of snow. With the harsh storm gone at last, the valleys were hushed in the night. One place in the surface of the lake was rough and uneven where the ice had been broken. An hour had passed, and it had refrozen.

A strong golden glow began to grow where the disturbed surface was weakest. Then the ice erupted, scattering fragments about. Adwen coughed up water as she hauled herself free of the cold lake. She crawled away from the gaping hole she had created, then collapsed. Her new armor struck the ice loudly with her weight.

Adwen breathed in deep heavy gasps, glad to be in the open air. She rolled herself over onto her back to relax. Everything was quiet, and the snow was soft. A snowflake touched her cheek, making her curious enough to look up.

Her mind became lost, as she gazed up into the endless drifting flakes. Thoughts were coming in the same way. Memories of when her inner self had seized control were becoming her own. She could remember everything. She recalled destroying the first of the Bloody Brothers, contending with Oryn when he was still a knight, and more. The thoughts floated into her mind to settle where they belonged, like the snow around her.

She didn't bother to dwell on all of the moments. One in particular had her captivated. While they had stayed at the Red Lily Inn, she had shared a few conversations with Oryn. The last of them was on a rainy night. She now perfectly recalled looking deep into his heart. Inside was so much pain, blotted out with anger. What she had discovered hidden deep under all of the harsh self-loathing was warm. His heart held a strong feeling for her.

A happy smile found its way to her face. Staring far up into the clouds, her bright and very blue eyes glowed.

Chapter 19
LESSON LEARNED

A day had passed since Oryn had returned with Jack to the Order. The black hound was not pleased to learn what had become of the key to his chains, and his overseer was not surprised that Jack had plenty to say on the matter. His comments were as abundant and immature as ever.

The removal of the demon parasite made Jack far more receptive. Once Oryn realized that, it pleased him, though there was nothing else to smooth the disdain. Parasite or no, Jack had still betrayed them.

Many knights who did not have important business gathered in the stands over the pit to watch. Word had spread quickly that Sir Oryn was attempting to train an underling. It didn't matter that it was Jack the Underhanded, as they called him. They knew that Oryn's method of teaching was unpredictable. Only one thing was certain: His lesson would be brutal.

Jack flattened his ears at the sight of their audience and grumbled aloud, "What did you tell them? This looks like they're here to see a major match to the death. I thought we settled this yesterday."

In human form, Oryn never glanced at the mumbling audience and shook his head. "What was settled was with the demon, not you."

"You said that it used me like a sock puppet. Do you hold grudges like girls do?"

Oryn ignored the childish prod and maintained a serious expression. "Spites can control you so long as you allow. It is possible to resist. They feed off of fear and other dark feelings. There are dated accounts of those who starved the parasite by not acting on such drives. You let the darkness control you, and that fact is inescapable."

Still trapped in hound form, Jack's nose was almost level with Oryn's piercing green stare. Guilt itched at the base of his furry neck, and denying the urge to scratch, he paused before grumbling, "Point taken, but you still have to work on your sense of humor."

"Jests fall short when actions are out of bounds."

The black hound grimaced and growled, "Thanks for cutting my feet out from under me. I'm just trying to lighten the mood and start making up for being a jerk."

Irritated by the humor, Oryn couldn't help but be slightly flattered. If the cur were truly attempting to make amends, he would have to do better.

"If you seek redemption, you have only to close your mouth. Adwen will return, and I do not waste time when waiting. I aim to teach you lessons in combat."

"Okay, but go easy on me. I feel stronger since you took out that nasty bug, but I get the sense you're still overkill."

Oryn said nothing and thought of how to begin. Sometime in the night, they both had gained an immense amount of strength. Oryn suspected that it was due to Adwen gaining in power, but he was unsure. She was still far north in the mountains. If their massive addition of strength were a clue to her recent gains, then he was not concerned. He could assume that she was doing well, as usual.

Taking a few steps back, Oryn instructed, "Upon my signal, you shall come at me however you wish."

"Okay, Cujo," Jack panted while taking a fighting stance. "Whatever you say."

Knights whooped when the hound made the first move. As he threw a swift and powerful punch for Oryn's head, it was easily blocked. Jack spotted a fist coming for his ear and barely ducked in time. However, he did not see a right hook flying in for his throat. The knights laughed and clapped, while the black hound yelped and wheezed.

Oryn wasn't going to end the sparring match yet. He quickly grasped one of the hound's long ears and slammed his other elbow forcefully into Jack's back. The hound dropped, gasping, as he was held nose down in the dirt.

Applause and whooping filled the stands.

"What was that for?" Jack whimpered. "You really are holding a grudge."

"Your pain is your own fault. Your defense was poor." Letting Jack gather himself up for a second round, Oryn grimaced. "What is that vulgar name you've been calling me? I do not approve of pet names from anyone."

He grumbled as he massaged his throat, "It's the name of a giant rabid dog from a scary book. Haven't any of your girlfriends ever called you cute names?"

Oryn maintained his stoic appearance and tone. "Keeping one's focus on the matter at hand seems to be another ability you lack. Be silent unless it pertains to the lesson. This shall be your one warning. Now are you prepared to continue?"

"Yeah," he panted and cocked his ears slyly. "After you tell me what pet names your girlfriends gave you."

Again, the crowd of knights cheered when Oryn moved at blinding speed. He struck Jack's esophagus for the second time, dropping him to his knees, gagging.

He stood over the coughing hound with a fist in case Jack might not have learned his lesson. Aggravated, Oryn glowered. "Do you ever learn? Stand and face me."

Some knights were laughing, as others began placing bets on how long Jack could go before evoking another beating from his new mentor. One called down through guffaws of entertainment, "You can't possibly be this stupid, beast! We can't understand a word you say, but we know the general wouldn't strike needlessly. Shut up and save your pride!"

Standing up and regaining the ability to breathe, Jack whined, "You're no fun."

Oryn's patience was beginning to wear thin. "Stop wasting time. Come at me."

More and more men called out, as Jack thought before moving to attack. Out of time to contemplate, Jack moved as fast as he could to kick his opponent's gut. The shot was sidestepped, and the black hound quickly blocked a punch, and then another. He thought he saw an opening and threw a fist of his own. Jack was not fast enough.

Before the hound knew what was happening, Oryn dodged the punch, grasped Jack's bulky wrist and twisted him around into a disabling position. The pupil yelped, as he was steered around and forced to kneel.

Even more laughter rolled around the stands.

Jack yelped in dismay, "Aw, come on! I asked nicely for you to go easy on me! I'm a cop, not a lethal weapon like you!"

Oryn sneered at the comment. As a form of punishment for still not learning to be quiet, he grasped Jack's elbow and used his leverage on the wrist. A second later, there was a loud crunch, and the hound was howling and crying, clutching at his dislocated shoulder. The observing knights winced and chuckled at the sound, and paid winning betters their due.

Oryn let go of the black hound and listened to him cry. To his mild surprise, Jack was able to reset the joint on his own. Oryn was then pleasantly surprised that he didn't have a comment on the issue.

"Shall we continue? You are a slow learner, but I have the mental stamina for students such as you."

Jack gathered himself up, massaging the ache. "I sure am. But I'm not stupid. You're a slow learner, Cujo. I have the know-how to help you out, too. Sooner or later, I'll get to teach you how to tell a certain somebody how you feel about them. What do you think?"

The betting men in the stands didn't have time to place new bets. Oryn's eyes burned dangerously. He clenched his teeth and small fangs at Jack. Sneering, he rushed forward and leaped.

Jack blinked and tried to avoid what was coming but failed to notice that he was at the length of his chain. He was cornered, as Oryn came down, planting a single fist into the top of his head. The blow caused Jack to collapse, completely unconscious.

Oryn crouched on top of him, shaking and breathing heavily. The nerve of what was said had made Oryn snap. A side of him knew Jack was being honest in trying to be helpful. It was subdued by the rage that he dared to speak openly with him on the topic. He regained control of his anger and stepped off of the rude creature. It would be a while before the lessons could start again.

Those in the stands were not as boisterous as before. There was some disappointment that the entertainment had ended, and others made harsh statements about Jack. As they were starting to disperse, counting their coins, three elders followed the high elder into the open.

They were about to call for Oryn's attention, but he had already seen them. He strode to the edge of the ring and leaped straight up to join them. Carefully avoiding the spiked rail, he cleared it and approached, respectfully crossing an arm laterally over his chest. The old men nodded in response.

"How may I be of service, High Elder?"

A look that reminded Oryn of his own fragile patience was on the men's faces. As always, the high elder spoke on the behalf of the other elders, "The council is concerned, Sir Oryn. Where is the heir? Why has she not returned?"

Hiding his own frustration, he answered, "The Tame One is in the mountains to the north. She forbade me to follow and gave direct instruction to return here. As to why she is there, that is a matter that she would rather I not divulge. It concerns her well-being and no one else's."

A heavier-set elder among them cleared his throat loudly, prompting the high elder to bring up another point. None of their expressions had softened, and they continued to grimace.

"When shall she return? Summons for help have begun to flood in from peoples closest to Castle Gailarien. They must have answers soon."

It was difficult for Oryn to disguise his own aggravation. He was quiet and closed his eyes, taking in a deep breath while trying to sense Adwen. Their link was getting stronger all of the time, and he attempted to sense her intentions. She was still hiking somewhere far to the north.

Sighing and eyeing the old men, he told them, "That is not certain. She will return with great haste once she finds what she is searching for."

Again, the stout elder made a guttural sound to prompt Mamalis, who frowned. "Can you not call to her? She must know of this."

When he was a knight, he would have kept a cool composure. Things were different now, and he had enough authority to deny the old men so long as he was following Adwen's will. Their questions tested his temper. His eyes shone brighter with anger, and the red and white robed men shifted but didn't step away.

A note of warning was in his harsh voice: "What she seeks in the north is of equal or greater importance. Rest assured, she will return quickly."

They continued to frown in silence.

"Is there anything else you wish to inquire?"

It eased Oryn to see the high elder swallow his pride. "There is not. Thank you for your time, Sir Oryn." They nodded, and he saluted to them, as the men turned to go.

He glared as the elders disappeared into a corridor. If they badgered him about Adwen like that again, he could be tempted to put them in their place.

That would not do, he told himself. He raked a set of fingers along his scalp once for the calm it would bring. As usual, it instilled some contentment. Jack would wake later and be ready to continue training. Being centered beforehand helped Oryn to ignore all of the foolishness. This lesson was learned years ago. It's impossible to teach if your student spends most of the time asleep or incapacitated.

Chapter 20
KING'S PEAK

Adwen lay in the falling snow for hours. She remained motionless, letting herself become lightly enveloped, gazing up into the dark grey sky. It was still night when the clouds departed and unveiled the moons and stars. Though the snow felt cool, she was not chilled. She relished the crisp night air and got to her feet.

For the first time, she studied her knew apparel. Silvery chain-mesh held white and golden guards to her legs and arms. The gilded ivory plates protected her extremities, while her body was wrapped with more chain-mesh and golden bands. The backs of her hands remained armed, only this time with three golden spikes raking forward to her knuckles. As always, her feet were bare, and the white cloth that the spirit of peace had gifted was draped around her neck.

Adwen smiled. The sense of wholeness escaped description. She sighed, glancing up where King's Peak loomed. Some ground had been lost during the battle. It didn't matter, she thought and shrugged. The feeling inside that had led Adwen this far was clearer and stronger.

Upon taking a confident step forward, her foot sank deep into the snow. Adwen blinked her bright blue eyes and scoffed at herself. There were no more enemies to detect her presence, and she decided to continue onward in her true form.

Adwen's body rose up into its slender white shape while retaining her new garments, with the exception of her white hood. Her eyes brightened, and the golden mark on her creature face shimmered. The symbol of the Andredan bloodline had taken the place of the blaze she bore previously.

The thought of testing her limits caused her tail to swing playfully. She could make out a faint glow to the east beyond white caps and chose to race the sunrise to the top of the mountain. Starting with a loping gait, she soon leaped far out and continued bounding on all fours.

Wind stoked the rising excitement, a bark escaped her, and she summoned up and drew out the power from her heart. Her white fur shone brighter with the increasing power she summoned, and she moved ever faster. Whistling air rolled over her jaws and down her back, tossing up flurries in her wake. Adwen was a blur, rushing between trees and soaring over the tops of powdery drifts. Dark rocks jutted out of the snow the farther she went. They didn't slow Adwen down, as she darted and avoided the largest obstacles, covering many miles in the minutes before sunrise.

Now that definition in the mountain was easier to discern, she realized that a great opening was near the summit. Lofty stone stairs were soon under her claws, and Adwen steadily stowed away her powers. The glow left her body, but she didn't slow until she was nearing the final steps. Once there, she stood, shifted into her more human shape and approached the vast entryway, flanked by two stone pedestals.

The commanding feeling that brought her to this isolated place became subdued. In her heart, she knew there was a reason she was meant to be here before sunrise. But she couldn't guess why.

Adwen's curiosity was first piqued by the peculiar stone altars that each held a crystal the size of a man's fist. It intrigued her to sense faint magic in the sunstone fragments. That's when she looked at the entire area and realized that twenty-two more stones were mounted on pedestals, scattered about the shrine.

Methodically, Adwen stepped past the broad entry.

The instant her foot touched down beyond the threshold, she paused. There was silence, as she suddenly became aware of the true power confined to the eerie shrine. Strong magic blocked the wind from reaching beyond the stairs. The air was still but fresh, when it should have been stale in the absence of a breeze.

A shallow groove was in the stone floor under Adwen's bare foot. She brushed away a thin veil of dust and found that the indentation formed a gently curving line. Adwen didn't bother following it further. Her sharp sight could see the line forming a giant circle surrounding her and the collection of crystals.

She continued to the center, admiring and investigating the mysterious layout. Where the twenty-four sunstones sat formed three rings of varying sizes flowering outward from a pivotal point. To Adwen, the ripple-like design was familiar. Since becoming whole, her knowledge of magic and power had increased relative to her strength. This was an ancient seal. While lost in curious ponderings, Adwen paid no mind to the coming sunrise.

Cream and orange hues sluggishly reached out from behind the distant landscapes. The brighter and fuller they grew, the more the daytime sky unfurled, consuming the stars en mass. The light reached over to touch King's Peak. Subtle rays found the crystals at the stair, refracting to surrounding stones.

Adwen instantly saw the beams of sunlight and stared in surprise. There wasn't enough yet to fill the entryway crystals and cross to the rest of the twenty-four. The sun was continuing to rise and the intensity of the beams with it.

Unafraid, Adwen reached out a gentle hand to touch a nearby beam of sunlight, and as expected, there was warmth. The first light of day always danced on her body, and this little ray was no different. It wove and swirled across her hand like fiery water, up to her shoulder, and then continued to the neighboring crystal, unhindered.

After a while of admiring the light, her heart urged her to stand in the center of the circle. Her gaze wandered to the spot where a larger crystal was imbedded in the smooth ground, covered in the same dust as everything else. Curiosity made her move closer. What would happen, she wondered?

As she passed through the beam that was growing stronger, it split, passing to her as it did with the crystals. The first sunrays blazed in the many facets, overflowing into each other. Warm beams connected with Adwen, dancing and weaving in waves and shimmering ripples. It was soothing, as she watched intently, waiting for the result.

The sun rose above the horizon, completely filling the crystals. Web-like beams of light turned to strong currents of gold. They struck Adwen hard, taking her breath away. She was paralyzed by the power of the gems, while they siphoned their light through her and into the stone at her feet. It shone brightly with the focused energy until the stone it rested in glowed hot red.

Then an explosion of light pulsed from the largest gem, knocking Adwen backward and launching the settled dust into the air. She barely regained her balance to avoid falling. It was quiet, and the cloud of drifting particles was impossible to see through. What happened startled her, and her curiosity turned to alarm.

Soft sunshine cut through from the cavern opening, while the sunstones dimmed and went out. She began to sense a presence and crouched low by a stone altar, listening for movement aside from her own. For a long time there was silence. Her eyes wandered, searching, while her keen pointed ears were pricked and ready for a sound. Someone or something was here.

The dust was mostly settled when she heard it. Out of sight, a figure drew breath and sighed. She felt the hair on her neck stand on end. Creeping around her small hiding place, she searched for the new arrival.

Peering out to the other side of the formation, Adwen spotted the shape of a man standing amid the pedestals. The air was nearly clear, and she realized he could see her hiding and stood. There was little point in being timid. Preparing herself for anything, she waited for the stranger to make the first move.

He didn't attack. Adwen braced herself, as he took three strong strides closer. The instant she saw his eyes, she froze. They were glowing bright blue.

The man was a few inches taller than her, and his hair was short and white, aside from a set of blond bangs. He appeared young. When Adwen couldn't pick up a scent, it was clear that he was not among the living. His build was strong, lean, and he was clothed in crimson. A few golden markings decorated his garments. Though his stance belonged to that of a warrior, his smile showed a child's heart. He appeared to be kind.

They stared at each other for a moment.

Adwen was suspicious and murmured accusingly, "How do I know this isn't a trick? How do I know you're not an imitation?"

Amused by her questioning, Darien arched an eyebrow and chuckled.

She blinked as the Master Knight shook his head, chuckling, and strolled toward the top of the stair.

Darien watched the day begin before saying aloud, "You know I am no imposter. If that were so, you would know in an instant. The Light Spirits chose you as their emissary. You know whatever they wish you to know in your heart." When she did not respond he beckoned. "Come. Join me a while. You have a few moments to spare."

Feeling silly and a little surprised to be meeting her ancestor, Adwen went to him. She stopped beside Darien at the edge of his perimeter.

Not being in a living form, he was unable to go beyond the markings on the floor. Standing as close to the outside as he could, the Master Knight savored the sight of the magical realm.

Adwen was at a loss for words. Once she found the will to stop staring at his face, she also looked out at the world laid before them. Her nerves were calm, and her mind clear when he spoke again.

"My purpose here is to see that you are truly prepared for what is to come. Long ago, I found this place called Dargadia. The same as you, I also found myself on the verge of death. If it weren't for the elf prince, I would have become nothingness." He turned to give her a smile and added, "We both owe that debt to the very same healer. It was also he who foresaw your arrival and wrote the secret texts given to the Kingdoms of Day."

Adwen said nothing and looked back with mild surprise.

He smiled and his eyes glowed brighter. "You're a tad shorter than I had imagined."

At that she couldn't help but laugh.

"I am glad that I have this time with you. I am also sorry. You are meant to shoulder a heavy burden. I was consoled that you would have allies far stronger than those I once knew."

He paused, and she took the opportunity to speak. "What am I? The others aren't quite like me. Am I like you are now?"

Shaking his head, he answered, "No. You have transcended."

"What?"

"Though your prior demise was unfortunate, it was meant to be. In order for you to become my true heir, you would have to become more than immortal. To transcend is to rise beyond the material world. The only part of your being that belongs to the living worlds is your skin. All of the rest of what you are is spirit. Your body is spirit in imitation of living flesh."

"That's why my blood isn't red anymore," Adwen muttered, shocked.

Darien nodded.

"How and why did I have to transcend?"

"You had my blood in your veins, Adwen. If the one who saved me from destruction hadn't given me a living form, changing spirit into living flesh, you would have never existed."

"What? Wait a minute!"

He raised a hand to stall her questioning. "Please. All you need to know is that I was once spirit before this. In a living body, I was powerful but incapable of what you are able to do. A body composed of flesh has limits. It can only contain so much energy before it begins to be destroyed. Secondly, for the Light Spirits to endow you with pure light, you had to become pure.

"All living things have light and dark in their souls. You had to be pure. By passing on and through to where the great white tree stands, you were purified. They then granted you a fraction of their power so that you may be their servant. It was they who chose you from my bloodline, and they who move you to mark your warriors."

A satisfied feeling settled on her. She really was not to blame for Oryn or Jack being marked. Without thinking, Adwen mumbled, "Thank you. I needed to hear that."

"Never doubt yourself. Doubt is the enemy of action. The Light Spirits guide you directly. There is no need for you to doubt."

"Okay," Adwen heaved a heavy sigh and then asked, "What else is there?"

Darien was quiet. His expression was solemn. Eventually he explained his silence: "There is more I must tell that I am deeply sorry about."

"Why?"

"I am sorry that I cannot make it otherwise. A very long time ago, I endured an incredible pain. You shall, as well. It will be far more intense than any pain you've ever known. Do not let it consume you, Adwen. It almost did me."

Seeing the fear in her was what he had dreaded. Shaking his head, he reassured, "No matter how dark things seem or become, do not forget those closest to you. They will be your anchor. Without them, you would be lost. Never let them go. Surely, they will not let you."

Adwen shed a few tears and quickly wiped them away.

"That is the first caution I was told to give. The second is of the demon general, Guillot. He is the one demon you must beware of most."

"What about Sycan?"

Darien grimaced at hearing the name. "Indeed, he you must handle with great care and with great distance if you can. General Guillot, on the other hand, you must pay heed to. You are resilient to curses and a great many things, but Guillot alone has the power to bring you lasting harm. The dreaded sliver may stop you."

Disturbed, she warily asked, "How?"

"Guillot, and only Guillot, has the ability to taint any soul. Beware his gifts."

Adwen was even more unsettled and shuddered. "Doubt I would ever accept any gifts from a demon, but note taken. I won't forget it."

Cracking a small smile, Darien said, "You remind me so much of her."

"Huh?"

He took a moment to cherish her sweet face. "The one I used to know."

A second passed before she realized that he meant the woman

before the ancient princess of Dargadia. "Oh. Thanks, I guess." Her cheeks began to blush pink.

Darien chuckled and added, "With her wild spirit in you, the enemy has good reason to fear. Once your four warriors are assembled, the demon lord Melanin will quake in his prison."

She recognized the name but didn't know exactly who Darien was discussing. "Excuse me, but did you say a demon lord?"

When he heard her, his brow furrowed, and he looked astonished. "Yes. Who else would have power enough to command both Sycan and Guillot? You really do not know what you are up against."

Adwen laughed a little, genuinely entertained. "When will I ever?"

He sighed and laughed as well. "Perhaps never."

Chapter 21
BEGIN AGAIN

It was the third day since Adwen went off alone. The sun shone brightly overhead, and for the umpteenth time Jack was twisted into an excessively disabled posture by Oryn. No matter how hard Jack tried, the powerful Holy Hound's sheer speed overwhelmed him. Oryn had claimed that Jack was showing progress, but Jack was convinced the training was a ruse. It was a cheap joke to get away with inflicting pain and embarrassment galore. Knowing the sure-fire way to strike back, he spoke up again.

Jack struggled against the rough grip on his wrist, as Oryn forced him to dance around, making the few knights who watched laugh. Through the pain, Jack panted, "If I didn't know any better, I would think that you loved dancing. Does Adwen know that?"

The question hardly got a reaction, as Oryn was growing accustomed to the quips and immature questions. Without so much as a blink, he swiftly jerked the black hound's wrist, dislocating it in an instant.

More men in the stands paid bets.

Not letting go, Oryn watched with mild satisfaction, as Jack dropped to his knees whining obscenities and crying out. He casually responded, "You showed fleeting promise to me moments ago. Impress me by being silent and presenting a challenge."

Ignoring the pain, Jack panted back, "Isn't this a challenge? Every so often, I figure out how to push your buttons, while you try to find new ways to pop my joints. Don't you think so?"

Oryn's pupil was indeed proving to be a challenge. Of all the times he had trained warriors, he could not recall one who withstood his torture tactics. They all had responded by shutting their mouths and using their brains. Either this student was talented at dealing with pain or simply did not have any good sense.

Oryn didn't feel like ending the hand-to-hand training just yet. His patience was wearing thin, but he wanted to see if Jack had notable skills in combat. Curiosity was the only thing keeping him within a hundred meters of the annoying creature.

"Do you know nothing?" Oryn released him. "There is little time to train before the Tame One's return. Do you think that incessant yammering will aid you in the future? Take these sessions seriously."

After resetting his wrist and letting it heal, the black hound grumbled, "You must be joking. If this was a real training session, you would be trying to find out what my skills are, not pummeling me until I figure out how to stop you. How about bringing lunch or something? I'm starved."

Oryn frowned. "You devoured a whole pheasant not two hours ago."

"So? That didn't even touch bottom. Is there anything filling here, Cujo?"

Oryn raised an eyebrow to accompany the frown. "At last there is something that matches your bottomless well of words."

"My words come from that bottomless pit," Jack grumbled. "How about a pork round to help shut me up?"

Disgusted and more annoyed, Oryn snapped, "Get up."

"I will, once you answer the question. Does she know you can dance?"

Oryn's eyes narrowed dangerously. "Why do you test me?"

Jack's hound face showed a look of entertainment. "It's nothing personal. I'm getting to know you better. If you really don't want to answer the question, I could ask another one."

Oryn's expression was of restrained wrath, while his voice sounded calm. "Toying with me shall get you nowhere you wish to be. I say again, get up."

"Have you kissed her yet?"

The light in Oryn's emerald eyes lit like fireworks.

As usual, Jack paid the signs of impending pain no mind. He thought it over when no response followed and continued in a nonchalant tone.

"What was I thinking? You would never kiss her. You're too afraid for some reason. She must have kissed you by now. Has she?"

To Jack's surprise, Oryn took a breath and gave an abrupt sigh for calm. Then he glared and cautioned, "I believe you could appreciate and even respect that my business is only my own."

The black hound's tail wagged beside him. "Nice recovery! I thought you were really going to lose it. But seriously, have you guys done anything cute yet?"

Even the gathered knights flinched at the speed with which Oryn rendered Jack unconscious. One second, there were four feet between the pair, and in the next Oryn stood over the brute's limp, twitching body. This training session was adjourned.

For what remained of the day, Oryn prowled along aimlessly through the fortress's many curving halls. His boots made echoing sounds like a strange heartbeat in the places where few passed by, breaking the silence. Normally he would be spending every minute sparring with the men or studying old texts in the higher library.

He was far too restless and distracted. This was the longest he and Adwen had been apart since her return from the dead. There wasn't any worry for her safety. The link between Jack, Adwen and himself would have warned them immediately. She was well. Yet the anxiety of not having her nearby left him lost.

He tried a few times to sense her location but was without success. The last attempt was as the sun disappeared behind the western landscape. Night came, and Oryn scratched at the back of his neck when no one was around to see. This time, he willingly did so for the calming effect. Adwen would be here again soon, he reassured himself. When no more orange dusk light glowed on the skyline, the green-eyed warrior wandered off to his personal quarters.

His room lay in the east wing and was far roomier than his old captain's accommodations. The bed set out for him was made with fine feather pillows and silk linens. In the past few nights, he found it much more comfortable sleeping on the ground.

After glancing at all of the lavish things, his sights fell on the open window. He couldn't help but think of Adwen mentioning how nice it was to sleep along a broad sill. It made him smile a little. Shaking his head, he found his favorite place at the bedside on the plush crimson rug, made from what smelled like sheep's wool. Both the scent and feel beneath him easily lulled him into a deep and sound sleep.

As he slept, a sound almost made him stir. It was a subtle sigh. Then her voice whispered in his ear and made him wake with a start.

"Oryn."

His eyes snapped open wide, and he turned his head. She wasn't there. Thinking that perhaps Adwen was playing games, Oryn got up and surveyed the room. There was no sign of her. Not even a scent led him to her location. He was certain that he had heard her voice beside his ear.

A soft tune reverberated in the air, confirming his hopeful assumptions. It was louder when he neared the door into the hall. Knowing it could only be her magical voice made his casual walk turn into brisk strides.

The new day was about to start, as the dim light of dawn was brightening the navy colors overhead. With the sun beginning to rise, Oryn made his way through the corridors' many twists and turns, filled with expectancy. Though this wasn't as wild as some of the songs she cared for, he had the feeling that she cherished this song more than the rest.

Again Oryn rounded a corner. He was on a higher floor overlooking the Ring of Trials and his searching eyes quickly picked her out. The sun's first light was on her at the topmost walkway. Bright molten rays made it impossible to see her clearly, but he knew very well who it was, and his stride threatened to turn into a run.

The sun finished rising by the time he reached her perch, and as he had hoped, Adwen hadn't stopped humming. Oryn quietly came out at the top of the stairway to stand a few feet way. She sat up high on the stone barrier, dangling her feet over the edge. Without the sun disguising the colors, he was able to study the intricate set of armor she wore. It suited her personality, as well as her shape. At last, her gentle humming ceased, but she did not turn to face him.

"I woke you, didn't I?"

Oryn didn't reply, as he moved beside her.

Adwen took a long, deep breath and sighed deeply in contentment. She chuckled. "You took out Jack's Spite already."

The statement caught Oryn off guard. He pondered for a moment before asking, "How long were you aware of its presence? You allowed it to be?"

She thoughtfully ticked her tongue. "Well, I wouldn't say I let it be. Then again, those kinds of questions are confusing. I did and didn't. She did. I don't know."

He was unconcerned with the strange answer. "Were you able to find what you were seeking?"

The new question brought a big smile to her face. "I don't know," she teased and looked over at him with bright blue eyes. "But I think I did."

Her eye color pleased him more than it surprised him. Until that moment, he had not realized how much he had missed her eyes being blue.

Adwen's happy look turned into a sly expression. "You knew who she was."

His own expression quickly became confused.

"You know. Back at the Red Lily." She smiled as various emotions played over Oryn's face. Unlike him, Adwen wasn't embarrassed. Changing the subject ever so slightly, she looked back out at the horizon.

"I can remember everything now. I can remember all the way back to the first time Golden Eyes took control. It makes a lot of sense. Only my heart, freed from my thoughts of insecurity, would be capable of doing what had to be done. Being whole again should help with that problem from here on."

Oryn listened and then asked, "How was it done?"

She laughed a little. "It was so simple, I feel dumb! All I had to do was accept that part of myself. Once I did that ... snap! I was whole. I got all the power that used to be locked away inside of me. Well, I'm not even close to my full potential, but definitely stronger. I even learned a few more things in those mountains."

Pausing, she was calmer. "I know what I am now. I've transcended. I'm not dead or undead. On the other hand, I'm not really living."

A sober look crossed her face. "I'm a ghost."

Oryn made no effort to comment.

"I have only one purpose now. I am what I am because of my lineage and the Light Spirits. I'm their personal emissary. They send me to do what they want done when they want it done. I'm forbidden from almost everything of the living. For example, because I'm transcended, I'm made up of spirit flesh. I can't really die, but I can be destroyed. I can bleed, but not shed blood. I can be with someone, but not be capable of ..."

She didn't finish, and Oryn drew the conclusion well enough. More than ever, he pitied her for her losses.

Adwen thought about those things. Then she smiled and shook her head. Glancing at her warrior, she saw his sad look. Her eyes brimmed with light, and she reassured him, "I'm happy. Even though I can't have everything, I'm contented. I have the chance to be more. Serving the light and protecting the innocent is more than anything I could hope for. That is, aside from being with family."

"You shall see them again, I'm sure." Oryn returned her warm look.

"Thank you," Adwen replied before composing herself. Correcting her posture, she gazed down to where Jack continued to doze. His clawed hands and feet twitched in his sleep. Seeing him dreaming amused her. "I better go down to say good morning."

"When do you intend to set out?" Oryn asked.

"Not sure. Either way, Jack is coming along." She waited a second before shooting Oryn a sly expression. "You're not going to argue?"

"It wouldn't be my place to argue."

She suppressed a laugh. "After all the times you did before, now you're playing second string? Why the big change of heart?"

Being called out as a hypocrite made Oryn uncomfortable. He avoided her gaze and stared down at the sleeping hound instead. "My feelings toward this cur have yet to change. He is beyond the reach of even my conditioning. All that has changed is my opinion on his usefulness. Aside from a lack of manners, tact, skill and resourcefulness, he shows promise."

"So you're saying you think he isn't dead weight anymore?"

"I'm saying that I am impressed with his ability to withstand physical pain. That in itself has uses."

Adwen's eyes glowed, and she giggled, shaking her head.

"I no longer see him as a simpering whelp. My experience says he shall prove to be invaluable, no matter how much it sickens me to admit the fact."

"Good to hear you're on board with my plan. How about you do what you have to before we leave? I'm thinking of making sure all loose ends are tied up, including having breakfast. How long do you need?"

"Not longer than an hour's time."

"Great. We can leave before noon."

She was going to jump down, but Oryn quickly added, "It is best you know that the elders have been asking for your whereabouts. They may be seeking an audience."

She groaned. "That just ruined my morning. Thanks a lot for the heads-up, though. Wonder if they have anything new to pressure me with."

"Only what you are already aware of, I'm sure." Oryn failed to hide a small smile.

The sky was clear blue with the last of the stars gone. Jack began to stir in his sleep. He lay in the dirt with the cold metal chain still around his neck.

Near consciousness, there was an itch on his neck that felt like a tiny bug. While keeping his eyes closed, he swiftly smacked at the irritation. The sound that followed was that of a bare hand striking bare skin. His mind was far too bleary with sleep to register that anything was amiss, and he groggily blinked at his filthy palm, looking for a smashed insect. Thinking his sight might be hindered, he blinked a second time in disbelief at his very human hand.

Jack quickly sat up and marveled at the recovery of his human shape. A broad smile lit up his face, and his mahogany eyes had a jubilant glow. He laughed in relief.

Then the wind turned.

He smelled Adwen and turned to see her standing a few feet away. For a second, Jack thought she might still be angry, but when those blue eyes brightened, the idea seemed ridiculous.

After removing the large metal chain from around his neck and setting it aside, he looked sheepish. "So how do I say I'm sorry? Do I roll over and beg?"

She rolled her eyes and scoffed. "If you want to look stupid."

"Look," Jack dropped his humor and went on to say, "I know how I've screwed up. There's no way I'm going to be a warrior like your main man."

"That's fine actually. I'm not expecting you to be."

He grimaced and tried to smile through it. "I can't say all of my hostility went with that demon bug. I still want to go home."

"Note taken, and I don't blame you."

Jack heaved a dry laugh. "How did I know you wouldn't?"

"Don't know." She raised an eyebrow. "Telepathy?"

It was Jack's turn to roll his eyes. "That would be a nice trick to have. What do we do now, lady dog?" The name got a friendly laugh, and it satisfied him.

"The three of us are going out to kill more bad guys. First I have a few things to take care of here. What do you think?"

Getting to his feet, he looked hesitant. "You really want to know?"

Adwen shrugged.

"Being left alone with your green-eyed monster was the worst punishment ever."

"Jack?"

"What?"

"Shut up and get something to eat."

His sense of humor was restored, and he smiled. "And that's in the record books as the best command you've ever issued! Thank you very much."

Adwen only giggled, and shook her head while leading the way to the open gates.

In the time it took Jack to find a suitable breakfast, Oryn had already eaten his fill and had gone to visit a few comrades. The two brothers, Raglan and Dynic, were both disappointed yet relieved to learn that their training lessons were postponed again. Jack hadn't been the only one to suffer a brutal education under Oryn's watch. Despite the bruises, they were thankful for his time and gave a handsome number of gold coins in exchange. He thanked them kindly and left the knights' armor lockers to look for his free-spirited commander.

The search for Adwen brought him to the Order gardens, where the men seldom wandered. Tall statues depicting the Master Knight and his four warriors towered over the tidy greenery and any visitors. Magic kept the elements from wearing away the intricate detail of the stony surfaces, leaving them untouched by time.

Star blossoms pervaded the air with a gentle scent. The smells might have thrown off Jack's nose or that of any common dog, but his caught the hint of Adwen's trail.

Strong sunshine cast hard shadows beside the statues and hedgerows. Oryn strolled casually along one of the many stone pathways and stopped. He sensed eyes watching and instinctively looked to the source. The base of a statue was beside him and threw its shadow onto a tidy plot of grass. Just as he noticed that the grass in the darkest part of the shade was disturbed, he was distracted.

High Elder Mamalis called out, "Sir Oryn. Now that you are not busy toying with the traitor beast, I insist that you speak with me." The old man dressed in red and white seemed annoyed and very determined.

Oryn quickly checked his own temper and appeared nonchalant. "How may I be of service to you, High Elder?"

Mamalis stopped a few paces away and frowned. "The council has grown restless. The Tame One led you into the mountain pass days ago and still has yet to return and report what took place."

"The heir will meet with you in all due haste. In the meantime, my report of what transpired shall have to suffice."

The old man lowered his voice to whisper anxiously, "It is obvious to the council that the Tame One might regard meetings with us as trivial. Whether she revels in or loathes our encounters does not matter. Lady Adwen must keep the council informed of her activities. The playing of games will not do well in gaining the support of the elders."

Oryn's green eyes revealed no sign of an opinion. "Do you hold as little faith in her character as the rest of the council, or are you simply giving fair warning, High Elder Mamalis?"

He grimaced and paused. When he went on it was with a tone of caution. "I am merely hoping to inform the Tame One on these matters. As for where I stand, I would be a liar to say I approve of her recklessness."

"And do you still detest what we are, High Elder?"

A flicker of discomfort crossed his face. "I would never detest any warriors of light. That is a ridiculous accusation."

Adwen's voice cooed in the shadow of the statue beside them, causing the old man to flinch. "Oh, you're a slippery talker aren't you?" She stepped out into the direct sunlight, where her magical hood could not keep her invisible. Lowering the soft, white cloth back to her shoulders, she folded her arms and cocked her head at Mamalis.

The high elder struggled with his surprise and gave a smart bow. "Forgive me, Lady. I meant no ill words."

She tossed Oryn a clever smile. "Why don't you go and see if Jack is finished eating. I left him in the feasting hall."

He formally bowed before leaving the two alone in the Order garden.

Once the nervous elder found the will to look Adwen in the eye, she broke the awkward silence.

"For the record, I don't like politics. It fosters the bad habit of lying."

Mamalis was appalled. "I wouldn't dare to lie in your presence!"

Adwen rolled her eyes. "The elder council knows I don't like them, and I know you don't think creatures like us deserve rank."

The old man looked as though he had bitten into a lemon.

"Aside from that little problem, I don't mind having meetings with you. Now, back to that part about how the council doesn't want to support me."

Mamalis swallowed to clear his throat. "The elders sense your lack of concern for formality. They would prefer you come before them with whatever news you have with regard to progress and losses. Even elders who learn new movements hold meetings before the rest of the council."

"Oh. Well, that's pretty simple."

"It would help a great deal if you were to appear before them regularly, Lady Adwen. Proving that their doubts to your nature are ill-placed will aid in future meetings."

She smiled sweetly. "Thank you, Mamalis."

Adwen's failure to call him by his formal title put a knot in his throat. Did he dare to correct her? He decided to take the chance because she surely didn't understand.

"If it pleases you, Lady Adwen, formality is very important here."

The sweetness of her smile became wry, and she shook her head. "Sorry, but I had to test you. What I wanted to know was whether you understood my purpose."

The high elder was taken aback. "Lady Adwen, formality is a sign of intellect and proof of merit. You must understand that at the least?"

"I do get it, High Elder. Don't get me wrong; I know what you're saying. The concept you're not grasping is something I think is much more important. I'm not respected by the council. You're telling me that it's because I'm not formal enough. I think it's because you and the rest of them don't respect who I am."

She continued before he could interject: "And obviously, if you and the council think I have to adhere to your personal requests, then there's a terrible misunderstanding. I know who I am, High Elder. I am complete now, as you can see by the blue in my eyes.

"As the heir of the Master Knight I serve one master. The Light Spirits are the only ones that are higher than me. I don't belong to the living worlds or the laws that govern them. If I follow the rules of men, it is my choice or what the great light wants. As for trying to bend before the elder council, forget it. I don't have to talk to any of you unless it is the will of the Light Spirits. I'm their loyal Holy Hound and not a dog for men to fit a leash on."

He showed genuine shame and replied, "Yes, Lady Adwen."

"Anything else you need to tell me?"

"A small number of the council argued as much on your behalf before, Lady. Nevertheless, even they hoped you would agree to frequent council meetings."

Adwen let a second of quiet pass and told him, "There will be council meetings with me, High Elder. What I want to make clear is that I will take part only when I choose. I can take requests, but don't ever let the council think that they have the right to force me into anything."

A weight was lifted from the high elder's shoulders. Less worried, he asked, "May the elder council request an audience today, Lady Adwen?"

"Not today. We have to leave as quickly as possible."

"And if you could forgive my asking, where will you be traveling, Lady?"

She smiled. "I personally don't want to do it, but I'm taking my two warriors to Castle Gailarien. Hopefully we can find a way to cleanse the castle and reclaim it."

"Thank you, Lady. The council shall be pleased."

"You can't tell them what I'm doing."

Mamalis was startled. "What good could come from hiding such a thing?"

"It's just a precaution. Remember how two vampires got in to try and assassinate the king? I don't want to take any chances. If the enemy caught wind that I was headed there, it would be a disaster. You have my word that when I come back, there will be a council meeting with me in the elder hall."

The high elder was not pleased with the friendly command. Knowing better than to disagree, he nodded. "As you wish, Lady Adwen."

Rare lamb chops tasted better than Jack recalled from back when his life was normal. Ashley had talked him into trying a platter full in a restaurant years ago, and he had not liked it much. Now they tasted like tender slices of candy in comparison.

He was glad to be in human form and did what he could to blend with the rest of the men in the feasting hall. Steel chandeliers hung along the vaulted stone ceiling, and even more torch brackets lit up the chamber. This space was not nearly as luxurious as the rest of the fortress but still pleased the eye with arches and sweeping stone designs across the walls.

Jack sat alone at one of the many oak tables enjoying the last of his meal. Once he had picked the last morsels from the bones, a sense of satisfaction settled in his stomach. It had been a while since he last took the time to enjoy a meal. He was picking at a stubborn sinew stuck in his molars when a young knight greeted him.

"Hello, sir. Might I join you?"

The question caught Jack off guard, and he studied the man's tidy facial hair before noting how many other tables were vacant. Four empty chairs were available at this table, so he shrugged and waved a hand at the empty seats. "Go ahead. I don't have any invisible friends sitting with me today."

The knight guffawed at his humor and sat beside him. Nearly

dropping his plate and mug of ale, he replied, "You are a funny sot! My name is Giessen. I'm very pleased to have found a jester to complete my feast with proper entertainment!" More laughter followed, as he began eating at last. He washed down a mouthful with alcohol and asked, "What may I call you?"

"Jack, but I'm thinking about a name change. Maybe I could be Fido. What do you think?"

He scoffed. "I'm sorry, but that jest is in need of work. What jokes do you know?"

"At the moment, I don't feel like being a comedian." Jack stretched and sat far back in his seat until it was balancing on two legs. He stared blandly at the ceiling. "I'm just not in the mood."

"That's a shame. Are you a stone worker of some kind? Your garb tells me you have nothing in common with me or my comrades."

He was still wearing the dragon-leather vest and matching set of trousers. The boots he recently claimed were very worn and scratched. All around were knights in clean white shirts and dark trousers with black or brown boots.

Jack shrugged in reply while amusing himself by rocking back and forth.

"You are a smart man," Giessen said. "Since joining the ranks, I'm having second thoughts on my trade. Things aren't quite what I imagined they would be." He pointed to a distant table packed with laughing men. "Those sorts are who confound me."

While maintaining his lazy rocking, Jack turned his head to see where the knight was indicating. A small crowd around a table was playing a boisterous game of arm wrestling with even louder betting. After spotting Sir Peregrine and his men in the midst of it, Jack tossed Giessen a confused look. "What about them? You don't like the art of gambling?"

The knight frowned. "Even I like trading coins to pass the time, friend. Those fools take sides with Sir Oryn and that brute creature chained in the Ring of Trials." Shaking his head, a scowl grew on his face. "How dare they call themselves knights, nay, men? No man in his right mind would dare call an inhuman creature a friend."

Jack let out a small explosive laugh at the irony. Deciding this was the perfect time to have a little fun, he played along. "They like the dog people?"

"Like is too small a word. They dote on the creatures."

"It's kind of funny. Think about this: They're doing tricks for dogs!"

Giessen's aggravation mounted. "Precisely. The one they chained is a perfect example! An animal will always be an animal! That can never change."

Suddenly Jack wasn't so amused. His smile faded, and he listened carefully. "What do you mean?"

"A dumb brute will forever stay a dumb brute, no matter how many years pass."

Jack struggled to hold a cool composure and avoided eye contact.

"Even if that coward were not a beast, his being a traitor is enough for me to know that my point is true."

"What if he changed?"

"Changed? A shape can change on occasion, but no man or animal can change inside. If they are born weak, then they shall always be weak."

"Like women?"

The knight paused to smile. "Yes, like women. I like your thinking. You're a good man. I'll bet you could be a better knight than any of those idiots."

Jack was sick inside. On the one hand, this man talked the same way he had when this strange adventure started. Stranger yet was that he couldn't disagree more. Then there was the fact that this was an obvious wife beater. Nothing made his blood boil more than a sexist bully.

The bottled up disgust and hostility brimmed in his gut until his eyes were glowing like hot metal. Turning his head to stare down the knight, Jack watched his smug expression melt. He broke the uneasy quiet with a tone of warning.

"Well, I don't like your way of thinking very much. You're not funny or smart."

The wary knight didn't have the mind to move, as sweat formed on his brow.

Jack sneered. "Get lost, scumbag. You're ruining my brunch."

Giessen quickly and cautiously left the table without breaking eye contact for fear that he may be in danger. The angry glow lasted in Jack's eyes until Giessen was out of sight down another passageway.

Alone again, Jack couldn't help but notice that the man had left his plate and drink behind. He gave the mug a sidelong look for a few seconds and shrugged. There was no point in letting it sit there. He drank it in a vain attempt to drown out the sober feelings.

The drink was gone when he set down the cup and pushed it away. A hushed burp followed. It served as a warning that the alcohol wasn't setting well. Jack wished he hadn't drunk it – almost as much as he loathed that the knight had joined him.

He was becoming depressed by his own shortcomings when a sense in Jack's mind distracted him. An inaudible voice said, <So he does know shame.>

Instinctively turning in his chair, Jack saw Oryn watching from a distance. He frowned and studied the calculating stare. Had he imagined what he had heard? Then again, had he heard anything in the first place?

When Oryn didn't speak or move he called, "I'm sorry, but did you say something? My hearing is a little off."

"If you are fed, then it is time that we departed."

Jack was confused. Getting to his feet, he could see that Oryn wasn't being snide or playing games. He quietly joined him in the corridor and asked, "Did you say anything when you were watching me?"

Oryn frowned back while taking brisk strides. "I am not the kind to murmur behind the back of another. I would take the matter to you personally."

"I'm taking that as a no."

Oryn gave his shorter companion an odd glare. "Are you fully prepared to set out?"

A hint of doubt lingered, and Jack pushed the subject once more. It was out of curiosity and a nagging paranoia that he really could be going insane. He knew that only Oryn had been within hearing distance. Had he spoken?

"I'm ready to go if you really didn't say something about me out loud."

A split-second later, his doubts were laid to rest as Oryn stopped abruptly and whirled on him in a fury. Severely irritated, he snapped, "Enough of these childish games! I said nothing while observing you! If you must insist on speaking, do so with respect to my honor! Act as though you are competent for your title of warrior and come along!"

They were off again at a swift walk with a tense silence between them. Oryn was outraged, while Jack was struggling to make sense of it all. The voice he had heard definitely fit Oryn, but it wasn't audible. There was no way that Jack could have heard another person's thoughts, was there?

Noon was upon them when they reached the hall of knights, where Adwen waited patiently to begin their next quest. Surrounded by thousands of tablets with names of knights who gave their lives for their kingdom, she was thoughtful. What awaited them at Castle Gailarien would be of the most sinister kind.

Her main concern was whether any demon commanders were stationed inside. The strength she gained in becoming whole had turned her into a force to be reckoned with, but the general or Sycan still had the potential to overpower her. If they controlled the castle entirely, then a brawl inside would put her and the others at a great disadvantage. There wouldn't be much room for evading attacks, and worse, there wouldn't be any light. Darkness inside the king's castle meant little chance of finding survivors or achieving Adwen's main reason for going.

The ancient texts about Adwen's coming couldn't be left in demon hands. It had to be reclaimed, and this was not the time to liberate the castle. The strength of her warriors and herself was not enough. Taking into account that the enemy likely knew she had saved most of the occupied towns, Adwen hesitated to imagine the defenses on the castle grounds.

"We are ready for departure," Oryn said while failing to hide his bad mood.

Coming back to the present, Adwen cocked an eyebrow. "What's got you so grouchy? It can't be the trip to kill more bad guys."

He grimaced and was silent.

Jack shrugged with a pleasant smile. The dark circles around his eyes were less noticeable but still there. "I think he woke up on the wrong side of the bed and won't admit it. My personal form of anger counseling doesn't seem to be working."

Oryn shot him a wrathful glare. "Your mouth could anger a simple jester!"

Before Jack could form a reply, Adwen interjected, "That's enough. I'm warning you now before we leave. Making him mad is one thing. But if you mess with me, I'm going to make you miserable. Is that clear?"

Her green-eyed counterpart gave a nonplused look, and Jack was sheepish. "That's cool with me."

Jack had submitted to her threat straight away. A weak dog whine escaped Oryn: "This must be a prank."

Jubilant laughter from Adwen echoed around the vast hall. After regaining control, she was smiling widely and catching her breath. "I'm sorry. I had to see that look on both your faces. I needed a good laugh. Thank you."

Oryn showed pure relief.

"Hey! So you'll use your power advantage over me if I make you or him mad? That's not even right!"

"Get over it already," Adwen said, rolling her eyes. "It's not like I'm going to treat you like Oryn does."

As Jack was receiving a frustrated stare from Oryn, he admitted, "That's what worries me. I was getting used to him. This is breaking my rhythm."

She giggled as her closer companion sneered. "Well, either way, it's time to move on. The question I have is whether you're prepared."

"How many times do I have to say that I'm ready to go? I'm ready."

Adwen searched his eyes a moment and magically summoned the two daggers out of nowhere. "I picked these up for you from the armory."

His face went from childish to serious upon seeing the twin blades.

"What's on your mind?" she asked. "If you like, I can carry them for now."

"I don't know." Jack licked his lower lip and studied the pair. "Why do I get to have them? I mean, I don't see how a guy like me should be using them."

Oryn huffed in agreement.

Adwen ignored the cynical sound and answered plainly: "Who has the right to anything worthwhile in this life?"

Jack's eyes snapped up to hers. He couldn't think of an answer. Thoughts of Ashley filled his mind. Jack knew he had let himself become as low as any criminal he ever hated in an effort to see her again. That fact was inescapable. Shame twisted his aching heartstrings, and his hands gently accepted the daggers from Adwen.

Taking a deep breath, he nodded and stated. "No one alive."

"That's right," she agreed with a wry smile.

Jack's clever expression returned. Pointing one blade at her while stowing the other, he murmured, "You know that excludes you, right?"

Blushing and dropping her gaze, she stifled a quiet laugh. "Are you ready to have a second chance, Jack?"

With the daggers secured at his thighs, Jack nodded. "Are you standing by that promise about me and Ashley?"

Her blue eyes shone brightly, and she beamed. "Absolutely."

"Then let's get this show on the road. What are we waiting for?"

Oryn rolled his eyes and grumbled, "For you to shut your flapping lips."

Adwen chortled. "Okay, you two. It's time to go."

Chapter 22
REDEEMING VALUES

To Oryn's satisfaction, Jack didn't have any opportunities to be an annoyance. The pace that the three maintained on the first day was far too demanding and kept him short of breath into the evening when they stopped for rest. They avoided the open plains in favor of the woods, going south before heading east to the castle and its city. One day's travel lay ahead.

Jack continued to pant after they found a pleasant meadow. A spring caught his eye, and he promptly washed the sweat from his face before drinking his fill.

While Oryn scouted the perimeter for security, their commander settled by the base of an old elm. She watched the stars and warned her lesser warrior, "Three of the moons are out."

Jack paused at first. "Right. Thanks." After a few nights of not having to worry, Jack nearly had forgotten about full-moon effects.

The cool water had been refreshing, and being rid of cotton mouth was a pleasant bonus. Sitting on the hard ground and reclining against the weathered side of a fallen tree, Jack took in the sights and smells. A light scoff came along with a smile, as a thought came to mind. "You know what? You're too nice. I don't get how you do it."

Adwen gave a skeptical look. "I remember beating you to within an inch of your life."

He shrugged and chuckled. "I call that being heavy handed."

"You were like a kid exploring his boundaries. As I see it, I was letting you know where you stood."

"I'm not like a kid anymore?"

"Nope. You've graduated to the rank of teenage punk. Enjoy it while it lasts."

Jack prodded again, but more playfully: "What if I don't want to graduate?"

Adwen smiled at the sky and folded both hands behind her head. "Then you'll have to take it up with my chief of staff, who is currently stalking the perimeter. Would you like to file a complaint?"

Jack felt a full moon rising and decided he was enjoying the banter too much to care. Eyes glowing softly, he replied with mock anxiety, "That won't be necessary. I'll take the promotion before more lessons with your green-eyed monster." That got a soft giggle from Adwen, and it eased some of Jack's leftover bitterness.

The fourth moon rose a moment later, stalling the conversation. Jack's body bulged and stretched quickly, causing him to gasp and buckle over. Cries of pain rang in the clearing for little more than a minute, while his form quickly shifted. The shortness of it all was a relief, and again, Jack was thankful to have dragon-leather garments. They fit just as well as before, and the only tear was to accommodate his thick tail.

Though the experience was far from pleasant, Jack heaved a sigh. Then his tail flipped beside him, and a look of curiosity came over him. As Oryn was strolling back to join them, Jack panted with cocked ears. "Does the promotion come with benefits?"

Adwen rolled her eyes and chuckled.

"I'm serious," he grumbled. "Would I get to choose when I change?"

Eager for a way to silence their companion, Oryn glowered. "If I am to stand watch, I require quiet. Your chatter could give a horde of demons enough cover for a sizable ambush."

Jack whined, purposefully annoying Oryn further. "Come on, Cujo. What's the secret? How do you control the change instead of letting the moons control it?"

While Oryn was busy glaring, Adwen explained, "You have to pass a test. The hard part is calling on the change during the test to seal the deal."

Jack was stunned by the simple answer. "You're jerking my chain! Okay then, test me first thing tomorrow."

"Sorry, but it doesn't work that way," Adwen admitted. "It's a test of heart. You have to prove that you're noble enough."

Jack stared blankly and blinked. One of his ears twitched. "I don't know about noble. Would being skilled and apologetic make the cut?"

Oryn growled through clenched teeth and went to sit a short distance away.

While he stalked off, Adwen was studying Jack's eyes. She sensed his need to prove himself. "To become a full Holy Hound, you must embrace your purpose. That is to serve the will of the Light Spirits. They are the ones who will put you to the test. One day, you will have to choose to be what you are in order to protect someone."

Apprehension lit in his eyes. "I have to choose to be a dog?"

She shook her head, and her tone was kind. "To be gifted."

Viewing himself as gifted rather than cursed was difficult to accept. Discomfort made him lower his gaze and think. "Thanks," he quietly replied and said nothing else. Jack had heard enough for now.

Adwen watched the black hound turn over to curl up and glanced at Oryn, who pretended not to pay attention. A few seconds passed, and Oryn looked at the brute and then at her in astonishment. His expression showed gratitude for finally making Jack close his mouth and go to sleep.

Her blue eyes shone, and she smiled.

The three woke to cloudy skies. Adwen led them at a lighter pace than before so that they would not waste much energy. No direct sunlight meant stronger demons during the day. It was crucial that they arrived at the castle with their full strength. Nothing could be left to chance.

Once the towers and flying buttresses of castle Gailarien were in sight, Adwen deemed it was time for a short break. It was the middle of the afternoon, the smell of rain was sweeping in, and extra caution had to be taken.

"Do either of you smell burning tires?" Jack asked. "This stinks on so many levels. It's going to rain, we're about to go where lots of demons are, and on top of it all, I'm starving. At least I won't have to transform."

"That's not necessarily a good thing," Adwen said. "The reason for your change is to provide added protection when creatures of darkness are at their strongest. Tonight you'd better hope for no clouds before we go in."

Jack toyed with the hilts of his sheathed daggers and asked, "Why don't we wait for that?"

"We have already arrived," Oryn said darkly. "The change of the weather is unfortunate, but to linger would be dangerous. This is not an assault. We are merely attempting to recover the king's book. It is sure to be in the private study."

"Exactly," Adwen agreed. "If we are found too soon, our goose is more than cooked. It's ..."

Jack interrupted: "Well done?"

Adwen raised an eyebrow, as Oryn threw a warning glance.

Jack chuckled to himself. "Knew you were about to say something corny."

"Anyhow," she continued, "once inside, we follow Oryn's lead. He knows the layout. You and I will be watching his back. Is that simple enough?"

"Sweet and simple."

"Good. No more monkey business. It's time to go to work."

The rain turned out to be a blessing for their endeavor. Sneaking into the city without being detected would have been difficult otherwise. A light downpour covered their tracks and blanketed their sense of smell. It left them to rely on sight and sound, which was more than enough for the task.

Deleon City's people did not wander the streets. Most survivors hid and didn't dare to go into the open. A demon occupation was not obvious, as the gates remained open and no black haze hung over the buildings. Their taking over the royal city was discreet to the point that commoners stayed, unsure whether to leave and too afraid to go about their lives. Fear prevailed.

The three darted from one narrow alley to another, moving the same way as the few people they spotted in the shadows. Soaking wet, they quickly and quietly went to the abandoned wealthy district. When just the towering stone structures separated them from the gate to the castle grounds, they ran out of shade for cover.

They stopped a moment at the end of the narrows, and Jack whispered, "Why not climb up and use the rooftops? We can jump across easily."

Oryn promptly corrected him by pointing to the sky. A minute passed and a drifting shape with enormous wings appeared and vanished between the clouds. The Dred hadn't seen them yet.

"Looks cute to me," Jack tried to joke through his own anxiousness.

Adwen wasn't laughing. "That thing has a wingspan of about thirty feet. Not to mention a good pair of eyes. We can make it. We just have to be patient." She gestured to the closest establishment. "Oryn, do these buildings have access to each other?"

After looking back for danger and finding none, he answered, "They do not."

"Lovely. Guess that leaves us one option." Adwen took a deep breath and darted to the nearest covered stoop, hiding in the safety of its shadow.

Before Oryn moved to follow, Jack stole a peek at the clouds. "Adwen's a lot tougher since she got back. Why not muscle our way inside? I'm betting we could break into the castle, find the book and get out without much trouble."

Counting out the few doorsteps with eves, Oryn muttered darkly, "Doubtful. The demons would have their strongest holding this position. To assume otherwise is to think our adversaries are fools. Be quick and don't dawdle about."

The second Oryn left the alley, Adwen made a beeline for the next closest position, three doors away. Both were light on their feet and careful to hug the shade. It was now the time for their third companion to move.

Jack's heart pounded and then fluttered as he muttered under his breath and dashed for the stoop. Rain pelted his face, and the others moved simultaneously to not allow time for the Dred to spot them. Panting heavily from the rush, Jack put his back to the door and prepared for the signal to run again. A wry smile flitted on his face. This felt a lot like a game he used to play as a kid, though he couldn't name it.

Seven blocks of homes across from hanging store signs barely had six covered doorsteps among them. Adwen and her green-eyed friend were agile, whereas Officer Towers worked hard to come close to keeping up. They only moved on her call, as she could sense the proper moment to do so. In minutes they were within reach of the broad gate to the grounds.

An empty watchmen's post sat beside the gate at the end of the street. One by one, the three of them snuck inside. Jack came racing in along with them. Then he slumped back against the booth interior, panting.

Neither Adwen nor Oryn was winded or disturbed by the week-old corpse at their feet. Jack coughed and hacked. Shielding his face from the stink, he exclaimed, "Wow! Please say I'm not hanging back with the stiff!"

Oryn glared, while Adwen growled softly, "Be quiet. We're almost there."

Jack stifled a cough. The smell alone was reason to be quiet. Speaking required opening his mouth, and the air even tasted of rotting flesh. Nausea threatened his gut.

Adwen was checking for their chance to move when Oryn saw Jack's ill expression. Clenching his teeth and long canines, Oryn growled in warning, "Hold your sick in. If you give us away, I will make musical strings from your bowels."

Jack managed to not vomit, as the flavor of bile rested in his throat.

He kept it all down, and relief set in the instant their leader gestured to leave. All three rushed out, around and through the open royal gates. Jack expressed thankfulness by not saying a word, as they leaped into a menagerie of unruly hedgerows, nestled in rampant vines. There the scent of greens immediately calmed his upset stomach.

That was where Oryn took the lead. He brought them to a statue overlooking a fountain, engulfed in more untended plant life. A stone worker's hammer rested at the side of a female figure, serving as a disguised switch. Pulling the small lever, Oryn opened an underground passage. They went inside, and the opening closed.

Everything within smelled of rodents and dust. Demon musk reached them periodically on small drafts of air, making Jack even more alert to shapes and sounds. They kept their footfalls light to avoid any echo.

The end of the passage reeked of darkness. It made Adwen frown, and Oryn's eyes glowed as he returned her glance. Gripping the side of the hidden door, Oryn cautiously forced it open. Thick dust fell from the edge, and tattered cobwebs moved aside, along with the marble slab, until a servant's chamber lay before them. A modest bed and writing desk occupied the space.

They entered, and Oryn closed the passage.

Adwen quietly cautioned her warriors. "No transforming from this point on if you can help it. The demons would smell the magic almost instantly and sound the alarm. Oryn, do you know how far we are from the study?"

"The ground floor is above. A stairwell should be close by. We head for the north wing."

She collected herself in preparation, clearly not thrilled to be proceeding. "Once we have the book, we're going out the nearest exit. Stay close and silent as the grave."

Jack rolled his eyes and whispered, "Thanks for that turn of phrase." The remark went unheeded in the seriousness of the moment.

Not even Oryn wasted time to give an exasperated look. He was far too consumed with opening the door to the hall. It came ajar without making a sound. This pleased him, but dark mist curdled in and about their legs, as the door opened fully.

The strange fog alarmed Jack, and he held back a gasp of surprise.

Their green-eyed guide briefly checked the scene, and when he moved, the others were just behind. Oryn, Adwen and Jack crept along the hall with light feet. The dark mist billowed in their passing like heavy smoke, rolling and tumbling. Their ears were pricked for the slightest sign of danger.

Many lifelike statues lined the passageway in individual alcoves within the wall. Eventually, Oryn paused at the tall stone figure of a duke. Adwen watched him examine it carefully.

While they were paying attention to the statue, Jack thought he sensed something moving up the hall. Looking back nervously, his eyes and ears couldn't catch a thing, but he felt it. For a second, he thought he might be paranoid. That question was laid to rest once the mist around the corner started to ripple like disturbed water.

His ears caught the distinct hiss, and his right hand reached for a dagger. It was stopped by Adwen's powerful grip, as she took his wrist and dragged him along. They had entered another secret tunnel. The entry closed quietly to hold back whatever may have been coming to meet them from around the corner.

Less dark mist and no enemies lingered within, as they ascended to the main floor of the castle. Together, the warriors and their commander rushed along the darkened steps. They emerged into the north wing, much closer to their goal.

Dozens of doors lined the red-carpeted north hall. Every torch had been doused long ago. They did not find demons lurking where they entered. All was seemingly clear, aside from more dark mist.

Oryn quickly brought them to the double doors. He opened one for Adwen and Jack, keeping an eye on the hall as they entered King Lorvan's study.

The first thing Jack saw, aside from the antique desk and chair, was the broad surrounding shelves. Stuffing them were hundreds upon hundreds of books. Every conceivable size, shape and age lined the study walls. The king's collection was overwhelming, and Jack glanced around.

Looking to Adwen and Oryn, Jack saw them cautiously approaching the old desk, covered in scrolls and empty inkwells. He followed their lead. None of the three spoke. They stood staring at the heavy binding of what could only be the book they were searching for. It lay closed, setting before the chair as if someone had been reading and left it there for later.

Adwen licked her lips nervously. Reaching out, she moved the leather-bound cover close. Then she looked at it a while longer. Something was wrong.

Both Oryn and Jack looked between her and the ancient text. They easily picked up on her unease. Listening to the sound of rain battering the tall window panes, the warriors waited in silence.

As her hand gently opened the cover, Oryn let out a small gasp and Jack stared, his shoulders sagging.

The pages were gone. Every last one was ripped out and missing. Adwen gazed horrorstricken at the ruffled shreds left behind in the spine. A single scrap of parchment was left tucked inside.

"We must leave this place," Oryn murmured. He was feeling uneasy.

Nonetheless, they stood by to watch her take the folded parchment from what remained of the binding. Adwen was hoping to find a hint to where the pages were. When it was smoothed open in her hands they found a single sentence.

What took you so long?

A chill coursed through the three, and booming laughter filled their ears.

Adwen dropped the note, and they each prepared for a fight.

The same bodiless voice called, "You're late!" Again, the maniacal laughing continued.

The parchment exploded at Adwen's feet with flailing tendrils of darkness. They were too fast and powerful for her to fend off. There was only a second to scream in frustration. Then she was roughly wrenched into a portal of darkness, as the tendrils turned in on themselves and vanished.

Oryn vainly lunged to save her. "Adwen!"

She was gone, and the voice was still laughing.

Both warriors bolted out through the double doors of the study. Once in the hall, they could hear roaring and snarling demons they had never encountered before racing toward them.

Fellons were twice the size of Wretches and ran on all fours. In the place of spikes on their backs, they had four very long ropy limbs with serrated tips. Several of the beasts came dashing around the corner, gnashing their long toothy jaws.

Jack's eyes bulged at the sight of them, and both knew that standing their ground would be a poor decision.

Oryn instantly transformed, grabbed an alarmed Jack around the middle, and made a hasty retreat. His larger body was capable of outrunning the shadow-belching monstrosities. Sheer speed gave them a solid lead in escaping. Oryn didn't know where Adwen had vanished to, but he doubted she had left the castle.

Jack shouted, "Have any ideas on how to kill those things?"

"We cannot leave without her. She must be found."

"I don't know about you, but I think being alive would help!"

They were entering the east wing and passing tall windows streaked with rain from the storm. Oryn stopped dead when more of the same demons started to appear ahead. Trapped, he set Jack on his feet.

Roars and unearthly cries echoed from behind, as roars of delight reverberated ahead.

"I'm serious!" Jack snapped. "Are any helpful ideas coming to mind?"

The towering Holy Hound's teeth were bared, and his hair stood on end. Ears flattened in an aggressive display, he growled dangerously, "Go now!"

Looking ahead and behind at the demons closing in, Jack went from being anxious to being frantic. "Go? Go where, genius?"

An instant later, one of Oryn's massive clawed hands struck Jack's chest. The force knocked the wind out of his lungs, sending him crashing out through a window. As he fell into the storm, his Adrenaline surged. Reaching out blindly for anything, his hand found a solid fixture and held fast. Panting, he flailed for a moment before getting a better grip in the slick conditions.

A loud roar and a series of cries reached him from the window somewhere overhead. The sounds made by Oryn's struggle helped Jack think more clearly. He looked up to see where he fell from and looked back into the face of a weathered gargoyle. Seeing the glaring face made his heart leap, but he did not panic.

After a minute passed, the battle cries ceased. He waited to hear Oryn's harsh voice call down and say all was clear. It never came.

Jack knew things had not gone well. When the realization struck him like the green-eyed hound's knuckles, he knew he was on his own. The rain continued to fall hard around him, and he looked down.

The sight of how far the ground was below gave Jack vertigo. A sick fear powered his will to climb. Two weeks ago, he would not have been able to hoist himself up so easily. With the brutish strength the police officer now possessed, along with a natural fear of heights, he reached a place to stand quickly.

He crouched low on the ledge behind the stone statue that had caught his fall. Glancing up again, Jack could see that he had fallen two whole floors. The closest windowsill was along a narrow ledge, and his shoulders sagged. He slowly stood and grumbled aloud, eyeing the distant opening. "That was a swell idea, Cujo."

Oryn barely remained conscious, while he was dragged away. He had known he would be defeated. The demons were far too strong for him alone. If he had summoned the Greatsword, the result would have been the same, with the exception that his weapon would have been taken. For the purpose of keeping it out of enemy hands, he delayed the monsters with tooth and claw in order to give Jack a clean getaway.

The gashes and stab wounds wept. As he was dragged by the creatures and wrapped in a powerful tendril, red smears streaked the cold ground. After a short time, he was dragged roughly down a flight of steps, released into the coils of a demon-steel chain, and suspended upside-down.

His head flooded with a rush of blood. It made thinking difficult, but he managed to examine his surroundings. The floor was fifteen feet below, or above from his new perspective.

The demons prowled away to their respective corridors. When they were gone, he took a better look around. Oryn's bleary eyes saw a heavy metal cage hanging a few yards away. Both long ears flicked once he recognized Adwen staring back from behind the thick bars. It put him at ease to know that she was relatively unharmed.

She had reverted to her hound self in order to avoid being burned by the demon-steel cage. Her form was cramped within the confines, and she gazed back with concern evident in her expression.

"Where's Jack?"

Oryn fought to stay awake and growled. "I cannot be certain. He was able to evade the attack."

"How?"

"I forced him out a window as they came upon me."

At first she said nothing. Cocking her head, the silky tail flicked by her side in amusement. "Well, if we can't get ourselves out, we're going to have to rely on him."

Oryn huffed loudly. "Is there nothing we can do but wait on that fool?" Turning his head up as far as possible, Oryn spied a lock on his own chains. "Why would they use locks?"

"There aren't any witches to command the chains. As for that note we found, I think that was a message from a great distance. Obviously, whoever was laughing wasn't actually in the castle. They would be here getting ready to kill us now if that were the case. What do you think?"

Oryn whined miserably at the pressure in his head. "I believe the same as you. Are there not more chains lying about?"

Her slender head with the golden Andredan mark turned this way and that. "Nope," she answered. "There aren't."

"Then our talkative friend may well be in more danger than we are.

They obviously meant to capture you in the cage. The chain was intended for the likes of me. For Jack, they have nothing. There are no more restraints. That means they have no need for more prisoners."

Adwen's ears flattened in dismay.

"If he is found, we'll not be seeing him again."

Finally climbing in through a guardroom window, Jack dropped down and scanned the space for signs of danger. No dark mist was on the ground, and the coast was clear, so he wiped some of the rain off his face and ruffled his hair. Better prepared, he checked that the twin daggers were set properly in their sheaths. His instincts told him he may need them soon.

Jack passed through the doorway and briefly looked over the dungeon cells. Only corpses loaded with maggots occupied the confines. The stench was repelling, and he turned his attention to the one exit. As much as he didn't want to face the demons, staying in a room full of decomposing bodies was far less appealing.

A thin layer of dark mist lay in the next passageway. Both his hands fiddled with the dagger hilts nervously as he inched along, ears pricked. A sharp turn in the hall before Jack made his heart pound. He had an idea that the low level of the darkness indicated that the Fellons were elsewhere, but he didn't take any chances. He sidled up to the corner and peered around to check.

There was nothing but another door and two empty torch brackets.

Jack felt silly, as he gulped down the anxiousness. This wasn't the time to lose his nerve, he thought. Being the daredevil was something he prided himself on. With that in mind, he coolly strolled to the door and stealthily worked the handle. It was not locked and opened into another hall.

The mist was a little deeper here. His eyes scanned the unlit corridor, using what little light remained to examine every detail. As useful as night sight was, the heightened sense of smell surpassed it. Along with the strong scent left by demons was the stench of rat urine.

"Oh, how lovely. It's a new monster lurking in the castle."

When Jack heard the juvenile male voice, he stopped in his tracks. "Hello?"

The voice cursed quietly beside him in sudden alarm.

Looking down, Jack saw a fat brown rat scurrying off as fast as his short legs could take him. At first Jack thought he was hearing things.

Then he realized this was not something worth passing up. Moving fast, he grasped the rat by the skin on its back.

The rodent squealed and bit into the meat of his hand.

Jack gasped at the sharp pain and took a firm grip of the rat's tail instead. He held the small creature high, staring it down. Had it really spoken?

The two gazed at each other for a long while.

He eventually swallowed his doubts and asked aloud, "Did you call me a monster, fatso?"

In reply, the rat squealed, "I said nothing of the kind!"

Jack was speechless.

The creature demanded, "If you take offense with my being well fed, I pity you. Just don't eat me. I have a big family."

"I don't doubt that," Jack said after finding his lost tongue. "Can you do me a huge favor, little buddy?"

The rat laughed. "How could I ever help the likes of you? I doubt I could even help fill your belly! I am small, and you are so big, you see."

"Don't try and flatter me," Jack scoffed. "I'm lost, and I need to find some friends of mine."

"Did you check the dungeon?"

"Those friends are a little dead. I think my friends are higher up in the building."

The rat chattered, "So why should I help? You don't smell friend-ly."

Jack could see this going nowhere. An idea occurred to him, and he thought it was worth a shot. "Have you heard of the Tame One? I need help finding her."

Laughing harder than before, the rodent was skeptical. "Sure. And I happen to be an only child."

He gave the rat a sly look and showed off the mark on his other forearm.

The small beast sniffed at the elegant shape. After examining the mark a long while, Jack's captive chattered, "Well this certainly is awk-ward."

"Can you help or not?"

"As it so happens, I just may. Do you know how to find the grand hall?"

Jack frowned and grumbled, "Do you know where it is, fuzzy?"

"Actually, it's Frunze. That was once my favorite place for hiding scraps. How about you set me down, and I'll explain."

Suspicious, he eyed the rat carefully. "Don't pull any tricks or you will be lunch."

The creature was pleased to be set free but did not dart off. Setting back on his haunches, Frunze continued. "Where the man king once sat now belongs to the dark beasts. I watched them summon a cage and hang it by evil chains." The rat shivered. "I'd bet they would keep the Tame One there. If you are ready, I shall guide you."

"You're serious?" Jack asked with a note of surprise. "You would help me get past the demons?"

Frunze chuckled weakly. "Can't promise you won't stumble across any. Those wicked monsters are everywhere. If you are prepared, follow me!"

He watched the rat go. Shaking his head, he was careful to keep the small escort in view. The demons had never showed interest in the castle's rodent population, so the two used this to their advantage. Frunze gladly served as lookout and scouted a short distance ahead. Once they reached the level below the ground floor, the dark mist was up to Jack's waist, making seeing his tiny guide difficult.

Knowing that the demons were near made both adventurers nervous. Frunze cautiously sniffed at every turn without exception. In more than one instance, the rat had to take Jack on a detour to avoid demons standing at their posts. Nearly to the main floor, Frunze brought his guest to yet another lobby. His small whiskers twitched as he sniffed, and his dark eyes scanned the space.

Just behind, Jack also took a whiff. Having breathed in the potent smell from the Fellons for so long, it was difficult to tell where they were. He assumed that their thick mist served the purpose of disguising their scent trails. With their odor laid everywhere, sniffing them out was rendered useless.

After a minute of waiting for the rat to press forward, Jack whispered, "What?"

The creature's tone was wary. "The demons we passed blocked the passages leading to the ground floor. This way is the last, and I'm afraid that it may be a trap. My nose has become dull, and my eyes see nothing but mist."

Greatly disappointed by the news, Jack murmured, "You're sure there isn't another way? No secret passages we can get to?"

"There are none without guards." The police officer was stepping into the open, and Frunze squeaked, "What are you doing? It's not safe!"

He ignored the rat's chatter. Upon entering the spacious lobby, Jack looked for the slightest sign of trouble. The bare walls were unexciting, and two statues stood at either side of the space, posing blandly. The stairway lay at the end farthest from him, with no suggestions of danger. Nothing could be hiding in the deep mist, as it was mostly transparent. Some anxiety lingered, though all seemed clear.

Jack turned back in time to see the fat rat's tail vanishing around the corner. He frowned after the little beast but said nothing. Outrage at the animal running away was soon smothered by a tingling in his mind. A second passed, and something struck the officer from behind, slamming him to the wall. The hit stunned Jack for a moment, and he whirled around, reaching for one of the daggers.

A powerful tendril reaching down from overhead slammed again, much harder than before. The force knocked the wind from Jack's lungs. While he was still in shock, the thing wrapped around his neck and threw him across the lobby.

The dagger tumbled to the floor where he was first attacked and was far out of reach when he picked himself up. Finally, Jack saw the Fellon coming down from its hiding place on the ceiling. Mist gushed from its jaws, while it seemed to guffaw.

Jack drew the remaining dagger and prepared to defend himself. The demon bearing down on him had all four tipped tendrils poised to kill him in an instant.

The monstrosity had other ideas. It stalked closer, like a lion cornering a rabbit. Slinking confidently with tendrils poised, the Fellon let out a low, croaking chuckle.

Jack was ready when one of the serrated tips knifed for his heart. He deflected the attack and staggered from the force. The demon's strength was alarming. Jack had hoped the dagger would harm the tendrils. It did not. More guttural laughter made the officer redouble his efforts, as the demon toyed with him.

A strike came again, and Jack made a quick decision to counter. The plan failed almost instantly when the demon shrieked in delight, blocking the advance. One tendril snared the wrist clutching the dagger, as a second coiled around his neck.

The strong scent of fear thrilled the Fellon.

Gasps of air stole through Jack's restricted esophagus at every opportunity. He struggled to free himself. Helplessness filled him, as the demon's grip worked to crush his arm until the second blade fell with a clatter to the stone floor.

The Fellon pressed him to the wall, and he gazed back while fighting for breath. The demon laughed at Jack's hopeless expression. It could kill him now but chose to gradually restrict his airflow and blood circulation. Watching the warrior die slowly was too enjoyable to rush.

There wasn't enough oxygen for Jack to think properly. Even though his vision was beginning to falter, he could see past the demon and across the room. His stare fixed on the first dagger lying where he had dropped it. Hearing the demon's dark chuckle stirred anger inside, along with a thought.

He wanted that dagger. He wanted it not just to escape, but to punish the demon for laughing. The desire to have the dagger grew, lighting his mahogany eyes to a brilliant shine in the gloom. Officer Towers' gaze never left the blade. Both eyes seemed to burn, while powerful instincts drove him.

He wanted the dagger with every ounce of his being. As the blade began to tremble on the ground, he maintained his focus. All thoughts and feelings aligned within his mind, honing onto the single object. The sensation of bottled energy burned in the depths of his eye sockets. A strained cry escaped him, helping to release the built-up power.

By that time, Jack was on the verge of blacking out. The demon could feel him slipping away. As it watched the light flicker in his eyes, it was distracted.

Then the dagger glowed and left the ground. The tip flew like lightning, driving deep into the middle of the Fellons' back.

A terrible screaming pierced Jack's ears. He fought to stay awake, hardly realizing what he had done or that the demon's grip was weakened. It released him to writhe and shriek, as his dazed body hit the ground hard. Instinct was still in control. He dove for the dagger beside him, narrowly dodging a strike from one of the tendrils.

The large demon staggered, struggling vainly to find the dagger in its back, but it was out of reach between the waving limbs. When attempts to take the sting from its body failed, all efforts returned killing the warrior. The demon lunged in a rage.

Jack flipped the other dagger in his grip and threw it hard before leaping aside.

The large demon collided with the wall, narrowly missing its target.

Officer Towers was back on his feet in a flash and about to dodge again, but the monster slumped and collapsed. The weapon was imbedded in the vile thing's temple.

Relief swept over Jack. He chuckled weakly, while his heart still raced. Pulling the daggers free, while the monster became stinking muck, he thought he must be lucky after all. Jack assumed that the magic dagger had flown to his rescue on its own. That was the explanation he could believe.

There was no sense of time for Adwen and Oryn. The Fellons left them to themselves in the dark of the throne room, pondering what to do. As he battled gravity in order to remain alert, she was cautiously optimistic. A feeling in her heart told her that they would not stay captives of the demons for much longer.

Oryn struggled to reach the lock on his chains but to no avail. Giving up again, his body swung as he panted. "Have you not tried the lock on your cage?"

The gaps between the bars were just wide enough for her hands to fit through, and she eyed the back of the lock. "To tell the truth, I don't really want to try it. Jack should be on his way."

"The cur likely needs our aid more than we his."

She didn't bother to argue. Very carefully, Adwen reached one hand outside to pick at the mechanism through the keyhole. No sooner did she insert a pointy claw than condensed darkness blasted from the lock. Adwen yelped, taking back her injured hand. The small explosion of evil energy had seared her, and patches of green and silver oozed on blackened skin.

Oryn was alarmed. "Are you all right?"

Adwen licked the magical burns, whimpering. "Picking the lock is definitely out."

"To the pit with these chains," Oryn growled. "I detest waiting on fools. You're certain he can make it safely to our location?"

"Yeah, I'm sure. We're getting out of this one way or another, and we can't get out by ourselves."

He growled at the ground in frustration.

"You don't think he can do it, do you?"

Oryn gave a sidelong glance. "I prefer not to place my trust in his hands."

"He's a warrior for a reason." When he gave an even more skeptical look, she added, "You spent some time with Jack. By now you know he has redeeming values."

"I loathe waiting for his rescue, same as waiting for him to show resourcefulness. No matter when it comes, it arrives far later than necessary."

"Aw, did you miss me, Cujo?" Jack whispered as he ran into the throne room on light feet.

The two hounds were glad to see him, though Oryn growled, "I miss the silence more."

"Excellent!" Adwen said, wagging her tail. "You didn't get hurt did you?"

Jack approached the underside of her cage, smiling. "Had a little party with a monster, but he didn't know who he was messing with. I didn't even get a scratch."

"A likely story," Oryn growled.

"Do you know how to pick locks?" Adwen asked Jack.

A proud expression lit Jack's face. "Do I? You're looking at a cop who used to be a thief. I was good at it, too."

Oryn growled again. "I should have recognized that about you."

"Over here, Jack." Adwen extended an arm out to help him up.

He was confident and tried to assure her, "It's all right. I can jump."

She whined, "No, wait!"

The warning came too late, and Jack's bare hands grasped the demon steel. He gasped and quickly let go. Adwen was quick and caught hold of his vest, keeping him level with the cage door, while he puffed at his seared palms and fingers.

Oryn was amused.

"This is demon steel," she said. "Are you okay?"

"Besides the fact that I feel like I stuck my hands in a grill, yeah, I'm great."

He did what he could to ignore the stinging and took up a dagger to begin working the lock. Wisps of dark energy seeped out during his twisting and prying inside the gears with the razor-sharp point.

Adwen and Oryn's ears pricked at the echoing cries of angry demons.

"You might want to open it faster," she urged gently.

"Don't rush me."

Oryn growled, "Time is running short, fool. Be rushed."

"Picking locks is an art," Jack said. "You should never force an artist."

A dull clink and a hiss issued from the keyhole.

"See?" Jack chuckled, stowing the knife.

Adwen climbed free from the confines. As she did, she helped the warrior onto her back and leaped, catching hold of the chains binding Oryn. They swayed as she brought Jack down to the lock, which he picked open in a few seconds. The much larger hound fell out of the heavy links, landing on all fours. The others were joining him when a roar came up from the corridors.

Fellons were rushing the stairs into the throne room.

The three raced away down another passage, following Oryn to the quickest exit. Jack stayed close and kept one dagger out just in case.

On their mad dash through the castle, a demon managed to cut them off. Adwen swiftly clapped to create a powerful flash, blinding the monster, while Oryn summoned his sword to cut it down.

Ahead lay a dead end with a lovely stained-glass window. The evil creatures shrieked at their backs, as they knew the trio was going to escape. Oryn dismissed his weapon and was first to jump, shattering the decorative pane, with Adwen and Jack close behind. Dozens of roars and cries of rage followed, as the monsters could not leave their territory.

Each of them fell through the rain and went sliding down along a steep granite grade. Jack was surprised to keep his balance on the way down and chuckled when they reached the bottom safely. "That was so much fun that I hope we never do it again."

"We're not completely out of danger yet," Adwen barked. "We have to get out of here. Did you already forget about the Dred flying above us? Come on!"

"You've got it," Jack exclaimed, suddenly anxious to get moving.

The large flying demon did not see them, as luck would have it. They headed away from the castle to the cover of the forest. It was daylight again when they eventually transformed into their human shapes and slowed to a walk. All of the morning's excitement had them alert, and its events kept them thoughtful.

While Adwen and her closer companion pondered about the fate of the ancient texts, Jack was stuck on the thought of how he killed the demon. There weren't many explanations. In the end, he knew Adwen would know the answers. Strolling alongside, he began his questioning, "How many more secrets are you keeping, huh? You never told me I could use magic."

Still walking, she raised an eyebrow. "What in the world are you talking about?"

"I killed one of those crazy things in the castle with magic," Jack said. "My dagger magically flew up off of the ground at the demon."

Oryn frowned and sniffed the air about him. "I detect no such thing about you."

The officer was insistent. "I know I made the dagger stab the demon! Of course I have magic!"

Adwen shrugged. "He's right. You don't have that kind of magical scent."

"Aw, come on! There's no way the knife flew by itself."

There was a long pause, as Adwen thought. Oryn was quiet.

Frustrated by confusion, Jack brooded over the event once more. How had he done it? He tried to figure it out but couldn't.

Sounds from chirping song birds were all around in their hike back to Plexus. The soft trilling filled the trees and Jack's ears. His head was consumed in a quandary, until an inaudible voice spoke.

<At last, he is silent.>

Jack instantly recognized it as Oryn's voice. Glancing over, he was about to make a remark but paused when he heard him again while no words came from his mouth.

<I may as well enjoy the peace while I have it.>

Then he heard Adwen and gaped at her, as well.

<Hmm ... This is getting interesting. Hah! I wonder how long it'll be before he figures out he's psychic!>

Jack stopped dead and exclaimed, "I'm psychic?"

The others also stopped and stared at him.

For a long moment, the police officer was stunned. But once the moment had passed, he grasped his head and laughed long and hard.

"I'm psychic! Holy cows and donuts, I'm psychic! This is the greatest thing that's ever happened to me!"

Adwen rolled her eyes and smiled, while Oryn wore a sour look. Oryn had hoped it would be a lot longer before this day came. They continued walking, not paying Jack's exuberant rant any mind.

"This is awesome! Oh man! And to think I was going to be a psychology major! This is incredible! I can move things with my mind and hear thoughts! This is going to be a blast hearing what people are thinking!"

The continuous stream of laughs and jubilant sentences was torture for the green-eyed warrior. He would give most anything to have it end. Gazing into the distance, he groaned balefully to his leader, "Can you not make him stop?"

She took a breath and sighed. "Working on it." On their stroll through the wood, she spied a short dead branch on a tree.

Oryn watched, as she casually snapped it off without missing a step. The branch was unremarkable in any way. Despite that fact, he was wary of her impish smile.

Jack was still rambling excitedly.

Not knowing what to expect, Oryn watched as she whirled around to confront the jabbering cop. Adwen began waving the stick before his face energetically, and to Oryn's astonishment, Jack fell quiet, and his eyes honed in on the branch. A blank expression came over him, as he followed the rapid movements, looking this way and that. Then

Adwen threw the stick far into the trees.

Instinctively, Jack started to go after it before stopping dead where he stood. He slowly turned back to stare at her smile, mortified. "You did not just do that."

Adwen burst out laughing and walked away.

Oryn had a satisfied look, as he joined her in continuing on with a very surly police officer close behind.

Jack spent the entire day exercising his newfound talents on his counterparts. While her thoughts were worries about what the demons had stolen, he could tell Oryn was fighting to keep him out. It was impossible to keep open thoughts private, and Jack became increasingly better at catching them. By the end of the day, he was capable of automatically hearing all thoughts that crossed their minds.

The abnormal quiet from him made Oryn wary. If the police officer was not speaking, it left to question whether or not he was invading Oryn's mind. When they settled down in a little glen for the night, Oryn took the opportunity to put distance between them and stalked the perimeter for dangers.

As one warrior went off to patrol and the other was finding a suitable spot to rest, Adwen had already reclined back against a tall stone. She watched the stars come out over them. The sight helped bring some contentment.

It was getting harder for Adwen to keep from wishing for home. A part of her wanted more and more for the dysfunctional family she remembered. Her heart ached to be with them again. One day, she told herself. One day they would be together and happy for once.

The sensation of a knot was in her chest. She wanted to go home. A need to go to the world she used to know grew inside like a chant.

Jack had been listening to the thoughts as they began. It bothered him that they were getting strangely loud. Concerned, he asked, "Are you all right?"

His voice broke her concentration, but the thought to go to the world of logic did not leave her. As she wondered why, she closed her eyes and focused on the powerful feeling. A message was trying to get through from the depths of her heart.

Oryn returned to see Jack gazing in astonishment. He knew he must be reading her private thoughts and glowered. "Let her mind alone. She does not need your prying. Leave her be."

Without looking away from her, he held up a hand, and his tone was in awe. "Something's happening. I think she's having a vision or something."

The news did not change the swordsman's feelings on the subject. Much angrier, he warned, "All the more reason to keep out of her mind. Stop pestering her, or I'll find a way to break your concentration."

Jack wasn't worried and shushed him.

Before Oryn could choose how to respond to being dismissed so easily, Adwen's eyes opened, and they were shining brightly.

As their blue glow softened, she gazed at the two warriors.

When she said nothing, Jack asked, "Well? What's going on?"

She thought of what to do to keep Jack from reading the answer in her mind. Grinning, she got to her feet and replied, "Follow me."

Adwen led them on a wild run through the woods, over rolling hills covered in green trees. Their swift feet carried them at a flying speed that Jack was only just able to manage. He tried hard to read the answer from her mind, but she did not think about anything except following a magical scent that continued to get stronger.

She brought them to yet another clearing full of old leaves and finally stopped. A shimmering light began to materialize before them, forming a world portal. The surface of the mysterious sphere rippled with rings of aquamarine, suspended in the air.

Jack licked his lips in hopeful anticipation. "Are we going back?"

Sorry, he heard her think and then say, "You have to stay here."

The old bitterness returned. He became angry and glared.

"It's not just that we have an arrangement to uphold," she told him. "You would be safer here. Stay within a few miles of this place to wait. Catch a deer while we're gone. It may be a day or two before we come back."

The explanation simply wasn't enough to ease his aggravation. Jack scowled and asked, "What makes you think I'm safer here alone than tagging along?"

"Because we are going to visit a jail."

Chapter 23
A NEW LEASE

Raucous chatter filled the modern jail. Camera systems watched the blue-clad inmates like hawks, looking for any hint of trouble or suspicious behavior. Among the congregated inmates were crooks of every kind and many murderers. The county jail food was cheap, as the flavors suggested. In spite of the poor quality, they took what they could to the tables and ate.

Experienced men knew that sitting alone was potentially dangerous. This gave the more devious groups a chance to pick an easy target. Though that was common knowledge, some inmates were simply not fortunate to have camaraderie. They sat at tables to themselves, quietly nursing their stomachs with the terrible tasting cuisine.

One individual sat eating his beef and corn, occasionally sipping from a cup of water. The beef tasted like cardboard, and the water had the flavor of something from a bathtub. Only the sweet corn was acceptable, as it had come from a can. There was little chance for the cooks to foul away that flavor.

The man with medium-length blond hair stared off at nothing. He ignored the chatter and didn't care whether he was in danger of becoming a target. A fight would be welcome. He was strong, and his height was an inch short of six feet. He could handle himself in a brawl, and having nothing left to lose made him even more dangerous.

Living in a jail was hard partly because there was so much time. For Alexander Greeves, it was mostly spent sleeping. He hardly ever left his bunk, so the others hardly took notice of him. When another evening came, and the blond man was already in his bed, no one cared. The lights eventually went out, and darkness covered them completely.

Sleeping on the battered mattress was too much like the cots Alex had known in the service. This meant that when his body became too stiff, he would wake up and turn over to find a more comfortable position. It would happen every few hours. Sometime in the night, it happened again. As he cracked open his bleary eyes, he shifted around on the mattress, then abruptly froze. The light in his cell was on.

After looking briefly about the small space, he saw someone and turned over in a flash. The doors were locked. No one could have gotten inside.

Leaning casually in the corner of the cell was a woman, dressed in a white business suit. The collared blouse under her golden buttoned jacket was sky blue with a daisy yellow ribbon in place of a tie. Her hair was pure white, aside from the golden side-swept bangs. The color of her skin was copper, and her supple lips were jet black. If he didn't know any better, he would think that her ocean-blue eyes were glowing.

The last odd detail he noticed grabbed his attention immediately: Her feet were bare. It confounded him that this exotic female would go through the trouble to buy such an expensive outfit and not put forward the money for decent shoes to match. Left without a reasonable explanation for her being in his cell, he locked eyes with her and waited for her to speak first.

Adwen smiled as she saw his eyes linger on her feet. Making her garments take this shape was meant to express a sense of business. Keeping things as simple as possible, she kept her fangs and pointed ears magically concealed. Having no shoes was the one detail she honestly could not avoid. Once his gaze rose back up again, she greeted him.

"I'm glad I could meet with you, Staff Sergeant Greeves."

Still shocked to see the woman, he frowned and paused. "Who are you, and how did you get in here?"

She almost laughed. "Sorry, but that is a trade secret. Depending on how this meeting goes, I will tell you, Staff Sergeant Greeves."

"Call me Alex or Alexander. I'm not a Marine anymore."

"Ah, but you are still a soldier. Not to mention the fact that you were honorably discharged."

Alex looked her up and down again. Feeling confused by the encounter, he grimaced. The shine of her eyes was unmistakable this time. Alex was disturbed but not any less interested in the conversation.

"What do you want from me?"

"I want a lot of things, Alexander. What I want is you and your skill sets."

Thinking of where the conversation must be headed, he replied, "I'm not anyone's gun for hire."

Adwen raised an eyebrow and gave a sly smile. "This isn't that kind of deal; not even close."

She studied his eyes while being careful not to look too deeply and paralyze him. Then she continued: "I'm offering you a new life, Alex. There's a war out there that's meant for you. We need you."

At this he scoffed, "I'm done with war."

She thoughtfully cocked her head. "This is different. There aren't children with guns in this war. I can't promise that you won't come to regret it, but I can promise enlisting with me is a better choice than staying here."

Alex's gaze narrowed suspiciously. "Who would I be fighting?"

She paused and her eyes glowed brightly. "Fear, Alexander. Your greatest enemy would be fear. By joining me, you will find the cause your heart has been searching for."

He thought about it for a few seconds before responding. It sounded like a hoax, and yet he felt she was being sincere. "What happens if I say no?"

Disappointment crossed her face. "You can if you want. All I ask is that you think about my offer. You have until tomorrow to decide. But if you choose to stay, they will kill you."

His expression hardened further. "Don't you watch the news?"

She listened patiently.

"Why would you ask for help from a murderer?"

Adwen's kind smile beamed. "I wouldn't."

It took a second for him to understand.

"Sleep on it. You can let everything end, or accept my offer."

He gave a small nod.

Adwen chortled. "Sleep well, Alexander Greeves."

The light fixture fizzed out, sending the Marine back into darkness.

Her sudden departure surprised him, as her appearance had, but she was gone now. Given his circumstances, he normally wouldn't consider the offer. The proposition of dying didn't frighten him. At this point, he didn't care either way. What confused him was why he gravitated toward accepting her offer. There was a night to decide, he told himself. In the meantime, he had to go about his business.

The next day began the same way as the one before: No sunrise could be seen, and the only cue was that they were let out of their cells for more foul-smelling food. Alex was not hungry, and he remained in his cell for many hours. He emerged and joined the others at noon, when lunch was served.

The jail space where he and about two dozen others stayed consisted of three hard plastic tables, several seats cemented to the floor, four pale walls and a single television with only five channels. Cable TV was all they had. When Alex reached the space, a storm of swearing voices came from around the heavily fragmented television images. The picture was beyond recognition, and the scoundrels were clamoring and cussing, trying to fix the connection. Then, as he took a seat, the picture became crystal clear.

While he emptied his mind of things odd or disturbing, the other inmates continued to channel surf. At first, commercials plagued them. They laughed and made crude jokes at the various scenes until the only show on was a news broadcast.

"Oh, here we are!" A brutish man admired the woman news anchor. "I could watch her forever. She makes big hair look hot again."

"I could watch your mom forever," another joked. The two began to bicker back and forth, while the news woman read an unseen teleprompt aloud.

"Four days ago was the arraignment for the trial of Alexander Greeves where he has been brought up on charges for murder in the first degree. Police are still ..."

One of the degenerates cussed at the other and pointed to the screen, oblivious that Alex was seated some distance away. "Look! I know that guy!"

Alex did his best to ignore them. Shutting down his emotions was second nature, but this situation tested his self control. Head empty of thought or feeling, he mentally closed out what followed.

The news woman continued: "The once-decorated Marine, who was presented with the Medal of Honor more than a year ago, is now the only suspect in the brutal killing of the late Emily Greeves. This story has stirred the nation, as so many are strongly supportive and others are outraged. A few are making a public outcry to the president to strip the veteran of his awards if convicted. Though it is not clear exactly why this tragedy took place, there is little doubt to how people are responding."

A man with a beard by the screen swore aloud and said, "That guy must have done it. I know a killer when I see one."

Another shook his head. "I don't know about that. I heard she was real hot and sweeter than cherry pie. How does a guy with a clean record suddenly flip and gut his wife like a fish?"

"Maybe he found her cheating?" One offered.

The burliest of the vandals chuckled and nodded to the back of the room. "Hey, guys. How about you ask him yourselves?"

All heads turned toward the stone-faced Alex.

He hardly noticed them looking and didn't react.

"Hey!" One cretin called out. "Was killing the little lady as fun as when you took out all of those rag-heads in the corps?" He began to laugh at Alex's lack of a reaction.

While the creep jeered from a distance, a gang member covered in tattoos of Nazi images went to sit beside the stoic Marine. He coolly took up a chair, leaning in closer to start a semi-private conversation.

Alex knew he was there and pretended to be indifferent. He hadn't been in the jail for long, though he had already heard of this inmate's reputation.

"Have you heard of me, brother? I'm the one the guys call Jackal." He studied Alex's empty expression with a blood-thirsty glint in his eyes. "I killed my oldest brother and ate his kidneys when he stole money from me. I got away with it, too, when the rest of my family was too afraid to talk to the police. They're all idiots."

Jackal shook his head and chuckled darkly. "I wouldn't have killed them. You see, they weren't the ones who pissed me off. It was my brother. You understand?"

The villain's banter didn't move Alex in the slightest.

"The rest of my family didn't do anything worth being killed for. They were all respectful. My other brothers and sisters know not to be disrespectful. A good man will always pay his dues. How I see it is: If you owe something, then you need to pay. What do you think, brother?"

More silence from Alex allowed Jackal to continue.

"You look as empty as any guilty man I've ever seen. Guilty men owe a debt."

At last, Alex glanced over into the sinister face.

A moment of quiet fell over them, as they sized each other up. The others watched, eager to see a fight break out. It seemed inevitable.

The Marine's eye for a threat was keen. In the moment Jackal reached for a shank in his pocket, the reason for Alex's doubt of his own innocence was triggered. His mind went numb, along with the rest of his senses. Alex could not see or hear, and, unfortunately for

Jackal, he couldn't feel anything, either.

Jackal's attempt to stab him in the throat was deflected by a swift and very solid arm block. Before Jackal could recover to stab again, Alex's other fist came flying in, breaking Jackal's nose and knocking him out of the chair.

The small gathering backed away, cheering and shouting.

Both were up now, and Alex rushed in, simultaneously blocking another deadly stab from the small plastic spike. It was followed through with a forceful elbow to the killer's jaw.

Recovering from being stunned, Jackal smiled and tried again.

Alex barely dodged the next lethal stab. His fist flew in for a direct hit, smashing his opponent's already broken nose. As Jackal reeled from the devastating punch, dropping the shank, Alex grasped hold of his throat. Blood ran from the broken nose, dribbling on Alex's wrist while he squeezed.

Realizing the danger, Jackal struck his attacker's elbow to break the hold. It had no effect, and desperation drove him to kick at the staff sergeant's head and throat. Yet Alex's grip did not loosen. Defiant rage lit in the murderer's face, as it seemed as though he was going to die.

The men were confounded into silence when nothing Jackal did affected Alex. They stood by, gaping and watching Jackal suffocate.

Guards came in the nick of time and used a stun gun to subdue the powerful inmate. Though Alex didn't feel the electric shock, it forced his body to spasm. He automatically released the man and toppled to the floor, convulsing and gasping.

Now that Alex's instinctive mind was stalled, he finally returned to full awareness and realized he was in pain.

Jackal moved to attack again but soon joined Alex on the floor, twitching and seizing from the stun gun's jolt.

Groaning at the unpleasant sensations in his face and neck, the Marine didn't resist being cuffed. He merely wondered whether he had dealt more damage than he had taken. While he was lifted and taken away, he saw the condition of the neo-Nazi. One look told him he was the winner, and no more questions were necessary.

Bothering to ask why he had blacked out was pointless. He had never found an explanation for the phenomenon. It always happened this way, dating back to his first scrap in elementary school. Once he knew he was in danger, or if he became outraged, all thinking stopped until it was over. Normally he was the one on top at the end rather than the other way around.

His throat and left eye hurt terribly. There would be bruises. The guards brought him to a solitary confinement cell, had him place his wrists back through a space in the door and removed the cuffs, and left him alone in the quiet. Alex coughed and sat back on the solid bedside. It felt like a park bench. Comfort was no concern with this space's design.

Alex rested his head against the wall. There would be no food while he waited for what would come of fighting with Jackal. Chances were that the psychotic menace who called himself Jackal would be locked away for a while in solitary confinement, as well. Whether Alex would receive punishment didn't really matter, he thought. Nothing mattered anymore.

That thought bred another in his aching head. That strange woman had seemed sure he wasn't to blame for Emily's death. Curiosity grew until another idea occurred to him: What if the woman knew who was responsible?

The thought sparked heated feelings. If she did have a way of knowing who had murdered his wife, then her job offer was his only chance. He sighed and decided that his choice may depend on the answer. The thought of avenging his wife was the one thing that would make staying alive worthwhile. Even if the strange woman with the powerful connections didn't know, Alex was sure she could find out.

Time was impossible to measure in solitary confinement. Would the woman know that he had been taken to another part of the jail complex? If she could get in and out undetected, as she had with the regular cell, then it seemed obvious that getting into solitary would be no different. Both were absurdly impossible.

Some hours passed. As he waited, he grew bored and lay down facing the wall. He was just beginning to fall asleep when the lights blinked, and two swift thuds came from the door.

Raising his head, he glanced over and saw the woman. She had gotten into his cell, just as he thought she might. Knowing it was impossible, he sat up and thought he must be having a psychotic breakdown.

"I must be going insane."

She rolled her eyes and reassured him: "You are not going insane."

"Prove it."

Adwen roughly knocked her elbow on the door twice, making the Marine stare back in shock. If she were real, then she was about to get herself caught.

A few seconds passed until a guard peered through the small Plexiglas window. First he looked at Alex, then at her.

Smiling back at the man, she asked him, "What color is my hair?"

Right away, he answered, "Your hair is yellow and white."

Adwen chortled and shook her head. "Close enough. Thanks, Joe."

The guard nodded and departed.

Grimacing, Alex asked, "Is your offer still open?"

"That depends. Are you interested?"

"I'm interested. I want to know why you think I'm not a murderer."

Adwen was taken aback. "That's a very different topic."

"I don't think so. I'm only interested in the job if you answer a few questions truthfully."

"Fair enough. If I had any ties to what happened to your wife, I wouldn't hide them from you. I'm very straightforward."

He narrowed his eyes at her suspiciously.

"Now here's the kicker," she said. "How is it that you know I'm being honest?"

Though he was about to argue, he hesitated. Something more than instinct said she was telling the truth. He believed her completely. It made him nervous to continue this discussion, but he forced himself.

"If I work for you, will you help me find the truth?"

Closing her eyes to think, she sighed. Then she looked back with sympathy. "I have a lot of responsibility. Once things settle down, or if it turns out to be relevant, then yes. One day I will try to help you find the killer."

"Then I'm in."

She eyed him closely and restrained a smile. "No second thoughts?"

"Better to find some justice than rot in a hole. What are the details, and what is your name?"

She laughed. "Later, once you're out. Even these walls might not keep enemies from hearing. If my name got loose here, there may be trouble. I'll take care of everything."

He nodded and replied, "If you say so."

Too quick for the man to see, Adwen recalled her enchanted hood and pulled it over her head, making herself invisible. When she slipped out of the cell by taking control of the computerized lock, the look on the Marine's face was entertaining.

A smile spread on her invisible face. A sensor would have otherwise alerted guards that the room was opened. Controlling the energy within the compound was easy. Being similar in nature, her energy could manipulate the extensive security systems. Adwen's body had become so powerful that she was like a magic generator.

The sixth sense kept her constantly aware that demons were lying low, waiting. The creatures hadn't detected her yet, and that kept them from springing into action. Once they knew she was here for Alex, they would stop manipulating criminals into killing him and try to finish the job themselves.

She used her magical energy to reach out and feel the currents of electricity. The neutral powers running through the walls bent to her will and flickered and sputtered, causing lights everywhere to blink sporadically. She needed to fully tap into the power for her plan to work. It would take just a few minutes to do so.

The odd strobe effect overhead was an annoyance to most of the jail staff. A few were leery of what it could mean. This was not normal, as the compound had its own generators. It was the cause for many hushed conversations in the compound.

As the Marine remained locked away, Adwen remained invisible and just outside. She leaned back against the partition between his private cell and the next. In a little while, it would be time to put her plan into action.

Alex flushed the toilet in the corner, relieved. After washing his hands in the tiny sink, he kicked back on the uncomfortable bed for sleep. Chatter from a psychotic inmate in a nearby cell reverberated clearly through an air duct, though Alex was not bothered. Being in camps with troops had been similar, with nearby whispers and distant yelling.

Flashing lights were a problem, as it turned out. For a few moments, Alex closed his eyes and felt as if he had transported back in time. He saw intense mental images of the day he got his scars and earned his medals. The flashes from the guns were all around, along with the imagined sound of automatic gunfire. Booming yells from the inmate became the frantic bellows and shouts of his dying platoon. Mortar shells kept them pinned in a rural Middle Eastern downtown plaza. He heard distress in the voice of a soldier calling for air support while cursing them out for denying the request. Their ammunition was on the verge of being depleted, and no reinforcements could reach them in time.

Suddenly it all fell away, as the lights went out. The air duct carried more crazed yelling in the dark, and Alex sat bolt upright. All of the power in the compound was out.

Alex went to the door to look in the corridor. It was too dark, but he heard the security team dashing along the hall, trying to find out what was going on. They could not communicate on their radios, either. The power being out was trouble enough. How had the separate radio system broken down, too?

When the guards were gone, Alex's cell door unlocked with a bang. It swung open, and he felt a hand grab the front of his uniform, pulling him out. He heard the woman's voice murmur among the muffled calls of other inmates.

"Come with me!"

It struck him as odd that she had said that when the darkness was complete and she already was toting him along like a lost child. Dragging him down a few halls, he staggered and stutter-stepped to follow.

She suddenly stopped, and he blindly crashed into her hand. Something sharp on her poked his chest, making him quickly pull back again.

Then there was a strange and horrible sound that made the hair on his neck stand on end. Nasty animal shrieks came from everywhere. He couldn't tell what they were, but it did not seem good.

An army of Clown demons was preparing to corner the two of them in the corridor. Adwen would not let that happen.

Giving a nervous laugh, she said, "Okay, time for Plan B."

She released the Marine long enough to lower her shoulder and smash through the side of the structure. Stones and dust flew everywhere, making her new friend cough and shield his face from the blast. Sunshine dazed him further at the same moment that the vile screeching rose then stopped. The light had pushed them back.

A second passed, and the alarmed Marine found himself careening out of the building and tumbled through the air. His stomach flipped, and he gasped. Reaching out for anything to grab, his hands found Adwen's shoulders. Panic made his grip on her like vices.

Wind caught her hood and pulled it back, as she swiftly changed her hold on the man's blue jumpsuit, grasping him firmly about his ribs. Controlling the fall was the next trick she would have to perform.

At the moment he realized he could see her, they reached solid ground. Adwen's feet struck hard, and her unearthly strength absorbed the impact so that her new companion landed lightly.

His face turned pale, and the breath was trapped in his lungs. The state of shock had paralyzed him. He didn't have the mind to respond, so he stared wide-eyed at his smiling rescuer.

"Come on!" She urged and tugged at his uniform again. "We aren't out yet!"

They both headed for the distant chain-link fence when two guards on the roof with nonlethal sniper rounds spotted them. The men could not reach anyone on the radios, so one fired at Alex's legs.

Adwen heard the shot and whipped around, striking it with the back of her armored wrist.

The hard rubber bullet rebounded and struck the shooter in the thigh, making him cry out and topple over. His partner did a double take, not knowing what to do in response.

Adwen laughed and sliced open the perimeter fence with her small hand blades. After slipping through, the sparse forest was open to them. They continued to run even farther from the disabled county jail.

Alex's lungs burned, and he managed to think to himself, I'm out of shape. It was almost a year since he was honorably discharged, and working out had not stayed a priority. He had gained several pounds and felt it now. Alex fought to keep the pace, racing far into the woods after the white-haired woman.

Then he heard the sound of another man running through the trees. A stranger came alongside, and Alex stole a glance at the tall man with brilliant green eyes. At first he wondered if he needed to defend himself, but threw out the idea immediately.

Adwen continued to lead both Oryn and Alex around in the arid wilderness, headed for a proper escape route. They had to hurry. If her senses weren't mistaken, a truck had been dispatched to chase them down. Her magical link with the radios had been severed moments earlier.

She shouted back to Alex, "We have to move a little faster!"

"Outstanding," he grunted. His body refused to go any quicker. A bad feeling was coming over him, and he sensed that they were being followed. Never looking back to be sure, Alex carried on with his dead sprint.

The terrain was mostly hills with bushes, trees and intermittent deer paths splashed with the orange of an afternoon sun. Adwen fell back to be closer to her company and matched their speed. They were almost free.

She smiled and told Alex, "No matter what, keep running."

As she spoke, a strange anomaly appeared out of nowhere straight ahead. A large glowing sphere, rippling with rings of light, took shape over the ground, and Alex was about to stop. It looked transparent but far too solid for his liking.

Oryn snatched the Marine up by the collar of his jail uniform.

Alex did not bother to fight off the stranger's grasp. They were too close, and he was too exhausted to put up resistance. In a moment they reached the mass and passed through. It disappeared, and they did along with it.

Instantly, Alex found himself and the others running up a creek, and he stumbled on the slick rocks, barely catching himself in a crouch.

Adwen came to his side. Concerned, she kindly asked, "Are you all right?"

Dumbfounded was what he was. Where had this creek come from? Taking a glance around, none of the scenery remotely resembled the woods they had been traversing. The mountains were farther away, and the three were at the bottom of a lush valley. Taller trees were coated in moss, further illustrating how different this place was from the one they had left.

The green-eyed stranger came closer and offered a hand to help Alex to his feet. Alex took a second to read him and accepted. This one's look made him think of the time he had met a Green Beret officer. He was cool, confident and likely to have good reason for both.

Following them to dry land was tricky, as the slick rocks made the going rough. Eventually Alex managed and was glad for some form of stability. Again, he turned to look over the man and noticed a few oddities. His ears came to elongated points, and his eyes were strangely bright. Asking about the medieval attire or glowing eyes didn't strike Alex as reasonable questions. Still shaken by the sight of so many unusual things at once, he looked to the woman who had helped him escape.

At a loss, Alex asked, "How did you do that?"

She chuckled. "Which part? Getting you out of the fifth floor of a jail, or taking you through a magical portal?"

He gaped at her.

"To be honest," she added, "the easier one would be explaining the portal."

Alex stared, and his brow furrowed to show his lack of belief.

Not missing a beat, Adwen gestured to her stoic companion. "I'd like to introduce you to Sir Oryn Conrad. Oryn, meet Staff Sergeant Alexander Greeves."

Both nodded to each other, and Alex muttered, "Hello."

"I understand that you have a lot to ask," she politely told Alex, "but we have to keep moving."

"Where are we?"

Adwen read the man's look of uncertainty. She was patient and answered, "We are in another world, and it looks like we are in the Kingdom of Dargadia. How many fiction novels have you read?"

Caught off guard by the question, he replied, "None really."

She sighed heavily and chuckled. "This is going to be more difficult than I thought. Okay, well I think it would be better if I let you get over being in another world first, and then I will tell you the rest. Let's get moving, shall we?"

Alex blocked her way and gruffly snapped, "Wait a minute!"

He caught a glimpse of Oryn's dangerous glare and was careful not to be rash. Looking back to Adwen, he chose to start small with his questions.

"What is your name?"

"Oops!" she felt silly for forgetting. "My name is Adwen. I'm sorry, but we really do have to get going."

The stubborn Marine glared at her. "I am not a child."

"Hopefully not."

"Don't play with me. I didn't just get off of the truck yesterday. There is no such thing as magic. I know all of what's happened is just smoke and mirrors, so where am I?"

As a response, Adwen crossed her arms and let her pointed ears and small fangs grow back out. She raised an eyebrow at Alex's disturbed expression. "You've trusted me this far, Alex. Humor me, and let this soak in for a while. Besides, it's not really in your nature to ask this many questions."

A firm frown hardened his face. She was right, but how could she know?

This time Alex did not stop them from walking past him and toward the thick of the forest. He stuck close by and studied the scenery. It was beautiful, and that was the only thing magical that he could see about this place. How had she done that trick with her ears and teeth? For that matter, how had she kept him alive after jumping from the fifth floor of a building?

He eventually murmured, "How can this be another world?"

Adwen was quiet for a moment, and Oryn studied Alex with a piercing stare as they walked along. She looked up high overhead and scanned the sky and pointed.

Alex glanced to where she indicated with a sharp nail and stopped dead in his tracks. A red crescent moon was hanging in the east. See-ing the eerie indicator sent a chill up his back. How could the moon be that bright and that color?

She called out without stopping or turning back, "That is one of four moons."

Her voice jarred him out of his shocked state. Quickly catching up with her and Oryn, he sounded alarmed. "Are we on another planet?"

Adwen was thoughtful and responded, "That would explain why the time flow here and there is the same. Either way, believe what you want on that count. It doesn't really matter. This is a magical realm. Logic takes a back seat in this place."

"Where are we going?" He was still shaken by the sighting of the red moon.

"We are looking for our other friend. He was supposed to wait for us here."

They reached the clearing she and Orny had left three days ago. The portal responded to Adwen's presence and shimmered into exist-ence. While Alex stared and was distracted by the large sphere, Adwen and Oryn looked around for traces of their mouthy compan-ion.

The Marine crept up to the glowing shape, curious. He didn't dare to touch it. Instead he examined it from a distance. This portal seemed like the first one she brought him through. If the jail were on the other side, then the last thing he wished to do was go closer.

Leaving the thing alone, he heard Oryn call to Adwen, "I've found something."

They both joined him, and she shook her head at a carved mes-sage on a tree. Alex read the short message and wondered whether it was a joke.

"Went to town. Be back in five"

Confused, the Marine asked aloud, "Who left this?"

"Jack did."

Berkley was a small farming village nestled in a valley where Dar-gadia's best ale was brewed. The sun began to set, and Jack felt at home in a tavern named Duncan's Beacon. This place had not suf-fered from demons despite being a day's ride from Deleon and Castle Gailarien. It wasn't far from the portal where Adwen and Oryn had vanished through days before, so Jack felt the need to visit town.

Word of Adwen and her warriors was everywhere, and once he

flashed the golden mark to the townspeople, a small party ensued. He was then swept off on a grand tour that eventually landed at the tavern. And during the one night without rainfall, the villagers were startled by his transformation, but they quickly got past their fear. This evening Jack was well aware of the coming night and did not care. He was in the middle of a game and having far too much fun.

Two men had taken the liberty of educating Jack on how to play Wretches and Widows. It didn't take long for him to catch on. Others gathered around to enjoy the terribly one-sided gambling spree, laughing as Jack's pile of winnings grew larger with every deal. They all thought he must be truly blessed by the Light Spirits to be so lucky. Those who thought he must be cheating didn't speak out. It didn't seem appropriate to openly accuse a chosen warrior of light.

Robbing them blind wasn't Jack's purpose. He wanted to exercise his mind-reading abilities. The more he used them, the more honed they became. Moving things with his thoughts turned out to be more difficult. Instead, he decided to first perfect listening in on people's thoughts.

He quickly learned how to climb into a person's mind by touch, but laying a hand atop someone's head too long was suspicious. The other more secretive means of reading a person's mind meant waiting for them to think what he considered to be loud thoughts. In a game of cards, Jack could pick up on any concentrated idea without trying. This was automatic after a while, making the game easy.

None of Jack's opponents had the willpower to give in. It was very frustrating to be so easily beaten by a novice player. Determined to regain their money, small keepsakes and retain their shoes, quitting seemed absurd.

Jack only had to wait for them to draw and methodically consider their hands. As they decided what to keep and discard, it was a simple matter of countering.

Again, the man named Jerome dealt seven cards to each player and set the deck in the center of the worn wooden table.

"Weep, and be widows or discard two and continue," Jerome grumbled.

The second man was Landon. He glowered at his own cards and huffed.

Jack heard Landon's thoughts. <It's only necessary to say that on the final deal, twit.>

Jack chuckled and then heard Jerome brooding.

<Keep laughing, creature. I'm gonna keep my shoes and kick you

with them once I win my coins back. Snide fleabag.>

Jack wasn't bothered. Jerome's mental muttering was what kept the game interesting. Most thoughts passing through people's minds were fleeting and not of any concern. This man's mind was constantly abuzz, wandering in odd, even disturbing, directions. He was a perfect subject for Jack's telepathy practice.

Landon was just bright enough to begin suspecting Jack of foul play. Grimacing, he grunted, "Funny that you only hold your tongue now that we're in a game."

Casually discarding what was necessary, Jack chuckled. "Is it funny because you're losing?"

"No one has the spine to say it aloud," Landon grumbled, "but you must be cheating."

One or two observers murmured nervously.

Jack heard the storm of anxious thoughts suddenly explode in the room, and he had to massage his forehead a moment. Sorting through the mental yammering, he knew they were afraid of him being offended. He played off the discomfort as awkward amusement and rolled his eyes. "Even if I could cheat in this game, why would I? It was your idea to give me five coins for starting out. Why are you so suspicious?"

The man glowered and was silent as he also discarded.

When the door of the tavern opened unexpectedly, another eruption of thoughts was accompanied by happy clamoring. The next few ponderings of his opponents were drowned out to the point where Jack could not tell who was thinking what. What he heard out of the many chattering minds and mouths was that Adwen was here.

He could smell his leader coming closer and picked her mental vibe out of the crowd. Unlike everyone else, her mind was focused. Those strong feelings of amusement and disapproval at finding him gambling were impossible to overlook. She stopped at the tableside and crossed both arms, but Jack pretended to be oblivious. When his fellow players were too distracted to play, he finally acknowledged her.

"Hey! What took you so long? This town is fantastic. It has good drinks, good food and a great atmosphere. You should have been here the first night. That was a party to remember, wasn't it?"

As his last statement was directed to the tavern occupants, everyone except Landon and Jerome smiled and laughed heartily.

Adwen said nothing. Her look expressed her lack of enthusiasm. As they quieted down, she finally spoke and gestured to his stack of gold and knickknacks. "What's that?"

"My haul. Want your half? There's plenty to go around."

The two card players kept their mouths shut, and their thoughts of outrage made Jack's smile broaden.

"Give it back," she coolly commanded.

"It took me forever to get all of this!"

"You know you don't need any of it. Wherever we go, drinks and food are free. Give these men back their gear and gold."

Jack's eyes glowed with mounting frustration at her spoiling his evening. "Or what? You'll make me?" Jack had almost forgotten that she really could make him, and his voice trailed off. Unease spread across his face, while he waited, wondering if she would take control of his body like a puppet again.

The whole tavern was dead silent.

Not uttering a sound, she slowly raised an eyebrow in mild astonishment.

Jack knew that Adwen would force him if he didn't do it voluntarily. His uneasy expression turned to displeasure, and he frowned.

"When you're finished sorting out the pile, come and join us," she told him. "Try to be nice."

As she left to rejoin Oryn and whoever else was tagging along, Jerome grinned and displayed rows of crooked teeth.

After listening in on the men's minds for so long, Jack had nothing bad to say about Landon. He was a hardworking family man. On the other hand, Jerome didn't have a sensible bone in his lanky, scabby body. Draining the scoundrel of every last thing he owned gave Jack satisfaction. Too bad for Jerome, he thought. Now he would have to come up with another way to make the dirt bag miserable.

Onlookers began to disperse with the game ended. Then the nasty man wheezed between fits of laughter. "Aw! The poor mutt! His master went and jerked his chain! What a sad pup."

Jack and Landon gazed in an awkward silence at the scummy fool, who continued chuckling like a deranged court jester.

A moment later, Jack also began to chuckle and smile, confusing Landon. Gesturing to Jerome, he told Landon, "He's sleeping with your wife."

As quickly as Landon's face turned beet red, Jerome blanched and stopped laughing.

Jack kept on chuckling and responded to the angry man's questioning look. "I'm not joking. He really is."

In a flash, the burly farmer pounced on the troublesome fool, while the mentally gifted warrior smiled, relishing the scene. His distaste for the smaller man was satisfied at last, and he sighed triumphantly. He could leave his seat feeling fulfilled.

Adwen shook her head at his approach. "Was that necessary?"

"Yes, it was."

His merry demeanor faded once he got a good look at the newcomer standing between her and Oryn. After sizing up the stony jail breaker, his tone was full of surprise and disgust. "Is it just me, or have your standards dropped?"

She stared quietly with both companions at her side. "His name is Alex. Alex, I want you to meet Jack Towers."

The Marine remained stoic, and the police officer could not hear any thoughts coming from him. Either he was mentally talented at resisting telepathy, or he wasn't thinking anything at all. Jack guessed it was the latter.

Unsure whether to be impressed or stunned by Adwen's new choice in a warrior, Jack was dismissive. "If you could give me five minutes, I think I need a very strong drink. Excuse me."

Alex was equally as unimpressed with Jack's show of immaturity. He glanced at Adwen and asked, "He's with us?"

She sighed. "Yes, and don't worry. He comes across as dumb, but he's smart."

Oryn added in a sour tone, "Once you've gotten past his constant need to blather and complain about whatnot."

At that moment, her attention was drawn by a group of town officials gathered by the counter. When she realized they needed to speak with her, she was reluctant. It was time to share more bad news and hide her internal awkwardness.

Before going to them, she spoke with Alex. "Stay in the tavern, but go ahead and mingle. Get a feel for the place. We're going to be a while."

He nodded quietly. For Alex, the concept of being in another world was still unacceptable. Even though he had seen the strange moons outside, this place seemed more like a third-world country. He studied the inside of the old establishment. Could two worlds have so much in common?

While Adwen and Oryn attended to business, Alex eyed Jack where he settled at a table to himself. Out of all the others here, this one seemed to have an entirely different perspective. Whether this was or was not another world, Jack was likely to say so. Being determined to learn the truth helped Alex ignore the poor first impression, and he went to join the disrespectful stranger.

Claiming a chair at their private table, Alex studied how Adwen's shorter companion drank. He did not nurse the pint. Jack practically poured the contents down his throat, clearly in a hurry to become intoxicated. Then he set down the empty container and sighed.

"What is all of this about?" Alex asked Jack.

The strong smell of alcohol wafted into Alex's face when Jack scoffed, "A great big figment of your imagination."

Nearly scoffing as well, Alex responded, "It can't be." When the now-drunken man raised an eyebrow, Alex admitted, "My imagination was never this good."

"What has she told you so far?"

"Not much. I got the distinct impression that I was brought here to fight a war."

Jack rolled his eyes and was less cheery. This conversation was an obvious buzz killer. "I don't know why she decided to trust you and bring you into this, but you have to wonder what she's hiding. There is a lot you don't know."

Alex glared. "I don't care."

The irritated tone grabbed Jack's attention. More serious than before, he replied, "You should. If you knew what to expect, going back to jail might sound like the better option. Adwen is hiding things from you. Doesn't that bother you?"

He was firm and answered, "I know when I can trust someone, and I trust her. I came here to follow orders, not to question why I haven't been fully informed. When the time is right, she will tell me what is necessary."

Brow furrowed, Jack was confounded. "You're not a very bright guy, are you?"

"I'm smart enough to know you have issues with being insubordinate."

Jack shook his head. "You sound like a classic military grunt." Then Jack was stunned as a revelation dawned on him.

Alex knew Jack recognized who he was.

Smiling back, Jack laughed. "I don't believe it. She brought in Staff Sergeant Alexander Greeves! Maybe she does know what she's doing."

It was plain to see that this knowledge put Jack at ease. How could he not be concerned with a murderer being let into the group? As a test, Alex asked, "You know who I am, and you don't think I might fillet you in your sleep?"

This got an entertained look in response. "She has this way of knowing things. I don't understand it, but she can look into people and see whatever is there. If Adwen thinks you are the right guy for the job, then I guess you are."

Then Jack added, "Not to mention the fact that I'm a cop, and I never thought that a man like yourself could be guilty of what you were accused. Men have killed their wives before, but not without a motive. Someone as honor-driven and soft as you isn't capable of outright murder like that."

"Soft?" Alex grimaced and then realized what was said. "You're a cop?"

"That's correct. Now that you've ruined my chance to be drunk by discussing where we are, I should tell you what I know. Adwen didn't lie to you about this place. She has brought both of us to another world. Did you ever watch those ring movies?"

"Don't try to tell me I'm in a movie."

"It would be great, but we aren't that lucky, jarhead. If you don't know anything about fantasy stories, then it's going to be harder for you to grasp this stuff. Still, you deserve to hear everything before it's too late."

Oryn had stealthily made his way over to investigate their meeting. Not pleased with where it was going, he interjected.

"The soldier has heard plenty for now," Oryn told Jack. "I'm aware that you are incapable, but try to hold your tongue for the time being."

Wearing a bitter frown, Jack's eyes glowed. "You wouldn't have changed your mind about working with her even if you had known what was coming, but neither of us benefited from being ignorant. The new guy should have the chance to make a fully informed decision, don't you think?"

"That is for Adwen to decide." Oryn glowered, his eyes glowing brighter. "It was her wish that he learn more only after coming to grips with what he has already encountered."

Alex took in their conversation and couldn't begrudge Jack for wanting to help but had to side with Oryn. Either way didn't matter. So long as he was not wasting away in jail, everything was fine.

Then Jack smiled and took off his boots. "Have it your way, Cujo, but you can't shelter him from everything."

Oryn glared down into Jack's defiant expression, but then both of them became alert. Adwen's voice was remarkably loud and reached them over the din. Her tone was hurried and commanding.

"Oryn, stand guard at the entrance! Jack, I need you to keep Alex close. They're sending in Creepers. Stay focused."

The townspeople within the tavern rallied by Adwen, as she had instructed, hiding around the counter. Their shouts and alarmed clamoring filled the air.

Alex understood that there was going to be an attack. Unarmed, he was vulnerable and had no choice but to accept Jack's protection. During the commotion, he never left the seat, watching people jostle for a safe corner to huddle down in. He was going to ask Jack what to expect, but the sight of his fevered condition made him pause.

Beads of sweat were all over Jack, while each breath grew heavier than the last. His mahogany eyes were bright like lit matches, unfocused as he endured great discomfort.

Alex was concerned. "Are you going to be ready?"

Jack took out the dagger on his right and gave another wry smile. "Yeah. What about you? Are you ready?"

Reaching over to feel Jack's left wrist for a pulse, Alex found it was dangerously high, as was his body temperature. This was not right. If they were going to be in the middle of a fight, there was no way Jack was up to the challenge. He was dangerously ill.

The Marine shouted for Adwen's attention. "Something's wrong with Jack! He needs to stay down!"

Jack's free hand suddenly clamped around Alex's wrist, taking back his attention. Alex tried to pull free, but the grip was astounding, and he could not get out of it. Staring into Jack's luminous eyes, he didn't know what to do.

"Watch me," he said without the usual tone of immaturity. "This is what's going to happen to you."

The full moon outside came out, and Jack's joints crackled. Bones and tissues warped simultaneously, as his wail of anguish turned into a monstrous howl.

Alex gasped and spat out choice words. Pure horror played on the Marine's face, as Jack's face quickly elongated into fanged jaws. Again, Alex attempted to free himself and pried at the man-creature's powerful grasp. The frantic efforts were pointless until the excruciating changes overwhelmed Jack into releasing the frightened Marine.

Finally set loose, Alex was caught off balance and staggered. As he was about to fall, his back found a solid form. Whirling around in surprise, he froze, gaping at Oryn's towering hound shape.

The beast's piercing green eyes only glanced down momentarily, and then he looked back to the front door, summoning a golden two-handed sword.

The magical appearance of the weapon snapped the staff sergeant out of his dumbstruck state. He back-peddled a few steps before a nearby shadow sprang to life, taking on the form of nightmarish creatures.

A pair of Creepers leaped for Alex, and Oryn slew them in a single stroke. Purple droplets of demon essence spattered across Alex's blue jail uniform.

Another team lunged to strike from behind, but Oryn was still the quicker. He pulled the blond man to his side and laid waste to the fiends, snarling.

Now Alex could see the tavern was teeming with demons scurrying about, looking for a clean kill. Adwen made short work of each wave of attackers, though the assault kept her too busy to pay attention to much else. Her elf-like form ripped through the shrieking things as a hot knife goes through butter, defending the huddled villagers.

Then Oryn roared in outrage. Half a dozen fiends clustered on his back and head, taking him by surprise.

The moment Alex was unprotected, a single Creeper pounced. He saw the man-sized thing coming, and both went crashing to the floor. The fiend was on top and very strong, but so was Alex. He had a hold of the demon's wrists, struggling to keep its horrible claws from cutting his flesh.

The hungry thing gnashed its teeth at his face and throat, eager for blood.

Getting away was impossible. Needle-pointed teeth repeatedly missed his neck by inches. The Marine kicked and struggled, but nothing he did fazed the Creeper.

A dagger flew in from the side, striking the fiend hard in the temple, bursting its head like an overripe fruit. The blade stuck fast in an overturned table, and the remains collapsed onto Alex as a pile of purple ectoplasm.

Stunned, Alex gasped and panted heavily at the rafters over him. All was quiet now that the battle was over. Alex's gaze followed Oryn, who had just shifted into his more human shape to approach Adwen for further instruction.

Alex's mind was blank except for one thought: What had just happened?

A subtle rumbling and claws on wood grew louder until the creature that was Jack stood over him. His ears and facial features were skewed in such a way that he appeared entertained.

Alex stared back.

Jack huffed and took the Marine up by the front of his soiled uniform, setting him on his feet. Then he retrieved the dagger and sheathed it at his side.

Alex gawked at the hound warrior. This was real?

People were beginning to cheer and praise Adwen for rescuing them. Before she could be swarmed by thankful villagers, four town officials came forward.

"Will they return soon, Tame One?" The elder asked. "How long will we have?"

Everyone listened closely, keeping silent to hear, as well.

This was the most relaxed Adwen had been in front of an audience. Still, she disliked so much attention. "They will be back in maybe two days."

The elder's powerfully built son was determined. "How may we kill them?"

Adwen frowned, shaking her head solemnly.

A few murmurs swept the room, and the elder spoke again. "Where shall we go?"

"Go to Plexus and the Order fortress. You will be safe there."

Most had never seen the grand home of the knights, and one asked, "Will there be enough room for us? There are so many."

"You are not the only ones I have told to go there," Adwen said with reassurance. "The fortress constructed by Darien is more than enough to keep the kingdoms' people safe inside. Go and settle in the halls. Do not stay here too long."

They thanked her and bowed before going out to prepare to leave their prosperous little valley home.

Oryn was still awaiting the next command. She saw his firm expression, but the glint of admiration was in his eyes.

Smiling, she called out, "Jack! Go with Oryn and make sure the rest of the town is safe. I'm sure the attack was only meant for Alex, but search around anyway just to be sure. We're spending the night."

With the two on their way, Alex was left staring out into space. Adwen called him to the counter, where he sat quietly, and she asked the bartender to serve a couple rounds. The Marine needed a drink.

As their leader had hoped, no more demons were lurking elsewhere in town. After seeing that everyone had made it home safely, Oryn and Jack returned to the tavern. When they got there, they found Adwen chaperoning Alex as he downed a fifth pint of brew. He was being handed another, and the two warriors claimed empty tables to wait.

The dazed look never left Alex's face. He was very drunk, though it wasn't making much difference. Again, he murmured, "This is real?"

Yet again, she nodded in response. "Yup."

He drank some more and set the flagon down. "This is all real?"

"Uh-huh." She eyed the inside of the container and gestured for the bartender.

The cheery man gladly obliged. This had been going on since Alex had sat down, and there was no reason to assume it would end soon. The bartender made a move to refill the flagon.

Then the sullied Marine stopped him, placing a hand over the top.

Adwen and the bartender watched his face show comprehension.

This time the Marine said confidently, "This is real."

A kind smile came over Adwen, as she watched Alex take in his own words.

He did not smell sober, but he looked it while staring back at her. "I'm here to fight demons?"

She nodded.

"Demons want me dead, and they were trying to kill me in jail?"

She nodded a second time.

After a pause, he glanced over to where the others were sitting.

Oryn frowned at Jack, who occupied his time by sharpening his claws with a dagger. The brute finished honing one hand and brandished it at his companion, who glowered and was clearly not impressed.

"Was he telling the truth?" Alex asked, gesturing to Jack. "Will I end up like him?"

Adwen waited a moment before answering. "If you accept the unwritten contract, you will become like us."

His gaze came back to her attentive expression. "Us?" Finally understanding, he asked, "What are you?"

"We are called Holy Hounds. Our job is to protect the living and aid lost souls whenever possible. I am a spirit being, while the others are bound to me with strong magic. If you accept one of the demon-destroying artifacts, this will be your new destiny, as well."

"What is my destiny if I don't?"

"An untimely death by our enemies. That is your destiny. You are one of the few who have the chance to alter it completely. I did not pick you for this. The powers that guide me said to find you and give you this opportunity."

He was quiet for a long moment. "Where is this artifact?"

Adwen smiled.

Chapter 24
DÉJÀ VU

By the time night gave way to dawn, a thin mist had settled over the earth. The morning was cool and pleasant, while the townspeople were hard at work, preparing for their trek to Plexus. Standing in the midst of the bustling folk were the three hounds. They waited for Alex in their human forms, as he put on a clean change of clothes.

Sleep hadn't come easily for Alex. His head was still spinning from the day before, when most of his perceptions of reality were shattered. Despite being dazed, he put on the secondhand clothing. The realm of magic existed, and he was being asked to protect it. In his mind, this was no different than signing on to serve his country – except, the last he checked, his country saw him as a criminal.

"Hey, stranger," called the smiling bartender. The man was nearly finished packing his belongings and could see that Alex was about to leave. "Count yourself lucky. This kind of opportunity is only available to a rare few."

That was what his recruiter had said when he signed the military contracts. For a different world, things were feeling more and more familiar.

"Thank you, and take care of yourself," Alex casually answered.

The man smiled, watching the blond warrior head for the door.

Out in the cool air at last, Alex joined the others.

Jack chuckled and remarked on his clothing, "Isn't that a little small?"

The two others eyed him, while the newcomer was confused. "These are the right size," Alex assured him.

"They won't be if you stay with us for long."

Adwen spoke up before Oryn could throw a punch. "Jack, not now. The staff sergeant already has the idea, so just shut up." Turning to the Marine, she was apologetic. "I'm sorry, but we don't have any more time." She shot Jack a frustrated glance and added, "We will do our best to help you adapt."

The military had never apologized to him for throwing him into a mess. This was one difference that was easy to accept, and Alex shook his head. "It's fine. I made it through the crucible to near the top of my division. I can take whatever you throw at me."

Jack couldn't resist and spoke again: "This isn't boot camp, Private Pyle. Sooner or later, you're going to eat those words."

Adwen and Oryn both glared.

Finally, Jack fell silent, as his telepathy let him hear Adwen's decision to trap him in hound form if he uttered another syllable.

The mouthy police officer's silence pleased her and satisfied Oryn, who no longer felt driven to knock the brute senseless.

With quiet restored, Alex asked, "When do we leave?"

"Now," Adwen answered. "We are going to visit the island country of Eskrana. Hope you like humidity because they have a rainforest climate. It's across the ocean, and we better get moving if we're going to reach it by noon. Are you ready?"

He had never heard of anyone getting across an ocean that fast without a jet-propelled vehicle of some sort. Choosing not to worry about it, the Marine nodded. "I'm ready to move."

This pleased his new commander. "Oryn will carry you until we find the portal to take us there."

At her gesture, the faithful warrior obediently reverted into hound form and knelt down, allowing the Marine to get on.

Oryn's transformation drew a gasp of shock from Alex. It wasn't like Jack's the night before, but it was still alarming. Climbing atop the large creature's back was a little nerve-wracking, as well. He grabbed hands full of the coarse fur that covered the large creature's back. A moment passed before Alex found that grasping Oryn's shoulder armor and broad neck provided the best hold.

The uncertain human seemed prepared, so Adwen led them out of town and deep into the wilds. She stayed in human form, sprinting with her company nearby. They flew across the terrain, bounding and darting through the trees.

Alex held on tight, as the hound's heavy breaths made him reminisce about steam-powered locomotives. This beast plowed forward like an unstoppable force, exhaling in quick blasts. For a moment, Alex considered just how fortunate he was to be on Oryn's good side.

Their newest member was conditioned enough to endure the rough ride, as Adwen led them westward to the coast. After an hour or so, the forest became sparse, and the land grew more rugged. Abrupt edges and windswept rocks forced them to go around or leap over obstacles. The beach was in sight, but the rocky earth did not smooth out or slope to the misty shore. Adwen found the simplest way down was by jumping along the stepped tiers of volcanic shelves. She pressed on, with Jack and Oryn just behind.

Alex saw the edge coming, and his grip redoubled. Heights were among his least favorite things. Another was jumping from them.

The Holy Hound unflinchingly left solid ground, and the man clinging to his neck and armor clenched his teeth. His stomach bottomed out from the absence of gravity, making him queasy. The landing was just a little jarring, thanks to Oryn's taking care to absorb the impact. Still, the man grunted upon touchdown, struggling not to fall off.

From there, the search was easy along the windy surf. Gales blasted across the peaceful shore, whipping their hair with bits of sand and salty spray. Even Jack found himself enjoying the strong winds and soft earth.

The male hounds noticed their leader slowing to glance around. Eventually Adwen came to a stop, and they followed suit.

Alex slid down from Oryn's back. Weary from hanging on so long, he wasn't bother by the sight of the hound reverting to human shape. Instead, the Marine stretched sore muscles, glad to be on his feet again.

Chuckling, Jack caught his breath and remarked, "Out of shape? We'll fix that overnight."

Alex ignored him, but Oryn was quick to plant a fist into Jack's left kidney.

Gasping and on his knees, the cop moaned. "Aw! Come on! Do you ever laugh?"

Oryn sneered in reply, "Do you ever think of comical things to say?"

"Enough, guys! Cut it out!" Adwen commanded, putting an end to the bickering. "I need to concentrate."

With silence at last, she went back to sniffing out a source of old magic. It was close, but there was only sand surrounding them.

Trusting her instincts, she crouched low and started to dig. The others watched her uncover more volcanic rock, buried under a foot of sand. While most of the dark stone was rough and porous, the center had a smooth impression bearing the Andredan emblem. A clever smile lifted her cheeks. It was smaller than the first of its kind she had come across. Fitting a hand into the shallow indentation, her energy reacted with the mark. A moment passed, as a small portion of her light powers built up, radiating from her palm before blasting into the stone.

The ball of energy flew straight to the cliff face off shore, sending a curtain of sand high up in its wake. Once it struck the wall of solid earth, the surface became like water. Stones and soil churned and rippled in on themselves, creating a broad tunnel. Torches inside came to life with golden flames, lighting the way into the depths.

Alex watched in awe, though he said nothing to express it. Instead, the Marine quietly followed Adwen wherever the magical passage would take them. Once the team entered, the entry closed at their backs in the same roiling manner as it had opened.

The air in the tunnel was silent, save for their footfalls and breathing. Soft firelight glowed on their faces, illuminating each of their expressions.

Adwen was thoughtful, contented in leading the way.

At her side, Oryn wore a stern look. He was still irritated by their shortest warrior.

The glow in Jack's eyes was more pronounced, as his power had grown since being rid of the demon parasite. His mind was brewing with ideas of things to say to the new recruit. Unconcerned with Oryn's mounting aggravation, Jack clapped a hand on the stoic Marine's shoulder.

Not surprised by it, Alex avoided eye contact.

"It's not too late to turn back, you know. You have the right to turn down the weapon and avoid all of the heartache it entails. Trust me when I say that becoming part of the team is excruciating. You have no idea what you're getting into."

Their leader whirled around angrily, and her yell echoed in the confines like a gong. "Jack! That's enough!"

A moment of quiet passed.

Jack stared back in defiance.

Rumbling growls reverberated from Oryn, while Adwen seethed.

Meanwhile, Alex remained calm, giving Jack a look of indifference.

Short of outraged, Adwen managed to use a restrained tone. "If you want to help the staff sergeant, there are better things to tell him. Watch your mouth, or I will force you to stay in your true body. Get it?"

Jack huffed. "I don't know about you, but I think knowing there are choices is helpful. What do you think?"

"I recall warning you when you were faced with the choice. Besides that, why don't you tell me what I'm thinking? You were good

enough to take advantage of those men in town using your telepathy."

Alex blinked and gave them curious glances.

Jack groaned. "There you go again. You're such a kill-joy."

"What am I not understanding?" Alex said, confounded by the odd argument.

"He's psychic," Adwen told him and scowled at Jack. "That is very useful information. Now shut up so we can keep moving."

Watching as Jack dramatically rolled his eyes, Alex inclined an eyebrow.

"Yes, I'm psychic," Jack admitted. "So that we're all clear, I used that nifty ability in town so that I can make it better. Just wait until I figure out how to use my telekinesis. Then you can complain about how I abuse my talents."

They continued through the tunnel, and nothing more was said. The end of the passage was a little farther, and the group came across a section of raised ground. It was empty and uninteresting until Adwen's presence activated the portal. Rippling light spilled out of nowhere to form a large sphere, hovering over the bedrock.

Being in a magical world did not alarm the Marine anymore, but not being familiar with certain aspects of it kept him wary. As the others casually approached the light portal, Alex stayed close. He did not want to risk being left behind. It was just a precaution that he felt was worth taking.

The first thing they felt upon passing through was a strong wind, laden with humidity and the scent of rich spices. Adwen and Oryn were familiar with the Kingdom of Eskrana, so they were not surprised to arrive in a busy square hemmed in by many stone homes and colorful locals. The dark-skinned Eskrani people gasped at the group's sudden appearance by the fountain where they came for water.

Jack and Alex stared at the strange surroundings. The people were friendly and curious. Then before either could relax, large shadows swept by and were followed by deafening bird calls. Both ducked then looked up in time to see a squadron of huge battle Griffins soaring past.

Some villagers laughed, and others cheered, watching the aerial maneuvers overhead. The riders atop the winged beasts directed their flight training elsewhere, as Adwen laughed out loud. She adored Griffins.

Alex gave Jack an astonished look. "Have you ever seen those before?"

He shook his head and laughed. "No, and I want one. Let's see if we can get a free test ride somewhere."

Many passersby dipped their heads as they recognized Adwen. Along the way to the palace, they passed trading stands selling fresh fruit, as well as fish caught in the early hours of the day. Seasonings and a variety of other goods filled the air with sweet aromas, inviting them up the cobbled road.

This kingdom had yet to deal with any demon threat. Since the civilization was on a small continent across the sea and atop colossal plateaus, not even the giant creatures of the jungle below posed a problem. The only worries they had were for tropical storms and the harpy tribes that attacked at random. Besides the fierce weather and fiercer bird-men, the Eskrani lived simple lives alongside their Griffins.

Guards in flanking watchtowers blew horns, while their winged companions fanned broad wings, signaling Adwen's arrival at the palace gates. As the sonorous sounds died away, the entrance opened wide to let them through.

The other side was lush. A garden lined the inner wall of the grounds with bright blooms of every shade and shape imaginable. Adwen only had a second to admire the variety of orchids before the palace doors opened. Isla, King Zulo's advisor, came sweeping out to greet her with his thick accent.

"Lady Adwen." He bowed low and stood again. "It is an honor to have you among us again so soon. What brings you to the home of the sky people?"

She nodded and smiled. "I have a new warrior who needs a weapon. Do you know where we can find the guardian? I'm sure there's one here in this kingdom."

Shaking his head, the advisor was apologetic. "I am sorry, Lady. I have no knowledge of such a thing. Perhaps His Highness could tell you. The king would be pleased to speak with you again."

"Thank you."

The richly clad official quickly ushered them into the palace. Across the interior was decorated with long, draping green cloth over blue stone halls, lined with statues and ancient pottery. Few others were seen wandering about. Those who encountered Isla swiftly stepped aside and gasped at the sight of Adwen by his side.

Isla brought them to the king's private guest room on the far side of the palace, overlooking a view of the sea. As he was about to leave, he bowed again and addressed them: "I will return with the king. It will not be too long to wait."

Adwen nodded, thanking him again.

The doors closed, and the four had the room to themselves.

While Alex and Jack looked around, Adwen and Oryn's gaze drifted to a familiar sight at the top of three stairs across the room. Upon the raised side of the king's lounge stood the tall, narrow frame belonging to the mirror of truth. It remained covered by the same red cloth that they recalled when they first looked into its depths over a month ago.

Naturally, Jack's telepathy detected the strong emotions. His mind was becoming like a radio tower, constantly picking up signals from close by.

Eyeing the concealed surface, he smiled and said, "You guys sure don't like whatever's under that red sheet."

Oryn coolly claimed a seat that faced away from the steps.

Shaking her head, Adwen replied, "That is the mirror of truth. I don't think you want anything to do with it."

Now both Alex and Jack were curious and eyed the frame.

Jack asked, "How does it work?"

Oryn remained silent.

"You look into it and see who you are on the inside," she explained. "Only you can see what it shows, while everyone else just sees a normal reflection. No one can look in the mirror without being affected, if you can imagine."

Jokingly, he asked, "Where's the mirror of lies?"

"No one knows," Oryn murmured and fell quiet once more.

Adwen continued to explain: "The mirror of lies is dangerous. Unlike this mirror, the other one is evil. It lures beings close with images of the one thing they desire most but can never have. If they touch the glass it consumes them."

"It eats people?"

"Yes and no. It consumes souls. Whoever gets sucked into the mirror of lies will be transported into an alternative reality created by their innermost desire. That place is a fabricated world where they will waste away. None of the food or water is real. Everything in that reality is a lie. You see?"

Alex finally spoke up: "So they starve to death and can't even tell its happening?" He seemed disturbed by the concept.

"That sums it up. The one way to break the spell is for the prisoner to deny the lie and desire something else even more."

Jack gestured to the mirror of truth. "So if this mirror is good, why not look in it?"

She paused before answering. "It shows you your true self. Some-times what people find is enough to drive them insane. It's risky. Not everything you see is nice."

Chuckling to himself, Jack nudged Alex with an elbow. "Want to look, soldier boy?"

"What?" The Marine was unsure of how to respond.

"What do you say, jarhead? Do you feel lucky?"

Adwen was in no mood for Jack's pestering. "All right, that's enough. Don't touch the mirror. It's a custom for the king to offer a look."

Jack's interest was then drawn to Oryn's mood since entering the room. The green-eyed warrior continued to wait, staring out into space. His mind was quiet, but Jack sensed his aversion to the artifact.

"What did you see when you looked in the mirror?" Jack asked Oryn. "Did you see yourself as a little lost puppy? I'll bet that image would be enough to drive you crazy."

Holding his stony composure, Oryn coolly replied, "I saw myself hog-tie your miserable hide and toss you in a pit to rot."

Adwen was growing impatient. With disgust in her voice, she mur-mured a warning: "That's enough, Jack."

Far too curious to drop the subject, Jack went closer and leaned against the back of Oryn's chair. Again, he attempted to provoke Ory-n's mind into thinking specifically of what the mirror had showed him. It was like a game to pass the time, nothing more.

"So if you didn't see yourself in the mirror as a puppy, what did you see? Did you see yourself as a love slave or maybe a ..."

Jack stopped in mid-sentence, as his ploy worked at last. Instead of getting a single image of the mirror's reflection, a stream of sights and sounds ran through Oryn's mind's eye and instantly poured into Jack's.

First there were the screams of Oryn's mother and father with flashes of their dismembered remains all over the home. Jack saw eve-rything, as if he had lived it himself, while ten-year-old Oryn's hands picked up his dead father's sword and ran after the monster responsi-ble.

Then the setting changed to the moonlit woods where the bloody werewolf was waiting. It charged, and the boy was barely able to sever its head in time. After crawling out from under the corpse, soaked from head to toe in blood, he stood over the head to watch it become human again.

That's when the memory of the mirror appeared, showing the boy Oryn standing over the severed head of his golden-eyed twin brother. The memories stopped as soon as Oryn spoke, snapping both of their minds out of the horror-filled moments.

The swordsman glowered, clenching his fists. "I saw nothing worth sharing with the likes of you."

Only Adwen and Alex could see Jack's face was blanched.

The cop was dazed. His stomach churned, as even the smells in the memories had found their way into his psyche. To keep down the bile and the large lump in his throat, he swallowed with some difficulty. Though Oryn's mind was no longer dwelling on the matter, the things Jack saw and heard still filled his own mind, haunting him. The telepathic ability suddenly did not seem as fun anymore.

Unsteady, the cop muttered aloud, and his voice faltered and cracked, "I think I need to sit down and be quiet now."

Unaware of the new bond between them, Oryn sneered, "At last."

With all that had happened between them both, Jack had come to like and respect Oryn. He only provoked him so often because it was entertaining. Now it wasn't anymore. It was no longer possible for Jack to taunt Oryn again without wondering if he might find something else horrible and soul crushing. Those memories were in his mind now, taking up a permanent residency.

Stealing a glance, Jack studied Oryn's stony expression. Though his face was blank, both hands were balled fists on the arms of the chair. Such a twisted childhood tragedy explained a lot – mainly the explosive temper.

Feeling guilty for causing the bad recollections to surface, Jack wondered if this were something he could possibly help Oryn deal with. He had been majoring in psychology after all. Perhaps this could be where he fit into the team. Other than being a cop, Jack had toyed with the notion of being a therapist.

A long silence hung over their heads. No one wanted to be the first to break it. Oryn was tense, Jack was thoughtful, Adwen observed them both, and Alex didn't dare to ask questions. For the moment, no one seemed to be in the mood for conversation.

The sound of the door opening ended the tense silence.

A very powerfully built King Zulo entered to greet Adwen with open arms.

"Lady Adwen," boomed his deep voice, "it pleases me to see you! Welcome back to my palace, and what may I do to serve you?"

Adwen dipped her head, as the king made a short bow.

Smiling, she replied, "We need to find the weapon that Darien left in your kingdom, King Zulo. I have another warrior who needs to claim it."

For the first time, he took note of the three men accompanying her. "You are making great progress, Lady Adwen. Two warriors already, and you seek to command a third! This is good news. It would be an honor to show you the way to the guardian's lair. Bring your warriors. I will take you there." Isla was waiting in the hall and joined them as they passed.

They all walked in brisk strides. The king led them to the far side of the palace and came to a tall pair of gold-inlayed doors. There he halted and proudly presented the entrance.

"This is the way into the cavern, Lady Adwen. You and your men shall be the first to set foot inside since these doors were set into their hinges hundreds of years ago. Take care. It is said that the way is dangerously narrow."

"Thank you, King Zulo." She nodded politely. "If this doesn't take too long, will you have time to meet with me afterward?"

"Of course."

They stood by as Adwen turned to the heavy doors and pulled them open, releasing a cold gust of cavern air. The blast ruffled their hair and clothing until it subsided, and the crew stared into the shadowy depths. She entered with an air of confidence, followed by Alex and Jack.

Oryn was just behind, but before he could enter, the king called for his attention.

"Wait."

Stopping for the dark-skinned king, Oryn waited to see what he wanted.

His face was full of curiosity and surprise. Then he chuckled. "Amazing. I had not recognized you until just now, knight. Continue on your way, Sir Oryn. I only wished to see if my eyes were playing tricks on me. I thought you were someone else."

Oryn blinked and replied, "I have become someone else, Your Highness."

The king beamed. "It is good to see you. Blessings be with you, Sir Oryn."

Oryn gave a small bow and went into the dark after the others.

For a long time after Oryn had departed, the king continued to smile.

Inside the ancient cave was pitch black. The one source of light was supplied by Adwen's body, as she allowed a portion of her power to radiate through her skin. More than anyone else, Alex needed the strong glow. The king had not been wrong about the path. It was precarious. They all had to sidle against the cavern wall, careful to not slip off of the meager six-inch ledge.

Alex's concentration was broken by a frustrated remark from Jack. "You would think they'd put stairs here."

The Marine muttered and struggled to hold his balance.

"Hey," Jack called past Alex, "how much longer does this balancing act last? Is there any place to walk up ahead?"

Adwen replied, and her voice echoed. "I can't see the end yet."

"I hate spelunking," Jack said.

Moving along was difficult for Alex, and he wished Jack would keep quiet.

Hearing the thought, Jack muttered, "Sorry, jarhead. I'm zipping the lips."

Alex's next step landed on a weak patch of rock. It gave way, and there was nothing to grab to save himself. He gasped, flailed and fell off into space.

Before he could cry out, a large hand caught him by the arm. Adwen had shifted into her armored white hound form in order to reach him in time. She balanced on the ledge, while the Marine resisted the need to panic. Red in the face from his brush with death, he looked back and gaped at the sight of her clutching his wrist. Panting and gasping, he held still and allowed her to set him back on the narrow path.

Jack's chuckle bounced off the stone walls like marbles. "Nice catch."

Feeling solid ground underfoot, Alex quickly flattened against the wall, panting heavily. After glancing at the dark abyss again, he stared at her in awe.

She shifted into her woman form and also hugged the stone surface. Chuckling nervously, she warned, "It's a big drop. Let's go a little slower."

Alex nodded and muttered weakly, "Roger that."

They pressed forward and were extra cautious. Nothing but darkness and Adwen's light were in view. She was able to make out the way only a few meters past her own light source. Shuffling very slowly made the journey feel much longer than it really was.

After passing two bends in the passage, they reached safer ground at last. Even Jack was quietly thankful. He didn't want to speak too soon and risk jinxing the occurrence.

Ahead was a soft flickering glow that came from around a turn. There they found an opening into the main cavern.

Adwen halted her company by the entrance. "Alex is the only one who can come with me from here."

Oryn took no issue, but Jack was frowning. They eyed each other in an unfriendly manner.

"Don't worry, Jack," Adwen assured the police officer. "I will make absolutely sure that the staff sergeant understands everything he's getting into. Okay?"

"As far as I'm concerned you've already gotten him into it without telling him what he needs to know."

Alex finally spoke up in Adwen's defense: "You need to learn to watch your mouth." Jack looked him in the eye as Alex went on, "If you're bitter over the cards you've been dealt, that's fine, but don't even think of trying to put that resentment into somebody else's decision. I'm choosing to serve a cause bigger than myself. If that's not what you want, then why did you decide to be a cop in the first place?"

Jack's expression didn't show it, but the question caught him to the quick. There was nothing he had to say in rebuttal. Instead, he said, "Then serve the cause. All I have to say is a warning. One way or another, you will get more than you bargained for."

Alex glared a moment and turned to face Adwen. "Lead the way."

She nodded and tossed Jack a stern glance before taking Alex into the guardian's chamber.

Unlike the tunnel, the cavern was bright. Highly detailed facets lined the domed chamber walls, creating a heavenly effect with the light reflecting in every direction. They went toward an arching stair, which led up to a golden box that could only be the chest containing one of Darien's artifacts.

There was no sign of the guardian until they were about to reach the steps. Both ducked down when there was a gust of wind, and the beating of wings filled their ears.

A giant golden Griffin cried out from its perch over the entrance behind them. "Stop where you are!"

It leaped, flew and pounced onto the stairway, blocking their path. Fanning its enormous wings, the guardian trilled angrily. "Name yourselves! What business does the likes of you have by coming here?"

Thinking fast, she stared down the creature and answered, "I am Adwen Andredan, and this is Alexander Greeves."

The guardian's lynx-like ears perked in surprise.

"We are here to claim the weapon left to you by Darien."

Alarmed by the guardian's size, Alex listened to her speak to it and waited to see if he should start running. When the creature fluffed out its feathers and chortled, he got the impression that the Griffin was chuckling.

"Ah! It is about time that we met, heir of Darien! Welcome, welcome. Bring your warrior close so that I may have a look into his eyes."

Turning to him, Adwen called him closer. "The guardian wants to see you."

He was uncertain and glanced over nervously before asking, "What for?"

"It's okay. He won't hurt you."

Obediently, though hesitant, the Marine went closer. Alex took the precaution of not making any sudden moves, just in case this creature turned out to be wilder than Adwen seemed to think. The Griffin guardian's razor-sharp beak lowered until its amber eyes loomed before him, sizing him up and looking through his very being. Alex was unaware that the spirit creature actually could see into his soul.

After analyzing the Marine, the guardian made a guttural tone. It set back its pointed ears in displeasure and addressed Adwen in a series of chirps.

"Are you aware of this human's poor condition? His heart is completely closed off to all. This will not do. How is light to enter him when there is no entry?"

She frowned. Growling so that he wouldn't understand, she replied to the guardian, "I am aware. It's because his wife was murdered a few weeks ago."

The guardian was not moved by the explanation. Angry, it cried, "No Excuse! You know what is to be done. Counsel him now!"

A grimace flashed on Adwen's face before she turned to Alex. She was firm when she found the right words. "Alex, there is something you have to understand if you are going to accept the weapon. How quickly you were able to accept this world for what it is demonstrates the point I'm about to make."

The Marine's brow furrowed as he listened, wondering what she meant.

"The true reason behind your wanting to join us is because you want an escape, a distraction from your one true fear. Remember, I told you that we face fear in this war. The demons aren't what I was talking about. You fear is accepting the reality that the one you love is gone from this life."

The statement provoked a silent rage in Alex's heart. His expression didn't show much feeling. He simply held his tongue.

Despite his self control, Adwen sensed his anger. Spending so much time with Oryn had made detecting the emotion second nature.

She continued, "It was easy for you to believe in this magical realm because you are running away from that reality.

"By accepting a weapon from me, you agree to serve the Light Spirits. In order to become one of their warriors, they must mold you and test you. What you want out of this war is not possible. Being a part of this team cannot be simple warfare. You will be pitted against your innermost fears, and if you are going to become stronger and carry the powers of light, you must open your heart. Face your fear, and grieve your wife. Face it soon, before the Light Spirits force you to."

His baby-blue eyes bored into her. It was not in him to deny an order from a superior, but when it came to personal matters, that changed. These so called Light Spirits had nothing to do with his following Adwen's command. As for dwelling on what happened to the love of his life, nobody physical or ethereal was going to tell him how to feel. Serving Adwen would always be just business. Nothing could make a war personal to him, least of all some spirits or a hokey deity.

Keeping a calm look about him, he replied coldly, "Give me the weapon."

Adwen let out a small sigh of disappointment, as the guardian chirped irritably beside her, "Such a stubborn, insolent man."

She said nothing and merely gestured to Alex to claim the weapon.

With their eyes on him, Alex walked past the Griffin. He could not understand the guardian's speech but did have the sense that it was glaring.

The Marine did not care. He ascended the steps to where the magical chest sat. Being told that this pact would never be what he wished it to be caused his brow to furrow. It contradicted a firm belief he held since his time spent in the military that anything could be what you wanted it to be; your time spent is what you make it.

Each stride brought him closer to the goal, where he stopped to analyze the metallic surface of the weapon's resting place. Meaning to find an opening when he could see none, his fingers caressed the gold, activating the magic it held. Alex froze out of surprise when the once-solid ripples churned like an ocean tide, parting in the center like two golden curtains being drawn.

As the weapon came into view on a crimson silk cloth, the shape and size of it struck Alex in the gut, like a fist. The blade's general appearance trapped the air in his lungs and would not let it out. Once it was in full view, he stood still, staring.

For a moment, his mind was taken back to a memory he had locked away, intending to never think of it again. His wife lay before him in their upstairs bedroom, splattered and drenched in blood, the machete deep in her heart. The very same blade he had used to save his men in war was through the breast of his love, like a pin mounting a butterfly on display.

Still stunned, Alex restrained himself from glancing at Adwen. Had she known the sight of the weapon would take his mind back to those buried memories? It did not matter, he thought. This was going to be impersonal. Nothing could possibly change that. Decided on the matter, he suppressed the recollection, determined to leave it lost for good this time.

Alex finalized his denial by taking the blade from its resting place. It was strikingly similar to his old machete, though it was far grander. This weapon bore the resemblance of a large feather. It was very heavy, and the edges were serrated close to the curving, engraved hilt.

Watching the Marine set the blade at his side by his belt, the guardian trilled to Jack and Oryn, "Wait no longer and join us! Hurry to my side, warriors of light."

Adwen called, "Alex! Come here quickly!"

The four stood with the lavish Griffin guardian, wondering what it had to say. Urgency was in its eyes and creature speech, while it fanned its wings.

"Your count may be four, but one more warrior must be bound to the descendant and merge with your combined strength. Only when you are five strong and fully bound will you be ready. Prepare! Make haste and prepare! The darkening time approaches. Even now the days grow darker. The leaves will fall in this land and as summer ends your enemies shall be nearly ready. The kingdoms' people must hurry! Go now with my final blessing. I shall quicken your way."

Light spilled out of the guardian, and glowing feathers materialized along with a strong, warm wind. It circled the group like a tornado, lifting them off the ground. Each of them gasped, caught by surprise.

Now engulfed in light, the vanishing guardian let loose a proud eagle-like call.

"Farewell!"

In a flash, the guardian burst into thousands of feathers and flecks of light that whisked them off. The four flew through the tunnel on the magical gale, in shock and awe of the event. Adwen laughed and whooped with excitement throughout their wild ride.

The flight back to the palace halls was short. In a minute they were brought to the threshold of the golden doors before King Zulo and his advisor. Adwen, Oryn and Jack were set down on their feet, but Alex was not as fortunate. The guardian's magic purposefully let the Marine fall at an awkward angle, landing hard on his backside.

Adwen and Oryn only glanced and she asked, "Are you all right?"

"I'm not happy, but I'm not damaged."

Looking up, Alex found Jack standing over him, offering a hand. They eyed each other quietly before he accepted and stood, holding a minor conversation with their eyes. Alex remained stoic, and Jack's face showed scrutiny.

When Adwen had warned Alex, Jack had gotten his first real glimpse into the Marine's psyche. Most of Alex's thoughts were far too repressed or vague to hear, but Adwen had touched a nerve, setting off a series of loud thoughts in his head like firecrackers. Jack had heard most of them loud and clear. For claiming to be patriotic in nature, Alex was proving to be quite the contrary. All of this was expressed by Jack's stony frown.

King Zulo's proud voice brought them back to the present. "You returned so quickly. Were you successful?"

Smiling at the king, Adwen nodded. "We found it."

Becoming excited, he asked with a hopeful tone, "Might I see it a moment?"

She indicated to Alex, and the king went closer. When Alex took out the blade, King Zulo's eyes showed great pride. Very gently, he took it from the Marine for an even closer inspection.

Finished, he returned it. "The father of my father's and the first to forge an alliance with the Griffins was the wielder of that weapon."

King Zulo studied Alex's eyes closely, judging his character. "You are very strong. You are also as brave as any warrior I've known." Then he paused and added in warning, "You will need more than that for this new path you tread. I only ask that you carry the Wind's Talon with honor, as it deserves."

Alex nodded promptly. "You have my word."

As the king smiled, a wreath of fire burst into being nearby. Out of the center came an angry bird trill, followed by Malik the phoenix. With a few beats of his wings he came to perch on a statue's shoulder calling to Adwen.

"What have you done, Andredan child! Do you possess rocks for brains?"

She was instantly distressed. "What did I do now?"

"Imagine if you will," the fiery bird hissed, "a few hundred peasants knocking on the Master Knight fortress's door, claiming you told them to leave their homes for the safety of the halls. All of this, without the prior knowledge of the elders, who are now confused, quarreling and bickering over whether to let them in or send them away to bed down in the streets of Plexus."

Adwen frowned and winced at the ugly picture in her mind's eye. "Sorry. I forgot to warn the elders that I had told the townspeople who were in the most danger to go. The place was built to be large enough to hold all of the Dargadian people at once. I thought it was time to put it to use."

Oryn was surprised by her claim. "No one has ever said that was the reason for the fortress's vastness. Who told you that housing the entire kingdom's people was its intended purpose?"

She kindly dismissed the question: "I'll tell you later. Malik, can you find out how to tell them to let the people stay?"

He chortled proudly, raising his head. "It has already been done. I thought it best to make you aware of this folly. Do not repeat it again."

Now Adwen was irritated. "You came all of the way out here just to lecture me about my communication skills! Are you kidding?"

Malik trilled loudly, "I have not and I do not kid! My true intent for this meeting is to bring a very serious matter to light. The Baron Bartholomew is in danger. His letter has only just arrived to the king and the elders, announcing his setting out to rescue the townsfolk of Deleon."

"What?"

"The letter assured that his men are armed with weapons as ancient as those that your warriors carry. They are not nearly as potent but can kill demons in battle. However, they cannot win outright in your absence. The baron sent his apologies to you personally for not having the patience to wait any longer. His son and daughter are among those trapped in the city. Make haste! He and his men should be reaching the city soon."

She swiftly turned to King Zulo. "I'm sorry, but we really have to go."

"Go if you must. The pleasure of speaking together must wait, it seems."

After taking a split second to nod in appreciation, Adwen took off with Jack and Oryn on her heals.

Caught off guard, Alex struggled to catch up. The three of them were so fast that it was impossible to close the gap. He tried with all his might to gain on them once they reached the next long corridor. There was still no chance to run fast enough, but neither was he going to give up. Failure would never be in his vocabulary.

Suddenly, Adwen stopped abruptly by an elaborate mosaic, where the Marine was finally able to join them. His breaths were laborious, coming in large gasps and coughs.

Jack couldn't keep from making a remark, though he didn't have the same childish tone. The talkative warrior scoffed, "You were a Marine? For a jarhead, you sure let yourself go. I would think you could run seven miles before breaking a sweat."

In between gasps, Alex answered, "What does a cop know about Marines?"

He smiled broadly. "For one thing ..."

While the two distracted each other, Adwen's keen instincts and intuition guided her fingers to the mechanism that opened the secret passage. The loud thud made by the door's movement cut off Jack's well prepared insult, and both men gaped, waiting for her signal to press on.

Oryn took the moment to glower at them. "End your bickering. Now is not the time for nonsense."

Adwen agreed, and her tone was hurried. "We all need to have our game faces on. If there is any chance of rescuing the baron and his men, we're going to have to stay focused." Then she frowned at Jack and let him hear a thought in her head.

Picking it up like radar, he chuckled. "No need to be so blunt, but no can do."

"What did she say?" Alex asked.

Jack smiled. "She told me to shut up."

With the hidden door opened, the hovering, glowing portal was in view a short distance away. The four quickly dropped the conversation and rushed through to the other side. Even Jack recognized that they were truly running out of time.

As soon as they found themselves in the southern edge of the Dargadian Plains, Oryn resumed his task of carrying the new recruit.

Again, Adwen remained in her smaller shape with Jack, as they headed southeast at a dead run.

Tree branches and trunks rushed past Alex on his wild ride through the forest. As things usually did, it took a while for him to think of asking where they were going. He had a firm enough grip on Oryn's neck and armor to allow his attention to turn elsewhere.

Calling to Adwen through the rush of wind, he asked, "What's happening?"

Pulling back to run alongside, she nervously told him, "We are going to a city that is heavily occupied by our enemies. If the baron's army is discovered it won't stand a chance. Baron Bartholomew is a friend and one of the strongest leaders in Dargadia. Without his help, our forces would be crippled."

"Wouldn't being your bigger self help us get there faster?"

Frowning, she replied, "Not really. Unlike the others, I'm about as fast in both forms. My real reason for not changing is because I contain so much magical energy that our enemies can detect it easily. The only way that I can go unnoticed by them is by being this way. In this body, my magic is much more concealed."

It was Alex's turn to frown. "But doesn't that mean you are less powerful and more vulnerable?"

At this she smiled grimly. "Save your energy. You'll need it."

The Marine watched as she put on a spurt of speed and reclaimed the lead.

An hour later, the spires of castle Gailarien were in sight, looming over Deleon. From a distance, all seemed as deathly silent as during their most recent visit. Adwen was uneasy and sensed something was wrong. She did not know whether the silence was a good sign or a bad omen.

As they approached from the northwest through the forest, they stumbled across a trail left by a squad of men. Among them was the familiar scent of the baron. Following it closely, they eventually reached Deleon's walls. Three ropes reached the top, where each was held fast by a large grappling hook to the stone ledge.

Adwen couldn't help but be amazed at the distance that the stout man had climbed. Glancing to her companions, she whispered, "Everybody ready?"

Alex nodded from atop Oryn, who growled in affirmation. Jack chuckled.

Adwen was pleased, though she did not show it. Her face was set into a harsh expression, as she took a firm grasp of the middle rope, starting to climb. Jack ascended by the second rope, while Oryn carried the Marine on his way up the third tether.

Adwen hopped down into the walkway and had to wait only a moment for the others to join. They peered down at the city together, looking for any sign of friend or foe. There was nothing but dreary streets and dead-looking dwellings.

Oryn gave a dark growl. "I sense a danger we cannot perceive."

Adwen frowned.

"I hate to say this," Jack murmured, "but I second the feeling."

Neither she nor Oryn were in the mood to give a smart reply. Instead, they moved on, with Alex on his own two feet. Soon after going down the stairway and reaching the city streets, Adwen kept Alex close to her side with Jack just behind him. Oryn was covering their backs. Bringing up the rear, Oryn remained on high alert, constantly scanning for hints of danger or human comrades.

Alex kept his golden weapon out, ready for anything. With one eye on Adwen sniffing out the baron's company, the other was on all possible ambush points. He shifted his gaze second by second, anticipating an attack. The Marine thought for a second that he was back in the desert city where he had lost his friends and fellow troops. His brain began to trick him into thinking that robed men with guns were lying in wait. The ragged murderers were here and were going to spring out soon to shred them with automatic firepower.

"Alex?"

Adwen's voice snapped him back to the present. "What?" he whispered.

She had stopped in an alley, and they were staring as if they thought he was losing his mind.

"What's happening? You were zoned out. I don't need to remind you to stay focused."

He felt a twinge of guilt and tried to fool her. "I am focused."

Adwen looked skeptical.

Then Jack scoffed and shook his head, frowning. "This is not the desert."

Alex's head whipped around, and he stared. Surprise crossed the Marine's face, and then he was angry.

The cop was firm: "You're suffering from post traumatic stress disorder. I'm betting you never filed for that in your separation disability claims, did you, jarhead?"

Adwen snarled through clenched teeth, "Enough!"

To Alex, she quietly advised, "We can tell that you are struggling with something. For future reference, don't lie. Do your best to stay here with us in the now. When there is some time, we can find a way to help you work this out. Keep it together."

He drew a deep breath before nodding firmly. "I'm ready to roll."

She nodded in response and led them down the empty cobbled roads and by many more shadowed corners. The baron's and his men's tracks appeared to be going to every hideaway that the townspeople might use for shelter. So far, their search appeared to have been fruitless.

The farther the trail led, the stronger the scents grew, spurring Adwen to quicken her pace. Even with the urgency, she was mindful not to outrun her human companion. They kept their positions in the search, which led deep into the heart of the wealthy upper district. White stone buildings dominated the location, though they seemed grey with the dark atmosphere bleeding out from the castle grounds.

Eventually, they came to Deleon's elaborate scholar's academy. Built of white stones and dark timbers, this structure was three stories tall with two wings that reached around the courtyard like extended arms to welcome an embrace. The windows were dark or closed, giving the enlightening landmark a mournful aura.

Slinking through the shaded courtyard walkways, even Alex could hear men's voices coming from inside the main hall. As they approached the stained glass windows and the large wooden doors, the talking ceased.

Calling through the doors, Adwen announced herself: "Baron Bartholomew? This is Adwen. We're here to make sure that you are safe."

A murmur echoed inside, as the baron ordered his men to hold their fire and called in reply, "Come inside, quickly now. I am not a fool enough to turn away your assistance."

As the team of four entered, Oryn took one last look around before closing the entrance tightly.

The stout baron came to greet them warmly while keeping his voice down. Suited in his personal armor, he resembled a large dwarf. His friendly demeanor was very misleading, as Bartholomew could handle himself very well in combat. Behind him were twenty or so of his most loyal soldiers, armed to the teeth with swords edged with a coat of pure gold.

The baron's voice sounded more serious than before. "It is good to have you with us, Tame One. There are more survivors than I had anticipated. We shall need all the help we can get in leading them out."

Adwen contained her unease and replied, "Did you have any trouble getting this far? How are your men?"

"They are hungry, but not as hungry as the lot we aim to liberate."

Taking one glance at the commoners huddled by the tables and scroll racks, she could not agree more. They looked starved. As many as fifty men, women and children looked back in fear. She didn't dare ask how long they had been trapped in this place.

Turning to the baron, she advised, "It is still daylight. If you take them soon and move fast, there is a good chance that the demons won't stop you. Even if they did attack in the light, they would be at a disadvantage."

"I believe you, but making them move will be a chore. They do not believe they are even safe in the day."

"Let me try," Adwen asked.

He joined her, while Oryn and the others remained by the entrance to wait.

The people's frightened eyes followed as she came close. They did not know what to expect. Their lives had been filled with horrors for what felt like an age.

Studying the dozens of tired, feeble faces, she took a deep breath and sighed. After mustering a little power into her voice, Adwen focused magic into every syllable in order to calm and fortify the weary hearts of the people.

"Please, I beg of you, do not give up hope. This cannot be the end. If this were the end, I could not be standing before you. So long as there is a flicker of light, there will always be a chance. The sun is still high. With daylight on our side, there is little to fear. The demons are not invincible. I assure you, the baron's men have swords that are more than strong enough for fending off the creatures. We cannot leave you here at the mercy of the darkness. Please, do not make these brave men who have come to deliver you choose between staying and leaving you behind."

There was utter silence. All stared quietly.

Another painful moment of nothingness passed and she asked, "What say you?"

Suddenly, one man stirred and gathered himself up. Conviction was in his eyes.

His motion was soon repeated by everyone gathered in the school building. The people were tired and very weak, but their stares showed a flare of hope.

The soldiers and the baron himself had not been able to get them to budge in the past hour. Thanks to the magic in Adwen's voice, they could finally go.

Baron Bartholomew was very relieved. "Well done, indeed. Thank you for coming all of this way, Lady Adwen."

She smiled, watching the commoners following the soldiers to the great doors.

The baron's scouts opened the door, scattering around the courtyard to ensure that the coast was clear. At their signal, Adwen and the baron beckoned the people to leave. Alex, Jack and Oryn stood with them at the threshold, awaiting her instructions.

Bartholomew watched the first few walking out and mused aloud, "You seem to have grown very powerful of late, Lady. I am surprised that you could have known to find me here at just the right time."

"I never would have known if you hadn't sent that letter to the Order about rescuing your son and daughter."

The baron did not respond.

Sensing that something was odd, she looked at him and saw a look of utter confusion and alarm. The feelings were contagious, as she soon felt the same.

Shaking his head slowly, he murmured, "My son is among the soldiers I brought, and my daughter passed on a week ago, Lady Adwen. I sent out no such letter."

Adwen's face became pale.

A shrill whistling split the stunned silence before an arrow struck Adwen just above her chest armor. The demon -weapon came from overhead and sank in deep, reaching within a hair's width of her heart. An unearthly scream ripped from her, Oryn roared in outrage, and chaos broke loose everywhere.

Thirteen of what remained from the Red Cult stood atop the lofty awning, launching a storm of arrows and red fireballs. Several of the baron's scouts were killed after the initial attack on Adwen that had signaled for the onslaught to begin. The rest of the scouts responded to the baron's call to retreat. Soldiers gathered the shrieking commoners back into the shade of the grand hall, as the last of the scouts forced the doors closed again.

Alex took cover behind a large wooden column, unable to do anything except watch. Oryn transformed into his elf-like shape, carrying Adwen away from the towering windows that were being punched out by a shower of arrows. The screams of the unarmed people rose even higher once the shafts came through with flames on their tips, setting the books and scrolls ablaze.

In all of the commotion, Jack was overwhelmed. His mind couldn't cope with so much bombardment between the screams in his ears and within his head. He remained undercover by Adwen, who was snarling and clutching at the arrow that refused to come out. The overload of thoughts and sounds made thinking nearly impossible, disabling Jack, rendering him as helpless as Adwen and the crowd.

A strange calm came over the Marine. He had seen this before.

When the incident occurred in the Middle East on his second tour, Alex had no recollection of what he had done to save the rest of the platoon. A battle had begun exactly as this one had. Some civilians were held hostage in a rural side of the city. The terrorist group had adapted to surveillance technology, finding various ways to hide from infrared detection. Alex and his fellow troops were pinned and caught by surprise. Everyone was yelling and trying to use repressive fire. Fighting back would have been possible if it weren't for the mortar shells being launched from a higher level across the plaza. Making matters worse, being in a rural location made it impossible to receive air support from naval aircraft. They were trapped, ammunitions were quickly running low, and support was not going to come soon enough.

Watching a similar scenario unfolding in the magical realm, Alex felt transported back to that unfortunate moment in history. In the seconds that he heard the radio man being denied reinforcements, his fear receded. After that, there was nothing.

Amid the magical flames and horror-filled screams of innocents, Alex's eyes no longer saw the present. His memories of that Middle East battle took over, and he felt compelled to reenact the forgotten choices he had made in the most fateful of hours. Numb to all emotion or feeling, the Marine took up his machete/short sword, mindlessly rushing for the door.

Adwen spotted her warrior heading out into the open. "Alex!"

Despite the power of her voice, he did not hear her call.

The baron also saw Alex open the door and leave. There was nothing any of them could do to stop him. Corralling the panic-stricken commoners was difficult, and the soldiers were not able to get a good position for retaliating with their own bows. Fire had claimed the way to the stairs, keeping them confined to the burning grand hall. With each second that passed, more of their shelter succumbed to the expanding blaze.

Bewildered, Oryn looked around and then to his leader. She was unable to use her powers with the arrow in her body. To even change shape would do terrible damage.

He asked above the chaotic sounds, "What must be done?"

Looking up into his gaze, she didn't say a word. Instead, she wore a pained yet determined expression. Then she closed her eyes and began to hum.

While Adwen used the one ability not hindered by the demon-steel weapon, outside her newest companion was lost in his own memories. Her voice carried throughout the grounds, filling the air with a powerful, steady tune. It slowly infected her other friends, as well as the people.

Ignorant to the song, Alex charged ahead with arrows whizzing past, all missing by inches. He thought they were the bullets he had dodged on his way to the stairs. His feet moved swiftly across the ground, over fallen scouts/Marines. An archer/gunman appeared at the top as he passed the final stair step, and he used his machete/short sword to cut him down with one swipe. The terrorist/warlock toppled to the floor, and Alex didn't slow his pace.

Two more along the same balcony saw him coming and redirected their aim. The two arrows flew, though the Marine thought they were bullets. The warlocks missed, but Alex's mind recalled one bullet grazing his cheek and the other passing through his left leg. It did not hurt in the slightest. He could not feel.

Gutting them both, Alex continued onward, laying waste to every cultist/terrorist in his path. After cutting his way along the third-floor balcony, all that remained were the fireball-slinging witches on the rooftop. In his memory, there were two left, using the mortar launcher, keeping his men pinned.

The Marine rapidly climbed the ladder. Once on the rooftop, he moved faster than ever. His blade drove into the first enemy he could reach.

Blood poured out like a dark spring as the rest of the enemies saw him and stumbled back, reeling at the sight.

No mercy was in the warrior. Alex saw the look of fear but was incapable of recognizing it. He could only recognize an enemy. The robed enemy fell to the shingles, holding up a hand in fear and pleading.

Alex was unable to understand or stop. A cowering enemy was still an enemy.

Inside the burning scholar's academy, Adwen's melody had taken hold of everyone, instilling calm. In spite of the mounting inferno around them, the soldiers and city folk were not screaming anymore. They were waiting for an unknown signal, a cue to go into action. The stillness of their minds also gave Jack some reprieve.

For the first time in the last few minutes, no more arrows or spells struck the establishment. Jack and Oryn watched Adwen sit up and finally wrench the witch's arrow free from her chest, crying at the pain.

With every eye upon her, she called, "Outside! Go now, everyone! Go!"

The baron threw open the doors, letting the frightened captives out of the great blaze. Timbers and rubble were starting to fall, but there were no victims left behind to be crushed. Adwen followed them with both companions at her side, ensuring her escape to safety.

Amid the clamoring for fresh air, Adwen found the baron in the crowded courtyard. She was weary from the damage done by the arrow but would not let it show. Her tone invoked even more resolve into the tired leader of the rescue party.

"Get them out of this city. Take them as far as possible, to the Order if you can and avoid the plains."

Bartholomew was concerned with her injury, which was weeping silver and blackened at the edges. "Will you not join in the march? My men will wish to repay the debt they owe by protecting you in your condition."

A smile flickered on her face, and she shook her head. "I still need to find my new warrior. I have to keep him close until he is marked."

It was Bartholomew's turn to smile. "I've already found him, Lady. Raise your gaze to the sky."

Alex had remained on the rooftop, standing still as stone. When he had rescued his men in the war he had found himself standing over the enemy who had been working the mortar shells. Though Alex had not been fully aware during the rescue itself, he had always remembered finding the bleeding body at his feet.

The last of the terrorist attackers was barely twelve years old. The Marine's heart had sunk like a stone, and his insides churned until he purged those feelings in the form of vomit and bile. Even though he had not been truly conscious, Alex had saved his men, but at the cost of taking a child's life.

Adwen was right, he thought. She had been honest in saying that this war was different than the one he had known. This time he came out of his trance standing over a real villain. The slain warlock bled blood as black as sin, wearing a smile that made even the Marine's skin crawl. This was not just a fallen enemy. Alex had a natural remorse for the taking of human life; an enemy was what the young boy had been. This wretched spellcaster was something else. At Alex's feet lay the remains of evil, devoid of mercy or redeeming values.

In taking this life, there was no reason for remorse.

With his same actions taken under entirely different conditions, Alex felt relieved. The relief came from feeling somehow released from the guilt for what had happened in the past. He couldn't have explained how, but his heart felt cleansed of the child's death. What Alex could not comprehend was the liberating feeling of forgiving himself for what had been out of his control.

Free from the burden, Alex looked down to where Adwen and the others were gathered. Some of the baron's men cheered for his gallant rescue, as he picked out the Tame One's kind smile among them.

The thought occurred to him to wave back and let them know he was unharmed. Deciding to simply go back down the way he came, Alex settled with smiling.

In a split second, the Marine was gasped by giant claws and whisked up into the sky with Adwen's cry of outrage echoing after him. The abrupt force with which he was ripped from the rooftop caused him to let go of the sacred weapon, his only means of self defense. Alex could do nothing, as he was carried off by what looked like a nightmarish dragon.

The appearance of the Dred had caught Adwen and the others by surprise. In all the excitement, they had completely forgotten that the thing had been circling high in the clouds since the last time they had been here.

Surprising them again, the massive demon flew by for a second pass. It banked hard, revealing the rider atop its back. Wind whipped Sycan's medium-length hair about his face, as he laughed at them all. The Dred beneath him bugled in delight, carrying him and their prize away northeast on the wind.

Alex's weapon tumbled through the air, and Adwen caught it without taking her eyes off of them. Snarling, she bid the baron a hurried farewell.

"Take care, Baron. Stay safe."

Watching her magically dismiss the weapon away, the baron's worried gaze followed her and the two warriors she still possessed. The trio raced out of the archway into the grounds, on their way to perform yet another rescue. Bartholomew's heart went with her, but his duties kept him grounded. Shouting so that all could hear, the baron announced their departure:

"Look lively you lot! The Tame One shall seize the day a second time. We must leave while the day lasts, or else her company's efforts here were for naught! Move quickly and carry your young. There is much ground to cover before nightfall."

Chapter 25
WHERE WE ARE BOUND

Desperation filled the trio, as they sped on their way. Adwen and Oryn were both in their true forms, even though her powers would be detected by nearby enemies. It did not matter. Their arrival was expected, and time was not on their side.

Jack struggled to keep up, as they left the city. Adwen took notice and did not hesitate to touch him in mid-sprint, shifting his shape in an instant. It jarred him a little, but he adapted and dropped to all fours, moving much swifter.

Wind stroked their bodies, ruffling their hair and thick coats of fur. As fast as the hounds were, it made little difference. The flying demon pulled farther ahead. It disappeared in the distance not long after the three lost sight of Deleon.

Adwen's chest brimmed with fear and anger. Though her strength was weakened, it did not hamper her abilities.

Letting loose a howl, Adwen summoned up the energy from deep within herself, and the two other hounds shimmered with golden light. In order to move as fast as possible, her light energy infused their bodies, allowing them to reach incredible speeds.

It came as a surprise to Jack, while Oryn was glad for the new pace. Their keen instincts drew them in the right direction. She and her warriors flew through the forests, hoping to reach their friend before it was too late. Sycan had something planned. It was fair to assume that it was something sinister.

Even with their speed bolstered, there was no chance of them beating the setting sun. A few hours passed, the daylight began to die, and the three eventually crossed the narrow neck of Broad River. A cloudless sky unfolded overhead, urging them to go faster. In the dark, their forms were shooting stars, blazing across the terrain. Where they were headed, they could not know.

Finally, their eyes found the silhouette of a narrow fortress against the blanket of stars. The Dred sat perched atop it, fanning its vast wings.

Fearing her light had already given away their position, Adwen doused it and continued to lead with stealth in mind.

Blades drawn, both Jack and Oryn prepared for a fight to the death. Once they arrived outside the foundations, she stopped to formulate a plan.

To Oryn, she growled quietly, "Do you know this place?"

"I do not."

"Not a problem," Jack panted.

They both stared and waited for an explanation.

"I can feel the minds of whoever is close by. Even better, I can tap into their thoughts just enough to find our way around."

Adwen thought it through, as he and Oryn waited for her decision.

"Okay," she growled. "You two will go around and find a way to sneak inside. I'm using the front door."

Oryn did not like this plan.

Jack didn't think going through the main entrance was the greatest idea, either, but didn't argue. "Whatever you say, boss."

She nodded and darted for the large double doors around the corner.

Oryn gave her a last glance and followed Jack, leery of this night's outcome.

Inside smelled of rats and dirt. This place had clearly been vacant for ages until recently. Sycan's scent was everywhere, intertwined with the smells of men and human blood. For the first few minutes of stalking the corridors, Adwen wondered what Sycan was doing by leading her here with Alex as bait.

Then there was an eruption of horrible screams and howls.

A full moon was rising outside, changing many werewolves within this lost stronghold. The sounds spurred Adwen to move faster. She ripped around stone corners, desperate to find Alex before anything could be done to him. As the howls were dying down, roars and snarls took their place.

At last, she came to the source of the sounds, and her way was barred. The end of the hall before a vast space was closed off by thick rungs of metal.

Peering down from behind the bars, she saw a very deep arena that had once been used for baiting bears. Now the enormous pit was home to nearly twenty werewolves. Small portcullis gates held them back, while they snarled and jeered at the morsel tied and trapped in the center.

Alex gaped and struggled to free himself, looking for a way out.

Eager to reach him, Adwen pried at the bars with all her might.

It was no use. After failing to budge them, she realized that these were a new addition to the structure. They were made of demon steel. Before she could react, a familiar face came strolling out into plain view.

Sycan walked along, deeply engrossed in a thick set of bound pages without a cover. Licking a gloved finger, he turned another page. Chuckling at the content, a devious smile curled his lips.

"I've read a lot of books through the centuries, and as dry as this one is, I have to admit that I just can't set it down."

A particularly dangerous growl thundered in Adwen's throat, as a snarl rippled her jaws and every hair stood on end.

Turning another page, his speckled white eyes looked at her. Still smiling, he added, "You are an engrossing topic, Adwen Andredan."

Taking hold of the bars, she grew angry and roared at the top of her lungs. "Where is Princess Eyrie?"

His raised his eyebrows, and his smile became one of bemusement. Finally closing the ancient text and making it vanish, he replied, "I admire tenacity. You certainly have that. After all this time, you hope to find the princess that you hardly know?"

Snarling, she glared, and her sapphire eyes glowed. "Where is she?"

"I like you more and more with every second." His eyes glinted before answering, "It should please you to know that my master and I had a change of heart. Simply killing the girl was too old-fashioned. The idea occurred to us not long after my somewhat successful murder attempt on you. Are you familiar with the name Melanin?"

Light flashed in the cores of Adwen's eyes; she knew the name. Disgust filled her growls and snarls. Melanin was the demon lord who had started the war Darien had won ages ago. He was Sycan's creator.

Sycan took note of her reaction and continued: "You see, it is so very hard for the more powerful of us to have presence in the living realms. For those who cannot manifest like the Wretches and such soldier demons, there is but one alternative. We must have a body of living flesh to occupy. Unfortunately, my master cannot take just any physical body. Most will not contain his essence without breaking down. He is too vast. The one he had successfully possessed was a dragon, if you can imagine. I trust that you understand where my explanation is going?"

He paused to watch Adwen's horrified reaction.

"A very long story short, the dear princess is with my master. She has grown on him of late, and he wouldn't dare let any harm befall her."

Adwen snarled viciously from behind the bars.

"I must digress," he concluded. "You and I have important business involving your new asset."

Alex sat tied and gagged in the massive pit, watching as Sycan came to stand at the edge. He did his best to ignore the monsters surrounding him and gave the vile man with a creature's eyes his most defiant glare.

"Your soldier is bold. The Light Spirits always know whom to choose for their battles."

Adwen attempted to draw his attention away from Alex.

Growling, she chided, "Our fight in the mountains was cut short. I've become whole since. Why don't we settle things in a more exciting fashion? Let's have a match – best of two out of three."

Sycan saw through the ruse. After laughing at her, he shook his head. "You are so new to this game. I would love to take up your offer, but there's no avoiding the subject of today's lesson. Please wait until after the lecture for all questions. Until then, let us hurry. It won't be long before your doting company comes barging in."

Frustrated, she glared and snarled, clutching the bars tightly.

"I've spent most of my years traveling the world of logic, playing games with the ignorant humans," Sycan said. "The spoken language here is elegant, but your modern lingo is very funny and versatile. Anyhow, I want you to listen closely. From reading the ancient text, I have come to a sad realization."

He shook his head and wore a convincing expression of pity. "My dear Adwen, you are a tool. You are a slave. Every whim of yours is not truly yours. The Light Spirits have chained your will and shackled your body completely."

In disgust, she proudly replied, "I am glad to serve them. If my will is guided by theirs, then I'm better for it."

A wry smile appeared on Sycan's pale face. "Just as you can puppeteer your warriors, the spirits control you. They guide your will, though they leave you your mind and heart. That is so cruel. To enslave one such as you is wickeder than any torture I could conjure."

She grew angry, gnashing her fangs. "If I am a slave, then I am a willing one!"

The demon was calm and patient. "That is because you are still naive. Think about it, Adwen. They took you from the things you cherish most. The spirits took your body from you. You are incapable of anything but destruction or healing. As a woman, you cannot ever be a whole one. They killed you by my hand to make you this way. And as an added consequence, your body cannot create life. How are you not a slave of their doings?"

Adwen's patience finally broke. Barking and snarling, she raged through the bars, "I am their sword for your throat, you despicable monster! Come out here and face me yourself! Let's put an end to this ridiculous talking and act!"

He chuckled. "I agree. Let us act. To finish this lesson, I shall demonstrate your entrapment."

While she barked and growled louder and Alex struggled against his bonds, Sycan strolled to a collection of levers. Each one controlled the gates holding back the ravenous werewolves lining the colossal pit.

Running his fingers across the levers, he said, "Unlike those bars, the bars of your true cage are hidden. You and I both know that, in your present state, those demon steel bars will hold you back no matter what. According to the text, when the Light Spirits take hold and force you to fulfill the unwritten pact, nothing can stop you."

No longer barking, she stood and growled louder than ever.

Sycan inclined his head, raising an eyebrow. "If that is so, then breaking through them should be like walking through water – that is, once I speed your chosen warrior to his impending doom. That is the only way you can mark them. The warrior must be a breath away from his last in order to be marked. You are a slave, Adwen. Do not worry. I know the way to set you free."

Using his dark powers, Sycan activated all of the levers at once and crowed, "Look on your own pitiful helplessness, Andredan! Woe to you, petty slave!"

The last thing Adwen heard was the clang of the gates opening wide before a deafening silence filled her ears, and her vision swam with bright golden light. Then what followed seemed strangely slow. As the light within her took control of her body, she was unable to resist or do anything else.

Her form lunged, tearing through the demon-steel bars as if they were spider silk. In a single bound, she darted down into the pit, immersing herself in the wave of werewolves.

She was moving much faster than they were, but the monsters were quick to notice her passing by. The crazed things buried their jaws into her neck and clamped onto her armor. Their weight did not slow her down, but their holds were mostly on her arms, forcing her to drag them along. No matter how many bit into her body, her eyes never left Alex.

Alex was gaping around at the sets of fangs closing in. She could see his look of dismay and fear. Charging forward with the beasts, Adwen's body leaped ahead of the swarm. In the blink of an eye, she bit into Alex's right shoulder and tossed him far out of danger. The Marine went careening up from the pit, landing hard at a painful angle on the stone floor.

Once he was safe, Adwen's senses returned, letting in the sound of Sycan's laughter. After that, the rest of the werewolves closed in. There was no time to escape.

On the opposite side of the chaos from the laughing fiend, a large timber door exploded as a fatally wounded demon was launched through it. Both the brown and the black hound warriors came rushing in, covered in purple blood spatters, ready for more.

Sycan stopped laughing and smiled, raising an eyebrow at them out of intrigue.

Oryn's jaws wrinkled into a snarl. Before Oryn could go after Sycan, Jack yelped in alarm at the mess in the bear-baiting arena.

Adwen's silver blood was everywhere. The last of the werewolves that had not accidentally poisoned themselves with it by biting her soon had their throats ripped out by her claws. In immense pain and in control of her body again, she leaped from the pit. Her strength was just enough to let her land solidly without faltering. Shaking off the worst of the blood in a shower of silvery droplets, she turned to roar at Sycan's victorious expression.

Laughing manically, the werewolf overlord ran for the nearby tower passage.

Anger and pain made proper thinking impossible for Adwen. In the heat of the moment, she raced after him, intent on finishing off the ancient demon.

His laughter rang in her ears constantly with the beating of her golden heart. She bounded up stairways and leaped through small corridors, always a short distance behind in the chase. By the time she came to the top of the tower, Sycan was atop the flying demon and already far out of reach. Even as he was disappearing like his fading laughter, she roared in outrage.

It echoed in the wind. A short time passed, taking away the last of her rage. While she continued to stare after the dwindling pair of wings, Oryn joined her. Paying him no mind, she could not keep from watching the demon escaping for a second time.

Oryn stood by her, noting the extensive injuries on her neck and back. The wounds were made by creatures of darkness, so the bleeding had not begun to slow.

Transforming into his elf-like form, Oryn did not allow his concern to show.

"I ordered Jack to take Alex to the forest and await our arrival. There are still more demons lurking. If we do not wish to fight them, leaving is the best choice."

She was quiet. Just when he thought she wouldn't speak, she growled in reply, "How is the staff sergeant?"

"He suffered a head wound, but it appears to be from falling. The only other wound was your mark, but it had already stopped bleeding when I last saw."

Another long pause came, and she growled, "I could have killed him."

Confused, he asked, "How could you have killed the soldier?"

"Not him. I should have been able to kill Sycan. Out of all the demons I've ever come across, this one needs to die more than the rest. Sycan must be destroyed before this war is over."

The monster and his winged mount were long gone, but Oryn looked to where they had disappeared in the sky. Thoughtful, he attempted to be consoling.

"The Master Knight himself was not even destined for such a thing. I deem that you came closer to it than anyone before you during our battle in the north. This war has only just begun. The chance shall come again."

Shifting into her own smaller form, she murmured, "I hope so."

They were turning to go when her strength gave out. From loss of blood and pain, Adwen collapsed, and Oryn was only just fast enough to stop her from hitting the floor.

He was alarmed by her passing out but knew Adwen would be all right. She was drained and tired. Gently gathering her limp body in his arms, Oryn carried her back the way they had come.

Preparations

Scarcely an hour passed, and Sycan's flight came to an end far northwest near the sea. With the most-decayed reaches of Dargadia at his back, the last of the first six werewolves commanded the Dred to land before the great arches of a long-forgotten castle. A smile of satisfaction lingered on his face, as he slid down from the demon's scaly hide. It took wing immediately, and Sycan began to whistle a demented melody.

With a skip in his step, he carried the tune on his way through many dreary halls, past smoking plates of nightshade incense. To him, the scent was sweet, while deadly for any would-be trespassers. Not even the witches he commanded were allowed to enter here. He passed one of their corpses and didn't give it a second thought.

Deep in the castle, he arrived at the high vault-like throne room. A few torches were lit with green flames, and he knew Guillot was here. The presence of the demon general did not kill his giddy mood. Seeing Adwen's blood spilled had him in high, deviant spirits. Almost nothing could bring him down from that high. But then he smelled something that did.

He was nearly to Guillot's side before their master's throne, and he froze. Stopping dead, he sneered at the shadows nearby. Growling, the whites around his pupils turned black.

A shriveled man limped forward, chuckling. The staff he clung to was his only means of support, while he steadily came closer. His hair was knee-length, wispy white strands against the darkness. The withered sorcerer smiled broadly. His left eye was such a dark brown that it appeared black, but the right eye was foggy like a mystic's crystal ball.

Sycan looked away and rolled his eyes in disgust and disappointment. Glowering, he sneered, "Why didn't I smell this sorry bag of dust and bones from the stairs?"

The question was rhetorical, but the old man replied, "You burn too much nightshade. Try something less pungent, my son."

"Through the centuries, you still have the nerve to call me that. I am no child to you, maggot farmer."

Guillot's fragmented face shifted, forming a crackling grin. To join in the torment, the general adopted their language, speaking in his echoing voice.

"This is a special occasion, brother in shadows. It is only appropriate to include our old friend. We know how much you adore dear Ozovath."

"As much as I adored the fool hag, Nadeen. That wench was useless until I used her to test my theories involving the golden heart. She always had a weakness for pretty things. As she laid a hand on the surface, her fate was sealed." A small chuckle chased away his bitterness toward the sorcerer. "The lore in the ancient texts was proved true."

Their master's voice surrounded them, ringing with impatience. In time with the tones, a woman's voice spoke from the throne, equally as malevolent.

"Silence! There is no time to spare for idle chatter. While the heir of the Neverborn still exists, our victory is impossible!"

The three bowed cordially, afraid of Melanin's wrath.

To the throne, Sycan spoke politely: "My research is completed. No lies are to be found within the king's texts. We now know what must be done to destroy the heir."

The dualistic voice was suspicious. "Is that so? This is not the first time you have come before me bearing news of the heir's imminent demise."

Again, Sycan gave the throne a sincere bow. "My mistakes were unforgivable. Destroy me at your whim, my Lord Melanin the Eternal."

The dualistic voice laughed lightly, entertained. "I made you from a piece of pure darkness and a fragment of myself. I cannot destroy myself for any faults, and I would never dream of dismantling my finest and favorite spawn. No. What is past cannot be undone. I ask of you now to sacrifice no more of your cult. Keep them alive and working to swell the ranks."

Bowing again, Sycan replied, "You are far too gracious, Lord Melanin. Your whim is my own. If I may ask, how was it that you were able to enter that body? Even I was unable to assist you with the possession. Please, do teach me."

"You should know the answer. In the end, I had to do so myself, but it was easy once the solution occurred to me."

"How did you do it, great lord?"

The slender form in the throne stood, extending both arms wide.

While their master's form had been seated, Ozovath was unable to discern the details in the dark. But now he smiled, recognizing the face that once belonged to young Eyrie, Princess of Dargadia. Her body was wrapped in black robes, as dark as the eyes in her head. The sweet, young face smiled back at them, expressing the demon lord's self-satisfaction.

Sycan was unaffected. "But lord, you said that because the princess's blood shared some in kind with Darien's that her body could contain you, though her soul could not be consumed. What was the way by which you entered? I must know."

Melanin gave him a haughty look. "The same way that you shall smite the Tame One. It is time to prepare, my servants. We are ready." Eyrie's head nodded to Guillot.

On cue, the terrible general turned to Sycan, showing a most hideous grin made of onyx splinters and shards.

A moment passed, and Guillot reached up to the mantle of razor-sharp spikes atop his head. Taking a gentle hold of one point, green light shone in his hollowed-out eyes before traveling to the piece he held. When the insidious glow reached the tip, he ripped it free, capturing the energy inside. The green light disappeared into the depths, and the demon offered the dark splinter to Sycan.

Sycan raised an eyebrow in curiosity.

"Take these fresh memories, brood of chaos. You will know how best to use what is within. Cripple her beyond healing that even the sun cannot mend."

When Sycan accepted the gift, a glimpse of the contents flitted through his mind. Instant and maddening glee lit in his face, twisting it into a far more sinister smile than even the general could make.

Chapter 26
HALLOWED GROUND

The rush of water over rocks was the first sound Alex recognized. It was nearly noon when he came to, with bright light in his face, forcing him to squint and shade his eyes.

Slowly sitting up on a plot of grass by a river, his head hurt, and he realized the sunlight was not the cause. Feeling his scalp, Alex found nothing. Then looking down at his fingers, he found old, half-dried blood.

"Not dead yet, jarhead?"

Jack stood a short distance away, wearing a more serious expression than usual.

"After your skull cracked open, I saw you really do have a brain in there. Lucky for you, she marked you just before it happened."

Alex tried to ignore that he had survived a mortal injury and asked, "Who was that sick-in-the-head maniac?"

A wry smile appeared on Jack's face. "Sycan. I'm guessing he didn't introduce himself before sticking you in a pit full of werewolves. He doesn't seem to be in the habit of swapping names on a first meeting."

Disturbed, Alex absent-mindedly rubbed his shoulder where Adwen had bitten. "That's what those men turned into?" He shook his head. "I'm glad to know we're far away from those things."

Curious to see how his arm had healed, the Marine rolled back the sleeve, half expecting to find a scar. Instead, there was a golden symbol. The sheen of the marked skin caught the light like metal, and he almost gasped.

Jack displayed his own matching mark, studying Alex's reaction. Jack was barely able to hear a whisper of the Marine's thoughts. It was difficult to make out, but there was no doubt that Alex was shaken.

Alex gazed out into space. Only now was the concept sinking in that he was going to be just like them. Thinking of when he had seen Jack transform put a hard knot in his stomach.

"Having second thoughts?"

Frowning, the Marine stared at the cop's cynical smile.

"Let me know when regrets come up."

Alex grimaced. Determined and frustrated by Jack's attitude, he countered, "Even if I do have regrets, I'm not biting the hand that feeds."

"Okay. Enjoy your last day of being normal." He left Alex alone to contend with the anxiety.

Jack was tired of waiting to move on. Seeing Sycan again had brought back bad memories, and Alex's comment didn't help. Jack marched up the small hill to where Adwen rested against a tree at the edge of the woods.

They were west of Broad River's narrowest point, where the distance from bank to bank was a little more than a quarter mile. Oryn continued to patrol in the surrounding area, allowing the others a much-needed rest. When Jack came to where she sat in the sparse shade, he expected to find her alone. He was a few yards away when he stopped dead, having noticed a strange girl with green skin and leafy hair whispering in her ear.

The dryad saw him and was startled, as well. Her face turned dark brown, and bark textures swept across her eerie body.

Adwen did not share the same reaction. With a tired glance, she acknowledged that her warrior was present.

Realizing that there was nothing to fear, the forest spirit flushed with green again and finished relaying a message.

Once the dryad had finished speaking in its rustling voice, Adwen nodded and thanked her for the information.

Smiling, the spirit vanished into the foliage nearby.

Jack moved to her side.

She watched as he folded his arms and tried to hide a bitter frown. "How is the staff sergeant doing?" she asked.

Shaking his head angrily, he replied, "This guy is full of it. I don't get how he can lie to himself and think he isn't affected by anything that happens. Not to mention the fact that I can barely hear what he thinks. How does he do it?"

Adwen was almost healed, though her strength would not be fully recovered until much later. Calmly, she explained: "He's shut himself down emotionally. It's the only reason Alex joined us in the first place. His goal is to keep going on without accepting reality. You can barely hear his thoughts because they are very repressed. It's the intensity of the emotions that allow you to hear the thoughts."

Jack rolled his eyes. "If he thinks that's going to last forever he's an idiot."

She frowned. "He's afraid."

"Of what? To cry? I know a thing or two about minds. The longer he avoids the problem completely, the bigger the issues are going to be when they do surface. This jarhead is a ticking time bomb. He's a hazard."

Calmly, she added, "Weren't you when you started out?"

At first he was irritated, but Jack found himself calming down. Her tone showed that she was forgiving him, and her thoughts confirmed it, bringing him a dose of much-needed relief.

Rolling his eyes and heaving a sigh, he asked, "When are we leaving?"

"My nymph friend just gave me an important warning. The demon riders in the plains have doubled in strength since their companion was destroyed. There are five now, and their territory reaches into the entire northern half of the kingdom. Traveling is going to be even more dangerous for everyone, including us."

Jack didn't know anything about the demon riders. Raising both eyebrows, he admitted, "That doesn't sound like good times to me. What's the plan?"

"At the moment, we don't know enough, so we'll go back to the Order. There we can find out what the next best move should be."

Oryn wasn't far away and heard as he approached. "I agree. That is wise. If the demon riders' reach has expanded, then traveling through the forests will be no safer than the plains. I advise that we take to the open hills, where our speed is not hindered."

She took a few seconds to think things over. "Okay, but Alex will be at his most vulnerable tonight. We won't reach the Order before nightfall, and that is a problem."

"I know of a place where we might take refuge on our journey," Oryn said. "On the day you set out alone to the coast, I brought Jack through a part of the plains. Magic on the wind drifted out from a place at its heart. We could be safe there."

This piqued Adwen's curiosity. "Have you ever been there?"

"I have ventured to most of my kingdom, but there has never been a need to visit the empty plains."

She smiled. "Obviously, they aren't completely empty. I like the plan. We'll do it."

Half of the day had passed, and this trek would first take them westward. After spending another night in the wilds, they would continue north to Plexus's welcoming gates. Adwen, Oryn and Jack were more than capable of racing halfway through the plains without stopping.

What they had failed to consider was that the distance they had to cover would take more than five hours, and Alex did not have the strength to ride that long. Their Marine friend was tired from the haphazard adventures with little to no food or sleep.

He was weak and weary to the point that they had to let him rest each hour. These breaks were unavoidable. Adwen knew they were pushing their luck, but if they were to force Alex to endure an extended ride and the demons attacked early, he might not be able to defend himself. Even with Alex well rested, they were still outnumbered.

Relentless winds were yet another element resisting them. Sunset was a short time away, and Adwen knew their friend was very dehydrated due to the unforgiving environment. She led them in search of a spring, knowing the night would bring incredible danger. The foothills at the center of the plains were in sight but far out of reach. Nevertheless, it was important to take care of the Marine before he passed out from a combination of thirst and exhaustion.

Eventually they found water bubbling out between a small patch of pebbles. It ran clear across the stones, deep enough for cupped hands to reach into. This place would be their final stop before reaching what Adwen and Oryn believed to be a sanctuary.

The three panted, tired from the hours of running.

Raising and clasping his hands above his head, Jack gasped for air, drenched in sweat. "All right, coach. I need a timeout."

While Jack joined the Marine by the water, Adwen turned to Oryn.

"You should stay with him and let me keep an eye out. If our friends turn up, I want you to carry Alex out right away."

Without a word, Oryn nodded.

Her eyes glinted as she smiled. "Thank you," she murmured under her breath and bounded away, changing into her true self as she went.

Knowing that Adwen was on patrol left Oryn feeling at ease. As keen as his senses were, hers were many times greater at detecting danger. They would not be taken by surprise, so he strode to where the two others rested by the spring.

Alex drank his fill, relishing the cool water running down his throat. Getting rid of the bad case of cotton mouth was an added relief. Though the spring could not stop the growling in his stomach or soothe his wind-chapped lips, the Marine chose to be thankful.

"Hey," Jack called to him, "how are you holding up?"

The concern surprised him. Brow furrowed, he asked, "I'm not broken, but I'll need to eat chow sometime soon."

Still tired, Jack laughed weakly. "Well, food can be arranged but not yet. In a few hours I can probably catch you something. How do you feel about fresh rabbit guts?"

Alex was unimpressed. A scoff escaped him. "You can't scare me with crap like that."

"Yeah? We eat whatever we can catch, and raw, I might add."

Staring down the cop with a calm composure, Alex replied, "Another Marine and I were once stranded in a hole where all we had to eat was rotting dog meat."

A queasy expression came over Jack.

"After we got picked up and brought back to base, I was sick in medical for a week. The other guy almost died. On top of that, we were given a full set of rabies shots just to be on the safe side."

Jack looked Alex up and down, disgusted. "You're one sick puppy." Noticing Oryn approaching, he added, "Hey! I think we can already consider this guy a cannibal!"

Having heard the entire conversation, Oryn shook his head. "He is telling campfire tales."

"No way!" Jack protested, "I would know if he were lying."

"You complained that you cannot hear his thoughts as easily. This soldier has just fooled you with a false veteran story in return for your constant blabbering."

Both turned to Alex, waiting for an answer.

He glanced between them and began to smile mischievously.

Jack was beside himself. "Wow! I've just been punked by a jarhead! You're still a sick puppy in my book."

Alex shook his head, chuckling. "I'm sick but not a sick puppy yet."

A brief astounded silence came over Jack. "You really aren't bothered by becoming one of us. I get why, but I still can't wrap my head around it. Have you actually given up on life enough to subject yourself to losing your genetic humanity?"

Alex ignored the question. For him, accepting the fact was no different than welcoming death. It was easy.

"When does this thing happen?" Alex asked.

Rolling his eyes, Jack replied, "Whenever a full moon is visible after sunset."

"But there are four moons. How often is there a full one?"

Jack barely contained an exasperated laugh. "Every night. Every night at least one of the moons is full. This is the world where the first werewolves were made. It never occurred to you that this was a frequent thing?"

Once the idea sunk into Alex's mind, he was wide-eyed and quiet. Then he uttered, "Oh."

Jack agreed: "Yeah. Oh."

Fighting back the unexpected feeling of alarm, the Marine thought he should ask a few more questions, just to be safe.

"Is there anything else I need to know?"

Smiling, Jack did a mock impression of an Asian bow with hands pressed together. "Yes, grasshopper. Do not, whatever you do, do not fight it. You'll only make it worse. The first time is the absolute worst, not to mention the slowest."

Oryn nodded to validate Jack's advice.

"I'm not sure about him." Jack pointed to Oryn and continued, "But the first things I felt were a fever and my blood vessels multiplying like crazy. It feels like fire."

Frowning, Alex asked, "Anything else?"

Jack became thoughtful. "I know there's something else, but it isn't coming to me. Anyway, there's still a little time to remember."

The Marine shook his head, smiling. "So long as it helps rather than hurts, I won't hold it against you."

As Jack was forming a colorful remark, Adwen's howl rolled out across the hills. It made the hairs on the back of Alex's neck stand on end, while the other two were tense. A split second later, Oryn shifted to his true self, lunged across the spring and scooped up Alex. Then he and Jack began to make a mad dash for the rugged rock formations.

From the Holy Hound's shoulder, Alex could see clear across the hills that were quickly being swallowed by the setting sun's shadows. Adwen's white form was bounding toward a sweeping, dark mass. It took a second for Alex to realize that the moving darkness was actually five demons on hellish horse mounts.

Having seen them coming, Adwen kicked up pieces of earth as her claws propelled her straight for the terrible riders. She snarled. The dryad had not lied. These demons had grown in power, and they would be very difficult to defeat. With that in mind, Adwen ran at them head-on, intending to slow them down and buy the others time to reach the safety of more rugged terrain.

The demonic knights saw Adwen coming. What little distance was between them rapidly closed, and she leaped, claws out and jaws open, flying for the rider in the front of the formation. But as she came down, they were prepared.

In a flash of dark energy, they each summoned a spiked shield. Her full weight struck the surfaces, and she was deflected.

A yelp of surprise flew from Adwen's throat, while she twirled through the air to land on her feet behind the fiends. She had suffered only minor scratches and punctures, which made her very angry.

The riders stopped to look back, and they laughed darkly to each other. Then three stayed behind to face her, while two continued on to deal with the fleeing warriors.

Adwen showed them a fearsome snarl, gnashing pearly white fangs.

Oryn did as she had ordered. He ran with all of the speed he could muster while still carrying the Marine. Jack was at his side keeping the pace. Once the Adrenaline surge had kicked in, the idea of being too tired seemed silly. Both warriors ignored the fact that they were weakened and ran full tilt across the plains.

Dusk had arrived, and the demons were stronger and faster as the last light of day faded into nothingness. Darkness fed the mounts, rejuvenating them to the point of swelling until they were much more muscular than before. Cackling at the power of their steeds, the two riders drew out their bows. Their targets were hundreds of yards out but were not out of arrow range. Notching multiple arrows made from their own dark energy, the riders took careful aim and released the shafts.

Alex saw the arrows coming in the dwindling twilight, though it was not soon enough to warn Oryn. Most of the projectiles missed by inches, only to strike the dirt around them, but one found its mark.

A black arrow struck the back of Oryn's leg, and he snarled. He went tumbling, trying to protect Alex from the brunt of the impact as he fell. Through all of the jostling, the hound lost his grip, and the Marine went rolling across the ground.

Dazed, Alex was almost to his feet when Jack came to take him by the arm, leading the way to any hiding place they could find in the misshapen land formations.

Oryn turned over and ripped the arrow free from his flesh with a mighty roar. The wound bled horribly, but the demons were approaching fast. They would run him down if he tried to escape. Then again, he thought and summoned his magical weapon, when was the last time he ran from a good fight?

The first rider approached to contend with him, while the other pressed on after Alex and Jack. Adwen's newest warrior was still vulnerable. If the demons could find him, destroying him would be a great victory.

The new terrain consisted of rubble and granite covered in thin blankets of grass and scraggly shrubs, crouched in random rocky shelves. Most of the steep mounds looked identical to Jack, who dragged the Marine along like a child, forcing him to move at a pace his feet could not keep. But when Jack's bright eyes picked out a small cave high atop one of the land formations, there was no second-guessing.

Jack gave no warning, and the staff sergeant felt his feet suddenly leave the ground. His stomach flipped, as the cop lobbed him up through the darkness. A second later, his back slammed down onto solid ground, knocking the wind from his lungs. The floor of the small cave was not forgiving.

He was still wheezing and gasping when Jack joined him, stealing furtive glances outside for their pursuers.

Very tired and battered, Alex turned over and used his first productive breath to ask, "Can that thing get up here?"

To Alex's shock, Jack whispered urgently, "Hurry and strip down."

"What?"

Jack approached from the cave entrance to say more commandingly, "Do it. Take everything off."

This request confused and disturbed Alex. "Not on your life."

"Fine. Tomorrow you can spend all day looking for a new set of clothes while running around bare-ass naked. It's your call."

After hearing it explained that way, no arguments came to mind.

Jack was at least courteous enough to turn his back.

With all of his clothes off and his now bare feet in the dirt, Alex felt awkward and exposed. "You better not be making me do this as a joke."

Jack shushed and whispered, "A demon is below us, so put a lid on it." Then he saw the sky and muttered, "Uh-oh. We're in trouble."

Alex was crouched low so that if Jack did look, there was nothing too private to see. "What's wrong this time?"

"Get ready for the worst pain in your life."

Before he even said it, Alex felt his heart beating faster than normal. Next came the burning sensation Jack had described, and he gasped. The feeling started in his chest before spreading to every inch of his body. Intense pressure rose inside, pounding in his ears. Blood vessels swelled and pressed in on his brain, making him groan, grasping his aching head.

Seeing Alex with his forehead pressed against the ground, Jack murmured past the pressure he also felt. Having developed so much in the long weeks, his wait for the change was only slightly uncomfortable.

"That thing will hear us. I can keep it back until the hard part passes. If you can hear me, I'll see you on the other side."

When the agony came, Alex let out a blood curdling cry. He remembered being told not to fight it, but that was his first reaction. Every fiber slowly splitting and ripping inside gave off the distinct impression that his body was attempting to reject this event. But once he tried to merely escape the pain, the changes were able to occur in rapid order.

Jack's transformation took seconds, but Alex's had just begun. Jack kept close to the cave entrance, watching the demon headed for their hiding place, drawn by the echoing sounds of anguish. It did not appear as if Alex would be ready to make a run for it.

Muscles stretched, joints crackled and bones extended in systematic fashion. As one portion of his skeleton grew, the tissues would compensate and fill in. For Alex, this process kept him wailing and cringing, overwhelmed by pain. His human face elongated with his neck, making it nearly impossible to lay his brow in the dirt. Then the changes in his legs forced him to topple over. With all of the internal shifts occurring, the sprouting of yellow fur went unnoticed.

Outside their cave, the demon smiled, dismounting at the bottom of the slope to eye the cave. It kept its shield ready and stalked up the grade, summoning a nasty spear into its free hand. With stealthy footfalls, the demon continued toward Alex's cries. His voice was already becoming inhuman, making it clear that a fatal blow would need to be dealt soon.

When the evil entity neared the mouth of the cave, the black hound warrior lunged, daggers swinging. He collided with the dark shield, and both went sliding and tumbling back down to level ground.

Jack righted himself but not fast enough to take advantage of the demon's surprise. Its nightmare mount reared, keeping Jack from reaching the stunned demon knight. Jack could only dodge the monster's shod feet, leaping out of danger. Once the rider jumped into the saddle, a snarl curled Jack's stout muzzle.

The demon laughed, brandishing his long spear.

Jack took a ready stance and growled, "Let's see what you've got, Chuckles."

His opponent was glad to answer the challenge.

Standing firm, Jack let them come close. At the last second he moved aside and slashed with both daggers for the mount's legs.

It was no use, as the demon leaped over the attack then kicked hard, connecting with Jack's lower jaw.

He was all but knocked out. The force spun him around, bowling him over like a lopsided spinning top. Fighting to remain conscious, Jack realized the rider was coming in for a second strike. It took every bit of focus he had left to roll out of the way and not be crushed by the rushing creature. The instant Jack dodged the attack, he scrambled to his clawed feet, sheathed the daggers and started bounding away. Remaining in a close-quarter fight with this enemy was not in his favor.

Maniacal demon laughter followed him, and the rider pursued, enjoying the chase immensely. Having something to run down was too attractive to pass up. Spurring its powerful mount, the demon rushed after the fleeing hound warrior.

Sounds of panting and hoof beats flew through Jack's long ears like the wind in his face. This was not what he had in mind when he chose to be Alex's diversion. His intention was originally to kill the rider in a matter of seconds.

"Wonderful. Sea Biscuit from hell is going to turn me into a pancake."

In an effort to evade the rider, Jack took sharp turns through narrow gaps between grassy monoliths. Nothing deterred the demon. It remained at his heels by leaping over or blazing along detours in order to continue the chase.

More dark, echoing laughter came from the demon, as it gained on Jack.

In the midst of the death race, Alex was still undergoing his first change. The grueling process was mostly completed when his hearing took in the sounds from outside like water into a sponge. Demonic laughter rang in his ears from some distance away, suddenly triggering something. One minute he was in crippling pain; the next, his mind went blank and unresponsive.

Jack's tongue lolled while he ran, turning in random directions. His telepathy could only pick up fragments in the demon's thoughts.

There wasn't much except for desires to spill blood and consume life. It was beginning to occur to Jack that there was not very much he could do to stop this demon.

Honing its aim, the demon knight prepared to drive the dark spear into its prey.

As the two passed back through where the chase began, the demon was knocked off its mount and to the ground by a heavy mass. Both fiends cried out, as the rider was destroyed.

The mount quickly came to a dead stop before angrily returning to take on the one who slew its rider.

Jack was first to know the demon was destroyed. The split second allowed him to turn back first, straight for the unsuspecting nightmare mount. He was much quicker in gaining speed and pounced. Daggers out, he plunged one into the creature's back for leverage, making the thing shriek. The second blade was then thrust deep into where the heart would be if there had been one.

Purple poured out the mount's mouth, splattering across the dirt, as the demon collapsed in mid run, sliding through its own mess.

Jack dismounted before the dead thing could deteriorate any further and get more slime on his fur than was necessary.

Elsewhere, Adwen was busy keeping out of reach from the three demons that chose to face her. When they sensed their comrade's demise, one paused, distracted.

The other two were not able to stop Adwen from taking that fiend by surprise, leaping and decapitating it in the saddle. While the mount reared to try to throw her off, she stayed on, slashing with her claws until it fell dead.

The remaining riders wailed in dismay to each other, calling a retreat. Their opportunity to weaken the Holy Hounds had failed.

Adwen found Oryn when she could no longer detect the demons' presence. He only had the arrow wound in his leg and a small cut on his muzzle.

Glad to see him alive, she shifted to her woman form. "Are you all right?"

He chose not to revert. His leg still bled, as he dismissed the sword away and growled, "My injuries are not severe. Daylight will come soon enough."

Adwen smiled and replied, "Whatever you say."

Oryn continued on all fours to compensate for the lame leg, escorting her in search of their two companions.

Alex regained consciousness crouched over a puddle of purple muck. It reeked like burning rubber and vomit, curdling his stomach. The first time he had smelled demon blood wasn't nearly as bad. He backed away, and it felt strange.

Loud barking echoed from one side, surprising him as he understood Jack's speech: "Thanks for the help, show-off. Bet you can't do it again." His panting sounded like laughter to Alex.

Instinctively, Alex examined his hands. The shock of finding short, coarse fur and claws on them made him lose his grip on the short sword, dropping it. The shining blade hit the ground with a dull thud, like the feeling in the pit of his stomach at seeing the changes to his body. Standing stark still, he gaped for a long while at his large, clawed hands.

Jack joined him, stowing the daggers. "And do you have to make me look bad all of the time? You must be a natural at this, judging by how you aren't falling over. It took me a lot longer to figure out how to keep my balance standing up."

Nothing he said got through. Alex was too stunned. It was a little longer before he realized his eyes were seeing in the dark. Staring around at the land that had been black minutes ago, it now looked like twilight.

The lack of response worried Jack. "Hey? How are you doing, jarhead?"

Alex's ice-blue eyes darted to Jack, showing just how terrified he was. His body was now seven-foot-eight and appeared to be even more weighted down by muscle than Oryn's. Brownish-golden fur was all across his form, and the scar over the left cheek remained, along with the blond hair, giving him a few similarities to a lion.

At last, the Marine spoke with his new creature voice: "This is unbelievable."

"Tell me something I don't know."

Adwen and Oryn came around one of the mounds into view. When she saw them, a laugh escaped her. "I knew the two of you would be great together."

Coming close, with one hand on her hip, she studied Alex a moment. "I have to admit, you're bigger than I thought you were going to be. How does it feel?"

Looking himself over again, Alex marveled. "There isn't much I can compare this to. It's like someone turned up the volume on all of my senses and shot me up with muscle-building steroids."

"Without the roid-rage," Jack added, tail wagging.

Adwen rolled her eyes. "Just for that, you can go get his clothes from wherever you left them."

Jack grumbled before darting up the rubble formation to the cave.

Observing Alex as he knelt to pick up his weapon, Oryn said, "I am impressed with your adaptability, soldier."

"I'm not adjusted yet. It wouldn't take much to make me fall over."

Oryn's green eyes narrowed suspiciously. "Then how is it that you killed the demon rider without being harmed?"

"That's my problem. I don't know how. Every so often, I black out and go into an altered state of mind. It's caused me a lot of trouble."

"Well, I doubt it's too much trouble," Adwen said and smiled. "There is the chance we might help you gain control of that so-called altered state." Seeing Jack returning with Alex's things, she announced, "The magical source Oryn was talking about is a short walk from here. Let's keep moving. The sooner we find it, the sooner we all can get some rest."

Yet again, Adwen's estimation was correct, and the special plot of ground was waiting for them through the maze of dirt and rock monoliths. They went along leisurely, as there was no reason to hurry. When they reached the hallowed ground, Adwen restrained a gasp, stopping cold.

Oryn was concerned and rumbled softly, "What is the matter?"

Her body was not of the living worlds, so she was far more sensitive to spirit magic. Setting foot where the fragmented body of power rested sent a tremor through her.

The three other hounds stared. Eventually Oryn lost patience. He growled, "What is wrong?"

Adwen's eyes began to glow brightly, and when they did, she saw what this place had been.

Hundreds of years ago, this was a wondrous basilica. Where the monoliths remained, spiraling pillars once stood. Everywhere was gold, marble and glass. The Light Spirits had commissioned Darien to build this place with his powers, protecting the purity of the magic within the earth.

The others watched wide-eyed as she slowly wandered farther into the open. Adwen seemed lost in a daydream, but Jack was tapped into her thoughts, in awe of the images she was seeing.

"Wow," he gasped.

Alex and Oryn gave him a glance.

Before they could ask, he explained, watching her meander about.

"She's seeing what this place used to look like. It's incredible!"

Adwen soaked in the scenes of glowing lights from lofty panes, relishing it all in its glory. Then her ears heard sounds from the past. Metal on metal echoed from some place close by, and she followed it.

Though she was alone in the magical vision, the three hound warriors did not leave her side. They followed her to a circular formation of stones that Adwen and Jack saw as an entrance hall.

A monk was fending off two dark assailants with a sword made by elves. Fine holes in the surface allowed every stroke through the air to create a shrill, piercing sound. The monk's hood was drawn, and the swordsmen fighting him were wearing masks, disguising their features completely.

As the combat went on, the monk wore down his attackers, but one of the assailants dealt a lucky blow. As shallow as the cut was, the blade drew a few droplets of blood. When they touched ground, the monk bellowed in horror and outrage.

The attackers did not relent. After another moment, the foundation shook, rocking every pillar of the temple.

Finally, the attackers stopped once monstrous pieces of rubble began to rain down on their heads with splinters of stained glass.

While the two fled out the temple entrance, the monk fell to his knees and wept, watching his home fall to waste around him.

As the vision receded, Adwen dropped to her knees, gazing at the ruins, a sad shadow of the temple's former glory.

Jack was also in shock.

Jack's silence was a pleasant change for Oryn, but the timing was horrible. Angrily, Oryn snarled and barked for Jack's attention. "Of all the occasions to be silent, you choose the one in which we need an explanation. What has happened?"

Jack watched Adwen sit on the worn stones and patches of grass before answering: "She was shown what happened to the temple. This place used to be pure, but it was tainted. As soon as blood touched the ground, the place just fell apart."

Oryn rumbled thoughtfully to himself. He had heard of things like this before.

"Was this the only temple?" Alex asked.

"There were three," Oryn answered. "A second temple ruin is hidden in a forest across Broad River. The third still stands to the north in Tanoaks."

"If this place is not pure anymore, then why is it safer than any other?"

Adwen answered when Oryn paused.

"The seal was broken," she explained. "The ground is still hallowed, but the seal that was placed here for Dargadia's protection was destroyed."

Jack joined in the questioning: "Did we see all of that as a warning? Are we supposed to go and protect the third temple?"

She shook her head. "No. This place was meant to fall one day. The magic in the ground simply wished to express its sorrow. When the third does fall, we will not be able to save it. That is not something we can prevent. It is destiny."

Alex growled quietly, "There's no such thing as destiny."

A long, tense silence hung about them until Adwen spoke. Softly, she murmured, "A good place to sleep is just around this hill. We all need some rest."

Chapter 27
WAIT FOR ME

Jack was second to rise in the early morning light. Turning over on the soft grass, he spied Adwen atop a crumbling arch, watching the sunrise. At first he thought she was in a serene mood. She was too far away for his psychic abilities to reach, while his sixth sense detected something close to apprehension. Adwen seemed afraid.

A welcome distraction presented itself when Alex stirred in his sleep on the other side of a large boulder. He hadn't woken yet, but would soon.

Gazing at the stack of folded clothes, a childish glint came into Jack's eyes, and he licked his lips mischievously.

Alex yawned, stretching while in a light stupor. The feeling of his exposed skin on leafy greens and gravel reminded him of the previous night's events. Eager to get dressed, his day started with a short search for the peasant garments. He did not dare to leave the shelter of the boulder. But then raucous laughter echoed from overhead.

Laughing hysterically at the Marine's frustration, Jack sat on top of a weather-worn wall segment. The clothes and boots were beside him, far out of Alex's grasp.

Forcing a chuckle, Alex called out, "That's a good one. You got me. Give my stuff back already."

"What's that?" Jack replied, holding a hand to his ear. "I don't think I heard a please in there."

After hanging his head a moment, Alex made an attempt to remain calm. "May I please have my clothes back?"

Jack's smile only grew. Looking about aimlessly, he cried, "I'm not sure, but I think somebody was talking to me. Sorry! I can't hear a word you're saying." Then he burst out laughing.

"What is your malfunction? Give me my clothes!"

The laughter continued. He was so lost in his own guffawing fit that he failed to notice Oryn leap up and join him on the wall. Before Jack could even sense the green-eyed hound, Oryn held him around the neck in a solid choke hold, dangling over the edge.

Gagging, Jack chuckled and smiled. "What's up, dog?"

"You interrupted my sleep."

Oryn threw him to the ground far below, where he had the wind completely knocked from his body.

As he collided with the earth, Oryn merely blinked before gathering up Alex's belongings. Against the wall segment was a slope created by years of erosion, which Oryn skillfully skidded along to the bottom.

Alex was grateful when the garments were tossed into his outstretched hands. Immediately, he began to put them on. "Thank you."

Eventually Jack came out from where he had been dropped, coughing. "Nice one, Cujo."

"My name is Oryn."

"What is that name supposed to mean anyhow?" Jack mused. "Angry one?"

Rolling his eyes, he replied, "I am named for a small green bird native to this kingdom. It is said to have a beautiful song. So tell me, what sort of name is Jack?"

"Glad you asked. That would be Jack the giant killer."

Alex was fully dressed and came alongside muttering, "Everyone is a giant to you, short stuff."

Oryn wore a small smile, as he watched Jack retort, "Shove it, Ole' Yeller."

"Right back at you ... Spot."

Caught by surprise, Jack slowly turned to stare, raising an eyebrow. Then he countered with, "Rufus."

Alex smiled. "Otis."

"Scooby."

"Scrappy."

"Lassie."

That got a complimentary groan from the Marine before he continued the game. "Toto."

"Clifford."

"Cujo."

Jack instantly protested, pointing to Oryn. "No, no! That one is off limits. That's his name."

Both warriors chuckled, as their stoic friend glared.

Before they could resume their friendly name-calling duel, an explosion of flames appeared by Adwen's lofty perch. Malik the firebird came soaring out, landing alongside her, and chortling and fanning his wings.

She and the bird were so far away, Oryn couldn't tell what message the creature could be delivering. It was reasonable to assume that this was serious and not a social call.

It was not long before the phoenix departed into another wreath of flames back to the Order. Adwen sat for a moment, gazing at the sunrise, deep in thought. Then she stood, leaped to the ground and started taking long strides to where her three warriors awaited.

When she was closer, she announced, "There's a change of plans. We're not going to the Order. A small pack of Hell Hounds has been set loose in the farmlands close to Plexus. They have to be killed as soon as possible."

Jack spoke, and Oryn couldn't agree more with his question: "What are we still standing around for?"

Adwen frowned, causing the three to listen attentively.

"That's actually the least of our worries. There is a very big something making its way through the White Sea Desert. If this undead transport gets to any of the three civilizations, the results would be catastrophic. It has to be stopped within the next three days."

Grimacing, Oryn suggested what he knew as the only option. "As you cannot be in two places at once, it seems time for our company to take two paths."

"Yeah," she admitted. "Because the mission in the desert is more dangerous, Alex, you will have to stay in Dargadia."

"Wait a minute," Jack interrupted after getting a glimpse of the plan she had in mind. "You're taking me with you on the more dangerous mission? Am I hearing this right?"

"That is correct, mongrel," Oryn said. "That should serve as reason enough to take more pride in your purpose. I shall not be present to be the heir's protector." Then he sneered, "As far as I am concerned, you are unfit for the role."

Adwen stopped him from saying anything further. "He gets the idea. Focus on your part in killing the Hell Hounds and protecting Alex." To be more consoling, she added, "We'll clean up the desert and be back in no time."

Her most loyal warrior huffed to hide a sigh.

Turning to Jack, she grew serious. "To get to the desert, we will have to make a short visit to the non-magical world. When we get there, I'll need you to stay close."

Showing his most innocent look, he held up his hands. "Hey, you got it, boss."

"Oryn, Alex, you both have a job to do. If all goes well, Jack and I shall return in no more than four days. Look after each other. Good luck."

He and Alex gave salutes before taking off at a run out of the ruins, headed due north.

Alone, she glanced at Jack. "Here is the challenging part: First we need to find a portal to the other side."

"What about the one south of here when you went to get Alex?"

She shook her head. "That one opens up hundreds of miles south from where we need to go."

"Perfect." Jack rolled his eyes. "Can't you instinctively find a portal that goes directly to the desert instead?"

An uncertain expression came over her, and she scratched the back of her neck. "Normally I don't even know where they are until I see one pop up or I come across a magical power source directing me to one. When it comes to things like this, I guess you could call it my inner compass that tells me where to go until I find something that helps."

"Okay," Jack replied. Fully understanding and being practical, he asked, "So what general direction is your compass pointing toward?"

She hesitated and finally pointed east.

"Awe, come on! We just came from that direction."

"I know. The feeling says that our intended path is actually a little more southeast. Are you ready?"

"Ready as I'll ever be."

Taking the lead again, she brought him southeast, back onto the plains. Without a human companion to slow them, crossing the open spaces took a little more than five hours. But after they had crossed, Jack needed a rest at the edge of the forest; he was winded by the long run.

It was past noon when the hour of rest began. He sat against a tree, gladly allowing her to stand guard. To pass the time, Jack let his thoughts wander to whatever Ashley could be doing – worrying about him, most likely. She was probably furious and scared.

Jack didn't anticipate feeling anxiety after merely thinking of his wife. Only now did it occur to him that they might pass through their home town. If Adwen were right about the demons, being spotted in the vicinity could put Ashley in danger. Making matters worse was that he was likely a wanted man by his own precinct, considering he had helped an inmate escape custody.

Then he reminded himself that the whole department was compromised. The officers were all under the control of some dark entity in some way or another.

That meant if cops were watching his house, waiting for him, talking with his wife to find his whereabouts, then Adwen was right; the enemy would hold Ashley like a worm on a hook, waiting for his or Adwen's slightest mistake. This mission was much more dangerous than he had originally thought. That realization put a sick knot in the pit of his stomach.

At the end of the hour-long patrol, Adwen approached to signal the resumption of their journey. She sensed his unease but decided not to ask.

"Let's go," she murmured with a kind smile. "I'm sensing the portal is just up ahead somewhere."

Jack's silence was ominous. It lasted long after they passed through the portal into a vacant valley full of oaks and pines. His heart ached for Ashley, and he longed to know whether she was safe. True to his word, he remained at Adwen's side, knowing that was best for both their sakes. Nonetheless, doubts and worries gnawed at him.

The internal guidance that Adwen followed led past farms and even around illegal crop sites. Any property that had security cameras was easy to avoid, though her powers could disable the video feed. Most cameras looked over driveways or yards, where neither planned on venturing. It was preferable to go completely unseen while passing through this world. Traipsing across a stranger's backyard would be counterproductive. They both clung to the comfort of tree cover.

Hours went by. Sunset came as they were traveling along a smaller mountain ridge. Jack had finally given up on the idea of seeing his old town sprawled out on the familiar valley floor. Darkness was upon them, and the last light died in the distance when he noticed a glow radiating off to one side.

Adwen also hadn't said a word all day since leaving Dargadia. When she stopped to gaze at the glow from the city, Jack did, as well.

He heard her murmur somberly, "I know how you feel."

Jack frowned and tried to listen to her thoughts. They were quiet, but he sensed epiphanies strewn with paranoia. Unable to tell what they were exactly, he replied, "I think you do."

Still watching the town lights blinking like stars, Adwen went on: "While I've been trying to save the magical world, my missions have brought me back through this valley more than once. Every time, it becomes more and more difficult to resist the urge to look for my family. I miss them. Obviously I know that finding them would make it easier for our enemies to locate them, especially because they are being hunted. Not knowing if staying away will keep them safe at all is torture."

When she paused, Jack's brow furrowed. "Are you saying this to make me feel better?" It was not working.

Adwen dropped her gaze. "No," she whispered. "To try to make myself feel better."

His reaction was one of surprise. "If this has been bothering you, why not talk to Oryn? He cares enough to listen to anything you have to say." Then Jack was apologetic. "Not that I don't."

She shook her head. "He wouldn't understand like you can."

Seeing Adwen in such an emotional state made Jack uncomfortable. If she started to cry, he didn't know what he would do. Whenever Ashley or any girl cried, he always felt awkward.

Now was not a good moment to be a comedian. In an attempt to put Adwen back into a stable state of mind, he shrugged and gave his best advice: "Worrying doesn't help anything."

"No, it doesn't. Nothing helps." Then she slowly looked back toward the lights and murmured, "I'm still scared."

Jack was going to say something more to try and calm her, but both of their sixth senses warned of danger from the shadows all around.

By the time his daggers were out, so was a swath of the colorful versions of Creepers. Clowns leaped from every angle, slashing with long red claws.

Acting fast, Adwen created a blast to destroy the closer attackers and stun the rest. The flash-bang did the trick, buying her a second to transform and allowing Jack to assess the situation. Both quickly slaughtered the enemies stunned by the explosion, as far more poured out from everywhere.

Stinking purple muck sprayed and splattered the surrounding trees and rocks while they fought. She snarled, rending demon flesh over and over, trying to keep the man-sized fiends at bay.

Beside her, Jack was faring well. To his relief, the ability to read minds made dealing with the monsters much easier instead of harder. When one was on the verge of reaching him, its simple mind would flair with excitement, instantly alerting Jack to its position. Having had so much experience in using knives paired with the telepathy made it nearly impossible for the creatures to do him any harm.

What Jack was only beginning to learn was that these low-level demons shared a hive mind; each one was mentally connected to the others. Once the collective minds of the Clowns realized that Jack was a difficult target, they changed their strategy.

Adwen was not an opponent they could hope to overwhelm, but a psychic being could be beaten by numbers and teamwork. Three demons leaped in from different angles for the warrior's legs, chest and face.

With the rest of the monsters assaulting him, Jack could only do so much. When they struck, he kicked away the one down low and stabbed the other flying for his face. But he was unable to stop the third tackling from behind.

He and the demon tumbled down the mountain, struggling with each other. Their wrestling match stopped on the surface of a granite shelf, where they grappled for control. It had his wrists, while he had one foot planted in its concave abdomen.

Jack sensed more coming down the slope through the demon's mind. He sensed them struggling with Adwen above and that they had her distracted.

Another series of thoughts ran through the network of demon minds. They terrified him.

<We kill the warrior here. We kill him, and our reward is the woman. The warrior's woman will taste sweet.>

Horror widened Jack's eyes, and desperation gave his body the boost of strength needed to override his opponent. Squeezing the daggers tight, he bellowed and cut off the demon's head with both blades.

"No!"

Adwen slashed, clawed and kicked at the attacking waves, growing irritated by their relentlessness. There wasn't enough time to waste on such puny vermin.

Performing a single flash-jump to dodge them, she made another flash-bang, annihilating what was left of the Clowns. Purple plasma coated most of the surroundings, which had fallen quiet now that the shrieking things were silenced.

It was too quiet.

Growing alarmed by the second, Adwen barked, "Jack? Jack, where are you?"

Jack's feet could not move fast enough to satisfy his urgency. After sliding and skipping down another steep mountainside, he darted through a small grassy lawn before vaulting over a tall, wooden fence.

On the other side, his feet found a sidewalk and a freshly paved two-way street.

Many times he could recall having patrolled these roads. It was a gigantic L shape on the town map, reaching from the top of a hillside directly west and south. Catching his breath after gathering his bearings, he took off again at a dead sprint along the westbound street.

The rapid beating of his heart made him think it might burst. Jack felt as if every step turned the world around underfoot. His reckless pace in the dark brought him to a pair of well-lit intersections. Whether the walk signals were lit or not did not occur to him. Few cars were on the road this late, but he wouldn't have slowed down if there was traffic. If anyone were to catch a glimpse of him running by, they would not be able to guess it was a man.

His frantic dash carried on down more darkened streets, past homes with lights out for the night. It felt more and more as if he were running in a dream world, a nightmare where everything was both familiar and alien.

Wind whistled in his ears, scents of gases and green gardens filled his nose. For a moment, he couldn't help but realize how strange his home world had become. The idea was too surreal, so he discarded it and put all attention into finding Ashley before it was too late. He could only hope he would find their wonderful two-story home before the demons started to spawn.

Towering maple trees blotted out the sky over houses like leafy umbrellas, and he knew he was close. Taking advantage of his nocturnal sight, Jack read the road names at the next intersection, just to be sure. Upon reaching the end of the final suburban block, he came to a stop, struggling to catch his breath.

Then he stared at a car parked behind Ashley's large pickup across the street from their yard. Once he spied the light attachments, Jack was far more cautious. It didn't surprise him to find a police cruiser guarding his home. Of course, they would be waiting for him to come back. As for getting inside unnoticed, that would not be difficult to manage.

Calling upon old skills from his past as a thief, Jack found a hidden angle of the neighboring home's roof and leaped up from there. Then he crept across the slanted surface to the gap between both lots.

He crouched at the edge above the gutter, studying every visible window for movement. A nightlight dimly lit the upstairs bathroom, and one light was on in the living room. If Ashley were in bed or out somewhere, she would never leave a light on aside from the one upstairs. This meant that she had to be home and awake.

Stealing a glance at the patrol car, Jack could tell those inside were totally oblivious to his being on the roof. Now it was time to combine his talents as a thief and a hound warrior.

The strength he possessed made him incredibly stealthy. Leaping to the other ledge, his weight came down, and he absorbed the shock completely. Drawing a dagger, Jack gently worked the screen loose and eased open the window, knowing that it was almost never latched. With that chore finished, he slipped inside.

Out of the many strange things Jack had experienced up to this point, he never thought sneaking into his own home would be one of them. The house was old but had been renovated before they moved in. This eliminated most of the squeaks of the floorboards. Jack remembered the majority of the noisemakers in the hall and stairway.

But when he was at the bottom of the stairs by the front door, overconfidence led him to forget the second to the final step. A portion of Jack's weight shifted onto the stair, and it sounded like a terrified mouse.

Freezing in place, he waited with wide eyes, his psyche catching frightened thoughts from Ashley, who had heard it very clearly in the other room.

Alarmed, the fair-skinned blond called softly, "Hello?"

No answer came, and her fear was overridden by curiosity about what had caused the sound. The police officers watching the house would have knocked first before entering. Setting down a large book by a lamp, she left the couch and nervously went to the front entrance.

It was dark along the staircase, but Ashley could see well enough to recognize nothing was out of the ordinary. No windows were around the door, and to be sure no one was outside, Mrs. Towers peered through the peep hole.

Jack was hidden just around the corner in the kitchen, listening to his wife's thoughts. As she looked outside, a twinge of sadness bit into her heart, as the hope of finding her husband there was dashed again.

When Ashley turned to go back for the living room, he had to make a move. Sadly, calling her from the shadows would not do. To avoid alerting the cops outside, he had to take her by surprise.

Once Ashley's back was turned, Jack swiftly gripped her body and covered her mouth.

Ashley's blood-curdling scream was stifled, but she began to thrash, terrified, fighting to get free.

Jack was too strong for her, and a grimace formed on his face at the distress he was causing.

"Ashley, calm down! It's me, it's me."

Suddenly quiet, she realized who had hold of her.

Jack's mind felt Ashley's mental stability return. Knowing she would be careful to keep her voice down, he released his grip.

The second Ashley turned around, she leaped into his arms, breathless and on the brink tears. As Jack moved their reunion to the sofa, she gave him a fervent kiss, expressing how much she could not put into words. She had missed him terribly.

After accepting the passionate moment, savoring her touch after so long, Jack knew he had to warn her. Very gently, he pulled back, looking into her eyes with the bright table lamp glowing behind her shoulder.

But Ashley spoke before he could begin. Dismayed, his young wife nearly wept. "Where have you been? The rest of your department couldn't find a trace of you anywhere, and they seem to think you're involved in something."

"It's hard to explain," he replied in a hushed tone. "I'm sorry. I didn't have a choice."

As he spoke, Ashley noted the changes of clothes and appearance. Confusion formed on her face. "What's happened to you?"

Jack froze, startled by the question.

Touching his cheek, she felt that his skin was smoother than before. Jack used to always have some stubble even after a recent shave. Ashley gazed at his eyes, stunned by their glow, despite the lamp light.

"What happed to your eyes?"

Reaching up to hold her hand by his face, he saw the book lying open under the lamp was their photo album. The pages were filled with images of him at the beach and the redwood forest.

Jack turned to look into the mirror over the table behind the couch. The face he saw was altered from that of the album. His constant five-o'clock shadow and pale complexion were gone. A healthy color had come into his skin. His eyes were almost as bright as Oryn's or Adwen's. Without Ashley noticing, he used his tongue to feel his teeth, finding both canines were a little longer.

Jack never realized how many changes he had undergone.

"Jack, what's going on? Why is the police department after you?"

Returning his gaze to hers, he took her hand in both of his. "The department is compromised. Someone manipulating them wants me dead."

Licking her lips nervously, Ashley was afraid to mention what was bothering her the most. "They said you let out a murder suspect, a woman. They also said that you went with her without any explanation." Tears swelled in her eyes. "They asked me all kinds of questions about you … if I thought you might be seeing someone else."

"No," he firmly replied, gently bracing her shoulder. "My partner tried to kill me. She … this woman … stopped him. And when I found evidence that the department was compromised all of the way to the commissioner, she got me out of there before they could try again. I wouldn't be here now if not for her."

"I don't understand. Why would they try to kill you? Most of them are your friends."

Jack grimaced. "I thought so too. They aren't anymore. I think if the ones controlling them are taken care of, things could be fixed at the department. If they knew I was here now, they would kill us both."

"What?"

"Listen to me. I stayed away because it was the only way I could keep you protected. But I heard some of our enemies talking. There is a chance that they could be on their way. It's not safe here for you anymore."

She didn't want to believe him. "But why? Why would they want to kill us, Jack? This doesn't make any sense. What did you do?"

Jack gave a wry smile. "They want me gone because … I'm one of the ones who can stop them."

"Stop who?"

"That's too hard to explain."

Ashley wouldn't give up on the question. "Who wants to kill you?"

Studying the determination in Ashley's eyes, Jack wondered how to answer.

Instantly, the back wall of the house and part of the roof was ripped away. Dust and splinters flew everywhere. Ashley screamed, and Jack shielded her as best he could.

Holding her close on the sofa, he looked out into the night. The piece of their home that was torn off fell down from a great height onto the next block with a mighty crash. While the last of the dust lingered, a giant winged demon came diving for them, shredding tree branches in its path.

Unwilling to leave a horrified Ashley, Jack watched it come barreling through the air and defiantly bellowed, "No!"

The pterodactyl-like creature reached for them with its long, serpentine neck and open jaws. When it was over them, ready to strike,

Jack saw Adwen's white form leap in and run up the fiend's neck.

Taking hold of a waving tendril on the demon's head, she wrenched back, clawing and snarling.

Ashley could barely make out the shadowy shape of the monster past Jack's arms but saw the Holy Hound clearly. It was on the monster's head, pulling at dark, shadowy flesh with sharp claws and fangs. The spectacle held her frozen, stunned.

"Come on!" Jack urged her to climb over the back of the couch and head for the door before the battle could get any worse. As he was reaching for the handle, Ashley broke free, retrieving her bag and keys to the truck. Then she finally allowed Jack to usher her out into the street.

The two police officers had heard the entire commotion of crashing and terror-filled shrieks. Leaving their cruiser, both saw Ashley come out of the house with someone alongside. Once she and Jack reached the light of the streetlamps, they recognized the fugitive immediately.

Gun drawn and aimed downward, the first officer bellowed, "Stop, Towers! Stop right there and get down on the ground!"

Through the barrage of commands, Jack yelled back, "Get out of our way, Lewis! Put that gun away and let us go!"

Ashley's pleas were drowned out by the shouts from all sides. Eventually Officer Lewis did stow his Beretta, but his partner came in from the other side. He took hold of Jack's wrist, putting him into a quick restraining hold. Both grabbed onto Jack, trying to force him to the pavement.

A few seconds into the struggle, Jack thrashed, throwing off one officer. When the other did not release him, he grabbed hold of his belt and lobbed him against the police cruiser, fifteen feet away. The man's head struck the panels, rendering him unconscious.

When Jack turned and his eyes glowed like hot embers, the other officer ran as fast as he could, disappearing around a corner. Only four blocks lay between him and the police department with plenty of backup.

When Jack looked at his wife, Ashley's face was one of alarm and awe.

Ignoring the reaction, he took her by the hand, leading her to the truck. The fight between Adwen and the strange looking Dred was indeed escalating.

They were tearing apart the house with their brawl. Adwen's ripping and pulling caused the elephant-sized demon to knock over the couch, launch the small table and lamp off to one side, and began to wreak havoc on the rest of the structure. This new variety of Dred had more armored skin than the original, making it harder for her to do more than make shallow scratches.

In an attempt to scrape Adwen from its head, the winged fiend flailed, smashing her into the remaining ceiling or any solid surface within reach. No matter what, the white Holy Hound would not be removed.

Because her claws were not making a difference, Adwen decided to be creative. She forced a condensed ball of light into a tight fist. When it was ready, she brought the punch down on the demon's armored head. A flash lit up the area for a moment, and the monster was knocked silly. It cried out in surprise, toppling over onto its back, knocking over another segment of wall.

Acting fast, Adwen leaped to safety, avoiding being caught beneath it. As soon as the demon was down, she scrambled to its angular chest. On either side was weaker armor her hands could pierce. She took hold of the demon's exaggerated keel and prepared to plunge one hand loaded with pure light from her heart. The blow would be a lethal end to the conflict.

While she paused to gather enough power, the demon's head reared. Adwen looked up in time to see the thing's mouth open wide. Before she could deal any damage, the demon spat a ball of slime straight into her face.

It burned like fire. Adwen howled in pain, blinded. Her eyes and face seared under the demonic acid, turning black and weeping green. The loss of her sight foiled her powers, canceling out the energy she was mustering in her hand. Horrified and injured, Adwen yowled in agony, holding out her claws to defend herself.

With the heir helpless, the demon struck. Long, ruthless tusk-like teeth buried themselves into her body. They sawed through chainmail and the silvery spirit flesh she was made of, impervious to the purity of the substance. The more it gnashed at her, the more she cried out, driving the demon into more of a blood lust. It was not going to stop until it had her heart in its maw.

Out in the street, Jack had to unlock the truck himself because Ashley's hands were shaking. She was climbing inside when he heard the first howl of pain.

"Hurry up," Ashley pressed. "Let's get out of here while we still can."

Jack stood before the open door, ready to climb in and drive off, but he hesitated. Then he heard constant yelping and cries from the house, as well as the guttural growls of the demon. Adwen was losing.

Ashley's husband had one hand on the wheel to climb inside, but wasn't moving. Instead he stood frozen, gazing down at nothing.

"Jack? We have to go right now!"

Adwen's animal screams continued to echo in his ears, piercing his heart with each high-pitched note. No matter how much he wanted to get in the truck, Jack couldn't bring himself to it. Suddenly the idea of leaving Adwen this way made him sick.

Ashley called out, "Jack? Can you hear me?"

Determination swelled in his chest. Meeting her eyes at last, he commanded, "Stay in the truck, no matter what you see."

Watching him leave, she screamed, "Jack! Jack, no! Come back!"

Pointing a finger at her to show how serious he was, he continued toward the house, yelling, "I'm coming back! Just stay in the truck and lock the doors!"

She did as he said, frightened of what may be coming next.

Jack continued at a run and jumped in through the house's open door. The majority of the mess was in the living room. That was where he found the demon, mauling Adwen like a lion with a fresh kill, enjoying tender flesh between its teeth.

She was weak, swatting in pathetic attempts to stave off the fiend's jaws. Her loud wailing had become wheezing gasps and whimpers, while the demon carried on ripping and gnashing at her abdomen and chest. The mouth of the creature was too bulky to reach inside for her heart. That was not going to stop it from trying.

To get the monster's attention, Jack snatched up a heavy bookend that survived the fight. Throwing it hard, he yelled, "Hey, fly boy! Come and get some of this!"

It hit the demon's jaw and bounced off, annoying the monster enough to give Jack a snarl. Then it continued to maul the wounded Holy Hound.

Angry and desperate to get the thing away from Adwen, Jack bellowed. He resorted to picking up the whole waist-high bookcase, lobbing it with all his might. It broke across the monster's temple, books exploding in every direction.

This was very effective at getting the demon's attention. A loud, outraged shriek issued from deep in the fiend's throat. Its red eyes darted to Jack. Digging out the golden heart could wait.

Dashing for the door, as the large demon gave chase, Jack pulled out both daggers. He ran to the sidewalk, while the creature came through the door, tearing out the face of the house with it.

In the truck, Ashley watched the scene unfold. Stunned, she stared as Jack faced what she saw as a red-eyed shadow.

He crouched low, brandishing his daggers. "Let me see what you've got!"

At this, the monster quickly reared and spat a baseball-sized mass of dark essence. It struck Jack's right hand, knocking the weapon to the ground, covering his hand and burning his fingers.

The warrior hadn't known the thing could do that. Pain and surprise caused him to yell, but when more demon venom came flying, his plan of attack turned to one of artful dodging.

It spat again and again, gradually following him onto the road. No more of the black blobs landed on their mark. By the time both combatants were in front of the neighboring homes, the demon began to run out of venom. Eventually the monster tried to fire again but issued only a light dribble from its lower jaw.

Taking this as his chance to strike, Jack moved in fast.

Before the warrior could leap at the beast's body, it also lunged. Striking like a cobra, the demon fitted its maw around Jack's waist from the right side. Twelve teeth the size of carving knives punched into flesh and bone.

As he cried out in agony, Ashley screamed from within the truck cab, watching helplessly as he continued to fight. She could see his blood pouring from fresh wounds.

Jack wasted no time when the creature contemplated biting him in half. He clenched his teeth at the pain, looking back into the demon's right eye. An instant later, the one dagger still in his grasp was plunged into the vulnerable, glowing tissues.

The demon shrieked, flailing like mad. It let go of the warrior before he could stab deeper and do fatal damage, sending him careening through the air.

Crashing on the unforgiving road, Jack accidentally lost hold of the blade and rolled. He could hear the demon roaring at the loss of the eye. Defying the pain in order to turn over, he supported himself with an elbow and braced on the ground with one hand.

The copper smell of blood filled his senses. In the moment before he looked up again at the carnage and ruin, Jack realized his error. The Clown attack in the mountains was a trap. Those smaller fiends were sent with the idea of feeding on Ashley on purpose. Not only had he taken the bait, his promise to Adwen was broken. He had failed her once more.

Staring at the forlorn man lying before it, the demon tasted his despair. Then it smelled fear from close by and turned to look back at the truck. Ashley's big, horrified eyes stared unblinkingly. She shuddered like a leaf, paralyzed.

Jack knew Adwen would not be the only one to pay the price for his selfish mistake. Even if the demon let Ashley go, her knowing about the conspiracy in the police department would ensure her death. They would kill her.

Then an odd stillness erased his thoughts. Jack's mind became blank, while a hot sensation swelled in his chest. Defiance overflowed his racing heart, and Jack's eyes burned brighter than ever. Sneering, he pushed himself up with one knee on the ground, struggling against the pain of his many injuries.

The demon recognized the expression. Arching its neck aggressively, a loud hiss escaped the fiend's open maw.

Eyes still aglow, Jack heard a sound like rolling thunder reverberate in his own throat. He reached within himself for his new identity and a very vicious snarl came out from behind clenched teeth. When he did find the power, he called it out with a mighty roar. As fluid as a crashing wave, his body shifted into its true form at once.

Ashley gasped at the startling change.

The demon gave a guttural shriek, goading the hound warrior to attack again.

With blinding speed, Jack answered its challenge. The black hound rushed forward, snatching up the dagger from where it fell.

Striking with crushing force, the winged fiend reached out to tear into his red flesh for the second time.

As the set of monstrous teeth flew in to meet him, the Adrenalin made it seem as if everything were happening in slow motion. Glaring at the wide-open mouth, Jack jumped, deftly avoiding the attack and landing on the demon's bowed back. It shifted beneath him, making him reach for a set of tendrils to hold onto. Once he was firmly anchored, the warrior raised the dagger, taking aim for a boneless section in the creature's anatomy.

It shrieked and arched its neck to strike at the hound before it was too late.

Muzzle wrinkled in a tight snarl, Jack drove his weapon deep down into the body of the monster. His arm was elbow deep in the purple mass, stabbing the infernal creature's twisted core.

The demon bellowed and writhed. Then it collapsed, vomiting dark ooze onto the pavement. Though it was severely wounded, the

fiend clung to life by sheer will, refusing to die.

While it twitched and scraped the ground with its clawed wings, Jack pulled the dagger free and slid down, flipping his grip on the weapon as he strode to the demon's head. Snarling, he thrust the razor sharp point into its brow up to the hilt.

Finally, the dark creature perished. Even as Jack sheathed his dagger, it began to disintegrate into foul-smelling ectoplasm.

Gaping and shaking, Ashley watched the black hound. It did not look at her as it shrank back into the man she recognized as her cunning husband. No matter how long she stared, she could not understand what was before her.

Having dealt with the demon, Jack's mind quickly returned to Adwen. The boots he managed to keep for so long were now destroyed, and his bare feet carried him back to the last place he saw her. Small shards of glass or splinters pricked the underside of his toes, but they were the least of his troubles.

Holding an arm over the collection of punctures across his gut and chest, his ears were pricked, and his glowing eyes scanned for the white hound. Upon spotting her, his stomach gave a horrible lurch.

Off in a corner left standing by the onslaught, Adwen's hound form struggled to stand, blindly padding her hands up along the wall. Silver blood covered most of her shuddering body where there were not green gashes. Across her eyes was burned black and continuously weeping more of the same green liquid like poisoned tears.

Silent, Jack went closer, horrified at what was done by the demon.

Her ears and tail hung limp. Silver blood dribbled from her nose and mouth. Unable to smell very easily, she could not detect Jack's presence. The pain kept Adwen trapped within her own mind, lost and afraid, not knowing where the demon had gone or whether it would return.

Jack set aside his state of dismay, and with both hands slowly reached out to help the white hound find her way.

At his touch, Adwen gave a start. She yelped, recoiling and crouching with a defensive snarl. There she shuddered and shook, growling.

Jack shushed and kept reaching for her but did not try to touch her again. Instead, he prepared to brace his leader with one hand and held the other before her black nose. It was apparent that she did not realize who was standing by.

Adwen caught a faint scent beyond the blood pooled in her snout. Sniffing more diligently, Jack's unique smell wafted into her sinuses.

Understanding that the danger was gone, the next wave of pain wracked her, sapping more strength.

When she did collapse, it was into Jack's arms. Though Adwen was large, he braced her body without trouble.

Cringing, Adwen let out a low and pitifully weak howl of anguish.

"You're going to be okay," Jack reassured her in a soft tone. "I've got you. Let's go this way. Come on."

After Ashley watched Jack disappear into the demolished home, ideas swam in her head. Was her sanity slipping away? Had she fallen into a psychotic episode and lost touch with reality? None of this madness could be true. But as her husband exited the gaping hole in their house, it was a sight she could not begin to believe.

The armored white creature that had dropped onto the shadow beast came with him, heavily relying on his strength. It was so badly hurt that it appeared to be on the brink of death. What was more alarming was that Jack was bringing this thing straight for the truck.

Adwen all but draped over her warrior's shoulders with one arm nearly dragging across the ground. She worked to keep moving, while Jack murmured encouragement.

"We're going to get in the truck. It's just across from the yard. There are only a few more steps. Come on."

With Adwen in such horrible condition, Jack was secretly terrified. This was entirely his fault. Everything depended on keeping her alive. At last, being one of the chosen four to serve the heir felt like an honor. In his heart he knew that this was what he was born to do; this was the calling he had hoped to answer by joining the police force. Then again, Jack thought upon reaching the truck door, he sure was screwing up on the job.

Oryn's going to kill me, he realized.

Looking into Ashley's terrified eyes, he called, "Honey, unlock the door. Backup will be here soon." When she hesitated, he calmly added, "Ashley, please."

She feverishly unlocked the doors and scrambled back against the passenger door.

Loading the wounded Holy Hound into the back seat turned out to be a challenge. Fortunately, the seat itself was just large enough to hold her.

Distant sirens were growing louder, as Jack closed her in and swiftly hoisted himself into the driver's seat. Keeping the truck lights off, he started the engine and didn't give the wreckage a second glance. They drove off, disappearing amid the many unlit streets before police cruisers flooded in.

An eerie quiet filled the truck cab. Aside from the purr of the diesel engine and Adwen's raspy breaths, no other sounds seemed to exist. Jack felt his mind reeling, desperate to form new plans of action now that he had the chance to think. Taking Ashley along into the magical world was out of the question. Doing that would make her fate uncertain. At least in this realm, it would be easy for her to disappear.

Ashley was in a state of shock. Blood trickled from wounds on her husband's chest that should have killed him. Though the sight of the injuries was unsettling, the light in his eyes had her attention. They were more luminous than the digital clock numbers on the dashboard.

Refusing to meet his wife's gaze, Jack focused on the more important task at hand. Adwen didn't appear to be alert, and he feared she could be unconscious if not worse.

He called to the back seat, "Adwen, do you hear me?"

She did not respond.

Panicked, he urged, "Adwen!"

A pain-filled whine met his ears, dispelling the alarm. "I hear you, Jack."

Ashley gaped, while her husband began to converse with the creature bleeding silver on the back seat.

"Where's the closest portal? I have to get you out of here."

After a short pause, she replied through heavy pants, "The park ... in the park."

Jack protested, "The park! Do you have a death wish? There is no way I'm going to carry you into the desert like this. We are going back to the Order, where it's safe."

She gasped at a fresh wave of pain. Once she regained her senses, she replied, "There is another portal. It's on the other side of the park. It's in the soccer field."

Eager to return Adwen to the magical realm, he began to strategically drive while sticking to the shadows.

All was quiet until Jack's thinking shifted to Ashley. Glancing at her handbag, he asked, "Do you have your cell phone?"

She snapped out of her stunned state and began rifling through the contents. Handing it to him, she warned, "The battery is almost dead, and I don't have the charger."

"That's fine." Taking a last look at the black screen and pink casing, Jack squeezed, crushing it as if it were an empty soda can.

Ashley gasped and cried out in surprise.

Dropping the useless mass of plastic and metal, Jack continued driving, explaining his actions.

"You have to hide, Ashley, and that means you can't contact anyone. Don't use any phones, don't use the credit cards. In the morning, go to one of the banks outside of town and withdraw as much cash as you can. After that, go north. Get out of the country until it's safe to come back."

Dismayed, she exclaimed, "You're leaving? Where are you going? Why are you leaving me again?"

"There's something I have to do," he answered. "If I don't go, we'll never be safe."

Confused, tears formed in her eyes. "Jack, please. Don't leave me." Looking back at the injured creature, Ashley continued, "You don't have to do this. It's not going to make it, Jack. Please let it go. It's just an animal."

Jack's heart stopped. His eyes bulged, and his foot stomped on the brake pedal, sending the truck squealing to a sliding stop.

In the back seat, Adwen yelped and cried at the pain of being jostled around.

Her sounds went ignored.

Ashley gaped at Jack, who was grasping the steering wheel like a lifeline.

Staring straight ahead, he felt as if he had been doused in ice water. Fear flooded his heart, sending sick sensations to the pit of his stomach. Did she mean what he thought?

Mustering all of the courage he possessed, Jack quietly asked, "Then what am I, Ashley?" Terrified, he looked at her, unable to breathe. "What does that make me?"

Ashley released a sob, tears running down her face.

Feeling her thoughts as she hung her head, he knew she could not understand. Forgiving Ashley, Jack reached and brought her face close. Their foreheads rested against each other, while he gazed sympathetically into her eyes.

"I love you, but I can't stay. When this craziness is over, I will come back. I promise."

A long moment passed, and then they shared a heartfelt kiss.

Jack pulled away only because he had to. No sooner had Jack reapplied the gas than he forgave and forgot Ashley's emotional outburst. She was too frightened and unwitting to understand. He braced his fresh wounds while he drove, passing through infrequent pools of light from street lamps. There was the chance that they could be spotted by unfriendly witnesses, but the risk was necessary.

Quiet pervaded the still air within the vehicle, constantly threatening to rekindle each of the occupant's anxieties. The question none wanted to ask was what will happen to us next? But when trees and green lawns were in sight, those fears evaporated. What came next would be moving onward.

Jack drove the truck over the curb onto the grass. From the back seat he heard Adwen whimper, "It's close."

The bumper of the pickup neared the white border of the soccer field, and Ashley gasped as a glowing portal materialized, suspended a few inches over the ground. It was not far from the western goal net, fluctuating with soft green hues.

Seeing it gave Jack a much-needed boost of confidence. Once they went through to the other side, he would take Adwen to real safety, where their enemies could not keep her from recovering. Leaving the engine running, he got out and popped open the back seat.

Adwen was as much a mess as before. Her strange blood was in puddles on the floor and soaking into the seat. Ignoring it, he leaned inside, helping her to crawl free from the confines. She could barely move, making the process all the more difficult.

To Jack's surprise, another set of hands came to his aid. Ashley took hold of Adwen's other long arm, offering support she desperately needed.

He only glanced over for a second before turning back to his mutilated leader. When she was standing on the cool, moist turf at last, Jack securely placed himself under Adwen's side, holding one arm around so that she could lean upon his strength. The sheer size of the white creature made him look even shorter than he really was, like a child supporting a lame professional basketball player.

Step by step, Jack guided their progress toward the portal with his bewildered wife looking on in silence.

Then Jack halted. Keeping a firm hold on the Holy Hound, he gave Ashley a baleful yet hopeful look. When he found his words, he asked, "Will you wait for me?"

Letting out a small gasp, holding back tears, she nodded and smiled.

Jack's heart leaped. His eyes glowed bright and warm as he smiled softly.

"I'll come back for you. I promise I will come back."

Too driven by high hopes to feel the pain of his injuries, Jack carried Adwen into the waiting portal, still smiling.

Chapter 28
DOGS OF WAR

Wind whipped over the plains, rolling tall grass like the surface of the sea. Unrelenting gales rushed into the faces of the two warriors running across the fertile landscape. No matter how the wind blew, both warriors pressed on in pursuit of this newest source of trouble.

As they ran, the sky turned steely grey, cloaking the sun with a veil of clouds. Farmlands began to appear, followed by swaths of smoke and scorched earth. Several acres of crops were burned to ash, as were houses and barns. They ran past three devastated plots before finding a survivor.

A lone draft horse harnessed to a heavy plow trudged away from the worst of the destruction. The beast was exhausted, unable to run with the large wedge anchored to the soil.

Approaching the jaded horse, Oryn instructed Alex, "Unleash him and stay alert."

As usual, the Marine did not ask questions. Alex sliced through leather bindings, while Oryn began conversing with the powerful stud. Only the green-eyed warrior's part of the interaction was intelligible to Alex's ears.

Oryn was direct: "Where are the demons responsible for this atrocity?"

"North," the horse panted, short of breath. "I was able to escape because my master left me afield. There was nothing to be done except flee."

Alex nearly had the harness off, and Oryn replied, "Are they moving quickly or taking their time in bringing destruction?"

The horse shuddered. "They were in no hurry. That is the other reason I live now to tell of it."

After the severed harness fell to the earth, Oryn thanked the beast of burden and left it to seek sanctuary elsewhere. On the run again, they could see flames flickering in the distance, a sure sign of their enemy's travels.

The farm still burned when they arrived. Part of the roof on the farmhouse was charred, but relatively untouched. Meanwhile, the large barn was a roaring inferno. At first they were perplexed as to why the house was intact but quickly discovered scattered remains of the family and workers. Alex was first to have his weapon at the ready. The carnage put him on edge. Where were the monsters?

Oryn kept his ears pricked, surveying the soil, searching for tracks. For all he knew, these fiends had moved on to the next unfortunate farm. His nose did not help him, as these evil things only smelled of ash and sulfur. Still, he continued to try sniffing out a trail.

Minutes dragged by. There appeared to be nothing to find and no discernable trail leading anywhere. Oryn could not seem to turn his attention away from the blazing barn. He took a few steps closer to the searing tongues lapping at the beams and trusses.

The Marine felt a sinking sensation.

Out of instinct, Alex called out, "Fall back!"

The green-eyed warrior realized the danger and jumped away. A jumble of fiery beams collapsed, landing where Oryn had been a second before. Cinders blasted in all directions, spraying bright orange flecks into Oryn's face, forcing him to recoil and raise an arm.

Finally, the demons struck. Two fearsome beings leaped from the flames, as if born from the blaze itself. Searing red fire was their flesh on a barbed onyx skeleton, mimicking the likeness of canine beasts. To say they looked like hounds or wolves would be a rough comparison, as they were more elemental than animal. Bred from pure darkness, the Hell Hounds lunged, drooling liquid fire and sulfur saliva.

Alex's gaze widened as it followed the monsters descending on top of Oryn.

One pounced as the green-eyed warrior raised his weapon in time, staving off the molten claws and teeth. He was knocked to the ground but transformed, tumbling backward and onto his feet. A fearsome light filled his gaze. Though the demons had used the element of surprise, they would not get that opportunity a second time.

Again and again, the Hell Hounds circled like herding breeds, flanking and striking repeatedly. Oryn's Greatsword was a blur, twirling and arching to deflect them. It was only a matter of time until a lunge made it past his defenses. One fiend managed to catch Oryn off guard, leaping in from behind.

A searing pain hit his side, making him roar and buckle. It was too late to repay the monster because it was already out of reach. The demons were fast and were going to rip him apart, wearing him down with unrelenting aggression.

Alex was shocked at the speed of the monsters, as well as the Holy Hound fending them off. He did not know how help without getting killed in the process. But when Oryn's blood spurted and ran from his side, the moment of hesitation ended.

The Marine had not taken two driving steps when a third demon jumped out of the blistering barn fire. It landed in his path, blocking him from Oryn's aid.

For a split second, Oryn caught a glimpse of Alex and the third monster. It was stalking closer, preparing to pounce. Before it did, he also saw the Marine's face become like stone, devoid of emotion. What happened next, he was not able to witness. The demons he was pitted against seemed tireless.

The third demon lunged with jaws wide open for Alex's face.

Holding his short sword tight, he swung hard. The edge caught fiery demon flesh, spilling boiling plasma across his chest and arms. He felt nothing.

The injured monster made an unnatural wail of agony, while its jaw hung freely from one side, useless. Angry with the nerve of the emotionless warrior, it reared up, swinging a set of sharp, burning claws.

Alex stopped the blow with one hand and did not let go. Fire from the creature engulfed his arm, slowly eating his skin and flesh.

The demon stared a moment, surprised before swinging with another other set of claws.

Alex never broke his empty gaze from his opponent's red pupils. In a flash, he cut off that arm, then immediately sliced down the demon's exposed underside.

Even more blood flooded from out of the Hell Hound, burning everything on contact. More spattered across the Marine when the monster fell backward. It writhed and howled, liquefying on scorched earth in its own fluids.

When it was dead, Alex's mind registered the pain of his grievous burns. Dropping the blade and collapsing as his enemy had, he wailed, gasping for air, while pain took it away again as screams. He didn't know how he had been wounded and was not able to ponder it. The sensations were so overwhelming that he was soon unconscious.

No more cries came from the Marine, and the pair of demons assaulting Oryn changed tactics to compensate for the loss of their third member. One kept Oryn on his guard, while the other moved away, coughing and retching. A moment later vomit came out as liquid fire, like water pouring from a spout. It made a seamless wall of flame, surrounding the other Hell Hound and Holy Hound.

After seeing what the retreating monster had done, a vague memory of reading on these things came to Oryn's mind. Though their ability to spit liquid fire was limited, it could be devastating. He had nearly forgotten they could do so.

The realization surfaced just in time, as his opponent opened wide to blast a stream of red-hot slime from its twisted insides.

Dodging the shot with a sideways tumble, the whereabouts of the second creature made him wary.

His search was short. The demon was stalking toward a vulnerable Alex some distance away. If Oryn did not act quickly, Adwen's most recently chosen warrior would be dead. Standing between Oryn and the downed Marine were a deadly demon and a very hot wall of hellfire. Options were few. Taking advantage of the closest demon's moment of pause, he did the only thing possible to stop the inevitable.

Oryn reversed his grip on the large sword, took aim, and swiftly lobbed it past the first Hell Hound. He watched it pierce through the flames unhindered and fly until the tip drove down hard, pinning the second demon to the dirt like an insect. It died almost instantly, inches from where Alex lay still.

The last Hell Hound looked over its shoulder and growled angrily at the additional loss. If it had had skin on its face, it would have been snarling as it returned its attention to the Holy Hound.

Again, Oryn found himself in a position with few options. Facing the Hell Hound weaponless was not appealing but better than letting the Marine die. His chances seemed poor, until they became downright bleak.

The texts telling of Hell Hounds had failed to mention everything they could do. To continue the fight, the fire and more solid parts of its being crackled and rearranged until it was standing upright, imitating Oryn's general shape. Its claws elongated to twice their previous length, flexing and turning bright as branding irons. The Hell Hound howled with delight and rushed to meet Oryn.

It swung searing claws for Oryn's throat, but he blocked with a forearm, following with an uppercut that rocked the demon's head back. The force did not, however, stun the demon at all. The Hell Hound swung again and again, while Oryn repeatedly blocked and returned a blow that did not seem to do anything. His wound still bled, weakening him as the fight drew on. Each time he blocked and repaid the demon with a punch that burned his fist on contact, more of his strength ebbed.

Out of desperation, he chose to make an unexpected move by not blocking the next swing. Instead, the green-eyed hound gripped the wrist, searing his palms in doing so. Then he flipped the demon, slamming it to the ground. While it was down, Oryn quickly turned to where he last saw his sword. He ignored the pain in his side, closed his eyes tight and shielded his face as he leaped through the wall of fire.

Terrible burns appeared on his feet, arms and legs when he passed onto the other side. To put out the flames still burning on his fur, he quickly dropped to the ground and somersaulted.

As he was coming out of it, the demon came for him. The Hell Hound brandished red claws as it emerged from the fiery ring.

Oryn stumbled when the burns and his weakness took their toll. He fell within reach of his weapon, the Rose Thorne. When the demon leaped to finish what it had started moments before, Oryn took a hold of the blade and turned over, holding it up with the pommel braced against the earth.

It was too late for the fiend to stop. The body of the monster fell onto the sword and then away as the warrior swung the blade to the side. Not even the searing fluids it released could reach him.

As quick as it had begun, the battle was over.

The sound and scent of rain pervaded the air. Tiny percussions of droplets on wooden roof shingles and shuttered windows carried on a constant chorus. None of the moisture, save for the humidity, reached the interior of the quiet farm house.

Waking was made unpleasant for Alex by the prickling pain in his many burns. First his sense of touch warned him to lie still, and then his nose detected herbs. His eyes eased open, taking in the wooden ceiling of the second-floor bedroom. The large bed for two was stuffed with very compact wool and cedar chips. Soft blankets under him made it much more comfortable.

Movement caught Alex's eye, and taking care not to move too much, he glanced over to see Oryn dressing his own burns. He was in his pointy-eared human shape, applying a dark green paste to himself. His forearms and side were the worst, even now smelling of burnt flesh. As far as Alex could tell, the same mixture was coating his wounds, as well.

Feeling eyes upon him, Oryn looked his way. Applying more paste, he asked, "Where is most of your pain?"

After thinking about it, the Marine gently moved to test his condition. Then he gasped when he hurt all over. Past gritted teeth, he replied, "My arm."

A few minutes passed, while Oryn quietly finished what he was doing. Closing the ceramic jar containing the herb mixture, he set it aside on a nearby shelf.

"Try not to move," Oryn advised. "I shall see if there are any helpful remedies in this place."

Alex licked his chapped lips and grunted, "Don't take your time."

The heavy rainfall dulled the noise of Oryn stalking the home for remedies. Vibrations from his footfalls could be felt through the bed frame. The pace was quick, but not rushed. If there were anything else useful, Oryn was sure to sniff it out.

In the meantime, Alex thought hard to remember what had happened in the fight with the demons. It happened so fast. One moment, two enemies were attacking Oryn and one was coming for him; then the next, he was in terrible pain and smelled of burnt ham. Obviously, he had experienced another one of his blackout episodes. He felt irritation at knowing the fact. Rarely had anything good come from it.

Oryn soon returned up the stairs with a vial. The contents were brown, like old tree sap, with the consistency of syrup. When he approached the bedside and uncapped it, he grimaced and Alex winced at the smell. A harsh, bitter stink came out like a hammer to crash with their sensitive noses. The chances of it tasting any better were miniscule.

"Are you going to make me drink all of that?"

Oryn struggled to keep his green eyes from watering at the odor. Dipping the rod attached to the underside of the cap several times, Oryn reassured Alex: "A single drop is all that is needed. The effect is far more desirable than the smell. Now open your mouth, so that the medicine may land in your throat. I wish to close this accursed concoction as soon as possible."

As instructed, Alex opened wide, bracing for anything unpleasant. He hardly felt the droplet's touch and saw Oryn was already closing the foul-smelling vial. When he stored it alongside the green paste, the wretched taste found its way to his mouth. It was like swallowing horseradish and ginger, but much worse. Before he could ask what the medicine would do, the pain began to fade. Tense muscles in his body relaxed in the absence of the aches and stings.

Also feeling relief, Oryn reclaimed his chair. He sat close to the bed at an angle so that the door and both windows were in plain sight. Alex couldn't help but notice the strategic position he chose.

Feeling somewhat drugged, the Marine asked, "How long have you been doing this? You seem like you've been at war all your life."

He was quiet and then answered, "In a manner of speaking, I have been."

Alex frowned. "I've met kids who never knew what peace was. It shouldn't be that way for children."

Raising an eyebrow, Oryn advised the soldier, "The medicine I gave you is potent. It has the tendency to make one speak more openly than one would otherwise. Such occasions have caused many a feud. Watch your words carefully."

Alex didn't care at the moment. "What happened out there? I don't remember very much, and it's driving me crazy. I want to know how we got out alive."

The question helped Oryn draw a conclusion he was waiting to confirm. A sly smile came to him. "When one of the demons put you in significant danger, it caused you to respond in a way that made your mind go quiet."

Shocked that Oryn could describe his problem with so brief a description, he almost gasped. "How do you know that?"

"I saw your eyes. As for what happened, you gutted the fiend mere seconds into the battle. While I was a part of the Order, I instructed one or two men with such a trait as yours."

All Alex could think to say was a surprised, "Oh."

"If you wish it, I may begin training you in controlling your skill."

"What is it? It's been a problem for a long time."

"Every race has a different name for it, but men call someone such as you a berserker. When faced with imminent combat, you lose consciousness and fight without emotion or feeling. An odd form of the trait is in you. The silent berserker is more difficult to identify, as the usual type is rather volatile and remembers seeing everything in red."

Alex became more curious. "Will I ever be able to remember what happened, or will I always forget the things I do?"

Oryn was reassuring. "You cannot recall the events, as you have not yet tapped into the side of your mind responsible. Once I teach you how, your lost memories will be returned to you. It should be accomplished in a day or two at most."

The idea was pleasing to Alex, until he thought twice. A sour expression came over him, and he fell silent.

With the added side effect from the pain remedy, the Marine was much easier for Oryn to read. "What is so unsavory about knowing your actions?" Oryn asked.

"I don't think I want to know all of them. One of them is something that would be too painful to have in my head. I don't see how I could go on living if it turned out to be the truth."

Oryn already knew what he was insinuating. The drug also seemed to dull one's ability to be elusive in conversation. Being firm, Oryn said, "You could not have killed the one you love."

Alex was irritated, as the medicine kept him from becoming outraged. "You can't know that for sure."

Looking firmly into the Marine's ice-blue eyes, Oryn went on: "The signs are undisputable. Your ability can only respond to a threat to your life. Even in such a state, you could not confuse a loved one with a danger. For added measure, Adwen says that you are innocent of the crime. What more proof could you need to stop thinking you could be responsible?"

A long silenced followed.

Looking away, Alex's mood matched the weather outside; it was grey and dreary. Nothing Oryn could say would improve it.

At last, the Marine said, "I was downstairs when I knew something was wrong. Even though I was so close to where it happened, even if I had not done it, the truth is that I wasn't there when she needed me. I failed her."

Oryn waited before changing the subject. "The medicine should ease you to sleep. In the morn, we shall begin the training."

The remainder of the night was filled with wind and torrents of rain. It washed away the flames, purging the farmlands of any remaining cinders. While Oryn stood watch, his mind drifted off to thoughts of Adwen and Jack. If something were to go wrong, ending with her death, he would hold Jack accountable. In the end, he would blame himself, no differently than the Marine.

Chapter 29
FRIENDS IN DARK PLACES

The flash of going through the portal lasted a second, engulfing Jack's sight as he helped Adwen limp along. When it dissipated and the magical realm opened around them, it came with the unsettling feeling of falling.

By the light of the moons, both fell several feet and landed on the side of a gigantic dune. Jack tumbled and bellowed on the way down. Stumbling to his feet, he cried, "Adwen, are you crazy! You can't save anybody right now. I have to take you back to the Order!"

That was when Jack realized his lack of balance was not due to the long tumble. Unable to see properly, all of his senses fluctuated, causing him to stagger as he searched for Adwen. Jack dropped to his knees, succumbing to the effects, lost in a confusion of hearing, sight and smell. A hot feeling in his core grew, spreading to the rest of him. When it disappeared, the world came into focus and in greater detail than he had ever experienced before.

Next he noticed that his leather gear was gone. It was replaced by light armor strewn with detailed line markings. The harness and daggers were missing, but the new clothing grabbed his attention. His gloves were open for his forefingers and thumbs, perfect for his specialties with knives and lock picking. Rubbing his thumbs and index digits felt so sensitive that he could feel every ridge in his skin.

After feeling his elongated fangs, he reached up to find his ears were now like Adwen's and Oryn's. They picked up every sound of the desert. In the distance, a lizard was skittering over the grains of white sand, hunting insects. Another sound was strange, making him look around, confounded by it.

The noises came from behind, and when he looked, his luminous eyes widened with alarm. Adwen's body was being dragged over the top of another dune, and he only glimpsed her head disappearing over to the other side.

Jack sprinted after her. As he crested the sandy peak, he found her on the northern face. Small worm-like demons were working hard, tugging at her with sharp teeth, as others burrowed under the sand to move her more quickly. Her body burned their skin on contact. Every few seconds, new worms would rise up to take the place of those that disintegrated from holding on too long.

Jack ran after the foul things, kicking them away, sending them shrieking through the air. When he wished he had his daggers back, they materialized in his hands. Jack took a split second to be surprised but went straight back to driving the demons away from Adwen. The last of them quickly retreated, squealing and hissing, burrowing down out of sight.

Only when he could no longer smell them did he dismiss the blades and turn to his leader. She was alive and barely conscious. By now Jack was over the frustration of Adwen not cooperating with his attempt to return her to the Order. Kneeling beside her, he was back to being worried.

"Adwen, if you can hear me, I need to know where to go from here. I don't see anything but tons of sand. It isn't safe."

A meaningless whimper came as a response.

"Adwen? I don't know where to take you. I have to know where to go. Wake up."

A sound like distant thunder rumbled underfoot.

Jack froze and slowly looked out across the empty sands. All was still again, though a feeling of terrible dread began to fill him. The desert became quiet, just as a forest falls still before a predator lunges for its kill. Even the wind stopped blowing. When Jack's sixth sense began to pick up a growing presence on its way to the surface, the need for Adwen to be awake redoubled.

She was beginning to come around, as the sand before them swelled and shifted. Two digging arms like that of a mole brushed aside more and more sand, drawing the rest of its enormous body into the open air. The sheer size of it made Jack stop breathing, for fear it would sense him. It was not unlike seeing a beached blue whale, except the height was more than a four-story building.

This thing's appearance was like a frog he had seen on education channels, with its back covered in pores for holding its young. This monster was much more bulbous and hunch-backed. The holes across its back and sides stretched between hundreds of tall spikes, opening and closing at random. When the titanic creature brought the rest of itself above ground, it took a deep breath and released a long, wheezing sigh.

While the look of the monster was horrible, the smell made Jack gag and flinch.

The stench was strong enough to even wake up Adwen. Blinking, her blind eyes appeared green like jade marbles. Closing them again, she quietly asked, "What is it?"

Crouching low under the shadow of the behemoth, Jack murmured, "You don't want to know."

"That bad, huh?"

"Look," he whispered, watching the monster's yellow eyes open to the size of car windshields, "I need you to change shape, right now. I don't think we can get away if you stay in this form."

The monster caught sight of them, making Jack all the more alarmed.

"I don't have very much strength," she whimpered. "If I change, I will be much weaker. I will be unconscious. There's the chance I may not be able to wake up at all."

"We're running out of time, and I don't see any other solutions."

As the giant monster recognized the beings as enemies, it leered and bellowed, whipping streams of sand in all directions with its rancid breath.

Jack hollered, "Do it now!"

It moved to snap them up in its wide, jagged mouth.

At the same time that Adwen shifted into her smaller body, Jack rapidly changed into his larger one. He then whisked her off, headed southbound as fast as he could.

The monster only found sand with its jaws. Angered by missing the morsels, it bellowed again. This time small flying demons spewed out like spittle carried on stale breath after the Holy Hounds.

Running had never felt so effortless to Jack. His strength kept him just out of reach of the small winged demons. They trilled and shrieked, beating the air as fast as they could.

Suddenly, larger worms came up through the sand, trying to strike Jack's paws and slow him down. His psychic mind gave him an early warning at each turn, letting him know when to dodge an attack. Each one erupted from under the sand, snapping its round mouth full of teeth. The chase went on for what seemed like forever. Eventually, the things stopped following and disappeared.

Jack surveyed the desert, seeing nothing but the same desolate landscape. A telltale pale light was in the east, announcing the start of dawn.

Jack had not forgotten how those first rays from the sun affected Adwen. The sands had leveled off, and letting her lie down would not keep her from feeling the light of day.

Gently, he lowered her to the ground with his large claws. She seemed lifeless. It frightened him, and he reached to touch her neck for a pulse. After waiting and feeling nothing, his nerves began to come undone.

A piece of sunlight fell across her face. The rays did not dance as they had always done before. Then, before he took his finger pad from her skin, a weak pulse began there. Following it, the light shone and swirled across her like solar flares. Relief washed over Jack, causing his new curled tail to wag contentedly.

A tingle of nearby thoughts alerted him again, putting Jack back on his guard. He crouched over Adwen, summoning his daggers, looking for the stalkers.

Just as he thought, several men were creeping out from behind inconspicuous mounds of sand. They had their swords out and rag masks across their mouths.

He growled and snapped, showing his fangs. "Keep back! You don't want a piece of me. I've been having a very rotten day."

They could tell the hound was not bluffing with his display of ferocity. It did not make them back down. Slowly moving closer, each studied the black and white beast in light armor.

Before anyone moved to attack, the leader of the team called out a series of sentences. All of the men stowed their weapons, surprised by what was said.

One came forward, pulling away the cloth from his face.

Jack eyed him closely, not ready to put down his weapons.

In English with a heavy accent, the man welcomed him and bowed, "Greetings, warrior of Adwen Andredan. We were scouting this place when we found you and did not know if you were friend or foe."

Then he saw Adwen and recognized her right away. Alarmed, he shouted in his own language, making the others agitated. "What has happened to the heir?"

Jack changed his form to better explain himself. "We were led into a trap. Where can we take her to heal after the sun is finished rising?"

"Come," beckoned the scout leader. "There is a hidden place near here."

The men brought Jack to a small oasis. A trap door was hidden under several layers of sand and a heavy cloth. Jack insisted that they let Adwen stay above their outpost until she was in better shape. Minotaur roamed this territory, and the scouts made it clear that she would need to be taken below soon.

As Jack guarded Adwen topside, he became aware that the light was healing him twice as fast as before, melting off aches and pains. It felt as though hands were gently stroking and massaging him, leaving behind comfort.

When the time came to retreat into the scouts' den, Adwen's eyes and most other wounds were healed. Down a narrow ladder, Jack found a spacious cave. Water from the spring above trickled into a stone pool, making filling flasks easy. Lanterns flickered, creating a maze of light and shadows across the floor. The men led him to a dry, level location, where a few beds were made. There he set her on the blankets to rest. The lead scout indicated that he would need to speak with her once she was awake.

A chair was given to Jack while he waited, still watching over Adwen as she slept. Hours dragged on, passing lazily with no purpose but to annoy the warrior. They could not stay here forever. He would feel much better if they were in Dargadia. That kingdom was dangerous, but this one was totally unfamiliar. At least if Oryn were here, Jack would not need to worry so much about keeping an eye on his leader. Being given this enormous responsibility made him anxious.

Eventually, his mind picked up a spark of activity from her. When she opened her eyes, they were deep blue again. Glancing at his relieved expression, she said, "Like the new look."

He rolled his eyes. "My face looks better than yours did a while ago. As for the clothes, they're way more comfortable than going commando in leather."

She laughed softly. "I'll be ready to move in a few hours. We have to take care of what we found in the desert."

Jack's grimace showed how he felt about the idea. "I would ask if you were kidding, but I know you're not. What was that thing?"

"An ancient form of undead transport. It's likely to be the last one. If they had more, they would have destroyed the desert kingdoms a long time ago. There's only one reason it would be summoned now. Somebody ordered the king of the undead to do it."

"Why?"

"Tactical reasons. They didn't know we would make it to the desert. Their plan was to kill us in the non-magical world. Sending the behemoth was meant to draw us into traveling through the portals. Icing on the cake would be launching an assault on the rallying desert armies. Since we've made it, their plan is going to fall apart." Adwen chuckled.

Irritated with the understatement, he retorted, "We almost didn't make it, you lunatic. You didn't have a pulse at one point."

She still smiled. "Sorry about that."

"I don't think you are. It's just the two of us on the other half of the world from the others, and if you had died, everything would be over."

"Now you're exaggerating. This is not the other side of the world from Dargadia. It's just a few hundred miles. Secondly, my heart was only on the verge of stopping. That doesn't mean the war is lost."

He was nonplused. "Can you hear yourself? If your heart stops, it doesn't mean the war is over? If your heart stops you're dead. D-E-A-D."

Raising an eyebrow, Adwen waited for him to calm down.

Suddenly, Jack was curious. "What are you saying?"

"It's time I told you a secret," she said quietly. "My heart beats to keep me in this world. If it does stop for too long, my presence will cross over to the spirit realm. I can return if I am called. Only Oryn can do it. Remember that, just in case we run into a complication."

For a while Jack stared. "Why him? Why can't the rest of us do it?"

She didn't answer, and instinctively, Jack knew why.

Adwen stepped back into her role as commander. "Could you please find the leader so I can talk with him?"

Jack was not sure what to think about this secret, as she called it. That did not matter as much as this task and returning to Dargadia in one piece, so he stowed the knowledge and did as she asked.

As she said they would, Adwen left with Jack an hour or so after meeting with the scout. The man confirmed some facts and provided some new ones. When it came time to depart, the scouts gathered outside to bid farewell.

Both Adwen and Jack transformed and took off on a bound, sailing over hot sand under a four o'clock sun. Their goal lay to the north, where dark stones crouched on the horizon.

"So," Jack panted, "What did you talk about with the guy in the turban?"

"You should have been listening. He said two different scouting parties went missing while on patrol. I brought up what we found in the sand and found out that it had been spotted from a distance at night. The behemoth can tolerate direct sunlight, but the demons inside it cannot. It's been moving along in the dark since the day before my phoenix friend let us know what was happening."

"What happens after we kill it?"

"Let me worry about that. Save your breath and be ready for the showdown."

Jack found the self-control to be quiet. Most of the questions he could ask were easy to answer just by tuning into Adwen's thoughts. While they ran, he sensed a building foreboding. The same mood he had picked up the day before at sunrise was gnawing at her again. Her heart was sick with fear of something she could not understand.

Once she realized he was reading her, the dark feelings vanished. She glared at Jack, though he pretended to focus on the journey

Reaching the area where the monster would resurface, the hounds relaxed and took the time to bask in what remained of the light. The last of their wounds mended, and their energy rose. It was sweltering hot, but neither was bothered. Before Jack could ask, Adwen sensed his question by thinking of the answer. Jack's body was now infused with powerful magic. No longer human, he was a creature of pure magic. Extreme heat or cold did not concern him anymore.

When night came, Adwen discussed a plan of attack.

Eventually, Jack asked, "So if Plan A doesn't work, what's Plan B?"

Adwen flicked her long ears and tail. "For Plan B, you stand back. Hopefully it won't come to that."

"How come you tell me my part without explaining yours? Where's the teamwork in that?"

Panting in the place of chuckles, she replied, "Can you ask one thing at a time?"

Again, a thunderous rumble shook the ground. They were ready.

Half a mile away, the wicked digging claws breached the surface, drawing the grotesque body out of hiding. Once free, it made the same gasping wheeze.

That was Jack's cue.

The black hound, with his new Siberian husky-like markings, took off like a shot, bounding into the wind. His body sprung and recoiled over and over, propelling him toward the grotesque behemoth. Having become a full-fledged Holy Hound, Jack could not help but feel somewhat invincible.

After last night's run-in, he knew the monster was rather slow. Standing upright as he approached, he barked for its attention.

The sluggish, ovular head turned, searching with glowing eyes.

He took his chance, jumping up high. Before the creature could understand what was happening, the hound summoned both daggers, and landed on the beast's shelf of a cheekbone. No sooner did the undead monster realize there was an enemy upon it than Jack slashed the eye open and leaped away.

Pain made the behemoth bellow. Rotting juices spilled from its face like water from a breached swimming pool.

Jack landed safely on the sand and barked, "Come and get me, stinky!"

It was clear that the monster was provoked. A belch of decay and small flying demons funneled out of its mouth, forming a dark storm. More burrowing worms spilled out from the bottom jaw, piling up before digging into the desert. All manner of vile beings spotted Jack and attacked at once.

Jack's tongue lolled in a brief moment of excitement before he had to start running. The warrior did not stow his blades, as so many flying things could prove too quick. He ran fast enough to keep out of reach and led the denizens from the belly of the beast on a chase into the dunes.

With Jack fulfilling his part, Adwen raced in for her attack. First, she went for the behemoth's remaining eye. Her white form lunged through the air, landing and catching a hold of the monster's clammy, sand-caked skin. She raked her claws across the weak membrane, blinding it for good.

It bellowed again in a fit of rage and pain.

Adwen held on, while the behemoth flailed its gargantuan head, trying to knock her off. When it could not, the pores on its back opened.

She looked over her shoulder just in time to see Wretches flooding out of the hundreds of pores like army ants. Killing them as they came, she stood her ground atop the behemoth's head. When time allowed, she struck the giant, working hard to reach a weak spot and bring it down.

After minutes of slashing and kicking, while Jack kept the smaller demons away, Adwen reached the behemoth's skull. The waves of Wretch troops did not end. She filled her hands with light and slammed them together, blinding and stalling the fiends long enough for her to punch through the behemoth's bones.

But when she did, her claws found an empty cavity. To Adwen's surprise, the behemoth's head had next to nothing inside. Roiling worms and flailing wings rushed into the space and flew out at her, forcing her to find a different way of defeating the huge undead transport.

Jack saw her jump down from the head, which was still moving. He sliced at demons that came too close, still running to keep ahead. In the midst of it, the hound warrior called out to her, "Is it time for Plan B?"

Adwen did not reply. After putting some distance between her and the behemoth, still crawling with large demons, she studied how the things never stopped coming out. They were beginning to crawl down to chase after her.

She hunkered down and howled out a fearsome challenge at the monster.

It answered, opening wide to gasp and rumble, exhaling yet more flying demons and black, squirmy grubs.

The behemoth did not close its mouth and kept blowing more demons at her, while she came bounding in for an attack. Small talons raked her arms and face. Nasty grub mouths bit into her feet, but none slowed her down as she sped on, straight for the blind monster.

Jack looked just in time to see her leap through the air at an incredible speed. She disappeared into the mouth, engulfed by a tide of writhing, flapping black bodies.

He yelped in dismay and kept running from his own attackers.

With a snap, the behemoth's mouth shut tight. It wheezed, satisfied by ending the battle. Then at once it began to wail and shudder, collapsing. Wretches yammered and shrieked in dismay, as the behemoth fell and bright white light came blasting out from every oozing pore, burning it from the inside out.

Before anything could escape, the whole thing exploded, shreds flying in every direction like shrapnel. A shockwave pulsed, knocking the rest of the surrounding demons senseless. Those that flew tumbled, and worms flailed. Jack stopped when they began to flee or burrow away.

Then his attention went to the decaying pile where the behemoth once stood. He dismissed the blades and bounded up to the behemoth's remains, hoping to find Adwen sitting someplace, smiling impishly as always. When he got there, he only saw dry, caked flesh. As he walked in it, he changed into his more human shape. Cooked pieces left behind crunched like dried river mud, breaking and crumbling under his weight.

Growing anxious, he called, "Adwen?"

There was silence until he heard crumbling sounds ahead. As he came to one of the largest mounds of crispy rot, the top of it burst open. Chunks were brushed aside, as his white hound leader dug herself halfway out. She stopped to prop herself up by her elbows on the outer edge. Shaking the dust from her head, the thin cloud drifted off, and she cocked her head at him, eyes shining excitedly.

"You were worried?" she panted.

Rolling his eyes in exasperation, he responded with an irritated, "That was your Plan B? It should have been Plan A."

She transformed into her woman form as she climbed the rest of the way free. "Where would be the fun in that? You wouldn't have had to do anything."

"I can't believe you didn't take that seriously. It was huge!"

Once on level ground, she walked with him and replied, "In my own defense, it had to be used as a last resort. I just spent half of my power in one shot. The only way I can restore that much energy quickly is to be in the sun. Our night isn't done just yet."

Jack froze in his tracks, watching her continue north. A troubled look came over him as he said, "You're going to make me go somewhere bad, aren't you?"

She shrugged, tossing him a nonchalant expression. "It's not as bad as you would expect. We are going to have a word with the guy who sent this mobile fortress in the first place."

Thoroughly unsettled, he shook his head and began to follow again. "That sounds worse than I expected."

They continued north, remaining in their current shapes. Running helped them reach the threshold of their destination in a timely manner. Jack liked the looks of this new endeavor less and less by the second. A dark craggy range of towering rocks took over the view. When the white grains of sand ended, Adwen and her warrior entered the darkest land known to any in the magical realm. Mortigad never saw sunshine or knew the warmth of day.

Upon entering the shadows, Adwen let her feminine body glow, pushing back the darker shadows. After some time traversing the many narrow passages and cavernous spaces filled with running water, pairs of eyes found them and watched closely. Some followed, stalking silently where Adwen's light did not reach.

Jack did not like the looks of the creatures. They looked hungry, and most did not have a scent. The human-looking beings that did have on odor only smelled of blood. Daggers out, Jack walked with his back to his leader, defending the shadow he cast. If he wasn't mistaken, that would be the way he could be reached. These beings looked very hungry.

Keeping an eye on their stalkers, he asked, "Hey, Adwen? Are these all vampires? It would be great for you to do something about them."

A few hissed, salivating ravenously.

She paid them no attention. "That would not be a good idea. These are civilians. If we start something now, the ones with bows and arrows will show up in a hurry. They won't tell the archers that we're here until we finish our business."

"Why not?"

"Can't you tell? They can't help themselves. You look and smell too tasty to resist."

Jack chuckled nervously. "That's nice."

She continued onward through the dark city that materialized around them. Hundreds of vampires saw them and watched from windows above, knowing better than to strike. To walk into Adwen's glow would be instant death. She did not smell edible, but Jack's scent was tantalizing to their senses. Seeing him walk in their streets was like dragging a beef steak down a dog shelter aisle.

The crowds that slunk in from the many alleys and doorways stayed clear of the light around the trespassers' feet. When one of them stood in Adwen's path, not crouching but upright and expectant, she halted.

One hissed and tried to attack, but two creatures jumped down from nowhere. Winged gargoyles standing almost as tall as Oryn's hound form swooped in and ripped the offender to shreds.

Onlookers hissed and backed away.

Jack was bold enough to relax once the crowds recoiled. He saw the vampire and his two powerful companions blocking Adwen's way. When the scentless being stepped forward, Jack was not concerned. But when the vampire entered the light and did not burn, Jack raised his daggers and yelled,

"Stop right there!"

The vampire did. Well kept and dressed in scholarly clothes, the pale skin that touched Adwen's glow gradually regained color. Quietly, he waited for Adwen to address him, not once looking at the warrior defending her.

She raised an eyebrow. "Is your name Evrox, by any chance?"

He smiled, dipping his head, medium brown hair falling about his shoulders. "No, I am not him. If thou wished to come by him, thou wouldst have to go far from here. I am called the Page, but my name is Geraldine Corbett Mesintine. Please call me Core."

Jack didn't trust him. These creatures had minds like the landscape – they were solid and unreadable. Not being able to access their thoughts made him uneasy.

"That's nice," Jack replied. "Now what do you want, blood sucker?"

The attending gargoyles did not move, but they narrowed their eyes and growled at Jack.

Adwen shushed her friend. Cocking her head at Core, she continued the conversation with a question: "What do you want?"

"My wish is to obey Darien's commands. He said unto me long ago that I must abide in this place, awaiting my time to aide his rightful heir. Wouldst I be mistaken by assuming you are her?"

Bowing a little, she replied, "I am. It's good to meet you, Core. What did Darien say that you were supposed to do?"

The two gargoyles exchanged glances, and the day-walking vampire looked slightly embarrassed. "It was a silly thing for which to wait an eon. I was told I must ask."

Jack scoffed in agreement.

"And so I ask you, how might I aide the heir in the dawn of the darkening time?"

She smiled kindly. "We are looking for the undead king."

Core grimaced. "Ah. You seek a meeting with him?"

Adwen nodded.

He sighed before bowing deeply. "It is an honor to be a light unto your path. He is this way. The king, as you may know, never goes anywhere. Come."

The gargoyles strode on either side of Core, while he served as a tour guide through the kingdom of Mortigad. First, he introduced his hardy companions.

"At my left is Shale the Swift."

The lean creature bowed his slender head. True to his name, the color of his skin matched it perfectly; it was striped in layers of brick red, mud brown and dark grey.

"At my right is Granite the Enduring."

The thick-skinned female bowed. Her body was peach with a network of black splotches.

"I raised them from eggs. It is impossible to know how long ago. Counting days has not been possible since the armies began to muster."

Jack started to treat Core with more trust. "What is this city? I doubt these other vampires built it."

Core's eyes were a steel grey with green centers, scanning over the crumbling structures. "It is true. Vampire hands did not make it. All that you see was once aglow. This was once a land of healing. When it became corrupt by the hand of the ancient coward, it turned dark. Those who took in his breath wasted away into walking dead. Whoever was touched by him and his began to thirst for blood of the living."

Gazing sadly at the vicious watchers, Core admitted, "I was once one of them, the first of the blood drinkers. Darien found me in the wilds, and he took pity. Willingly, he gave me his life blood, making me forever satisfied. As a gift, he gave unto me freedom of mind from hunger and let me back into the sunshine."

Raising a skeptical eyebrow, Jack asked, "What about the guy responsible?"

Core stopped and pointed up a high stone stairway into an ominous pantheon. Ragged banners etched in faded emblems hung from either side of the pediment. Cold breezes reached miles from the sea, rustling them like somber waves.

As the group stared, Shale bent down to Core's ear. A soft trilling came out before he whispered, "We must go."

He nodded and turned to Adwen. "Before I depart, is there anything else I may do to aide you?"

"Yes. Get out of Mortigad. Find a safe place in Dargadia near the Order of the Master Knights. I'm not sure how long you will have to wait, but when I make it back, I will have more work for you there."

Core's young looking face showed astonishment. Smiling, he replied hopefully, "Would I be performing scholarly duties once more?"

She nodded.

"You are too gracious, child of Darien."

Shale trilled more urgently and warned, "We must leave now."

He climbed onto Granite's back and whispered, "Farewell, Andredan and warrior."

All three of them quickly vanished without a trace into the endless pitch black.

"Come on." Adwen ushered Jack up the stairs, leaving behind the hissing mob of vampires. None went after them into the stone landmark.

As they ascended, Jack had yet another question: "Who was the coward he mentioned?"

"The Great Coward is the king of the undead. A demon named Melanin found him and made a deal. The man was so terrified of death that he gave up his soul for what he considered immortality. He was also promised an army."

Jack reached the top with her and looked back at the city, veiled in darkness. "It sure looks like he got it. Did he know he was getting a dead army?"

"Not sure. In a second, you can ask him yourself."

At the end of the grand hall, two torches with green flames dimly illuminated a throne made of black marble. It was polished to beautiful perfection.

The work of art was a stark contrast to the occupant. Boney with baggy, sagging skin around his neck, arms and calves, the king wore a fur-lined cloak and deteriorating silk robes. Pustules under the fine fabrics oozed, showing through as damp spots of varying sizes. After sitting in one place for so many years, decaying moisture from his bodily crevices and sores leaked and ran, leaving trails down his arms and the front of the throne. His foggy eyes wandered aimlessly, half blind.

As they came closer to the rotting being, Adwen stopped with her sphere of light a short distance from the carpet under the king's feet. There she stood with Jack alongside. Seconds passed until the undead face began to show signs of expression.

When the eyes narrowed, he spoke in a soft, raspy voice. "I smell warmth. I smell blood that is not teeming with parasites. Who dares come into my presence with no offering of succulent flesh?"

Adwen responded with a harsh tone, "Greetings, Nasogus Vard."

Briefly surprised, he soon became indifferent. "So, the brood of the Neverborn has come? What could one such as you want from another immortal such as me? I'm afraid that all I have to offer is rack-of-goblin at the moment."

Jack was busy holding his breath. The stench from the throne was unbelievable.

Adwen tolerated it. This was not the moment to show a weak-willed nature.

Shuffling sounds started coming from nearby. Two zombie servants limped lazily, groaning as they carried gold platters of goblin meat and goblets of dark fluids.

Adwen glared in disgust. When the undead were about to pass her to deliver the sick pleasantries to their ruler, Adwen swiftly expanded the reach of her light. It caught the fragile undead, vaporizing them and sending the platters and drinks clattering to the floor.

Nasogus gave a pathetic bellow of outrage: "How dare you? They take forever just to draw the blood into goblets, let alone bring it to me! Curses on you, girl."

Her glare fell on the king and intensified until Jack felt anger radiating from her body as a sizzling heat. He took a step back, unsure whether she was going to have an outburst of some kind.

The king could barely see but returned her look. "You wish me gone, so why don't you do it and be done? I will not stop you."

"No. I don't think so."

Jack was fed up with the sight and smell of the rotting king. "I'll do it."

Adwen extended an arm, holding him back.

He stopped and saw the king chuckling.

"You have a hasty little insect for a warrior, girl. I ask again, what is it that you want? Why have you come all this way to see my eminence?"

Before saying anything more to the king, Adwen sent a silent message to her psychic companion. She warned that powerful magic was binding the king to the pantheon and the rest of the black mountain range. If he were destroyed, everything would come crashing down.

Jack got the message, and his eyes widened. That sounded much worse than staying where he could smell the stink. Jack tried again to hold his breath, studying the king with fascinated horror.

"You sent the behemoth loaded with demons," Adwen said. "I'd like to discuss that with you for a moment."

"Moments are all we have, girl," sneered the king. "What of that giant toad creature? It was the last one I possessed. I don't much care here or there, so long as it reached its destination. That, I can only assume, would be why you wanted to see me."

"It was halfway there when we arrived," Adwen said. "Who told you to send it?"

The king gradually clenched his teeth and scowled. "Blast you to oblivion, girl." Then he spat and missed her feet by inches. "Who do you think? As you said, demons were what it contained. So who else could have told me to send the thing out?"

"Melanin?"

"Yes, Melanin."

"Why would he do that?"

Nasogus was astonished at the stupidity of the question. "Are you simple, girl? Why else would he tell me to send a behemoth laden with an army? He ..."

The truth finally dawned on him, making him twitch and fume with rage.

Adwen smiled.

"To the pit with that demon," Nasogus spat and sputtered. "He's twisted me like a top for the last time! Use me and my forces as cannon fodder, will he? Tell me, were my forces used as bait to draw you into a trap or not? I know you cannot lie."

"Yes, they were."

"Then they see me as disposable," he murmured to himself.

"They?" she asked.

In a fit of anger, the king yelled weakly, wheezing as he did, "Is this why you've come? You came here to mock me in my own chambers! How dare you? Damn your pride, girl!"

Now angry, Adwen yelled back, her voice empowered with magic. It echoed everywhere in the far corner of the black city: "I did not come all this way to laugh at the smell of your green flesh and pus! Sending the behemoth has drawn my attention to you, as the demons probably wished in the case that I survived. This is a warning. I now hold the power to make you suffer, but I will not. When I come back, it will be to kill you, and your cowardly curse on the dark stones will not take me or my warriors."

Dimming her light to almost nothing, she rushed forward and slapped Nasogus enough to turn his head to one side. When he started to wail and shriek, she gave her parting words. "I will see you again soon, Vard the Coward."

With a burn in the shape of a hand on his cheek, the king of Mortigad let out a resounding wail. Unlike the sounds he had made before, this one had power.

Thousands upon thousands of similar wails answered from outside the pantheon.

Jack whirled around. "Adwen, I think we should go."

The king started to laugh. His croaking guffaws became more and more out of control, as the thundering of footfalls grew in the dark streets.

Adwen replied, "Me too," as she quickly restored the glow around herself and Jack.

At a run, they left the throne behind and came to the top of the stairs, only to find a churning ocean of undead creatures waiting. Faster vampires were already storming the steps, eager to feed on Jack's red blood.

"Come on!" Adwen urged, leading the way to a distant rooftop.

Leaping to it and then to each rooftop that followed, they raced to keep ahead of the hungry vampires hot on their heels. Some fired arrows dipped in demon's blood, but the Holy Hounds were agile enough to dodge them. Both dashed to and fro in order to be elusive targets.

When a few from the street jumped up to cut them off, Jack gasped, and Adwen blasted them to dust with her light. Then they kept running.

After getting somewhat lost amid the maze of shelters, they found themselves cornered with only a high ledge to jump to. Vampires with swords and bows funneled in to bring them down, but Adwen and her warrior were already sailing up to their new escape route. The monsters' cries of anger echoed after them, echoing off every stone in their narrow tunnel out of the cavern.

"We're out scot free now," Jack laughed.

As he spoke, the tunnel path ended abruptly. They were forced to stop at the edge of a drop so dark that their eyes could not see where it went.

Taking back the claim, he said, "My bad."

Loud shrieking from overhead and behind made them look all around. No other path could be reached from the finger of stone they stood on.

Jack was going to ask what to do, but by then Adwen was in her hound form.

Fully transformed, she began to punch the ground between them and the tunnel, which was quickly filling with monsters.

Over and over, she hit the stone.

"What are you doing?" Jack yelled.

Winding back her arm for a final attempt, she loaded her fist with a piece of light powers. When she struck the ground this time, a loud crunch came from it. She shifted back into her woman form, and both braced themselves as the ground dropped an inch.

Corrupted gargoyles and all manner of undead were bearing down on them.

Adwen crouched low, turning her back on them. Jack mimicked her without thinking, and she smiled. "Hold on."

Another sickening crunch later, the two fell away from the masses, sliding down on the stone fragment. They gripped the terribly small crevices as best they could. Jack screamed in terror, while Adwen seemed to be squealing with delight at the ride.

The black stones curved and bowed every which way, scooping up their rock, sending it in and out of tunnels and natural troughs full of rain water. Soon they were seeing stars between gaps in the formations. Wind whipped their hair, and Jack was almost out of breath from hollering. The momentum of their black slab began to slow as they were nearing the edge of yet another drop.

"It's time to evacuate," Adwen crowed. "Jump!"

They both leaped just before the black rock went tumbling over. Adwen and Jack went rolling in the sand, followed by a massive explosion, caused by the boulder striking the earth.

The stunned and exasperated warrior lay splayed on his back, staring at the early-morning sky. In a few minutes the sun would be rising. What his leader had just put him through had him wonder why he was even seeing sky at all.

Adwen jumped to her feet laughing. She whooped and shook her fists. "That was awesome! Quick, let's do it again!"

He let his head loll in the sand to stare at her vacantly.

This got another bout of giggles and a fit of dancing in response. He thought she was absolutely nuts.

Chapter 30
No One

With Oryn's help, Alex was well enough to travel in the morning. The portals leading back to Dargadia had a tendency to be in the east, close to Broad River. He did not want to leave too much to chance and took the Marine far from the farmlands and neighboring plains. They ran throughout the day at Alex's pace, coming to stay in the forest near where Oryn recalled that there was a portal.

When night returned, the training began. Oryn waited for Alex to go through his second transformation and went about teaching what he knew of mental control. The very useful technique for breathing in battle allowed a knight to block out distractions. Another technique helped soldiers who were dealing with berserker issues. Often, berserkers lose all control and get themselves mortally wounded. Knowing how to begin and end the episodes kept them alive while still making them a force to reckon with.

Right away, Alex noticed a difference. Normal men needed months to perfect it, but those who shared the Marine's trait found almost instant benefits. In a few hours, Alex was fighting toe to toe against Oryn, holding his own. Even when a blow landed, it had no effect. Then as the sparring sessions ended, the Marine recalled every second.

When it came time to sleep, the green-eyed hound kept watch, and the yellow one dreamt of the past. The promise of remembering old occasions when he blacked out was kept. He even recalled the one time it happened in high school. A bully had tried to take his pocket change. It ended with the boy in traction.

Meanwhile, Oryn sat watching and listening to the forest.

In his vigil, his heart and mind wandered to thoughts of Adwen. Was she safe? Would she return tomorrow as she had promised? He wasn't sure what he would do if night came again without Adwen.

The next day, Oryn insisted to an exhausted Alex that they continue training.

He prodded him awake from behind, as the Marine had fallen

asleep in his other form, leaving him nude.

"I grow tired of waiting," Oryn said. "Dress yourself, and be quick. You have more training to do."

"I'm awake. Give me a chance to grab my things."

Without a word, Oryn stalked off to allow the Marine privacy. Oryn knew that his impatience was not about Alex's training. Alex was taking the brunt of Oryn's anxiety over Adwen. It would not last, Oryn knew, because training was his way of avoiding worry. Once Alex was prepared, Oryn could deny any accusation of being fearful or concerned about Adwen's whereabouts.

As it turned out, training did not help with the anxiety. More than once, Oryn snapped at Alex angrily, pushing the Marine beyond his skills with a sword.

By the afternoon, Oryn was unable to focus on training.

Fed up with Alex's inability to perform a complicated sword tactic, he growled then spat, "Enough! Put that blade down and go practice your breathing! Your incompetence is trying my patience."

Alex was also irritated. He snapped back in reply, "She'll come back, so get hold of yourself."

The Marine blinked, and Oryn's face was already in his, with the force of his speed brushing wind against the Alex's chest. His glowing green gaze was fierce.

The Marine almost gasped, but he did not flinch. He stared straight back, as he had with his superiors in boot camp. The one difference was that he never made eye contact with them. Alex stared down the hound warrior, not willing to back down.

A rumbling growl could be heard behind Oryn's cool, collected words: "Mind your tongue, Greeves. I am not one to suffer those who talk too freely."

Oryn was his superior, so Alex responded softly with a subtle condescending tone, "Yes, sir."

Before anything else could be said or done, a familiar male voice yelled from across the clearing.

"Hit him in the nose, Cujo! I know you want to!"

Both turned to see Jack and Adwen come strolling into view. As they approached, it was clear that the shortest among them had changed.

To clarify that Oryn's bad attitude was because he had missed Adwen, Alex covertly watched his reaction upon seeing her again. The tall warrior's expression instantly softened before turning to Jack. This was enough for Alex. Perhaps he could let go of how he had been treated today.

Oryn worked hard to keep from looking relieved. To do that, he scrutinized Jack. His enchanted garments suited him. He wore a leather vest with a thin section of short fur across the shoulders, much like the jacket he had upon arriving in this world. In fact, the whole ensemble was a vague reflection of his old attire.

Placing his hands on his belt, much like the cop he used to be, Jack chuckled. "If you have something to say then say it."

Oryn inclined an eyebrow. "It defeats the purpose when you already know what I am thinking."

Dismissing the knight, Jack turned to the Marine. "What do you think about my new look, jarhead?"

Alex smiled. "I almost didn't recognize you. You're so short, I thought you were a Keebler elf."

Adwen burst out laughing, while Oryn was confounded.

Jack rolled his eyes. "Nice going, Blondie. She's been laughing all day."

Alex replied, "At what?"

"Don't ask."

By the time it was dark, they found a more secluded place for rest. Oryn was contented to remain at the campsite, while Jack took a transformed Alex on a moonlit hunt. They intended to find a deer and bring it back for Oryn to skin; he was much more skilled at the task.

On all fours in the brush, Alex followed the trail, sniffing.

Jack's panting was loud, representing a human chuckle.

Alex growled, "What?"

"You're naked."

"Shut up!"

Twice, Jack spooked a deer by provoking his friend. It was entertaining that the yellow hound couldn't seem to learn after first making the mistake. Jack was eager to see whether he could make Alex scare off the deer again.

Their hunt led up and down hills, past boulders and toward the waterfalls that lined the northern border of the kingdom. They could hear the dull roaring. It covered the sound of their movements. Soon they found the deer again at the top of a ledge, staring at one of the waterfalls.

With the animal distracted, Alex shifted his weight to pounce. He was adapting to the new instincts well, but some of his clumsiness interfered. Without any help from Jack, he snapped a heavy branch under his claws.

The spooked doe looked back in a flash and bolted.

More of Jack's heavy panting followed. "You're a natural." Then as they plodded after it, Adwen's scent passed under his nose.

"Wait up," Jack growled.

Alex saw him sniffing, but his own senses weren't quite as keen. He moved next to Jack, and both ended up staring out at the falls.

It was a long distance away, but there was no mistaking the feminine figure standing on the black rocks under the pounding cascade. Once they realized she was not clothed, they did not know what to do.

Unaware of witnesses other than wild animals, Adwen back-flipped into the deep cold pool and vanished.

"What is she doing out here alone?" Alex asked.

"It's called skinny dipping."

Alex growled, "I know that, but why isn't she doing something else?"

Watching her resurface for a breath of air before diving down, Jack replied, "Beats the heck out of me."

Then they heard a voice from behind. "I shall too, if you do not explain yourselves."

The hounds flipped over onto their backs, and Jack swiftly shifted into his human shape. They gaped at the knight hound's human face. He was frowning, which was a rather obscure expression for Oryn. There was no way to tell whether he was feeling murderous or simply testing their nerves.

Naturally the more daring of the two, Jack answered, "We were hunting for fresh meat. How about you?"

Alex's eyes widened, and he nudged Jack's ribs with a large, furry elbow.

Jack closed his eyes immediately after using the bad turn of phrase. When he opened them again, Oryn was glaring. That was a bad sign. His thoughts at the moment were bouncing between skinning and impaling; once he thought of doing both.

With his notorious deadly stare, he glowered. "I present you both with an ultimatum: Leave now and never speak of this again, or I rip out your tongues and shove them down your throats."

Jack's eyes shifted from side to side, as he thought it over. Giving a weak chuckle, he knew they would get out unharmed. Then he asked, "Which tongues would go down which throat again?"

Oryn's green eyes burned brighter than the stars over him.

Quicker than the doe, the warriors darted off.

When they were gone, Oryn did not look to the falls. He knew what was there.

They finally caught the doe, and there was some confusion as to who really killed it. Jack insisted that he had pounced first to keep Alex from scaring it again, while Alex stood by his claim that he gave the final blow. In the end, Oryn told them both to be quiet, and the venison provided much-needed nourishment. When Adwen did not join them for the meal, they assumed it was because she went to catch her own food. When the blood was cleaned from their coats, the trio settled in for a deep sleep. Adwen would be close enough to keep an eye out for danger.

Oryn's dreams had been becoming more colorful in the past few weeks. Adwen was in each one. Her face swam into his hazy imaginings, smiling dreamily. This time he dreamt of holding her close. They were in the pool below the waterfall together. She felt so soft in his arms

It was morning when Jack woke up with a start. His face plastered with confusion that he was having Oryn's dreams. Even now that he was awake, the intensity of the dream that the warrior was experiencing invaded his mind.

He got to his feet, holding a hand to his head in an effort to force the visions out. They would not leave; worse, they were intensifying.

Going to stand over Oryn, Jack thought perhaps he was just going insane. Maybe this wasn't another male's dream playing in his head.

Then as he saw the real Oryn smile and the dream turned more exciting, Jack hollered and kicked him.

The yell woke the unclothed Marine, and the kick momentarily stunned Oryn before he rebounded, snarling.

Oryn came at Jack, who was quick to hold up both hands, trying to calm down Oryn long enough to explain: "I know what you're thinking. Now hear me out."

"You have ten seconds to talk or start running!" Oryn fumed, red in the face, though not from the attack. "Choose wisely."

"You would kick me too if you were having my dreams!"

Outraged, the knight bellowed, "What did you say? Keep your filthy thoughts away from mine, cretin!"

"That's what I'm trying to explain! It's you, not me!"

Now he had Oryn's attention. "Speak, dolt, and be quick."

"When someone thinks, I hear it like a whisper. But if the thought is very strong, it's louder to me. Some thoughts are just too big for me to avoid. I can hear her thoughts when they focus on things that are important to her, like family or saving this place."

Jack pointed at the Marine, dressing himself behind a tree. "I can barely hear anything in his head for whatever reason."

Returning his focus to Oryn, he shook his head, at a loss. "You are driving me insane because you are driving yourself insane! You can't stop thinking about her. Now it's to the point that your dreams are showing up in my head, too. There is no way for me to keep it out. If you want to keep those things private, and I would love to help you do that, then something has to be done."

Oryn huffed. "What do you propose?"

"Trust me on this; I'm educated on these things. You have to say how you feel out loud."

"Fine. I believe that you are a simpering fool looking for a way to die."

Jack's eyes rolled. "No, not me; her. If you don't stop avoiding the subject of your feelings for her, I'm going to keep waking up to your out-of-control thinking. I don't want that, and you don't want that. Tell her how you feel about her before we both go crazy."

A fraction of a second later, Oryn's fist smashed into Jack's face, knocking him out cold. Alex came out fully dressed and froze when that deadly gaze turned his way.

Adwen skipped down an embankment onto the scene. She took a moment to analyze a red-faced Oryn, an unconscious Jack with a bloody nose, and a stunned Alex.

She looked disturbed. "Okay then. I won't ask. Oryn, you get to carry him again because I know you did it."

Oryn shot the Marine a warning glance before saying, "At your command."

The journey back to the Order was slow due to Alex being on foot and Jack being incapacitated. Adwen was not interested in carrying anybody, and Oryn's hands were already full. By noon, Oryn began to wonder whether things would be better with Jack awake and able to function. That way they could move along much easier.

A long day of casual running made it possible for Jack's advice to sink into Oryn's stubborn thought process.

This set his mind into motion deciding how to go about express-ing his feelings. Saying them aloud would be difficult; saying them to

Adwen would be nearly impossible. The others saw that he was lost in thought for the rest of the afternoon. He was thankful that they did not ask why. Knowing the right words to use would be imperative. As night fell and they were in another cozy clearing, he was ready.

Jack was pleased and knew he was victorious, as he had returned to consciousness during their trek and simply pretended to be knocked out, letting the disgruntled warrior carry him the rest of the way. If Oryn had known he was awake, he would have been too busy hiding his thoughts to focus on how to express himself to Adwen. Any other time, he would have admitted it just to get a rise out of the knight, but this little nugget of information could be saved for a better occasion.

Adwen stuck around into the evening to ease Alex through his transformation, as a way to give him a break. Afterward, she departed for a break of her own.

She watched the sky, counted shooting stars and tried connecting those that stood out. No monsters were here, and the falls were not far from the tiny encampment. The need to go for a swim nagged at her until she decided to give in. Silently, she crept farther away for the seclusion of the forest.

Going around a giant willow, she found Oryn and stopped in her tracks.

He was leaning back against the tree, arms folded and looking ahead at nothing.

Finding him here confused her. "What are you doing over here?"

His answer was plain: "I am wondering the same of you."

Adwen's gaze dropped, embarrassed at being caught.

Before she could say anything, he asked, "Why do you enjoy swimming?"

At first she was alarmed that he knew, but she got over the shock. Thinking about the answer made her activity seem less strange. "It makes me feel peaceful. The sun does, too, but not like swimming does. When I'm underwater, it feels like I'm in the spirit world again; there is no sense of up or down, and I feel free. That's where a being like me belongs, I guess."

When she tried to come closer, he left the tree to stand, maintaining his distance.

Adwen pretended not to notice and took his place against the bark.

Not looking at her, he murmured, "I see."

It was obvious that Oryn was tense. Not knowing what else to say, she gently asked, "If you don't mind, I would like it if you came to sit with me by the water."

In a flash, he roared, whipping around and shifting unintentionally as he slammed both palms against the tree over her head. "Stop it!"

It frightened her, and she froze, eyes open wide. His large jaws hung by her ear, and she heard a small whimper amid the deep, strained breaths. "Please ... stop."

Adwen blinked a few times. She did not know how to respond. Swallowing the knot in her throat, it seemed best to walk away.

At first, he let her go. When she was a few paces away, he took his clawed hands from the tree and found the courage to stop her.

"Wait," he whined.

Not taking another step, she listened for more, and nothing came.

Oryn tried hard to say what he wanted to say, but the words had left him. Instead, he stared pathetically along his muzzle at her, hoping she would turn back around.

She hesitated but did look back into his baleful expression. Another long moment passed with no words spoken.

Frowning, she murmured, "How can I make this simpler for you?"

The hound felt defeated by his own useless tongue and hung his head.

Adwen went closer, careful to make no sudden moves. He could not harm her, but an element of fear came after his outburst.

Not wanting to make another horrible mistake, he held still, listening as she moved closer. Soon she was face-to-face with him. Only then did he look her in the eye. That was when they both sensed each other's fear.

"It's all right," Adwen soothed. Going slowly to where she could lay her cheek on the side of his jaw, she gazed up into his big green eyes. "It's okay."

Her hands felt along where his jaw line met his strong neck, barely moving the short, coarse fur on his skin.

The touch made his heart ache as though it was being crushed in a vice. He wanted so badly to hold her and struggled to deny the desire. As he fought the intense need, one of his big hands hovered inches over her arm, shaking feverishly.

When she noticed, she gripped the unsteady wrist, guiding it to rest on her shoulder. By doing so, it helped set Oryn free from the hound shape he had put himself into like a cage. Now that he was a proper size, the knight gently wrapped his arms about her, and she returned the tight embrace.

Adwen felt relief at feeling him hold her at last, though Oryn wished he could say the same. Fear tortured him. He had not said what was on his mind. It had to be done; he had drilled himself in preparation. His baleful expression remained, even with his change in shape. If he did not say it now, then it would be too late to do so again.

Unknowingly, she helped him to start: "Why are you so scared?"

"Because this cannot be. It can never be."

Shocked, she muttered weakly and fought back tears. "Why?"

"Because one such as you should only ever be alone. It would be best."

Adwen tightened her grip, as her voice cracked. "But why? I don't understand."

"Because ... no one could ever hope to deserve you."

A sharp pain struck as he said it, making her gasp while drawing out tears.

Knowing his words were true, he made himself let go and step back. Doing it left his heart feeling empty. He took a deep breath and heaved a sigh before walking out into the night without another word.

She watched helplessly as he left her standing in the dark, feeling lonelier than she ever had in either lifetime. Tears streaked her face, bringing her to her knees by the winding roots in the soil. Not even the feeling of being in the spirit realm could alleviate the pain she felt inside.

When Adwen finally transformed and ran, howling at the sky, Jack shook his head from his vantage point between the trees, growling. This was not at all what he had in mind.

Chapter 31
DREAD

Oryn eventually returned to sleep alongside Alex, but Adwen did not. Throughout the night, Jack remained awake, working his brain to dissect what he had heard in order to fix what the knight had completely ruined. It was no mystery that she wanted to be more than friends, but Oryn kept the psychology major guessing. By morning, it was clear that the knight thought he was not good enough for her. The problem was whether Jack could figure out how to make the stubborn brute see that he was wrong.

After dawn, Jack sensed the knight's mind waking. Jack wanted to be there when he did.

Taking Jack's advice helped quell Oryn's wild dreams and sporadic thoughts. What Oryn had not counted on was waking up to the same sense of emptiness that had started the evening before. It was a calm, cold feeling, but at least he could think clearly.

Then he detected a presence standing over him. Opening his eyes, he glared up at Jack, who stood with arms folded, looking disgusted.

"You're an idiot," Jack sneered down at him.

Growling, Oryn stood, replying, "Many words have been used on me, but idiot is not one of them."

"Okay, how about fool?"

That word got under Oryn's skin in a flash, making his eyes gleam.

It mildly surprised Jack to not get another fist to the face. He remained firm and continued: "She trusted you. Adwen gave you her heart on a silver platter, and you crushed it. How does that not make you a fool?"

Oryn's fist flew, but Jack deflected it, surprising the knight, who scowled.

"I'm not finished yet. Hitting me isn't going to make you feel better."

"It always has before. Leave me, worm."

"No it won't; not anymore. And I'm not leaving you alone until you understand what you've done. Emotional stuff is not your strong suit, but pain is." When the knight's scowl vanished, replaced by a frown, Jack knew he had struck a nerve. "You need to hear what I have to say."

Oryn gave Jack a sneer before turning to go. "This conversation is over."

For a moment, the determined hound-cop lost his temper. Though he was in human form, a series of barks and snarls jumped out from behind his gnashing teeth as he darted around to cut off the knight's escape.

The explosive sounds woke Alex with a start, and Oryn stopped cold, wearing an even icier glare.

Jack was alarmed by his own animalistic behavior but got over it quickly. He swallowed to stymie the growls in his throat and picked up where he had left off. "I know why you think what you did was good, and I have news for you: It was a mistake. You think that because you are the subordinate that things will never work out, so you put up your emotional wall. Did it ever cross your mind that you were putting all of us at risk?"

If he did not have Oryn's attention before, he had it now.

"Our strength is somehow tied into our wellbeing. Yes? Think about it. If that is true, and if some of our strength is drawn from hers, what do you think you did? You hurt her, and there is no question of that. There is no telling how long she will be hurt. Because you are too absorbed in feeling sorry for yourself, you couldn't see that your choice would affect us all. You weakened us. Don't you feel it?"

It was true, but Oryn remained stony.

Fully dressed, Alex came to try to assess the argument. Having only just woken up, his bleary mind was still struggling to grasp things.

Coming between them with hands up to keep the two warriors apart, Alex interjected. "All right, this needs to stop. What in this crazy world is going on?"

The two did not break eye contact, but Jack coolly answered, "You know how Adwen feels about this big nimrod?"

Brow furrowed, the Marine blurted, "Yeah. So?"

"Well, you see, this guy here had a heart-to-heart talk with her last night, and he told her that there was no way that it could ever happen."

Alex threw Oryn a shocked and disgruntled look. A second passed, and Alex replied, "Please tell me you called him an idiot."

"Already did," Jack murmured darkly.

Growing angrier, Oryn snapped, "This argument is pointless!"

"Maybe it is, but unlike you, at least I'm willing to try! Your only good argument for breaking Adwen's heart was that she's better off without you, that any relationship would put a strain on this team. With that debunked, what other stupid reasons do you have?"

"You cannot understand!"

"Make me understand," Jack bellowed. "Ever since I got here, you have been saying how I can't understand. Now it's you who doesn't get it! There is nothing you can say to make what you did to her okay."

Oryn was quiet.

"All right then," Jack went on. "If you won't tell me anything, then I'll just help myself to your memories."

He reached to touch Oryn's hairline, but his hand was batted away.

"Keep off me!"

"You're such a self-centered moron! Let me see so that this can be over. I want to know the answers behind your actions. I have to understand so that I can show you just how much of a fool you really are!"

Oryn's eyes blazed as he yelled. "You want to see, do you? Is that all?"

Alex stepped aside completely, knowing that if they wanted to fight, they were too strong for him to stop them.

"Yeah!" Jack shouted through more involuntary growling. "I do want to see."

Jack finally got his wish. In a fit of rage, Oryn decided it would be easier to just give him what he wanted and roughly took Jack by the wrist. A split second later, his palm was against Oryn's temple.

The memories came in a mad rush like having a waterfall suddenly dropped on him, smashing his mind under the weight. When things came into focus for Jack, he saw them differently than Oryn had. This time, it was as if he were a bystander rather than being placed in the knight's perspective.

In the first flash, Jack saw a frightened brunette with bright blue eyes and a collar hanging around her neck, standing with her back to a dark manor. He did not catch what she was saying but knew it had provoked the pale-looking knight in armor. The old Oryn came at her and delivered a nonlethal stab with his knife, forcing her to recoil.

The sight made Jack wince.

Then he was transported to another place and time. The brunette was ill, slouched back at the base of a tree. Tears filled her eyes as the knight was holding a dead rabbit in her face, outraged that she was making them lose time because she did not want to feed on bloody kills. Despite starvation, she was struggling to retain the last fragments of humanity she possessed, and he did not pity her in the slightest. He threw down the limp thing into her lap and stormed off.

Last, Jack saw the knight pull out his knife again, forcing her back against an old oak. With the edge brushing against her throat, he leaned into her face and sneered.

Everything fell away, and the rushing of thoughts sent Jack spinning. It ended as Oryn lifted Jack's hand so that it was no longer touching his head.

Jack was disconcerted.

This made Oryn feel justified. Releasing him, he turned to stalk off.

Quietly thinking over what he had witnessed, Jack eventually scoffed dryly and muttered, "That's not you anymore."

Oryn stopped and whirled around. "Don't," he warned.

Much calmer, Jack did not give the caution any credit. "You didn't deserve her, and you don't think you ever will. I can't argue with you there."

The hound knight was almost taken aback but realized that there was a point he didn't quite see yet. He kept his guard up and listened.

"I was right, though. You are self centered. You think that keeping your distance is what is best for Adwen. I would agree with that, if it weren't for the fact that you can't stop using your past mistakes as excuses. Take yourself out of the situation before you decide what she deserves."

"What I have said cannot be unsaid," Oryn replied. "I am a beast at heart, and she deserves better. I ask you, what is it that you think is right in regard to Adwen?"

"To be honest," Jack admitted, "she needs to be with her family. I know I do, too. She thinks about them every day. What they can do that you can't is show her love. It's what she craves. It's what keeps her going in all of the insanity."

Dropping his gaze, Oryn took in the words.

"Here is where I'm most concerned: Tell me, what will you do when she needs you to be more than just Oryn the servant?"

For a second, the thought frightened Oryn. Giving Jack a stern look, he murmured defiantly, "That will not happen."

"I hope not," Jack said. "But I think it will. When it happens, what will you do? Will you be there to catch her, or will you watch her go down in flames?"

A long silence followed the question. Oryn could not say. He did not want to answer, as it felt like doing so might make it prophesy.

The three stood like statues waiting for an artist, pondering what was to come. No solution could be easily reached, and they continued to stare, wondering about a terrible something that could happen that was enough to force Oryn's hand. It was possible, but none had the stomach to predict what would come in the end.

Rustling brush announced Adwen's return. None moved as she came strolling into view. She had expected to come back to find Jack knocked out for some reason, but seeing him up and without a bloody nose gave her relief. The fact that the warriors were standing still and doing nothing did not escape her notice; rather, she did not care. It was strange, but she was far from being in the mood to tolerate much of anything.

Clasping her hands, she breathed an exaggerated sigh of relief. "Good. Everyone is awake and unharmed. Let's get going. Plexus is only a few hours away."

When no one moved, she was a little annoyed. "What is wrong with all of you?"

"Nothing," Jack lied. "I just finished schooling Oryn a bit."

The partial lie was enough to fool Adwen at the time.

"Fine. How about we move the class along?"

They each began to shift their weight in order to break out of the dark mental cloud that had enveloped them.

Then a wreath of flames roared in the air overhead, spitting out the phoenix, Malik. He was shrieking madly with urgency in his rapid wing beats. This time Alex understood what the creature was saying.

Soaring back around to hover over Adwen, the firebird trilled and shrieked: "Child of Andredan, you are needed! An attack has come! You must go immediately!"

"Where?" Adwen snapped impatiently. "Just tell me where!"

"Eskrana! Eskrana is under siege! Hurry to the closest portal, child! Run!"

The bird vanished back the way he had come, and Adwen lunged for Alex. When she touched him, he rapidly changed into his hound shape. The swiftness of it stunned the Marine for a second before the rest changed form on their own. His clothes were damaged, and the shirt was shredded, while the trousers miraculously remained whole.

"Keep up with me!" she barked.

They were off like a shot, bounding out of the clearing and into the woods. The hounds raced between the many obstacles of the forest until the plains opened up before them. Then Adwen used one of her abilities for speed. She let loose a howl, sending some of her own power into their bodies, making them glow gold. Now the four hounds pressed on at an unnatural pace, sailing across the landscape to the coastal forest.

They had to cross the whole of Dargadia to get there. Nearly an hour had passed when the smell of sea air met their senses. Reaching the sheer volcanic cliff face, each of them leaped out into space and down to the windswept sand.

Adwen found the indentation on the beach straight away and shifted into her woman form to activate it. As it did the first time, the energy from her hand was thrown under the sand to the cliff, opening the secret tunnel. They disappeared into the passage and soon collided with the permeable surface of the magical gate.

When they did, the other side was full of roars and screams. Darkness swirled in a daytime sky, blotting out the sun over the home islands of Eskrana. Dreds swooped in aerial combat with the Griffins, Wretches assaulted foot soldiers, and a few Fellons stampeded, destroying everything in sight.

Immediately, the Holy Hounds sprung into action.

"We have to take down those Fellons!" Adwen snarled to the others. "Those are the most destructive and are the hardest for the enemy forces to replace."

The closest one decimated another home, killing anyone who might have been inside.

Jack played decoy, drawing its attention by aggravating it. He raced up to the monster and sliced off one of the four tendril blades from its back.

As it roared, belching purple fog, Oryn leaped high and came down with the large sword driving through the demon's back. It fell immediately, and the duo continued to the next one.

Adwen and Alex cut down a few Wretches on their way to one of the ten Fellon attackers. Upon reaching it, she blinded it with a flashbang, and she and Alex struck hard together, bringing it down as quickly as Oryn and Jack had theirs. They received a cut or two from the flailing limbs but were relatively unscathed.

This continued until the last of the larger demons was killed by combined efforts from Oryn, Jack and some of the Eskrani soldiers.

As much as they were needed on the ground, the battle in the sky was going worse.

The heavy Kaluka Griffins that used sonic-boom voices in combat were strong, but they were not equipped well enough to fight a Dred. Their blasts could only stun, and their raptor-like talons had yet to be coated with molten gold to allow them to do damage to the demons. Those that kept their distance bombarded the monsters, but any who met a Dred head-on soon fell back to earth, raining blood.

Gathering her warriors together, Adwen howled to the Griffins overhead.

A small formation swooped low, gathering up the male hounds by their shoulders, while she reached up to grasp a giant talon on her own. They were then flown over one of the massive winged demons.

She barked loud enough for her company to hear: "Trust the Griffins. Just let them get you to your marks, and they will catch you when it's done."

Oryn barked in acknowledgement, and the others hid their unease.

Dozens of Dred soared over the city, spitting acid and wrecking structures. When Adwen let go to drop onto the back of one, it turned to spit in her face.

Taking a hold of the monster's back, she moved aside to dodge and plunged a handful of claws into the fiend's body.

It writhed, flailed and began to fall.

In the nick of time, a Griffin snatched her up to go after another Dred.

Alex, Jack and Oryn followed suit, dropping onto unsuspecting Dred. A few of the monsters saw the attack coming and flew in to tear them down.

Adwen and her Griffin swiftly whisked her in to stop them. Once she got a good grip on any of the fiends' leathery backs, they were as good as dead.

The battle persisted. Ruined bodies were cast over rubble like toys discarded in a nursery. Red and purple fluids painted the streets, reeking of death. Regardless, the brave fought on. Soldiers with weapons prime for fighting demons resisted and pushed back enemies on the ground now that the Fellons were destroyed. The number of Dred remaining was dwindling, and soon Griffin-mounted warriors were the greater number.

Another demon fell, and then the dark flock turned away without warning. Nearly twenty remained to flee to the east. Cheering filled the air over the capital.

Then a desperate scout flew in to find Adwen, shouting in his native tongue. He was frantic.

To his mount, she barked, "What is he saying?"

The creature trilled, "The king! The king is chasing down the demons alone! You must save him! They killed his eldest son and took the queen!"

Frightened and outraged, Adwen howled. Her warriors and their own Griffin mounts rallied to join the rescue, flying like mad after the retreating forces.

In order to catch them, she had to lend some of her remaining energy, making them glow gold and soar like arrows to the target. A minute passed, and Adwen could see the king atop his brownish-golden eagle Griffin, chasing the demons in a vain effort to stop them.

The dark shroud in the sky made the demons much faster and stronger, and that made catching up more difficult. When Adwen and the rest reached them, the forces were over the eastern island and its single plateau. To conserve her power, she had no choice but to relinquish what strength she was giving her comrades. The glow faded away from the Griffins, and the aerial battle began anew.

In the chaos, King Zulo and his feathered friend were fierce. They flew headlong into the fray, straight for the demon carrying his wife. She cried and screamed, as he came to her aid.

The Dred that had her in its grip saw him and had a malicious gleam in its red beady eyes. It dropped her.

Putting away his saber, the king cried out in horror as his Griffin went into a steep dive. He did not see the Dred coming down after them.

As the king and his Griffin caught her before crashing on the plateau, the demon was over them, ready to finish them off.

Adwen and her Griffin tackled it, knocking it away. The brave beast with her had to swoop away, but she stayed, scrambling along the monster's neck to its unprotected head. Her claws ripped skin, and her teeth sunk deep into the demon's face. It flew and flailed awkwardly in a fit to remove her. She ripped its throat, spilling purple liquid like mixed paint, and she crashed with it into the ground.

The hard landing stunned her at first, but she shook it off and bounded away to find the king. After running through the trees and into a wide clearing, she found him and his wife huddled beside the golden Griffin. It was badly wounded but continued to shield them with its wing.

When Adwen arrived, she shifted into her woman form and came to a stop beside them. Fearful, she asked, "Are you all right?"

Holding his sobbing wife close, the king nodded and replied, "We are not harmed. My friend has broken a leg but may still fly. If we are to escape, it will be difficult. For him to take wing, he must now jump from a ledge."

A terrible wailing shriek echoed from across the clearing, making them all turn to look. A mob of Wretches was coming out of the jungle.

Without changing, Adwen ran up to meet them.

In the sky, Oryn saw the scene. "Get down there now!" he urged his Griffin.

Adwen blinded, kicked and scratched the Wretches one after another. Her size made it hard for the monsters to fight back. The speed with which she moved confounded them to the point that they could do nothing. On the other side of the skirmish, Oryn joined in, dropping down to the ground to use his sword. The pair worked together in destroying the small legion.

In the midst of the fight, Adwen twirled and vaulted over and around her opponents. More came out of the jungle, but they did not stand a chance against two Holy Hounds.

When she had a second to spare, Adwen yelled to the king, "Get out of here! Go now, and the squadron with escort you back!"

In a flash, a long chain shot out from under the soil and turf. The end of it ensnared one of Adwen's ankles, grounding her. She quickly reached to try to fight it off, but another lashed at her from the opposite side, restraining her by one wrist.

A Dred swooped low and spat a small glob directly into her eyes, burning and blinding her. She tried to summon her powers but was unable. The demons knew she would not be able to fight back once blinded. As the chains began to coil around her body like demon-steel snakes, she screamed.

Oryn heard, and his eyes widened with fear. He whipped his head around in the instant that a much larger Dred took to the air from a neighboring grove. The chains that had taken hold of Adwen were in its talons as it climbed higher, ripping more of the lengths free from their hiding place under the dirt. Before Oryn could move to stop it, Adwen's bare feet were already being lifted from the ground.

When she screamed again, he bayed in a mixture of alarm and fury, dismissing his sword to chase after her.

On all fours, he bounded, claws kicking up clods in his frenzied race to save her. As the demon flew, she was several yards over the ground, fighting against the restraints as they burned her skin, searing it with black and green. Oryn could feel her pain as if it were his, spurring him to move faster. The desperation he felt made his mind feral, fixated purely on taking her back from the enemy. He could barely hear laughter coming from atop the Dred. It was Sycan.

The chase took Oryn up embankments of rock and jagged outcroppings. As the demon continued to ascend, the hound warrior gained. His powerful body flexed and lunged as he jumped higher and higher after her. He was nearly to her.

As the highest ledge was about to end, Oryn leaped. His claws reached for the chains, but he was a breath away. He fell back to earth, his gut wrenching at the moment of failure. Colliding with the sheer side of the embankment, he tumbled a short distance before instinctively reaching out to catch something solid. Gaping after Adwen beneath the demon and its rider, Oryn roared long and loud enough for the entire ocean to hear.

Chapter 32
GUILLOT'S GIFT

When the others came with their Griffins, Adwen was already gone. Oryn had climbed back to the top of the ledge, where he appeared to be in a wild fit. He paced to and fro, roaring and snarling at the dot in the distance, disappearing on the strong sea zephyrs. The dark veil went with it, keeping the sun out during its journey.

Alex and Jack stayed on their mounts, who they had befriended in the recent battle. There was no need to ask the green-eyed hound what was happening. Instead, Jack instructed another Griffin to give him a ride. With the demons gone and daylight restored in Eskrana, survivors on the island made sure that their king and queen reached the city safely. It was left to the three warriors to save the heir now.

Jack shifted back to his elf-like shape and yelled at Oryn when he failed to notice the Griffin standing by. "Stop it and get on the bird-cat! If you want to get her back, you're going to have to fly, idiot! Get on it, and let's go!"

At last, Oryn climbed on the Kaluka, but he did not shift into his smaller shape. This made it a little more difficult for the beast to carry him fast, but there was nothing to be done. He could not control it. All he could think about was her.

Over an hour of flight passed. The dark cloud with the demons had disappeared from sight, filling their hearts with growing dismay. Alex, still stuck in his yellow hound form, came alongside Jack.

"Where did they take her?" he asked Jack.

"You don't want to know." Across the sea was Mortigad. Jack had hoped not to revisit that place so soon.

Then the Marine indicated Oryn. "What's wrong with him?"

"What do you think? He loves her, and they took her away. Who knows what they will do to her before we catch up."

"No," Alex explained. "Why is he stuck like I am."

"I'm not sure. But I think I can guess. He's prone to being controlled by his animal side more than the rest of us. I think he's out of control."

To that, Alex responded, "He's going to get us killed!"

"Not if I can help it."

Eventually, the nightmare land loomed before them with its range of black spikes, arching over each other like colossal slivers from the netherworld. The closer they got, the more apprehension built up in the newest warrior. Jack had warned Alex that he did not want to know this place. He was right.

The Griffins glided on wind gusts along the outskirts, staying clear of rocks jutting from the water. Their tips were sharp as razors. They found an entrance and a place to land. When the beasts let down their riders on solid ground, they took off to hide themselves close by.

Oryn bolted for the opening of a dark passage, and Jack was ready. He cut him off and transformed, blocking his path.

The green-eyed hound roared.

Jack roared back and snarled, "You don't know what's in there! I do. If we are going to find Adwen and make it out alive, we all need to be in our right minds!"

Oryn regained enough sense to respond with more than just angry sounds: "Get out of my way!"

Jack avoided his large, beastly punch and shoved him back from the path. Changing back again, he snapped, "Get ahold of yourself!"

Rumbling dangerously and baring his fangs, Oryn warned, "I have ahold of myself, and I will have one on you if you do not stand down!"

"You may be a higher rank than me, but I'm smarter, and I have a higher pain tolerance than you. You are out of control, and we cannot let you get us caught before we can save her. I figured out why your feelings for Adwen are driving you insane."

"We're wasting time with nonsense! Step aside!"

"Say it!" Jack shouted, "Say it aloud. You have never said how you feel about Adwen. If you want to be prepared to save her life, you have to get control. Now say what you feel about her!"

Stupefied by the situation and outraged, Oryn was at a loss for words. He could not respond. He gaped with open jaws at the fellow warrior.

With both hands, Jack pushed him hard and asked, "Do you love her?"

Still stunned, Oryn staggered back.

Again, Jack pushed him back, closer and closer to a tall rock beside the ledge.

"Do you love her? Do you love her? Say it! Do you love her,

Oryn? Say it! Say it!"

Then Oryn's fur-covered back slammed against the solid surface, and Jack stopped.

An unearthly wailing came out of Oryn. "With all that I am!"

Alex and Jack were both frozen in shock.

The warrior's body then melted down, becoming human. When he was in his smaller form, he glared and said, "Ever since the first moment ... I loved her."

Both stared in silence.

Irritated, but more or less under control, he sneered, "Are you contented?"

Jack nodded. "Yeah. Let's move."

Deep in the darkness of Mortigad, Adwen had been taken to a fortress built long ago by demons for Sycan's personal use. It was large, foreboding and quiet as a graveyard. Fellons patrolled the court-yard, and halls brimmed with an army of Wretches, expecting visitors.

The halls were large, like a cathedral to everything vile. Depictions of pain were everywhere. Nothing inside that place inspired hope.

Adwen hung from her wrists, with a second chain linking her shackled feet to the floor far beneath where she was suspended. A narrow stone stair lined with candle-sized flames, led up to where she was bound. Creepers stalked about, skulking in the gloom. They watched her and waited for the fun to begin.

Wicked smells crossed Adwen's nose time and again. The shackles on her wrists and ankles had stopped burning her. Her skin was black and oozing where the metal touched. There was no part of her flesh remaining in contact that could be harmed. Soon she heard boots on steps coming up the rise.

Sycan's devilish smile gleamed with delight as he chuckled and looked her over. "That looks rather comfortable. I shall have to try it out for myself the next time I want to be tortured." Approaching Adwen, he wiped a hand across her face, taking away the burn and restoring her sight. "I would very much like it if you could look me in the eye during our meeting."

As a show of defiance, she did not raise her head. When he lifted her chin, his glove smoked where it touched. Adwen glared into his white pupils, flecked with black like a strange animal's. She did not flinch at his presence or show any sign of fear.

In a familiar tune, he sang, "Who's afraid of the big bad wolf?"

Then he chuckled and removed his hand. "I spent many a year in the world where you were born. I know so much about technology and strange jargon such as yours. Most people there are either superstitious or utterly skeptical. I suppose you could say I got away with murder."

She said nothing and gazed angrily at the steep stairs.

This amused him. "I have been around for a very long time, and once or twice I made it into history books, though you wouldn't know it was me by name. A friend of mine, an apprentice of sorts, helped to destroy the last czar family ruling imperial Russia. That one sure did turn out to be a talented necromancer."

Adwen knew who he was referring to but did not want to play along with the demon's sick game.

Sycan thoughtfully mused, massaging the end of his chin with a curled finger. "What was his name again? Ah! Rasputin. He did eventually die, but that was old age. I didn't bother to teach him to defy time, just all manner of weapons or disease. Drowning didn't do much more than slow the man down."

Sycan moved gradually closer with a casual pace, as a politician does when on stage in front of voters. Using dismissive or emphasizing hand gestures in his gruesome monologue, Sycan elaborated on his favorite past experiences in the non-magical realm.

"Over the hundreds of years, I had killed in so many ways and saw all matter of destruction. At one time, I entered a tidier phase. I was curious to see how neat I could be. London became my new stomping ground, and their populace was like a market, ripe with unwitting prey. During my stay, I was imitated by a human who wanted to get away with killing a few tarts, as he called them. I disposed of him before he could draw too much attention to my work. My goal was to kill, leave little evidence, and toy with the minds of those who tried to unravel the truth. My reason was the same for anything else I do: fun." Leaning in close, he whispered like a hiss past his lips, "I am Jack the Ripper."

Adwen puffed, unimpressed. "I'm not afraid of you."

He blinked and tilted his head. "That's fine. It does not matter to me. What I want is your scream. Everyone has a true scream, and I have not heard yours yet. I'm sure that by the time you truly scream, your warriors will be close enough to hear it, as well."

A sly smile split his lips. "A little birdie tells me that your first warrior is deeply in love with you, Andredan."

At this, she failed to hide bitterness in her expression.

A mock look of surprise and concern came over Sycan. "You don't think he loves you? How sad. Believe me: He adores you with every fiber of his being. I can show you just how much he loves you."

The demon was so close that she did not see his hand summon a demon-steel sword. In the blink of an eye, he ran it through her abdomen, the suddenness making her gasp.

In the pitch-black tunnels and enormous caverns, the three warriors were running, following instinct alone. Alex's claws made little noise compared to Jack's and Oryn's boots, but none of the nastier inhabitants had taken notice of their passing. The feeling that time was running out nagged at them.

When they were in another long, narrow corridor of misshapen rock, Oryn suddenly felt a sharp pain through his middle. It felt as though he had been stabbed, and he buckled. With a yelp, he tumbled and rolled before colliding against a hard corner. The others felt something in their stomachs at the same moment, but nothing as intense as Oryn had. Jack and Alex went to his side.

Oryn felt like a blade was twisting in his flesh, making him yell at the top of his lungs.

To stop him from alerting enemies, Jack quickly covered his mouth. When he did, Oryn bit down because of the pain.

Then Jack also had to struggle to keep from crying out.

Adwen winced and shuddered, while Sycan twisted the weapon in her body, watching her facial expressions of anguish.

Eyes wide with excitement, he coolly asked, "Does he feel that, Adwen? I'm certain he does. You are connected with each other, but he is so attached that he feels your pain like it is his." With his deep demon voice, he chuckled. The white around his pupils turned black. "You can thank me later for showing you just how much he loves you. Don't worry. I'm not done yet."

The fiend let go and left the blade where it was. Adwen struggled to breathe, and her fingers fidgeted against the shackles, burning as they touched the metal. With her head hanging low, she watched her ruined essence come out green and run along the blade. It rained down into a shallow pool.

Onlooking Creepers cackled and hissed.

While she bled, Sycan summoned out the pages of the stolen text.

He flipped through them, searching for a particular place. "This has been very helpful, but one part caught my interest. Here it says: 'Any who may so touch the golden heart meets a swift end. Any who may so dare to love the golden heart risks oblivion.' I can only assume that there is a riddle to it, but I can't help but think that the Light Spirits are putting more restrictions on you than necessary. Tell me: How can you be a willing servant to such a controlling master?"

For Adwen, ignoring him was made easy by the intense pain.

He waited a few seconds longer before looking sidelong at the dripping of her blood. Raising an eyebrow, he said, "We don't have much time. Let me help speed things along."

The demon tossed aside the pages and drew out another sword imbued with dark magic. He plunged it in deep.

Oryn had gotten back up and resisted the pain while they ran. Later, when the second sword cut into Adwen's body, he bellowed but did not stumble. Instead he roared and summoned his sword, as his inability to be silent would draw attackers. All of the warriors sensed enemies honing in on their location. Not only that, but their sixth senses told them that their search for Adwen was nearly over. They could feel their strength being sapped as hers dwindled. This quickened their strides.

Two swords drained Adwen's blood twice as fast. It pleased Sycan, and he was contented to carry on his banter.

"I'm sure you've noticed by now that I'm taking out the majority of your essence. Call it blood if you like, but you don't have any. All that you are is ethereal, besides your pretty exterior. To kill you properly, I first have to remove as much as possible. That liquid essence protects your solid essence and your heart from impurities. Without it, any kind of weapon of ours can destroy you for good, ripping you from existence. When the bleeding stops, it should be time. Do you have any questions?"

Adwen breathed in shallow, uneven gasps, while green droplets fell from her nose. She appeared to be trying to speak.

Curiosity made the demon come close. With a hand to his ear, he leaned in to hear her. "I'm sorry. I can't quite make that out. Speak up."

Once enough wind was in her chest, Adwen used some remaining strength to spit in his face.

Her green blood sprayed him lightly, and his eyelids fluttered. Wiping some away, he examined it on his glove and clicked his tongue repeatedly. Shaking his head, he scolded, "That was not very ladylike."

In ragged breaths, she wheezed, "You'll fail. I will still be alive when you die. The Light Spirits just showed me your death." A fit of coughing ended her short speech of defiance.

Sycan shrugged and looked disappointed. "You're so boring. I already know that! Don't you think I'm of a high enough intellect to know the nature of the universe? My kind crave destruction, and in doing so, some of their actions bring about their own ends. I do not care about living forever. My only wish is to be the one who takes the most lives. That is my solitary desire. Bringing up obvious things in conversation makes it awkward for those involved. Try to bring up more interesting topics next time. What about your health?"

Adwen shuddered, growing ever weaker.

Planting a palm to his forehead, Sycan corrected himself. "I'm sorry! That's probably a sensitive issue at the moment."

A flicker of hope returned to Adwen, as her heart detected the warriors closing in.

Sycan saw the look and knew as well. He smiled.

The three leaped up to where the foundation of the evil fortress sat, leaving behind a swath of hungry vampires below. Before scaling the wall, Oryn and Jack transformed. The green-eyed hound lobbed the yellow one up, as the tall outer wall was too high for him to jump in a single bound. When Alex landed on the walkway in a mess of Creepers, Oryn and Jack quickly followed. They were powerful enough to make the jump and helped take out the small patrol of fiends.

Shrieks from the dying creatures alerted the Fellons in the court-yard. They wailed, sounding the alarm to the whole fortress.

Oryn was first to leap down. With sword poised, he shrank back into his human form at the last second, making him a smaller target for the deadly tendril blades. He cut off a Fellon's blocky head, then fended off several strikes from another.

Jack and Alex pounced before it could land a strike.

There was no time for relishing the clean kills. They raced past more enemies and charged into the main entrance.

Inside was filled with black-on-black decor. The only other colors were those of the many monsters guarding it. Shrieks and hungry howls greeted their arrival.

The trio gritted their teeth and fangs, and grasped their weapons tightly. Pushing farther into the fortress would not get easier.

"Your kind always keeps their promises," Sycan mused. "So do I. My promise to you is that you will scream before the end. Trust me. I'm a professional." He laughed at his own dark humor.

Adwen's dim eyes fluttered, as she was barely conscious.

Taking a second to study the rate of her bleeding on the blades, Sycan saw how lightly they weeped. A drop or two fell every second, a cue to his next step in the terrible process.

"I'm glad we had this time to talk, Adwen. Let me be frank: You are not the funniest company I've had. Before I send you on a short trip to the land beyond, there is a gift here from an admirer."

Sycan snapped his fingers, and a sharp black stone fell into his grasp from out of nowhere. "Even if I do fail to kill you, maybe this will help with a few pesky problems. You see, this is a very special gift. My friend had been doing a lot of traveling in the other realm, and instead of a postcard, he insisted that I deliver this. It's a cure for hopes and dreams, and may even set you free from your bondage. Most of all, I just want to see how you react when you get it."

The demon relished the pause as he approached, and Adwen glared, prepared to at least try to resist. Unable to move, she was help-less to watch, as he raised the sliver high and drove it deep into her brow line. It disappeared under her skin immediately.

The pain of it entering did not reach Adwen before the memories. A flood of blood and chaos crashed through her mind. Scenes of many gory deaths and murders smashed her resistance to pieces. She saw her mother, brother, sister and father. Then there were her aunts, uncles, cousins and grandparents. Car wrecks, gunshots, blood sprayed at the meeting of a knife point. There was only torture and death. All of them were found, and all of them were slaughtered with-out mercy. No one remained.

Every memory entered her simultaneously, and the agony of the truth hit her weakened heart like a lightning strike. It overwhelmed her completely, and she let out the last of her energy in the form of a blood-curdling cry. Then she was struck with a third sword, and she went limp and quiet.

Sycan's smile widened sadistically.

The hound warriors had made it past the first hall and were still wading through a river of Wretches. In the midst of fighting, they heard a scream of anguish and horror. When it stopped abruptly, each of them felt Adwen's presence vanish with her pain. Jack had to help Alex, as he had returned to his human form without warning, and Oryn's face blanched.

Sensing Adwen's location at once, the three resorted to running and dodging the demons as best they could. Oryn sliced his way through the mobs of claws and teeth with the others at his back.

Rounding the corner and heading to towering double doors, they broke through the ranks into open ground. To get inside, Jack transformed and leaped far ahead, tackling the line where the two doors met. They burst open, revealing the tall altar.

As Jack tumbled beyond the threshold, Oryn saw Sycan raising a dark dagger and aiming for Adwen's heart.

Oryn stepped onto Jack's shoulder as he righted himself then leaped high through the air, headed straight for the demon. The sight of what the monster had done enraged him until he yelled in a mixture of a beastly howl and a scream.

In that moment, Sycan paused. He knew that sound. Looking to see who it was, his eyes met those of the green-eyed warrior. A sick smile came over the demon as he turned his dagger to block the Greatsword swinging in to strike him down. They collided and went careening from the top of the stair for the stone floor.

In the descent, Oryn gnashed his teeth at the villain, who was smiling jubilantly. Creepers scattered to make way as the two fell and tumbled before getting to their feet. Both found each other's eyes again and stared, sizing up each other.

Alex and Jack arrived and slid to a stop between Oryn and the demon. The black and white Holy Hound barked, "Go take her down. We've got this."

As Oryn nodded and dashed for the altar, Sycan smiled and tilted his head. "Jack! How lovely to see you. Are you here to help me again?"

Jack snarled, "Fat chance!" In addition to the reply, he launched a dagger for Sycan's vile face.

The werewolf lord was so fast that he caught it with his fingertips. To mock Jack further, Sycan held it up while it burned his hand and laughed.

This angered Jack so much that something in his mind broke loose. Reaching out at the blade, he snarled and urged it to return. As a result, a purple hue surrounded the weapon a split second before it flew out of Sycan's grip, landing hilt first in Jack's grasp. Then the light diminished.

Alex and the demon gaped, awestruck.

A thin line appeared on Sycan's cheek, and blood wept from it where the dagger had cut him. A second passed, and the expression he wore contorted into one of bloodthirsty rage. Black surrounded his white pupils and spread to his mouth, making his pink gums turn pitch black around his white, pointed teeth. All of him except for his teeth, eyes and his slanted scar turned dark as pitch. Then he roared and attacked.

Alex stepped in the way and swung his weapon. Before he knew what had happened, the Marine was flying back through the air and striking the wall.

Jack deflected a few strikes from the demon, who had instantly grown out his long, sharp claws to tear him to shreds. Then he too was hit by a speedy blow and thrown across the grand hall.

Slumped against the stone blocks, Jack shook his head to stop the spinning.

Beside him, Alex was weary and asked, "Do you have to make everyone hate you?"

Jack only had a second to shrug his furry shoulder before Sycan came sprinting at them. He swiftly pushed the Marine out of harm's way and leaped aside.

Sycan's foot hit where the two had been, exploding smooth stone blocks and sending a large crack up the wall to the ceiling. Sycan roared again and went after the retreating warriors.

While Jack and Alex kept Sycan busy, Oryn quickly pulled the swords out of Adwen's lifeless form. They clattered on the ground, splattering green across the stone floor. He used his own sword with perfect aim to shatter the ankle restraints. The chain fell away into the pool.

At last, Oryn broke the shackles on her wrists, and she dropped. He leaped after her, letting go of his weapon to catch Adwen in his arms. Landing on his feet, the vat of sickly green fluid splashed about them. Holding her tight, he snatched up his sword and barked to signal the others to make a speedy retreat.

Jack and Alex had some difficulty keeping out of Sycan's reach.

He was far too powerful for direct combat. So when they heard Oryn's call, there was not a moment's hesitation. The two avoided more furious swipes and sprinted after him out into the halls, as Wretches and Fellons came flooding in.

There were too many to fight, so Jack helped forge a clear path to a lofty glass window. They leaped along the tops of sinister statues and artifacts. With his body, the dagger-wielding hound crashed through to make way for the others, who quickly followed. Their escape to the roof made the demons wail in aggravation. Sycan also roared after them into the darkness.

Once outside, the three saw a sea of undead around the fortress.

After a moment of searching, Oryn spied a set of large rocks, far above the hordes. "There!" he yelled.

Seeing the Holy Hounds make their way along a path that was out of reach, the vampires shrieked in hungry desperation. Their feast was getting away.

The many towering formations gave the warriors a means to travel out of the immense cavern to yet another. A weak draft met them, hinting that their path was the right one. Oryn led the way, carrying his sword in one hand and holding Adwen's body in the other. Her head lolled, as the rest of her limp form made fleeing all the more difficult. As a knight, Oryn had carried dead weight before. It was never easy to keep hold of a body with no life left inside. The dead always wanted to slip away.

To make matters worse, the denizens had not given up the chase. Corrupted gargoyles and vampires that could fly darted through the air.

Jack watched their backs, striking down monsters that came too close.

Alex stuck close to Oryn, struggling to keep up.

The passages were uneven and rough. Spikes lined the walls in some corridors, while other tunnels turned into narrow land bridges, making running precarious. They were all becoming winded. Not even Jack could hold off the pursuers forever.

Then another draft came, bringing fresh salty sea air.

With hope of escape restored, the warriors mustered what was left of their determination and ran even faster. Clean winds pushed against them, but the taste of it drew them out of the intense darkness, filled with echoing howls and shrieks. Around the hundredth and first corner of the dim maze, they saw daylight and dashed out to meet it.

The sea roared against black rocks, as the three Griffins swiftly came to collect them. All the commotion from inside had made predicting their arrival simple. They dipped down, letting the warriors jump on their backs and carry them west on the gales. The screams of Mortigad stayed behind.

Chapter 33
WHAT SPANS WORLDS

Wind moaned in their ears as it rolled down the backs of the Griffins. It howled at the Holy Hounds, rushing past like a bad dream. Jack and Oryn had dismissed their blades when none of the monsters dared to fly into the sunshine.

No one spoke. Alex let his mind remain still, as Jack kept a close watch over Oryn. The knight sat astride his Griffin, clinging to Adwen, bracing her against his chest. His mind was almost as blank as the Marine's, though he was more in a state of shock. A part of him hoped that the wild beating of his own heart might revive hers.

It did not.

Adwen knew this place. She had been here before. A dark grey sky was above. Beneath, the great white oak was locked in the center of an endless dead forest. On this plane of existence, time had no sway. The pale glowing refuge for innocent souls stood alone to catch Adwen when she appeared and drifted down into its sweeping boughs.

Her semitransparent form came to stand among countless shimmering, silvery souls. They passed into and out of each other, swaying like autumn leaves. Before the memories of what had brought her here could return, a collection of souls gathered. The balls of gentle light changed, taking the shape of who they had been in life.

Gaping at one of the familiar smiling faces, Adwen gasped, "Mom?"

The sweet woman went to her, while the others watched.

Sarah brushed her child's cheek with a ghostly hand. "It's okay, honey. We're all right now. They can't hurt us anymore."

Adwen trapped her mother in a firm embrace, shuddering, as tears did not exist in this place. "I'm sorry I couldn't be there to save you. Forgive me. Forgive me. I couldn't save you."

After allowing the girl to release her grief, Sarah pulled back to look her in the face. Gently, she said, "We forgive you, but you did not do anything wrong. You did what you had to do. You're saving people. We are all very proud of you for being so strong." Adwen looked away, but Sarah touched her cheek again to make her look back again. Smiling, she continued: "You need to go back."

"I don't want to go back. I want to stay with you."

"Please." Sarah frowned and pleaded, "Please, baby. You have to. If you don't go back soon, you will start to forget. The light has let me remember long enough to tell you. Go back while you still remember it. He loves you, baby."

Adwen blinked in confusion.

"Who?"

Oryn dropped down from the Griffin's back. On the uninhabited island, they found a cave where they could stay the night. Jack had urged Oryn to let the Griffins take them back to the capital, but it was no use. The knight refused to wait another hour to see to Adwen.

Laying her down on the earth in the gloom, he brushed Adwen's messed hair from her blood-splattered face. Then he felt her neck, searching vainly for a pulse, which he knew did not exist. At a loss, Oryn stared, quietly begging her eyes to open again.

Jack went to his side, and Alex remained by the entrance. The Marine did not want to see this. The whole scene threatened to bring back his own painful past.

The hound cop knelt beside his better, waiting for him to do something.

Licking his lips nervously, Jack asked, "What are you waiting for? Call her."

Filled with hopeful disbelief, Oryn gave a quick glance and looked back to Adwen. "What are you talking about? She cannot hear me in this state. She is gone."

Frustrated, Jack answered, "I don't know. That's what she told me you would have to do. She didn't explain it."

After giving Jack another look, Oryn took in the vague instructions. Speaking to her couldn't be the answer. With all that had happened, he was still not good at riddles. Once it crossed his mind that he had to call her in another manner, he did the only thing that made sense.

Closing his eyes, he took her back into his arms. Kneeling in the stillness, Oryn rested his brow against hers. Using the strong feeling at his center, he called out her name from inside. Oryn called her name over and over, hoping beyond hope that she could hear him on the other side.

Sarah was almost to the point of begging. "Please, don't forget. I understand how hard it is, but you have to go back. They all need you, but he needs you the most. You can't let them down now. You've come too far to give up."

Shaking her head, Adwen refused. "I'm tired of hurting. I don't want to remember anymore. None of it should matter. I'm here with my family."

"Yes," Sarah replied. "We are your family, but you have to see that now your friends are family, too. Go back to them. Go back, baby."

From somewhere above, a voice called. At the start, it was difficult to make out.

Adwen and Sarah looked and listened to the sound as it grew louder, echoing in the quiet world. It said the same thing over and over: "Adwen. Adwen."

Confusion made her squint, as she searched for the source. "What is that?"

Sarah knew and smiled. "It's him. He's calling you."

Looking back at the loving family, Adwen paused.

"We will be waiting," Sarah reassured.

Shaking her head, she wrapped her mother in her arms again. "I can't leave you again."

Several minutes passed. Jack stayed close, waiting to see if it would work. When Oryn raised his head, even Alex looked to see what was happening.

Never had the knight felt such stillness. The world around him seemed to be holding its breath, watching and waiting for her to stir. Another moment went by, and his heart sank. Adwen had not heard his call. Along with his heart, his hopes broke into a million pieces. She was gone for good.

Oryn's face was blank. Losses had always left him empty instead of wrenching with grief. Tears had never been shed for any deaths he had known. This was no different. Rather than crying, another part of his soul died instead.

A spark of warmth entered the three warriors, making them gasp and look on in anticipation.

Adwen's eyelashes flickered weakly, making Oryn gasp. When her deep sea-blue eyes opened, the first thing she saw was Oryn. His eyes were glowing bright and beginning to overflow with tears.

The breath caught in the knight's lungs as he wept, holding her to his chest. She had come back to him.

Adwen did not stay conscious for long in her state of weakness. While she slept, the warriors and the Griffins stood watch, and Oryn kept her in the sun to heal until nightfall. The worst of her wounds mended, leaving behind shallow scratches. After sunset, Jack and Alex took turns keeping watch, allowing Oryn to stay with her the entire time. He slept beside her, unwilling to leave her unattended for a second.

Early in the morning, when the sun was just returning to the sky, a terrible feeling woke Oryn from his slumber.

His eyes snapped open wide. The place where he last saw Adwen was vacant. In a flash, he was on his feet, searching urgently for her whereabouts. At the cave entrance, he found Alex and Jack. Both stared out at the sunrise together. They appeared wary of something when he joined them.

Looking out the same way, all he saw was Adwen gazing at the horizon.

Oryn moved to go to her, but Jack swiftly blocked him with an outstretched arm. After shooting him a deadly glare, he waited to see what had them so disturbed.

It took a moment for Oryn to realize something was amiss. When he saw it, he gaped.

The sunlight was not dancing on her skin.

Brushing Jack off, Oryn went forward.

"Wait," Jack urged. "Something's not right." His warning went ignored.

As Oryn went closer, he noticed that the grass in a wide ring around her was wilted and curled. Defiant of the bad omens, Oryn stepped into the space.

A force suddenly came down on him like a heavy weight. It was difficult to breathe, but his determination to help Adwen overrode the need to go back. Taking another step, he came to a stop. This was not pressure, he realized. This was her pain. It was so great that it was pouring out of her onto anything within reach. Even the flora underfoot was reacting to the intense negativity she emanated.

When she did not move or say anything, he murmured, "Adwen?"

The grass rustled, as the energy lifted, letting it stand.

He was also alleviated.

Adwen spoke softly with a tone of apprehension: "Did you sleep well?"

At first he paused, wondering if he should answer. "Yes."

She was quiet. Then she asked, "Do you remember when we talked about what we would do after this war? I never asked what you would do. What will you do when everything is over?"

Oryn knew what he wanted but said, "I suppose what you guessed. It is possible I could return to serve the Order. Why does that matter?"

The silence that followed made him uneasy.

Afraid of what she might be talking about, he was urgent. "Adwen?"

She gradually turned. Eyes cast down, Adwen glanced over one shoulder. Dark circles had appeared under her eyes, and the subtle frown was haunting.

When her eyes met his, in a single moment, visions of men, women and children being burned, stabbed, crushed and dismembered hit him like a fist to the stomach. Becoming white as a sheet, he shuddered. There was no need to ask who the victims were. It was apparent by the look she wore, and his heart ached.

She finally murmured, "It doesn't matter."

Oryn flinched at the coldness of her statement. This was not like her.

To try to undo the damage of his prior answers, he added, "I had hoped you would stay with the Order, as well. The Order halls were erected for you by your predecessor. It would only be right if you claimed your place in them. Would that not be so?"

Adwen blinked solemnly. "No."

Once more, Oryn felt like he had been smacked. "Why? Why would you not wish to stay in a wondrous place such as that? Is there no reason you could think for being in the Order?" He held his breath for her answer.

Bitterly, she said, "Nothing in this world could make me stay any-where."

Oryn could not breathe again, but it was not because of magic or powers.

"I want my family. Being with them is where I want to be. If I could, I would go there now and never come back."

"Then what was it that brought you back," he whispered breathlessly.

"I don't know. It doesn't matter now. I'm here with no reason to be."

Bitterness stung him, as her words bit like a hornet at his insides. It wounded him that she would rather be dead than in his company. A hard frown formed on his face.

Before he could reply, she said, "Let me go." With that, she soundlessly jumped off the edge into the dense jungle.

Wearing an angry grimace, Oryn turned away to storm back to the cave.

Jack was aghast. Running up to the knight, he snapped, "Why did you let her go? What is the matter with you?"

The reason surfaced in Oryn's mind and leaped to Jack's, making him freeze. Then he reevaluated the situation and went after him again.

"You can't do this! She needs you!"

Oryn stopped with his back to him and glowered. "I should have known a heart of gold has no warmth. It is just as cold as metal. There is nothing I can do for her now."

Jack was about to tell him off when Alex spoke up.

"Hey! Where is she going?"

Whirling around, the cop pointed at the thick foliage and tall trees. "Go find her and stop her. We'll be with you in a minute."

The Marine nodded and disappeared over the side into the vegetation.

Bringing his attention back to the stubborn knight, Jack was beside himself.

"How can you not get it that she's hurting? She didn't mean what she said because she's in pain! Her family meant the world to her!"

Snapping back, Oryn bellowed, "She said she would rather be dead and with them than alive and with me!"

In response, Jack punched Oryn in the jaw, making him pause and glare.

"Listen to me," Jack urged in a serious tone. "That can't be the truth. She told me that you were the only one who could call her back to this world if she crossed over. Don't you see?"

Oryn was red in the face with rage but refrained from beating Jack to a pulp. Jack's point was not clear.

"She loves you so much that she could only hear your voice from across the worlds. On top of that, she left her whole family there for you, you idiot!"

More contemplative than before, Oryn considered Jack's claim.

Alex needed to remember to use his nose once he got lost in the trees. Tracking Adwen was not difficult after that. He sniffed out her trail and followed it wherever it led.

The Marine pushed aside giant ferns on his way, eventually using his weapon to cut them down. He was hacking another to pieces when he spotted her. She was just going behind another enormous tree in the distance.

Adrenalin flooded him, and he lunged after her. She was still walking away when he caught up and kept some distance between them.

"Wait!" he shouted, but Adwen did not wait. "Stop!"

Coming to a halt, she gave him a sour expression. "What do you want?"

Not knowing why he was nervous, he wet his dry lips. "You need to come back. Oryn is just being an idiot. Come on. Jack is straightening him out."

"Why do you care? You have no more reason to care than I do."

Seeing the look in her eyes, he recognized the pain of loss. Becoming somewhat consoling, he insisted, "You've lost someone. I understand, but the mission is not completed yet. You have to face the fact and finish the mission, or they died for nothing."

Anger lit in her bright blue eyes. "How dare you? What a hypocrite you are to accuse me of not facing the truth. You haven't even begun to face your own truth yet. I believe it is high time that you did."

Raising her hand to point a condemning finger at the Marine, she looked in his eyes and ripped away the wall he had built around the final memories of his wife.

Absolute loss hit him first. Feelings of horror at how he had found his beautiful bride dead in their home took hold of his heart, squeezing it hard until he thought he was going to die. The Marine wanted to die in that moment, if only to escape the reality and the pain. Blinded by it, he wailed and fell to his knees, languishing with his thoughts.

By the time he recovered from the storm of terrible memories he had worked so hard to hide, Adwen was gone again. The Marine realized this and gathered himself up, forcing his body, weary with grief, to continue on. He had to find her.

Beginning the search anew, he quickly deduced that she was no longer walking. Alex had not been down for long, but she was much farther away. Her fresh scent took him even deeper into the jungle. Nearing the end of the trail, it brought him to the hidden entrance of a natural underground passage.

The Marine held his sword tighter, as he did not know what else could be in the dark other than his bereaved leader.

Water dripped from limestone stalactites, falling into dark pools. His bare feet padded downward, to where he could not guess. His nose guided him farther, gathering more of Adwen's smell as he continued. He was getting close.

His toes came across the start of stairs she had used, and he was further unsure of this situation. Should he have waited at the entrance for the others to catch up? It was too late now. Turning back was not a viable option.

Light from below signaled the beginning of another cavern. Something was illuminating it, and he arrived at the opening to see what it was.

Two crystals the size of fists rested on metallic stands, shining on Adwen. She rested on her knees gazing deep into a broad mirror in a silver frame. As he went nearer, he saw that the tarnished metal was imitative of a spider, cradling the reflective disk as a real spider does an egg sack; or its captured prey.

Going closer, he saw that Adwen was sitting just before it, sobbing. Alex could only see her reflection, but he suspected that she saw something else. While she wept at it and smiled weakly, her hand hovered shakily over the surface. She wanted very badly to touch it but tried very hard to keep from doing so.

Carefully, Alex crept to her side and soothed her: "It's all right. Come with me. We have to get out of here." Then he looked into the Mirror of Lies and froze, unable to turn away from what he saw.

Emily, his wife, was there. She was smiling, washing dishes in their old kitchen. She gave him a clever look. That was how she always used to tell him to hold her.

Stunned, he dropped his sword with a clatter. Alex slowly raised a hand, hoping to reach out and find her under his fingertips.

He never found her there. A rock-hard fist smashed into the side of his head, bowling him over like a rag doll.

Surprised by the sound, Adwen turned to see Sycan and his devilish grin.

At that moment, Oryn and Jack came into the lit part of the cavern. Before they knew what was going on, the werewolf lord grabbed Adwen by her hair and slung her into the mirror. It consumed her, and she vanished from sight.

Oryn roared, and Jack snarled.

Sycan's demonic laughter filled the cave, reverberating in their ears.

As Oryn lunged forward, the monster leaped into the wicked looking glass.

Jack called after him, but it was too late. The knight was already jumping in after them both.

A swirl of colors filled Oryn's vision as he tumbled through space. When he came down, his feet landed on a boulder. Wind tossed his hair, whistling in his pointed ears. Looking all around, he saw that he was in the wilderness on a riverbank.

Whirling around and around, he shouted her name: "Adwen! Adwen!"

The roar of the river was the only sound he heard.

...To be continued.
...Sorry.